SUMMER IN TERMUREN

LOUIS PAUL BOON

TRANSLATION BY PAUL VINCENT

DALKEY ARCHIVE PRESS

NORMAL · LONDON

Originally published in Flemish as *Zomer te Ter-Muren* by De Arbeiderspers, 1956
Copyright © 1956 by Louis Paul Boon
English translation copyright © 2006 by Paul Vincent

First edition, 2006
All rights reserved

Library of Congress Cataloging-in-Publication Data:

Boon, Louis Paul.
    [Zomer te Ter-Muren. English]
    Summer in Termuren / Louis Paul Boon ; translated by Paul Vincent. — 1st ed.
       p. cm.
    ISBN 1-56478-414-2 (pbk. : alk. paper)
       I. Vincent, Paul (Paul F.) II. Title.

PT6407.B57Z313 2006
839.31'364—dc22

                                                                      2006040272

The translation of this book was funded by the Flemish Literature Fund
(Vlaams Fonds voor de Letteren—www.fondsvoordeletteren.be).

Partially funded by grants from the National Endowment for the Arts, a federal agency,
and the Illinois Arts Council, a state agency.

Dalkey Archive Press is a nonprofit organization whose mission is to promote
international cultural understanding and provide a forum for dialogue for the literary arts.

www.dalkeyarchive.com

Printed on permanent/durable acid-free paper, bound in the United States of America,
and distributed throughout North America and Europe.

Wildly comic, inventive, and disturbing, the fiction of Flemish writer Louis Paul Boon (1912-1979) was far ahead of its time. Born in the town of Aalst to a working-class family, Boon quickly transcended his early devotion to a pedantic, socially committed realism to produce some of the world's first and finest "postmodern" novels: works that couch his scathing and satirical brand of humanism in a relentlessly idiosyncratic style. Using almost no capital letters, running bold, journalistic headlines at the start of every chapter, layering multiple narratives on top of each other, and never flinching from frank descriptions of sex, violence, and hypocrisy, Boon was pilloried and misunderstood by both the Left and the Right, but eventually became one of the most respected—if scandalous—figures in Belgian literary history. Virtually unknown outside Belgium, Boon now may come to be recognized as one of the twentieth century's most important writers

Picking up where his novel *Chapel Road* left off, *Summer in Termuren* is, among other things, the story of Boon himself, a struggling novelist who wants to write "the novel of the individual in a world of barbarians": a novel that will change the world for the better. This fictional Boon in turn tells the story of Ondine and Oscarke, a young married couple living in the "1st grimy houses" of the mill town of Termuren at the turn of the century. This story is meant to show the truly awful conditions the working class lived in before the era of reform—but Ondine turns out to be a cruel and manipulative woman, determined to be "someone" no matter whom she destroys in the process; and Oscarke, an aspiring sculptor, is beginning to develop an unhealthy fixation on underage girls.

Meanwhile, in "real life," Boon's friends (Tippetotje the painter, who's "bagged herself a baron" to pay the bills; Johan Janssens, the socially-conscious poet and reporter who's forced to work as a housepainter to support his family; Tolfpoets, with his "2 gold teeth," who'd rather crack cheap jokes than help Boon with his epic; the bureaucratic "Mossieu" Colson of the ministry, who hears ghosts in the walls of his apartment; and the academic Music Master, who tries, without success, to teach his students common decency) won't let him write in peace. They bicker over, and comment on, his increasingly hope-less novel, adding their own sections and even suggesting other stories that might serve his purposes better. In the end, Boon finds it's not so easy these days to tell the barbarians from the individuals; and he, Ondine, and Oskarke must all decide whether to persevere in their dreams, or else retreat forever from a life of disappointment and regret.

A panorama of modern existence, from its tiny, daily indignities to the over-whelming terror of war, charting the destiny of a few small lives as they struggle to survive in the wake of history—*Summer in Termuren* is as daring and innovative today as when it was first published in Belgium in 1956.

So this is the 2nd book about chapel road—the second book about ondine and oscarke, about her brother valeer and all the other characters you already met in the 1st book about chapel road . . . but with lots more besides, like ondine's daughters, judith for instance, and mariette with her big mouth, and their brothers maurice and leopold who grow into such a pair of crooks! They grow up around ondine and oscarke, who get old and have to wear glasses and a truss for a hernia or some such thing. The children spring up around them like mushrooms and along with those mushrooms other strange things spring up: technology and mechanization, unemployment, fascism, and war. And see, as they slowly grow old and start to resign themselves to many things, they approach Our era . . . approach the age in which johan janssens lives, and boon and kramiek and tippetotje, and god knows who else. The novel of our heroine ondine and the novel of our other hero boon come closer and closer together . . .

And then—oh dear it's another ocean, a chaos and then some, I'm really sorry—but it's not so much a novel of socialism anymore, it's more the novel of the individual in a world of barbarians: this book is dedicated to you, this book was written for you and no one else—you, the individual, in this world of barbarians.

THE FIRST CHAPTER, WHOSE TITLE IS THIS
RATHER STRANGE THOUGHT OF ONDINE'S:
ONLY THE PRECIOUS LITTLE MOMENT COUNTS

FOR ELISE

You're just sorry you can't write music in words, can't pour out sounds, because then you'd start with that silvery trippety-trip with which little elise comes tripping along . . . comes tripping into beethoven's melancholy life. And you imagine little ondine tripping along chapel road with her two braids down her back . . . past the long wall of the Labor Weaving Mill, and beneath the gray rainy sky and the smoking chimneys of the Filature Spinning Mill . . . ondineke, who comes tripping into your life as a writer and is not content to be a proper novel heroine . . . trippety-trippety-trippety-trip, her nimble feet dance down chapel road, and her laugh is a silver bell heard by the long long wall of the labor weaving mill. And gradually she takes shape, because as he constructs that life, sketches that body, composes that laugh, the writer collects everything he hears and sees about the laugh of the ondinekes . . . to the point where the writer's wife, to her dismay and irritation, sees the photo of some ondineke or other on the corner of the desk. Because ondineke is taking shape and stirring in the writer's life . . . and the writer is only human—trippety-trippety-trippety-trip—and ondineke trippety-trips over the writer's heart, with her nimble feet she dances over his tired and pierced and torn heart, she laughs silver bubbles in his tired tormented and tortured head. But the pepperpot creeps along chapel road and shadows ondineke, and devours her with his eyes, and looks right through her trippety-trip skirts: he hides in the patch of wood when ondineke thinks no one can see her, and slips off her chemise and goes for a swim in the castle pond: he stands behind the ancient hedge there by the first grubby houses behind the labor, and leaps out when ondineke comes tripping along. Oops, ondineke. And now you should be able to pour out sounds instead of words—oh your great useless regret that you're not beethoven but just boon—beneath that trippety-trip the darker sound would enter—dadoomadoom. And the pepperpot, the writer, the collector of photos of ondineke: the hymn to ondineke becomes brooding and dark, burdened and charged. Oh, he wanted to keep it so pure, so light and earthy: an angelic little girl with a mocking laugh and nimble little trippety-trip feet—dadoomadoom. And the writer who wanted to keep the motif light and pure: he stumbles and falls and falls in love with his own little heroine: he would like in the depths of his desire to be a god in order to destroy the pepperpot who's stalking her, to demolish the long wall of the labor weaving mill, and to purge the gray rainy sky of the filature spinning mill. But he

is human—dadoomadoom, dadoomadoom—he's human and stumbles and falls
. . . but gets up and leaves ondineke untouched by the pepperpot, unmoved by the
gray squalls of rain, and undaunted by the long wall of the labor weaving mill:
trippety-trip. And ondineke strides on through life, but beside her walks the writer
heavy-footed and with a darker heart—and her motif soars high as a lark above
the motif of boon who loves beethoven: dadoomadoom.

TO ONDINE

The reason you write "for elise" is that beethoven's motif happens to remind you
of your story about ondineke . . . of your book that was supposed to change the
course of things, of your life's work, your swansong. And god, what's become of the
time when you went round with such reckless and absurd ideas? In the meantime
ondineke has grown old . . . that is, in the reality of your life, in the reality of this
age the woman who was your model for ondineke has grown old (she's already
a gray-haired old woman who stumbles down the street and recognizes scarcely
anyone anymore, and only when you say: "hello madame ondine," looks at you
intently and replies with her toothless mouth: "oh, hello little louis boone my boy,
and how's your mother?") but not only in the reality of today, but in your story
itself too ondineke is starting to grow old, in your story she has grown so old that
she has got married to pathetic oscarke, and so is no longer the little ondineke who
wore her two dancing braids down her back and is comparable with beethoven's
little elise.

Yet . . . hey, how old would beethoven's little elise be today? She's gone, she's
long since ceased to be a woman and is a skeleton crumbling to dust. Meanwhile
beethoven's hymn to little elise is still played. Oh, you know full well, it's all so
futile—maybe it would be better if you went on looking for a little farm to plant
trees on—and a bit of orchard and a bit of woodland to sit in. Just sit. In your
book ondineke has grown into a young married woman, who rents a room above
the café that serves the 1st grimy houses . . . but in real life she's become an old
woman, with severe glasses and no teeth. And what about you yourself, how old
is little louis in your book and how old in the reality of the present? Only the
moment counts, the precious little moment . . . the little incalculable moment, for
instance, of this day in june: you should come and sit in a bit of woodland, and
listen to the rustle of leaves, a poplar, a willow, a silver birch. Only the precious
little moments have counted in the life of little ondine, only a few peaks that she
still remembers, having become very old and short-sighted and toothless . . . that
she still remembers, having just got married in your book. A few little moments of
deep happiness, a few little moments of deep pain . . . an evening in the company
of rich gentlemen, who had got her drunk . . . a few hours of which she still says:
lord, it was such a hoot! . . . a night when she once cried terribly and passionately,

and moved the heart of her god with her tears—when her little god inside became as big as the god outside. Which is to say . . . well, no, it's not to say. Only those moments count. And those moments in your life pass by without your noticing, without your being touched by them. If someone asks you what moments you remember in your life, you'll have to reply: I don't remember any moments, I've written every moment of my life, I've written off every moment of my life. Written off. Oh, what a cruel phrase has suddenly appeared on the paper in front of you, piercing you like a dagger: so have you, yes YOU, written off your life?

THE YOUNG MARRIED WOMAN

There sat ondine, looking out of the window of the room above the café serving the 1st grimy houses . . . she looked out at the yard that was an air shaft, at the back of the labor weaving mill, and at the wonderful june sky spread above it. That's right, she was married . . . she was married to oscarke, and vaguely and strangely and annoyingly somewhere inside she had the gnawing sense—no, not the sense, but something that could easily have grown into a sense—somewhere a strange and gnawing worm told her she had thrown her life away, that she had somehow gone astray. What was I really supposed to do in this life? she wondered, staring at the chimneys of the labor weaving mill, which were again belching out their smoke and blowing soot into her room . . . when I was young it seemed as if I was put here to set a few things right and sort them out once and for all—and all the while she was drumming her fingers on the rotten windowsill—and now, I can't properly imagine those things from my youth anymore, I came to serve god and live, to become a saint and make the world ashamed and repentant . . . and afterwards it seemed to me as if I was put here to serve men and let their seed grow in my womb, to strangle them with the monster of socialism . . . and now . . . and now? Ondine was married to oscarke and lived in a room above the café that served the 1st grimy houses. And whether or not she remembered the most beautiful and cruelest moments in her life, a difficult period began for her of cheating and lying and begging . . . of buying things in stores where she wasn't well known, and pretending that she'd forgotten her purse. She returned to her parents' house and saw her brother valeer still hanging around . . . he hadn't gone back to brussels after her wedding but hung around here, ostensibly to help his father, if required, to repair the guttering at the castle . . . but wasn't he far more concerned with getting drunk? She got him to haul the stove from father's shed and bring it to her room above the café—she herself sold her gold bracelet and bought herself a coal-scuttle . . . bought, but on second thought didn't pay for it, because she couldn't bear to part with even a fraction of the sum she'd received: "I'm keeping it for a rainy day!" was her alibi. And she told oscarke that everything was bought and paid for . . . why, she didn't know herself . . . perhaps That was her real role *in life: to cheat and lie to everyone. She sometimes met people from termuren and told them: I live in a house in town now . . . and sometimes she met someone from town and told them: I live on an estate at termuren. And suddenly she met her old school friend monique, who was married to mr van wesenborgh, head book-keeper of the filature spinning mill. Oh, what a conflagration of competing pride: my husband's been promoted from head bookkeeper to commercial director of the mill, you must come and see our house, our paintings and oriental rugs: we have a reception every thursday. And ondine went one thursday evening, armed with her parasol but now without her gold bracelet: oh goddammit, having to sell it off Now of all times! She apologized for the fact that her husband had been unable to come . . . especially to see the paintings, since he was an artist . . . but he liked solitude although he was famous, and the parks in brussels were full of sculptures he had done. And suddenly she remembered dear mr brys . . . mr brys who had been the first socialist and had had to flee to england . . . mr brys who was the uncle of this stuck-up bitch, and hence the black sheep of the family. And she asked after that mr brys and how he was doing. Monique answered sweet as pie that he was in england and occasionally wrote: things weren't too wonderful over there, he was working in a mill in manchester, and was learning english and hoped to get an office job before long. A mad rush of satisfaction rose to ondine's head . . . she had felt more or less uncomfortable in this drawing room—that is, uncomfortable because it was not Her drawing room, because She had not had herself married off to a bookkeeper with no balls but now, hah, mr brys was in england and dirt poor, and hoped soon to be promoted to some dingy office! And it was as if the ondine that one knew, sitting in this drawing room, suddenly disappeared to make way for Another ondine . . . a god, an avenger . . . and full of her own sense of self-worth she looked round this house, where just a moment before she had been able to venture only a glance clouded by regret and envy . . . she looked round and saw a pale child sitting on the oriental carpet, a snail from the cellar, a head of chicory grown underground. And of course she couldn't wait to bring up the subject of the child . . . she remembered gloatingly how monique had once explained that her husband was going to let her have her way over everything, especially over this fundamental precondition: that she mustn't get pregnant! And ondine smiled down on that head of sun-starved chicory on the carpet . . . smiled down at her wrist, where the gold bracelet should still have been: a gold snake slithering through engraved flowers.*

AM I SCREWING UP MY LIFE?

And tolfpoets enters and bares his 2 gold teeth in a grin: I'm here, it's a long while since you saw me! And he doesn't notice that actually there's a hint of horror round your mouth . . . because are you going to start filling your book again with stuff about tolfpoets and his jokes, about the music master and his rather comical solemnity, about johan janssens and his career as a house-painter, weekly journalist, and whatever else . . . about mossieu colson of the ministry who mixes up his files with his poems? Are you going to start all that again, and write a 2nd book about chapel road? Goddammit. And in comes tolfpoets and bares his two gold teeth in a grin: here I am, and I'm wondering if you need me to add some shallow humor and frivolous jocularity to your book, just as you put salt in soup and sugar on hemorrhoids . . . or is it hemor-rhubarb? And he laughs and tells me he's bought a piece of land the other side of termuren, beyond the unmanned railway crossing, and has put up what he calls a villa . . . I live there now with my wife maria, nature girl, who's putting her frivolous ways behind her, but is surrounding herself with cats and a crazy young guard dog, and shrubs and bushes and flowers . . . and she's also dying for a blackbird that she can have shuffle about on gray rainy days, and she's also dying for a lark that she can have soar into the air on yellow summer days . . . but can I plant a blackbird for her the way I plant a pear tree?

Right, you accept tolfpoets—tight-lipped, and, if the truth be told, reluc-tantly—and if the truth be told you allow him into your book feeling a bit of revulsion. And you ask what he Really thinks of life . . . because he laughs and tells jokes and skates over the rough edges, he avoids the depths and the heights and stays on the ground floor with his witticisms . . . but what does he Really think about life? Why are you living your life, tolfpoets, and what do balls and pussy, bread and disaster and death mean to you? And don't you have the feeling of wasting your life, just by steering clear of heights and depths and telling jokes about it . . . just as I'm wasting it by writing about it? And for a moment tolfpoets turns into a child on the point of tears, having been told that it was just playing around, that its life has been nothing but play, that there's something quite different looming up behind it—tolfpo-ets becomes as sad as a child, and recalcitrant now that you've asked such a thing, and he says evasively: it's summer and june and hot—shame about the wind—and women are walking around in light clothes with plunging neck-lines and translucent flowered dresses . . . yesterday I noted down everything that entered my field of vision: first a young woman who approached me with the sun behind her shining right through her clothes, so that she was coming towards me as if naked—a naked silhouette—and then a young woman who got off her bike and raised her leg high . . . and then . . . Which doesn't mean that Those things are all I pay attention to: I also hear the loudspeakers booming away for the elections, and I see the deluge of manifestoes. But I don't listen to what blares from the loudspeakers, or read what's printed in the manifestoes, just as I don't chase after the young women who pass me in their veiled and laced-up nakedness.

And you nod your head, slowly and pensively: right, I believe you . . . but what do you really think? Do you really not have the feeling that you're somehow messing up your life? And tolfpoets gives you a look, surly and recalcitrant, and, in fact, sad, like a child being taught about the terrible seriousness of life, and he makes a gesture with his head, as if to say: Whatever could have made you think of something so crazy?

THE LONG ARM

Suddenly it turns into an evening when we get nothing but stories about the long Arm . . . you know: the law has a long Arm, but its legs are too short . . . or: someone with a long Arm will get me a job. And it happened for the simple reason that tippetotje had turned up again . . . she had turned up again from the jungle of brussels, bringing a bottle, and around the bottle hung the good news that you had a chance of winning the state literature prize, that someone with a long Arm had announced he would do something for you, that you were going to be able to publish novels and novellas in foreign languages, and that some joker—a viscount—was extremely interested in your work. But, 1st question: what will be left of all this good news once tippetotje's bottle is empty? And, 2nd question: didn't tippetotje used to be called "the ship of lies"?

It's this long Arm that's blinded everyone . . . and sickwit the student says that actually he also met someone with a long Arm once . . . but that this person regards boon's work as evidence of a pathological case . . . and so he'll only help sickwit out on the condition that he has nothing more to do with boon.

And tidelomba, the young lawyer, is also sitting there, by tippetotje's bottle . . . and tells us he's passed his exams with flying colors and is now on the street: no clients, no practice, nothing cooking in any ministry or branch of the civil service or any non-government organization—although someone with a long Arm had said that he would find something for him: and in the meantime tidelomba was giving French lessons, 3 lessons a week at 150 francs—making 150 a week, making 600 francs a month.

And suddenly there's your wife's comment: that recently she's heard nothing except stories about men with long Arms . . . and that she believes there are no men with short arms left nowadays.

And yes, sickwit told us something else, but what was it again? Oh nothing, I remember now . . . it was me that answered that all those men with long Arms are whores. Although the question immediately came up of first defining what a whore is: and a prostitute is at least still a working girl, whereas not even that could be said of all those long Arms.

But tolfpoets, who never quite manages to hit the nail on the head, also came up with a story about the long Arm: about a woman he knows who brought up her child with a long Arm . . . that is with beatings and threats: behave, or else! . . . And now her little girl is terminally ill, and the mother looks on helplessly, since she can't cure her with beatings and threats . . . she can't say: stop that nosebleed, or else! . . . Her long Arm falls short.

And finally there's the dream of johan janssens's young son—jo, who's 10—about a shadow that was following him, and how he kept vaulting down these enormous stairways to escape the shadow . . . and then saw his father walk casually by in the distance. And after he's told us about his dream he gives his father an embittered look: because his father doesn't have a long Arm that can help him in his dreams.

No, the end is like this: johan janssens suddenly asks whether all the stories about long Arms stem from the forthcoming elections? Because if you read the manifestoes they're Full of long arms, offering us a golden age on a platter.

ECKERMANN

It's summer and june and fine weather—shame about the wind, which is still blowing from the north, the north or the east or the west, but in any case whips up blinding dust clouds . . . where on earth does that wind keep coming from? Ha, and you suddenly remember mossieu colson of the ministry, who was once preoccupied with people's idiosyncrasies, with every idiosyncrasy of every person, and who said: where do all these idiosyncrasies keep coming from? And You remember mossieu colson of the ministry, and that very moment he looms up, that very moment he's sitting there beside you with his silent smile and calm hands, and he says: for elise, for ondine, am I screwing up my life? You write things like that, and you also wonder whether you have any further use for me . . . whether you'll go on using the music master and johan janssens and myself—mossieu colson of the ministry—as the foundations of your 2nd book on chapel road. Because you're definitely going to write it . . . you'll write till your last gasp, write till it becomes time to lie down forever . . . and even Then you'll still say: mossieu colson of the ministry, hand me my pen—give me a moment so I can write something down before I go. And by now I feel like eckermann and write down a lot of the things that you let slip in your most despondent moments, in your sunniest moments, in your moments of peace and quiet and calm—all the things you forget to say in your books—you keep writing that you're writing off your life, that tolfpoets is screwing up his life, that ondine has the feeling that she's gone astray somewhere . . . but where in your books is the reflection of the courage with which you're looking for a meadow, the courage with which you talk about the election propaganda as something that makes you seasick . . . of the joie de vivre with which you write about women in their light summer clothes . . . of the love with which you surround your household . . . of the precious humor with which you raise yourself above the gloomiest moments in your life? I hear and see the things in your life, but do not find them reflected in your books. And yet they should be there: the beauty and the humor and the courage and the humor of the individual, amid the frenzy with which society is rushing to its doom. You need us, you need the music master and johan janssens and tolfpoets, because without us your book would be a black snowball, growing fatter and gloomier and more dangerous, and would plunge into the abyss even before our disintegrating society does. I feel like eckermann beside goethe—though I write down many things incorrectly, and though I lash out more than I soothe—but in that way, like eckermann, I feel as important as goethe himself. Drum up all your heroes and heroines, question them, call them to account, and you'll hear and see that they're all vital to your 2nd book on chapel road—and when you drum them up, don't forget tippetotje again, whom I met yesterday over in brussels, and who asked me: what's this about that bottle? He writes that I visited him, bearing a bottle! And it's not true: I didn't visit and I'm not even allowed to drink out of bottles because I've got stomach ulcers. So drum up all your heroes, and they'll say that you're inclined to see everything blacker than it is, to give into a kind of despondency, a wrong-headed tendency to give up the fight—ondine and oscarke always tend to say: oh come on, that's how it is, why try to change it? You'll go on writing till your last gasp, but it will always go on raining in your books, if I, mossieu colson, don't hold an umbrella over your papers, and don't inform the reader that it will be fine again tomorrow . . . it will always be gloomy and dark, burdened and loaded, if tolfpoets doesn't make the occasional quip . . . you'll shut yourself up too much in the bitterness of your heart, if the music master doesn't come along and throw open the window of your mind . . . you would retreat from the battle far too quickly if johan janssens, housepainter and weekly journalist, did not bring you back again and again to the thick of the battle for Existence.

THE MEADOW

And you ask your heroes whether or not they are going to be involved in your 2nd book on chapel road . . . you ask the music master but he waves his hand dismissively as he starts to negotiate the unmanned railroad crossing over there: I've no time, he shouts, I've got to go to the meadow that I've bought. And as you hurry after him he tells you: looking for some kind of farm, where you wanted to write your 2nd book at your leisure, you wondered if it would become a life Outside of life—but what difference does it make to me whether it becomes a life Outside of life?—you turned my head with that "some kind of farm," and I started looking too. And I found a farm, but it was an ugly house that had taken off from the center of town flapping its wings and, scratching itself, had landed in the middle of the fields. And when I went to see it, I made a mistake, and accidentally looked at a very beautiful and ancient farmhouse that I immediately got excited about, and so started haggling with the farmer—but then I found out that I'd got it wrong: the farm for sale is over there! said the farmer. And I looked with revulsion at that ghastly eyesore of a city bird perched there, and some time later tolfpoets said to me: but you're looking everywhere for some kind of farm, and no one ever bothers to go and look at my uncle amadeus's farm, which is also up for sale! But I didn't go and look at it, because I suspect in advance a farm connected to tolfpoets's family will be far too humorous a farm, full of unexpected jokes and novelties - apple trees that produce pears and cows that lay eggs. And how it happened I don't remember, but I, the music master, incited by you, longed for some kind of farm . . . though everyone connected with me and my life talked not of a farm but of a meadow: the music master wants to buy a bit of woodland, they said first . . . and afterwards they talked about a bit of meadow: we happen to know where there's a nicely located meadow, they said. And I went and looked at that bit of meadow and met a troublemaker of a farmer who owned the property next to the woods and may have poached rabbits or chopped firewood there . . . I don't like trouble and I didn't go back. And then they took me to the meadow of a horse dealer, who persuaded me that the land was full of loam and even fetched a spade. But did I want loam or solitude? And since he couldn't dig up solitude with his spade, I left. Oh, because I longed for solitude they took me to the top of a hill, that is, to the side of a hill . . . a dream, a solitary dream of a dream, from where I saw the sun sinking below on the horizon, and where I heard the blackbird in a neighboring wood singing for rain. This is where my dream is, I said. And they nodded and said we thought so, it's just a shame that this hillside is not for sale. And I slunk off in shame, and in revenge bought another meadow . . . a meadow that was not my dream, but that (as these things go in the world) I might be able to make into my dream, provided I worked long and hard, provided I closed my eyes, and provided I toned down my expectations. I bought that bit of meadow solely because it turned out to be dirt cheap, something that someone was giving away for nothing, as it were, so that I rushed to the notary in too much of a hurry, for fear that someone would beat me to it. And when I got to the notary's office, in the presence of the farmer selling the land, the notary's clerk, and the lender, the price suddenly grew into a sum I'd never even heard mentioned before . . . let alone one I'd ever have agreed to: there were registration fees, surveyor's fees, duties, commission for the notary, 5% for the lender, 12% tax, and now I'd better shut up, because the more calculations I do the more is added on. And there I stood and couldn't afford the meadow: I was standing there buying something I didn't want—and at the same time I couldn't even afford.

And the music master goes quiet, crossing the distant railway line beyond termuren . . . and extends his arm and says: that's my meadow over there, look!

FOR FREEDOM AND PROSPERITY

So there lies the 1st book on chapel road and johan janssens is just leafing through it with a certain disdain, and equally unsolicited is just pronouncing a disdainful verdict on it: very briefly summarized, the book reads as follows: *in 1800-and-something, when ondineke was still a girl with 2 braids bobbing on her back, the bloody battle for prosperity and freedom began . . . and if ondineke had not enjoyed the protection of mr derenancourt of the castle—a special protection, let's call it—she'd have had go to work at the age of twelve in the filature spinning mill, she'd have stood there from early morning till late at night, she would have had no vote and no old age pension for the time when she was old and worn out, she wouldn't have belonged to a workers' medical plan . . . but if she had been good all her life, she would have been allowed to go to heaven.* At the same time, there's another thread running through the book: the present day, when people are starting to forget the bloody struggle for freedom and prosperity and to sink back into that cesspool from which our parents emerged, with blood and dirt under their bent and torn fingernails, with sweat and dust in the furrows across their faces, with tears of rage and pain in their eyes. And we their children live on, as long as appearances are kept up and we don't hear the grinding of the clapped-out machinery. And the end of the book: where we, a few frugal individuals, go in search of a farmstead, a refuge of our own, to go on working there quietly, all alone. But isn't that fear of life and flight from life? Because on that bit of farmstead won't we, the last of the mohicans, surrender ourselves to the existentialist joy of the present moment? Won't we start saying that only a few moments count in our lives, a few moments of deep happiness, contentment, beauty?

And johan janssens, after pronouncing that disdainful critique of your book on chapel road, stares out through the window at that chapel road—eternal subject—where the festive banner of the victorious party hangs (true, it's hanging limp and listless in the july heat, but it's hanging there nonetheless), and johan janssens can't help adding: I can go along with your leaving chapel road, but only on the condition that you continue your struggle on your bit of a farmstead, the struggle for . . . for . . . And he falls silent. Johan janssens, who was probably going to say "for freedom and prosperity," falls silent . . . And afterwards he says, perhaps a little too theatrically: our forefathers fought for all this, their faces covered in blood and tears . . . we were hated and had the bread stolen out of our mouths and were refused holy communion and locked up in prisons—and those who jeered at and kicked our fathers . . . and were forced to concede the right of association with suppressed fury, countenanced education in impotent fury, reluctantly recognized the 8-hour day and may day . . . they themselves have now paid millions for an election battle in which—with loudspeakers, cars, and planes—they have defiled the beautiful slogans our fathers perished for: for freedom and prosperity. They themselves locked freedom up in prison and wrapped prosperity in rags, they made the people work 10 and 12 hours a day, they kept the people poor and ignorant—and now they are bellowing everywhere: for freedom and prosperity! And while those poor, blind, ignorant people return to slavery, you on your little farmstead can celebrate the beauty of the moment . . . the blackbird singing in the rain, and the rustling of the leaves in the poplars. But will it be a book . . . or garbage?

YOU CAN'T MAKE AN OMELETTE . . .

Stop, wait a minute! cries mossieu colson of the ministry . . . wait a bit before you draw a line under "for freedom and prosperity," because I've got news from the election front: that bunch on the right, the victors, who bellowed from their cars and planes and loudspeakers that they stand for freedom and prosperity, have also published a manifesto featuring the photo of an apache, who is of course meant to represent the image of someone on the far left . . . wait, I've got the photo here with me: and do you know that man? It's the squire of the castle, the owner of the filature spinning mill, the son of the clerical minister and party leader, the brother of his holiness the illustrious dignitary monsignor and bishop . . . but he's put grease on his face and pulled on a cap at an angle—of course he didn't need to imitate that leer, since he has it naturally. And after we had studied the photo with more and more disdain, mossieu colson adds this: and below this fake photo they put the following caption: they excuse their crimes, murder included, with the saying: "you can't make an omelet without breaking some eggs," their methods are constantly changing, but the dominant aim remains the same. And they don't write this of themselves but of the left-wingers . . . who to judge by their thinking must all have greasy faces and wear their caps at an angle. No, just as they photographed themselves, they wrote a descriptive piece about themselves . . . but they subsequently hung it up as a portrait of the others.

15

And tolfpoets nods—tolfpoets who worked for the liberals—and he says: that's what the clericals do, that's right . . . but do you know what the pinkos did? they touched on the 50-year struggle just in passing, with a drawing of the ragged proletariat, and the wealthy socialist prime minister who gets them out of their rags and gives them a nice suit—as if that were the end of the struggle, as if it was He who took things this far . . . as if He were one of the socialist leaders of the past, who perished and died in the bloody struggle for slightly higher wages and a more human life. And everyone looks at tolfpoets, because for once, quite by accident, he grins at the right moment . . . but tolfpoets goes on unperturbed: and do you know what the blood-red reds did? in the last few days they walked themselves to a standstill along the muddy river into which the labor weaving mill and the filature spinning mill discharge . . . they walked there when the factory whistles signalled the end of work, to nod and nod to the hero of the century—the factory worker—and now if you go past the long long wall of the labor weaving mill, look to see whether you can't see a head lying anywhere, one that simply rolled off a scarlet torso with all that nodding, a head that literally nodded off.

OSCARKE HAS TO FIND A JOB

When the days had passed in all kinds of scheming, ondine would lie down beside oscarke in the strange bed . . . oscarke scarcely touched her, he was disgusted by those things, he couldn't handle them and had no urge to do them—yes, it was just as his father, and his mother too had said: despite everything he was still a child. He had gone home to fetch his potter's clay, and now he wanted to start by modeling her . . . but she had no time to sit, she had to go farther and farther in search of little shops, hunting for coffee and sugar and salt. And anyway, modeling her . . . she just couldn't sit still from the agony of the bedbugs: it seemed to her that people would be able tell from the image how it had been made in the midst of stinking poverty. If it were exhibited, everyone—mr ludovic gourmonprez from the labor, and that fat glemmasson, and even the commercial director van wesenborgh—would spot the poverty and the bedbugs in the sculpture. And she'd counted off the rich acquaintances of her youth, but she hadn't listed Him yet, the ideal of her youth: mr achilles derenancourt. And thinking of him . . . always thinking of him but never mentioning him . . . thinking of the man who had set her youth on fire, with whom she had lived in the castle and to all of whose strange whims she had catered (lain down naked by the fire, spoken french, and made herself the scandal and laughingstock of the whole of termuren) crying, stamping her foot, suffering with headaches, she could not forgive him for taking monique away from school . . . it was ok for him to ravage her, ondine, morally and physically, but ONLY her, not the whole of madame berthe's school. She found it even more difficult to forgive him for passing monique on to an office manager, a commercial director . . . while he'd left ondine with her hair blowing out of the window—as people said, with some justice, in termuren. She'd let him defile and besmirch that youth of hers, and as a reward had become a desperately poor woman . . . had come here to a room above the café of the 1st grimy houses, where the bedbugs were having a field day . . . god had deceived her, the world had deceived and ridiculed her. And she rushed at the living crucifixion and burned it, she cursed herself, and she cursed oscarke sitting over there next to a shapeless lump of potter's clay . . . and she knocked the styluses out of his hand and squashed the clay till the whole face was distorted . . . and the mouth, on which he had worked . . . or, to be more exact, had messed around with for three days . . . was obliterated. Messed around, yes, that was more accurate. You'd do better to learn your trade, because you haven't much of a clue, she said. And for that matter, that drawing! . . . and she took out the drawing he'd once made of her, over on the heath . . . that had been folded inside her French missal . . . she took it out: now does that look like me? she asked. And viewed critically it looked less and less like her. Get out of my sight, she shouted, and tore up the drawing. She must stop now or else nothing in the room would be left intact. Then she collapsed and started crying . . . but that too was just an act . . . because when she'd finished crying she asked oscarke to look for work, temporary work, as a farmhand somewhere. He nodded his head, since he was ready to do it, he was ready for anything . . . so what on earth was wrong with him that he had no opinion of his own about anything, anything at all? She started looking for work for him, because there was nothing for sculptors, for that he needed to be in brussels, she was told. How about going to brussels to look for work? she asked him. And again he nodded his head. At least he thought he had nodded, or she thought so . . . in reality he sat there staring at the ground without saying anything, listening to words that made no sense. To brussels for example . . . what was that, brussels? He had never seen brussels, he had never worked, he had just copied some plaster statues in clay at the art school of this little town. Off you go then . . . she said. And she gave him some money, not much, and looking on innocently he saw that her purse was bulging. But that was the money from her gold bracelet, though he didn't know it. He got up, though he had no idea what he was supposed to do once he got out into the street downstairs . . . so there he stood, staring blindly at the fronts of the 1st dirty houses, but something behind him drove him on . . . it was as if ondine were standing behind him invisibly and pushing him towards the station: he looked round, and sure enough, there she was at an upstairs window looking at him.

THE LAST WEEKLY

Johan janssens, the poet and weekly journalist and housepainter—soon you'll need a whole sheet of paper to list all his professions—comes walking along on this hot day, his arm held in a clean handkerchief: what's wrong, johan janssens, why's your arm in a sling instead of filling the weeklies with copy? And johan janssens looks gloomily at his arm, and tells us that he was bitten by nothing more than a simple mosquito, but my arm's swelled up and paralyzed and ulcerated, it's already cost me 500 francs in doctor's bills and loss of work hours . . . hold on, soon you'll be thinking that the weeklies pay me more than 500 francs, and by the hour too . . . no, it's the old painter and decorator who lives over there on the corner of thrift street who pays me by the hour, to help him paint houses. Because the weeklies, don't talk to me about them . . . if I write something that's intended as a criticism of the ultra-crimson socialists, it's automatically barred—because in matters of politics and social sciences they are omniscient and infallible, like the pope in rome is in matters of faith and morality—and so the criticism finds its way into the weekly of the pink socialists, who are delighted with it and say: johan janssens is no longer an ultra-marxist. But if I happen to write something that does fit in with the line of the ultra-crimson socialists, they print it with a lot of hoo-hah and big headlines . . . and say to the pink socialists: you see! And I, johan janssens, who don't belong in either camp, but try to speak my mind freely and independently, am put in a bad light, and regarded as a whore, who in the pink weekly is pink and in the poppy-red weekly is poppy red. No, I prefer painting house fronts for the old painter and decorator from thrift street . . . even though I always get the most difficult and dangerous jobs, since I'm the youngest and therefore supplest, the lightest and hence the first up ladders and scaffolding. But I like standing on ladders and scaffolding, because it gives me a broader view of the world.

And johan janssens looks at his arm, and arranges it a little more comfortably in the sling: and now realize once and for all that the weeklies of the pro-vatican party, the clericals and fascists, are thriving and proliferating, becoming bigger and bigger both in size and length, and that they're gaining more and more readers . . . but that the puny organ of the poppy-reds has scarcely 4 pages, and that its flame is fluttering like that of a candle in the draft of an open door . . . and that the weekly of the pink socialists, bless them, is on its last legs: people are ready to lower the blinds and give it a civil funeral. And then . . . on my way to brussels I meet tippetotje who supposedly turned up at your place carrying a bottle . . . and who no longer remembers turning up at your place carrying a bottle because she said to mossieu colson of the ministry: your writer must be dreaming, because I never drink anything out of the bottle, I've got stomach ulcers . . . and so I meet tippetotje as she's strolling along with the baron talking about hundreds of thousands . . . talking about millions . . . about an art show, about an artistic salon, about an art club, about a gallery for works of art. And I tell her that the pink weekly is on its last legs . . . it can happen any moment, tippetotje, I say with restrained sorrow. And tippetotje replies: I'm pleased about that, because that pink weekly wasn't really the real thing. And I also tell her that the crimson weekly won't publish my articles if they're not 100% to their liking . . . and tippetotje replies: they're right, they're the only ones whose knife cuts on that side. And I ask her: but imagine that there is only 1 red organ, are they only going to publish what is 100 percent in line with their viewpoint, irrespective of whether my work gropes honestly for the core of things? And tippetotje replies: we're not democrats who allow themselves to be forced into a corner. And I left tippetotje and her baron standing there with their millions, knowing that I won't be allowed or able to write for any paper, and won't be allowed or able to receive so much as another centime from any editor.

LETTER FROM TIPPETOTJE

I'm writing to you because I've met johan janssens . . . oh I meet so many people, I meet your mossieu colson of the ministry and I meet my baron and I meet bromme bast, and the editor-in-chief of the ultra-poppy-red weekly . . . I'll soon be meeting myself again in my mad rush, and I'll bang my forehead against my own forehead . . . and actually I'd like nothing better than not to have to meet anyone, but to sit down and be allowed to paint . . . oh the joy and pain of being allowed to paint . . . but instead I rush around and meet myself . . . sorry, who was it again? . . . oh yes, johan janssens. Anyway, it was about johan janssens that I was going to write to you. So I'm running around and I meet him in my mad rush in search of myself . . . I met him as he was walking along with his head between his legs . . . and I heard him say that wherever he goes he gets kicked in that head hanging between his legs. And I . . . I, tippetotje . . . gave him an extra good kick in that head, because it pains me to see him going around being the same poor prick . . . maitre pots the lawyer has come to brussels and is advising the baron, and I tippetotje the painter have come to brussels and am driving him crazy by going on and on about an art exhibition . . . and meanwhile we're both kissing his ass, but can have ten thousand conversations . . . and that's why I gave your johan janssens an extra kicking, so that it would make him mad and he would go and kiss some baron's ass for himself. That was the only reason I kicked johan janssens, while I was taking my baron for a walk . . . so that he wouldn't do his business indoors but against a tree in the park . . . yours, tippetotje.

p.s. . . . I've heard a rumor that oscarke also went to brussels to find a job . . . a shame his story takes place so far in the past, otherwise I could have given him a kick too.

DOESN'T EVERYTHING COME IN ITS OWN GOOD TIME?

Last sunday tolfpoets, the music master, and johan janssens went to the town of the 2 mills, across a carpet of manifestoes, to vote, to do their parts. I'm going for the liberals said tolfpoets, because a voice cried from heaven: votez liberale under no. 4. And I'm going for the pinks, said the music master, for I have only one god and only one wife and I want to have only one ideal—but as he was saying that he may have been thinking the opposite: I don't believe in that 1 god, and that 1 wife is all women to me, and that 1 ideal is only for want of anything better; and johan janssens said: anyway, I'm going for the far-left scarlet reds, because although the world they're going to build is not My world, they're still a counterweight to the far-right world, which is even less my own.

And that was, as was said, last sunday . . . but now it's a new sunday again and they take a completely different direction: away from the town with the 2 mills, onto the road that is supposed to take them far beyond termuren. And johan janssens is just about to say something about the recently concluded election . . . something significant but gloomy . . . that again a greater shift to the right was acceptable . . . he is just about to say that, when the music master with a grand gesture shows them his meadow. And all of them look at the meadow, silent and visibly disappointed, and johan janssens says of the meadow what he was about to say of the elections: it's like our society and just like the wavering masses that are coming down more and more on the side of the right: dry and shriveled and shaved clean for the last time by the farmer. I'm well aware of that, says the music master in defence of his meadow . . . I'm well aware, but you're just seeing my meadow as it is now, while I can already see the dream I could turn it into: over there at the back a bit of a wood that turns imperceptibly into a bit of an orchard that turns imperceptibly into a bit of a wildflower garden. And johan janssens starts to see the dream too, and jumps up and rolls up his sleeves: let's get started right away then, let's plant those woods and those fruit trees and those christmas trees . . . And let's stick flowers on the bushes and hang pears on the christmas trees, laughs tolfpoets. And mossieu colson of the ministry . . . who had fallen a bit behind because his blood is too thin . . . mossieu colson of the ministry arrives just in time to hit johan janssens over the head: and have you never wondered, johan jans-sens, whether in your struggle for a left-wing society, perhaps you shouldn't be planting now, but that on the contrary you should have planted long ago? . . . that on the contrary it's time to leave what you planted in peace . . . that on the contrary it's time to harvest? . . . that on the contrary it's time to sow? that on the contrary it's time to feed or harrow or plough? . . . that on the contrary it's time to make plans and set dreams down on paper, just as the music master is now making his paper-meadow into an earthly paradise? And johan janssens, disheartened, sits down and tolfpoets hits him over the head even harder: last sunday at the elections your left-wing friends also strewed the streets with leaflets and stuffed letterboxes full of manifestoes, but for the rest of the last 4 long years I've never seen a leaflet lying in the street or found a manifesto in my letterbox . . . and now your left-wing friends are disheartened and say very comically: the working class is not worthy of what we do for them. According to my tolfpoetsian logic I must have also have found manifestoes on Other occasions too . . . once one that showed the music master's meadow as it is . . . and some other time one that showed how working people lived 50 years ago, and then one with a list of everything that could be changed and improved . . . and then another with the plan for his dream of an earthly paradise . . . because the wavering masses of tolfpoetses, of which I am one, is slow to learn things, but very quick to forget . . . I forgot again how bad things were 50 years ago, and I don't notice whether we have it better now . . . I am a bush and need planting in october and watering in july: who'll buy me a beer?

THE DREAM ABOUT THE PIPE

And you wake up in the night, and around you things seem to have a secret life of their own . . . that is, you have the feeling that a moment ago they were in some way living, but were alarmed by your waking up and are now waiting passively in an attitude of life caught by surprise. You know, it must really be your own fault . . . just now, while you were asleep, they must have been living in your dream. You've woken up and have the feeling that you've seen an infinite number of images, or that you've seen the same image countless times, as in facing mirrors that reflect things to infinity. And you sit at the window in the night and smoke a cigarette and suddenly remember: it was a pipe—you were busy carving a huge pipe bowl from a block of wood, but the wood was hard and the knife was very blunt, and something was upsetting you beyond measure . . . it was your towers of strength, mossieu colson of the ministry and the music master . . . they were standing too close to you and kept pointing out your mistakes, they kept touching the pipe with their hands and getting in your way and trying to grab the knife. And now you remember precisely: you were just on the point of smashing the pipe to pieces.

And if dreams have a meaning, doesn't that mean that you should no longer use these interfering heroes in your book? And you sit there at night-time at the window, and feel that inanimate things are standing there in an attitude of life caught in the act . . . that is, that the moment you woke up they assumed this dead attitude, and are just waiting till you fall asleep again in order to go on living in your dream. That dead telegraph pole outside, that stretch of wall lit by the moonlight, that shadow on the wall:

they're all waiting to come to life . . . to nestle up to your dream and start living a double, quadruple, hundredfold life . . . just as the things placed between mirrors live a hundredfold life. And that pipe just now . . . there was something about that pipe . . . didn't you try smoking it? The bowl was much too narrow and there was a crack somewhere . . . Ha, and you had just said: that's what you get when you keep buying cheap stuff. And smoking your cigarette at the window at night, you feel the same sickly saturation with nicotine that you also had in your dream: it was a tasteless pipe: it was the poor taste of someone who smokes too much.

And if dreams have a meaning, does that mean you're smoking too much again?

There was a crack where the stem met the bowl . . . right next to the beard . . . ha, and now you suddenly see the pipe again: it was a Mr Right pipe, an Oriental man with a turban and a pointed beard. And you think how odd that is, to be smoking a pipe in your dreams, whereas in reality you never smoke anything but cigarettes. It was a Mr Right.

And suddenly an image from your youth pops up: as a growing kid you smoked a pipe like that for a while, a Mr Right, a man with a turban and a pointed beard . . . it was an inferior, inelegant pipe . . . and if you remember correctly: sure enough, it had a crack, just like in your dream. And you ask yourself how it's possible for all those dead things to go on proliferating in you, like objects between mirrors that reproduce themselves ad infinitum. It's been, let's see, 20 years now that that pipe has gone on living inside you.

And if dreams have a meaning . . . but perhaps they have no meaning and it's just like this: all those dead things your memory frees itself from take revenge by coming back to life at night in your dreams, and multiplying a hundredfold as in a hall of mirrors.

TOLFPOETS'S TRICKS

And suddenly you're sitting there in your study without enthusiasm . . . there is repugnance, disgust, reluctance in you . . . your room has become almost like a cell, with walls concealed by rows of books, *thicke bookes*, yet still vain and empty—your ashtray and wastepaper basket are overflowing but the sheet of paper in front of you is blank . . . and you run away through the unmanned railroad barrier, far beyond termuren, and to your amazement you see a new house there in the middle of the countryside: it's tolfpoets's so-called villa. And tolfpoets chases off his stupid young guard dog, and bares his 2 gold teeth in a smile, and shouts over the fence: would you believe that you were rather reluctant to go on using us in your work . . . and now you yourself have come to visit me, to ask, to beg me to go on collaborating with you . . . I'm prepared

22

to go on collaborating, but now on one condition: I must have a different role, or a bigger role . . . I must have the occasional corner all to myself, where I can play my tolfpoetsian tricks . . . anyway, I'm not always the man you make me out to be . . . I do tell jokes but I don't always tell jokes, I also concern myself with strange and mysterious things, just as the story of your pipe was mysterious . . . theosophical matters I could call them, although they have nothing to do with the religion of andré the theosophist . . . no, rather more in this vein: when I had only just met my wife maria, she wanted me to go to her family's place and ask for her hand officially—may I have your daughter maria's Hand there, mr what's-his-face—and on my way to her place I got the houses mixed up . . . she said: we live at 117 . . . and by mistake I walked past it and rung the bell at 127 . . . yes, you can laugh, but what happens? At 127 the front door is opened by my maria, because she's always in and out of the neighbor's house. That was my first story, and now I give you my second story: walking through the town of the 2 mills with my wife maria, *I suddenly think of your heroine ondine . . . who by now must be old and toothless and virtually blind . . . and I think of her husband . . . what's-it, what's his name again? . . . and I ask her: whereabouts do you suppose what's-it lives, maria? And maria stops and gives me a quizzical stare: are you pulling my leg or what, asking me where what's-it lives just as we reach the house where he lives? And I stop too and look at the house, and sure enough, what's-it comes out of it . . . what's his name again . . . oscarke . . . a quiet guy with a tuft of gray hair on the back of his head.* And tolfpoets looks at you with a strange smile, leaning over the garden fence of his so-called villa . . . and because you stare at him in silence and are expecting something more he throws in the following tolfpoetsian trick: if you overlook some of my idiosyncrasies you'll see that I can knock a story together as well as the next person . . . but you mustn't mind if I keep getting figures and numbers wrong . . . I'm no good at that . . . and you mustn't mind either if I keep forgetting the names of things . . . things are all things to me . . . a tree is a thing and oscarke is a thing . . . but naturally you must spell Thingumee with a capital letter to indicate that it refers to a person, as opposed to just things, which are only things. Ah, and I remember a joke about that: I was once in a shop when Thingumee came in and asked for a thing for a thingumee.

And you hurry away from tolfpoets and his so-called villa, you hurry back home, to your study, and regret lending an ear to that tolfpoets stuff . . . *and it's true, how could he talk so comically about things . . . eh, about oscarke?*

I DIDN'T FIND WORK

By the time oscarke made it to the station it was no longer all that early, since the train was full of students and clerks and travelers . . . he felt desperately alone

23

. . . or no, not desperate, just alone. He felt alone in the train, and he felt alone in the overpowering gare du nord in brussels, where all the others immediately rushed off: they knew where they were going, they all had work . . . but he didn't, he would never find work in brussels, and he looked up at the great house with his small, timid heart: how could they possibly need a sculptor here? And he sat down on a bench with the botanical garden behind him, and in front of him he saw streetcars and soldiers and notre pain baker's carts . . . he didn't understand brussels, it was too big, it spoke a language that was alien to him. And he sat there just as he did at home, looking at the ground and listening to his inner voices . . . he ate his sandwiches and dozed off for a bit, and didn't dare leave the bench for fear that he would never be able to find his way back to the gare du nord. What a crazy idea of ondine's this had been! It was easy for her to say: find work in brussels. Like she had said: and apply for a worker's season ticket, that's cheaper. And he'd applied for a worker's season ticket, but he had been sent from the station to the town hall for a copy of his birth certificate signed by the mayor. How could they ask him to go to the town hall, just like that, and say to the mayor: could you just sign a job-seeker's certificate for me? Still, he had gone . . . but what a surprise he got when he found a whole line of people waiting their turn . . . and what do you know, he didn't have to see the mayor anyway, there was a man with a goatee—just like his father used to wear . . . was this man also in the habit of spending his whole salary on feeding frogs' legs to whores?—and he signed the form: oscarke could then clear off and make way for the people behind him. And now, here on the bench in the botanical garden, he wondered what had become of those men . . . had they just come for a form saying they were job-seekers? And they were job-seekers, weren't they? Finally he stood up, and finally had to leave the bench . . . his bench . . . where he'd grown stiff and numb with sitting. What was he going to say to her back home? He didn't know, he longed to be on the train, and to be back home quickly and to be left alone and to go on playing with his clay. But at the gare du nord he was stopped at the barrier: this was the exit, not the entrance . . . and when he found the entrance it wasn't for workers' season tickets . . . workers' season tickets were further on over there, or else at a different station, the allee-verte. He didn't understand what they meant, he thought they were trying to keep him prisoner in brussels and pushed his way through, between madame with parcels and madame with children . . . he found a niche on the train and listened to a workman who explained where the other station was and advised him to take the 4.05 train the next morning: that was a workers' train.

Ondine looked at him, but he did not look at ondine . . . I didn't find work, he said. Once again he only had plain bread to eat, because she hadn't cooked, she'd been out marauding all afternoon, buying all kinds of goods without paying for them, and singing the praises of her husband who had been summoned to brussels for a big commission, a statue. Oscarke pushed away the bread and the coffee and

24

got straight to work on the clay . . . he tried to repair the mouth, which she had squashed . . . but he worked without much enthusiasm, since he would have to turn in soon to be ready very early the next morning.

FROM THICKE BOOKES

It's certainly true what mossieu colson of the ministry says: that everything you write is too heavy and too ponderous, that it gives no light and no hope . . . and that it doesn't even manage to point to any consolation—it's a consolation but a small one, said victorine. But look, it's july and summer and you should be at the seaside or in the ardennes, you should be in kempen, or in paris or prague, but instead of that you're by the sickbed of your wife, who once again is having a nervous crisis. A crisis brought on by a badly functioning liver, or a badly functioning liver brought on by nervous strain—not a single doctor seems to know which—and so you sit there, and what else can you do but pick up some thick book or other, and shortly afterwards put it down again and look at the thick dust sticking to your hands . . . because what you happen to have in your hand is a book on mental disorders: a mighty-looking book on the outside, with gilt edges, and if you dare open it you'll find that science knows All about mental illness . . . but that if someone is mentally ill, they can't be cured. And you clean the dust sticking to your hands and select another book, a history of art, equally impressive and gilt-edged . . . and you open it by chance at the page on the metsijs family, quinten, jan, and cornelis, but all you find are the commonplaces we all already know about quinten . . . no, there's something about his son cornelis too: how he included lusty peasants in a landscape painting. And that's that. Really: period. Not a word about jan. Although you know that jan was banned and outlawed by the clerics, and that his work went up in flames at the stake because there was nothing in or about it that related to religion. And you remember that one rare work by jan metsijs is still hanging in a brussels museum, something that did happen to have a religious subject . . . but that, unnoticed by the inquisitors of the day, is actually as irreligious as it is great: a chaste susanna, but so beautiful, as cold as if it were by delvaux . . . a woman awakening from a dream, in a landscape that belongs to all ages and is hence timeless . . . although it's slightly reminiscent of a greek landscape . . . rough, wild mountains, with cold attic columns in the foreground. And in this landscape the woman awakes, and gazes uncomprehendingly around her. Yet this woman is in fact too pagan, simply too pagan, to be called modern . . . jan metsijs's hope and confidence lies quite simply in the pagan world, but our hopes and our confidences are too severely shaken every day for us to be simply pagan . . . there's not only sick fear and equally sick despair in us, but there's also sarcasm and eternal skepticism. Fear and despair, skepticism and doubt have taken root too deeply in our blood for us to be simply pagan, as jan metsijs was in his single remaining canvas. Nowadays one paints a naked woman . . . but even the blind, inanimate point of the brush approaches the canvas full of fear and skepticism, paints the nipple in despair, since no one knows whether by the next day that nipple will have disintegrated into atoms. But all that aside, the solitary surviving work by jan metsijs makes up for all those dying christs, all those christmas cribs and adorations of the magi: it is close to us, it belongs to Our world. And in addition, it belongs to our world by the very fact of its having depicted that woman, that woman waking from a pagan dream under a misleading mask:

>red thigh—oh god is great
>red ass—oh great is god.

And the writer of today who sees his books banned and burned still has to work in the same way:

>red ass—oh democracy
>red nipple of a burgeoning breast—oh social situation of
>some other place where things are dire, but not here.

Because no one is great enough to embrace the world and the age, and as we all advance towards a very great and very distant goal, the best work, the most liberated work, the work that comes closest to that aimless goal, is repeatedly banned and burned . . . and writers and painters are eternally compelled to mask their forbidden truth beneath a permitted lie. And you clean the gray dust off your hands and put those thicke bookes away . . . since they contain nothing but dates and lies . . . the emptiness of the vessel and the rattle of the skeleton. For the rest you must make sure you cure yourself of your nerves, and discover the living beauty of the past for yourself.

I HEAR THE EVENING POUT

I hear the evening pout, said the poet gazelle . . . and every time you were lonely at the campsite and the evening silence fell around you, you muttered that one sentence almost like a prayer . . . I hear the evening pout . . . and what could be more beautiful or more exact? But now you're sitting at the open window gazing at chapel road in the twilight, while your wife lies on her sickbed behind you . . . she has bad nerves that must stem from some kind of grief, some fear, some turmoil . . . and you're at the window alone in your calm, from which you can hear the evening pout: we're all lonely and alone. And over there in the evening twilight a figure comes walking along—isn't it johan janssens?—johan janssens, you're alone too . . . alone with the turmoil of your bad nerves, or alone in your calm, from which you hear the evening pout? Neither, says johan janssens . . . or, that is, with both, since I'm filled with turmoil and regret and irritation, but on the other hand I'm also filled with the beautiful joy of a new discovery . . . I've just come from the flemish library that we've reopened, professor spothuyzen and I . . . an ugly old room where you have to fight heroically against the layers of dust collected from all the years of decline . . . and a catalog with hundreds of works we've all been looking for for years but have never found . . . only empty bookshelves, from which all the books that we've been trying to find for years have disappeared. Disappeared: perhaps stolen, perhaps lost, perhaps burned by the germans, perhaps left behind during one of the 120 moves from one stuffy room to another, or else casually borrowed and just as casually never returned . . . how should I know? . . . a lopsided old room with the dull thud of horses' hooves behind the wall, since there's a stable around the back, I think . . . a cracked ceiling, and lumps of plaster falling from time to time onto you and on the books . . . on the few books left that we sardonically call: the Remnants. The last remnants that were not worth stealing or burning or forgetting to return. And professor spothuyzen and I wiped the dust off those last remnants and listed them in a new catalogue. But no one came . . . no one except 2 boys and a girl who had got the wrong room, and looked around in bewilderment: isn't this the Ping-Pong room anymore? And just came in and messed up the bookshelves a bit, thinking it was kind of like Ping-Pong and laughing spitefully at some dirty joke or other they told in the meantime. So, that was my regret and irritation. But there was also a beautiful joy in me, because suddenly I discovered a friend, a writer, a man . . . p. f. van kerkhoven . . . I'd never heard of him, but he was a contemporary of prudens van duyse, of hendrik conscience (who supposedly "taught his people to read") and de laet and karel lodewijk ledeganck . . . but all his life he attacked those quacks and punctured those windbags . . . he wrote novels that paved the way for zetternam and vuylsteke. A great man then . . . dammit, he taught his people to swear properly. And that's the reason for my beautiful joy this evening, joy tempered by regret and irritation because no one knows him, no one has read him, because on the one hand people are still mesmerized by that old windbag conscience, and on the other hand they've got the wrong room and want to play Ping-Pong. And johan janssens leaves you and you're alone with your beautiful joy, dampened by equally beautiful regret and irritation . . . and your wife lies behind you, alone with her nerves, and you remain alone at the window, in the calm from which you can hear the evening pout.

THE DARK

And then it's night . . . it's night and dark and quiet . . . and in the silence of the night and the darkness your wife wanders about with her nerves: she bangs her head against the walls, and against the mirror. And you switch on the red bedside lamp and rush to help . . . you hug your wife, who is blundering around and bumping into everything with her head and her nerves. But is it nerves, or is it . . . ? No, it's best not to say these things, it's best if some things remain unsaid, that some things are not born as words, if they do not even become unspoken thoughts. It is best if some things remain unborn, remain in Nonexistence, in the silence and speechlessness of the night . . . in the Dark. She is walking around like a little, scared, crying child, she looks at herself in the mirror and holds her hands in front of her face to protect her . . . I'm frightened, she wails, like a small, scared child wails . . . and you put your arms round her, around her cool, bare shoulders, and you ask *what* she's afraid of . . . what are you frightened of, my little love? And she raises her hand to protect herself and screams . . . no, wails . . . she wails on and on like a small scared child: I'm frightened. And you put your arms more urgently round her cool smooth arms . . . round her cool smooth neck, around her fading but pounding breasts . . . oh, where are the days when you wrote poems about your lover's breasts . . . these breasts are fading . . . they are breasts whose youth has gone, which have withstood fear and heartache and hunger and bombing, which are fading and whose nerves are shot. I'm frightened. What are you frightened of, my dear little darling? And she wails and cries, and the tears drip over you, over your hands . . . oh, I don't know where I am anymore . . . I don't know who I am anymore . . . I'm FRIGHTened. And you hold her in your arms and calm her fear, her turmoil, her grief. Because she is also sad: I think of you, I think of our child that I love so much, and I'm afraid. You mustn't be frightened, my darling little love. And you calm her and take her to bed and give her a pastille, a pill, a powder . . . or 20 drops from a bottle in a glass of water . . . or something else, always something new, always a miracle remedy, a special cure, something costing over 100 francs. And she swallows it and calms down a bit, she goes on crying quietly while her heart hurts a bit, and her wrists. Tomorrow she'll say: I think I was a bit tired, I've been overdoing things a bit lately, or else: perhaps I should have more to do . . . I drink too much tea and coffee and eat too much greasy food, or perhaps I don't eat enough fat. Tomorrow the doctor will come and write a new prescription, something costing more than 100 francs . . . and he'll say . . . well, nerves . . . and he'll ease himself into his car and drive off. And suddenly, at night when it's quiet and dark, you wife starts wailing again like a scared little child: I'm frightened.

But you, my wife, what are you actually afraid of? And when you ask her that the day after, when the dark and the black of night have gone . . . she says nothing.

It was still dark at 4 A.M., when oscarke had to leave for the station . . . in fact it was still night . . . and he thought it was stupid, how was he supposed to find work in the dark, when he couldn't find any in the daylight? It was a train full of workers, all the ones who had lined up for their forms the day before, and oscarke felt rather ashamed when he thought of yesterday's train, where he had sat with higher-class people. He looked round and wondered if these people too had a goal in brussels like his, and also thought of his bench, far away in the botanical garden. But there were two young men on the train who had been to art school with him, and who were also looking for work . . . they were laughing and enjoying job-hunting, they made fun of everything they saw on the train . . . They had been the same at art school, always laughing and breaking plaster figures and throwing pellets of clay at the ceiling. He, oscarke, had not been like that . . . he'd always been amenable, always meek . . . from home to art school and from art school back home. But it did him good to meet them . . . and they too were glad to have someone around to boost their hopes: we'll walk all over brussels, they said . . . we'll go to the covered market, we'll go and look at the slaughterhouses in cureghem. Oh, he could feel his temperature rising, perhaps they'd find a sculptor for him on their way. But the train was getting later and later, and it was almost broad daylight outside . . . we won't even be there by evening at this rate, someone said . . . there's been a train crash, said someone else. And oscarke wondered how this person knew. Later a guard said that two trains had collided head-on at jette and that they had to get off: their train wasn't going any further . . . two groups formed that continued on foot and would try to head for a streetcar, but oscarke's two sidekicks wanted to go and see the crash up close . . . in their lives they wanted to see everything that was broken and disrupted: they traveled on as far as they could and goggled at the smashed carriages. Their train returned to where it had started from, they were the only passengers left, the three of them had the whole train to themselves: they thought the whole Belgian rail network was theirs. They crawled from carriage to carriage, they lay full-length on the seats, climbed up into the luggage net, and could see through the windows that the whole railway was in disarray: here was a train that could go no further, here was one traveling back: they whooped and laughed and were happy about it: they smashed a window and pulled the emergency cord and then quickly ran to another carriage. And they said to the guard who came hurrying along, they said: we saw him jump out of the window, he ran into that wood . . . and the stupid guard chased after that fiction through the woods, followed by the fireman and the driver. They, in the train, roared with pleasure . . . oscarke did not, he had remained the same, he was afraid, he was always afraid . . . he was always cold, and now again he was huddled in the corner: to be able to crawl into a corner was all he longed for in life. They came

and sat beside him and asked what the matter was . . . and he apologized with
some incidental excuse, some incidental lie; that it was fine for them to laugh, they
were young . . . but that he was married and had to look after a wife. And that
made them laugh too: they thought that being married was a joke . . . they asked
him things that embarrassed him: what it was like with a woman? And he didn't
dare answer, no, on the contrary, he couldn't *answer, because he knew nothing*
about it himself. They started on about the girls they'd laid in the grass, and he
was all ears: these were things he would never have suspected.

He told ondine that there had been a train crash . . . and he tried to sweep his
guilt under the carpet by making it sound as though he'd nearly been in the crash
himself . . . but ondine asked him why he hadn't continued on foot . . . he was
almost there, he could have caught a streetcar. He looked at her in bewilderment,
and thought of the people who had done just this . . . and he couldn't shake the
feeling that ondine was somehow all-knowing, that she could see from her room
who had acted correctly . . . and who on the contrary had had some fun and
smashed some train windows. You have to find work tomorrow, she said: if not,
I'll go and have a look. And she didn't say another word all evening.

SICKWIT THE STUDENT'S CAT

A little while ago the evening was like an oven . . . but now night's fallen
and it's still as hot as the boiler room of the labor weaving mill when camiel
the boilerman levels off his fire. It's murderous, that's all you can say about
it. And while the lightning flashes in the distance and indoors the standard
lamp is on, the windows are wide open to the scorching night so that all
the mosquitoes and even a late-night pedestrian can look inside. A late-night
pedestrian . . . no, there are 3 of them: tolfpoets who with his wife maria can
no longer stand it in their so-called villa in this outrageous heat, and sickwit
the student, who's on vacation. I'm on vacation, says sickwit, but where should
I go? . . . I've been invited to cycle to Luxembourg, and I've been invited to sail
to Ireland on a cargo boat carrying cattle. And tolfpoets blurts out unasked:
so one trip would be by bike and the other by cow. And he also blurts out:
and you might even learn to moo, but brushing the flies off with your tail
will be a bit trickier. But sickwit doesn't recognize tolfpoetsian humor, all
he knows about is sickwitted sarcasm, and he answers tolfpoets: I think a
cow is an insufferable creature that's far too much like a human being; it lets
itself be driven into a field surrounded by barbed wire, and on top of that
lets itself be milked. And sickwit considers the dog a stupid animal too—it's
far too gullible and loyal, it begs in the corner for a lump of sugar, and then
defends its owner's wealth with its life. This is held up to schoolchildren as an
example of good conduct . . . And at school they're also told the fable of the

grasshopper and the ant: the ant who goes through life dumb and blind and works itself to death is praised to the skies, while the grasshopper is ridiculed for being a poet. They're taught how faithful the dog is, and how patient the cow. I, sickwit, would much rather hold up the example of the cat . . . I would point out that the cat is always on its guard, that it always stops in the doorway so that you can't open or shut the door . . . that it turns away when you call it, and refuses the meat it's offered. It's indifferent to flattery, but is brave in danger, courageous when defending itself and its young . . . it has a well-balanced cerebrum and always lands on its feet. In my view the cat must be incredibly old . . . that is, must have a very distant history behind it, since otherwise it's incredible that it should act so cautiously and sensibly. I'm not sure, but in my view the cat must have a much longer history than man, for example. Men and dogs and cows and ants are not that old, they're still unsuspecting and stupid and industrious, and trust blindly. The cat has unlearned its blind trust in the multitude of disasters it's been through, in the ice ages it's experienced, the deluges it's survived, the nuclear fissions from which it's escaped. But just as the spiral development of history put it through these hellish epochs, it also gave it some heavenly interludes . . . the cat remembers not only the ice age, it also remembers the golden age, in which there was no need to be so industrious and frugal, or to struggle so bitterly for existence. The cow, the ant, and the bee know nothing of golden ages . . . all they do is gather, they work themselves to the bone, and in that blind and ignorant faith they would make a new golden age possible . . . were it not for man the exploiter, who robs all their stores, all their surplus. The cat *does* remember the golden age, but remembers even more clearly that such a period is always followed by dark ages, where snow and ice hold the upper hand and squeeze the life out of everything . . . and for that reason it doesn't believe so naïvely in heaven, where there'll be rice pudding for all. It takes a very superior view of that rice-pudding-heaven that people and dogs and cows believe in. And so it also takes a superior view of people and dogs, who are not as old as it is and whose naivety it knows all too well. It takes a superior view of men, who have a lot to learn before they reach its level . . . and it takes a superior view of dogs, looking up to man foolishly and with blind faith. The cat has no master, it is its own master . . .

But the cat does have one thing in common with us, says tolfpoets, interrupting him. And sickwit looks down from the heights of his sarcasm at that funny tolfpoets person: and what might that be? And tolfpoets looks at his wristwatch, which shows 2 A.M., and says: that it also makes the most noise at night. And having said this he disappears into the scorching night with his wife maria, in the direction of their so-called villa. And only sickwit stays seated, and he tells you something else, about his stomach aching all the time.

Far away tolfpoets disappears into the night with his wife maria, in the direction of the lightning in the distance . . . and sickwit the student who has
stayed seated round your standard lamp and watches their disappearing figures, says: the foul weather is coming closer, And you smile, because though
he's a philologist he keeps using odd language, just now he was talking about
hay and stray, and now he's talking about the fowl weather. I don't give two
hoots about grammar, says sickwit, because just try looking it all up, about
belgian dutch, about *le mot juste*, about stylistic and poetic exercises . . . read it,
and it's scary, because they're chopping a living language into dead firewood.
A while back I went to see that so-called villa of tolfpoets's, and in the distance across the fields I saw a sandstone cut into the shape of a cross, and there
was a date carved into it, 1700, and it said underneath that there had been a
"reverse" there at that time. And that stonemason in 1700 must have been
someone like me, thinking that "reverse" is the opposite of happiness, the
reverse, turnaround, around, reversion, happy and unhappy chance, fair and
fowl weather, welfare and ill-fare. So what the language experts say leaves me
completely cold.

And as the storm comes nearer, and the sheet lightning is no longer sheet
lightning but lightning followed by approaching rumbles . . . as you say to
sickwit: I don't think you've got a great deal of confidence in scholarship!
Boom, and the lightning strikes somewhere, and at the same time there are
cracks and crashes, and the rain slaps the ground with a thousand flat palms.
I'd have confidence in scholarship says sickwit, if there were no scholars . . .
because it's them I don't trust, because I know them like I know myself: I've
had a stomachache for quite a while, and the doctor says it's a duodenal ulcer
and then gives me an injection . . . and now I have strange dreams at night, I
dream I'm a woman and my breasts are hurting, and I go back to the doctor
who gives me another injection and I tell him about my dreams . . . I tell
him about them, for no special reason . . . and he replies: it's not really all
that strange, because I'm injecting you with female hormones. Boom: that
was another lightning bolt and a crash of thunder, and rivers of rain flooding
down. Female hormones, I ask the doctor, isn't that dangerous? No, says the
doctor, they're very good for stomach ulcers. They may be good for stomach
ulcers, but I'm asking if they're dangerous. And he looks me up and down
as though he'd heard distant thunder, just like we can hear the thunder in
chapel road at the moment: if it's good for stomach ulcers, it's good . . . and
if it's good then it can't do any harm. You don't understand, I go on, I'm
asking if they can harm the whole complex apparatus of the organism . . .
you think a human being is made up of assembled parts, of a heart that must

be given strychnine, plus a stomach that can be surgically removed, plus the liver into which up until now it hasn't been possible to make incisions . . . but you're wrong, the heart and the stomach and the liver are interlinked parts of a complex mechanism . . . and aren't you confusing that mechanism by injecting it with something essentially alien to it? And the doctor shrugs his shoulders, like this: half thoughtful, half dismissive of his nascent doubts . . . while pursing his lips: no, I don't think so, I've never heard anything about that, I don't suppose it's true, or likely to be, I mean . . . but you know what . . . if I were to inject too much, it's possible that your mammary glands would start secreting milk. And now do you see, says sickwit the student, why I don't trust those guys? . . . my stomach ulcer hurts less, but my very nature is in turmoil, soon I'll turn into an abnormal creature who has to be locked up somewhere . . . because night after night I dream I'm a woman, and in my dream I heap curses on the head of that doctor, and cry out: look what you've turned me into!

And sickwit the student looks outside, at chapel road, where rivers are flooding down in the darkness, and he says: it's raining even harder . . . I'll be off home, to bed, to my weird dreams.

THE BLANK WALL

All night long new rivers have poured down, and in the morning it's chilly and rainy and forlorn—sure enough, it's raining again in your books—and johan janssens the housepainter walks past. Laden with cans and ladders and brushes: where are you off to, johan janssens, surely you can't paint houses in the rain? No, I've got an indoor job, I've got to put emulsion on a couple of ceilings in that so-called villa of tolfpoets's. And he puts down his cans and ladders, and starts telling you about sickwit the student who dropped in to see him . . . That's not possible, you say, he was at my place till 2 A.M., it was fowl weather and it was pouring down . . . That's right, says johan janssens, he turned up at 3 A.M., and he was soaked to the skin. I expect he talked about his cat or his stomach, you venture. And johan janssens replies: no, he talked to me about rilke . . . you know, that poet . . . johan rilke . . . no, my mistake, rainer maria rilke. He's got to write a study on that rilke for his thesis, and after he's been through piles of thick books about that rilke, he's realized that there isn't much to add—anyway, that rilke doesn't interest me, he said—and I asked him if he had ever connected rilke's work with that of rodin, the sculptor. What do you mean, he asked. Well, I said, read rilke carefully and underline the images where he makes plastic images with words . . . take the very first page of malte laurids brigge, where he describes a pregnant woman—a pregnant woman is groping her way along a blank wall—and if rilke hadn't learned to see through rodin's eyes, he would never have had that woman grope along the wall. Why must she grope along that wall? . . . there's no earthly reason. Another writer, first and foremost, would never start that page, that journal, with the image of a pregnant woman . . . but he would, because it's plastic, because it's monumental. Another writer, if he *were* to start his book with a pregnant woman, would not have the woman grope her way along the wall . . . at the very most the woman would walk past the wall—a pregnant woman, next to a blank wall—because that says more than enough for the writer . . . it even says more than enough for the painter. But rodin has her grope her way along the wall . . . why? . . . once again, because as a hewn image it is more monumental . . . because, carved in the stone, it forms a single whole . . . because, modeled in stone, it is necessary for the various parts to remain connected. Rilke the writer could not free himself from the methods of rodin the sculptor and made the woman form a single whole with the wall. Besides which: it's a blank wall. Why did the wall have to be blank? . . . again, because a sculptor sees a wall as a block and he would never destroy the monumentality of that block, for example by carving windows into it. So, that's what I said to rilke . . . sorry, to sickwit the student . . . at 3 A.M. when he turned up soaked to the skin. And sickwit the student shook his head and said: actually I should never have studied literature, because the more I learn about literature—which is a re-creation of life—the more hostile I become to the way it's taught as a subject. Can you see me, in my thesis, starting to write about sculpture? . . . and can you see me submitting that thesis to the profs?: they'd look at me as though I was a hunchback and laugh themselves silly.

And johan janssens loads his cans and ladders back on his shoulders . . . he'll be getting a hunchback himself soon . . . and heads off to tolfpoets's so-called villa. To put emulsion on a couple of ceilings.

I'VE GOT WORK

The next day oscarke met his cronies again in the dark station . . . they'd been looking for him everywhere: today we're going to turn the city of brussels upside-down, they said. And sure enough, they went much further than his bench by the botanical garden, they took a streetcar to god knows where . . . through street after street . . . till the train reached the end of the line and went no further. And then they went further on foot, they ate their sandwiches in the country on a grass verge, and oscarke wondered if this was still brussels: he could see the gray city way out in the distance. They played around with a pile of straw . . . they drank a pint in a pub, and ran out without paying . . . they stood relieving themselves by a hedge and adopted obscene positions when a young girl passed. No, those two cronies of oscarke's outdid each other in pulling the craziest stunts. But aren't we going to

34

look for work then? asked oscarke . . . and they looked at him, and they considered the fact that he was married: we'll find work for you, they said. And they looked round as though they could suddenly see a sculptor in need of apprentices appearing in front of them. Well, oscarke was also astonished by the fact that they all always talked about apprentices, *whereas ondine always talked about* assistants. *They kept walking and fooled around and forgot about it, but then they came to a cemetery: they're bound to need a stonemason here, they said . . . and sure enough, there was a new avenue running from the cemetery into town, and on it was a newly-built house, with trees planted round it, and there were streetcar-lines, even though there was no streetcar service yet . . . and on the corner of that lonely lane lived a stonemason. Gravestones stood in a fenced area next to the house, the gate was open, and a girl . . . of about 13 . . . was skipping. Go and ask in there, they told oscarke . . . and he looked at them, looked at the gate, and didn't know what to do . . . they pushed from behind and couldn't understand why he was hesitating . . . they went inside and called out in funny carnival voices, asking if there was any work. The stonemason arrived. He had a moustache that was too heavy that he had to keep brushing upwards with his hand as though it were weighing down his face . . . he looked pensively at oscarke and said something that sounded like: bah. Oscarke didn't understand, and showed his certificates from art school, 1st prize in modulation and 1st prize in torso and classical figures and art history. Bah, said the stonemason, and he went in with oscarke, to see his wife who did not even have time to say bah, being busy baking flan. You can start tomorrow then, they said . . . and he didn't know what to say or do, did oscarke, whether to cry or laugh or thank them and take to his heels. I've got work! he said to the others. And they just nodded, they couldn't understand that it was such an unbelievable fairy tale for him . . . they went on chatting and carrying on with their antics . . . but he walked along beside them silently, listening to the words inside him: I've got work, I've got work . . . He couldn't get to the station soon enough to get home, but his cronies wouldn't hear of it: shouldn't we find work for us too? And then they talked seriously about it to each other, but they weren't sure what kind of work they would accept. He left as soon as he saw a streetcar going in the direction of that gray thing out there . . . he had only 1 fear: that he wouldn't be able to find the spot again, that lonely avenue in the countryside. And taking his bearing from every street corner, he managed to find his way back to the "allee-verte," but in his haste he bumped into a factory girl, a young thing with budding breasts, and she swore like a fucking laborer, asking him to keep his hands off her tits. The train didn't go fast enough, he couldn't get home fast enough, get home to the little room there above the café of the 1st grimy houses . . . as he was going upstairs the landlady said that ondine wasn't there: she's gone to brussels. To brussels? . . . oscarke sat pondering silently on the stairs . . . but although he had plenty of time, because evening was gradually coming in, he still couldn't fathom what on earth had taken ondine*

35

to brussels . . . most likely she'd also gone to find work for him, and equally likely she'd have found some . . . and he would have to go there: he'd have to go where a laborer was needed, and wouldn't be able to return to that sunny avenue where he was seen as an apprentice. And he was also distracted by other, secondary thoughts: that landlady from the bar, for instance, with her translucent black blouse . . . he shuddered, it reminded him of ondine's nakedness in bed . . . and speaking of nakedness, he also remembered the young factory girl in the "allee-verte," whose pristine breasts he had touched by mistake . . . for Christ's sake can't you keep your hands off my boobs? And he felt no disgust at all, now . . . on the contrary, sitting there on the stairs, he found himself turning into something of a hero: he thought he might, perhaps, meet her again tomorrow. And at the same time, he went through agonies . . . constantly repeated agonies, wondering whether his cronies had found their way back to the lane and asked for the same job . . . instead of oscarke, who had said he had won first prize in life drawing, when it wasn't true.

So it got late before ondine arrived . . . she had gone to see her cousin about the other 100 francs, and had not said that they were living in poverty, far from it, she had bragged so much about her husband, who was an artist, and who already had several statues ready for the triennial exhibition . . . and she'd lied so much and so outrageously that she'd begun to believe it herself. She also scouted around for work for him here and there, but had found nothing but a mop factory, where they needed a few extra hands . . . they took down oscarke's name. And she saw him sitting on the stairs like a dog waiting for its master, she flung open the door of their cubbyhole without a word and went in. He followed her, and she immediately started accusing him of being a worthless thief and a bastard, of having deceived her and of not being a sculptor at all . . . and when was he going to have an exhibition? and his mother still hadn't paid her father. He couldn't understand the meaning of it all: I've got work, he said. She turned towards him abruptly and gave him a searching look . . . she asked what he would be earning, but he didn't know: he didn't know what time he started work or finished or how much he would be paid, he just knew that one thing, I've got work. No, he just let her go on about madame wesenborgh, who hadn't followed her heart like she, ondine, had done, but had married a man who had risen to become a managing director . . . he let her go on about mr brys in england and about the last election in which the socialists had again made giant strides . . . he was thinking about over there, wondering if it would be work where he could be his own master, and soon he'd fallen asleep before he even realized it.

THE LAZINESS OF SICKWIT THE STUDENT

That evening, beautiful and mild, the music master comes cycling along on a gleaming bike . . . and he looks at the children who have built a tent by chapel road out of bits of packaging, on the gravel and tough, tall grass, right in the spot where in the depth of winter woelus's fairground wagon stands. Children and fair-stall holders turn a nondescript piece of ground into Heaven, says the music master from his gleaming bike: you can see, I'm laden with pots and pans as if I'd been out in the wide world camping, but I could just as well have made camp here. And parking his gleaming bike he comes in and leafs through the 2nd book on chapel road, and exclaims: but what is it with you and that sickwit! What do you see in him that you've got so much to say about him? He's someone who goes on and on studying and never gets anywhere, he takes digs at masters and graduates and doctors and professors so relentlessly that it can only be because he wishes he were a doctor or a professor . . . he pours scorn on them all, because he's frightened he'll never make the grade himself . . . he'll never make the grade, and do you know why?: he's too lazy. And this conclusion of the music master's is almost triumphant, as if he's summed it all up, beginning to end, from a to z, and there's not a single word to be added. Sickwit the student is certainly lazy, you say to the music master . . . and no one knows better than sickwit himself that he's lazy: it's scarcely comprehensible how lazy I am, says sickwit . . . I'll fix a time to finish my work in and when the time arrives I'll start wriggling like an eel to get out of it . . . I run as hard as I can to get away, and fool myself by fixing the next deadline the following day . . . just putting it off . . . and with me putting it off is letting me off the hook. Actually I'm scared of work, says sickwit: looked at from my perspective my laziness is Not the be-all and end-all: all of you are scared of being lazy . . . around you, above you, and under you there is emptiness and you're all scared of that emptiness . . . you work and study and get degrees and positions, and that's because you're afraid of the emptiness of doing nothing . . . Because you just don't dare to actually sit there and let the emptiness above and below and behind you sweep over you. Sickwit says that we never study anything in depth but are far too quick to express a judgment about it and then never revisit the judgment for fear of having it demolished . . . he says we rid ourselves of things by writing about them for fear of having to consider them too long and too closely. And sickwit is mainly lazy, mainly afraid because he doesn't know how that emptiness can be filled with anything positive . . . perhaps man was put into the world to fill the emptiness of the universe with something positive, says sickwit . . . but none of you fill the emptiness, you work and get degrees and close your eyes . . . you flee the emptiness, you make it greater with all your negative work. I, on the contrary, says sickwit, try to make the emptiness smaller by looking it in the eye, getting to know it and getting to the bottom of it, and by reflecting on how all your negative work could be replaced by positive work . . . all of you are out there trying to pump a basket full of water, thinking you're doing hard and useful work, but I on the other hand can't possibly join you and help pump. And the music master leafs through your 2nd book on chapel road, and reads *the bit about oscarke: I've got work. It's true, oscarke has work. He starts tomorrow with a stonemason in brussels. But oscarke is* not sickwit the student: may the empty universe save us from being, all of us, sickwits.

MAN

And the music master, going back to his gleaming bike, tells you about the thing that's remained with him longest from out in the wide world: that they fished in a stream, that eels and pike are cruel creatures . . . if you saw them with their jaws open you'd get a real fright . . . and we, frightened or not, ate all those cruel creatures right up.

IN THE PACKAGING TENT

And so on those cinders and that tough grass, in the same spot where in the winter woelus's wagon stands, the children have built a tent: they sit in it in their underwear, which they think are bathing suits . . . there are 4 boys and 1 girl in there . . . and the girl crawls into the tent, perhaps to undo her petticoat for a moment and 1 of the boys lifts up the side wall of the tent and cries out: I can see her boobies. And the other 3 kids kick and fight in order to get in the tent too, until the tent collapses and all 5 of them are trapped under it . . . and there's laughing and giggling, and you hear one of the boys: will you take your panties off too . . . And suddenly the smallest of the boys crawls out from under the collapsed tent, and goes and sulks a long way off . . . and from over there he yells out: I'm not playing anymore.

THERE'S NO ARGUING WITH A FACT

And on that beautiful summer evening, the evening on which the music master tells you the most special thing from His wide world, and the children of chapel road sit in Their packaging tent . . . on that beautiful summer evening mossieu colson of the ministry and johan janssens, the housepainter, sit opposite the 4 villas . . . they're sitting on johan janssens's doorstep, and the latter moves a matchstick up and down between his lips: take that matchstick out of your mouth or I'll choke instead of you, says mossieu colson. And johan janssens replies, be careful about making that kind of statement, because the feeling that one is going to choke instead of someone else is often cited as a sign of mental illness. Ow, and mossieu colson soon shuts up . . . shuts up and sneaks a look at the paint that despite lots of brown soap still clings to johan janssens's hands . . . shuts up and sneaks a look at johan janssens's mouth, which on this peaceful evening remains closed. But tell me honestly, johan janssens, if you look back with regret at your career as a journalist on an extreme left-wing daily? And johan janssens looks straight ahead for a very long time, as if he hasn't heard, and then intently at the children and their packaging tent and finally says: what kind of useless and unnecessary word is regret? . . . in fact the whole story of the extreme-left daily doesn't exactly leave me indifferent . . . my heart is left-wing, mossieu colson . . . and also I can never forget what was once such a big part of my life . . . but one has to be able to accept some things as an indelible fact. I still sometimes get a late letter from an old reader, I still get the occasional letter from someone who's doing his bitter duty, and I still get the occasional letter from someone who would be doing his bitter duty if he hadn't been thrown out on his ear . . . thrown out because of god knows what petty bourgeois politically correct decision? I get a letter from someone who was taken on after me as editor . . . summoned to brussels . . . had to go to brussels with his wife who was pregnant and had to squat in a tiny apartment costing 1,100 francs a month . . . and was fired just as summarily as he had been summoned. Fired and out of work, squatting in a tiny apartment costing 1,100 francs a month with his wife and her tummy. I get a letter from someone who's working himself to death and says that out where he is they've worked 7 days a week year-in-year-out . . . not 5 or even 6 but 7 full days . . . that is, monday tuesday wednesday thursday friday saturday sunday monday tuesday etcetera . . . and that person writes to me that they may well be working for Freedom and Prosperity . . . for Justice and Freedom there, but it sure looks like it's for the birds, though god moves in mysterious ways, and so he carried on in the pious illusion like emmanuel. And you know that when emmanuel carried on he fell asleep. And I get a letter from the guy who did my job after me because he was summoned by the party—no, I'm not putting it right, he hadn't been summoned by the party—and he did his duty towards the party, but felt like a pale imitation of johan janssens . . . he wrote and he wrote, and in a certain sense people were pleased with him, because in a certain sense he turned out to be a perfect idiot . . . and so he signed his articles p.i. and despite everything he wasn't ideologically pure enough—with his column "great minds" for example people asked why he always had to write about dead people when living people are a better ad for the party. And finally he quit of his own accord whereas I had the ideologically-pure courage to wait till I was kicked out . . . they'll have to kick me out before I abandon my job, I thought. And after that perfect idiot, another one came in, one who didn't know a thing about the johan janssens era, and so didn't have the feeling of being either an imitation or an underminer, but on the contrary felt like a Dragon Slayer. And that one told them to get lost after three weeks and that was the end . . . that was that with the intellectual life of the party. Do I have regrets? Well, I have regrets because working people are again sometimes misled by the arrivistes in the party . . . no, by the party itself . . . because yet again yet again yet again people have to serve a party or a faith or a religion . . . and it will almost never never never be the other way round. I regret that. But as for myself, I have no regrets, for at the moment I'm a housepainter and leave it at that.

IS THE SPHINX HOLLOW?

And sitting there on that beauteous summer evening—and even if, as you can see, you use old-fashioned words—sitting there on that evening, you see mossieu colson of the ministry and johan janssens the housepainter get up and you hear then ask: are you coming with us? We're walking over to tolfpoets's so-called villa. And off you all go, and over there in the field beyond termuren you find tolfpoets in the so-called garden of his so-called villa: you've got a nice place here, you say. And his wife maria, who has taken off her ribbons and bows, and instead has a crazy young guard dog draped all over her, adds: maybe, as you say, we have a nice place here . . . but I don't care about that . . . having a place, that's always been both my hope and my fear, ever since I worked in an apartment rental agency in brussels, at a time when there was a terrible housing shortage . . . we hung lots of ads in the window: attractive apartment with so-and-so many rooms, in bosvoorde . . . and the people who came over from antwerp or liege, where everything had been flattened by the flying bombs, almost demolished the door of our office . . . but that apartment in bosvoorde had already been rented, and my boss said: pay a deposit of 200 francs and we'll let you know if something else comes up . . . and all those people dug deep in their pockets, and even gave me a bit extra, if I let *them* know first . . . of course there was never anything going, not even a garret, not even a gutter . . . all I did was copy the ads from the daily papers onto cards and hang them in the window—nice apartment with such-and-such many rooms, in bosvoorde—and it was shown to people: now we've got something for you! And then when they went to see that apartment in bosvoorde, it had been rented before the last war, or it was simply a figment of someone's imagination, or just bait being put out by a competing office where they said: pay us 200 francs and we'll keep you posted. So you see how it was, says maria the nature girl, and since then I've always lived in a panic about finding a place to live. And tolfpoets laughs, baring his 2 gold teeth, and is about to make a comic remark . . . but his wife maria goes on: having a place, just having a place is the main thing for me, and that's why it leaves me stone cold when people say our villa is just a so-called villa, that the plan of our villa was just a tolfpoets-type plan, full of wisecracks and clever little subtleties . . . he sat drawing evening after evening, doors that close by themselves and locks that have to be opened with a knitting needle, banisters that you can slide down, and a chimney with a built-in nest for a blackbird . . . night after night he drew, and night after night he thought up new jokes . . . but our so-called villa is here, and we're living in it.

And on one of those rare times in your life you step outside your role of observer and ask maria the nature girl directly: so for you things themselves matter most . . . not what kind of place, but the fact that you have a place . . . not how you live, but *the fact that* you're alive? And maria the nature girl looks at you for a moment, thinking about what you're actually getting at: that's right, *the fact that* I'm alive, she finally says hesitantly. And you smile at her encouragingly, in order to wheedle out of her a little more of the secret of her life—that is, the purpose and meaning she attaches to life. That's right *the fact that* I'm alive, she repeats again. But she gets no further than that, she reveals no further secrets. And all you can do is ask yourself deep inside the question at the beginning of this section.

THE FACT I'M ALIVE

And as oscarke went to catch the 4:05 train early that summer morning, he listened to the things around him . . . he listened first to the hum of a telegraph pole, to his own steps in the echoing street where everyone was still asleep, and really enjoyed the sounds. He arrived in brussels and found the streetcar to take him to the stonemason's . . . but when he arrived, they were still asleep: he stood and waited at the shop on the corner, and they laughed at him for being so early . . . no, he couldn't join in the laughter yet, he didn't realize yet that life can have its sunny side too: he wanted to know what he could get to work on. Oh, they had to measure up a new tombstone . . . but not right away, in a bit, after their breakfast had settled . . . and he had to try their flan and give his opinion, but all he could do was roll his eyes a bit and lick his fingers. And then, returning from the cemetery, they went for a pint: it was rather different from what he'd imagined . . . working elsewhere, working in brussels, it had always been an atrocious specter. And now he had lunch at their table, they didn't want him to bring sandwiches anymore . . . he told ondine in the evening, but she wouldn't hear of it: he must take his sandwiches and eat then in the workshop, otherwise they'll dock your wages for lunch. Bah, he said . . . and he didn't realize that he was using exactly the same expression as they did over there . . . bah, why would they do that, they're different people from us here. And apart from that he said nothing. She looked at him in surprise, it was the first time he'd allowed himself an opinion of his own . . . she threw her arms round his neck and told him she was the unhappiest person in the whole world, and that he must help and protect her. But it was only playacting. She was afraid . . . well, she didn't really know herself what she was afraid of, but she became afraid because he had met some other people for a change. She, ondine, was almost all calculation, playacting, machination . . . it was difficult for her to be spontaneous like other people. He comforted her and promised to stand by her always and felt quite someone and so took his sandwiches: he ate one sandwich on the way there and threw the rest out of the train window on the on his way home . . . once the men who left with him from the "allee-verte" were enraged by this: they watched the pack as it fell and mowed him down with their eyes. It was dark in there, it was badly lit and badly ventilated, and the smell of their dreadful tobacco made him cough and cough . . . they talked about socialism, and they were all in a union and were reading their own daily, Justice and Freedom. *They swore and smashed the windows, yes they were that kind . . . but under the dim light in that stinking smoke, when oscarke heard them singing about the red flag, he couldn't keep his heart from pounding along with the beat . . . he asked if he could have a look at the paper . . . one couldn't really call it a paper, it was so small . . . and he said to himself in amazement: so this is the newspaper that I saw ondine get so furious about. But now he saw proudly that it contained a description of the "allee-verte," about the people who went there on their wooden clogs, and sat in the dark, and so on . . . and they pointed out to oscarke the guy who'd written that: he probably thought it was a gentleman, no, no, it was one of them. He looked, and it was the student . . . but he was no longer a student, he worked in brussels in a stove factory . . . oh, he sat among them and said that they must be united . . . one day the sun would rise . . . and they didn't understand literally, but they knew what he was getting at . . . he also said that bryske had been asked to came back from england, to attend the open-air meeting on the canal, to mark the party's anniversary. Oh, they talked of nothing but their party . . . party comrade, they said to each other. Oscarke bought their newspaper everyday, he carried it in his coat pocket to work and read it to those people over there at lunch . . . they were as Christian as could be, and so were stunned that he was a socialist . . . of course people in brussels no longer thought that socialists were men with blood-streaked faces and knives between their teeth . . . but it was still a shock to learn that someone was a socialist. And they were a bit snooty about their socialist, and told everyone that they had one working for them . . . well, it wasn't really brussels over there, it was just a suburb . . . or not even that, it would become a suburb in a few years' time perhaps. At home, though, he wasn't a socialist . . . or not yet, he just sat by the stove from ondine's father's workshop and felt his feet aching . . . he was a long way away, by streetcar, train, and on foot, and then back again, on foot, streetcar, and train . . . it was time to turn in, soon, soon, after he'd had a bite to eat and looked from a distance at his own lump of clay, over there in the corner.*

And as you're about to leave tolfpoets's funny villa, when the others are already out of the garden gate . . . tolfpoets stops you because he wants to tell you something. He smiles awkwardly—or should you write immaturely?—baring his 2 gold teeth, and looks at you uncertainly: you've now heard that for my wife maria having a place is what matters most . . . but it's not for me, I have to live in the country, have to have a few but very spacious rooms, with amusing things in them that always bring a smile to my lips . . . because as I've already told you, there's also something contradictory in me, something strange and incomprehensible . . . a fear of ghosts, I'll call it . . . a fear of finding myself in a house where I'll get lost, and suddenly being in a room THAT HAS NO DOORS OR WINDOWS . . . houses are always an obsession in my nightmares. I dream again and again about the house I lived in years and years ago . . . the house where I spent my childhood. And I drew and drew in order to build myself a house that no longer resembled the house of my youth at all: a funny house, a so-called villa for tolfpoets. But now, the day before yesterday, I dreamed once again that I was being brought to that feared and abhorred house: in the middle of the countryside, a long way outside termuren . . . and in my dream, that house is my so-called villa. And at that moment there's a split in me . . . in my dream I am suddenly split into my tolfpoets-self and my dream-self . . . and my tolfpoets-self protests strongly, protests but can't get a word out and just wails, wails like the child I once was . . . that's not nice of you! my tolfpoets-self wants to say to my dream-self . . . and my dream-self stands there hesitantly, on the road that leads to the countryside, and it says: actually I can't go to your so-called villa NOW, I've still got to take you to the house of your childhood NOW. And suddenly I'm back in my childhood house after all . . . or no, it's actually THE house I'm afraid of, the house of my anxious dreams that in some ways recalls my childhood house, but is nonetheless completely different . . . and my tolfpoets-self tries to put one over on my dream-self: it hastens to lock the doors and to isolate itself in 1 single room, UNTIL THE DREAM IS OVER . . . but again it's my dream-self that's the more powerful, that put one over on my tolfpoets-self: I lock the doors, but there are more and more doors, now bigger and bigger doors that begin to resemble church portals, now smaller ones that turn into dollhouse doors . . . doors that lead into other rooms, into appallingly empty rooms, into rooms where even more appallingly there is only 1 chair . . . 1 chair in the middle of an empty room . . . and I run to the window . . . or I'd like to, but can't run, I've got to stay on my guard and especially show that I'm not getting scared . . . but I hurry to the window that should be there but soon won't be, or if it is there will have no contact with the ordinary world but look out onto a closed courtyard that's empty and lonely and in semi-darkness, or look into long corridors with different new doors, or simply into another room that's the mirror-image of the room I'm standing in. And suddenly another strange new element is present: time, time that's running the wrong way . . . it seems to me as if I lived in my tolfpoetsian villa years and years ago, and as if this house, this abhorred dream house, is the end result of all my comic plans. And my tolfpoetsian self tries to be brave, and says: years ago I wasn't frightened in my so-called villa, so why should I be frightened in this house now? And I go forward bravely, although cold sweat clings to my temples, and I pass through all those rooms, now ascending a staircase that climbs up an infinitely high wall and suddenly vanishes into a peephole that's miles up in that unending surface . . . but is also the mouth of a pipe and so I wriggle through the pipe and then have to descend steep stairs, spiral iron staircases and then worn wooden loft stairs that end in a plank across the awesome abyss of an enormous chasm. And then . . . long-awaited, long-feared . . . suddenly I sense in a corner the invisible scratching—teeming—of unknown things. And I shout: for christ's sake what's in here? And at the same instant it's on my back. But at the same instant too my wife maria shakes me awake and says: you're swearing in your sleep again. And I lie there bathed in sweat, in the funny bed in my so-called villa.

THE TRUTH COMES OUT

And maria the nature girl comes and listens to what her tolfpoets has to say for himself at the garden gate . . . and tolfpoets laughs and bares his 2 gold teeth and says: I'm telling him about how I sleep. And he turns to you and asks: how do you position yourself when you sleep? And you look at him searchingly, and he is able to tell you that you usually wrap your big toe round the Achilles tendon on the other foot. And he looks at you and smiles. You're right, you say, I do sometimes sleep like that. And he sticks up his finger and says: ha, that we used to be so comfortable sleeping in the trees is something darwin forgot to mention.

THE PEPPERPOT'S CONFESSION

You walk back to termuren all alone, to chapel road, and the sun sinks behind the castle wood, casting pink highlights over the gray of the evening . . . and you stop for a moment and look at this pink and gray world, and as you stand there watching you hear rustling next to the castle stream, and to your astonishment you see the figure of a man: it's the pepperpot, who in turn gazes at you in astonishment. And the pepperpot emerges from the gray and pink of the gathering dusk and asks, quietly and despairingly: did you see? Did you see him standing there with his fly open, watching for prey? And the pepperpot buttons his fly in embarrassment then runs his hand across his forehead, across the hot groove in his forehead: during the day I can be a normal person who does a normal job, and then that other stuff in me seems very far away, it seems nonexistent . . . but a woman can't ride past on her bike without my eyes being glued to the hem of her skirt, to catch a flash of what's going on . . . I mean, what's down there. A girl, a child-woman, can't go by without my eyes boring through the opening in her dress to batter themselves on her breasts, to know what's there . . . I mean, what's going on in there. A young woman can't bend down without my eyes darting towards her ass. And if there's no one out in the street, then my eyes search the windows, always in hope of catching some little glimpse: a woman bathing, going to bed, getting dressed or undressed. A woman can't sit down, stand up, walk, run, lie down, without my pursuing her most carnal details: in my life I've looked very little at women's faces, for me a face is a distant, unknown land, a smooth deserted plane, a faceless face. And the closer it gets to evening, the more heavily all those moving skirts pile up in, I'm filled with a sea of moving skirts, a mountainous landscape of veiled breasts . . . a forest of breasts and a sea of skirts . . . a sea that roars and boils, that draws me in and engulfs me in its surf. I have the urge in me to live more deeply than a man really can, to live more diversely, more passionately, more intensely, hornier, harder, to forge ahead in life, to bore through life entirely . . . to bore ever more deeply, harder, and more passionately—to be engulfed completely by that sea of skirts, to stray through the landscape of an ass, to wander through the mountain of a budding breast. A saucy skirt and beneath that the hem of a petticoat, and beneath that a flash of thigh: woman must be pierced. So when evening starts to fall, I creep around, the pepperpot in me awakens and bellows at life, is hungry and thirsty for life . . . I hang around here by the stream behind the castle and wait for some girl or other to come along, some very young girl who as yet knows little to nothing about life, and whom I shall astonish with my taut, hot flesh . . . whom I'll upset with the sight of flesh that is bigger and hornier than life itself . . . oh, I do go on . . . and I stand there and can't say go away: I shudder and shiver and am dismayed, I'm dead inside, but the pepperpot lives twice as much inside me, lives on my behalf . . . I have a face-less face and the girl has a faceless face too . . . I'm not a human being, but a ghost that's been taken possession of a human being, and the girl is not a girl but Life . . . I am a ghost in search of life: 1,000 dead people in me pushing me towards the woman in order to get back to life. You can't understand what that's like. But those dead people tug at my fly and make me stand and wait shuddering and shivering, in order to be able to return to life . . . *through* ondine, through jeannine, oh, it doesn't matter what they're called, provided their names have an "in" . . . in in in and the surf sucks me in, forces and pounds and pushes me deeper and deeper, to a more and more fanatical life.

And meanwhile the pink of the evening has died away, and only the gray is left . . . the pink of what's to come, and the gray of what's already died . . . and that gray comes a small step closer, and the pepperpot goes even grayer in the face than the gray of the evening . . . and his hand strokes his thigh unthinkingly . . . but he remembers that you're sitting next to him, that you've listened to his confession, and he disappears into the evening, he creeps off like a startled ghost, like a ghost caught red-handed . . . like a ghost terrified of people, just like a human being is scared of ghosts. But in a while, when you've gone, he'll loom up again behind his bushes until night has fallen fully.

FINALLY JEANNINE APPEARS

Oscarke didn't dare take the newsletter out of his pocket at home, it was ondine herself who found it . . . there happened to be an article in it about the filature spinning mill, and mr derenancourt who fed off the sweat and blood of the poor and wanted to become mayor: a policeman can't run a spinning mill, but the chief of police could run a spinning mill . . . but it won't happen, we socialists will put an end to the most outrageous this and that . . . Yes, it was all about him, mr achilles, to whom she had given the glory of her youth. They slandered him again and again in that rag, they talked of hunger and deprivation, about the children working in his mill—what nonsense that was, hadn't children always worked in mills?—but her rage was directed more at him over there, at oscarke, who read and believed such stuff: that's what little, gullible men were like. And what pained her the most was to have to endure such a gullible little shit in her immediate vicinity . . . how could the mills compete with foreign mills if there were no children on low wages working for them? . . . and pregnant women, what kind of stupidity was that, why can't a pregnant woman work the same as anyone else? Oh, said oscarke, that wasn't the point, but there's the article about the allee-verte, that's definitely true: it IS dark and it IS cold, and we'd prefer something better than a cattle truck to come back home in, evenings. Ondine replied furiously that he thought he knew everything because he happened to have had a close-up view of it once, but that one shouldn't see things close up: one should be able to see things from a great height. He said this and she said something different and finally they went to bed and they lay next to each other like corpses, though it wasn't really any worse than on other nights . . . except for the times when she was friendly for a change and said, sleep tight, oscarke . . . and he answered, sleep tight, ondineke. And he wondered whether she would leave him in peace. But she did:

she was reluctant to ask him about the things that everyone talked about on the streetcars. Of course, she sometimes wondered if he was always going to be like this . . . if he was going to stay an innocent child all his life . . . but she didn't mind, it seemed as if her sex life had also been removed to "a great height." But naturally oscarke couldn't stay a child forever, one day he had to wake up, however backward he might be in this regard . . . constantly coming into contact like he was with the lowest of the low, the scum of the earth . . . those conversations about women . . . and especially the women themselves, who at the slightest provocation hitched up their skirts and showed their bare fannies: it was if he were stuck in a kind of hell, in a hothouse, where his sexual maturity would be artificially cultivated. And suddenly, one midday over on the lane, in sun and silence, while he was leaning against the side wall looking at the unused streetcar rails . . . when the stonemason's daughter came to skip by as usual, and he noticed that she was starting to grow out of her dresses . . . only yesterday and the day before he had played with her, child as he still was . . . and now, suddenly: he saw something different in her. Actually he didn't yet know that he saw something different in her . . . it was difficult to explain, but he looked at her legs, which were strong, and he noted to himself that her flesh was taut under the skin of her legs . . . and thinking about that flesh he looked at that flesh: suddenly something was born, while something else died in him: he was a different man . . . he was again that oscarke who over in the allee-verte had accidentally touched a young factory girl . . . a girl who'd sworn and asked him if he couldn't keep his paws off her boobs. At the station he'd looked out every day for that girl . . . and now . . . here in the sun sat the stonemason's daugh-ter, and he scarcely dared play with her, and it gave him a headache to look at her. Oh, he longed for those dark, chilly mornings, for the train that would take him to her . . . and he hated the return journey, especially because it took him to ondine. And when it was Sunday, and he looked through the window at the 1st grimy houses, at the blank wall of the labor, and at the people going to church . . . how long that Sunday lasted and how far he was from jeannine. And he became ashamed, he gradually realized what was happening to him: he killed time on sunday afternoon by starting to work on the potter's clay . . . he had to dig out his stylus and his wet cloths, because ondine had already put his equipment to other uses. It was a girl's head that he wanted to make, and the lips must be slightly parted in a smile . . . a smile? . . . wasn't it for a kiss? That was what ondine asked: who is she kissing? And it shocked him. It was understandable that having become a man he wasn't going to look for Woman in the person right beside him . . . he knew ondine too well, she meant something different to him, she'd taken him away from his mother, and in so doing she'd become another mother, so to speak, a mother who'd promised him that he'd be able to go on sculpting, but who had not kept her promise. He discovered woman . . . but he discovered her far from home. He tossed and turned in the restless night, in the stifling july summer night

47

. . . he thought of that sweet little thing over there and finally bent over ondine. Night after night he was like a sex-starved devil, so that ondine finally could not help realizing that something strange was going on . . . she felt, so to speak, that in embracing her he was embracing someone else, nailing her dumb and speechless to the bed . . . that there was another person between her and him, she even looked around and asked if the door was closed: she thought someone had come in and was standing there watching. He spent all his evenings on that head in clay . . . and jeannine, gradually came to be a better likeness . . . especially that mouth of hers, exactly as she sometimes looked at him . . . that mouth that ondine thought was in the middle of a kiss. He stood in front of the clay head, and he'd no sooner taken up his stylus than it was time for bed. Ondine nagged at him to come to bed, she was cold in bed, all alone, and the light was too expensive . . . and there was an unpleasant memory troubling her, since he had visited madame van wesenborgh, and had heard that mr brys was coming back: in a letter mr brys expressed the wish to see his country again, he was feeling homesick . . . but I expect it was because the atheists were growing and growing in numbers here, and he probably expected to be surrounded and protected by them. And thinking of that she looked at oscarke's work . . . she got out of bed and went up to him: I really don't think that mouth is quite my mouth, she said . . . my mouth is like THIS and she stuck her finger into the clay. No, she couldn't show it properly . . . from the bed it seemed as if she only had to stick her finger in to make the sculpture perfect . . . but now it wasn't her mouth or any other mouth: it had become a lump of shapeless clay: it had become a face with mouth cancer. Oh, his hands were paralyzed with the shock . . . he wanted to remove that ulcer, that dreadful mutilation . . . he dug his stylus into it, but it only made it worse . . . in his nervous haste, he worked at it without seeing what he was doing: it was as if he were trying to grope blindly to recover her mouth, jeannine's mouth. It became an impossible task, fever raged in him, the thought that it might be irretrievably lost drove him crazy. No, it was destroyed . . . but god in heaven, how long it took before he could admit it to himself! It's fucked it's fucked, he cried loudly and repeatedly. She tried to console him by saying that he could start again tomorrow . . . start again modeling her . . . but he was inconsolable, he simply couldn't forgive her. It crossed his mind that others, in his position, might have murdered her . . . but however much he imagined all the possible ways of committing a murder, he knew he would never do it.

POVERTY IS NO DISGRACE

And however much I imagine all the possible ways of committing a murder, I know I'll never do such a thing . . . whispers johan janssens to you as he watches the others who are discussing this and that in your house. *Oscarke has found work, johan janssens continues . . . and to begin with he was happy, happy*

48

as only a child can be . . . but soon his happiness will be more about the fact that his work in brussels is far from ondine . . . but enough of that! . . . up to now he's happy and he can show what a real man he is: finding work in brussels all by himself! And then there's sickwit, johan janssens continues . . . and sickwit is frightened of all the useless work perpetrated in the world. But it's not about oscarke or sickwit, it's about me . . . the world revolves around an imaginary axis, and that axis is imaginary, pure and simple, everyone imagines that They are the axis . . . and I, the axis of the world, of my own world, I'm walking round empty-handed, dying for a bit of work like the fields beyond termuren are dying for a drop of rain. I wouldn't be proud of the work I had to do in the world, like oscarke . . . and I wouldn't be afraid of all the useless work I had to do in the world, like sickwit: I'm dying for work because of the paltry wages I get. And you'll say that I'm never satisfied, that I've got work as a housepainter right now . . . you'll say: paint walls, paint doors, paint faces if you have to, and in your spare time you can write columns, shit columns about whatever you like. But you're forgetting that house painting is also a hopeless chain, a chain in which I'm the very last link: if an eccentric occasionally pops up having come to the strange conclusion that the front of his house needs a lick of paint, he's immediately engulfed by a swarm of every man around who's ever held a paintbrush . . . and he's promised colors distilled from the rainbow, from the setting sun, from dewdrops, from rose petals . . . and on top of that he's promised that they'll keep far below the going daily rate and do it practically for nothing. And if it's actually reached the point in the chain where the old master-painter has been chosen, over there behind the 1st grimy houses on the corner of thrift street, I still have to wait and see if the old master-painter and son can get along without me, johan janssens, the last loose link in the chain: and if not I can finally make my entrance. Alas only in a tiny non-speaking part: to paint the top gutter. I was a journalist, but there are no daily papers left that I can or am allowed to write for. I'm a housepainter, but I'm only allowed to paint the occasional unusually difficult and perilously high gutter. And having said all that with suppressed sadness, johan janssens concludes: there are people who have only to reach out for something and it turns to gold in their hands . . . but the moment it's in my hands that gold turns straight back into . . .

But at that moment all the others in your house, who've been discussing this and that, have reached an agreement . . . and the lovely lucette comes over to the corner where johan janssens made his woeful confession to you, her eyes shining, her voice polished, and is about to ask him if he . . . if he . . . but she hears his last sentence and stammers: that's a shame, because we were just going to ask you if you'd come with us to the banks of the ourthe for 10 days or so. Oh, lovely lucette, who in punishment for your beauty are

49

a little lacking in sensitivity, proving that one excludes the other! And johan janssens withdraws even further into his corner and says airily: why shouldn't I go? . . . if you take the train, I'll use your music master's gleaming bike, if you all stay in a hotel I'll borrow tolfpoets's bed, and if you all go out to eat somewhere I'll make myself a camp fire and cook on a skillet. And the lovely lucette claps her hands with delight and repeats everything johan janssens has said . . . she repeats it to her music master and to mossieu colson of the ministry, she repeats it to your wife with her bad nerves, and she repeats it for the last time to herself. And everyone looks away in some other direction, and no one has heard. Only your wife . . . only your wife might be prepared to say: I'll pay for your train, johan janssens . . . she might be prepared to say: I'll pay for Everything, johan janssens. And look, she goes up to him, she puts her hand on his shoulder . . . a tear glistens in her eye like a beautiful pearl . . . but, she says nothing. She says nothing and turns her head away. And as she turns her head away, she notices that you, her own husband, have to steal a cigarette from johan janssens's packet. Poverty is no disgrace, for christ's sake. No, it's a crime that must be punished . . . but however one imagines all the possible ways one could commit a murder, one knows one could never do such a thing.

ON THE BANKS OF THE OURTHE

Just look at the gang, mossieu colson of the ministry, the music master, johan janssens and his son jo who's 10, your wife and the lovely lucette who's pregnant—and whoever else . . . hallo, hallo, anybody else—as they flee the flat lands of termuren and plunge head over heels into the solitude of the ardennes: silence, the pungent smell of pine, clear water, and a stream that conducts long murmuring conversations with itself, flames of the campfire late in the evening, the screech of a night owl with a plaintively peeping bird in its beak, perhaps a fox as well, perhaps a squirrel. Alas: johan janssens is obliged to pitch his tent on the banks of a tortured ourthe that twists and turns through a fairground of tents . . . an ourthe where the banks are covered with tents the size of castles, equipped with double roofs, pavilions, dining rooms, living rooms, and bedrooms . . . an ourthe along which the engines of cars and motorbikes with sidecars and vans and trailers roar . . . an ourthe with crusts of bread floating in it, ripped packaging and used sanitary napkins and opened cans and broken bottles in it. Oh, don't worry, says the lovely lucette . . . who doesn't have to camp in that teeming fairground anyway, but is renting a room from a farmer . . . don't worry, these are people who just come for the weekend and the day after tomorrow they'll all be gone. Fine, they'll be gone in a day or two and johan janssens pitches his tent, in the last empty spot, he trips over the guy-ropes of the other tents and apologizes and withdraws to the furthest corner of his tent. And what he sees taking place on the banks of the ourthe is the following: a fashion show in which the gentleman from tent 7 walks around in his underpants with the lady from tent 17, who's in shorts—the gentleman who came with the lady from 17 is meanwhile walking around with the increasingly amorous daughter from one of the farthest tents—and where they swim together from 10 to 12 and play funny games with a rubber ring: the lady throws the ring and the gentleman has to catch it . . . and from 12 to 3 the gentleman goes about in an open sports shirt and the lady in a flowered crepe dress and they go for lunch together in "l'air pur" or "beau rivage"—that is, the gentleman from tent 7 lunches with his own lady and the lady from tent 17 lunches with her own gentleman—and then from 3 to 5 they sunbathe, with the gentleman and lady dressed in nothing but a pair of sunglasses—that is, the gentleman from tent 7 is back with the lady from tent 17 and the gentleman from tent 17 with the increasingly amorous daughter from one of the farthest tents—and afterwards they walk round in evening dress, the lady with bare shoulders and long skirts, and the gentleman . . . Wait, johan janssens's social hobbyhorse refuses to note something down here: as dusk falls the lady withdraws behind a hedge, and the gentleman creeps closer on his hands and knees on the other side of the hedge, because though he's already seen her dressed only in her sunglasses . . . and what's more has helped her dry off after swimming and throwing the rubber ring . . . while she in her turn helped him dry off after swimming and throwing the rubber ring . . . but he hasn't yet seen her while she's had to squat behind a hedge . . . so she's sitting there and suddenly spots the gentleman through the gap in the hedge: she laughs, she coos, she protests faintly . . . she lets him look more closely, provided he doesn't repeat the game the next day with the increasingly amorous daughter from one of the farthest tents, and provided that he has a look round to see that no one from the other tents is approaching the hedge . . . both conditions are met, and the lady gives a close-up demonstration of what is called: relieving herself. And it is only then that the lady puts on an evening dress, before visiting a bar—with her own gentleman this time—where as a joke the record player is playing "home on the range." And late at night johan janssens is woken rudely from his sleep by the returning campers: they are laughing and singing at the top of their voices, breaking the fences round the fields, so that the cows escape and plod around in alarm on the main road in the headlights of cars . . . an orchard is plundered, a forest destroyed, a haystack goes up in flames. And at 6 in the morning johan janssens sits at the entrance to his tent with his head spinning, while the others have only now fallen into a deep sleep: it's only for the weekend, says the beautiful lucette, but johan janssens has been here for

7 days now, and still new cars and motorbikes and vans are arriving . . . have camp beds and stoves and bulging wardrobes onboard, a table and six bourgeois chairs, as well as their bourgeois mentality of behaving disgracefully here where they are complete strangers. So johan janssens sits at the entrance to his tent at 6 o'clock, and notices that the woman next door is already up—a serious person, a decent person—and she puts her hands together and raises her eyes to heaven, and says what a mess it is here: it was quite different last year, there were twice as many tents, but they were all in a neat straight line. And mossieu colson pays a visit to johan janssens, and rubs his tortured brow and says: it's only 6 in the morning and I'm already on my second aspirin: and I haven't heard a single bird singing in the whole of these seven days. And johan janssens replies: you might not hear any birds sing, but you sure do see birds swing.

WHERE IS SOLITUDE?

You fled the banks of the ourthe down there, and when you unlocked your door you found a letter from tippetotje: I don't know where you've got to, but I went to see the exhibition of modern art with my baron . . . and I assume that some people never find a solitary spot anywhere in the world, never discover a place where it's so quiet that they can bring their dreams into the world alive—like mammals bear their young—I assume that some painters prefer to depict a strange, nonexistent landscape: a surrealist landscape, a cubist, expressionist, futurist landscape . . . yes, even an abstract landscape. But it always makes me shudder, I get sad and constricted around the heart when I see people trying to populate those landscapes with Woman. They keep forcing woman into that chilly abstract or ghostly surrealist landscape as a human element, as if she had to be there in order to confront what is alien. And none of those painters realize how cruel they're being, how cruel and cowardly . . . cruel and cowardly like the germans for instance with their concentration camps: a cowardice that stems from fear. All those painters create a world that has nothing to do with the human world . . . and those who support modern art say that it is the courage of pioneers setting out to discover new lands, and those who are opposed to modern art say that it is the cowardice of weaklings fleeing the human world. A cowardice that stems from the fear of those who have become too weak and tenderhearted in this world . . . a fear of those who in this world live only among glass and steel and concrete and many other things that slice and chop up and crush human beings . . . fear because on the one hand the world is becoming ever sharper and on the other hand man is becoming ever more sensitive to pain. And becoming hypersensitive to pain under the monstrous pile driver that the world has become . . . some painters dream up another landscape, Another World, where it is lonely and silent and dark. And they are driven only by cowardice. And on the other hand there are painters who set out to discover the Other Landscape, the Other World with the courage of pioneers . . . but who, arriving in the world of their dream and their mind, are also seized by cowardice and fear. Because it is a strange country where man doesn't exist yet. It's the country of the surrealist imagination, or it's the country of the abstract spirit . . . so it is not the fear of being crushed by one's fellow men that prevails, the fear that prevails is the fear of standing face to face with the dismaying Unknown. And so they send their guinea pig into that country, they send that tender creature, woman, into that country of pain and silence, into the world of killing loneliness. But I'm getting worked up for no reason . . . I, tippetotje, realize that those who paint those landscapes just happen to like to flee the world for a while, in order to be different. Yet I also wonder if there isn't again another deeper reason underlying it, I wonder whether in their fear they haven't a vague presentiment of a land that is bound to come: cold and chilly and lonely, and populated only by Woman . . . the landscape of a world split up into atoms, in which only the odd block of concrete is left standing, a stretch of railway line that has been uncovered by the wind after being buried for years under sand and weeds . . . and in that cold chilly and atomized landscape, nothing but: a wandering woman. Your lonely tippetotje.

And as you are folding up tippetotje's letter, you hear your wife calling from your patch of garden: come and look, while we were looking in vain for a bit of solitude, here in the solitude of our coal shed a cat has given birth to 2 tiny kittens.

THE LONELY LAND OF OSCARKE

Oscarke left home silently in the morning, while ondine was still asleep . . . that was best: even just saying good morning would have hurt, just hearing her speak would have reopened the wound. At lunchtime over there he started again on his sculpture: he asked if she would sit for him, and he modeled her full length . . . it wasn't a bad likeness and that was the main thing for the stonemason and his wife . . . and he was satisfied too, it soothed the hurt even though he was aware his new effort was only an academic exercise. The other head had been something more, a fragment of life, a piece of soul trapped in the clay . . . and it had been something else besides: even if he modeled and modeled those lips 100 times, more and more beautifully and expressively, it would still never be like what he had done in his room: the image of burgeoning sexuality. He began to depict her again, now with her arms raised upwards reaching for something behind her, so that she had to twist her torso: his boss told him to copy it in stone, even though there was a job on: the wagon had to be taken out, and a stone at the cemetery had to be polished and sanded white, but the stonemason did it himself and let his apprentice hack away at the block to his heart's content. Oh, the mason was just a craftsman, who could put in a marble fireplace and do a bit of rough work, but if a customer wanted a motif carved, then his only way out was to say that such things were out of fashion, or wouldn't look right, or some other pathetic lie. But that oscarke had landed here out of the blue, with his pocket stuffed with 1st prizes . . . and he had said to his wife: let's take him on and if any delicate work comes in he can do it. They were happy to have a real sculptor with them, an artist, an artist a socialist a prodigy . . . and oscarke was paid for carving the girl, stretching, reaching out, they didn't know for what, but they would put it in the shop when it was finished. He wanted the sun to stand still and for it to never become evening: he loved that empty, deserted lane, those 3 or 4 houses that had just been built, the sun that shone down on them and the people who were different people . . . he loved all that, but especially he loved jeannine, who still danced there and skipped with the skin growing tauter daily round her dear dear flesh: it was heaven there, that's what it was. And when he was there and possessed that heaven, oh, then he thought of ondine as winter, as october and september and rain and wind. Yet . . . staying here and saving his money, not saying that he was married, living with jeannine, never returning to that termuren with the stinking river dender and the smoking chimneys of the labor weaving mill and the filature spinning mill, to act just as if he had died . . . no, he couldn't do that, because She over there was something in the nature of the omniscient god . . . he suddenly realized that very clearly: she was omniscient and would come and unearth him here: she already knew that there was a girl here, and that in possessing her, ondine, he was possessing jeannine. And would also know that he was thinking of leaving her, but that he would never dare do such a thing. He returned home in the evenings, with a bitter line round the mouth and sad eyes, he sat in the train and read the socialist newspaper, and on sunday mornings he went to church, in the parish of the 2 holy mills, and listened to the priest who happened to be preaching a sermon about socialism . . . just as if he knew that oscarke was there, because he was looking right at him . . . the following sunday, however, it was about illicit relationships, and again the priest looked at him as if he knew that over there oscarke . . . But oscarke could hold his head high, since he had never laid a hand on jeannine. And something deep inside him wept BECAUSE he had never laid a hand on her, even though it would have meant his damnation. And the thought also gnawed at him that the truth might well be just the opposite: the life the priest was trying to make him believe in might well be hell . . . and the life he dreamed of, in sin and socialism and illicit relationships, might be heaven. The thought scared him . . . although something else in him, his intelligence . . . or the devil—or were intelligence and devil 1 and the same . . . was stupidity and goodness god, and reasoning the devil?—but no matter, something else in him pointed out that the priest never preached about the allee-verte station, or about the stove factory where pregnant women have to push wagons about. Nevertheless, it was totally out of character for oscarke to say: he may preach that you must bring children into the world but he doesn't preach about what you're supposed to do with those children in the mills. No, he wasn't malicious, but still would have liked occasionally to hear the priest preach about the badly lit and ventilated trains . . . he talked about the moral decay in the big cities, so he knew about that . . . but he didn't say that common people stank because it was badly ventilated. Ondine asked him if he'd heard what was said at mass, and he nodded . . . he couldn't say, did not dare say what he thought about it . . . and anyway, how was he supposed to explain: for me hell is heaven and heaven is hell? . . . ondine would have had him thrown in the madhouse.

ABOUT THE CRAZIES

We tell a few jokes about crazy people—e.g., the one about the crazy who writes himself a letter but doesn't know what's in it, he'll only know tomorrow when the postman comes—they tell a few of those jokes and johan janssens's little son, who's 10, listens very intently and then says: oh, I wouldn't put anything past those crazies. And johan janssens's wife looks very intently at her son in turn and says: listen kid, I wouldn't put anything past the others, the ones who Aren't crazy.

And, of course, there's a ring at the door and it's dr mots who's come to give johan janssens's wife an injection for a fee of 50 francs . . . and with his syringe in his hand he sees johan janssens's messy papers on the table; the papers themselves and everything else that belongs with the papers: pen holders, newspaper cuttings, cigarette butts. And as he prepares his syringe, he says: artists, they're all crazies. And johan janssens's wife nods in agreement. And johan janssens also nods in agreement, but: so are doctors. And he also says: looked at from your point of view artists are most likely crazy, because they work and work and work and even then don't earn enough to put one slice of bread on another. And dr mots gives a carefree laugh in the process of injecting the content of his syringe: do you perhaps mean that we, doctors, are just raking it in? you've got it all wrong. Work it out: for night calls I get 75 francs . . . 75 francs is 75 francs, you may say, but again you've got it all wrong: first and foremost the State will deduct 40 francs from that paltry sum . . . and so I'll have got up in the middle of the night, had a bite to eat, smoked a cigarette, got my car out of the garage and lost a night's sleep . . . would you do all that for 35 francs? Ha, I'm prepared to help a person in need, but I don't want to make the State rich with my work. You just want to make yourself rich, adds johan janssens with a low, mocking laugh. He also says: and that proves that doctors aren't crazy, but it still doesn't prove that artists are. But dr mots says nothing as he is engaged with his most important task: collecting his 50 francs. And after he has done so carefully, he says: no, by artists being crazy I mean that they're really crazy, pathological cases, schizophrenics . . . otherwise they couldn't possibly write such insane books and make such insane paintings, like, look at picasso, isn't he crazy? Instead of replying, johan janssens looked among his scattered papers for an opinion on picasso . . . the opinion of dr c. j. schuurman, a psychiatrist: only great tensions in picasso's unconscious can explain such a caricature-like but accurate picture of our time . . . I see him as a creative artist who has managed to express in an astonishing way a lack of integration, which is the essential characteristic of our time . . . there are insane people who obviously experience the world in a rather analogous way, but the work of Picasso, although showing some similarity with the stiff, mechanical element in the artistic work of such patients, nowhere exhibits the typical distortions and absurdities . . . this therefore constitutes his greatness, to have depicted the insanity of our age without himself having been insane. And johan janssens, having read that article, observes dr mots very closely: the artist is not a madman, but someone who observes this crazy age closely and tries to render it and explain it in his work.

And that would have concluded the story of the mad, had not johan janssens's wife added something after seeing dr mots glide off in his car: that's all very well, but you know, he's still got the 50 francs.

THERE'S TOO MUCH IN LIFE

Your house is empty and smells stuffy when you return from the banks of the ourthe . . . and well, to continue about the cat that gave birth in a portion of your garden during your absence . . . just as you try to give birth to your dreams . . . to continue about the cat: your wife walks round with her bad nerves, and wonders whether those two kittens aren't cold or hungry or . . . like, what else could your wife dream up about the kittens to torment herself? And she fetches old curtains, and milk and soaked bread, and some fish for the mother. And at night the mother comes and takes her kittens away and to thank us shits all over the flowerbeds . . . all over that herb that we call rice pudding, she dumps her own rice pudding and scratches the rest to pieces, supposedly to conceal her crime. But these are just the worries of your wife with her bad nerves. Your own worries are in tippetotje's letter on modern painting . . . because what if it were really true that the world will one day collapse, and nothing but a little sand will rustle around the last remains of—by way of an example—the palace of justice or the "allee-verte" station? . . . there is no modern painter who doesn't put lonely expanses of sand on the canvas

56

with rubble and the shadow of a woman, and there isn't a modern writer who doesn't talk about fear and more fear. And you see the rapid shadow of johan janssens gliding past, laden with cans and brushes, and His worries must be about something totally different, about less reflective matters, let's say. And you wrench open your front door, and at the last moment tread on the shadow of a ladder, and ask: what are your worries, johan janssens? And he puts down his ladders and paint cans and replies: oh, my great worry is that I can never really worry about anything . . . life is too quick for me . . . the things that should be noted circle around me like swarms of birds, and if I managed to shoot one of them down, the other 99 would fly Far away. For a few days I've been back working for the old master-painter, who has his work-shop over there by the 1st grimy houses . . . and while painting a elevator car with him I hear the weird story of madame, who tells the old master-painter about her milk . . . her milk isn't good, she says. And he stands nodding his head good-humoredly . . . sometimes our milk is no good either, he thinks. No, it's not good and that's why I have to have it drained off. And so the old master-painter is a bit alarmed but remains polite and says: what do you mean? And when the lady has gone he says: what was all that about . . . about her milk? And look, says johan janssens, as I continued painting the elevator car, I thought what a nice article one could write about it. But no sooner had I started to put it together in my mind than the old master-painter's son started a conversation with me . . . about all those newspaper columns I write. But what kinds of people do you write about in those columns, he asked . . . about mossieu colson of the ministry, and the master and the rest . . . they're all intellectuals! And he pronounces that word with fathomless contempt. What kind of people are they? They're not people, they're intellectuals! And sure enough, says johan janssens, it hit me harder than you can imagine, that for a young apprentice painter intellectuals aren't people. And on the way home, at midday, I thought of writing a column about *that* . . . but when I got to the bar on the corner, over there by the 1st grimy houses, there's a truck and they're unloading coal into the cellar . . . and I watch the man emptying a sack from his shoulders, a nervous guy with thick owl-like specs, but with an American army cap on his head . . . good god, it's the poet johan brams. And the poet johan brams, who's working as a coalman, strikes up a conversation with me, johan janssens, who's working as a housepainter . . . and he boxes the air and jumps from one leg to another, as he normally does, and cries out: well, that's a sign of the times! And what do you know, it went through my head like a lightning bolt that I should worry about *that*, that I should write a column about that. But no sooner had I realized this than johan brams, heaving a new sack of coal onto his shoulders, said the following: what do you know . . . someone's attacked you in the daily paper!

And johan janssens picks up his paint cans and ladders again, and worries about the fact that there is too much in life to be able to worry about One Particular Thing.

THE LAST DAYS OF MANKIND

Walking on a beautiful Sunday morning to the country outside termuren, to tolfpoets's so-called villa, to the music master's meadow, mossieu colson of the ministry says the following to you in confidence: of course I'm an enthusiastic supporter, but just between us, when I see you writing about life Separated from life . . . that meadow of the music master's, that cat of sickwit the student's, and all the rest, then I'm inclined to call your work: the tragedy of isolation. When I read everything you write, I always think of karl kraus, who died in june '36, and who like you, it seems to me, was an artist who did not believe in historical development, in the forces of the future, if I can put it like that. Certainly, he was an exceptionally violent opponent of modern social conditions, who hacked away at the always-rampant tendrils of corruption and debased culture . . . but his ideology, as it is called, his literary oeuvre, as it is known, broke in two at this point: he too proved incapable of seeing what he was criticizing as a historically inevitable period in the development of society, which will eventually give way to other, higher forms. If I were to list your titles, they would show a striking similarity with the titles of karl kraus: downfall of the world . . . the last days of mankind . . . etcetera, that show that his criticism of present-day society became bogged down in a deep pessimism without hope of a better future: kraus was stuck in negation, just as you will be if you don't change. I don't know, I haven't read that book of his myself, but I found something about it yesterday, leafing through a very old magazine, and the critic discussing it called it a very one-sided book—after saying that when it appeared it was totally ignored, he added in his turn that that it was an extremely one-sided book—and he managed to say the following about that extremely one-sided, that deeply pessimistic, that negative book: in these scenes, where more than 500 characters appear, we find only one good person: in the 38th scene of the 4th act the following happens: a soldier is first tied to a tree in a temperature of 30 below zero by his company commander, and then thrown half-dead into a stinking hole . . . and when he begs for a drink, one of his comrades, who has to guard him, says: this is more than a man can stand, I'll hold a snowball to his lips. And that is the only time that a touch of humanity is depicted in a tragedy of 743 pages . . . 743 pages in which all classes of society take the stage . . . from streetwalker to emperor . . . one sentence of humanity and compassion, amid the rest that depicts nothing but stupidity and corruption, nothing but deceit and brutalization, nothing but lies and baseless pride . . . a single humane soldier, amid an army of incompetent officers, venal politicians, war manufactures amassing fortunes. And in those last days kraus depicted not 1 type but 20 and more, for the reader must not be allowed to think he was being shown an exception: that's what they're all like, and that's why kraus presented numerous examples of each type. You see, that's karl kraus's book, the book of Negation . . . the book that you'll probably run right off and look for and read . . . because I know you, you'll probably honor him as a predecessor, and try to continue the tradition of his work. You mustn't hunt for that work and immerse yourself in it . . . in my humble opinion you should retain only the following from it: that kraus shut himself up in his bitterness, that he sought out the music master's meadow and tolfpoets's so-called villa, in order to live there Outside life: that he experienced the tragedy of isolation, and gave not a single glimmer of hope for a better world. Because where you see disruption around you, it's really the quite normal signs of winter and death, they're just rotting leaves which must turn to manure and provide nourishment for the coming of a new spring. These are not the last days of Mankind, but the last days of a certain kind of humanity.

THE LAST DAYS OF ONDINE?

For oscarke then everything began to stand on its head and hell was heaven . . . but what was heaven for ondine, who had wanted the most impossible things in life? and who had seen all her desires, 1 by 1, go up in smoke? They had all been dreams, dreams and dreams, and the only tangible thing was the days in the room above the café of the 1st grimy houses, the broth, and her own modestly growing belly. These days were too strikingly similar to those other days, in her youth, when . . . when . . . when a child had fallen into the toilet, which she had never dared to think of since. Again she wandered round in her nightdress, and since she'd lost the curling tongs her hair hung in bunches . . . however small the room was, everything got lost, she had to hunt for hours for everything . . . and she didn't feel like hunting: it was a mountain of chaos that she couldn't possibly shift. What was it with god, that he tested her so sorely? Sailor and mr brys and all those other socialists were doing well . . . look at how happy mr brys was over there in England, he could even afford to feel homesick, he was coming back to his old homeland as if he were one of the aristocracy, while she in her struggle against this godlessness didn't retain slightest trace of prosperity. Yet she did not dare to rebel in those days. And on top of that, how could she lose the curling tongs . . . they couldn't just run off on their own! Actually she didn't dare look for them, actually she didn't dare curl her hair, because she was thinking of the child, the other one, that had never been christened and that no one had ever seen . . . and which in her

59

thoughts was ALIVE: after all it had a soul, and that soul was haunting chapel road over there, where it was lonely, despite the villas that recently been built. Ondine scarcely dared stay alone in the dark any longer, as soon as evening fell she sat down at the window and looked over at the district round the 1st grimy houses . . . she waited for oscarke and listened out for the footsteps of the people due to come from the train . . . but each moment the silence grew more painful and frightening . . . she left the room backwards, on tiptoe, as if she could deceive and mislead the thing she was afraid of. Then she slammed the door and hurried downstairs . . . and once downstairs she had to giggle at her own crazy fear, she talked the fear away, she had just come for a glass of beer, a glass of brown ale with a lump of sugar in it. Yet she was back there the next evening. She started to get a taste for that beer, and could no longer do without it . . . then oscarke would arrive and find her downstairs in the bar, and was allowed a sip from her glass . . . and as they went back to their room she did not admit her immense fear of being alone, but did admit her immense desire to get drunk . . . drunk, drunk . . . so that she would no longer know where she was in the world. But the same night she woke up, bathed in sweat . . . again she felt the same pains as before, after the birth of the child, when a raging fire had consumed her insides. And it was not just because of the pains themselves that she sweated blood: it was mainly the thought that they were leading to something involving death. She wasn't really aware of mumbling: it definitely can't have gone right with the 1st one, I'll have to pay for it, you'll see. Oscarke probably didn't understand her garbled words, he looked for a candle, and by the light of that flickering flame he lit the stove and warmed cloths to put on her belly: and to see her sweating and squirming, with her skinny bird's face, with her hair in tangled bunches, it wasn't a pretty sight for him. She groaned and asked for something to put her to sleep: if the pain rises to my heart I'll be dead, she said. But she didn't want a doctor, she was frightened that the doctor would find out what had happened in the past . . . but she couldn't explain that to oscarke, she couldn't explain it to anyone: it was something she just had to bear, and she asked the lord god for strength and willpower; to conceal the fact that she had murdered a child: god knows what she had already blurted out! She asked oscarke what she had said just now. Said? asked oscarke . . . he thought about and thought it might have been that she wanted to get drunk. Yes, that was it, she said . . . get me some drink! He slipped down the dirty stairs and groped his way round the bar which was dark and smelled of spilt beer and cigarette butts . . . he did not want to wake up the landlady . . . that is, he did not dare go and wake her, he was afraid of her overabundance of bosom and buttock . . . and feeling his way round in the dark he found a bottle on the bar: I'll get ondine to pay for it tomorrow, he thought. But of course he would forget tomorrow. Ondine first poured some of the bottle into cracked coffee cup . . . they had nothing but cracked coffee cups, not a single beer glass, not a single measuring cup . . . then she put the bottle to her lips while oscarke watched it empty, gradually empty in astonishment; and from the bottle he looked in bewilderment at ondine. But she didn't finish it completely . . . she collapsed like a lump of lead, the bottle escaped her hand and rolled across the bed: ondine, ondine! said oscarke in amazement. He picked up the bottle and looked at the small amount remaining by the light of the candle . . . he drank it up . . . at first it was sweet in the mouth, but then it started burning . . . he became strangely lightheaded: he felt like the night and fog that he saw clear away every morning through the train window: in this station it was still dark and there was an arc lamp on, and in the next station the pathetic light of the arc lamp had already become useless along the morning platform. That was how he felt now. He was bewildered because not one of his problems remained . . . for example his doubts about god and socialism: he saw quite clearly that the priest was wrong: god wanted what was good, and socialism was good, because it wanted comfortable streetcars for the workers . . . and so god was a socialist . . . christ had been a socialist: we must start praying for everyone to become socialists. And it was like a revelation as he stood and looked at ondine lying there as if dead, that he realized that she was not part of god but part of the devil: she understood, she fathomed people, she knew all about what he was feeling and thinking in his haven over in brussels . . . and so he had first assumed that she was something like god: but it wasn't true, she and the priest and that abnormal religion: they were something devilish. That became clear particularly in terms of the problem with her over there, with his dearest girl, with the dearest thing he knew of under the sun: god could surely tolerate there being 1 thing that was joyful in his life: god wasn't a torturer, and so he had allowed a human being to be born, a being who had said: come unto me all ye who are heavy laden. And he was heavy laden, and behold, god forgave him and brought jeannine, put her in his path. I am not bad, I want to be like a father to her, all I want is to serve my art through her. His art. And he wanted to go over to the bucket of clay, there in the corner, but his legs failed him . . . his mind was like a trap, but his legs were like rags. What was wrong with ondine, who had drunk the whole bottle? He began to think she was dead: it was impossible that it hadn't killed her. He undressed and blew out the candle, and as far as he could he moved closer to her and tried to get hold of some of the covers: he lay there with his eyes open and was afraid of having to touch her, for fear of feeling her grow cold.

NIHILISM BUT NOT REALLY

The music master has been to see his bit of meadow, the meadow that he has bought way out beyond termuren, and is now walking along the winding path, lost in the country . . . and as if it was meant to be he bumps into the last landscape painter still putting a stream and a tree on canvas, and enjoying himself mightily in doing so. And the music master rubs his glasses clean and says: you can enjoy yourself reading a book and you can enjoy yourself putting trees on canvas . . . but in my opinion it's not serious work: it's recreation, not Labor. And while the last landscape painter bows his head in shame, the music master raises a solemn index finger in the air: in painting thou shalt labor and not enjoy thyself, since amusement is always destructive while labor is something constructive. And having said this, the music master feels himself grow by 3 centimeters. But the last landscape painter replies, quite casually: when I read what all of you wrote in the book about chapel road, that's certainly labor . . . but your labor is more dangerous than my amusement, because it's destructive labor: all you can do is demolish without ever building anything, all you can do is deny but aren't able to put any new faith in its place. And the music master stands there with his 3 centimeters . . . but he scratches his musical ear and conjures up some piece of sophistry: even though we have nothing to replace it with, at least we are offering Nothing instead of the totally erroneous. And to this the last landscape painter replies, quietly and modestly, but effectively: if you offer nothing but Nothing, then you're Nihilists! Ow. And again the music master stands there . . . he who himself has so often said that our book on chapel road is far too nihilistic, hears himself called a nihilist in turn by this landscape painter seeking nothing but enjoyment . . . and as he treads on his musical toe, the penny drops: you can plant trees in the middle of the jungle, he says to the last landscape painter, and in the same way you can build ever more powerful engines for our society that is hurtling towards the abyss, and all that seems to be constructive work, but it's not true. And having said that he rises like a lark into the sky and cries out: in this case constructive work would be: felling trees in the jungle, shutting down the engines with which our society is hurtling towards the abyss. Seen in that way our nihilism is not nihilism but a constructive razing to the ground. And placing himself right in front of the last landscape painter, he tells a story about children playing in the street, on the slate steps of the church . . . and the little girl suggests to the others that they go into the church and say a prayer to baby jesus . . . but the slightly older boy asks if she has any money . . . and the little girl stares silently at the slate steps, the ironclad door, and that towering building. And he tells a second story, about a little boy who has learned at nuns' school how christ was laid on the cross, and nailed to it with great thick nails . . . and as soon as he gets home he climbs on a chair to look at the copper cross more closely, and then the nihilistic miracle; he says: hell, this one's been screwed on. And you see, says the music master . . . you see, I put my hope and trust in the girl who looked up in disappointment at the lofty door of the church, I put my hope and trust in the little boy who was able to test his faith against reality—and for as long as I put my hope and trust in something, you have no right to call me a nihilist—those children will have both feet on the ground and look at man as he is: a being who preaches love and justice in order to take advantage, to become vastly rich, to control the world more quickly . . . those children will demolish the world that was built on false assumptions, that was built from an arbitrary point, far above or far beyond the earth . . . and is hence a castle in the air. And so they will finally succeed . . .

Very true, said the last landscape painter . . . very true, but would you mind getting out of my way now, so I can go on amusing myself negatively for a bit by putting that stream on the canvas?

TRUE NIHILISM

Man, I went as white as a sheet, says johan janssens, when I read that bit about nihilism . . . first of all the music master has gone up into the air again, just to make that last landscape painter doubt himself—since anyone who really believes in himself has gone down the drain—but I went pale most of all because it's pure fabrication that he was lost in the country walking there and met the last landscape painter: that country road isn't lost at all, but ends in a proper road: a road that runs through the countryside: a street which older poets would say lies strewn and lost, and which younger poets would say is an outpost of the advancing city. But it is neither one nor the other: it's just that land is a bit cheaper there, it's cheaper to build yourself a cottage. And doing a job for the old master-painter in that street going nowhere, I didn't meet either the music master or the last landscape painter . . . painting a house-front I only saw two men who had grown some potatoes and beans close-by and were chatting . . . one was a retired railway fireman, and was constantly weaving the railways and His train into the conversation and the other was a man who works at the labor weaving mill and was constantly talking about his machine . . . they both talked about Their machine, but they each meant a totally different machine . . . but apart from that they understood each other very well. And meanwhile a woman with a fat belly had come and sat in the shade of the house, and also joined in the conversation . . . but she kept talking about what might be going wrong: I'm already 3 weeks overdue and nothing's happening. And suddenly a stranger appeared and turned to the two men who were talking about their machines: they've just called me in about my father, who died in the clinic, a brain operation. And all of them together, the 2 men with their machines and the woman with the belly and the stranger, continued the conversation, but now operations were the main topic: the brain is something They still can't quite get to the bottom of . . . operations are always successful, but it's the complications that kill us . . . we're guinea pigs.

They lure us in and cut us open and the rest is gibberish . . . but you have to pay. And the man whose father it is, says nothing and thinks: it's my father. And the retired fireman goes on about His train and operations, and thinks: it's not my father. And the man who works at the labor weaving mill goes on about his machine and about operations, and about something that isn't in the least relevant: the resistance—what, what's that got to do with it?—I'm glad, he says, that I was never in the resistance, I was too smart and my father-land wasn't worth it . . . besides which, the resistance is something that only emerged after the war . . . during the war no one talked to you about the resistance, and after the war everyone told you they'd been in the resistance. And the retired fireman nods and says he knew an engine driver who was also in the resistance and now needs a brain operation: and I told him so, says the retired fireman. And the stranger nods and says: I told my father too, but what can you do? And the woman with her belly . . . yes, she suddenly goes inside, and another woman comes out, shouting for them to hurry: it's a girl. And the three men interrupt their conversation for a moment and start nodding and congratulating. Congratulations! says the retired fireman, and he goes on talking about operations and mishaps and His machine. Congratulations! says the man who works at the labor weaving mill, and goes on talking about the resistance that in his view did not exist during the war, and about mishaps and about His machine. And johan janssens concludes: and so, there in that road going nowhere, it was a lot different from a conversation about supposed nihilism . . . it was true and unvarnished nihilism itself.

JANPIETERSEN JUNIOR

Over by the 1st grimy houses behind the labor factory there's a fair and a barbecue, and you stand at your front door on this beautiful summer evening, and hear the tortured music from the loudspeakers . . . and see the people from the fair and the barbecue quickly finding their way to chapel road: the men with the overconfidence of their sex just stand there and the women squat down and look left and right. You stand there and occasionally toss away a smoldering cigarette butt, and that's all there is to be seen of your inner drama. Only mossieu colson of the ministry comes to keep you company for a moment and to toss his cigarette butts alongside yours. Worries? He asks, staring at yet another shadow seeking a dark corner . . . and you nod and you ask him whether he has read your latest chapters, and whether he has any criticisms. They are . . . they are . . . he starts hesitating. But you cut him short and say flatly: they are not worth a damn. And that judgment, worthless, so alarms the dimness of chapel road that the shadow over there in the corner hurries back to the light and the fair and the barbecue. They are worthless

. . . you are all standing around me to point out my futility, my work is not becoming the broad stream, the mighty breath, the all-embracing fresco that it should be. It's something that's just been knocked together, hesitant and dead . . . when I read the last few pages a smell of death fills my nostrils. *I should let that novel about oscarke and ondine go its own way*, and only occasionally interrupt it with an observation, an occasional section, an occasional short sentence, a trifling remark, just a few words. Now, on the contrary, it's becoming artificial, like the window of a clothes shop, a tailor-made suit, a wax dummy with a price tag: a column for the weekly papers. And mossieu colson wants to speak, no, no, you check his words: be quiet and let me look the truth in the face for once: I find that novel full of nooks and crannies as repellent as cold porridge—as the proverb says, though I'd much rather say as hot porridge, since in my view porridge should be served up cold—I'd much rather start on something new, a novel of daily press clippings . . . as I've kept up with the papers for the last 3 years and cut out everything that was affecting and moving, and I can go on and on reading them like they were a masterpiece: it just needs structuring a little, pruning, clarification, with a bit more emphasis, with maybe a thread running through it maybe with some story of some family, let's say the story of everything that the members of that family have got up to, resolved to do but did not do, did but never thought that they would do, said but didn't mean, thought but immediately forgot.

Yes, I can hear it, says mossieu colson of the ministry, within you burns the eternal flame of the creative human being, who wants to edify, who can't go to sleep at night if he hasn't picked up 970 ideas during the day and piled them into a structure, a wall . . . and you're forgetting that there are people who likewise can't go to sleep without having demolished a wall during the day and strewn it along the road, 970 scattered stones: look at the museum for the poet janpietersen junior. How do you mean? You ask. And mossieu tells you that the museum in question was being inaugurated, and the curator, a walloon, invited all his friends . . . also all walloons . . . performed a french medieval play in the open air. But since it was ostensibly partly also the museum of a flemish poet, they started looking for a fleming to say a few words about janpietersen junior himself. And quite by chance they came across kramiek, who after the french open-air theater and the french speeches added a few words of flemish about janpietersen junior. And I, mossieu colson of the ministry, asked kramiek a few things about janpietersen junior, and kramiek replied: actually I don't know him that well. I only gave the talk to do the curator a favor because I fancy his daughter.

And you gaze at mossieu colson expectantly. As if some explanation is still to follow . . . but no, he says nothing more . . . and you ask: right, but what are you actually getting at? And he looks at you with a skeptical grin and says:

well, just suppose that you're neither the walloon curator, nor his daughter, nor kramiek . . . but quite simply the poet janpietersen junior himself! And gazing at yet another shadow slipping away from the discount fair in order to spray the dusk of chapel road for a moment . . . gazing at that shadow you nod your head in agreement: indeed, imagine after all your labors, all your self-criticism, after all your inner dramas that your were only that poet, janpietersen junior.

OSCARKE LONGS TO SEE CLEARLY

Oscarke lay next to ondine with his eyes open and was afraid to touch her, feeling her go cold. A moment ago everything had been clear in his mind: god was good, god was just . . . and everything was as good and bad as it could possibly be. But now it was yet again no longer the case, because ondine was dead. And that meant he was glad she was dead, and at the same time was frightened because he was glad: no, these ideas of his weren't so simple. He couldn't get to sleep—I won't get any sleep all night, he thought—and went on looking at the ceiling, and suddenly started awake: he had been sitting next to ondine in the train and ondine was dead, he told everyone not to touch her, because she was already cold . . . and suddenly the train stopped and there was no train, just a dark tunnel, and a man in a gray uniform and a rifle over his shoulder came towards him slowly out of the darkness . . . oscarke looked at him and sat as if paralyzed, as if death itself, or something far worse, were approaching. He started awake and felt his heart pounding as if it were about to burst: still, I was able to close my eyes for a few moments, he thought. It wasn't true, though; he had slept right through, and the tinkle of the alarm was what woke him: it was 4 o'clock, he had to get ready and run to catch his train. And ondine? He had not dared look at her . . . the way she had lain there, the way she would be lying there just the same when he got home: cold and stiff. And yet, was he happy? On the contrary, his conscience was troubled and heart was heavy . . . he was cold in the train, he was even cold out there in the new lane, although the weather was still very nice for these 1st few days of october. But when he came home after dark, she was still lying in bed . . . but dead?: it looked as if she could endure tremendous punishment, and so doing would inflict tremendous punishment on him, but she would never die. Her head felt fit to burst from having downed that whole bottle, but her belly was still hurting too. And would he have to get a new bottle every night until she was an out-and-out drunk? She was silent and thought of that night when she had hung a blanket across the window before throwing her shame down the toilet. Now everything would come out! She thought: if he talks about a doctor, it'll be proof that a doctor must come, everything must happen as god wills it. But oscarke did not mention a doctor, he sat silently thinking about himself . . . and a little later, when he heard a terrible fight going on down in the bar, he remembered that the bottle had not yet been paid for . . . well, ondine would settle that when she was better. She called him over to the bed: oscarke, she said, what do you think . . . should we get the doctor? He stood up and took his short overcoat off the nail in the wall. Oscarke, she repeated. A very weak sound came from the bed . . . he turned back to her . . . she grasped his hand and cried. Well, what's wrong? He asked. But could she explain that it was only a question . . . and that it was up to him, him alone to make a final decision? For her it would be a sign from god . . . but to him that "oscarke" sounded like the feeble cry of an animal in distress and he didn't know how to answer the cry. She thought she was going to die, or that in the worst case she would be thrown in jail for murder . . . degenerate murder . . . years ago young mother threw baby down toilet . . . and she wanted to confess, she just couldn't bear it alone any longer. But gathering all her strength she whispered: if the doctor comes and says things . . . things implicating me in heaven knows what, don't you believe it . . . I've always been fond of you, oscarke, will you help me? . . . you'll help me, won't you? . . . you'll stand by me, won't you? He nodded, pulled his hand from hers . . . it was clammy, that hand of hers, and as skinny as a bird's claw . . . and as he went down the stairs into the bar he could hear that the argument was long since over—upstairs it was ondine and her eternal belly, and down here it was the landlady and her eternal arguments—only a drunk stood outside leering at the closed door: and the next time you think you're a bottle short, count them first . . . count them. Oh, it suddenly dawned on oscarke that they were talking about a bottle . . . a bottle that had been stolen . . . and that He was the one who . . . and he went bright red in the dark night, walked off hunched, pounding his way past the house in search of a doctor; he thought: ondine and her belly, that bar and that fight and that bottle . . . and me, and jeannine. And as he looked for a doctor he went unconsciously towards the house with the big window, where at the beginning ondine had talked him into believing they were going to live . . . he saw again the slate under the windows in which a decoration had been carved seemingly in the shape of a woman's breast. He suddenly realized what ondine had wanted back then: in that stone she had wanted to show him her own breast, he felt it now and found out that ondine had been lying: it wasn't her breast, it was jeannine's breast. Jeannine, that stolen bottle about which there'd been an argument in the bar, the landlady and her eternal squabbles, ondine and her eternal belly, a doctor. He rang the bell and wondered what he was supposed to say . . . he wondered what the doctor would say in reply, especially when he realized he was being called out to some poor folk's garret, that someone had the audacity to get him out of bed to look at the belly of a poor person. And oscarke became servile and humble and made ondine's illness sound like something fearsome . . . and later, when it all turned out to be nothing serious, he would show the doctor that he had just been an anxious and ignorant idiot, but that his respect for and trust in doctors was boundless. A little later the doctor was already walking with him down the street in the dark and even said that it was nice weather for october, shame about *the fog. And oscarke agreed that it was a shame about the fog, and chatted on a bit, about this and that, about how he was so used to seeing this town of the 2 mills at night: I leave at about 4 in the morning in the dark, and I come home in the dark at about 10 at night . . . and you may laugh, but I long for just one thing . . . And as they walked on he looked at the doctor and waited until he answered: the doctor looked at him and said that he wouldn't laugh: well, said oscarke, it's to see this street in daylight for a change. And the doctor could not help laughing softly . . . and oscarke laughed too, firstly because he did not dare kick up a fuss, and secondly because when he put into words, it did sound rather ridiculous. Still, it hurt him, and stopped him from going on pouring his heart out . . . and it also made him reflect that that a rich man can never be a brother to someone who has to commute backwards and forwards to brussels.*

I JUST CAN'T BELIEVE IT

When you suddenly see woelus arriving over there in his fairground wagon to claim the spot where last week the children of chapel road pitched their tent . . . no, you just can't believe it . . . you just can't believe that he's back again from his journey through the land of the sun and fairs: because it means that the winter is about to begin, it means snow and ice and rain and wind, it means hibernation and death across flanders. And from your threshold you stare at woelus and his wagon, and you say to mossieu colson of the ministry: I just can't believe that that's the end of all that sun, all those girls in their light summer dresses, those children in their packaging tent, and that once again gray skies will extend over chapel road. And mossieu colson nods reflectively and says: you could write a poem about it like karel van de woestijne: again the smudgy light of the asters will bloom, again autumn approaches . . . but you'd have to change those asters into woelus's fairground wagon. And you confess that it would indeed be like that, if it were not for the fact that instead of a poet, you're just a cheap hack: you write something, and it's only when it's been set down that you begin to see what's wrong with it. You're an eternal doubter and an eternal unbeliever, concurs mossieu colson. Just recently I received some printed pages about the death of my sister jeanneke, you say . . . in which I wrote that I no longer believed in god and his wizards the priests, nor in science and its white wizards the doctors. You're an eternal doubter and unbeliever, repeats mossieu colson . . . and apart from that, the driving idea in your work doesn't shoot forward like an arrow from a bow, but on the contrary creeps along tentatively like a vine on a brick wall. I can't help that, mossieu colson . . . I no sooner think *of allowing ondineke's father vapeur another chance to say his piece in our novel about ondineke . . . of having her father vapeur say that god is going to be replaced by science—the time*

68

will come, ondine, when people will have to pray by inventing things—and no
sooner do I think of having vapeur say that than I start doubting science too.
Vapeur believes that science will oust god from his throne . . . and I, who had
vapeur say such a thing, begin that very instant to see science as a new god
that I have to doubt as much as the old. I imagine that the time is actually
approaching when science will be ousting religion . . . in the past religion
had indicated vaguely and blindly a point in eternity, and said that this was
man's ultimate goal . . . and then science came and denied that the blind spot
in the distance existed, but continued groping around in turn: this is a stone,
this is an atom: and what if we explode that atom? And as it investigates the
tree of life and knowledge, science ousts religion, but scientists become the
modern high priests, there's no questioning their omniscience. We've replaced
the incomprehensible symbols and mysteries of faith with the equally incomprehensible symbols of geometry, and the mysteries of higher mathematics.
Science has become a religion, and those who don't understand it must be
silent and believe . . . those who weren't satisfied with the vague and super-
natural goal of religion—where a human being could no longer be a human
being, but had to become an angel—helped science to oust that faith . . . but
now science has become a religion in turn, spreading its omnipotent tentacles,
dissecting and reassembling things, making man into something that can be
split up into atoms and using those atoms for the benefit of society and indus-
trial concerns. And what will become of science in this way? No more and
no less than a new dishcloth to replace the old: the god who was worshipped
was a capricious god, a being that was believed to exist, a hypothesis . . . and
the god hypothesis is simply being replaced by a science hypothesis . . . science
becomes something dogmatic, something that commands us to believe blindly
without allowing us to doubt whether its goal is the True goal, without being
allowed to question whether it brings more harm than good. And we, who
doubt science just as we doubted god . . . we shall be denied salvation a second
time: tomorrow or the day after science will have its own inquisitors, its pope
and its gallows . . . and man will again be reduced to slavery, believing that
he was put on earth to serve and praise science.

And mossieu colson stares at woelus's fairground wagon, which has
appeared in chapel road . . . that has returned from the land of sun and fairs
to seek shelter in chapel road from black ice and snow and rain and wind.
And he in his turn shakes his head and stammers: I can't believe it.

FENCING OFF

With a protective hand on the pocket with his sparsely filled purse in it, the
music master proceeds from the lumber yard to the hardware store . . . and

when he meets johan janssens on the way he stops for a moment and says: a man may dream of turning a meadow into an earthly paradise, but if you want to make the dream a reality, then your 1st priority must be: putting a fence round that earthly paradise. And johan janssens has no time to mount his social hobbyhorse and join battle: the music master is too quick for him: no, don't say I have no social conscience because I want to reserve that dream for myself alone. No it's something else . . . I could plant fruit trees, and I wouldn't mind a bit if one fine day all my apples and pears were gone . . . for me the most important thing is that the trees I've planted should blossom and grow and bear fruit according to their nature—as it says in the book of genesis—and whether or not that fruit benefits me, the rightful owner, really wouldn't matter that much to me. But I know to my great regret that other people aren't so concerned with that fruit, that it's not their intention to steal other people's fruit for their own use, but on the contrary just to take something away, to prevent you possessing it. Not out of desire for an apple, but so that someone else should not have that apple . . . so that they can savor the german word "schadenfreude" as you stand there sadly contemplating, that not only has your fruit has been stolen, but your trees have also been violated, branches cracked, stalks damaged, the trunk snapped. And to think that it's all out of hatred and rage at Possession . . . that they were furious because they are poor as can be and can't call a single fruit tree their own, while other people can consider building themselves an earthly paradise . . . if only it were out of hatred, out of the noble hatred of the duped thin man for the dishonest fat man . . . that they had got the wrong idea, thinking that I—I, a music master with savings—am an estate owner living off their sweat and blood and poverty, so that they break and crack my young trees: that'll teach you to be rich! But it's not even that, because go by the castle wood, go by the gardens and orchards of the castle of mr derenancourt, the catholic mayor: you won't find anything stolen or destroyed: no, they're left alone because people are scared shitless, terrified of the catholic mayor mr derenancourt of the castle: he would get them fired from the filature spinning mill, he'd have them thrown in jail, evict their parents, and have their children excluded from heaven. They don't hate mr derenancourt: they're afraid of him. And so it's the trees in the town parks that are mutilated and vandalized and torn down, it's their neighbors' trees, it's the trees of all those who are on the same bottom rungs of the social ladder: it's their own trees that they tear down. Because they have such an urge to destroy, and they don't destroy what stands in the way of progress, they destroy their own property, their own rights, their own happiness and prosperity and peace and freedom . . . and defile and smash up the property of those who are near to them, of those who belong to their own class. They destroy themselves, and respect and fear only those who look down on them like a catholic gendarme, a catholic priest, a catholic lord-god with a flaming beard. And the music master has pronounced that harsh judgment like a rhapsody. You must really hate working people, johan janssens is about to say astride his social hobbyhorse . . . but the music master doesn't give him time: you might think that I hate working people, but that's not true . . . I'm furious with them, I could weep and stamp my feet because of them . . . because look, not far from my meadow the chief engineer of the filature spinning mill has bought himself a piece of land and is going to build a house . . . he's the son of a poor guy with a social conscience who in his youth took part in the class struggle, and who in that noble struggle won something for his children: his son has now become chief engineer in the mill instead of a spinner, and now walks around in a gleaming white topcoat. Thanks to the contributions of the first socialists, and thanks to the socialist workers' college, he was able to become an engineer, and can walk round the factory in a gleaming white topcoat. And now . . . now his father, the veteran socialist fighter, is proud of him because the whole workforce is scared of him: he tells everyone, his chest swelling with pride, that his son is a hard taskmaster to the workforce, quick to haul them before mr derenancourt of the mill, and gives them 8 days' notice . . . yesterday he was in the factory canteen and he dressed emmerance down for saying prosper instead of sir: our prosper doesn't care two hoots that emmerance used to live right next door, and he's quite right: there's only one master.

And johan janssens stares speechlessly at the music master from astride his social hobbyhorse, and he hears him ask in the wood yard and the hardware store for posts that are not too heavy and wire that is not too thick. Do you think perhaps there's still the ghost of a chance that they'll reform? asks johan janssens. They may reform, but the reason I don't want too substantial a barrier is that I've got to watch what I spend.

THE NEW NOVEL

And as you stand there on your threshold still staring at woelus's fairground wagon, you see woelus himself, who says hallo with a wide sweep of the arm from the steps of his caravan: there's something about him, something that's traveled with him from the land of sun and fairs, and that he'll lose soon, lose once it starts turning from october to december over chapel road . . . and mossieu colson returns that greeting together with you: good to see you, woelus, but a pity you herald the winter like the crows. And turning back to you mossieu colson says with a smile: and that he brings the rain with him into your books . . . soon you'll be making it pour down again! And you answer, also with a smile, that our book is quite simply the record of this age and these people and this weather: I'm not happy about it, but I started with a chapter called "spring in termuren" and now gone on with "summer in termuren," I have to continue the series . . . I have to write autumn and winter in termuren too: that's the problem with a novel. And apart from that, novels are more durable and enduring than their writers . . . they're pages and pages long, and they take you years and years to write . . . but can I write about nothing but you, mossieu colson, for years on end? Or about woelus with his fairground wagon who returns every winter like van de woestijne's aster and the winter aspirin ads? No, I'm sick of it, I'm absolutely sick of it . . . I'm going on with the novel simply because I've started it, but yesterday evening I just couldn't go on writing: it was thursday, and in the fog and darkness a couple came along and started courting with their back against woelus's wagon . . . and while I watched that eternal game recommencing, he pressing her against the wagon, she unwilling and said no . . . as I watched I wanted to write a piece about it . . . and I also wanted to write a piece about that eternal game people play, not aware of what they're doing, living blindly and blindly obeying laws, never thinking but more or less Feeling things . . . I wanted to write pieces about all that, mossieu colson, but I couldn't . . . something in me wanted to go on, that person who's not yet a person but is more or less alive, more or less obeys laws, the laws that make the sphere roll when you kick it, and which stop it rolling if opposing forces come into play. And you'll say that by not writing that piece, I am still obeying a law, the law of inertia, but it's not true . . . oh for christ's sake spare me that sarcastic smile! . . . let me believe I'm not obeying the law of *at first being enthusiastic about something, and then gradually getting sick of it* . . . no, it's just that as a human being I'm too aware of my impotence, aware that this book of mine should have been finished long ago, and that I should already have started on another book, a new book: my book of press clippings. I didn't write that column—a column a day, I tell myself, until I've turned into a column myself—I didn't write it but read back through my novel of press clippings: oh, mossieu colson, what a wondrous novel it is! About a trip through the brazilian jungle, people who were recruited and promised the earth, and had to tap rubber trees in the forests of brazil and died there . . . and all, thousands of them, died without anyone saying a word. Oh, the things that are in that book of clippings from the daily press, and I imagine drawing a thread through it: the story of a family, as I once told you . . . and what better family could I choose than my own family? My own weird family from which have come heroes and cowards, a saint martin and a bandit of a baekelandt, a mata hari and a vincent van gogh, consumptives and lushes, nuns, politicians and freemasons: a multicolored mishmash that I can write about till I get writer's cramp, but my heart and my mind would still go on crying: go on, go on!

And mossieu colson of the ministry answers that everything you say is absolutely true: you said the same thing at the start of your last novel, he says.

NOT A NEW NOVEL, BUT A BUSINESS

Oscarke went silently up the stairs above the bar with the doctor . . . the candle flickered in the draft of the open door, and there lay ondine shivering with fear: she was praying and praying. Don't be afraid now, said the doctor . . . he threw off the covers, sniffed, and said that they had bedbugs: something had to be done about that, because they brought disease with them . . . and he looked at ondine and said: especially when there's going to be a baby in a little while, it couldn't be too clean . . . bedbugs are capable of eating it alive. And so her tummy was hurting her?—and he looked at her belly—he could believe it; how long is it since you last went to the toilet? He asked how many months pregnant she was and ordered ondine to lie flat on her back and rest and especially to ensure that she purged herself quite soon. Ondine began to pluck up her courage . . . so he couldn't see it at once, an exultant voice said inside her, he didn't mention it . . . and now she wanted to know if it was noticeable, she was drawing him out as it were, she wanted to tempt her fate and ask whether he noticed anything wrong with her belly. What on earth is wrong with my belly? she asked. Oh, a belly is a dark cellar. Then she fell back laughing softly . . . a belly is a dark cellar . . . and who, entering a cellar, could see what had happened there years before? No one, no one, no one . . . and she went on laughing softly, although she was in unbelievable pain, although the pain would never ever subside again, of that much she was sure. So she stayed in bed and waited for her time . . . she occasionally walked round the room with laborious steps, or sat at the window on the only, hard chair . . . she put the pillow on top, but it was soon squashed flat, and then she was given a wicker chair, a woven seat, by the landlady. She was also given some linen for tearing into strips and sewing into baby clothes. Occasionally the doctor with his silent laugh called to reassure her . . . he sat next to her at the window and looked at the bustle over at the 1st grimy houses, and talked about his boys that had smashed a window somewhere, and where on earth do you see a doctor's sons playing in the street and smashing windows? And the more the doctor told her the sadder ondine became . . . she knew he talked about things like that to bridge the gap between them, and to win her confidence: he was a rich man who was trying to put a poor person at ease: oh, it hurt her terribly that people could see nothing in her besides just another poor person. She started talking about her childhood, she dragged up the old lie of her mother, her mother who had served in the castle and had taken a child away with her . . . she, ondine was that child—and anyway, a lie? Who said it was a lie? But . . . she had lived in the castle that autumn . . . with achilles? An abyss suddenly opened up that she dared not look into: in that case she would have lived there with her half-brother, she would have committed incest. She fell silent . . . and also broke off her train of thought, which had raced ahead of her words . . . and stared at the doctor with dismay in her eyes. Well, what then? he asked gently. Oh, said ondine . . . and she gave a different slant to the story: she told him how she had been an intimate friend of fat mr gourmonprez—and she tried simply pass over mr achilles derenancourt in silence, but it was impossible—and her sudden admission, against her will, that she had been incredibly in love with achilles derenancourt, incest or not, was forced from her, she could do nothing about it: no sooner was it said, shouted aloud, than a distressing and unprecedented blush spread across her face. And as if she could erase this confession she was about to rattle on quickly about lots of other things . . . like her faith and hope and struggle in those days . . . but what good would that flood of words have done? she asked herself, with firmly clenched teeth, looking closely at the doctor, wondering what hidden power might be hidden in his silent laugh. He just sat there, and smiled benevolently, and yet he wheedled out all her secrets: soon he would fish out the fact that she had broken the offertory box in the chapel many, many years ago . . . and that one night in the box room she had . . .

She shivered, despite herself. She sat straight up in her chair. And the upshot was that she said: and so you see how I wound up here! He nodded and went on looking at the bustle over by the 1st grimy houses and at the high back wall that obscured the whole view. So that you have to sit looking at that wall all day long, he said. Ondine looked up in surprise: that wall there was the back wall of the derenancourt mansion. So that they dominated termuren with their castle and they dominated this small town with their 2 mills and their mansion. Ondine suddenly began crying. He comforted her, advised her to get back on her feet as soon as possible . . . she must save, not throw her money away on fancy rubbish or drink . . . and she must be clean, poor but clean, and those who were clean could save . . . and she must try to earn some money too, 2 wages and only 1 child, then they could get ahead quickly . . . but she mustn't leave her money idle, because even with the best will in the world it was no good trying to keep it together: it went as fast as it came: no, she must go into debt for a house of her own, then her money would go into that . . . before she knew it, she would amass a small fortune . . . set up a small business, keep a shop while you husband works: you'll see how you get on. But he had prattled on for too long to be able to convince her . . . meanwhile she had had time to study him like a cat with a saucer of milk, with half-closed eyes, weighing up her chances: she asked him if he would advance her that first sum of money. But if she was shrewd, he was just as shrewd . . . though in a quite different way . . . he sat there still laughing and maintained he had no money to spare with those rascals of his, they were both going to high school, the eldest was preparing to go to university, and the cost of that you just couldn't imagine. And as he sat there dreaming, she realized that he was thinking of His time, and how he had got where he was with hard work . . . it dawned on her that this couldn't be a real rich man: he was a saver—a model bourgeois. They looked at each other, and each one had weighed the other up in a couple of seconds: he wasn't going to lend her money because he could see that saving wasn't in her blood, while she wanted to talk the money out of him—just to have, to give the impression that she was rich, to play the lady at the expense of this stupid bourgeois. But . . . actually it wasn't a bad idea to start a business: she went on thinking about it long after he had gone. Once she could manage with the child, she would get started.

WITH TIPPETOTJE IN PARIS

Stop, cries mossieu colson of the ministry as he charges in, almost knocking over your lamp . . . stop writing a novel in articles, writing about today's world, because you don't know the world till you've seen paris: go to paris, and revise everything you've ever thought and said in your life. And you adjust the lamp and say: I'll put down my pen and go on strike with arms folded till I've seen paris through your eyes. You'll see through my eyes everything of paris that I've seen through the eyes of tippetotje, says mossieu colson. And he looks for an easy chair by the standard lamp, and tells me that he had long wanted to go to paris with tippetotje . . . but you know what tippetotje's like . . . first it was in the baron's car, free of charge, but it was quite possible that she would be going much further than paris, to spain, to morocco, to the jungles of africa . . . all in that car that wasn't even hers, with everything absolutely free of charge . . . and when I asked long afterwards when she was going to drive to africa, she replied that it was next week, but that it was quite possible that she would drive on to the moon . . . well, you know tippetotje, you know that tippetotje has a dream and that she's been chasing that dream all her life: finding the spot in the world where the sun never sets, and where the mountains are made of chocolate, and where at night you can read the book . . . The book . . . that describes why everything is as it is . And finally tippetotje rang me to say that she was going to paris after all, though not in the baron's car but on the train . . . and not with the baron either but with me, mossieu colson, all alone, just the two of us . . . and so not free of charge, but full price. And then I spent 4 days and 4 nights constantly running and running with tippetotje and turning paris on its head—or was it rather tippetotje who turned me on my head?—she ran round and wanted to see picasso and jean-saul partre . . . no, I got it wrong in my haste to dog the heels of tippetotje in her mad dash . . . it was What's-his-name that she wanted to meet, le club du néant, aragon, the booksellers along the seine, henry miller with his bald head . . . and I had only one fear in her mad dash, that tippetotje would meet herself, run into herself, smashing their foreheads together, still searching for what she's been searching for all her life. And I who followed panting in her wake begged her to stop, to have a bit to eat, to catch up on some sleep . . . but tippetotje sped across the streets and boulevards, forcing the cars to brake: we'll get some biscuits in a bit, she said . . . and in a while we'll sleep on a bench, like tramps. And stumbling after her with aching feet, I asked her how much further it was to where What's-his-name lived. Scarcely ten more minutes' walk, called tippetotje over her shoulder . . . and she was already much further on, across streets and boulevards, and I stumbled after her and asked her who we had to see. And tippetotje stopped running for a moment, and said that she didn't know herself Who she actually had to see and didn't know either what she actually had to know: I run and I run and expect that one day I'll bump into what I'm looking for . . . one day something will happen, a thud, a blow, a light and a 1000 stars. But I, mossieu colson, could go no further and collapsed on the spot.

And you uncross your arms and take up your pen again and you ask: and what did paris teach you, mossieu colson? Paris, I didn't see it, he answers . . . all I saw was tippetotje's back, her nice legs . . . and yet, and yet: you've got to have been there and chased around like a madman, if you're going to go on writing columns.

THE CHILD . . . NOT WORTH THE TROUBLE

So the baby arrived, a girl . . . and ondine was rather listless, she cried a little, although oscarke was terribly excited, she thought of the other one, who might also have been a girl. Oscarke's mother, that gray mouse, was going to be godmother, and so it was going to be called judith after her, yes that was a real name for a mouse . . . and ondine couldn't help thinking that everyone gets the name that suits them. Oh, the whole family sat there in that little cubbyhole above the bar, and everyone acted as if there had never been any fighting . . . valeer was there too and looked loutishly at the baby, he was rather flushed and ogled at his sister ondine . . . her father vapeur got talking and told then about his invention: as they approached, the train wheels must make contact with the grooves in the rails, and some ways past the contact must be broken . . . but he would have to study electricity to know more, he had already bought a book, l'électricité et ses applications pratiques. He looked happy, did vapeur . . . since the marriage of his daughter ondine, his son valeer had not gone back to brussels, and he helped his father with the difficult jobs . . . and as he explained the mysteries of electricity to oscarke, who was actually not listening anyway, the gray mouse did her best to make fun of ondine's poverty. It made ondine furious, she could see that the ugly old bat was relishing her son's plight, and so she answered haughtily: no, oscarke doesn't regret having married, because now he can warm himself at the stove as much as he likes, and eat as much as he likes . . . we're not the kind of bourgeois who try to poke out other people's eyes . . . nowadays oscarke sometimes says: it's a bit different from home, where we were hungry and cold! . . . and anyway, poverty . . . actually the whole house belongs to us, the bar downstairs too, but we let it out to the people downstairs. And as if she were thinking about things generally, she continued dreamily: but not for much longer, because I plan to run the bar myself. And oscarke looked up in surprise . . . he knew that when she said things like that, she did them.

So, she'd like to run a bar! he thought, that day and the next. He got back from brussels and out of the train window her saw the october fields with a strange green and red evening sky above them . . . he was trying to direct his thoughts of jeannine a different way, since his hunger for her young sweet body was becoming more intense and disturbing by the day . . . today she had been wearing that blue dress again, in which he couldn't look at her without wanting to tear her open with his rock-hard cock . . . and looking at those hills with the autumn evening stretched out over them, it seem to him suddenly that a field was a woman, a woman about to go to sleep . . . and it moved him and suddenly paralyzed something in him, something that had been hyperactive for the last few days; his struggle suddenly seemed futile; nature was flesh, was assaulting, killing, and procreating. The whole earth was jeannine who was lying there calling to him. And now that he saw this, it became stupid to avert his gaze back home when the baby kicked her legs in the air . . . while here on the contrary, through the train window, he reveled consciously and indulgently in the sight of a huge belly. Ondine and the priest and his mother, the gray mouse, all jumped to their feet and said that it was sinful, to love his own dear jeannine and her young belly . . . but it would never occur to any of then to find it even more sinful to love and posses the belly of this earth. With these thoughts in his mind he climbed the stairs of the bar of the 1st grimy houses . . . but he was astonished to find their room empty: smiling and radiant ondine stood behind the bar. But there wasn't a single customer . . . at first he thought it was a joke, but no, their own wretched little stove was there, and from the kitchen behind the bar he could hear the crying of little judith. Ondine couldn't stop talking . . . there had been an argument again . . . there had been a burglary somewhere around town, and someone had also climbed over the long long wall of the labor weaving mill to steal something, and all the stolen goods had been discovered behind this very bar . . . the public prosecutor immediately took charge and they took the landlady away in her torn black petticoat . . . and she, ondine had hurried to see the brewers, and had taken the place of the landlady.

And so the child had arrived, a girl named judith, and oscarke had rejoiced a little and ondine had wept a little . . . but the main thing was that she had taken the bar by storm.

And yes, something else was the main thing too . . . the main thing just for ondine . . . someone had come into the pub with the news that mr brys was back! And ondine had left the place on the spot, and without giving a thought to little judith she had rushed to monique's: there too she landed in the middle of a disturbed ants' nest: monique among the chinese vases in her drawing room talked about her uncle, mr brys: how super-shrewd those socialists were, he had convinced people that his old bones were longing for his homeland, so they had actually lent him some money for the crossing . . . and now, it had leaked out that he had only come over for the anniversary of the party. Ondine was beside herself . . . the anniversary! . . . they were already celebrating, they had forgotten the days of their arduous rise, back at boone's . . . they no longer remembered the day when they came to smash boone's windows, smear shit over the walls . . . ondine talked about the celebration with everyone she met en route, she put her hands together and turned her dismayed eyes to heaven, as if surprised that no fire and brimstone and pitch were descending from it. But the people from these 1st grimy houses were a little different from the people in the hamlet of termuren . . . true, they were a little uneasy and nodded whenever ondine said that this kind of thing should be banned: since when were murderers and cannibals allowed to take to the street and hold meetings and even celebrate? But she wasn't surprised that the people went about their business and ordered a kilo of salt and kilo of dripping in the shop, just as if . . . just as if the world were Not about to explode that afternoon at the socialists' party. She was pathologically curious about it, she wanted to have a close-up view . . . she went along the canal and looked out over the water; the whole quayside over there was full of that sort: they were in their clogs and swore and spoke loud and filthy factory language . . . mr brys came and stood at a window and presented them with a red flag—where were the days when he would never have dared do such a thing, for fear of the priest, who would have snatched away his ticket to heaven—and ondine also saw lots of people standing round him who in those days had betrayed him . . . Indeed, had jeered at him and smashed up his chairs. But he was an old man with a weak heart, standing there weeping because he'd been presented with an album containing all the portraits of his party comrades: it was ridiculous. And ondine actually did try to laugh at it . . . but it didn't work very well, on the other bank it was full of hurrahing socialists, and on her own bank there was no one, no one.

And so the baby, a girl called judith, lay all alone back in the pub . . . she was crying, and she was of secondary importance in ondine's life.

On a beautiful Sunday morning the music master wanders round like a lost sheep. And calls at johan janssens's house, just like that, without knowing what he wants to do or say . . . and johan janssens comes to the door, with a palette and three brushes in his hand: the music master is so shocked he almost falls over: do you paint too! he exclaims. And he's not called the music master for nothing, saying: and what's happened to your columns in which you were adapting reynard the fox? . . . you forgot them long ago, perhaps you don't even remember you got stuck halfway through, after isengrim the wolf had accused the fox of assaulting his hersinde from behind . . . you stopped at once, and at the same time you stopped all your art criticism, your articles on picasso and salvador dali and delvaux . . . you started painting house fronts, and now you're standing there with a palette and three brushes in your hand: johan janssens, journalist, editorial secretary, housepainter, and artist . . . close your door again and goodbye! But on the contrary johan janssens opens the front door wide to let the music master in: at first I did write art criticism, certainly, and afterwards I certainly painted house fronts . . . and so I was able to test the theory against the practice, and then I got to work . . . let that reynard the fox stew meanwhile, let isengrim go on explaining how the fox assaulted his hersinde from behind, let them get on with it, I'll revise and make a fresh start on that trial all in good time . . . but for now I'm painting, come in, see, and be convinced. And bringing the music master into the small living room, which has a window looking onto chapel road, he lets him admire his painting: joke among the ruins. My starting point was delvaux, says johan janssens apologetically . . . because you got to start from Somewhere, and you must model yourself on something . . . and apart from that it's only the bunglers and rubbish painters who dare not admit any influence . . . my starting point was delvaux, that is to say his colors and presentation, but what I have to say is something quite different. Here you can see an endless path and it's the path of life, the path of humanity along which for the moment not a single person is traveling, and on which not a sign of life can be discerned. The sky looks red, an unusually ghostly red, it doesn't come from the setting sun, but is there of its own accord; you see nothing on either side of the path, that is to say you see only a couple of ruins on the plain: the town, the things made by human hands: they have just been atomized: the sky is ghostly red, the town has gone, the path along which people once traveled is empty. And here you can still see a bit of a statue, a piece of a plaster female torso, a broken stone arm holding a stone flower in its stone hand: man succeeded in making flowers out of stones, but the arms lies broken and the flower stands there turned towards Nothingness as a last witness. But look, my little son comes along, hesitantly, skeptical and uncertain. He is naked like the greeks, an innocent nakedness, a doubting and uncertain nakedness . . . and he sets his hesitant foot on the path down which human beings once went, and in his hand he holds a living flower, a living branch: the living branch of the naked joke meets the stone bloom of the broken arm. And the music master stares at the painting, and cleaning his glasses he say that it really is a splendid work: you're a poet, johan janssens, a writer, an artist . . . the only shame is . . . that you can't paint . . . the only shame is that you didn't write it like huxley in his latest book, where the apes wage war against themselves: 2 groups of opposing apes, and each group stands facing the other, and each group has a mascot, but on both sides the mascot is the same: one group has einstein as its mascot and the other group also has einstein as its mascot . . . and the two einsteins meet in the heat of battle and look at each other sadly, saying: are you here too, albert? And turning back to the painting, the music master says: but if you had been able to paint, this would have been even greater than huxley: that gesture of your joke's, that tentative step of your joke's among the ruins: it suddenly gives me fresh courage.

And johan janssens, moved, puts down his palette and 3 brushes and says: the trouble is, that I lack that courage myself, because yesterday afternoon a young man came past on his bike and he whistled a tune . . . and I abandoned my palette and 3 brushes to stare after him hurriedly: what does THAT mean, I wondered, that he's whistling a tune?

ALSO A RIFT

After his day's work johan janssens, the housepainter, sits there in chapel road at the door of one of the 4 villas . . . and he is lonely sitting there . . . he sits there so patently lonely that you can't help putting your work aside to go and sit beside him for a moment. You're right, I'm sitting her all alone, says johan janssens, actually I'm sitting here like the mouse-dog that tolfpoets caught over in the fields behind his so-called villa: neither a mouse that can play with the field mice nor a dog that can romp around with the other dogs in the street. I don't know what you're talking about, johan janssens, you say. No, you don't understand, and that not understanding is the source of all my loneliness . . . because look, as a housepainter I'm always around bricklayers and joiners and floor-layers, cabinet-makers and plumbers . . . my workmate is the son of the old master-painter, and when he talks to me about all of you, he says contemptuously: they're just a bunch of intellectuals! And it hit me very deeply that for a working guy an intellectual is not a human being, just as it has always struck me when intellectuals looked down contemptuously on—or showed exaggerated interest in . . . which amounts to the same thing—a workingman.

And talking to all of you about the working class . . . talking to the music master and mossieu colson and tolfpoets about the working class, I heard that you were all most offended by their lack of rationality, their lack of intellectual energy, their fear of seeing an argument stripped down completely. The working class doesn't dare think, most of all doesn't dare pursue a train of thought, you've said that a lot . . . it's like the proverbial ostrich putting its head in the even more proverbial sand, you said, and this ostrich is inexplicably alarmed by things that require reflection, where a decision has to be made, their brains are just rudimentary organs, they just drag them around as ballast, something they stick a label on, a label with a skull on it: danger.

And sitting there lonely on his doorstep, johan janssens says: thinking about their assertion, I can't help admitting they're right . . . I who sharpen my intellect every day on a different subject wander around lost among those plasterers and joiners and plumbers, and usually don't know what sort of conversation I'm to have with my workmate, the son of the old master-painter. But what happens, the music master asks me will I help him put a fence round his meadow, and I arrive at his meadow on sunday morning about 8 o'clock, ready to work and work . . . but he himself turns up at about 11 o'clock, without a hammer and without an axe, and he looks round a bit and says: I'm off to lunch soon, but then we'll pull out all the stops. And he actually does come back that afternoon, and with mossieu colson and tolfpoets at that—tolfpoets in a spotless white jacket, and with his crazy young white guard dog on a leash—they arrive like a regiment of labor and a squadron of duty, about to move the universe . . . but instead of moving, they sit down: the music master sits with the post that he wants to cut into a point . . . mossieu colson sits with a hammer that's too small, waiting for that one post . . . and tolfpoets remains on his feet and plays with his dog. And as they sit there they talk about work, they have important opinions about work: they're intellectual, witty, and entertaining, but they achieve nothing that could actually be considered Work, they're afraid of using their hands in the same way that a working man is frightened of using his intelligence to measure up an idea. According to the son of the old master-painter an idea, a poem, or a book are things one cannot take seriously: it's a game, it's something that has no real meaning in this world. And for mossieu colson or the music master work is something one never has to think about seriously: it's a game, a relaxation of the mind, something that has no real meaning in this world. And I, johan janssens, who can't behave like a brother with the son of the old master-painter, and can't ask or tell him anything about all kinds of problems . . . can't behave like a brother with the music master either, because the things that for me have meaning and significance, a hammer and an axe, a nail and a stone, are beyond his comprehension.

And sitting there by the front door, next to johan janssens, you ask him: and could you manage to get the son of the old master-painter over his fear, to think about some problem or other? Couldn't you succeed in getting the music master over his fear of doing work with his hands? And johan janssens replies: I don't know as yet, all I know is that I feel like that mouse-dog; or like a bat, neither a mouse nor a bird; or like a whale, not a fish but a mammal.

THE BLACK SHEEP OF THE DERENANCOURT FAMILY

The other side of the river dender had been full of cheering socialists, and there had been No one on ondine's side. Was it any wonder then that she became a thorn in the side of everyone in the whole world? . . . that, once she got home, she decided not to bother about anyone anymore, but to go her own way in life: sitting there in her pub and not feeling like she was in the right place: not in place with the rich folk who had forgotten her, and not in place with the people from the 1st grimy houses who patronized her pub. She felt like a bat that's not a mouse and not a bird, just like a whale is not a fish but a mammal. The pub, for instance, what kind of shit-hole was that? . . . she had to be able to turn it into a place the rich would come for entertainment, but for that she lacked the starting capital . . . and without a second thought she hurried to brussels to their cousin maria, who still owed her 400 francs. On her way back, among the people getting on the waiting train she spotted a derenancourt face . . . she would recognize such a face among thousands, and her unreasoning heart began racing: she hurried to be able to get into the same compartment with him . . . foolish woman that she was not to realize that he, the god of the filature spinning mill of termuren, of the town of the 2 mills, would be traveling first class. But no, her heart was racing too unreasonably, and so she was deeply disappointed indeed to find a derenancourt in the third-class compartment: only norbert. Not achilles. Only norbert, with his spiritualism. And at the last moment she got into another compartment: no, she had nothing in common with this norbert, in her youth he had frightened her too much with his ghosts and spirits. But he must have been in league with the devil, because a few days later she was sitting at the window in the pub, and she saw him coming up to their front door: he must be bringing news of achilles derenancourt: so achilles derenancourt had not forgotten her AFTER ALL . Or . . . was he coming of his own accord, on his own account . . . who knows what murky business he was going to propose! And despite everything she was fatally curious about occult things . . . she thought of the prayer to the devil, in the book of the dead he had read aloud to her. But God forbade these things, but confusing god with the priest, she reflected that after the devil she could go and see the priest . . . that she could make herself useful there too and put in a word for the common good. And thinking about the common good, she meant HER good, HER interests . . . and something deeply spiteful in her said: a good bitch must be serviceable from the front and from the back, by god and the devil. Ondine hurried to open the front door for him . . . but he stood before her as a perfectly ordinary drink salesman, about to start praising his wares. Was he so poor then that he had to practice such a lowly trade? . . . had he fallen so low that he had to beg the local pubs to buy a bottle of booze from him? She stood staring with her slightly mocking smile . . . she could imagine it: very probably he'd been stupid enough to allow his crutches to be found by the other derenancourts—those crutches he used to show the ghost at night in chapel road—and he had been thrown out, disinherited! Her face should have brightened, since god had been victorious yet again: a sun should have started shining in her heart! But no, on the contrary she was sorry. After all, he wasn't such a bad chap . . . she had taught him what love was against the hard, cold wall of the labor, and he—oh, she had to smile with tenderness still—had been so clumsy and helpless. And afterwards, yes afterwards they had felt the same disgust at the world and at people. And finally, remembering that he indulged in spiritualism: wasn't the devil also a fallen angel, for whom one should feel pity? . . . were we not all fallen angels, in our way? And again but much clearer now, it dawned on her that that man was himself the devil . . . that many years ago man had stood before god's throne, and had become rebellious, and had been cast down. He, norbert, recognized her at once . . . but still pretended not to recognize her, perhaps because her was a little ashamed of his humiliating position: he packed up his things, and was about to leave: but ondine barred the way and kept him there. She blocked the door right enough . . . but it was thrown open from outside and the landlady appeared: she wore an expensive coat over her torn black petticoat, and immediately opened wide the sluice-gate of her mouth: I've been in the slammer for theft, and the brewer denied me the lease of this pub, but now I know who the dirty thief is: you. You hid the stolen goods under my bar, and you also came and stole bottles of booze! Yes, ondine had to admit to taking the drink . . . but it was only 1 bottle. And with that she turned to norbert as if nothing had happened . . . she wanted to know what had happened to him, his brother, mr derenancourt . . . she wanted to know how the whole cheerful gang had vanished. But the landlady wasn't satisfied with that: you took that bottle? Why? Oh, oscarke took it and forgot to pay, said ondine . . . and then she turned back to norbert . . . but the landlady started shrieking again: it was impossible to have a conversation. Pay me then! shrieked the landlady. And ondine fumbled in her pocket, but her hand came out empty . . . she thought of the baby, of the christening party she had had to buy ham and biscuits for. Come tomorrow and I'll pay you, she said. Norbert looked at her, and she looked at him: they understood one another—they were two of a kind.

And you also wander along to the music master's meadow where there is a world in the making . . . an earthly paradise in the making . . . tolfpoets is also strolling about with his crazy young guard dog, the music master is begging johan janssens not to work so hard and so feverishly and johan janssens is telling the music master not to be so useless . . . the last farmer in termuren leans over his harrow, watching and providing age-old advice. And mossieu colson, who is listening to the last farmer and to johan janssens, doesn't know which way to turn . . . and he sees you coming along and shakes his head and says: It's all slapdash work here. And you're either a writer or you're not, and you take out your notebook and write: slapdash! It's a nice expression, you say . . . I wonder where it comes from? And johan janssens says at once: I think it's a derivation of slaphappy . . . and that would mean: happy-go-lucky. And mossieu colson immediately asks sadly why we can't leave the expression as it is: I think it's actually an onomatopoeia . . . a slap or a blow or a thud: slap: missing the point like a blind man who can't find an egg: slap. And you write all that down in your notebook, but the music master says pityingly: what you're getting involved in there is useless, because recently we had to buy a book for school to regularize language . . . and the inspector says that we're obliged to refer to that book when the children do an essay . . . and whenever the children have found a nice word, like slapdash, we have to cross it out right away and deduct a mark. So they're not allowed to write "up-country" anymore. They must write: "down in the country." And we who live in hilly and undulating brabant, or the flemish ardennes, or koekelberg or kluisberg or on the old mountain have also got to say: I live down in the country on the kluisberg. Nor can we call that old farmer leaning on his brake a philosopher. You call someone like that: the smartest man in the village. And so a philosopher from the marolles in brussels, from the docks or the spinning mill is: the smartest man in the village of brussels. And we must not say anymore: I'll give you a good *dragooning*. Because the word comes from the foreign powers who trampled belgium underfoot, from the austrians whose soldiers were dragoons, or heavy cavalry . . . so we say that anyone who fell into their hands got a good dragooning. But our language reformers know nothing about that, and the children have to write correctly: give you a good hiding.

And everyone who listened to the music master . . . johan janssens and mossieu colson, tolfpoets and his crazy young guard dog, and even the last farmer in termuren . . . is indignant: what kind of uncultured idiot has taken it into his head to write about material he knows nothing about? And how was he able to get sponsorship from the ministry of education for such an uncultured book? And does that give him the right and power to level out, mutilate, and kill our language? It's another social mistake, says johan janssens: someone like that should have had better career advice and seen that he has no feeling for language, but was cut out to be a mathematician instead. In mathematics there's also rhythm, feeling, and music, which he wouldn't have understood, says tolfpoets. And just imagine an idiot like that coming into my garden, shouts the last farmer in termuren . . . imagine him coming in and cutting my flowers and putting figures and triangles in their place. And tolfpoets's dog growls viciously. And mossieu colson says: just yesterday tolfpoets made a nice remark about that track of houses out in the country . . . there are still gaps in the track, and in-between there are bits of wasteland, so tolfpoets made the comment that each of these houses was a slice of street sausage . . . how nice and how accurate that is: a slice of house? But the music master raises his hand anxiously: be quiet, because tomorrow I have to correct their essays, and if I see anything like slapdash or like slice of house, I have to cross it out in red and give the child a talking to.

MISTAKES

It's gotten to the point where you're writing "summer in termuren" . . . and since it's been a wonderfully long summer, it should be an appropriately long chapter. Sadly, that is a mistake. Because with the summer and the fine weather andreus mottebol has had to paint house fronts from early in the evening to late in the morning—ow, another mistake—from early morning till late at night. And master oedenmaeckers has taken advantage of the fine weather to set off on his gleaming bike. And mr brys, what has he done? . . . maybe nothing, maybe he thought that his blood pressure was too high again and so he had to have a rest. And now it's got to the point where woelus has suddenly returned from the land of sun and fairs . . . back with his wagon and his wife and dog—and, good god, a child too—while roundabout hangs the sad halo of black ravens and chilly rain, and howling wind. And you stare at woelus, that prophet of bad weather, and think about the mistake of your book: summer in termuren: *everything that ondine and oscarke will think and then forget again, resolve to do and then not do, what they will do when they hadn't even the slightest intention of doing it . . . it will all happen in a rainstorm, in a fierce wind, on a carpet of fallen leaves . . . and all the same it will be called Summer in Termuren.* And over your shoulder master oedenmaeckers also stares at that mistake in your book, and he says: take comfort from the fact that we're not the only ones who make mistakes . . . let me tell you that there's a teacher at our school, who lives way Way over at woubrechtegem, and has a difficult connection between trains and so has to leave in the chill of the early morning and comes home in the deep dark evening . . . and he applies to be transferred to the school in waaiberechtegem itself: and suddenly he receives the good news that his application has been received and that he will be transferred instead to the school in rotterhoecke, though he doesn't know where it is on the map. And would you believe it, the teacher who lives on the very same street as the school receives the news that he's being transferred to the waaiberechtegem school.

And mr brys is also looking over your shoulder at your mistake and he says: take comfort from the fact that we're not alone in our mistakes . . . let me tell you that in the ministry an under-director is being promoted to director-in-chief, and so the people in the office wanted to give him the news . . . alas, he was nowhere to be found . . . He wasn't to be found in the ministry that had appointed him, and he wasn't to be found in any other ministry or service or nongovernmental institution either: there wasn't a single director who was This director, and as a result it was discovered that a certain person had for years been erroneously considered as an under-director . . . and had been receiving the appropriate salary! And leaning over your own shoulder at your mistake too, you say to your friends: let's take comfort from that we're not the only ones who make mistakes . . . let me tell you that the governor and chairman and the members of the permanent provincial council have founded something they call a cultural committee, and are now organizing something that they call cultural ceremonies: ministers of state, the great and the good, and permanent delegates talked at the council about art and culture, a literary society performed a play by a Southern German author, and a priest won the inter-provincial prize for literature. And yet! you say to them . . . it was a priest who wrote children's books. But I don't want talk about that, you go on, I should tell you that in addition occasionally an artist HIMSELF received an invitation to attend those cultural ceremonies . . . the old master-painter, among others, received an invitation . . . the old master-painter is now going on 65 and for 20 years he's practiced the honorable trade of housepainter, and now he receives through the mail an invitation to come and listen to what the VIPs have to say about art, and to watch a priest being awarded the inter-provincial prize for literature. Actually it was from the old master-painter that I heard that the permanent delegation instituted something in the nature of a cultural committee—I, who have sat hunched over my novels for years, did Not get an invitation . . .

And realizing in this way that in fact the world is made up of mistakes, you turn back to the chapter of your book "summer in termuren" and go on with a clear conscience writing about the wind and the rain.

The day after, norbert derenancourt visited her again, and the following after-noon he brought fat glemmasson with him . . . ondine was surprised to see those two extremes together . . . and all the same in her surprise there was something that seemed familiar and rang a bell: she had seen those 2 together in the past, and had been amazed even THEN. When had that been? she tried fruitlessly to remember. It must have been in a dream, she thought. And in the same instant she remembered the dream . . . the nightmare, when she had given birth to her 1st child over in her parents' house, and out came the blood streaming from her body. Oh, she remembered everything that had happened that night . . . she remembered how norbert and fat glemmasson had positioned themselves round her deathbed. Mr glemmasson was a little less fat now, but his smile on the other hand had got even greasier—though he too had fallen on hard times . . . that was probably through horse-racing, and women . . . he had also lost his jester, but he still acted as if he were the Bee's knees. They came into the pub, and ondine left the baby and sat down with them . . . she made a double chin, and though she'd been longing for them for years, she had nothing to say—if she'd had vases or paintings or rugs in the house, she would have shown them now, or if she had read books she would have talked about them now. As it was, though, she had nothing and knew nothing. Unless . . . perhaps . . . and she fetched a wooden box that oscarke had carved, 4 little mice formed the feet, and a larger mouse sat atop the lid: they asked her what it was. Ondine said in a whisper that it contained the gold bracelet that—He—had once given her.

Alas, alas . . . that gold bracelet, hadn't it been pawned long ago?

Scarcely a day went by now without the sound of fat glemmasson's greasy laugh and norbert derenancourt's sniggering being heard in the pub by the 1st grimy houses—sometimes they brought others with them, if they'd gotten drunk elsewhere—and then they said: come on, let's drop in on political ondine. And then they filled the empty pub with their shouting and slurred talk—the empty pub, because the folk from the 1st grimy houses stayed away now—they crept out of the dark aristocratic houses to this traditionally suspect pub, they asked ondine at the tops of their voices when she was finally going to show them her mouse: and to loud laughter, she showed them the chest with the wooden mouse on the lid. And then on a wet and windy october night, they knocked over the stove while ondine was out getting some meat pâté . . . she came in with a shawl over her head and saw the impossible happening: there were norbert derenancourt and fat glemmas-son busy mopping out her filthy pub. That wasn't all: as it happened another pair of jokers had forced their way into her kitchen and were bringing baby judith's little wooden cot into the pub: they were singing a requiem as if they were carry-ing a coffin. Ondine was speechless.

It's October and it's windy . . . it's so windy that on master oedenmaeckers's meadow the newly planted trees are hanging all askew, so that everyday he runs through the howling fields to push them straight again . . . and when he gets there it's swarming with children frolicking over and through his newly planted hedge and pushing his lopsided trees even further over—in the past there were never any children to be seen, the meadows and woods were lonely and no one knew them, and now he plants trees and a hedge and for miles around children spread the word: come one, come all, there's something for us to destroy over there . . .

It's october and it's windy . . . and mr brys is in brussels where he works, and among those towering houses round every sharp corner, he encounters the equally sharp wind . . . he meets tippetotje, who belonged to the proletariat, and meets the baron who belonged to the aristocracy—and both of whom, having met each other, don't belong to Anything anymore—he collides with the thundering and merciless life of today . . . but the wind dissipates it all, and in the evening when he arrives back in chapel road exhausted from all he has heard and seen, he falls straight asleep, while his wife asks him: is as windy as this in brussels too?

It's october and it's raining and windy . . . and andreus mottebol the house-painter still has a job to finish here and there, a glass roof to repair, an outside door to varnish, but it's raining and windy and he can't start anything . . . he stares out of the window, and is of two minds, and isn't sure if it'll clear up this afternoon, yes or no: there's no point in sitting by the stove in the corner and writing a piece for the paper, and there's no point in starting a painting . . . the old master-painter may come in any moment and ask where he's got to: you're staying at home because of that little bit of wind? And if he goes to see the old master-painter himself, he runs the risk of his asking: are you crazy, wanting to work in this wind?

It's october and it's windy . . . and you yourself, boon, should really go on with your book, with your chapter "only the precious little moment counts," but you can't write about ondine and oscarke, you're sitting somewhere in a slow train where it's dark and stinking and dirty, with the notes for a reading in your raincoat: you're going to read about your characters who are scattered all over the place—yes, where has sickwit the student gone to, and professor spothuyzen, and dr mots?—and you get to waaiendijcke or woubrechtegem and you read from your work . . . you read a *fuck* by accident or by an even greater accident you read about the baron's ass, and you suddenly hear silence in the auditorium, as if everyone is disconcerted, so that you can hear the howling wind in the streets of woubrechtegem very clearly: everyone is wondering how you can dare write such a thing . . . and why you don't use a euphemism as other writers do so brilliantly: it's like the october wind, we know it's there but we don't talk about it. And it strikes you that it's becoming more and more difficult to talk to people, on the radio you can't even say anymore that not even a cat believes in some pie in the sky, and in the auditorium in waaiendijcke there's something else you can't say: soon everything will be forbidden: no laughing, no crying, no howling along with the wind. And soon it'll also be forbidden to appear in company with bare hands, soon manual labor with be something indecent in these times of mechanization, electronics, and atomic science . . . you press a button, and the world will explode, but you'll have to wear gloves . . . hands will also become an unmentionable part of the body, they'll have to stay hidden, tucked away in darkness, covered with a leather sheath, so that the indecent digigenitalia are hidden . . .

And the slow train brings you back to the little town of the 2 mills, and you arrive in chapel road in the howling october wind, and discover that that you've left your notes behind somewhere: your handwritten indecent novel: it's lying somewhere between waaiendijke and woubrechtegem, and will end up being strewn about by the wind.

QUESTION TIME

It's a shame I'm having so much trouble with my trees blowing over there in my meadow—or should I say my bower, my garden, my eden?—says the music master . . . because otherwise I would have come much sooner to put some questions to you: for instance, what's got into you all of a sudden, changing my name just like that and starting to call me master oedenmaeckers? My lovely wife stares at me occasionally during the day and bursts out laughing: master oedenmaeckers? But I can't see the joke: I don't wear an at, sorry, a hat . . . and on top of that, you're not content with calling me atwearer, you have to go to extremes again and make it oedenmaeckers: wasn't calling me music master enough for you? And with a hint of humble apology in your voice, you can only answer: I don't know anything about a change of name . . . and what's more, I don't even know where the manuscript itself is; it must be strewn about on the slow train between nattedijck and kouwaaieghem . . .

But at that moment tolfpoets and his wife maria come walking down the winding country road, tugging on the leather leash of their crazy young guard dog . . . and tolfpoets calls from a distance: hello, master atmakers! And master oedenmaeckers is angry and awkward and vicious and says: just you wait, if boon's head gets even more confused he'll change your name too . . . you may end up being called polpoets instead of tolfpoets . . . polpoets and his wife paula . . . hello paula! And maria, covered in bows and ribbons, gives a sort of laugh, while at the same time getting rather annoyed: olala, are you all going mad with the wind like our dog?

But at that moment mossieu colson of the ministry arrives and asks what's has been going on lately: there I am reading a weekly I don't subscribe to, and I see articles about us . . . and what's more, I see something written about me, but I've lost my name and am called mr brys . . . and I'm not protesting because I've turned from mossieu colson into mr brys—one's the same as the other, really—but be careful! . . . remember there's already a mr brys in our novel! . . . in the story of ondine and oscarke there's mention of a mr brys who without knowing it became the 1st socialist in the town of the 2 mills, and had to flee to england . . . and who's now come back to install the flag of the socialists . . . and suddenly that mr brys is no longer the Only mr brys, but there's another: me, mr brys of the ministry. I don't think that's very nice of you, you must be sure to make a distinction: mr brys no. 1 and mr brys no. 2. And you stare in bewilderment at mossieu colson of the ministry, just as you did with the music master oedenmaeckers: someone must have found the manuscript that blew away, and muddled everything up!

But at that moment johan janssens, the housepainter, arrives, laden with tins and brushes and ladders: he asks if you all know each other by name, or if you perhaps address each other as paulapoets and her husband mr oede-nmaeckers? And all of you rush up to him and surround him and squeeze him like a lemon: and you extract the following: he's not getting much work these days from the old master-painter, and has agreed to write a column in yet another weekly . . . but he can't write about the same characters you fill your articles with in another weekly . . . so he changed the music master into master oedenmaeckers, and rechristened himself, johan janssens, as amadeus mottebol . . . he only had problems with mossieu colson of the ministry, he couldn't think up a good name for him, except for one we already had: mr brys. But between you and me, says johan mottebol, hasn't it a brought a breath of fresh air into the book?

THE COALITION . . . ON THE ONE HAND

When oscarke got home from work, and was cold and hungry—it was almost november . . . the priest talked of the increasing moral corruption on the workers' trains, and he still hadn't mentioned that there was no heating on those trains— oscarke found a drunken ondine at home surrounded by gentlemen slurring their words, and a certain mr glemmasson who had rediscovered his old pastime of pull- ing chairs across the floor till they screeched. Oscarke hurried through the pub to the back room, where judith was bawling for all she was worth—she was dirty and when he unwound her diaper he saw that the skin of her bottom was chapped:

he powdered her and took hold of her and shushed her. That was just about all he could do. He also learned how to make some baby food for her, after he found a tin with some directions on it, and he even learned how to rock her to sleep . . . even though that was by far the hardest thing of all: to have to compete with all the howling coming from the pub. It was wonderful how well he sang . . . he sang mostly military songs, the national anthem, and o river scheldt, and the 1st socialist song, the red flag—little judith was calm by then, and he thought: as soon as she quiets down I'll start to clear a bit of space for myself there in the corner, where I can do some modeling. Because he had a new idea: a sleeping girl. With the wind and rain over there in the new lane, jeannine had caught cold and had fallen asleep by the stove—he had stood looking at her, with his hand like so, as if to take hold of her, or—if he wanted to deceive himself—to start modeling her right away. But he got no further than putting out his styluses on a chair: it was as if little judith knew—and it was also as if he only came home from brussels to walk around with that child in his arms, to sleep a bit and then to rush back to the train. What, sleep a bit? More likely he'd give rein to his awakened lust, to imagine that the earth was a woman he could keep underneath him and impregnate: so that ondine again stood behind the bar with a swelling belly, listening to the gentlemen's nonsense. Yes, their nonsense, she realized all too soon . . . because her understanding of life and people and time had matured: in the past she had seen gentlemen as the fonts of omniscience, but now she could hear and see every day that they were quite ordinary souls. They talked about exactly the same things that preoccupied ordinary people, the socialist cooperative, about kaiser wilhelm and a war lowering over germany and france—they just used slightly longer words, with a sprinkling of french—they also always held exactly the opposite opinion of ordinary people, it was easy, that way they didn't have to think, they just needed to say white if the folk from the 1st grimy houses said black. But mostly they talked about girls . . . or more precisely married women, because they had matured too and their former sweethearts had all married some ignorant lug—and what they like most of all was playing dice, or a game of cards they called "banker": they played for amounts ondine had never held in her hands since her father had built the 4 villas. Sometimes she was drunk, and she laughed with the women who let themselves be fooled around with: you mustn't feel sorry for those married women, she said . . . but sometimes she was sober, then she became furious that they never talked about more serious things: that none of them ever looked at the world, really thought about things. About what things? they asked her. About god and the devil and hypnotism, which was a new miracle—oh they were terribly interested in miracles—and about electricity that the whole world was talking about, and about the international situation that was tense, and about the alarming growth in the number of those . . . those men on the quayside. She got worked up and had red blotches on her cheeks, but they weren't looking at her face, they were looking at the belly that she had forgotten about in her excitement . . . they laughed at her and said that she hadn't changed a bit in all those years: do you know we used to call you "political ondine"? And though it had been more or less a term of abuse, she couldn't hold it against them: on the contrary, she was pleased, her heart swelled with pride: she forgot that they'd come to her place to drink and gamble and give their demons free rein, and if she wanted to talk politics, well she would have to go and see achilles . . . achilles ate and slept politics, he was probably going to be mayor. She was seized by nostalgia, nostalgia for him and her youth: she was much quieter than usual that evening, and also drank more than was good for her: she wept drunken tears and blurted out the secret of that autumn in the castle: whether he was my lover or my brother, it didn't matter, together we were capable of transforming the world. She asked why he never came, but they laughed at her: however late it was, he was at his desk, he was going to succeed his father as managing director of the filature spinning mill, as a senator, and he might even become a minister—she had to understand that someone like that couldn't sit and drink in an ordinary pub by the 1st grimy houses with an ordinary ondine—however hard that truth was to take, she must learn to face it—and she understood, she had taken so many knocks that one more blow more or less made no difference. And to tell the truth, it wasn't like a slap in the face: she thought it was wonderful that he was hard both on her and on himself in his struggle. But she couldn't get over the fact that he couldn't assess her share in the struggle at its true value: she talked of the socialist menace . . . and looking at norbert and then fat glemmasson, she asked why their liberal friends never came along: if they could gamble together, why couldn't they join forces against the common enemy? What mr achilles derenancourt, despite his hours of study and sleepless nights, could not accomplish, she tried to achieve here in her pub: a coalition of catholics and liberals, which had always been her dream, even as a child.

THE LAST OF THEIR AGE

When the wind drops it will rain, and if it rains it will be for the good: it will mean winter. And in your imagination you can see andreus mottebol's household adjusting to winter: the light is on, his son joke comes out with his well-known dogmatic comments from the kitchen, his wife has picked up her illegal knitting—over the years everyone's tried in vain to guess what it's supposed to be—and he sits there with the illegal book that he's been knitting . . . no, writing for years. You made another mistake, and let's hope that andreus mottebol is not making a mistake too, by continuing to write his wife's knitting. And you hurry through the rain and wind to the other side of chapel road: andreus mottebol, I'm worried about you and your illegal winter work! And andreus mottebol has cleared the kitchen table, but is sitting there with all kinds of reproductions—reproductions of renoir—pictures representing paris as seen through the eyes of renoir. And pointing to those pictures, he tells that he loves everything really beautiful, really honest . . . but I know that though I'm looking at those coaches driving through the streets of paris in all their pomp and glory, they are the last of their age. Renoir painted them in all their glory, decorated with blossoming women being driven through the streets of paris . . . and I think of the books of emile zola, when baroness sandorff and nana and laura d'aurigny sat in those carriages with their bare, powdered shoulders and had themselves driven to their ball and entertainment and their sunday mass. And lo and behold a spoke broke, or the bodywork was scratched, and the carriage was sold to a Belgian lady who owned a castle near waaiendijcke . . . and she in turn sat in it in a dress full of lace and folds and had herself driven through the streets of brussels where she owned a mansion. And the coach was repainted and the crown on the doors disappeared, and the coach was bought by a rich gentleman from the town with the two mills—by mr derenancourt from the castle, by mr gourmonprez of the labor weaving mill—after that the coach was bought by the well-known coach-hire specialist wildepennings, who had 25 coaches and 9 horses . . . and then, oh how should I know, but it was refurbished and repaired, the rims were retightened by the smith and the cushions checked by the upholsterer and the paintwork touched up by the carriage painter . . . and all those craftsmen reminisced about the days of coaches, and inspected the undercarriage—the train, as they called it—and examined the top section—the imperiale, as they called it. And the years went by and the coaches disappeared, and now you occasionally see an old landauer trundling down chapel road, *one when ondine from termuren took her first communion, one when she married oscarke, and one when she was buried.* And yesterday a coach was brought to the old master-painter to patch it up a bit and strengthen it with a coat of varnish . . . and scratching the hub of the wheel he discovered a copper plaque and cried out: look at that: carrosserie renoir, paris. And sitting down next to andreus mottebol, you see the old coaches in their glory days, when no one yet knew that world wars and split atoms were on their way: they were driving along and thought they were going to convey bare, powdered shoulders through the avenues of paris forever . . . and they had no idea they would end up one day in chapel road, with staf spies, hauler and coal merchant . . . that they would stand in his yard in the rain and the wind, paintwork dull, with 3 scrawny chickens and a limping cockerel between their wheels, looking for some Spanish wheat—they didn't know that staf spies would say to the old master-painter: give them a last lick of paint, because it'll be all saints' soon and they're going to rack and ruin out in my yard.

And andreus mottebol's wife lays her illegal knitting in her lap for a moment and says: we're all glad those days are over, but are sorry they've been replaced by a new age: yesterday I was waiting in the chemist's, and the chemist's wife is gradually going blind—and while her husband sells modern science by the boxful, hormones and pernimont forte and calcium cedrille, she goes to him and says: remember, tomorrow I'm going on a pilgrimage for my eyes. And andreus mottebol's little son says: perhaps she can hire staf spies's coach, to take her there.

POEMS FOR WORKERS

During the festival of all saints' johan janssens rushes around delightedly, clutching under his arm the verses of young people singing the praises of the hero of the century: the worker. And he passes the verses on to the music master . . . but the music master gives them right back, and is able to say that this kind of thing is not his cup of tea: they blame everyone for being an individualist, but they are the greatest individualists I have ever read: they're obsessed with the compassion they have for the hero of the century, the worker . . . and they make a show of their own great compassion in a way that no poet before them ever dared make a show of his own petty sentiments—though they are poets only in the pettiest definition of the word, versifiers of what is most in fashion: the hero of the century: the worker.

And johan janssens puts the poetry collection back under his arm, thinking that they are not to the taste of the music master; for him all that matters is what one could call: Classical Beauty. And johan janssens gives the verses to the son of the old master-painter, who is a working lad . . . but he also gives them straight back, saying that they're not his cup of tea: what are they good for anyway? There's nothing in them that teaches me how to behave in these times and among these people . . . there's nothing in them that consoles me or shows me the way, or that makes me say: wow, that's beautiful. It isn't a call to arms, a manifesto, a message—it's just someone who, I think, says he feels sympathy and pity and compassion for the working man . . . and he needn't feel that for me: in waaiendijcke the priest has a dog, and it shits compassion. You shove the poems at me and said that they are poems for workers, but it's not true: you'd do better to give them to your music master. And johan janssens replies: but the music master told me I'd do better to give them to you! But the old master-painter's son shakes his head violently: no, no, for me a poem must be a song, like the one about the signalman who derails a train in order to save his child who is playing on the track . . . like the one about the drunk who promises his wife that he will turn over a new leaf—and as the man talked of a new life, he breathed his last. You laugh at that, but for us there's something behind those things that is real and true: those ballads are made by our own people, and tell in a rather exaggerated way the story of our

94

own lives . . . and though it may not be art, it's something meaningful: about man tossed between reality and his own desires. And do you know the songs of the 1st socialists? They were beautiful songs because they were true songs: about the engine-driver and the fireman driving the train through the night, while the "rich" on their pillows were cursing the working man: but the man without sleep tends the engine! And also, have you noticed that even street songs characterize the age and people's attitude to life? Look. Before the war it was "vivat boma" or "our hundred francs must be spent," and when the troops were sent off it was "parting brings sorrow," and in the war "there'll be a new day tomorrow" . . . and now after the war, it should be something like . . . like . . . And he stops talking, waiting for johan janssens to say it instead of him. But johan janssens doesn't know, just as the poets of our time don't know. Well, says the son of the old master-painter, that's what those poets should be singing to me.

And johan janssens stands there with his verses, not knowing who to give them to: those who read verses ask only for beauty, and those the verses were written for ask only for simplicity and truth.

THE COALITION . . . ON THE OTHER HAND

A coalition of liberals and catholics: even when ondine was a child it had been her dream: she was exultant, she was happy, and after she had closed up the pub and oscarke was able to warm himself by the stove, she told him about it. He was deeply shocked, and told the student about it as soon as possible, the next morning on the train. Oh, they still called him the student, though his hands were now in a terrible state from working in that stove factory. The student was pleased to have the news and replied to oscarke that they would take countermeasures . . . because if the liberals entered into a coalition with the catholics, they would enter into a coalition with the socialists, that is, a sort of secret alliance. The others on the train looked at him quizzically, and he explained that We, socialists, would not yet have enough votes for a seat in parliament . . . but that there would be a socialist on the liberal list, and that all party members would have to vote for that liberal list, next to the name of Our candidate. Oh, what a struggle it was! . . . a struggle that only a few people could make head or tail of . . . something about which there was whispering on both sides, no, on All sides. But the people on the train had confidence in the clear head of their student; they winked and thought: it'll be all right. Oscarke returned home in the dark and sang his battle songs—he forgot "sleeping girl" and sang judith to sleep with "the red flag," while next to him in the pub people were taking measures to nip socialism in the bud. To say that he forgot his "sleeping girl" was a bit of an exaggeration: it was still at the back of his mind—but when he had claimed that he had done life-model classes at art school,

it had been a lie: his mother had forbidden him to take the class, she had said that
one should not look at naked people, and now he lacked the technique—he had
wanted to buy an old magazine to find a "reclining girl" in it, but ondine would
not let him do even that: again they had to save (and again just when oscarke
needed something).

THE SINKING DOG

Along the canal that cuts the town in two . . . with the labor weaving mill
on this side of the town and the filature spinning mill on the other . . . along
with that stinking canal, in which the dying fish float to the surface and in
whose surface the gray smoke from the mill chimneys is reflected . . . along
this canal then, the music master is finally on his way to work, on his way to
his pupils. To his pupils who are products of this age: little creatures believing
in nothing, doubting everything, living for themselves. And on his way to
work along the canal he thinks of them, of how one or another of them will
say again: no, I didn't reread that poem, and you shouldn't talk to me about
poems anymore because I don't need it anyway: later beauty of a poem won't
be any good to me in the future. And on his way to them along the canal his
heart is heavy and his spirit oppressed, and he wonders how he'll be able to
temper their urge for luxury and pleasure, so that it doesn't become a passion that will dominate all their thoughts and feelings . . . so that they don't
become wild animals in search of gratification, but human beings in search
of happiness. Yes, wild animals in search of extravagant luxury, wild animals
that kill in a cruel and cowardly way in order to steal . . . and even worse, kill
for the sake of killing . . . and most gruesome of all, kill for pleasure. Kill for
pleasure? Hey, where does the music master get that from? It's because over
there by the side of the canal a man is drowning a dog: he's stuffed his dog in
a sack and tied a stone to it . . . but the dog has fought doggedly for its poor
dog's life, chewed through the twine and bitten a hole in the sack, and is now
swimming to the bank with the fear of god in it. And would you believe it,
there stands the man who tried to drown his dog and is seeing his attempt
fail—and he shouts "shoo! shoo!" and throws stones, so that the dog has to
swim to the other bank, to the bank where the filature spinning mill is—and
as it arrives with its last desperate energy, there are children who in turn shout
"shoo! shoo!" and drive it away with stones. And the dog swims back to the
bank where the labor weaving mill is, where the man who throws stones is.
The dog swims back and forth, the children laugh, the man laughs. Finally
the dog sinks. And the music master arrives at school with a pained heart and
an oppressed spirit, tells his pupils about it, and waits . . . and sure enough, his
pupils begin to laugh. They have the same smirk round their mouths as the

man on the bank: they smirk, they look around from one to the other. Their smirks mean that they're sorry not to have come to school along the canal, because now they've missed yet another spectacle: again the music master has been present at some incident that's provided him with the material for a boring lesson . . . and they who could have fully appreciated the game with the dog, they sadly missed it. A game. And the music master tells them more about killing as a game: we are on the spinning mill side and amuse ourselves by putting a dog in a sack and throwing the sack in the water—but what on this occasion happened to be a sack with a stone tied to it might just as well have been a car racing along and driving into a crowd of people at dusk . . . it could just as well have been a pilot releasing his bombs. A game with the object of committing murder, unpunished. But we've now reached a danger-ous point that's never before occurred in history: mankind is capable of com-mitting murder on the world: by dropping 3 or 4 atom bombs it can amuse itself by murdering the world. Write me an essay on the subject.

And the pupils stare at their music master in dismay.

THE ESSAY

Write me an essay on the cruelty of mankind, said our music master . . . but actually he didn't mean it, it was just a way of finishing his lesson, it was a way of waking us up at our desks, it was to shake us out of the complacency with which we drown dogs and run people over, and will drop the atom bomb yes or no. And we come to class and we've done our essays . . . and they're not about the sort of cruelty he imagined, cruelty with which civilizations are first built up in order to be smashed down again with twice the cruelty . . . or about the cruelty with which as he said *the derenancourts had broken the first socialists, and knocked mr brys down into the gutter.* No, they're about our own cruelty, cruelty that's petty and cowardly: once I'd caught a sparrow, I was 12 and the brand-new trap had knocked the little creature unconscious between its gleaming brass jaws (this may be about cruelty, but looking back I can't help feeling sorry, and so now and then I'll write *the little creature*); between my hands I revived the little creature by breathing on it, and I tied a length of string to the sparrow's foot and let it fly up: it couldn't go further than the length of the cord and flew round in a nice circle—the sparrow went round and I went round with it, and now and then I gave a tug so that the little gray creature came towards me and fell towards the ground . . . but before it hit the ground it straightened out and the game began all over again. The sparrow tired of the game but for me it was only just beginning: I picked it up and let it dangle on the string, then I took it to our cat and let it flap its wings helplessly above its head: the cat jumped up at it but the little creature fought for its life, and although it was dead tired it kept flying up as the cat pounced. I who am older than I was when I was 12 and caught the sparrow, I now have to write an essay about cruelty, and have to say that I in my cruelty understood nothing of the little creature's fear (an essay is an essay after all, and at the end of the essay I'll be able to say that I finally understand the little creature's fear, and that therefore we shouldn't be cruel to animals), but if I remember correctly it was precisely the fear of the sparrow that I enjoyed: it might have been someone who tied Me to a cord and made Me jump about, and then I would have been afraid! When one is 12 one is cruel to people, says our music master . . . at 12, I was cruel to my little sister: once my father had killed a chicken, I grabbed the bleeding head by the comb and held it up to my sister's face, she screamed and started to cry. I was 12 at the time, now I am 15 and I read in the daily paper that in Idaho the body of a 7-year-old girl was found, and that the murderer, the 16-year-old student butterfield, had tried to reach the pacific coast by car . . . he admitted having struck her with a weight before throwing her in the water . . . he said: I only killed her in order to see someone die. That is my essay and the lesson is: in human life people are cruel out of . . . out of curiosity, and from something else, something that, being 15, I can't yet describe properly.

And the music master puts the essay in his briefcase and returns home, along the canal that cuts the town of the 2 mills in two, and meets mossieu colson of the ministry: what do you think of this essay? he asks. And mossieu colson dodges the question with another question: what are you planning to do with that essay?—because however cruel it may be, you still have to give a grade: so how did he do?

LONG LIVE SOCIALISM

No, oscarke wasn't allowed to buy any old magazines, to find a "reclining girl" somewhere: ondine said that they had to save, that doctor goethals's idea had to be put into practice: whenever the doctor had been by, she started in about it . . . and went on about it for 2 days. He came quite often, doctor goethals, as there was constant trouble with her belly, and there were constant problems with little judith who lay crying in her little wooden cot all day long: because in the evenings ondine had no time to look after the child, and during the day . . . Well, during the day she had to go out: via norbert, mr achilles derenancourt had given her the task of gathering as much information as possible about mr brys—and she had already found out that in the evening he kept the books of the cooperative without receiving any payment. She wanted to find out more about those books . . . if it was possible she wanted to make contact with him: the first sunday afternoon that came along she went there, but he didn't open the door. But that didn't matter, there was nothing so awful for her as to stand in front of a closed door—she stamped her feet, she imagined that everyone she knew was going to come round the corner at any moment and survey her on the doorstep with a sarcastic smile (it was a stupid false fantasy, as she knew very well, but she couldn't get it out of her mind) her nerves got the better of her, she looked around unconsciously to see if there was anything to kick, or to destroy in blind rage. It was an old street where a cankerous lime tree cast its shadow on a saint andreus, which sat lonely in its niche crumbling and decaying . . . and as she looked at the statue she was again busily trampling the whole earth underfoot: she who was in contact with the cream of the town, had to stand outside the house as if she were a beggar woman: mr brys and the square and saint andreus should be smeared with filth, yes they should. And since there was a gathering again at the pub that evening—and they were on the lookout for something to do, something that would be a good laugh—she suggested daubing saint andreus with filth and then saying that the socialists had done it: dammit, yes, we'll do that, said fat glemmasson. Norbert hesitated and mentioned his brother, perhaps achilles wouldn't like it . . . but the real reason was that, believing in spiritualism, he was frightened of mocking images or symbols. We'll ask your brother, said fat glemmasson—they got into his coach, which was waiting outside, and a few moments later they came back with beaming faces: he agrees, said fat glemmasson. But the others didn't believe them. It's true, said norbert . . . he said that we, or you at least since I'm not coming along, should give the statue a good bashing. So off they went—but they still weren't satisfied after they'd given vent to their animal instincts: they went to the printing shop of the local paper to compose an article about it, and they also went to the police station, although that was entirely unnecessary—the chief of police had been among them and had done his very best: he'd knocked a hand off the statue and stuck it upright in a pile of filth. And the next day the police were waiting at the workers' trains to arrest the leaders of the socialists: they had to go through the town in chains, and the people jeered at them: why shouldn't that sort, who didn't respect saints' statues, have their own hands cut off?

The election victory was celebrated in advance at ondine's pub, they stood round her in a circle, and raised their glasses . . . but suddenly the front door opened, and he himself, the mayor-to-be, the managing director of the filature spinning mill, and possible future minister, came in: he insisted on coming to congratulate her personally and expressing his thanks for all she had done regarding information on mr brys, regarding the rapprochement between liberals and encyclicals—and he also spoke, admonishingly but smiling, about a certain statue that that been destroyed by the socialists. He spoke french, and the others listened with heads bowed . . . he finished his speech and shook her hand: he called her "madame ondine." It was an honorary title; it was the reward for her years of restless toil. She wept, and turned away so that he shouldn't see her swelling belly. But this wasn't the crowning triumph: they saw him off, since he couldn't stay long . . . and on reaching the door of the pub they saw someone coming by really drunk: it was mr brys: he had accepted the job of bookkeeper in the local cooperative, and while he'd done the job for nothing he had been honesty itself . . . but now that he was finally a paid employee of socialism, he'd taken to drink . . . and was probably drinking up the money of the cooperative. They stood on the threshold and jeered at him, he turned round and shouted, slurring: long live socialism . . . but they laughed at him and threw stones. The stones missed, but in trying to avoid them he lost his balance and rolled into the gutter.

HAMLET IS IN CHINA

Now come winter evenings with rain and fog and howling wind: it is the time when the people of termuren group closer together, at the spinners' ball, at peace rallies, at a lecture on china with slides. And meanwhile you yourself sit in a slow train to agterdenbergh, to give a reading from your scattered papers and on that same train is professor spothuyzen, who's going to give a lecture on hamlet—well, if it isn't!—and you start a conversation on the train: look, in the summer, with the fine weather, the people of the town of the 2 mills are scattered at the seaside or the kempen or in the ardennes, they're seeking their own individual happiness, solitude, being left alone by the others—but now the pendulum has swung the other way, and winter is coming, and people are seeking communal happiness, protection from loneliness, help from outside . . .

True, but what are you getting at? asks professor spothuyzen. What I'm getting at, you say, is that you could also find a rule, a law in this: in periods of fine weather, prosperity, security, man tends to retreat . . . in periods of bad weather, disaster, and danger, man tends to crowd. In happiness man wants to be alone, in danger he wants to know that there are other people around him. In times of disaster and danger he's obliged to take measures to avert or overcome the danger . . . but alone he's frightened of doing anything, it might be the wrong thing, which makes the danger greater and brings it even closer. But together with others, he *does* dare to take a step: if he fails, then they'll all fail with him . . . if he perishes, they'll perish with him.

And professor spothuyzen takes his briefcase from the luggage net and from his briefcase the papers for his lecture on hamlet, and reads: physically exhausted by the constant fighting and mentally exhausted by numerous defeats, the remaining nationalist troops wander about the deserts of south china like heaving wrecks . . . without leadership and without communication between them, without provisions and without pay, their only hope is to be taken prisoners-of-war . . . the generals no longer obey the orders of their commander, who has lost all the prestige of leadership . . . a leader is only great when he allows himself to be led by the wishes of his followers, he is only powerful to the extent that he formulates and expresses those wishes and imposes them on his adversaries . . . he is only fit for his office when he has the courage at all times to take responsibility for his decisions: the present leader no longer has any of those characteristics: in despair and desperation he has retired into seclusion, after having issued orders and counter-orders for months, which contributed to the general collapse.

And reordering his papers, professor spothuyzen asks if you remember the newspaper report, over 10 years ago now, in which the same leader announced to the world that we were on the eve of a universal collapse: "the moment has now come when every serious person must reflect and ask himself what is happening to the world." And this leader is like your people in termuren: in times of emergency they lose their heads, they reflect on it being the eve of some general catastrophe: when the end is near, reflection comes, but it always comes too late. This leader sees the catastrophe through his own eyes, i.e., through the eyes of those who are among the declining classes . . . and so he says that Everything is now going downhill, and is unable to make a distinction between half-built and half-demolished walls: it's clearly all half to him, and hence all rubble. He reflects, but reflection is something futile, it's a fungus, a morbid growth of the brain . . . his reflection evokes only phantoms, which bring doubt, turbulence, despair, and fear with them. But no faith! In times of winter and bad weather, emergency and catastrophe, man seeks help and comfort: in the first place he seeks a Faith, which can ward off the danger . . . and then he seeks out him who was appointed to take action, though never knowing where his acts will lead us . . . and this is either someone who just gets stuck in his position, or he's someone who has doubts and is frightened of doing the wrong thing—hamlet in china.

And we, professor spothuyzen and I, are a pair of quite ordinary phonograph needles, who can only reproduce a lecture . . .

And professor spothuyzen smiles as the train reaches its final destination, and the porter shouts: agterdenbergh! . . . he smiles and says: so you see, you're wrong about that, we're all people from termuren: homogeneous, consistent little hamlets, right off the conveyor belt.

AGTERDENBERGH STATION

With the papers you've just been reading from under your arm, you're waiting at the joint station of agterdenbergh-braemenbosch. But who in belgium can describe those brick walls, standing in the sweltering heat beside the tracks with their blossoming brush, standing in the chilly winter rain beside the track with their blossoming signals . . . situated at the edge of the 2 villages of agterdenbergh and braemenbosch, for the benefit . . . of belgium, with the benefit of its joint stations and its unmanned crossings. And you come from agterdenbergh, about which you read in our book "summer in termuren," and are sitting on the bench in the waiting room, exactly as if you'd been on the train for a while. And from braemenbosch comes professor spothuyzen, who has given a talk on hamlet there: the two of you sit there in a station serving two villages. And professor spothuyzen says: which of the two villages do you think the stationmaster comes from, and which of the two talks do you think he went to listen to? And you reply: as is usual nowadays, I expect he belongs to both villages, and attended both talks, simultaneously . . . he probably got everything scrambled under his stationmaster's cap and thinks our book "summer in termuren" is about hamlet. Perhaps it *is* about hamlet, says professor spothuyzen . . . perhaps you're a hamlet yourself, looking and looking and writing everything down, but not drawing any conclusion . . . perhaps in your book you're gazing noncommittally at the evolution—or the confusion—of our age . . . perhaps you sympathize with the man who doubts and doubts, and hence plays into the hands of chaos . . . and perhaps you're afraid of the man who does not doubt, but imposes a certain idea on the world, forces it to take a particular course, and doesn't ask himself if that particular course is a good one: sometimes you think it's dangerous to think too hard about anything, and at other times you think it's wrong to follow an arbitrarily plotted course . . . and meanwhile there you are sitting in agterdenbergh station, as the train hurtles past . . . you sit there and think that it's better not to go anywhere. You start from the assumption that people have always imposed arbitrary goals on other people, simply so that they shouldn't be unoccupied. Once the goal was an unattainable heaven, and an even less attainable god . . . and subsequently the goal consisted of man himself, in the course of countless centuries, becoming his own god—eating of the tree of the knowledge of good and evil, but also eating of the tree of eternal life—and subsequently the goal was the ideal community, which was attainable in a foreseeable period of hundreds of years . . . and subsequently the aim was the immediately attainable ideal State. But what do you see when you look back over the first book on chapel road?: that people turn away from everything connected with ideas, from everything to do with goals to be attained, from everything that leads to a particular course, because beyond that point they always find themselves disappointed . . .

But at that moment the stationmaster of agterdenbergh-braemenbosch comes into the waiting room, and tips his cap: excuse me, he says, I went to hear the talk and felt that it was just the other way round: people believe that they'll wind up disappointed because they no longer have the courage to press on in the service of ideas. Well, whatever, says professor spothuyzen, in either case people turn away from ideas . . . well, the book asks the question: WHY CAN'T PEOPLE JUST LIVE, LIVE WITHOUT A GOAL? Why can't they just stay where they are? No, that's not possible, says the stationmaster of agterdenbergh-binnendenbergh . . . it's impossible to stay here, just sitting here.

I don't mean your actual station, says professor spothuyzen, I mean that man Is, that man Exists . . . well then, leave him be, let him exist! And then existence itself would be the ultimate goal: man would exist, and his only concern would be to continue existing, his only concern would be to exist with as great-as-possible-a-degree of relative happiness and relative freedom. And then it would be wrong, criminal, to make man sacrifice his relative happiness and relative freedom for an idea: for god, the community, or the State. But then the first book on chapel road says as follows: that isolated individuals who start thinking in that way will be driven into a corner by idea-obsessed people . . . but that's nothing, they don't mind, they regard that little corner as their refuge, where they can start living for themselves, once and for all, once and for all win their freedom . . . and, as far as possible, extending their happiness and freedom out from that corner, from that refuge, offering it to other people . . .

And the stationmaster of binnendenbosch-agterdenbergh turns to you appalled, and asks: did I hear you read That?

UP AND DOWN?

It's down in black and white now what professor spothuyzen thinks is the meaning of your book, and you look a bit sheepish: did I make such learned material out of my bits and pieces? You're too perplexed to be arrogant. But that's the way it goes and always has gone, one thing leads to another, and next comes sickwit the student who for the moment is a soldier . . .

Forgive me for being a soldier, says sickwit the student . . . and forgive me too for wanting to go on playing a part in your book . . . but permit me to reply without being asked: that final thought in your 1st book on chapel road, of living in a refuge where you would constantly extend the circle of individual happiness and individual freedom . . . well, that in turn is just another ideal community, an ideal utopia. To the extent that I've worked at the factory of universal intelligence and have listened carefully, I've been able to draw the following conclusion: if we want to trace lines and laws in history, the 1st law should be that of the pendulum movement: tick-tock says my wristwatch, and tick-tock says the wristwatch of history too. And man too obeys that law . . .

man is constantly lured from the place he's in: just as he always longs to Be something he's not, so he also longs to be Where he's not.

That's true, you say to sickwit the student, looking at your wristwatch in turn.

But sickwit doesn't want to know about your being in hurry to get away: man longs again and again for what he doesn't possess . . . the monk hungers and thirsts for a carnival of vanity, and the jazz singer sings in all his songs about the solitude of nature . . . the individual obeys the law of the pendulum, and all individuals together also obey a much wider pendulum-motion: containing the grain of sand in the desert, the water droplet in the sea, the blade of grass on the prairie that wants to be another grain of sand, etc. . . . and all together they obey the law of mass: the law that makes blades of grass flower and fade, drives the sea from low to high tide, that slowly makes the deserts shift position. I assume so, you reply to sickwit, just as I have assumed so many other things . . . but what has that got to do with our refuge? It has to do with the fact that in human history there is both a high and low tide, a flowering and fading, a general shift: at one moment there's an urge to bury oneself alive in monasteries, and then there's the urge to seek communal prosperity, peace, and freedom . . . there's on the one hand the urge towards saber-rattling, the smell of gunpowder, and the last judgment of the atomic bomb, while on the other hand no one is interested anymore in hitler or jesus or marx: people shut themselves away in a refuge. But there too you'll see the pendulum of history swing back, you'll see that your wife and friends-cum-characters will grow restless after a while . . .

But as if a hole were growing in sickwit's brain, he strokes his forehead and thinks for a moment: what did I say? he asks. They won't be satisfied even there, you reply, because satisfaction is another word for end or death . . .

No, it was something else . . . oh yes, about history: that the wristwatch of history also goes tick-tock, as far as we can ascertain anything about history—since history itself is also imperfect: man has investigated only Those things that benefited him financially, and neglected everything else: self-knowledge, the meaning of his existence, the meaning of his progress through the centuries. He hasn't asked himself where he came from or where he's going . . . i.e., he's never asked himself anything, really, scientifically, Honestly . . . there were always a few individuals who wanted to lead the masses to a goal, and They made history, they made Their history . . . they twisted and turned certain facts and put them in their most favorable or unfavorable light, depending whether it suited them to present those facts as beautiful or ugly. And so human history is something unreliable, and we know little or nothing about what really happened. Yet, to the extent that some things can still be established, a pendulum movement was their principal characteristic: from right to left and back again from left to right. And so, said sickwit the studious soldier, it actually seems wrong to me to push the pendulum in a certain direction . . . because the further you push it to the left, the more powerfully it'll strain to go back to the right, Even in your refuge . . .

And you're just about to ask if you have to write That too in your 2nd book on chapel road . . . when master oedenmaeckers comes charging up with his hands raised in supplication: wait a bit, wait a bit! And in his haste not to be late he trips over a stone and falls, and is late anyway.

ONDINE: A LADY

The day on which ondine had been called Madame by mr achilles derenancourt became a milestone in her life: something that put the events of the past in a different light: her view of everyone changed, her life was measured by a different yardstick. She no longer wanted to be called plain ondine, she defended her title of Lady as if it were a coat-of-arms. It seemed impossible to her that the days could fall back into the same old routine. It made her happy, that "madame," and in a way that was comparable to the happiness of her youth: back then they had been only inconstant joys, back then she would have leaped up and danced, and her eyes would have started to sparkle and glow—but now it was more a controlled, inward joy: as a result it was also a more intense joy, a happiness that seemed capable of defying the years. Seemed. Because in the days that followed, one by one, it became clear all too soon that her happiness was not yet completely under control: it seemed as if she would never reach its highest summits. She wondered if she were not too impulsive—she was calculating enough when it was a matter of making a profit, but alongside that, separate, there was another ondine, completely dependent on her emotions, to put it in the gentlemen's high-flown words: she was shrewd, and she was brave, but those damn emotions! Nor did she have the gift of simplicity . . . a gift without which she would never rise above herself: in those days she was in the street more than anywhere else. Sometimes a coach drove past, and the window was lowered and people greeted her. Good day, madame Ondine! fat glemmasson would call out . . . and norbert derenancourt's echo called the same, but fainter, because, well, since fat glemmasson no longer had a jester he had to have Someone sitting next to him. Ondine thought he hated loneliness, was afraid of her . . . after all he had always prided himself on having the blood of the medieval crusaders in his veins, . . . but in that case he had not only their cruelty, but maybe also their fear of ghosts. Ha, and that norbert! He was just the right company for him. Norbert was his shadow, and in as much as there was any space to see around that fat head of glemmasson's, norbert looked through the window and then called out: hello Madame ondine! . . . or raised his hat behind the other. And once when ondine had to pass the station . . . actually to find out what a workman's season ticket cost, because she would have had a fit if she found out that oscarke was cheating her out of so much as a centime . . . and she was coming back and passed the red-light district, a woman came out of one of the houses and nodded respectfully: good day, madame ondine! So, people she had never met in her life knew her and were talking about her: she was something well-known and famous, she was something like electricity that people never tired of talking about, she was something like the approaching war, about which people argued whether or not germany needed to invade belgium, and whether belgium . . . so she was something like that, something great, something that filled peoples' lives and about which people spoke, not just like the bad weather, but with emotion and passion. She lived in an intoxicated state, it was as if she were drunk with megalomania. And even knowing that that woman was a brothel-keeper didn't diminish her triumph . . . no, it enhanced it, it added to its relish: it was a proof that gentlemen only went to that woman . . . well, to have their dirty linen washed, as it were, to kill the worm gnawing away somewhere inside them . . . while people came to her on the contrary as if to a source of higher life, that would refresh not their body but their spirit. It was proof of her greatness, she had only to open her mouth and speak and she could make something be or not be.

THE FANTASIST

In these december months johan janssens is silent and introverted . . . he doesn't join in your arguments about man's mission, the value of society, or the future of this world: it's all far too complicated and academic stuff that doesn't achieve anything, he's reluctant to let slip that in fact those centuries and centuries of squabbling haven't taken us one step further or even added 1 decent thought to our stock, but on the contrary had made things more complicated and constantly led us from one mistake to another. And with a smile you let johan janssens inveigh against all those assertions and strange thoughts of professor spothuyzen and sickwit the student and heaven knows who else . . . for you know him as well as you know yourself! But as he walks on beside you, he suddenly turns the full breadth of his attack on you: and you, you go along with it! He bursts out: you yourself get involved in those arguments about the mission and the greater-good and heaven knows what else, though that's not in any way your job. Every human being has his job, the one he's best suited to, and your job consists of observing things carefully . . . it was your job to go round with your eyes and ears open, and to sift and separate what you had heard and seen . . . to discard the unimportant and to put what was important down on paper, to reject the impermanent and transform the permanent into art . . . your job was to look and look, and to reproduce what you had seen as accurately and simply as possible. And it is

Not your job to sit there arguing about the purpose and function of art. Let professor spothuyzen and sickwit the student and the music master pontificate all they like, let them go in search of man in their own way . . . but you look for him in your own way, as you always used to do: by looking at him closely, and by carefully re-creating his image. All the rest is rubbish, a theory prepared in advance that's used more or less like a mop . . . or no, like a mop with which the pavement of theory must be kept clean.

And johan janssens's outburst in this month of december hits you like a bucket of icy water over the head. My son jo has been so ill . . . johan janssens continues more quietly and more self-possessed after his outburst. He'd been ill, and on his first day back at school I went with him, because you know what fathers are like: the child is the arrow from the bow . . . and the bow is concerned about the destination of the arrow . . . and going with him to school we meet a boy who's also in his class, and who starts telling us a story. He has an intelligent face, but has a big bump on his forehead . . . and there's also something odd about the eyes; they're eyes that stare vaguely into the distance. And he tells us that he has to be good at home or else he gets a walloping from his father: he kicks me, he gets a chair and with the chair leg he drives me into a corner and goes on kicking me. And I . . . johan janssens, who can't imagine such sadism . . . I say, appalled: but that can't be true . . . I think you're telling fibs! And his abstracted staring eyes smile vaguely and distantly, and he goes on: no, it's not true . . . but he puts his hand into his sneaker and keeps thwacking the rubber sole against my cheek. And I'm so appalled that I forget to ask my son jo who the boy is . . . but for days afterwards I'm tortured by the thought: what a strange creature man is that the bow could abuse its own arrow out of a lust for power . . . and if these were just the thoughts of a little fantasist, what kind of child is it who Likes making up such things? is it that it would actually want something like that to happen to it? And you answer johan janssens: man . . .

Of course, I know, replies johan janssens . . . in theory man is this or that, or something else—but instead of listening to all those theories, you'd do much better to go round and hear and see and write down stuff like I've told you here.

THE SPIRAL MOTION

There in the station, master oedenmaeckers comes along, out of breath . . . but it's not on account of the last train at 11:05 P.M., it's because of the most recent statement of sickwit the student, that the world does not undergo any kind of evolution, but that everything goes up and down . . . tick-tock . . . like old paerewijck's watch with the hour hand missing. And arriving out of breath, master oedenmaeckers trips on a stone and falls, but as he falls he straightens and shouts: excelsior, onward and upward! And sickwit the student bursts out laughing, but master oedenmaeckers raises his eminent forefinger in the air and says: according to you, all we can discern from history is a pendulum movement, but you're wrong about that . . . you hit the nail on the head by saying that man has twisted and distorted his own history—arguing that truth was constantly sacrificed whenever it was necessary to lead the masses towards some goal or other . . . Did you say lead or bleed? asks sickwit, interrupting him . . .

It's all the same, says master oedenmaeckers: leading them to a goal, or making them bleed for it . . . but the main thing is that man knows little or nothing about his history. For that matter, what *does* he know anything about? Man is too short in stature, too short-lived—with inadequate eyesight and a deficient brain—to be able to really grasp anything . . . and with his weak and slightly cross-eyed gaze he thinks he makes out a vague pendulum movement, and immediately cries out that there's a pendulum movement. But couldn't it just as well be a spiral movement? A spiral that extends further and further into space, and up to now hadn't been discernible by human beings. Man has always miscalculated how high or low things were . . . a miscalculation that stems from his average height of 1.65 meters, so that something 300 meters high is "high" and something 0.4 millimeters high is "low." But however and in whatever way he develops, the Fact that he develops means that he evolves.

But that doesn't mean that evolution is an improvement, observes sickwit the student . . .

No . . . but it *is* a change, says master oedenmaeckers: ostensibly everything stays the same, death always follows life, and new life is always born from death . . . and this remaining the same in the face of constant change is confusing for us because we can't see what endures eternally even inside of what's constantly changing . . . and so we can't see what's constantly improving in that which endures eternally. A gnat lives for just a short summer, and only sees how the summer slowly grows less warm and becomes chillier and rainier . . . and from its point of view all life must be coming to an end, according to its calculations the world must be going under, there must be a general catastrophe, a hopeless loss of all values. And life must be just as pointless for a bacillus that lives just a few hours: the smaller you are in relation to your space the more senseless that space must seem. For man, that pale limpet measuring 1.65 meters, the cycles of centuries has no meaning: it's impossible for him to imagine that the succession of nights and days, of summers and winters, could be extended into eternal circles: into the rise and fall of centuries, into the rise and fall of series of centuries. And since religion was too quick off the mark in embracing eternity, and we found the insubstantial image it had of it wanting . . . and since science is too slow in its splitting and reconstituting, and has been found wanting in turn, and in turn is becoming a monstrous excrescence . . . now man has tried 2 times and failed 2 times, I don't see why he should despair . . .

But a 3rd time! says sickwit the student. And he grabs his poor head: is it still here under my student's cap—or no, under my soldier's beret—or is it over there in the madhouse?

USE MAN

And sickwit the student says: man . . . But you cover your ears with your hands and don't want to hear any more of this learned nonsense: only what your eyes have observed about this world and this age and this mankind, and that you must put down on paper: this is your strength and your fame, your rock that will endure the storm: leave me alone, professor spothuyzen, master oedenmaeckers, and student sickwit . . . leave me alone with your far-too-intellectual nonsense that distracts me from my real goal: to see, and write down what I've seen. But sickwit laughs pityingly, and from a distance you can hear master oedenmaeckers laughing pityingly, and from even further away you can hear the echo of professor spothuyzen's laughter: more brains, for god's sake! And filled with revulsion, spilling over with disgust, you have to listen to things that give you a splitting headache. You have to listen to professor spothuyzen who says that the individual is turning away from ideas, from god and community and the ideal state, in order to achieve his own happiness and his own freedom. To sickwit the student who afterwards comes up with: human history as far as it can be traced has always offered the same spectacle, an up-and-down movement, a longing for first this, then exactly the opposite. To master oedenmaeckers, who on the contrary says: we are too small to be able to say with any confidence that everything is a pointless up-and-down movement: perhaps it may be a spiral—the 1st turn of the spiral: the belief in god, which we had to abandon after a while . . . the 2nd turn: belief in science, which we'll also have to abandon after a while . . . the 3rd turn: in search of some methodology that doesn't see the perfect knowledge of what surrounds us as its highest aim, not technology or mechanics, but the knowledge of man himself: man has made himself understand everything around him, everything that can serve to help him achieve whatever goals he's set himself . . . but he's overlooked the most important thing: who he is, and what he's on earth for. This is what man should learn, first and foremost: and if he should discover that he himself is the only point, that his own freedom and happiness is the only Positive Thing, then he should subordinate every god or science or idea to that freedom and that happiness.

And you rub your hands together because they're finally all in agreement, because they'll finally leave you in peace and spare you their claptrap . . . because you'll finally be able, in your own freedom and for your own happiness, to go on writing about what you enjoying writing about, about oscarke and ondine, and the things to be seen in chapel road, but you're mistaken, because no sooner has master oedenmaeckers put his most beautiful and rounded period after his last sentence than sickwit the student—who's now a soldier—has to add some hairsplitting qualification: the more man comes to know himself, the more That knowledge will impede his happiness and his freedom. But he can be sickwit as much as he likes: from the chill that comes creeping into your head, from the sadness that comes creeping into your heart, you know that it really will be like That—or that there won't be much knowledge in it at all—the gaining of knowledge means the loss of freedom, says sickwit, because for man, knowledge of those laws unhappily means the use of said laws . . . and the more laws he knows about, and hence uses, the more he'll become a slave to those laws, the more unhappy he'll become in applying those laws, the more dangerous the use of those laws will become: it's in his nature to always want to intervene, to feel the best and the cleverest, to set himself some goal or other . . . and to use all the laws that he knows in order to achieve that goal. And just as he uses fire and water and electricity to serve his own ends, in this 3rd turn he'll come to know himself . . . and use that too.

And as you try to slip away, *to your story about ondine, to the downfall of mr brys who was used by his fellow men as one uses an object* . . . as you're slipping away, master oedenmaeckers grabs you by the coat, in order to use you as an argument against sickwit, and he asks you skeptically: why should a human being use another human being, anyway?

USE MAN (encore)

Yes, ondine only had to open her mouth and speak for something to be or not to be . . . because when she looked around, what did she see? She saw that the cooperative was collapsing . . . something that of course was not only due to her, but in large part to the socialists themselves, who had more than a few fortune-hunters in their ranks, scum who took advantage of bryske's gullibility, cheating him and stealing from him so that his books didn't balance and so took to drink . . . that idiot of an oscarke might think that bryske had started drinking because he couldn't stand the joy of seeing a dream become reality . . . it was far more likely that he saw everyone around him stealing and cheating so that he saw how useless it was to sacrifice oneself all alone, and how much better it would be for him to grab his share and run . . . and also, it was quite possible that the interpretation she gave of it didn't hamper the oscarke's interpretation at all: those different, completely contradictory explanations could All be true, could All be psychologically correct. One truth didn't stand in the way of another. But . . .

Oh, she had let her thoughts wander off again . . . she'd only wanted to remember: remember that bryske drank, that the cooperative had collapsed, that oscarke was good and willing, so it seemed that a special gift had been given just to her: what did it matter if that monique was married to the person she was married to? What monique had in life she'd gained by pulling the wool over a man's eyes . . . but what she, ondine, had, she had got by her own efforts, she'd fought for it against god and the devil, against temptation and despair. She'd had to wrest it away inch by inch, fight fate itself as it were, digging diversionary canals for that fate to flow into . . . Oh but it made her breathe oh so deeply with something that pride was not a big enough word for: she'd managed to divert bad luck onto the heads of others, and she laughed about it, silent and proud. Secretly, she longed to observe those victims in their struggle, perhaps a life-and-death struggle. And she also wanted, with that madame van wesenborgh especially, to see to what extent they were fundamentally different: she wanted as it were to measure, in spiritual terms that is, how great the difference between them was . . . and ringing monique's bell, and again taking in all that luxury, those carpets and paintings, those vases full of flowers, it still pierced her to the heart: it's spiritual, spiritual! she kept repeating inwardly, whispering to herself but almost weeping. And as she sank into a sofa she thought: she earned this with her fanny, making do with an old man's office stool and meekly obeying the gentlemen's whims and being their slave. And she tried to look down on monique with a fine sneering smile round one corner of her mouth: you're a common whore, while I on the on the contrary am a dominatrix. Or no . . . why did that word "dominatrix" keep sounding in her head . . . she meant: an intelligent woman, a creature who was no longer bound to stupid natural laws like some ignorant animal, but who had a will and an intelligence of her own. So let her have slightly more comfortable chairs here—my time will come, she thought: everything I wish for will come to me if only I wish hard enough.

She contented herself with asking about bryske, and saying that she had seen him . . . and she showed a degree of sympathy: poor devil, where are the days when he used to write poetry? And after all those years she remembered one of his poems: ondine, yes, stick it right in! Did he really say that? monique asked in surprise. And ondine was going to nod, but finally did not, deterring her with this rather blatant lie: oh no, she said, I was only joking. And almost with pity—it sounded so much like pity she wondered whether it wasn't actually the real thing—with feigned pity then, which was almost Actual pity, ondine asked how bryske could have sunk so low! And when monique made excuses for him . . . because he was her uncle after all, whichever way you looked at it (although she herself cursed him and didn't give a damn . . . and yes, even in her prayers, in her frivolous prayers at the late sunday mass, which people attended mainly to be seen, where they made rendezvous and listened contentedly to father vanderlincke who preached so marvelously about vice that one couldn't help but succumb to a very severe vice that very afternoon . . . there, in her frivolous prayers, she asked for bryske to be hounded into the lower depths as soon as possible), but now, to ondine, she made a special case for her uncle brys. What he had done was only human: hundreds, thousands, would have succumbed in his place: he'd had to do without everything in his life, almost like the lord Himself he had not had a stone to lay his head upon . . . who, for example, would have had the courage to emigrate to england in his old age, and to work in a factory, when he had always been a bookkeeper? . . . and now, sitting with the socialists day in, day out, he finally saw that they were scum—something for that matter that his family had told him in every possible way—now he saw it for himself. On the anniversary of the party, for example, a few walloons had come to celebrate . . . but what did that rabble on the quay do? . . . they got the Walloons drunk and stole their wallets. Her uncle had wept with shame, and he had paid back the stolen money from his own wallet, and yes . . . because he couldn't make ends meet, because he didn't have much himself, he took money from the cooperative, intending to pay it back as soon as he received his salary. But in the cooperative itself he had uncovered fraud upon fraud: the man in charge was lining his own pockets, and the man under him in turn took advantage of his goodness . . . so he was unhappy and had started to drink, and so of course because he had no money of his own, he'd started drinking with the cooperative's money. No, she hoped that he would die soon: he was getting old, and he couldn't just go on drinking and wandering round the streets drunk without something terrible happening to him.

And as monique bided her time and felt almost content, ondine too felt content . . . they sat there opposite each other, each with their smile: ondine with a smile in the right-hand corner of her mouth and monique with a smile in the left-hand corner. Ondine finally went home and was content, since the final massacre of that poor-people's party couldn't be long in coming . . . the movement was going to collapse with an earsplitting roar, and another of her childhood dreams would be fulfilled. And smiling, her head held very high as if she we searching with a mystic's eyes for something miraculous in the gray sky above, she didn't feel the rain that fell now in long, hot streaks.

EAT MORE MAN!

No, not even with a clout of the flu—clout, what kind of dialect is that? Does it mean a bout of the flu, or the kind that knocks you out, a bad infection?— but it doesn't matter, even while you're buried under a pile of blankets, shivering and burning by turns, they can't leave you alone: professor spothuyzen, sickwit the student, master oedenmaeckers. They pursue you even into your restless sleep, the tormenting demons. And vaguely, from very far away, you hear master oedenmaeckers asking: why should man start using man, eh? And from even further away comes the laughter of professor spothuyzen and the laughter of sickwit the student: hasn't one man always used the other? And much farther back, when man was still going round with a club and cramming snails into his mouth—for god's sake stop that disgusting stuff while I'm lying here with the flu—even while he went around with his club he peered with distrust at every creature who resembled him . . . he observed him from the bushes, his own mirror image . . . and then beat out the brains of the creature that frightened him because it was Too like him. And talking of meat, you always hear how opposing armies make mincemeat of each other: from one dish to another: allow a little butter to brown thoroughly, add some salt and pepper, chop up everything and put it in the pan: eat more bread, eat more fish, eat more man. And you hear the laughter of the student spothuyzen, of professor sickwit —no, that's another mistake—but still, you can hear their laughter, and you hear the laughter swelling from centuries ago, the laughter of everyone who made mincemeat, and were made mincemeat of in turn: who is man's greatest enemy? . . . and you hear the reply too: man himself.

And full of the flu, you try to escape your tormenting demons, you toss and turn under the blankets, and try to toss and turn away from them: be quiet, because you're only torturing my brain, but you're messing up my book on chapel road: *what will my heroine, ondine, say when she hears you say that man is his own worst enemy?*—ssh, quiet!—*because ondine has already discovered that the devil outside doesn't exist but that she herself is a devil, a devil of a human being . . . and later she'll also discover that the god outside her doesn't exist and that she is also her own god: that she carries a god of man inside her.* But now . . . that man is supposedly his own worst enemy, man will be driven from the earth by man, that man will pronounce the last judgment on man! *Be quiet, because if she hears That it will be the end of my novel.*

But what's the point of your protesting? Your demons can't hear you, they just hang there like puppets assigned a role, who rattle off their parts without mechanically: man is his own enemy; while he thought he was opening the gates of heaven, all he was doing was casting thousands into the abyss of hell, into the dungeons of the inquisition . . . while someone was concerned with freedom he was sitting in judgment and pushing all those not willing to enjoy his freedom and equality under the swishing blade of the guillotine. And this was just the good ones . . . if these were the green wood, what can we expect of the dead wood?

Eat more man! And each generation in turn is driven to school to have every doubt and every bit of skepticism, every difference and every quirk of personality cut away with the pruning knife . . . in the schools the mind is systematically poured into the same mould, every human desire is kneaded by the church in the image of the same wax statue, every human aspiration is fit into the same template by society: a standard type has to be created to populate the schools, the church, the recruitment offices, the ministries, the mills, the cinemas, the pension funds, the universities, the insurance companies, the army, the daily press: all have to feel the same hope, faith, love and remorse. That's always been the real aim: to channel everyone, to be able to make everyone into the same mincemeat.

And you toss and turn in order to escape you demons, your enemies, because they're gradually beginning to involve you in their conversation, dragging you towards the great god Pan.

BRYSKE'S CHAIR

So she didn't feel the rain that fell in long, hot streaks: there wasn't a soul to be seen in the street, she walked down it alone, soaked to the skin. But she paid absolutely no attention, since there was a sun shining inside her. And yet . . . and yet . . . she looked at the rain, and kept saying: there's a sun shining inside me . . . but she repeated it more and more slowly, because as she walked along and thought—or rather felt, because she was as she was—a slight irritation, a slight discomfort surfaced. Back there she had sat in a comfortable chair, and at home she had nothing but a hard chair . . . or if you like, the wicker chair that was falling to pieces since oscarke had shaken it while rocking little judith to sleep . . . it was still held together by a few strings, and had come to look like someone's lap . . . but it was a complete eyesore, a poor-person's lap, and she hated hated hated everything that smacked of poor people. She had to pass a shop where they sold comfortable chairs, and she stood for a long time by the shop window, with her nose against the cold glass. Then she thought: shouldn't I nose round a bit and see if there's an auction going on anywhere? At home she sat with her hands round her knees dreaming and brooding more and more, and little judith would cling to her skirts and say: pick me up. Pick me up . . . ondine didn't hear, all she knew was that life was going to become impossible if she didn't have a comfortable chair—though, really, she had no paintings or carpets, she had no expensive leather-bound books, and none of that bothered her at all. So had she simply kicked off her clogs in the mud of termuren to compete for honor and wealth . . . without any appreciation for wisdom and beauty? No matter, all that mattered for the moment was the chair—though it wasn't just about having a magnificent item that could make other people's eyes pop out in jealousy, it was going to be an increasingly necessary piece of furniture, something to lie down on whenever she wanted to rest from the struggle. Besides, mariette would soon be here . . . since ondine had no doubt at all that the second child was going to be another girl, she could bring only girls into the world, she thought . . . the other one had been a girl too, how could she have worried so much about it? And now zulma, her crazy mother, wanted to be godmother . . . but ondine didn't want another zulma to come into the world: one was enough. And now, mariette . . . mariette . . . she savored the name again and again, there was music in it, there was beauty in it. And so, After All, perhaps she did know what beauty was, perhaps she simply didn't want to bother herself about things that would be impossible to attain for another few years. She was a wonder, she was an incongruous mixture, she was a web that was almost impossible to unravel . . . so that people could say what they liked about her, it was always partly true. With her, one might well start believing that psychology was nonsense . . . because look, she turned her thoughts round again and again, she turned her opinions on their heads, and still they all remained partly the plain truth, and partly the most beautiful fabrication. And as had happened so often in her life—that she looked for something without being able to find it, and then when she gave up it fell right into her lap—so it happened now too: someone told her that mr brys's furniture was being sold at public auction. Or, anyway, bryske's furniture . . . because before he went to england he was mr brys and since he'd come back he was just plain bryske . . . as if people could tell just by looking at him that he'd worked in a weaving mill over there in manchester. And now, one sober day he had felt remorse again and wanted to start his life anew: he was going to confess and make amends, return all the money to the cooperative. There was a cabinet with artificial glass windows containing books. And although apart from her lives of the saints and grammaire française *she had never read a book, the cabinet dazzled her, though she had enough self-control to turn away . . . she walked round and tasted the pleasure of touching and contemptuously assessing the furniture that this old person had spent his life with, as if she were touching and judging his very soul . . . or rather, his body in its most intimate and private places. But she didn't forget to look around for an easy chair . . . she found one, but to tell the truth, she found it rather old-fashioned: the upholstery had faded over the years, and there was even a hole with some horsehair sticking out. But . . . how ridiculous, even monique's chairs had to be filled with something . . . if a man knew what was inside a woman, he would no longer find her desirable—oh, that's the way it was with everything. And she put her hand over the hole, and muttered something under her breath: but what offended her most was that hollow there in the back, you could see that bryske had leaned against it for years and years, had sat reading or having a midday nap: it had gone black with his sweat . . . and now she would have to lean her head against the same spot! She shivered, trembled . . . just like that night when she'd had to sleep in that strange bed for the first time. I can wash*

*it, she thought . . . but she knew that washing wouldn't be enough. I'll take the
material off, and have it reupholstered, she thought. And she told someone who
was also looking the chair over that she wanted it for an invalid . . . for a sick old
creature who lived with her, in her own room, and hadn't much longer to live.*

TIPPETOTJE'S ALIVE AND WELL!

The postman does his rounds along chapel road, and throws printed matter
through the door with a grand gesture—a manifesto from the association of
fairground booth holders—and slings a letter into woelus's fairground wagon
with the same élan. And woelus turns the letter over and over in his hands. A
letter from tippetotje . . . I don't know any tippetotje! says woelus. And it soon
comes out that there's been a misdirection of correspondence: woelus disappears into his wagon with his manifesto, and you tear open tippetotje's letter:
      dear, I regularly read the failed epistles on the aim and purpose, the rise
and fall, the spiral motion . . . but you're forgetting the main thing, the decline.
And having read all this I've actually read nothing: I've wasted my time on
those stories about ondine, that story about bryske, and those stories about the
how and why of the Because: I could waste my time much more pleasantly
at my baron's side. So as I sit here with your book of bits and pieces, appearing here, there and all everywhere, in dailies and weeklies, in monthlies and
annuals, I wonder why you too—yes, you!—don't waste your time more
agreeably by the side of some baroness (I write "side," but I mean something
else). You introduce all your friends to your characters in order to escape the
dead hands of those increasingly hysterical lunatics, in order to buy a bit of
meadow somewhere, a bit of woodland—a refuge—to be able to retreat to
that refuge, and from there resume the fight for freedom and happiness . . .
starting first and foremost with your own freedom and your own happiness.
And if one of your friends really started on that project, if one of your friends
finally did give up serving and praising god, re-educating the people, bringing art closer to the people—if you know any more good slogans, you can
tack them on here—then you'd cry pathetically: tippetotje, are you going to
abandon me too? You're talking nonsense . . . you say something, but don't
do it . . . you no longer believe in any of those things, and yet you still strike
the pose of a proud frankish warrior. Soon I'll start hating you . . . soon I'll
start accusing you of following the bandwagon like the rest . . . no, soon I'll
start being disgusted by you. You were born a writer and you'll die a writer
by the devil or by the balls of adhemar or god, who's telling you that you have
to go on writing for . . . for . . . come on, why don't you write me something
about baekelandt or cartouche, or better yet write me the story of that robber
chieftain jan de lichte . . . jan de lichte seen through your eyes, described

by your pen. Oh, I dream about that every evening, after I've tucked in my baron, pocketed my tip: I dream about sitting by the standard lamp a little, with a cigar and a large glass of gin, reading about the gang of jan de lichte, as written by boon. Christ, if I weren't so lazy, I'd write it myself, I'd write the masterpiece of our age myself, a page every evening: jan de lichte founds his gang . . . jan de lichte meets a baroness . . . jan de lichte addresses his gang . . . and last of all: jan de lichte in his lighter. Your tippetotje.

And you close tippetotje's letter and everything feels empty and gloomy: it's easy for tippetotje to dream about a book on jan de lichte: but you, boon, aren't a jan de lichte. And the main thing, you can see . . . writing in the evening, next to the baron's bed, with a glass of gin in front of you . . . the main thing is that you don't have to worry about readers understanding your plays on words: jan de lichte in his lighter! For tippetotje a "lighter" isn't a boat but a coffin: in termuren a coffin is called a lighter. And you also don't have to worry that your pieces or those of johan janssens won't be published anywhere: tippetotje writes for her own pleasure. But we don't: we must strike and soothe, we must go out and look around us and make the best of what we see.

DOWN WITH KIERKEGAARD!

One evening at the end of december, you stroll with mr brys through the avenues and squares of brussels: live fir trees have been chopped down and now line max havelaar boulevard, nailed to two cross-slats . . . there are garlands of mistletoe and electric lights . . . and meanwhile mr brys talks to you about The same things sickwit the student talks about: the spiral movement of history. What a spectacle! You hear mr brys talking about the course of thousands of years . . . and meanwhile you see a shop window with a real oven and a real baker in it, and you see a shop window with an automated loom . . . but whatever one does these days, it's all electronics and mechanics and chemistry: nothing in my hand, nothing up my sleeve, hocus pocus: science. And meanwhile mr brys is talking about the history of man, saying that in the outward rotation of the spiral something is always lost, but that the return always brings something different and new: something you come to believe in unconditionally, as though it were the greatest good, something that gets hyped up out of all proportion and becomes a bubble in our brains that grows bigger and bigger till it explodes with a pop. Everything the egyptians discovered was harnessed to the service of magic, spiritualism, and the knowledge of death; everything the greeks discovered was harnessed to the service of reason and beauty; everything we have discovered is harnessed to technology. Man has never had a sense of proportion, says mr brys. And meanwhile—don't forget—you're strolling down max havelaar boulevard, past the torn-up firs with their garlands of electric lights: they're growing again there, they flower with a new, artificial life . . . they live, like us, in a nature beyond nature, sustained by electricity, by chemistry, by money. A life in the outward rotation of the spiral, where for the first time in human history we've found the pivot from which the earth can be torn out of its orbit: what a shame that the marquis de sade never lived to see That, he would have forced the handle into juliette's hand. And you stroll on past the shop windows and find that all this technology and electricity have Fashion as their only true aim: the woman who wants to live again with her dress trailing over the ground and her completely bare shoulders, wants to live again in the year such-and-such. You observe this—but mr brys goes on talking about the rotation of the spiral . . . about the bubble of technology that has reached its greatest possible diameter, and will soon explode with a bang. And he talks to you about the fear that haunts the minds of the people of this age . . . about books and literature which deal again and again with fear, fear, and more fear, about kierkegaard and heidegger and jaspers who are the center of attention. Fear has become a part of our essence—and meanwhile you see the shop windows filled with the fashions of the year such-and-such. The best among us are permeated with fear, says mr brys . . . but they stick their heads in the sand, or turn the clock back by dressing women as they were in the year such-and-such.

WASTELAND

And wandering through the avenues and squares of brussels with mossieu colson of the ministry . . . on this evening in december, when the fir trees live their artificial lives . . . he puts a hand on your arm and says, in a friendly way not intended to offend, that you live far too lonely a life back there in chapel road: you should experience more of the life of these avenues and squares with me: those who walk these avenues have blood that flows faster, hearts that beat louder, and brains that work faster. Back there in your chapel road you think more, that's true . . . but it's equally true that you think too much and too long: you study things for so long and so closely that they start to blur in front of your eyes . . . you think until, like hamlet and the marquis de sade, you see suicide as the only way out: your heart is a beat behind, like the existentialists you only talk about fear and fear. I know, fear is boundless, but it's not nameless. Instead of giving in to your panic, you'd do far better to wander round in search of the causes of this fear . . . and you'd soon find out that it's only the fear of the sword of damocles hanging over the world: we invented god, and use him only to engineer disasters and evil, poverty and shame, enslavement and the eternal fires of hell . . . and then we invented technology, and also used it to unleash poverty and disaster and eternal fire . . . and now it's happened for the first time in the earth's history that a creature that was produced by it is capable of destroying it. The earth itself is afraid, and communicates its fear to some of us, to those of us who are linked to it by more delicate fibers, to those who probe it with more sensitive feelers, to those who eavesdrop on it with more refined antennae. The earth itself is afraid, because it was able to destroy its dinosaurs and brontosauruses, it could destroy the Neanderthals easily enough, but now it's no longer capable of destroying modern man without causing itself to disintegrate. That's the cause of the feeling that lodges somewhere between your heart and your stomach, and that back there in chapel road you call Fear—but if you were to come out here and feel your blood and heart beating louder, your mind working faster, you would also find out that this feeling of ours is actually greater than fear: it's something that outgrows fear, just like how in times of danger a coward can suddenly emerge as a hero. The hero is only someone who feels his fear grow into something greater, something more, who sees his fear outgrown by courage. Nothing is lost and nothing is too late: our coward's fear can still turn into the courage of a hero.

And ambling through the streets of brussels—on this december evening, when the christmas trees grow with Another life, with a life removed from nature and almost mechanical—mossieu colson of the ministry stops and reads a story to you, a short story that he's written about the metropolis: behold these 12-story buildings, banks, the headquarters of insurance companies, offices of steel, and uranium trusts . . . and at the foot of those towering buildings, a small unsightly patch of wasteland . . . and on that unsightly patch an old fellow has grown some vegetables: and now he brings his friend, another old fellow, to that unsightly patch of ground and proudly shows off his paltry few vegetables, and says: look, these peas will go to waste!

And you stare at mossieu colson, just as the one old fellow must have stared at the other: with joy and in admiration, because, despite all the setbacks, all is not lost.

THE CHRISTMAS TREE

Along comes sickwit the student . . . But you sneak out the back door and hurry across chapel road, across the unmanned termuren railway crossing, and without realizing it you are already sinking into the mud of the country path that leads to the earthly paradise of master oedenmaeckers and the so-called villa of tolfpoets. Oh, oh, in this rotten weather you've forgotten master oedenmaeckers's garden and tolfpoets's so-called villa all over again! How is it possible that in the summer you live and laugh, and in the winter you forget all about that laughing life, and do nothing but sit by the stove brooding about decay and death? And sinking into the mud, just in front of tolfpoets's so-called villa, somebody else is sinking with you: a gardener, with a spade and young tree over his shoulder. And polpoets comes rushing out to offer help, and after him comes his crazy young guard dog, and behind comes the child of nature maria, hung with ribbons and bows . . . and polpoets calls out to them: two birds with one stone: our little tree and our little boon! And the little tree gets a place in the garden, and little boon gets a place in the living room under the mistletoe—while outside the gardener sticks his spade in the mud, and in the living room polpoets tells his christmas jokes. His first joke is about the earthly paradise of master oedenmaeckers, which lies there desolate and abandoned, and in which he, polpoets, sometimes takes a walk . . . and yesterday doing his rounds he sees that a fir has been chopped down by somebody or other wanting to celebrate christmas. And the child of nature maria interrupts him: I should add only a few firs and a cedar had even been planted, and now one's already being sawn down! It's not there anymore, says polpoets . . . it's BEEN sawn down and it's GONE. And he smiles, baring his 2 gold teeth: a stroke of luck that the crafty bastard didn't get it wrong and saw down the cedar instead . . . but it's not too late, there's still a day before christmas. And at that moment the gardener puts down his spade and muddy clogs by the garden door, and comes inside in his stocking feet: yes, he says, we still have a day till christmas, and I live over there by the unmanned railway crossing at termuren, and if you need a christmas tree you shouldn't wait: they're piled up in the street, they've practically buried the whole front of my house: for ten francs you can pick whichever one you like. No, no! laughs polpoets . . . I get no pleasure from a christmas tree purchased legally, I have to have stolen it Myself and chopped it down Myself . . . chopping down and sawing, stealing and plundering and destroying, those are the sort of things that have to be bound up with a christmas tree if I'm to get any pleasure from it. And the gardener looks in alarm at tolfpoets's 2 smiling teeth: so has man been put in the world to saw and chop down, to mutilate and steal everything around him? he asks. Has man been put in the world to dismantle everything, exterminate everything and finally remain all alone? you ask.

But tolfpoets smiles, baring his 2 gold teeth, and tells his second christmas joke: about a lady who wanted nothing more than to have a nice house, who went and cleaned and scrubbed for rich people to get money to make her house even nicer—and so, in order to have a nice house, could never spend any time in that house—and so she went and cleaned for a man with only 1 leg . . . and suddenly one christmas night, This hidden, destructive life also burst out there: she had planted a christmas tree in her living room, and invited the man with 1 leg to celebrate christmas eve with her and admire her nice house . . . and there they sat, having a dram or two, getting nicely drunk

. . . and once he's drunk he starts leaping around on his 1 leg and knocking everything over with his crutch . . . he knocks over the chairs and smashes the vases, he smashes the mirror and knocks the bottle off the table, all the while ranting and raving: look, look, I'm knocking the legs off everything! And the woman shouts and laughs with him: yes, knock the legs off everything . . . knock the legs off the chairs, knock the legs off the christmas tree.

And polpoets smiles and bares his 2 gold teeth, and says that he's written this story down and given it a title: "the world without legs." And the gardener looks at him, appalled, and you cry out equally appalled: enough of your creepy jokes, polpoets—imagine me having to write a story like that, "the christmas tree without legs" . . . no, no, this is bad enough as it is!

HAPPINESS? WHAT'S THAT?

So oscarke came home that evening and found valeer on the kitchen floor repairing a chair . . . he wasn't taken aback, he let all of ondine's tricks just wash over him—but he couldn't understand her, it was as though she was from another world. He was as far from ondine as ants were from people . . . his love and hope and remorse and all his other human things were over there at the stonemason's place, and here he felt only indifference, here he lived among strangers whose fate he could contemplate without being moved. Now, for example, he sat silently ingesting his warmed-up supper and staring at valeer without seeing him . . . between valeer's hammer and nail he saw Her head, and he thought of what would happen if she, jeannine, became pregnant some day: he saw her walking over the chair that valeer was sitting next to, with a belly like ondine's. He had to tear his eyes away, because however much he longed to see her like That—with ondine it was appalling, it was monstrous, but with her it would be . . . oh no. He couldn't even imagine how terribly moving it would be—he would never be able to See it, he wouldn't be Allowed to see it, because it would mean the end for him, dishonor and prison. But as he turned towards his food for a moment and then looked up again, he saw the chair itself, which was rather old-fashioned, and which had a leg missing: valeer had just attached the replacement; a square piece of wood, black with age, alongside the other, elegantly curved legs. And he also saw valeer himself, fiddling and tinkering around, trying to stretch new material over it: he had to pull down the material with his mutilated hand, push in the nail and then hit it, but the nail kept flying off, or he didn't hit it straight, or the material came loose: he'd long since learned to carry out 2 operations with 1 hand, but 3 was too many. Without a word oscarke got up and sat on the floor next to valeer to lend him a hand . . . he found it rather strange that he'd never seen a man's face, the face of a fellow human being, so close up before . . . he started in bewilderment at valeer's features, he must have only looked at him superficially in the past, forming a vague, indifferent picture . . . because now, sitting on the floor next to him, he seemed almost to have become a different person, someone who no longer corresponded to that image in the least. Those eyes especially, he saw that they were ondine's eyes—and that mouth would also have been ondine's had it not hung open with such a lack of will. And he hid the thought that valeer could have been ondine, had he been a different sex and put together a little better, he hid this thought by simply saying: it's easy to see that you're ondine's brother! Valeer nodded his outsize head—ondine didn't have That either: it was there behind the seam that his head was so thick, as if the fontanel had stayed open for too long. And oscarke, who recently had started to wonder whether all people weren't fragments of a disintegrated god, just like the earth and moon were fragments of an exploded sun, now wondered what kind of human being he was: malevolent or loving, a thinker or a doer—a little villain like his father, or a big one like ondine and her ilk, who spent every evening in the pub. And he realized that he had a little bit from every category in him: he was good and bad, malevolent and loving, capable of building something but also capable of immediately demolishing it. Everything is represented in man, he thought—man is a part of the great whole and the great whole is as we are, good and bad together: I say god and devil, but in reality the two are one. As though it was meant to be, his father-in-law vapeur had come over one evening to talk to him about electricity—because his invention was ready in broad outline, he just needed a clean draft to make blueprints from, but he was too nervous to make a start, he walked round chattering about the most insignificant things, and didn't realize . . . really, he didn't see . . . that everyone was making fun of him—and he explained to oscarke that the principle of electricity was based on positive and negative poles, which attracted or repelled each other. You see! oscarke had cried . . . and had begun a confused argument that Everything in the world was like that, man and woman, day and night, high and low tide, life and death, everything had a positive and a negative pole: and it's the same with god, but we call the negative pole devil and the positive pole god, because we don't understand that the whole system stands Above god and devil. And through this theory he felt himself rise in his own estimation: ondine, he had said, was a creature of action, a small ignorant particle attuned to one pole, while he on the contrary was a creature of thought, a fragment of the other, god pole. And perfect happiness must therefore consist of becoming part of the ultimate principle itself, beyond god and devil. Oh, he had been happy with his newly discovered theory—but what he didn't realize yet was that this happiness had its origin in the fact that he had begun to Live, that he'd forgotten god and devil and the priest and ondine and had finally grabbed hold of jeannine. Because that was true: tears, sickness and sorrow came by themselves, but happiness had to be fought for. And valeer, who had gone on nailing the cotton material round the chair and had also sat thinking about oscarke's words "that he was like ondine's sister" wanted to say: externally like her perhaps, but internally she is different, she acts, and I'm more of a thinker—but just as he'd distilled this thought into a reasonable sentence and was about to speak it, oscarke came up with something else: happiness is something that has to be fought for. And valeer looked at oscarke in astonishment. You've got the socialists, said oscarke . . . since it's a movement that wants to bring a little happiness to human beings, it has to shed blood, sweat, and tears at every step in order to achieve anything, but something that keeps the world in darkness, in misery, grows all by itself, effortlessly . . . just look at weeds, don't they grow by themselves too? Valeer agreed with that . . . but about socialism he wasn't sure, hadn't he heard that it was something bad? In which case, according to this new theory of oscarke's, one ought to believe that socialism and atheism and immorality grew by themselves, but that the true faith must be preached and preached again. Not that he cared about faith or atheism, no that wasn't his business, he liked smoking his pipe in the evening, and watching the card players in the pub . . . and whether the world was good or bad or just or whatever, well, the world would have to decide for itself . . . because how long does a man live?—ha, so it was stupid to act as if you, Along with the world, were going to live for ever. And with a nail in his mouth, and his finger raised as though he had made a great discovery, he said: your happiness is something you must fight for. But that's what I said myself just now, said oscarke almost in a whisper. Valeer conceded this, but surely that didn't stop him from discovering it himself as well?—right then, and was going to put it into practice! And as he went on nailing, he talked about putting a strip of edging over the nails and finishing it off with nice brass studs.

HAPPY NEW YEAR

You meet andreus mottebol on the day you go around wishing everyone a happy new year . . . and you say it to him too: happy new year, andreus mottebol . . . I remember how in my youth I was guilty of writing a novel that began: happy new year, there's a bit of black ice, the postman falls and breaks his leg, happy new year. And andreus mottebol replies that in one's youth one only has in mind the opening pages of novels yet to be written: one is brimming over with novels that could, might, should be written, one would like to write 70,370 novels even—and one writes only the first few pages of them—and that if you were able to see those first few pages again later, yellowed, and in a handwriting that isn't quite yours, you'd notice that they all have the same content, but in slightly different words and each in a different key: because all of us write only one novel in our lives: our own novel. And in dismay you answer andreus mottebol that mr brys gave you a hard time over christmas: merry christmas, you're sitting brooding in that chapel road of yours far too alone—merry christmas, meanwhile giving me a good kick in the shins. And now you wish me happy new year, and meanwhile you kick me in the ass by saying that all my books are the same. Happy is the man who at this time of new year still has friends who dare tell him the truth, says andreus mottebol . . . and happy especially is the man who dares listen to that truth—like at home, where my son jo (who's eleven) has written a new year's poem about his mother: you fear no harm, you're always calm, like a candy bar, on the desk by my schoolbag you are. And you smile, because like father, like son: it must be a nice home where the child praises the mother because she has no fear in her struggle to keep house and can remain calm and serene, can be luxuriant and tasty as a candy bar . . . and congratulations on your son, who sings so beautifully in rhythm and rhyme and sound: on the desk by my schoolbag!

Absolutely, says andreus mottebol . . . but once I asked him to write something about me, just like that, out of curiosity and fear—as with everything we do—out of curiosity to see myself as my son jo sees me, and out of the fear of seeing myself as I really Am. And he wrote: dear dad, in fact, you use words to act, whatever you want you can do, write articles, fill pages too. And when I saw him write that down just like that, without thinking, I knew they would be unconscious truths . . . look at that phrase like a flaming sword: you use words to act, someone who just sits there, and thinks and frets, and can only act in words. So my son sees his father as a man of our time, who is infinitely tired, and hopelessly old, and can only change the world on paper—so that the world remains the same, and the only result is some filled pages. And listen to the mockery in "whatever you want you can do." Someone who can do whatever he wants, and hence can't do anything, but can do everything more or less, a so-called everything . . . someone who can play a bricklayer and housepainter, writer and journalist, world reformer and clown . . . and is perhaps none of them, except probably the last. And a little more quietly andreus mottebol adds: and I heard that praise is being heaped on me again and I had the painful thought that you can be pushed down a hole by being raised up on high—like the proverb: vivat, raise him up high to let him fall—like in reynard the fox: long live reynard, he has a nice coat that'll come in handy—like today when people wish you a happy new year and meanwhile kick you in the shins.

And while andreus mottebol has been shaking all this from his mothball of a head, you're standing at his front door, and then you go in for a drink and to wish his son jo all the best: happy new year, you're young and write lots and lots of beautiful poems! And jo mottebol sits there, like his father andreus mottebol, just sits and sits, as you yourself just sit and sit—and the boy talks like you yourself talk, oh boy, I'm actually an old man of eleven! And while andreus and his wife start to laugh you stare silently at jo mottebol because he is a parody of what you Yourself are: a person with too little hope and still less courage: happy new year.

HOW OLD ARE WE?

On christmas day you went to see polpoets in his funny villa, and you can't help going for new year's too, to wish him many happy returns—although you really don't give a damn whether he has many happy returns, because you really only go for your own sake: because it's so solitary and pleasant to be out there in the middle of the country, far from modern people, far from the age in which those people live. In polpoets's funny villa there is no time, he sits in his pleasant study making notes from old archives from the year 1750. Happy new year from the year 1950, polpoets! And polpoets smiles and reveals his 2 gold teeth, and wishes you a happy new year from the year 1750: there is no time and no old age, he says . . . it's just like that jo mottebol said: oh, I'm an old man of eleven. And he said it as a parody, to pull his father's leg . . . to pull your leg, writer of ondineke of termuren: you feel old and tired, and write and think like tired old people think. And that's because you're actually far too young: those who are young can afford the luxury of feeling old. It's only when you start to grow old that you pride yourself on feeling very young, Deep in his nihilistic core man denies the existence of every value, of every epoch, of every age. And I, polpoets, feeling myself centuries old, just as you and andreus mottebol feel centuries old, go pale when my wife maria says that at the new year that I'm only 38 . . . and I'm glad because I feel myself growing younger every year. And while I sit hunched over these archives from 1750—from the time of the robber chieftain jan de lichte, whom tippetotje wants so much to write a novel about—I feel younger every day. In these papers I read the description or "portrait" of a thief and arsonist and highwayman who they couldn't catch— do you think that he's still on the run today, in 1950?—and his description is as follows: about 5 and a half feet tall, beer-colored hair, very slight and thin in build, dour-faced, thin-legged, usually wearing a greenish cassock, about 20 or 21 years old AND EVEN YOUNGER IN APPEARANCE. And I, pol- poets, read that and feel myself growing younger and younger: well, that guy burned, robbed, and stole, and so you'd think he would be someone . . . well, a bandit, a legend, a creature with no age. And you discover that he's someone like you and me, someone who's old, old in what he writes and thinks and does, but who despite all his old, tired thoughts is slight and thin in build, and "even younger in appearance"! And polpoets laughs because there's no time, because he sees everyone growing old, but not himself: everyone grows old but I myself have nothing to do with time and age. With regret, with sadness, with oh, for christ's sake, I once saw that my father was starting to grow old

. . . but when I went to wish him a happy new year he vented his spleen on his neighbor and said: that stupid old bastard next door! And I, polpoets, realized that my father sees other people growing old, but not himself . . . realized that everyone says of other people: that old so-and-so!—but sees themselves becoming younger and younger all the while.

And you admit that polpoets is right, you wish him a happy new year and see he's getting old . . . but on the way back to termuren, you realize that it's all self-deception on polpoets's part: walking along, your face looking even younger, you feel old and tired like andreus mottebol's son . . . and you stammer, with regret, with irony, with parody: oh, I'm already an old man of 38.

THE END

No, this is not the end of the world, it's just the end of the chapter "only the precious little moment counts" . . . and before writing the final section, you quickly leaf through the manuscript, and you realize that it's mainly about people who have lived on the fringes of society—true, andreus mottebol doesn't tell us any more about reynard the fox, but on the other hand polpoets sits hunched over the archives describing the trial of jan de lichte—and noticing that this chapter is mainly about tramps and vagabonds, you feel that something's not quite right: walking round here and there you encounter an old poet, with eyes and a mouth that remind you a little of chaplin (charlie chaplin, also a vagabond and a tramp, who again and again is cast out by society)—(ha, something else about chaplin, something unconnected with our chapter, but still very beautiful: a friend of ours wrote somewhere, MY THOUGHTS WALK LIKE CHAPLIN'S FEET), and that old poet then, who reminds you of chaplin, not because his thoughts go in all directions, but because you can never decide whether his smile is hiding disappointment or contempt . . . that old poet says to you: look, tippetotje's "gang of jan de lichte" is the book that I should like to write Too. And you meet a young novelist and talk to him about tippetotje's "gang of jan de lichte," and he smiles and says: don't take my smile the wrong way, it's not that I look down on that stuff as a topic, but because I myself had been thinking about writing about the life of baekelandt . . . and you know, then I met the most emiment of all writers and poets, and he said to me: I'd like to write a play, but with a rather odd theme: the gang of cartouche.

And you laugh, because it's funny to find out that we're all walking round with the same idea, and yet are all worried that our peers will find it odd. But on the other hand it makes you sad, for the very same reason: we think we have brains like steel traps, and it's not true: there's just some fog, some gas, some mist and miasma floating round that penetrates our brains through our ears and eyes . . . we don't think, we just feel a little . . . we experience things faintly and distantly, and something in this society, in this age, in these people around us fills us with fear or puts us on our guard: we all retreat into our refuges, and our dreams gravitate towards those who have lived outside the law: tramps and vagabonds. But we Ourselves dare not or cannot be like that, and so we write about them . . . we dream and write about those who succeeded in escaping from society: about baekelandt and cartouche and jan de lichte. And you go to see polpoets, where he sits ransacking the archives in his so-called villa, as if he were the only person concerned with jan de lichte—and you see him taking notes intently, classifying and ordering . . . and he waves his hand: don't come in here and hypothesize about my pastime, please, he says . . . don't come along and state that I'm the victim of a general phenomenon of the age . . . of this age, which is particularly scared of this or that, which particularly wants to escape this or that—like women want to escape by dressing like they did in 1750, believing that they're living in 1750, and so can't be harmed . . . and like writers, whose minds rush back to the days of 1750, writing about vagabonds and tramps, thinking that they've managed to escape the society of 1950. Don't tell me all that, because I don't want to know . . . I'm alive, I smile and show my 2 gold teeth, and (for the end of your chapter) am going to describe a few men to you who were part of the gang of jan de lichte . . . members of his gang who were never caught, but who could only be hanged, broken on the wheel, branded, banished from the land, or sent to the galleys "in effigy," as it were. There's . . .

And all you can say is: stop, polpoets, you're too late, a line has been drawn and the end of our chapter has really arrived: only the precious little moments count in life.

THE REAL END

Your happiness is something you have to fight for, said valeer . . . and apart from that he talked about the chair, about finishing it with big brass studs. Oscarke nodded his head. But, he said, happiness, perfect happiness will only be found in the world when all nations, at one with the great principle, live in brotherhood— and actually it was a slogan of the student's, because he talked every evening in the train about his brotherhood of all nations—and it didn't fully express what oscarke meant, but he said it because nothing else happened to come to mind. Oh, that brotherhood of nations was something that valeer didn't understand, or only partly, but because he was busy arguing, feeling the equal of anyone else, he brooded a while and then found a reason to go on arguing: brotherhood between all nations? Hadn't he heard that a war was coming between germany and he'd forgotten what other countries? Why did oscarke talk of brotherhood, if germany goes and attacks us surely we can't go on regarding them as brothers! That's just It, said oscarke . . . That's just the point. Although he himself didn't understand exactly what the point was . . . or, at least, he understood this much, that he heard everyone talk about germany as though they were talking about a creature, a human being or an animal, although it was a country just like here, a country where young socialists dreamed of the same kind of brotherhood, but he couldn't articulate it clearly, so he said something approximating it. Yes but . . . replied valeer, who after an even longer search had found another clumsy argument, since because he had little or no intelligence he considered himself the smartest guy around. He had a very large head, but there wasn't much in it: on the contrary, that abnormal head was probably responsible for his stupidity. And sitting there arguing, neither of them cared about understanding the other, they simply tried to get the other to admit he was wrong. Meanwhile they tugged and dragged the piece of material, stuck horsehair here and knocked in nails there—and the chair turned into something ghastly. Ondine may have said: this is how it has to be . . . but it was easy for her to draw a few lines in the air with her hands: what did it mean to valeer who'd sat patiently watching? He'd had to guess, and as a result he paid attention not so much to her hands, moving from left to right, but to her mouth which had gone on chattering the whole time. He had nodded, since couldn't he see for Himself what needed to be done to the chair! Put on a new leg, nail some more material over it, no more than that. And when ondine came into the stuffy kitchen and saw that monstrous thing there, that rough length of wood beside the three elegant legs, the flowered material that wasn't stretched taut, and was creased in some places and was baggy in others, was this the pièce de resistance to put in the pub? Was that the thing she'd dreamed of? It was too horrible even to . . . to . . . And look at those two clumsy oafs, staring up at her from the floor, she Couldn't blame them . . . it was actually herself she should be blaming, herself, the world, everything.

A NEW CHAPTER, BUT WHAT TITLE SHOULD WE GIVE IT?
PERHAPS THOSE AWKWARD WORDS OF VALEER'S:
YOUR HAPPINESS IS SOMETHING YOU MUST FIGHT FOR

VALEER'S CHAIR

No, it's not easy . . . our book is called "summer in termuren" and look how that summery book got written in the winter . . . and because you respond to the things around you, and thus respond to the weather, it rains and rains, it hails and snows in this book. But it doesn't matter, because the idea is much more that *ondine, your heroine, is in the summer of her life—and that summer goes on for many years . . . and only after she's fully involved in bringing up her children, and those children gradually grow up, could it become "autumn in termuren."* It's not in the weather where the mistake lies, but in something much more important, in the spirit of the thing: because leafing through the 1st chapter, quickly, quickly, before going on, you were thinking that it was about people living on the fringes of society . . . about people who retreated onto a refuge, about people who bought a bit of meadow to dream of an earthly paradise on, about people who withdrew into a so-called villa, a funny little villa . . . about women who start dressing up in the style of 1750, thinking that they can escape 1950 . . . about vagabonds and tramps, like jan de lichte and baekelandt and cartouche. And in a certain sense this is true, it is about them . . . *but in addition it's about oscarke, that skeptical little guy who still goes on thinking courageously . . . oscarke, who takes the train to and from brussels where he works for a stonemason, and meanwhile searches for the meaning of life and death, god and man and society, about socialism and how to make a more beautiful world. And this while his wife ondine figures out that there's no such thing as the devil, unless it's the devil inside her . . . discovering that she herself is her own devil, and later discovering that she's her own god as well. Husband and wife both go on thinking courageously, but without knowing anything about each other's thoughts. Because between oscarke and ondine there's a gaping chasm, the gaping chasm between left and right. And oscarke figures out for himself that he's god and the devil rolled into one, that he's good and bad, malevolent and loving . . . capable of building something but also capable of demolishing it immediately thereafter. And most of all there's valeer, that oaf, that impossible brother of ondine's . . . who goes on thinking courageously too—however difficult, how indescribably difficult Thinking is for him. And he has the honor of making a discovery in the final pages of the last chapter: he discovers (after oscarke makes it very easy for him) that happiness is something we have to fight for. And then he says, naively and simply:*

ALL RIGHT THEN, I WANT TO PUT THAT INTO PRACTICE. And you've got to admit that something like that could've been a very nice start to a new chapter . . . but no, it wasn't enough for you, you had to go into it in greater depth: once again you needed to get right to the bottom of things, to take them to a climax, to a pinnacle. *And that pinnacle consists of valeer just going on working at what he happens to be doing—repairing a chair—and he goes on hammering nails, talking about putting some braid around, and finishing the chair up with some nice brass studs.* It happens to be a chair, but it could just as well be a chapter of a novel. It could be anything in the lives of the people of this modern age: whatever happens, let's not rush back to 1750, but go on fighting for our happiness . . . let's go on hammering nails, talking about putting some braid around, and finishing up with beautiful brass studs.

OSCARKE'S CHAIR

But how could ondine blame the world for anything . . . how could she throw Everything in the face of anything—as if Everything were a creature, a human being, with a face? And while her intellect continued to fight against the nerves that were trembling, burning, itching, in her body, she looked for something, anything, even an old, torn bag of garbage to throw clattering onto the floor, to give vent to her mounting fury. But since I've got that child inside me, it wouldn't do me any good to get violent, she thought . . . I've got to concentrate on something else, I've got to, I've got to. And looking round she realized that it stank to high heaven in that tiny kitchen . . . judith had done something in her diaper, and those two oafs with their idiotic questions hadn't noticed—so she took judith out of the cot and unwound her diaper, and looking for more names to call the men she saw that there wasn't a single clean diaper left, they were all rolled into a ball by the back door, and the other ones were down round the stove in the pub, drying and stinking. Yes, she should have started doing laundry the day before yesterday, but washing, pissing, and cooking—they were the concerns of every ordinary woman, weren't they? Had she stormed the fortresses of her youth only in order to wind up as a domestic pet? Had she made herself like a wild sea in order to run aground? . . . oh, what terrible metaphors she was using, but really, hanging out piss-soaked diapers? That was a job for people like oscarke! And growling and cursing to herself, she nevertheless began looking for a bucket and a washboard, stepping on a nail of valeer's in the process: she was so bitter she didn't even want to take off her stocking to look at her foot: she just gave her brother a slap in the face. She cursed this life of hers among these stupid people: why on earth did I get married, she wondered . . . why this and why that? And there was no sign of that special sun in her heart. And she blamed everything on that drip of an oscarke, who sat silently in a corner fuming because valeer hadn't understood a thing about his theories, all the while putting on an arrogant expression like he was the smartest guy around. He said nothing, oscarke . . . and ondine, who went on blaming him (and even went so far as to imagine what he might have said in reply to her, had he dared to respond) suddenly shouted: go fuck yourselves! So that they both looked at her in astonishment. Then she began to laugh, and then they looked at her in even greater astonishment. The two oafs didn't understand her, of course . . . but she'd started to laugh because she'd shouted "go fuck yourself!" to the baby along with the rest of them: if you can piss all over them, you can learn to dry them too! And then in her strange, convoluted imagination she really did see the infant judith standing by the washtub and rinsing her own diapers. No, it wasn't the first time that at the height of her fury she'd thought of something absurd and started laughing . . . But this was particularly terrific stuff: she laughed at the crazy image, and meanwhile instead of terrible pain because of the chair and the nail, she had tears of laughter in her eyes. Go fuck yourselves! she shouted again, and out she went, into town.

Oscarke sat silently shaking his head and wondering what the matter was with her: you could say she's gone soft in the head, he said to valeer, but then how could you explain her being so sharp? For instance, I might think to myself: next week I'll save up some of my wages, but, you know, if she gets wind of it, she knows immediately what I'm planning and starts telling me all about the sorts of people who save up their wages: and you certainly wouldn't do that, would you, oscarke? she says. Is that madness? what do you think? Valeer replied: oh, I know her, she's so subtle you wouldn't believe it, I saw that enough at home . . . I don't think she kicked up a fuss this evening because she didn't like the chair: from a craftsman's point of view the chair is a masterpiece, she knows that, but it's just a pretext to pick a fight and run off—if you could follow her now, you'd see she Has to go somewhere anyway. And his eyes, those eyes as gray as ondine's, started twinkling in his fat face: why don't I follow her! he suggested. Oscarke didn't know why he said "no" so quickly, he said no when in fact he probably meant yes . . . and chewing his fingernails he realized that he was afraid of Knowing whether or not she had a goal, a destination, yes or no . . . let her get on with it! he said, and he put little judith on his knee. But he couldn't take his eyes off that crazy valeer: that idiot! he thought. And at the same time he doubted that valeer was as crazy as all that either, he couldn't shake off the secret fear that valeer had just "pulled a blindfold from his eyes." But smiling calmly, as if he were omniscient, as if he himself was feeling like a great fragment of the exploded god, he started refuting all of valeer's ideas . . . at first he spoke without sense, searching for his thoughts, but as he talked on he arrived at a theory that was acceptable: she doesn't have an easy time, you know, she has her pub where she has to receive people and hide their poverty, she had to cook and wax and water . . . and apart from that, the new baby would be here in a few days' time. And grateful for actually having found a good reason, he repeated what he'd said: let her get on with it. Valeer nodded his fat

head, he knew nothing about women in the last stages of pregnancy—he still had
the same fear he'd always had of everything even remotely connected with sex, and
so he quickly conceded that it must be true. You see! laughed oscarke . . . but he
didn't believe it himself. No, ondine had gone into town with a goal in mind! With
difficulty oscarke tore himself away from these thoughts and turned his attention
elsewhere . . . it was strange: if he was thinking about something too much, he only
had to turn his eyes in another direction to see all his thoughts disappear.

Bah! he said . . . It was the word that they used Over There, over in brussels at
the stonemason's. And as he thought of over there, he was content, happy.

ONDINE'S CHAIR

It was too good to be true that valeer's chair should turn into the climax of that
first chapter. It's true that he'd discovered a beautiful thought in his monstrous
wobbly head . . . and that having made this discovery, he went on working on
the chair anyway. It could actually have served as a motto for his life, for our life,
for our book, for this world and this era. It was Too beautiful, something had to
happen to it, something terrible. And you'll see what in a bit: oscarke is sitting
next to him and has to avert his eyes because the chair reminds him too much of
ondine, who stands in the way of his happiness. And ondine too has to avert her
eyes, because what valeer is doing to her chair is gruesome: besides the 3 elegant
legs he attaches an unfinished length of wood, stuffs horsehair into enormous
lumps, and pulls the flowered material so that it's either baggy or creased. No,
those beautiful brass studs he's going to finish it off with won't be enough to save
it. And ondine doesn't know what to do, swear or cry or slap his face or throw
things on the floor. And after all, he's not to blame, she thinks: it's herself, it's the
world, it's Everything. As if "everything" has a face you can spit into, eyes you
can scratch out, a mouth you can punch. And you know that something like
that would be much more suitable material for the real and definitive end
to your chapter: because you yourself also occasionally think to yourself that
happiness is something that you'll fight for . . . you yourself may occasionally
be satisfied with your work, no matter its state, which you'll want to finish off
with braid and brass studs: but that doesn't mean that other people will be
satisfied, that Everything (as ondine says) is going to be satisfied. Everything
is a strange word! In termuren they have the saying that in everything you
can find some chicken shit: something good and something bad, a sunny side
and a shady side, some sunshine but also the occasional shower. And apart
from that, if we knew that there's nothing else to do in this world than fight
for a bit of happiness, and other than that nothing to do but go on working
and whistling . . . there wouldn't be much of anything to fight for, or even to
go on working for. Because what would you work on? First and foremost not

on this next chapter here, because then there'll be no more questions, and so no more answers will have to be looked for. We fight for our happiness, and go on whistling over our chair . . . no, go on working on our chair, whistling as we work. That would be the alpha and omega, the beginning and the end. But what will we do with the woman who's started to dress up in the style of the 1750s, who's now walking around with bare shoulders and long, creole skirts . . . are we going to let them go on walking around like that in our book, like the women in delvaux's paintings, in clothes from 1750 but with the frightened faces and shocking language of 1950? And what are we going to do with the ghosts of baekelandt and cartouche and jan de lichte that we've evoked as examples of people who've learned to live outside society, who've escaped time and the world by pushing themselves beyond the law. No, all of this must be put in order . . . we must entreat the women in our books to again dress as befits the women of 1950—we must restore order to the case of jan de lichte and his gang members and either revise them in such a way that they can find a place in our society again . . . or else change our society so that the gangs of baeckelandt, cartouche, and jan de lichte can again fit inside it . . . so that they're no longer called thieves and arsonists, but people who for the sake of individual freedom have fought for a little happiness.

That is ondine's chair: a chair she doesn't like. That's the end of one chapter, and the beginning of a new one: chapters you won't like either.

1750

Arms raised, polpoets cries: how dreadful social conditions were in 1750, in the days of jan de lichte! And you immediately interrupt him, you want to shut him up by saying that he has to stop going on about the years around 1750, because what will the reader think in the long run? First we wrote a book about 1800-and-such-and-such, with commentaries from the present day—and now that ondine and oscarke are gradually approaching our own era, we on the contrary flee back to 1700 (and change)! And polpoets drops his hands, lets his arms hang down by his sides, and says, indeed, the reader! . . . but how woefully mistaken he would be in his all-too-hasty judgment, and how ashamed he would be if I were to show him these trial papers, these archives, these documents of circa 1750 . . . if I could convince him what a tremendous novel, what a masterpiece could be written about it. And you look at polpoets in surprise because he's starting to wax lyrical, and so forgets to smile and bare his 2 gold teeth. Yes, laugh at me, says polpoets . . . but if I were to write my novel, my masterpiece about all that, I would first of all focus on historical background: the austrians and french trampling all over us, each in turn, robbing and burning and killing. And if the situation in france were the same as it was here, it's no surprise at all that the people gradually revolted, and that the cannons and the battle hymns of the revolution could already be heard as far as the horizon. And look, in my novel I'd also make a comparison between france and flanders: how the people of france resisted the same abuses, unfurled the red flag, and added a magnificent page to history . . . and how the people of flanders just grumbled a bit, waved the red flag listlessly once or twice, and just turned into a gang of thieves . . . and yet I love those people who turned into a gang of thieves . . .

Oh, you can see already! And you shut him up, polpoets that is, because it won't do to start singing the praises of a bunch of tramps and thieves and murderers . . . look how they attacked lonely farmhouses, stabbed the farmers with their bare bodkins, stole their money, and set the stables on fire. And polpoets interrupts you: I'm not singing their praises, I'm just defending them—like maitre pots I am an advocate of the poor and I just can't believe that they were only a bunch of scoundrels, a handful of villains who were too lazy to work, and preferred to drink and carouse, preferred to gamble and organize paupers' orgies. No, no . . . just look at the yellowing trial proceedings I've collected, and count the women who were part of the gang: and lots of women between 60 and 70 too—they weren't all witches and devilish old women but more likely old frumps who had to steal a pair of socks here and there, or a skirt, a piece of meat, a loaf of bread, because they were hungry and cold and absolutely wretched. And look, there were also loads of women between 16 and 20 who fenced stolen goods, or stood guard while their husbands or lovers pulled a raid somewhere—were they All young sluts, were they All degenerate sluts? No, no, I can't believe that. And even supposing they were all old witches and young sluts . . . what kind of life, what kind of world was it when every young girl had to become a slut, and every old woman a witch, in order to earn her living? And afterwards . . . after all those women were arrested and imprisoned and "lashed till the blood flowed" (that is to say, they were stripped and lashed across their lovely bare backs till they started to bleed . . . that is to say, they were branded on their lovely bare shoulders with red-hot irons . . . that is to say that they were then banished from the country, chased off like dogs, skinned like rabbits, and left to their fates, branded forever), it turns out that a lot of the girls of 16 and 17 and 18 and 19 weren't lashed after all, because . . . they were pregnant. So, now, what does that mean? Who did the most wrong? What kind of world was that back in flanders in 1750?

WOMEN

You'd like to write about a thousand things at once, but you can't help it: polpoets and his documents from 1750 intrigue you. A novel he said,

136

a masterpiece. And your pulse beats slightly faster, your mind works more feverishly . . . and before you know it you're sitting next to him again, making notes and absorbing facts: so the young women were left to their fate, polpoets? That's right, said polpoets . . . the women were, but the men weren't . . . the men were broken on the wheel, that is, all their bones were broken with an iron bar, and they lay on the wheel till they died—every judge was his own marquis de sade. And in addition all of their possessions were seized and sold in public—every judge his own thief. And if you were to write that book about jan de lichte, that novel, that masterpiece . . . perhaps you could shift it forward in time a little to when joseph fouché was minister of justice. Imagine, the biggest thief and fraud of all time, a chief of police . . . So the poor exploited people, the lumpenproletariat, joined together into one big gang of thieves. Joseph fouché versus jan de lichte: the marquis de sade let loose on the pariahs.

And then all those women in a gang of thieves . . . girls of 16, beautiful and luscious and sometimes already pregnant . . . and all those old women: skinny and crooked and cross-eyed, bent with humps—oh polpoets! You don't know how you're making my mouth water, how you're making my pen itch to start writing. But polpoets continues imperturbably: you've got for example a certain judoka spruyte, about 27 years of age, who was the wife of a gang member, and was charged with having incited her husband to steal, and with having led a generally indecent life. There's anne-marie de clerck, about 23 years of age, the sweetheart of a gang member, who was one of the ones who couldn't be lashed because she was pregnant. And here's the nicest one of all: johanna morels, who had no idea where she was born, and was charged with consorting with and committing vagrancy with thieves and rogues, and who was under serious suspicion of having stabbed a rifleman of the french army with a knife, in the parish of godtveerdeghem. And my polpoetish heart quivers a little, because maybe you can also guess why a woman would defend herself with a knife against a foreign soldier—long live johanna morels, who didn't mind consorting and cavorting with thieves and rogues, but still stabbed a foreign rapist. But despite this heroic courage she too was stripped and flogged till the blood flowed, branded with the letter V and banished from the country. And here is little anne-marie bleecker, 16 years old . . . and here's sars hendricks the bohemian girl, 16 years old, charged with having crawled through a hole and opened the door for the thieves. And I can also mention maria vlieghers, who gradually became used to being flogged, branded, and banished, since although she was only 29 it happened no less than 3 times . . . I could also mention isabella spruyte, maybe the sister of judoca spruyte, who'd seen her husband hanged a few days before . . . and there's also an anne-marie van de wiele, born in aspelaere and only 16 years old, and a maria brunincks who (what kind of a world was it, anyway?) didn't know how old she was or where she was born . . . and had already seen her two children hanged for stealing a piece of meat. And then there's johanna opsomer, françoise cauwaerts, maria van dorpe—and, and—all of them pregnant on the day they were supposed to be flogged and branded . . .

But your pen's already burned to and fro across the paper so many times that you've got writer's cramp: stop, polpoets, I can't write anymore. And polpoets asks: what kind of world was it that our women want to return to 1750? But you answer him with another question: but what a book, a novel, a masterpiece—couldn't you write about that?

THE DEAD DON'T SPEAK

And ondine herself? Yes, she wanted to go into town, but she had no goal, except to be called madame . . . and even that, was that really enough to fill her life? The day before yesterday they'd raised their hats to her in greeting from a coach, and yesterday a lady from down by the station had greeted her as she walked past—but what had remained of that, aside from a vague impression? There was something else she wanted to achieve in life, but just like before, she couldn't remember Now what had to be achieved. And anyway, why would she have had a goal in town: she still had no real goal in life. She just walked around aimlessly, and the cool of the evening soothed her throbbing temples—she forgot the crazy image of the baby at the washtub, and gradually started thinking normally again . . . She had to make a list in order to assess the situation: that chair, she said . . . true, it looked awful, but if necessary it could go in the kitchen, and could serve as a bed for Judith when the other baby arrived. Certainly a bed would be better—what if she were to suggest to valeer that he move in with them and bring his bed along? He could find work somewhere and give her his pay . . . and yes, in the evenings he could build a wall in the pub together with oscarke, so the stairs didn't lead straight into their apartment, and so that people wouldn't have to pass through the little kitchen when they wanted to go to the bathroom . . . so people would no longer have to see oscarke and his soppy sculpture, and judith's piss-soaked nappies, and two or three days' dirty laundry. And she could also ask for a reduction in rent from the landlord then, for improving the pub by the 1st grimy houses. She walked through the dark streets of the little town of the 2 mills, and went on and on linking things together: it turned into a closed circuit, a circle in which one person exploited, lied, stole, and all the proceeds went back to her: the world was a beehive that lived and died for her, the queen bee.

A wall then . . . and something else, some drapes for the window on the side facing the street. That chair, she could write that off, but some drapes, a heavy top curtain, That she had to have . . . she would have to manage to get it cheap somewhere, but oh, if it had to be expensive, it might as well cost a little bit: after all, she couldn't have Everything for nothing! And she stopped in a lonely back-street where there was no one around, and there she quickly reviewed all the plans she'd concocted. She counted it on her fingers: valeer, the bed, the wall, the heavy curtain . . . and she looked round to see if she had forgotten anything—and she suddenly noticed that there Was someone with her in the backstreet after all, a man standing in a dark doorway and looking at her: a jolt when through her; so the man had heard her talking aloud, and even worse, had seen her counting on her fingers. She turned round and, and hurried, hurried away . . . she was going a bit further anyway, so to speak, no she couldn't Wait, she started in again about valeer and the bed and the wall and the heavy curtain. Right, a curtain, not only because it gives an impression of wealth, but for another reason too, ha, for Another reason too . . . fat glemmasson had paid for drinks a few evenings ago and ondine was giving him his change, but looking in her purse she had fished out a sacred medal of saint antony instead . . . it was unexpected, she had thought it was half a franc, and they'd laughed till the place shook, or do you still believe that when you fall in the water that saint antony will keep you afloat? No, she'd answered, but are you catholic or not? Oh, the gentlemen shrugged their shoulders: being catholic meant something quite different, for example that you supported the status quo, but not that you believed in blessed tin gewgaws and paternosters. There was Nothing, fat glemmasson had said . . . death came and it was all over. And flaunting his knowl-edge and looking round the pub, he saw norbert giving him a cold little smile. After death it's all over, glemmasson repeated stubbornly, but less certain of himself . . . and everyone stared at norbert, who kept on smiling. Turn the light off for a minute and we'll listen to what the dead have to say about it, he replied. Ondine waited with baited breath: do it, do it! she said. And with embarrassment she'd remembered the evening, long, long ago, when she ran off in fear . . . but, well, she had been that young, little ondine, scarcely 16 then (although she remembered at the same time that Then too she had recovered her composure and had said to him: they're only hallucinations). But now she had matured, she wanted to know: at once, at once: was glemmasson right or was norbert?—was death the beginning or the end? No, said norbert, neither . . . death and life don't exist, it's all illusion: there's nothing but movement, change, distortion. And he had gone over to the gas lamp and turned it out . . . but it wasn't dark, there was a lamp hanging on the back wall of the labor that sent its pale rays into the pub by the 1st grimy houses. There should be a thicker curtain over the window! norbert said . . . And then he had turned the light on again. There they all sat, and you could see by the look of them that they, all of them, had expected something wonderful. Only fat glemmas-son recovered immediately . . . he laughed, greasily and heavily! No, that's good! he said. But ondine, whose nerves were taut as an antenna, heard that his laugh was . . . not false—that's too strong a word, but still a little strained. A heavy curtain *then—that was all that stood in the way of being able to investigate the secrets of life and death. And she had sat down beside norbert and asked and pestered him to explain to her the principles of the occult . . . but glemmasson called to her from a distance: oh, he's told me all about that stuff too, but none of it can be proven. And ondine whispered: if you believe in ghosts why did you need crutches, why did you have an iron brace? Norbert shrugged his shoulders grumpily: those were things for my far-too-lonely youth, he said . . . and it has nothing to do with the dead, just like a scapular has nothing to do with the catholic party.*

WITH A DRAWN KNIFE

Kramiek enters . . . kramiek who once came out with the proverbial slogan that literature is the flag under which we perish . . . he comes in and surveys you rather aloofly and says: I've come to tell you that it can't go on like this: soon you'll actually write that book about jan de lichte, soon you'll lower yourself to the level of starting to write a popular novel. And you're astonished that things should have gone this far with the literary crowd. Come on kramiek, you don't know what you're talking about . . . You don't know what an honor, what a delight, what a wonderful task it is to be able, to be allowed, to be compelled to write a popular book. Sometimes, kramiek, sometimes in the evenings I can worry for hours on end over why I didn't follow in the footsteps of eugéne sue, the wandering jew: writing about the secrets of the common people, the seven deadly sins, the mysteries of paris. And then, kramiek, I could have written my book in installments, and would have given a heading at the start of each chapter: in which the reader makes the acquaintance of joseph fouché, and the father of jan de lichte, joseph de lichte . . . in which the reader sees that big thieves have always caught and condemned little thieves . . . in which the reader can add to the saying "honesty is the best policy," that honesty is best for getting rich. And, kramiek, I would inform my readers if there was to be a change of character or setting: the reader now leaves the 16-year-old marianne bleecker in a state of pregnancy to follow us and meet maria van dorpe, who does not know where she was born. But kramiek protests with every ounce of his littérateur's being pleads and begs you from now on to only follow the paths of Art.

But now it's you who survey kramiek rather aloofly, and dig out the notebook containing the things that polpoets has collected for you: information about a certain francies meulenaere, about 22 years old, who stabbed a certain lieven van der steen deliberately and without any motive in cosentiens straat, with a knife that he hid under his vest . . . and who in addition was arrogant enough to drink brandy with a certain francies bracke and to have threatened to cut her throat with that same knife because she wouldn't consent to his going to bed with her daughter . . . and with the same knife gave her a deep cut in her left cheek through which her tongue protruded. You see, kramiek, that's francies meulenaere . . . and when you hear and see all that, how do you picture him? And kramiek says: I imagine him as a knife-fighter, a bandit, a no good . . . well, I expect they broke him on the wheel? Sorry to disappoint you, kramiek, they only strung him up with a rope, kept him up there until he was dead . . . although he had a number of other counts against him, because on whitsunday, at scheldewindeke, between 8 an 9 in the evening, he helped murder a certain jan de vriese (and this jan de vriese, kramiek, was an informer who planned to betray jan de lichte to the french soldiers), and together with adriaan vagenende he dragged the body to a well, to hide the remains there . . . after first removing its clothes and taking them for them-selves. And I certainly see him, kramiek, as a knife-fighter, a tall, skinny lout with a cruel face, perhaps with a blue scar beneath the eye, and a mouth that was sharp and thin and bare, just like his knife.

OSCARKE AND HIS INDIFFERENCE

And now, walking through the evening streets, ondine shivered—not from fear, because she longed for the evening when the ghosts would be summoned up . . . she hungered for it, in fact—but she shivered from simple cold, since a fog had started to rise. She hurried home, and slamming the door of the pub behind her felt the clamminess of her clothes. She stood warming her hands at the stove, and said: look, valeer, I've been thinking, how much pocket money do you get from father at home? Well, replied valeer . . . and he looked away, in order to nod and say "well" again: he named a ridiculously small amount of money. She grimaced: he got nothing at all. Well, she said, I'll give you double and you can come and live with us, but first you'll have to fetch your bed from home yourself . . . tell father that I'm ill, and that you've got to look after me: it's not All lies, because you can see how I am, it'll be starting any moment. She also turned to oscarke and she gave him a friendly tap on the knee as he sat tucked away in a corner: and I'll give you pocket money as well. He let it sink in, nodded briefly, and went on staring at his knuckles. She gave him a long look: is there something wrong? she asked. No, what could be wrong? he asked in turn, She looked deep deep into his eyes, as if to penetrate the world of his thoughts . . . but oh, he was probably thinking noth-ing at all, he was just indifferent again—he was even indifferent to her caresses (admittedly they were rather artificial caresses, since she sometimes acted on the principle that, after all, he was her husband, and had a legal right to some love): he hadn't even reacted to that, even That left him cold. What was wrong with him? Another woman? She found it difficult to believe, unless it was some piece of baggage from the train, or . . . and she had to fight back her secret sneer . . .

wouldn't the logical thing be to have said: as long as it wasn't one with a disease! And she raised the subject that very night, of men who work in brussels and go around with other women, and how one can never be sure: they came home with diseases, they make their whole household unhappy and even went mad: it was the kind of disease that led to madness. And he, there, in the darkness, thought again that she was must be aligned with the devil (positive pole! he thought) but he was also upset because she had compared jeannine to a woman with a disease. Not always, he said. What do you mean, not always? she asked. But he didn't go into it any further: you just be careful with all those rich, foulmouthed customers in your place, he said, that they don't bring their own diseases. Oh, she was suddenly moved, she thought she'd found the key to his apparent indifference: he was just jealous. So he was still oscarke, with whom (how long ago!) she had lain among the brambles beyond the railway line, and who was perhaps still dreaming of carving her in stone. And she pressed up against him, against the oscarke from the old days: I don't give a damn about those rich customers, she said, I just want their money and their influence. In the darkness she told him of her desire to . . . well, she didn't quite know how to put it . . . but her desire to be something more than just an ordinary person: why, there was a customer who could summon up spirits! It had been a long time since she had wanted to be so close to oscarke, but then, how stupid . . . he was no longer the oscarke of over there among the brambles . . . she ran right up against his eternal . . . yes, After All, his indifference.

All the things you're listing there don't bring happiness, he said. She asked what did bring happiness. I don't know, he said. But he did know, or at any rate he thought he knew: she heard it from him often enough.

OUTSIDE THE LAW

You meet johan brams, the poet . . .

Stop, we have to stop writing these fairy tales, dishing up these sweet lies to the world—what do people think a poet is?: he's someone who writes verses from morning till night, feeds on manna, and is a little crazy—he's someone to whom the statutes, the regulations, and the old-age pension do not apply—in fact he's someone who lives outside the law. And so you meet johan brams . . . a man among men, who occasionally—sometimes late at night, sometimes on sunday afternoons, sometimes during a boring train journey from woubrechtegem to nattendijcke—cooks up a poem. But what does johan bram do when it's Not a lost evening, Not a lost sunday?—but when it's monday tuesday wednesday etcetera? The poet johan brams walks around and feels cold, feels hungry, and knows that his wife has caught the disease of our age—nerves—and knows that his son, joke brams, needs money to buy his schoolbooks. Of course, the answer to his problems is simple: johan brams should get a job like the rest of us, go out and work in a shoe factory, occupy a desk at the offices of the water board . . . anyway, what else can you do?

And it's true enough . . . But imagine if all the johan bramses of the world go underground in shoe factories, or take desk jobs in the offices of the water board . . . and then on sunday afternoon you sit down quietly in your chair, you've worked all week and now want some relaxation: you open your sunday magazine, and . . . no, you can't find anything to read anymore, because the magazine is empty and blank: johan brams is working in a shoe factory and no longer writes. Well, that's up to him, and you throw the empty magazine away, you write off all the magazines, which no longer exist anyway now that johan brams has a job like the one you do. By there are other things you can do to amuse yourself, and so you turn on the radio . . . but you can't hear anything, you hear only the hiss of the ether: because johan brams, who lived outside the law and tried to earn his supper by singing a song for you, by writing a radio play for you, by putting together an evening variety show for you . . . But that's all over now, he works 6 days a week, like you, at meyers and meyers, the insurance company. Or, in a nutshell: a world without any poetry, without any beauty, without any diversion, without that little something extra, without any color. Right . . . and after a little reflection you'll say (and again you'd be right) that all those poets, those living-outside-the-law types should band together as we've banded together, should fight for higher wages, should go on strike. But who the hell could care less about a few poets going on strike, a few singers refusing to let anything issue from their throats, a few painters refusing to exhibit? Who will care, I ask. You? . . . me? The managing director of meyers and meyers? . . . the arts minister? And imagine a few johan bramses banding together and making demands to the magazines: how many young, up-and-coming artists, wanting to see their names in print, wanting to be Famous, will give their pieces away to the magazines for nothing?

And so johan brams goes on living from hand to mouth and his wife will have to get rid of her neuroses on her own and his son will have to try and see if he can get his schoolbooks for free . . . and in the event that he can't get them free, he'll have to learn without books, or else go fuck himself. Right, and johan brams goes on writing his stories, goes on singing his songs, goes on painting his canvases, and tries to make ends meet . . . he tries, but he doesn't always manage. And you, you who work for meyers and meyers, and who will perhaps rise to become deputy office manager, if you pay attention and behave yourself, you'll enjoy child-care benefits, accident insurance, a reduction in medical coverage, old-age pensions. But there goes johan brams, outside the law . . . because he's not working for meyers and meyers, limited—he works for himself, he's a freelance professional, and must bear the fateful consequences of that choice . . . or perish.

Look, johan brams has just told you all this with a wry laugh. And you adopt his wry laugh and ask: but why don't you just join jan de lichte's gang?

THE SENTIMENTAL GENTLEMAN

It's actually true that you met johan brams . . . and he also told you the following: of course other people have a right to everything I've learned, if they've become an ordered and subordinated part of society . . . pensions and compensation and insurance policies . . . I've been excluded from those things, and so I have no right to them and don't really know what they're all for. I'm the poorest and most needy person in society, but I have no right to this society's consolations. But so be it, I go on singing my songs, I yodel, I write rhymes, I write funny anecdotes, I write plays, I live and hope for the best . . . I tell my wife she has to ignore her neuroses . . . I tell my son that he mustn't feel hungry: what right has a boy of 10 to dare to say he's hungry! . . . and I go on singing my songs. But the most irritating thing about my case is that all my sporadic incomes are so unreliable, so much in the air, so unstable: this month a magazine is coming out that wants to take two stories of mine, but next month the same magazine will only want one story, or won't want any stories, or the magazine will have ceased to exist . . . and so I look for another magazine, but there they take advantage of the occasion and pay me only half my going rate, or I oust johan krams and johan vlams, who Also write stories, and now have to go without. And then there's suddenly a magazine that asks for over 20 stories, immediately, Immediately . . . and just where am I supposed to get 20 stories overnight? I go round racking my brains (and don't forget, those stories themselves are just a sideshow, something that has to be done now and then to earn a little something . . . because my main job is writing poetry, is writing a novel, writing a masterpiece, is looking round and weighing things up in order to represent this society as accurately as possible . . . and meanwhile these stories are something that you have to do once in a while, to make a little money, and so you suddenly have to deliver 20 stories about love and devotion, about blood and shame, about sopping tears and innocence triumphant—because that's what those magazines want. . . no, demand . . . sentences bristling with clichés and just oozing with romanticism. And you go round racking your brains, searching for a new, pining, warbling innocence that unmasks and destroys all its persecutors, and then marries and lives happily ever after. And so you look in an old issue and draw your inspiration from old stories of robbery and unfaithfulness and blood and guilt.

But now (forgive me for suddenly changing the subject), now there's now an exhibition on of the painter van gogh, and an old, lovable, and sentimental gentleman . . . wealthy, seriously wealthy . . . visits the exhibition and is devastated at the fact that such a man always had to live in poverty, and he says: if van gogh were alive, I would support him. And having said that he returns to his comfortably appointed house and his cozy armchair and opens this magazine and reads the stories of johan brams, stories about innocence triumphant and long-sought happiness that finally comes to the worthy. And the gentleman remembers having read another such story in the past, and he writes a sweet, endearing letter to the publisher: sir, I read this story 5 years ago, but then the heroine was called emmy, and now she's called anny . . . and then it happened in a coach but now it takes place on a plane. And the indignant publisher refuses to accept, publish, or pay for any other story of yours.

And johan brams again has holes in his socks, and says to his son joke brams: you're hungry? Well, I'll make sure I meet jan de lichte tomorrow and discuss the situation with him.

BRUSSELS IS BRUSSELS

The next day everything went just like ondine wanted: she'd just come to the front door to take a look round when valeer arrived with his bed on a handcart. It was the old cot the two of them had slept in as children. And while she helped him bring it inside, she looked at him, surprised: we slept in there together, she said. She knew that she was not going to be able to find work for him immediately, and so she put her suggestion on the table right away, suggested making a start on the wall. A wall? asked valeer . . . and he looked at the place where it was supposed to be, as if he didn't understand how such a thing could fit into the house. She laughed and said: I suppose you think you can buy a wall just like that and put it in anywhere? No, it's got to be built, stone by stone: go to the filature spinning mill and ask mr achilles for some stones from a demolition! And since the cart was still outside the front door, he got going again right away . . . she watched him go without much hope, and actually was rather surprised to see him come back with the stones, and with a bag of sand and cement, and even a bricklayer's tub. She'd sent him off to the filature spinning mill, after all—it was very doubtful whether he'd get anything at all . . . but, obviously, she had not been forgotten: she had only to speak and people leapt around to fulfill her every whim. What did mr achilles say? she asked. Oh, replied valeer . . . I didn't see anyone, so I just wheeled the barrow onto the site to find what I needed round the back. She looked at him in astonishment: then no one knows about it? she asked . . . and she had to shake her head, annoyed but still smiling at the idiot. Exactly, it was exactly like oscarke had said last night: money alone doesn't bring happiness—something else is needed, something with no name, a tic, a word that hadn't been invented yet, to designate that special condition: you experience happiness the same way you experience that new scientific discovery, electricity: it was there all around them but no one could say what it was like. She helped valeer, she kept the cart balanced while he unloaded everything and took it inside . . . she drew a chalk line across the floor: up to here, she said. And what's that? he asked. Ha! You see? Ha! she said: you see? . . . that's the space for the door, because I know you, you're quite capable of bricking us up so that we can't get in or out anymore. She'd been squatting on the floor and suddenly felt that her time had come, and picked herself up with great difficulty . . . and the wall, those lines on the floor, suddenly they didn't have the slightest importance. Make sure you finish the mortar nice and smooth, and find an old door that you can smarten up, but first go out and get doctor goethals, and don't forget to cook oscarke's meal tonight, she added. Then she went to the bedroom, but from there she called to him again: and look after judith! All her orders made him nervous as a sparrow, he ran this way and that, and got everything wrong: he couldn't pick anything up without it clattering to the floor . . . he heard her calling, she probably thought he was breaking something, but when he went and listened to what she was saying, it was only more orders. Oh, go fuck yourself, he muttered . . . and he started on the wall, he mixed the mortar in the small courtyard, and since he had to keep going out back with a bucket of water, and always forgot something, all the doors were open . . . there was a draft and little judith was crying her heart out, and in no time at all it was the biggest mess imaginable. When oscarke got home in the evening he had had to cook his supper for himself, but first he had to go for the doctor . . . because ondine had already asked him a couple of times where the doctor was, and he'd just shrugged his shoulders stupidly: but it soon came that valeer had forgotten to call him. The doctor finally came and shut himself in with ondine while oscarke and valeer squatted by the chalk lines on the floor, arguing endlessly about how a wall should be built. And jumping from one subject to another oscarke started talking about brussels . . . he described it as if it were heaven, as if every street in brussels was a piece of the world of the future of which socialists dreamed, and as if every woman there were a jeannine. Valeer on the other hand said that it was just the same there as here: I've lived in brussels and I've lived in termuren, and now I'm living in the 1st grimy houses and I can tell you This: the world is the same all over. That's because you're not alive, said oscarke . . . for a dead man it's the same all over. I'd like to know how you're more alive than I am, asked valeer . . . I'm here in the pub bricklaying and looking at stupid stones, and you're in brussels in a stonemason's workshop, and what do you see? . . . only stupid old stones there too! Ha, so it all remains the same! But oscarke, who in his blind love for jeannine was about to let something slip out, looked at him and said: I . . . But something in those eyes of valeer's stopped him: oh, you're like your sister, he said . . . you're far to clever for me! Valeer smiled. And whether he was really shrewd—or just so stupid that he felt happy when someone called him shrewd—was impossible to tell. He picked up a stone and, after nearly an hour had passed, started trimming it . . . but then he put it down again. Maybe you mean that one person sees more than the other, he said . . . that one person is blind to what the other notices? Exactly, that's it! said oscarke. Well, valeer went on, let me tell you, that's all just talk, let me tell you that you're a dreamer . . . brussels is brussels and those who are dreamers see their dreams and those who are not dreamers see brussels as it is.

THE BANK MANAGER

Johan brams is still sitting in front of your stove, slurping down all your coffee and smoking all your cigarettes. And you say to him: it's obviously easier, johan brams, if you're employed by some company or other, a big bank or an insurance company . . . but the way you live now you're much freer. Stop it, says johan brams . . . because that freedom is romantic nonsense: I ask myself why the factory manager, or the permanent secretary of the ministry, or the primary shareholder of the comptoir et credit bank, why do they get to enjoy all the social benefits that the worker thought he was acquiring for himself . . . why can't a little bricklayer, a poet, or a housepainter enjoy them? They do work where they're their own boss, that's true . . . if they want, they can stay at work an hour or two longer, that's also true . . . but they're usually without work all winter, and don't enjoy anything at all in life, and that's even truer. The working man has fought for social benefits, and it may be coincidental that only those who were working for someone else had a rotten little morsel tossed to them . . . and that all those who are still more or less free were left to their own devices. But I'm much more inclined to think that it's a conspiracy: the only ones who get a pension are the ones who're prepared to be a cog or a screw in the monstrous machine: those who have sought work in factories, banks, and ministries, where one's name is on a card that's numbered and can be checked at all times. Down with the small farmer, the small craftsman, the peripatetic artist! And I, johan brams, sign that manifesto, and add my shouts to the rest in the march: down with them, we can do without a few extra potatoes and vegetables, we'll all become civil servants, we'll all become employees of the monstrous apparatus that puts things on cards! And I, johan brams, go and visit the bank manager to ask for a job. And there he sits at his desk, enjoying all the social benefits of which I have been deprived up till now, smoking his fat cigar and killing time by reading the comic strip in the daily paper. And luck is on my side: he agrees to give me a job: he needs someone who knows four languages, and can read and write fluently, and apart from that he has to be able to fit in around the office almost immediately . . . that is to say, he has to be someone who you don't have months of trouble with before he gets the hang of the job—no, he has to be someone who's able to do everything right right away, all at once

. . . and who can do something completely different the next day with just as much ease: it has to be someone with energy, daring, and most of all someone who can make decisions at lightning speed. Of course, he'll be a hard worker, very hard . . . it may even happen that he'll have to take some of his work home in the evening, but he won't mind that—and he won't come and ask for afternoons off: the bank manager can't handle all these requests for time off: What the hell is this? Are they working or what?

And I, johan brams, sit there in the presence of the bank manager, and ask myself if I meet these criteria: can I speak and write four languages fluently, do I have willpower and daring and energy, can I make very rapid and at the same time excellent decisions, am I capable of working very hard and never asking for an afternoon off? And I look at him, and ask in a whisper what such a person would earn . . . the salary, that is . . . because that's what matters to me. And the bank manager answers in a bored tone, suggesting that it doesn't matter at all: oh, a good wage, I ask the maximum in work, but I also pay the maximum in wages: I'll give you three thousand francs. And I johan brams thought about saying: yes, that is the maximum . . . the absolute minimum wage for the absolute maximum performance. But I did Not say that . . . and I went away saying that I would think about it. Oh yes, I thought about it . . . but not about whether or not to accept his starvation wages, but whether or not to join jan de lichte's gang, to try an armed robbery at the bank.

WHO IS MR VREEKANT?

With a sarcastic smile still playing round his mouth, johan brams says: you have it easier too, writing about cartouche and jan de lichte, about men who squat on the edges of our society and say philosophically: even if we don't earn very much, we still have a nice life . . . you write about them, but I'm one of them, That's the difference. And just like reynard and jan de lichte used to prepare as evening fell to terrify a hare or a lost traveler, so I prepare in the morning after I've read the want ads in the paper. A while ago I found someone who was looking for a young man, familiar with modern child-rearing techniques, very high salary, write to the newspaper offices. I wrote in and the next day I received a postcard on which it was suggested in very beautiful handwriting and an elegant prose style that I go on a particular evening to brussels, to the poisson d'or café, and there ask for mr vreekant. And I johan brams turned the card over and over and noticed that there wasn't the slightest hint of any return address on it. But I reasoned as follows: right, let him hide for the time being, perhaps he's a person of quality wanting to entrust a backward child to a private tutor, and wants to meet in person before showing his hand. But whatever he had to hide, even if he'd been jan de lichte or the prince of saxe-coburg in person, I rushed to brussels and found the poisson d'or to be just like I'd expected, it was one of the largest establishments in the capital, with a bar in the front, followed by a restaurant, with all sorts of bells and whistles . . . a string quartet was playing, a number of waitresses were moving between the tables, and I estimate that there were over 60 people present. Which of these 60 was mr vreekant? In order to save myself a lot of bother I went straight up to a waitress, and asked for the guy I was after. Monsieur Free . . . Freek . . . oh, ici! And she took me to an old-fashioned gentleman from the provinces. So this was him? He stood up, gave his tie a tug, and began rather nervously: as I wrote to you, sir, I was a schoolteacher, fully instructed in modern pedagogical theory, and I'd like to hear about the the position in detail. I stared at the slightly deranged little man. For a start he hadn't written to me that he himself was a teacher . . . and in addition in the paper there had been talk of a post being offered, at a very high salary—a job I myself would have liked very much. . . But immediately the deranged little gentleman looked at me in dismay: but you're mr vreekant . . . aren't you? he asked. We looked at each other. I tried to picture the situation as it actually was: so this gentleman had also written to mr vreekant, and had come and sat in a corner here to wait. Well, I'll be off then, said the gentleman rather gloomily . . . since they were asking for a young man, you're bound to be given preference anyway. No, why don't you stay, I said . . . after all, you were first and so you have precedence. Anyway, I began lying, I've got lots of offers to chase down . . . I only came here because this one sounded so mysterious. The old gentleman from the provinces seemed to have exactly the same idea, but had been attracted more by the name: vreekant. For him it evoked something like a small, sunny village . . . he imagined vreekant must be someone who lived in a villa with a big garden . . . where they wanted to entrust some backward child to the care of a private tutor.

Oh, he was such a sweet old gentleman that I would have felt a swine if I'd stood in the way of his dream for a second longer. I thought: let the old chap have a happy old age in villa vreekant—I'll find some prey elsewhere. So, ordering a new cup of coffee I said: right then, you're welcome to the job . . . but allow me to sit and wait here till this mysterious mr vreekant shows up . . . just out of curiosity, you understand?

A BITTER JOKE . . . A SOCIALIST JOKE?

And johan brams continues his story: I gradually found it more and more odd, why did he place an ad for one and the same job in two different papers, and why had he taken such pains to ensure that neither of the two applicants discovered his real address? But it was only privately that I made these observations, because the old gentleman agreed to everything in advance . . . yes, yes, he kept saying with his full and easygoing mouth, drinking his pint or sucking at his pipe. But I kept a careful watch on the rapidly revolving door, and all at once I saw a nonchalant gentleman enter and speak to a waitress. I'd have bet my life that that mysterious gentleman was vreekant! So we were finally going to know where that village or that peaceful, sunny estate was located. And the waitress, thinking hard, brushed her temples, remembered us, and took the gentleman to our table. We both sat up and shook his hand: he looked much less mysterious than his antics would lead one to assume. On the contrary, he was rather nervous, produced a postcard, and asked which of us was mr vreekant. Which of us . . . So, unfortunately, this was the third contender for the crown. While the old gentleman, at my request, began going over the whole story again, his pipe comfortably in his mouth, I began looking round the café with growing suspicion: who was to say that mr vreekant wasn't in the bar, gazing at us with well-concealed pleasure? But no, a little while later a stiff gentleman came in, immediately went to see the manager, and while he occupied a seat in the center of the bar, the loudspeakers started asking for monsieur fléka . . . fléka or frékan, it was hard to hear exactly. Still, I got the message: the loudspeaker actually meant mr vreekant, and I informed the old gentleman that a fourth candidate had appeared. Our teacher stood up, holding his pipe in his hand, and went over to invite the newcomer to sit at our table. Are you also acquainted with modern educational methods, sir? I asked sarcastically. He immediately went white with rage, thinking that it was us who had played the joke. It took only a few seconds to inform him of the situation . . . he sat down next to me and followed my furtive glances round the bar: it's quite possible that that so-called mr vreekant is a woman, I observed. And then we began to survey everyone in the room still more carefully, still more frantically. You know what, said the teacher: yes, yes, I'm leaving, because I'm gradually beginning to see a completely different meaning in that name . . . it's quite possible it's not peaceful and sunny, but a "wreak-hand," a hand that will wreak vengeance! And he was gone, immediately, with his pipe, his faded jacket, and his rather worn-out shoes. For a split second we felt sorry . . . although I couldn't help laughing at his "yes, yes." Vreekant . . . the revenge-wreaking hand. No, it was impossible, it must be some kind of joke, and I wanted to stay put till I found out who could dream up such a thing. I agree, said the nonchalant chap. But, I went on, if he placed a 300-franc ad in four different papers—because we all saw the ad in a different paper—then it's a joke that had cost him, or her, a good 1,200 francs! We sat there until I'd almost missed my last train, but we didn't see the slightest trace of a Vredekant or a Wreaking Hand.

And johan brams looks at you with his sarcastic eyes, and asks: but can you imagine that in this society such sinister characters go round and can spend over 1,000 francs on an evening's amusement, by bringing together four people looking for a job . . . just like at the fair you pay 5 francs to see a wild man eating fire? And you answer johan brams: I can imagine that there really are sinister characters like that running around, but I find it difficult to believe that they get any real pleasure from what they buy.

THE WALL

Those who are dreamers only see their dreams, and those who are not dreamers see things as they are, valeer said. Yes, that was something they could argue over for hours, but then the doctor came into the pub and looked down at them . . . they looked up at him, and since they had nothing to ask him, he left without saying anything. But from the back room they heard the weak cry of a child, and oscarke cocked his head . . . And ondine was already calling him, so he went and looked, and it really was another girl: it was mariette. Make sure valeer puts mortar between the stones, ondine said. Every evening when he came home, she asked about the wall, how high it was, if it was nice, whether the staircase looked like it was in a real hallway, if they had remembered the opening for the door . . . she lay there in bed, but she was still living with them in the pub. Oscarke said no more than ah and oh, because god, it was like a whole world being created downstairs . . . the whole house was full of lime and sand and cement and piles of stone dust—there wasn't a single customer, because what could they do, it was damn cold down behind the half-built wall, since the stove stood there burning to no avail against those wet stones with mortar bulging out as thick as a finger. Shouldn't you get rid of that mortar? asked oscarke. We'll do it later, valeer said. And they started arguing about something else, every evening they had a different subject, the war that everyone was talking about, socialism, and electricity, which was now being put in many homes . . . but they never talked about girls, though oscarke's heart was full of them—and, for that matter, what was wrong with valeer? He was a man too, wasn't he? But he avoided the subject completely. And no matter what oscarke talked about valeer pooh-poohed it . . . it was all the same everywhere, nothing was worthwhile: oh, that's going easy on yourself, said oscarke—in that way you never have to think about anything, you say it's rubbish before you even know what it means. And then they started arguing about that. Still, without understanding how or why, one evening they ended up reaching the same conclusion, and valeer raised his thick head towards oscarke in surprise: that's a shame, he said. What's a shame? asked oscarke. That we agree, said valeer. One sunday oscarke had suggested that they go on working, since he was home for a whole day they could make some good progress . . . but it wasn't so much the work, it was those conversations he wanted to continue: at certain moments over in brussels by his block of stone, he thought of home and that wall and valeer, and he felt homesick for them: happiness there with jeannine was something that he had in hand, and for precisely that reason he longed for the happiness that he didn't have, he longed to be somewhere else and to talk about his happiness there: I really will start talking about her soon, he told himself at these moments. And now it was sunday and now he was going to start . . . but for valeer, on the other hand, who was there in the muck day in and day out, it wasn't sunday at all. And besides, they had only just got started (because despite their endless orations they'd already reached the point where they could lay the stones standing up), when ondine walked in. Yes, there she was, out of bed, a bit slovenly, a bit drawn and aged, and probably not having the slightest idea that she'd changed: she went around and tormented people, got ill, and then got back on her feet, just like everyone . . . and in that way her life was running out, her cord unwinding, it wasn't too clear in her mind: almost imperceptibly her life was declining and her death looming larger. No one really noticed . . . but oscarke thought: she's starting to look like a bird. And she thought the different feeling was just because of the things around her: that wall, for instance. And she looked at the half-built wall, just as she'd looked at that chair . . . she shook her head and she knew once again that she'd expected too much: those lumps of mortar, didn't I tell you to smooth those out? she asked. And her voice had a dull sound, as if she still felt too tired to really enter into battle with valeer, with life. They'll go, said valeer. Think so? she asked . . . and no one saw the resentment—the hate, perhaps, in her eyes. Of course! said valeer with conviction, how could she doubt something so obvious? But it turned out that he didn't really have a clue about bricklaying—what Did he have a clue about?—because all that mortar had already set and had to be chiseled off. And that there will that come off too? she asked, pointing. Certainly! replied valeer . . . and he had no idea what she meant. He followed her extended finger and saw that she was indicating a huge bulge in the wall. He looked at it, surprising himself, because though he'd made sure that the stones were running in a reasonable zigzag course, but it hadn't occurred to him to make sure that the wall was perpendicular. Oh, that'll be covered up when it's . . . plastered, he said hesitantly. When the job was finished, the result was grotesque, it was beyond comparison with the chair: there was a layer of dust centimeters thick on everything, mortar had been daubed everywhere, on the stove, on the fireplace and the coffee pot and the cups, to say nothing of the floor . . . Ondine had to avert her gaze, or else she would have grabbed hold of those idiots in a wild fury and cracked their heads together. But miraculously, she managed to restrain herself . . . she said, so calmly that they looked at her in astonishment: put a coat of plaster on it and clean up the mess, so it'll be finished.

Oscarke the sculptor . . . though actually he's only a stonemason who travels up and down to brussels, and usually has to fit a marble fireplace, or cut a slate doorstep, or clean the encrusted dirt off a tombstone in the cemetery. Meanwhile, like you and me and all of us, he goes on building his dreams, his view of the world, his ideas about human existence. And sitting in the train everyday, with a packet of sandwiches and his coffee, he cherishes his eternal hope that he will be Able to embody these ideas, avoiding his eternal fear of never being Capable of embodying them. And you yourself, who empathize with your heroes, occasionally see sculptures, and wonder: could this dream carved in stone be oscarke's dream? And usually the answer is negative, because while what you see is sweet and beautiful and even startling, once and a while, and sometimes astonishingly modern, or else sometimes classically patriarchal, it remains a piece of stone, a block of marble, a log of wood, a lump of clay. It neither grows nor lives nor laughs, it asks no questions, it gives no answers. No, oscarke would never make anything like that: he'd much rather go on chipping away at his doorsteps, because if that kind of work is neither more beautiful nor more ugly, it is at least something of use. But then suddenly—oh, the rarity of that "suddenly"!—you see work in which everything that oscarke has ever dared dream and imagine has been frozen . . . but then you have to ask yourself: could he, oscarke, really make anything like that? You see, that's the tragic thing about our lives: the work that oscarke could do just as well, indeed even a little better, is not worthwhile, is far too small to express his thoughts . . . and the work that on the contrary expresses Everything that he's imagined, he would never be able to make. That's how he is, and that's how I am, I who write about oscarke—and how about you? But look, suddenly, unexpected as a thunderbolt, as an exploding bomb, he's rooted to the spot when he sees the work of marini in brussels . . . or is it marino . . . or is it the two together, marino marini? Oscarke is too overwhelmed to check more carefully on the name. But what does it matter, here is someone who's made something that reaches further than our little feelings, that probes deeper than our little thoughts, that transcends our little dream: little bronze men on bronze horses: they're small and unattractive, they have round squashed heads and have arms—far too short—that open out into the elusive space to their lefts and rights . . . the space that they try to grasp with their short, fat, sausage-like fingers. They can scarcely straddle the horses under them with their too-short legs—the horse: the animal—they're not even in control of their animals, and yet their sausage hands clutch at vastness. And see how beautiful and pure that gesture is kept: this effort to embrace both the animals beneath them and the space that surrounds them. Beautiful because those hands aren't

raised to the heavens above them but to the space immediately around them
. . . and pure, because only their heads, their globular and squashed heads,
with the beady eyes of rats, dare look up to heaven. Their beady eyes reach up
to heaven, their sausage hands into mundane space . . . and beneath them the
animals, with their long monstrous necks, with their cruel monstrous heads.
And oscarke scarcely dares look at them . . . because isn't it an unnaturally
long phallus that they're riding, stretching dauntingly from between their too-
short legs? That long and cruel and monstrous thing that stretches its head
forward with bared lips to leer at its prey? *And oscarke sees that, and knows that
he will never be able to make such a thing.* That is his tragedy, and mine . . .
and perhaps yours too?

THE END OF THE WALL

*Throwing a scarf over her uncombed hair ondine went out. But to say that she'd
been able to restrain herself was actually far from the truth: it was much more
the case that she'd not been Able to get angry. When she reviewed the scene in her
mind, she saw that she had only shaken her head occasionally—and apart from
that? Apart from that she'd felt only a strange indifference . . . or no, because
between the indifference of oscarke and her own frame of mind there was a world
of difference: it was more a kind of revulsion at having to deal with all their
nonsense: today it was this and tomorrow it would be something else, and it was
never what she Wanted. In bed for all those long, long days, she had lain there
calculating and adding up and combining: valeer's bed that would serve for the
children, the heavy curtain that she could pick up for a song, a wall she was
having built for nothing. And now, what was left of those castles in the air? . . .
a mutilated chair, a wall that no one could look at without bursting out laughing
. . . a wall just like the man who had built it: grotesque, with a huge, fat head
and a withered hand . . . yes, that's the kind of wall it was. To say nothing of the
house itself, which was no longer a house, since every floor had been damaged.
And yet still she went on, and there in bed she had calculated and made lists, she'd
constructed her castle in the air . . . and although she realized, better than anyone
else, that all the calculations were wrong, that her castle was collapsing, she went
on finishing the plans that after all had already been made. It was stupid, she
knew, but what else could she do? . . . give up and let the world go on turning?
She couldn't do it, she was only human . . . she was just ondine, destined to kick
up a fuss, to live life and at the end to collect god knows what new nonsense. She
dropped in to see the landlord and told him about the wall, which had made a
real hallway in the house, a real stairwell, and which also freed up the kitchen
. . . well, which in a word had finally made the place habitable. Oh, she told him
about the wall all right, but she didn't go into detail about valeer's handiwork, she*

described the ideal wall that only existed in her imagination . . . but the landlord didn't understand exactly what ondine was getting at, so she had to spell it out: she'd thought that there might be a reduction in rent now, since she'd increased the value of the house. But he had all kinds of impossible objections: certainly, his house was worth more now (at least if she was telling the truth, he'd have to come and take a look for himself), but so what? He saw no reason to reduce the rent. On the contrary, he said a couple of times. On the contrary? asked ondine . . . in a moment you'll be claiming that I'll have to pay more because the house has risen in value . . . soon you'll be evicting me in order to put someone in who's stupid enough to pay a higher rent for that dump! And because he smiled and said nothing, she saw it as a confirmation . . . she straightened up and sighed: oh, fucking christ, she said . . . And she was saying it more to everything and everyone than to the landlord alone. And although there had been days in her life when she would have smashed skulls over a setback like this, again she couldn't manage to flare up . . . she was furious, with a greater raging fury than she'd ever known, in fact, but she couldn't manage to erupt and start kicking and flailing: her great indifference that was not indifference . . . but would be better described as dejection . . . spread through her entire being. She turned to the landlord, and with her hand already on the doorknob, said in such a flat voice that he looked at her in astonishment: I'll knock the wall down! Woman, he replied, I think you're losing your mind!

She went down the few blocks to her home, and said a number of times to herself: he thinks I'm going mad. She wasn't exactly mad, but she couldn't think properly . . . she was indifferent, yes, that was true . . . in her place another person might have longed to be able to cry like a child, but when she thought back to her childhood . . . imagined that childhood again, and then thought of all she'd been through since, she felt even more ill than she already was. Her condition may have struck that blood-sucking landlord as abnormal, but when she shook her head silently it was not at herself but at the others who didn't understand her: I'm going to knock that wall down, she repeated . . . I must have said that I would be taking the wall with me when I moved away, I must have said This and I must have said That. And when she got home, would you believe it, there were those two idiots back sitting on the floor, each with a scrubbing brush in his hand, scrubbing the mortar off the floor . . . each with the scrubbing brush raised and chattering away to each other, arguing about the most incredible nonsense.

DOWNHILL

And you read the last few pages, about oscarke and the wall, while mr brys is hanging around your house without too much to say for himself . . . after you've read about the grotesque wall with lumps and lumps and daubs of mortar, mr brys sits for a while nodding and saying nothing, before suddenly coming out with: art is going downhill. And of course you don't quite understand him: does he mean that your own writing isn't very good, or is he indignant because oscarke, who after all is a sculptor, can't even build a decent wall? And you reply that art certainly is going downhill—when you go to people's homes and see the grotesque things they're surrounded by, the pots and pans they use, the frames they hang on their walls, the statues they put on their sideboards, the books they devour, you can't help but notice. Art is going downhill; you hear some people saying to you, for example: up to now I've written poetry, because it was easier, but I don't know . . . after all you do reach a wider public with a novel. As if the poet were a pork butcher, a hairdresser, who wants to satisfy his customers: a shave, sir, or a haircut? Art is going downhill: when you meet kraniek holding a book, he looks at the outside and then the inside and then puts it down again unread . . . and finally says that he's sorry not to be an englishman or an american: only the english and the americans write things that are part of world literature. And who therefore thinks it's just a matter of language . . . or else, if abraham hans had written in english, he would have produced a lot more masterpieces.

And in addition you say to mr brys: but everything we've summed up there, is it art? Or things that have nothing to do with art? You like to believe rather that it's these things and people that are going downhill, while here and there a solitary person who paints or writes looks on in dismay. A person who writes, you say . . . because you don't like saying "writer," because things have reached the point where people see a writer as a comedian, a jokester . . . and you don't like saying "artist," because it's reached the point where people confuse an artist with a dirty old man, with some crazy with long hair who acts weird, an exhibitionist trying to attract everyone's attention. And so although here and there the odd person who paints or writes looks incredulously at the things around him, and has to shake his head at them in disbelief—and then transmits his astonishment in his books or on his canvases, having to experience it anew everyday . . . meanwhile things are certainly going downhill, but not with the art of these people. Because all of those other people who go on rushing downhill at a furious pace, they see on their way down the occasional rare, pure, human work of art, and zoom past it as they zoom past the trees lining the concrete highways: they wonder what the use of such things is, what they mean, what good they are? They just stand there making the curves dangerous, and smashing our skulls when we crash into them at 120 kph.

That's certainly true, mr brys: things are going downhill . . . but man himself, who occasionally makes a work of art proclaiming this fact, is not responsible.

I was in amsterdam, says andreus mottebol to polpoets . . . to give a talk about jan de lichte and his gang—because we've all been talking about jan de lichte, but none of us have been able to bring himself to actually become a bandit as yet—and there in amsterdam there were a few things to do with art and artists going on, but I don't like that kind of thing: don't bring me face to face with all those people who are connected with art in some phony way or other. Well, a well-meaning friend took me to a pub frequented only by artists, performers, comedians, and actors. And that kind of spectacle makes me sad, when I see that stampede for success, and the way they all try to attract that success. If you'd seen it, polpoets, you would have grinned and told them that they should creep up on that success quietly and sprinkle some salt on its tail . . . the way you convince children they can catch sparrows. And I remember that lawrence called that kind of thing "la déesse-chienne" . . . and can you think of a phrase in your polpoetsian flemish that would be a good translation of that? So there's this young man who wants to make a name—as they say—with a notorious novel or a epochal volume of poetry, but since for the moment he's not capable of writing them, instead he attracts attention by wearing a strangely shaped beard round his chin. Then you have the eternal painter with some actual talent, copying first van gogh and then de chirico, always dressed in a thick woolen sweater, or a fisherman's wind-breaker, because permeke or picasso once wore one. There you have the young poet who constantly gets other people to telephone him at the pub—telephone call for the poet mr jan klaassen!—and conversations dry up all over the place, everyone looking round to see if mr punch the poet is there. And who's to say if mr punch the poet isn't on the other end of the line himself, having himself paged? And then there's that gentleman with the awfully long hair and the face that's no longer a face at all but a thing frozen into a mask of pride . . . and if you ask who that might be, no one has the vaguest idea: he's someone, they think, who might play a bit of piano, or maybe he acts or plays the oboe . . . but at any rate, he plays, that's the truth: he plays the artist: he's in heat for the bitch-goddess fame.

And while amadeus mottebol has been expressing his revulsion, polpoets started to laugh, and his laughter has become more and more expansive: he sees all this as a joke anyway: that's how it's always been, amadeus mottebol! he says. Here and there you find someone, a rare and beautiful human being, who makes soap, or works himself to death on a daily paper, and carefully sizes people up, and has to shake his head at them . . . and sometimes, maybe once every three years, he writes a poem about it. Those are the poets. That's art. And the rest is just a bunch of circus clowns running round with a huge saltshaker trying to make it big. The rest is an army . . . no, a horde . . . that wants to climb parnassus just to have themselves photographed, to hear their names shouted down the telephone line, to strengthen their positions.

And because that's how it's always been, says polpoets with a laugh to andreus mottebol, you shouldn't get bitter about a centuries-old stupidity, and shouldn't forget to smile and bare your 2 gold teeth at that bunch of clowns. You write and talk about jan de lichte's gang, amadeus mottebol, instead of joining his gang: you ought to storm parnassus yourself to drive out all those moneychangers, instead of encouraging them in their stupidity and profiting from it.

L'HOMME

The very same day—or no, the next day—andreus mottebol receives an express letter from tippetotje in which she writes that polpoets is absolutely right. And this letter of hers also contains a catalogue of everything one can buy in big american department stores, a catalogue of plastic objects such as: lampshades, curtains, vases, statues . . . below which a caption reads: very Artistic. Very artistic, like books and films and plastic sculptures—surrounded by such noisy and expensive advertising that everyone eventually comes to believe that it is indeed very definitely Artistic. And tippetotje writes: you'd do better to resign yourself to all this, andreus mottebol, and accept the situation as it is—you'd do much better to become a sort of jan de lichte of art. Look, all you'd have to do would be to dress up in an odd way, with an amiable mask for a face, perhaps with your hair parted down the middle, combed out on both sides so that it starts to look like a wig . . . you could learn a whole string of words off by heart, like "components of a sublime concept" . . . and as you pronounce the sublime word sublime you'd go up on your points like a ballerina, stick your thumb and forefinger in the air as though you were holding the sacred host, and make your amiable but comic mask assume an exalted, heavenly expression. You could hire a room, a kind of cenacle, an artistic sacristy, on which all the snobs would descend to declaim their rhetoric. You'd ask young artists to make something along the lines of dubuffet or zio-zito—and if they don't want to, you simply start making them yourself—and you palm the product off on the snobs. And to a different sort of public you'd sell plastic sculptures of bambi, and show how at the push of a button you can turn them into ashtrays or lampshades or coffee-grinders—very Artistic—and meanwhile your mask is concealing only one real gift: cunning. Cunning would be your watchword, the horse you bet on, the banner under which you'd fight and die . . . but like an embezzler, you wouldn't be able to show that horse, that flag to anyone—but in public you'd maintain that you followed quite different ideals, for example the rather obscure: long live the marquis de sade. Since no one has actually read de sade, no one knows what you actually mean. Or perhaps you could choose something else, something that sounds just as stupid, and preferably with numbers in it: 2 and 7 equals 27. Or maybe you could take that last unsullied symbol: l'homme. Your tippetotje.

And because andreus mottebol is a poet and weekly journalist, he can't help but imagine himself for a moment in the place of one of those charlatans, those pirates, those jan de lichtes of art, and nods benignly: l'homme . . . mankind. Hell, he immediately writes a reply to tippetotje: dear, my destiny would follow me even there, into charlatanism—when all I'd want would be to cheat fools, my first customer would happen to be one of those rare and precious beings: an animal that's learned to walk upright, that actually thinks and no longer assents mindlessly to everything he's told. And what am I supposed to do, tippetotje . . . palm some plastic off on That being of rare beauty?

HOT AIR

They hadn't realized that ondine had come home, and valeer was just replying to oscarke that there had always been poor people and rich people: and if those socialists ever got into power, they'd line their pockets too: you're a sucker, he said to oscarke . . . just wait till that student has some weight to throw around, you'll see him stuffing his face. And oscarke replied that it wasn't true: you don't know the student! And he painted a picture of the student that made him look like the risen christ . . . though he himself knew that the picture was false: he was simply describing the socialists as he saw them in his finest dreams, and he said nothing about the sailor and the guy with 1 hand and all those other specimens that he knew were just scum. Because that wasn't the point, just like it wasn't the point that the apostles of christ were poor fishermen—you only had to go down to the canal to see the kind of people who worked the mussel boats, and they were probably the same way in christ's time—it was only the doctrine that mattered: the brotherhood of the working people of all countries, and the completely new world that was on its way. And so valeer must not tell him that the workers were only such and such, oscarke knew the workers better than anyone: if you want to learn about them, you should try lining up on the allee verte with them everyday. But that meant nothing to valeer of course, it was just one more proof without substance. And ondine, who was behind oscarke's back, said: do you really think that? Oh, he didn't know she was there, the blood drained from his face and he saw the wry mockery on hers—he saw her contempt, he knew that she looked down on him like he was a limpet, but that didn't prevent him from saying: certainly I think that! He got up. And if you don't believe it, try traveling up and down to brussels everyday, he said. And the tuft of hair that always stood up on the back of his head actually trembled . . . it was hilarious at that moment how like a dog he looked, a dog whose scrap of food someone was trying to steal. But ondine couldn't laugh, nor did she feel capable of arguing with him . . . sure, she could point out that he was getting all worked up about a movement that was going to turn the world upside down, that he was giving his sympathy to the poor scum who were the same the world over, thieves and lazy bums and foulmouthed scoundrels— because she'd heard it said that they sang the filthiest songs imaginable on the trains—but that he never thought about his own family, which was his principal duty: asking for a raise, fixing things around the house, helping Her live a life a little more worthy of a human being . . . No, what he felt was altruism, which was a disease like any other, a kind of madness: don't you know they can stick you in the madhouse for it? But no, she didn't say any of this, she just thought it—and looking at him her train of thought continued: I can say all that to him, but I don't want to. And she simply threatened something ridiculous instead: I'll get the priest to come round! But in fact what she felt even more strongly than usual was that oscarke was still a child, a mindless child that it's better to frighten outright rather than reason with. Fine, call in the priest! cried oscarke, who'd never contradicted her before, but who was getting bolder since he'd realized that it wasn't the end of the world if he had to bare his teeth once and a while. Fetch the priest! . . . and more to the point because it was so incredible, something she would never do. Right, ondine said, and she actually went. Valeer was shaking with laughter . . . now you're going to have the priest on your back, he said. I'm not scared of the priest, oscarke said. At that moment he wasn't scared of anything: for example, if war were to break out, he said, the war that everyone's talking about, like they're glad there's going to be a war . . . how ludicrous, since there's been peace for years, and no one really remembers what war means anyway . . . And so as he was talking about the approaching war he gradually forgot about ondine and her priest . . . I'd volunteer right away, he continued, if it wasn't for the fact We are against the war, à bas la guerre! And as he was about to start talking about jean jaurès, the door opened and there, sure enough, was ondine with the priest. They looked at her flabbergasted: I think you're going nuts, said oscarke. The priest talked to oscarke the way one talks to a naughty schoolboy: what's this I've been hearing about you, oscarke? Like he thought the world was one big youth group, a well-behaved sunday school without factories where people worked for starvation wages, without mines full of methane, without workers' trains like cattle trucks. He managed to tell oscarke that in the beginning god had created poor and rich people, and that the responsibility for all the misery in the world lay with those two first humans, adam and eve, who had eaten of the forbidden fruit. And since it was his job to speak about those things—just it was oscarke's to carve stone, and only a hobby to talk about those

things—he stole oscarke's thunder right away. Oscarke couldn't cope with it: cer-
tainly it might be true about adam and eve, but that didn't stop the workers' trains
being . . . There'll be a change in those trains too, said the priest: the pope himself
had come out against socialism, and had said that the life of the working man
had to be improved by setting up christian groups in which the employers could
reach agreements with the workforce—and wouldn't it be far better to join one
of those, once they've been set up? The socialists, well, he realized that they were
poor misguided souls, but did oscarke know that they wanted to abolish religion
entirely? He also talked about our traditional faith and morality and opened his
eyes wide as if the heavens were collapsing and all the sparrows were falling out
of the trees. He, the priest, pulled one way, and oscarke pulled the other . . . but
politely, and both of them saying things that weren't quite true—because oscarkee
knew perfectly well, but didn't dare say, that the church should concern itself only
with religion, since they couldn't care less whether a poor man believed or not, but
they Did care whether he was going to stay stupid and servile. And oscarke also
thought about how he would never dare to say: how can you, little priest, know
more about god than we do? But the priest talked on and on, wasting more and
more words: saying that it didn't matter whether someone was rich or poor, but
that it did matter whether they were going earn a place in heaven while here on
earth. Be a good man now! said the priest, and oscarke replied that he had never
been anything but good . . . and they stopped their argument, and the priest went
to see the baby, and talked about the christening, and it had all been nothing but
hot air.

YES

It's the sunday morning when the people of chapel road are going to vote
whether or not they want their king back . . . whether or not they're for the
feudal lords, the bishops in their purple robes, and the gentlemen with their
castles . . . if they're for the iron heel and the whip. And as you, together with
mr brys and master oedenmaeckers, when you see all those people trooping
meekly past, you know the answer will be Yes: we'll have to get hit in the
face again, get beaten up outside the factory gates, yes we'll bow our heads
respectfully to the ground and doff our caps—yes, we know who and what
our masters are . . . but we've got to put up with it, after all: we're not a nation,
we're not people, we're just servants—yes, we've got to listen to our masters
bawling out their orders, and they don't like our looks, we've got to take it
on the chin. And mr brys turns away from the procession, which is starting
to nod in unison—and picks up the newspaper, where they write so nicely:
you'll vote No because you're not a yes-man nodding at everything the great
and the good undertake on their own authority as if they were ruling over

slaves. No, never! And mr brys wonders how brave that man will manage to remain in future, when he could just as well have written: you will vote Yes because you've been a yes-man since you were a child and will stay one all your life . . . because you've scarcely any reason or understanding, because you've lived life with blinders on, because you're ignorant of what the great and the good undertake everyday on their own authority, because you want to remain a people of the lame and the blind . . . because you're slaves, now and forever more, amen. And the blind and the crippled go on a pilgrimage for the glory of their king, and murmur and mutter Yes, as only a race of servants and maids can . . . slaving and toiling from early morning till late at night, moaning and whining all the while: my master's a dirty bastard . . . he beats me! And other maids, other servants reply proudly: that's nothing . . . mine kicks me! And the beaten and kicked arise and go out to vote Yes—it's just a shame they can't say amen too. And after mr brys has said all this, with rage, with sorrow, and also with bitterness, master oedenmaeckers asks whether it isn't all *our* fault . . . asks if we're not a vanguard that's ventured too far forward . . . asks if we aren't rather like the band in front of the parade, a band that marched straight ahead and realized too late that the procession behind them couldn't keep up, and so wandered off, marching around aimlessly . . . perhaps now led by a faux band, a clown orchestra, only miming their instruments, and who are leading us back into the ditch from which they came. Master oedenmaeckers wonders whether we haven't just brought the blind out into the daylight, which only burns their dead eyes . . . he asks whether we haven't given the cripples their freedom, when freedom is something that terrifies them.

And then . . . sunday morning is over: the race of servants and maids has gone to vote: and half of them have already dared to say no.

ONDINE ALSO NODS

And what the priest had said, and what oscarke had replied, once again left ondine as indifferent as that glass of water by their bed. I think you're going mad! That was the second person who'd said that today, the second person who didn't know the state her mother was in, and so didn't know what indescribable pain they were causing ondine: because in a mad person's house you don't ever say to someone that they're going mad. Was she like her mother after all, then? Still, when she retraced her thoughts, her actions, they were normal . . . or perhaps they only seemed normal, perhaps she no longer had any sense of what was normal or not, and in other people's eyes everything she did seemed completely insane. What surprised her most, though, was that because of her indifference, because she felt so distanced from the conflicts around her, oscarke and his ridiculous socialism had been emboldened. But . . . even if it were her fault, she still couldn't bring herself to say: there are things that should be kept quiet, however much truth they might contain. Certain things were allowable—like the time she'd broken into the offertory box as a child. But did that mean that everyone who wanted should be allowed to break into an offertory box too? She realized that they were missing the point, oscarke and the priest, each thinking to himself that he was indisputably right, and the other absolutely wrong . . . the reality was that they were both right. But they didn't realize it, and because she, ondine, did, they thought she was mad . . . because she towered above normal people, they thought she was abnormal— abnormal, certainly, but not in the one sense of the word that they were capable of understanding. And because she kept silent, and stared at the three of them . . . her brother and oscarke and the priest . . . simply started at them and went indifferently along to see the baby and talk about the christening, the priest asked her: but, are you a believer yourself? And ondine looked right past him—right through him, so to speak—and replied: perhaps I'm the only real believer left.

DAGOES AND DRAGOONS

And on that sunday morning when our race of beggars and servants goes to the polls, johan janssens writes this column for the weekly paper: since 50 percent of us have always been yes-men, agreeing to everything the gentlemen in their castles ask . . . and since 50 percent of our people know nothing of their wretched origins, let's leave the world of today and cast a quick glance at history. Follow me, dear reader, and see the gloomy landscape that surrounds us . . . don't be too alarmed, those fires you can see on the horizon are just small farms, farms over which foreign soldiers have made the red cock crow. That wheel over there, set high on a pole, is nothing . . . true, it's not the wheel of fortune, but it's "broken" as many people. Of course it was only criminals, thieves, and tramps who were put on it, and who then had every bone in their bodies broken with an iron bar . . . then, high on that pole, they were turned with their face to the sun, to lie there till they died. And now you'll think, reassured, that these were the same scoundrels who set fire to those farmsteads there on the horizon, who've now reaped their just reward and are lying on the wheel with their limbs smashed? No, reader, you're jumping the gun a little. Let's be clear. Foreign soldiers set fire to that little farm, robbed the farmer of everything, stripped his wife naked, raped his young daughter, and then rode on. That's all. That has nothing to do with the man on the wheel. Because the man on the wheel: he's a tramp. He no longer has a fixed abode. Imagine that! And he was a thief too . . . look, we can find it here in the old chronicles: accused of having stolen a piece of meat. But don't you worry your head about that, dear reader—let's save the worrying for later.

So you've taken in the landscape properly now, you've shuddered a little and you're glad you're not living in the world of 1750: people are content with so little . . . readers' hands, like children's, are easily filled. And so you clap your easily filled hands and cry out: but what kind of world was it then in 1750?

And yes, that's just what we wanted you to ask! 1750 was a time of famine, plague, cholera, and smallpox, and lots of foreign soldiers. There are still ruins standing left over from the time of Spanish rule, and the body of the last drowned hero has not yet fully decomposed. One can still hear the dreadful groaning of all those who weren't catholics and whose hands were naturally chopped off in consequence . . . and the dull thuds of the heads of the resistance fighters can still be heard, severed from their torsos by razor-sharp axes and rolling off their wooden platforms. I won't tell you, dear reader, about the blood that spurted up like a fountain, the blood of the resistance fighters . . . the blood-fountain of the people of flanders, who were too poor to even dream of freedom. Poor little resistance fighters, poor little iconoclasts, poor headless wretches, poor wretches without hands. Suckers suckerorums, the priest still says in his church, and the crafty man knows why. But enough about that.

Enough about the time of the catholic dagoes. They've gone. There they are disappearing over the far horizon, while on the opposite horizon the austrians appear—and we can still hear today words that the spaniards used and which our people remembered but did not understand. An "abbeladoe," for instance. An abbeladoe is a poor wretch, a sucker who walks about with his skinny backside showing through his torn trousers—it comes from the spanish "hablador," beggar. How many times the spaniards must have slung that word at the bowed heads of our people for us to still remember it! But we've already said: enough of that. They disappear over the horizon, so that the austrians can appear over the opposite horizon. Between those two armies are fields that have been laid waste and trampled flat, ruins that were once farmhouses, and skeletons dangling from the gallows: now the austrians are here. And a word from their occupation has also survived: the word "dragoon." I'll give you a good dragooning. An austrian soldier was a dragoon, and the thrashing he gave you was therefore a dragooning. Think of all the dragooning our people must have had to endure in order to remember that word for so long! The austrians looked at our people, kicked the shanties apart that the people had only just cobbled together from the remains of their farmhouses, and before mounting their horses and riding away, they gave us a good dragooning.

SOLDIERS OF LOUIS XV

And johan janssens also writes: we know, dear reader, that you are probably one of the 50 percent who voted "no" . . . but what I write is intended more for the other 50 percent: I told them about the dagoes who were catholic and murderers, I told them about the austrians who gave us a good dragooning. But now other troops appeared on the horizon—other and better, as the proverb says! Alas, way over there where the sky looks ghostly red, and where you see thick smoke rising, the troops of louis XV have appeared: the king of france ousts the empress of austria, and the french maréchaussée takes the place of the austrian dragoons. Unfortunately, though, there isn't much left to set fire to, and there isn't that much left to steal and haul away; there are only some girls who are too young to be assaulted, and women who are too old to want to assault. There are only a few trembling magistrates now, a few cleaned-out merchants, a few dirt-poor farmers to massacre—and thumbscrews are used, and dying prisoners have their feet put in the hearth, all to find out were the last few pennies are hidden, the last coin rolled in a sock, the last savings for a rainy day. But you, dear reader, who've cast a fearful glance at the falling darkness, at the dangling skeletons on the gallows, who are indeed starting to look a bit grisly . . . you'd prefer to hurry on and get off the roads, to reach this little town before nightfall. Well, consider the town carefully: it's empty and desolate, it is scarcely 6 o'clock and already everything is closed—people are silent inside, spooning down their potato soup, and no one dares talk too loudly or unbolt their doors, because the drunken soldiers of the french king are roaming round and amusing themselves by battering them down, smashing up the houses, and stealing the last few pennies from the inhabitants. And look, besides the soldiers of louis XV, alongside but opposed to them, an army roams flanders and brabant, a horde of nearly a 100,000 beggars and tramps: in france the revolt against the king will take the form of a revolution . . . but in flanders that same revolt begins, alas, a few years too early, and doubly alas, only in the form of a gang of thieves.

NOTHING BUT WIND

Oscarke on the other hand had squatted down again to go on scraping away the lumps of mortar—and looking at valeer, he said: why did you have to make such an effort not to burst out laughing just now? And valeer, who was now dying with laughter, laughing till the tears ran down his cheeks, replied: couldn't you smell it? So that was it! And oscarke felt everything around him growing empty, empty . . . ha, so that's how they were—valeer was the same as his sister—she too had stood there and looked at him and not said anything . . . and you'd have thought: she's thinking things over, weighing things . . . but no, probably she'd just farted, like her brother, and said nothing, thinking: no, they won't smell it. So that's how the world was: the priest was trying to turn him into a god-fearing soul, and meanwhile just farted. Apart from himself, everything could be reduced to a malodorous but insignificant fart—that's how the world was. And he also thought: god, we have to have ideals, because we'll quite simply fall over if we don't have anything to hold on to! And looking around he found the loveliest example: he was squatting against this wall, but what kind of wall was it? An awkward pile of stolen stones, an unsightly mass of lumps and daubs of mortar, but what else had he to squat against? That's how it was with socialism too, he believed in it because it was simply necessary to believe in something—because it gave his life some content with which he could argue with valeer—because it warmed his heart a little, though he knew that the cause he was toiling away for was only a so-so cause—though he knew that his arguments were wasted on valeer, because what did valeer do? he farted, and struggled not to burst out laughing. But strangest of all, as he looked at valeer wiping the tears from his eyes, he thought of what the priest had said and perhaps meanwhile hadn't smelled—and he had to laugh himself, a long sustained laugh, such as he hadn't laughed for ages. They stood shrieking with hilarity and holding their bellies when the priest went past. And what will the priest think? Christ almighty, let him think what he likes! said oscarke. After all, there was only 1 thing in the whole world that was truly sacred to him, and that was between jeannine's thighs.

But in practical terms, what was the upshot of all his theories, how would it affect his behavior towards ondine and the others? Not at all probably: all he had to do was stay the same—he was oscarke, a small piece of humanity that lived somewhere and would die somewhere, but whatever he said or did in the future didn't have the slightest importance . . . god, it didn't even have the slightest importance to himself. All he had to do, all he Could do, was to stay with the children, with judith and now with mariette, in the stench of shit and piss-soaked diapers. Hanging around in the stuffy kitchen in the evenings, and letting his hesitant, contradictory thoughts fight it out in his mind, he'd cleared a corner for himself to sculpt a head of christ . . . he tried to see himself in this christ, not god but the son of god, the suffering human being, the human being who had moved his interests beyond narrow self-sufficiency, who did not fart or laugh about it, but who on account of his abnormal notions of goodness and justice was mocked and kicked and crucified. The rough block of wood stood there, the chisels were hanging nearby, but still he did nothing but stumble up and down the room, from the unsightly chair where judith was crying to the wooden cot where mariette was crying. And speaking of the suffering human being, no, he wasn't that completely—or rather he wasn't that day in and day out: he was also sometimes the human being capable of enjoying himself. He experienced these two extremes all at once, he experienced christ and he experienced jeannine, and it was only a few weeks before ondine was expecting again.

And johan janssens goes on in the weekly paper: allow us, dear reader, to leave this world of today for a short while longer in order to have a look at the work of the executioner in earlier days. He's busy stroking, in his odd way, the back of a young woman . . . called johanna morels, tramp and beggar, suspected of having defended herself with a knife against a soldier of louis XV. His bared arm goes expertly up and down—and the drops of blood, which appear here and there on her flesh under the whip, become more numerous: soon this drop here on the shoulder blade merges with a couple of others that are already softly gleaming further down. Then and only then has what—in the minutes of the trial of jan de lichte—is described as a lashing "till the blood flows" come about.

But, "expertly," we said . . . as if the executioner were an Ubermensch, someone who's risen above his fallible humanity to become a demigod in the service of justice. But let's leave the broad path of gullibility for a moment and begin to doubt that fairy tale of the executioner's perfection. It often happened that one of us was sentenced to have his head chopped off—right, we walk in our nightshirts behind the tumbrel, our hands tied behind our backs, and our bare feet stumbling on every loose cobblestone . . . hundreds of people line the streets to enjoy the spectacle of a delinquent taking his last steps. And although at the eleventh hour we want to rub ointment on the king's beard, and give a kiss to the priest's crucifix every five feet, it won't help us a bit: we only hear dogs barking as a caravan passes, and from a window an indignant catholic throws one last stone at our heads . . . and although we duck instinctively, so that the stone hits the priest, we can't even snicker about it anymore. Something else awaits us—something that we won't elaborate on at the moment. We are in our underpants, because it's well known we still might shit in our pants at the last minute. And then, dumb and blind and silent, we climb onto the wooden platform. If we've remained in this bitterest hour the same kind of person we always were, we will not deign to look at those around us. However, in this hour of our death, our cowardice erupts (because we are human beings, dear reader, and beneath our bravado we always kept a little terror hidden), and our fear starts to grow, we will beg god and all his saints and also the honorable members of the court for mercy. You never know.

But enough of that. Our head is put on the chopping block, and the executioner does his work. And here we come back to our starting point, dear reader: what happens if the executioner gets his work only half-done? If in his clumsiness his chopper goes astray and only catches part of our head? That's impossible! you'll exclaim. Well, you're wrong, it's more than possible: joseph de damhoudere, a jurist from the time in question, writes in his "practice in criminal cases": executioners bring hatred on themselves and their office by not performing their duties with the appropriate humanity: they often abuse the condemned person, they jerk and drag him along by his chains, they kill him, murder him, slaughter him so contemptuously they might as well be dealing with beasts. And look, dear reader . . . if you can believe this learned gentleman, the executioner missed with his ax because he didn't think that it was a human being lying bound at his feet: he thought it was a pig, a slug, a cockroach. But again—you must learn to doubt everything—another writer of the period adds that it was not always contempt, but that the cause also lay in a simple lack of knowledge of the craft. Ha, well that's something differ- ent! Those who knew their trade abused us, murdered us as contemptuously as though we were beasts—thank god that today we no longer have to deal with such bestial executioners, but with the more humane ones . . . the only trouble being that they don't know their trade. And we lay our heads on the chopping block . . . our anticlerical heads, our resistance fighter's heads . . . and he strikes. The blood spatters in all directions, but we're still alive—and we see our more humane executioner lift his ax to strike again.

BURNT PORRIDGE

And johan janssens continues in the weekly paper: we've been struck a bloody blow by the executioner, dear reader . . . and now we're lying there on the scaffold with half our head sliced off. It's unbelievable! you'll say. But as we lie there, bathed in our blood, we have no trouble believing it ourselves. Once the executioner of mechelen was ordered to decapitate a condemned man with a sword—the good fellow missed his stroke and grievously wounded the sub- ject without killing him. The common people, who attended the execution en masse, weren't satisfied—they stoned the executioner and then finished him off with cudgels. But what happened to us—what of the victim, what were we thinking about while we were lying there waiting? Of course it's nice that the executioner was finished off by amateurs . . . but what sort of condition were we in while we waited for the coup de grace? A little later 5 guys were sentenced to death in gent: the executioner didn't succeed in finishing off even one of the five with a single stroke . . . which is to say that he botched each and every one of them, slicing off a piece of skull here and a piece of chin there. A few years later he was deft enough to need only two strokes—but his successor was so clumsy that he feared for his own life . . . which doesn't mean that he was so clumsy that he actually endangered himself, no, but that he dropped to his knees before the crowd, asked forgiveness, and promised that it would never happen again . . . but he lied, adds the old historian.

And so you'll now draw the very wise conclusion, dear reader, that it's best never to face such severe charges, or at least not to flaunt your position as a resistance fighter in public, so that you can only be sentenced to the gallows. There's something to be said for that—but here too, as always, there's a "but" ... The ladder is kicked from under your feet and you fall, but the rope keeps you in a vertical position. However, it can happen that the rope breaks, and you drop down, and look around in bewilderment, and have to climb the ladder all over again. It may equally well happen, however, that you hang dangling from the rope, and for whatever reasons are still far from dead. And what happens if you just hang there twitching your hands and feet? Was it a dress rehearsal? No, the sentence was officially carried out in public, the honorable gentlemen withdraw, the common people have had their money's worth and drift off: only two people are left who know that you're not dead: you yourself, hanging there, and the executioner who hanged you. And then the executioner cuts you down surreptitiously, tightens the noose a little, and strangles you for good by standing on you neck and stamping on it. That's what it says in the old chronicles.

And then, dear reader ... we can count ourselves lucky not to be a woman, sentenced to be buried alive. She was lowered into the pit and the earth was packed down on top of her: a neat and discreet burial, that's true. And like meetje mie said in her simple innocence: I've bought a stone for my husband with "dead and forgotten" carved on it. Dead and forgotten, dear reader. But in this case the situation is a little different: the woman is already forgotten but is not yet dead. And then the executioner comes and stamps on the earth until not a single stifled scream reaches his sensitive hearing. Then he goes home and eats his rice pudding. And it's here that the reader will have to hold his nose, because to tell the truth, the rice pudding is slightly burnt. Burnt rice pudding is not good to eat. And so he goes back to the dungeon and beats out a strange rhythm with his whip on the back of the young woman johanna morels, who defended herself with a knife against the foreign invader.

But we, dear reader, now beat a hasty retreat to our world of today, where 50 percent of the populace want to return to all this.

EVERYTHING IS SOMETHING

Ondine was a little surprised to find herself pregnant yet again . . . she wept a bit, but in the evening when her old friends came around, she said: oh, if only we didn't enjoy It so much. And that became an in-joke among them. It had just slipped out . . . she looked rather perplexed because people saw more in it than she'd actually meant. Joining in the laughter, she said afterwards that it was all very well for them to laugh: but I'm stuck with it . . . and that's not all, but valeer

169

is wandering about too and can't find a job. If he's as funny as you, he can have a job with my sister, said fat glemmasson . . . because she needs a manservant. A manservant, someone who would eat and sleep in her house? Oh, and she thought of his bed, which would finally be for them . . . she and oscarke could sleep in it, and the children could have the old bed, the old bed with the bugs. And she couldn't wait to leave the bar and go to the room where valeer slept, and look at her childhood bed. It was a bit small. Oh, how small this bed is! she thought with feeling . . . was that the vast space, were these the heavens, the abysses, where she had once lain dreaming on sleepless nights? She touched the bed for a moment and couldn't shake off the thought that by going back to sleep in this bed she would again become her old indomitable self: every night I'll remember those years long ago, perhaps I'll dream again that that I'm hanging on the neck of a horse and charging down chapel road. And she leaned with her hands on the foot of the bed and breathed deeply: that will be the end of my strange, oppressive indifference! she said. Then she hurried back to the pub, to her customers, and as soon as they'd gone she sat with her feet on the stove, scorching her shins—valeer stood next to her, and stretched his hands out, as if he wanted to fill his pockets with warmth, and she looked up at him and smiled . . . smiled at him and oscarke, at the unsightly wall and the heavy drapes with the daubs of mortar on them. There was sunshine in her heart again . . . for the umpteenth time she'd filled herself with dreams, with mirages. I think I'll pop over and see my father at home some day soon, she said with a smile . . . and she looked only at valeer—deliberately ignoring oscarke—because she suspected that he would now want to go and see his mother too, idiot that he was. I wouldn't go just to visit him . . . oh, what's the good of that? As a child you think that your parents will remain your parents till you're dead, but when you get on in years and start to learn about life, you realize that your parents were just something coincidental, a doorway that you've passed through . . . no, I'd like to go for you know what! And now she did look at oscarke, but only fleetingly. Perhaps I can pick up a few things that they don't use anymore but that we're badly in need of here. Because she was cunning enough to know how she had to deal with these two idiots: she was going to steal from her parents again and in that way she was also going to steal from valeer . . . but winking at him and involving him in the plot, she twisted and turned things until it looked as if she was only stealing from him for her parents' sake. And he, with his sheepish smile, didn't understand. But oscarke did understand: oh, he said, then I'll go home for a visit as well, perhaps they'll have something that's usable too! Because it was true that he missed his mother, and also his father, however much they'd all blackened the image of that father . . . actually he missed the life he used to have, though back then he still couldn't live the life he wanted to live—couldn't, wasn't allowed, didn't dare to (yes, that was it, didn't dare)—and compared to which this life here with ondine was six of one and half a dozen of the other. But ondine laughed with her loud, false laugh—oh, he'd come to hate, hate that fake laugh of hers: when she nagged and did crazy things and was spiteful and under- stood nothing of his inner self (although when they were young she had intimated that she understood and empathized with everything about him, his dreams, and his inexpressible longings), then in a human sense she was still bearable: she was ondine, she could be forgiven. But that loud and phony laugh wounded him to the depths of his soul. What could you get out of them? she asked, still laughing loudly and spitefully . . . have you forgotten by any chance how they treated us? Have you forgotten that they were never able to pay for anything? Have you forgotten how cold and hungry you were there? And because he shrugged his shoulders with his—in her view—eternal indifference, she said: have you forgotten that your father once made me, your own wife, an indecent proposition? Oh, oscarke said reluctantly . . . an indecent proposal! And he withdrew into his corner, with his face averted, so that it was difficult for her to follow him into his fantasies. Is that nothing? she screamed. Certainly it's something, he replied, but everything is something . . . the fact that you want to crush my desire to go and visit my parents—that too is something.

THE EXHIBITION

Stop all that writing, cries mr brys from the ministry . . . stop filling page after page without asking yourself whether you . . .

And you put down your pen and wait in resignation to see what gross flaw mr brys has found in your novel this time. You write, he says, *about the friends of ondine, who all came from the upper class . . . including fat glemmasson, who's in the catholic party and doesn't believe in god. And meanwhile you write about oscarke, who takes the train up and down to brussels, and is a small, skeptical guy.* Well, those two circles you've drawn are too far apart . . . they never intersect in your novel, as happens in real life all the time, in an appalling way. *Oscarke, for example, sometimes goes into the palais des beaux-arts on his lunch hour, to look at the sculptures he'd like to Be Able to make himself . . . and as I see it, at the same moment that fat mr glemmasson should also be there. And so you take up your pen in order to describe fat glemmasson as he enters the room . . . but you wonder what he's actually come for: he's rich and votes catholic, he's without morals and flouts god and all his commandments, he bets on the horses and has three mistresses, but art and beauty are nonsense to him. And with your hesitant pen in hand you say: I can't see, mr brys, how I can get that fat glemmasson into the palais des beaux-arts. So mr brys shakes his head and thinks: what kind of writer are you! . . . and he says: describe him while he's having his afternoon nap, or while he's playing cards for high stakes at his club . . . someone comes along and talks about painting to him, about the palais des beaux-arts, about some poor slob of a painter who through a stroke of luck, through knowing the right people, through a bit of talent, has got into the palais: and do you know what, glemmasson, if you play your cards right, you could do some good business there! And fat glemmasson puts his cigar down, just like you just put your pen down, and sticks a fat sausage finger in his nose: what ism does this painter belong to? he asks. And the other man says: oh, I don't know much about it, but I read the reviews carefully and it seems he'll be someone who'll be famous after he dies . . . you see? whose work we can buy for a song now, and after his death can sell for millions—but apart from that, brr!, he paints women I wouldn't dare go to bed with!*

And fat glemmasson pulls his sausage of an index finger out of his nose, grabs his cigar again, and says: buy them all. And lo and behold, the exhibition is closed, the paintings are packed up and taken to fat glemmasson's castle . . . and there are packed up just as they are, stored in the attic.

NEON LIGHT

With his hands raised like a surrendering soldier, like a madman convinced that the sky is falling, andreus mottebol comes forward and says to you: are you out of your mind, starting to write things without the slightest understanding of them, like a mammoth purchase of paintings by fat glemmasson? Yes, look at me with your innocent face, but don't you realize that the palais des beaux-arts is now being stormed by all these up-and-coming painters . . . that they're fighting out their various isms at the entrance, and that they're flipping coins to see who'll be the first or last to exhibit . . . all in the hope that they'll be bought up by fat glemmasson, bought, packed, and banished to his attic. The day before yesterday it was the pablo van gogh's turn, and when I asked him how his work was doing, he replied in a disappointed voice: I suppose your writer was playing an april fool's joke on us with that fat glemmasson story—because tomorrow's the last day of my show, and I haven't seen anyone show up ready to banish me to an attic and speculate on my death. And when I asked him if that was really what he wanted, he said: I paint because it's simply my vocation and my passion—not being able to paint means not being able to live—but apart from that I don't give a damn where my canvases wind up: whether they're purchased by the state to give me a little encouragement, or by some snob because supposedly no one else understands what it represents, or by some sweet old lady because she feels a little sorry for my thin face, or by fat glemmasson who thinks he's making a good investment: the main thing is that I get money for it and can go on painting.

Well, you say, interrupting andreus mottebol . . . is that a reason to come to me with your arms raised to heaven? Or do you think the world's coming to an end because writers and painters no longer have their silly heads in the clouds, filling their bellies with nothing but beauty? But andreus mottebol won't allow you to interrupt him: he keeps his arms raised to heaven and says: and since pablo van gogh had to go to bruxelles nord station that evening, just like me, I suggested we walk together—I like strolling through the streets of brussels in the evening and falling in love with the city, just like with a woman . . . and again it was beautiful with all those lights, so I became poetical, lyrical, and began to speak in free verse: see, I said, how beauteous the city is as evening falls . . . pause with me for a moment and look (look with your eyes, not with your watch), at the front of that tall building there, with all its ocher and wealth of shadow contrasting with the purple-colored sky . . . and look how around the whole front of the edifice there stretches a fine green ribbon of neon light! And so I go on coaxing more free verse from my lyre, and the painter stops too and looks at the neon lighting and says: that must have cost them a bundle!

And while you, straining to control yourself, nevertheless burst out laughing, andreus says with fathomless disdain: you see, that's what you get, you with all your bitter descriptions of oscarkes who dream of beauty on the one hand . . . and fat glemmassons on the other, who breed painters and writers like people breed goldfish and white mice: as a commodity.

YOU'RE ALL THE SAME

And because oscarke said that Everything was something, she laughed again with her false, piercing laugh. Stop laughing like that! he shouted. Going home to mom, home to mom . . . she cried, laughing louder and louder, more and more crazily. What do you think? asked oscarke sadly, to valeer . . . and valeer replied that she'd always been doing things like this at home too: you'll see, she'll spend the whole day in bed tomorrow. And he looked at his sister then with all the stupid bluntness that came naturally to him—but leaving that aside, it turned out exactly as he'd said: the following day she didn't get out of bed, and yet she didn't want valeer to get the doctor . . . no, she just lay there, lay there staring at the ceiling—and valeer said to the bewildered oscarke: oh I knew, I've seen all that before, our mother has it just the same! I never thought of that, said oscarke rather flatly, suddenly alarmed, although really he'd thought about it a thousand times before, and had kept putting it out of his mind—and meanwhile he stared straight at the floor with raised eyebrows. She should pay attention in future! said valeer with a visible sense of superiority. So it was madness! Oscarke jerked round to look at her as if he thought he would see a totally new ondine lying there—he shook his head slowly, he was on the point of making a momentous discovery and adding it to his theory . . . but he was rather too hasty: madness, he said . . . she's always been like a devil to me . . . Yet he saw immediately that it wouldn't work to say: the devil in man is madness, a defect in the brain. I'll think about it more thoroughly tomorrow, he thought—but naturally, the following day he pretended he'd forgotten.

And besides, the following morning ondine got out of bed in order to carry out her resolution and actually go to termuren—it wasn't as far away as it had always seemed to her: it was only chapel road that stood between her and her parental home . . . and it struck her as rather strange that all she had to do was to shout fairly loudly from one end of chapel road to the other to reach them, and yet it seemed as if they were a whole world apart. Just look at that muddy road, she kept saying to herself . . . just look at that muddy road! And she looked at it, but there was nothing unusual about it: it was the same mud, with all the same clog-prints—and if she looked closely she would find hers still among them. She entered her parental home and simply said hello, as if it hadn't been four years since she'd held their door handle. Her father looked at her, and said hello too . . . and because she came closer and sat down by the stove without being asked, he looked at her again, and said: oh, it's You! Didn't you recognize me? she asked . . . and since he didn't reply, she realized at once: his eyesight probably wasn't too good anymore, sitting by the paraffin lamp night after night drawing and calculating—but the possibility that in those four years she herself might have changed, aged, didn't occur to her. Why don't you move closer to the town of the 2 mills? she asked . . . at the other end of chapel road everyone already has gas lighting! And she also told him that she was considering having electricity installed at home . . . but she stopped talking about it just as suddenly as she had begun, because in fact she'd come to complain, to get something out of them, but her mania for outdoing everyone had again tripped her up without her realizing. And anyway, talking about electricity suddenly made her think of something else . . . of her father's peculiar hobbyhorse! How far have you got with your invention? she asked . . . and since he said nothing she stretched out her hands towards the stove, and looking at those hands, she began ranting: these inventions of yours, and that sculpting of oscarke's, oh, I'm sorry I'm not a man . . . because you men never have to see things through: you're all far too dreamy . . . like you and your perpetual motion, I was talking about that to someone who's cleverer than all of us put together and he had a good laugh about it! He also asked if you weren't trying to make gold out of lead, or were going around with a divining rod? Vapeur looked at her hands too, he stared at her fingers that she bent and stretched again as though she were playing a game. Well, you tell this person who's cleverer than all of us put together that the old alchemists were far from stupid, far from stupid, you hear? There'll come a time when we can really make gold from lead, and much more besides—and as far as that perpetu . . . oh . . . And she stroked his forehead: as far as those unmanned crossings are concerned, they were finished long ago: I sent them to the railway company. And he went and fetched a miniature train, with rails and a barrier and a signal box . . . he fetched all the books, german and french books all mixed together, and pointed to the pencil marks he'd made in them—she really did look at them, and tried to understand . . . she bit her bottom lip, her hands now hidden under the table. And she said hesitantly . . . were you going to make gold out of This? And when he saw her eyes, he couldn't help laughing bitterly . . . he closed his books and said: you're all the same. And he put on his clogs and went into his workshop.

THE BARON

I've already written to you about my life with the baron—writes tippetotje—but I've never written anything about the baron himself, what sort of person he is, what he looks like in his baron's clothes, or what he looks like when he's taken off his baron's clothes and stands there like a perfectly ordinary beast of a man. And you've always written me a letter in reply, about your work or your friends, and you've never asked me anything about the baron: that's noble of you. Well, he provided me with money so that I could furnish a studio—I'll describe that studio another time—and he comes and visits me there occasionally. He comes and goes, but never on foot, he always has his car . . . and he sits in his car with his trousers open and that thing hanging out and drives in that state through the jungle of the city of brussels . . . and that's how he drives up to my studio, but before getting out he takes care to observe the traffic in the street, and the moment there's no sign of anyone around—apart from a couple of schoolgirls, apart from a schoolboy, apart from a young woman with a dog or a child—and, as I said, the moment there's no sign of anyone around except a person from this list, he throws open the door of his car and very slowly starts "adjusting" his pants—correcting his absentmindedness—so slowly that he might as well be opening them further. I've seen him, with a schoolgirl, just pop right out of his car, right in front of her, walking to the door that leads to my studio . . . the schoolgirl looks at him with interest, and he looks at her . . . and when she, growing slightly paler, doesn't feel like letting him drive her to school, he hurries into my apartment. And since I haven't described my studio to you yet, suffice it to say for now that it has its own bathroom. Well, my baron comes into my studio, sees I'm not there, and goes into the bathroom, opening the window wide and positioning himself right in front of it, supposedly to adjust his pants one last time—the bathroom window looks out onto the back of an enormous apartment block . . . so here there's a woman beating a rug, and there a woman is watering a flowerpot—and he stands in the window stroking his thing like you'd stroke a child—but whether he's talking to it and teaching it to say dada I don't yet know—but he caresses it so that the women beating the rugs or watering the flowers look up from their work and start staring at my bathroom window. I enter my studio and see this spectacle through the open bathroom door . . . I go over to the radio and turn it on, and music streams into my studio . . . I cough . . . so the baron knows I'm there . . . and a few moments later he joins me, very correct, very distinguished—a baron, in fact—and makes a courteous bow and asks how my work is going. And how's your work going, my love? Why, my work is going just fine, I say . . . I'd like to paint rats.

RATS

I sit in my studio—writes tippetotje—with a newly stretched canvas and brushes and tubes of paint: this is the moment I daydreamed about hundreds of times when I was younger: premature easter sunlight would fall on my easel, but still I would've stuffed the stove full of crumpled magazines, and even a few books no longer worth keeping . . . and in front of me there would be the white canvas, and my brushes would be lying ready, my dreams would be lying ready. I daydreamed about that scene, but it never came true . . . there were always the mugs of the nouveaux-riche to be painted: war profiteers, grand ladies, and men of achievement. And you who know everything about me know that there were even worse things, which I Couldn't talk about in polite company: dressed in dirty overalls I stood on scaffolding painting houses, I hung from dizzily high gutters on wobbly hanging ladders, I . . . but now the momentous instant has come, I'm sitting in my studio, I can paint what I like, I can live out my daydreams: he, the baron, has had a studio fitted out for me, he brought in housepainters to give the walls a soft gray color I picked out—I went to have a look while they were working, supposedly to see if I liked the color, but actually because I was consumed by the urge to see those who Haven't managed to find themselves a baron, and have to bow to the whims of the rich, grand gentlemen who want their walls painted a soft gray—the baron ordered carpets, a grand piano, a polished bookcase containing gilt-edged editions of books on the catholic index of forbidden books. The april sun shines . . . a lot of books, not worth reading, are lying in the stove burning pleasantly . . . I stare at the area to be painted. And at this momentous instant (that I've imagined hundreds of times, Differently and more appealingly), I hesitate and think of you, and write you a letter to ask: what shall I paint?

I imagine a ruined house, a house whose front has been demolished, by whom or what I don't know—it may have been the bombing, it may also have been the henchmen of the marquis de sade . . . it may have been god himself, roused to anger on mount sinai, or it may have been the devil prowling the earth at night . . . or it may also have been fate, which has always hung over the heads of mankind, and it may have been the end of the world, which is to say the end of the world as inhabited by man—and so that house stands there with its front missing, like a man with his face torn off, and you see the caves of the rooms where those strange and long-extinct creatures, human beings, lived and loved and harbored their strange anxieties. But that was a very long time ago, because the pile of rubble outside is no longer rubble but has turned back into earth, has silted and muddied up into dirt where weeds take root. And the caves of the rooms have long ceased to be bleeding wounds, but are petrified wounds, black with age—and in these black wounds, across those cankerous beams, hollow rafters, and crumbling walls . . . there are rats at play. They sit on the beams and look around with their intelligent, beady eyes and their cruel snouts, and they let their disgusting tails hang over the beams . . . and other rats hoist themselves up on those tails, their bodies . . . squirming and wriggling and looking round, cruel and intelligent. And yes, that's what I, tippetotje, would like to paint in my studio—in the studio paid for by my baron, and where there are thick carpets on the floor, and where there's a grand piano, and where there's a polished bookcase with forbidden books in deluxe editions. Your tippetotje. PS: are you still writing books for the ennoblement of man?

THE CRAZY DIRECTOR K.

You write a reply to tippetotje—you see her sitting in her studio in front of the blank canvas where she'd like to paint rats . . . you know all about her polished bookcase of forbidden books, and you know her stove is fueled with worthy books . . . and at that moment she gets your letter: tippetotje, I am indeed still writing my books for the ennoblement of man. But recently as regards technique I've been under the curse of kafka . . . I've always lived under the curse of someone else's writing, and it was only to escape that curse that I wrote things that were mine. Now I'm writing, but only to escape kafka and his hero k.—I write, I rewrite, and as I write I correct everything that kafka wrote . . . and so I conquer the kafka in myself: as I rewrite him I discover his faults or I add elements to his work—elements that he (how stupidly!) didn't think to include. I live in his labyrinth of administrative systems, offices, papers, documents, and files. A simple clerk, taking up his pen to write an insignificant letter filled with perfectly ordinary words, is an event. A messenger delivering this letter, a doorman who knocks to hand it to you: they are omens, harbingers of the horsemen of the apocalypse: this letter may, with its quite innocent appearance, contain the fatal word that will bring Everything to an end . . . and this knock on the door by the clueless doorman with his drooping mustache may be the signal for D-day. And then, tippetotje, we penetrate into the corridors and are the bearers of blank paper . . . we see to our dismay a clerk take up his pen to write the irrevocable word, we see the deputy office manager pointing his finger ominously at the document in question, we see with horror how the office manager is about to add the document to a file. And then we finally see the director—he sits there, he asks for an explanation, his finger points to a redundant comma . . . or, even more alarmingly, to one that is Missing, one that was forgotten amid the irreversible movement of fate. And suddenly the director erupts in a wild rage, grabs a handful of pens from a box and sends them clattering against the walls . . . his face is in a paroxysm, there are small flecks of foam in the corners of his mouth, and the right-hand side of his face (the side we call the sociable side) is contorted and askew. And the pens, crackling like machine-gun fire, ricochet and fall on the waxed floor of his office. Hang on to your hat, tippetotje . . . because this director k., this eminent gentleman who occupies a position of trust, is . . . a madman! But look. He recovers, wipes the flecks of foam from the corners of his mouth, and with a trembling hand smoothes away the crazy contortions of his face, and returns to the letter in question. His finger glides towards the forgotten comma: correct this error! he orders. It's an order, but it's given in a tone of entreaty, as a weeping child would give an order, or a kicked cur, or a cornered rat.

So I describe to you the crazy director k., tippetotje . . . but don't laugh at this presentation of a character that might have been presented by kafka, at whom madness was always gnawing . . . don't laugh, tippetotje, because everything that kafka wrote was fantasy, and everything I write is the bitter truth: you paint rats that live where people once lived . . . I describe people who still live where the rats have already become king. PS, tippetotje: and the best bit is that all those subordinates—doormen and messengers and clerks—greatly appreciate the director's madness, and think: if I were the director, I'd do even more . . .

THERE'S A RAT IN THE TOILET, TOO

No, stay a bit longer! ondine said to her father . . . and she began to explain that he shouldn't just see her as a woman like any other, but . . . she twisted and turned her words, she turned every word over and over so he wouldn't realize that, in her desire for money, she really was like everyone else—or actually even worse—and she told him about valeer, that she'd had him come over to her place because she understood what a burden he was here: he had the appetite of two people, but didn't earn enough for even a half a person—and she told him about her husband, she wasn't going to say a bad word about him, it wouldn't do any good, but, well . . . and she was expecting her second, no, her third child, and wasn't it a sin against the holy ghost that one person could make gold and that another had to bring her children into the world in hunger and poverty. I can't make gold, said vapeur. No, but you can send your inventions off to the railway company! she replied. Again he was silent, as in the beginning . . . she looked at him, he seemed older, his hair had gone snow white . . . and that curl around his mouth (because she couldn't imagine her father without seeing that little peculiarity around his mouth, that little feature that the folk of termuren, and the priest of termuren, and mr derenancourt of the castle, and she herself couldn't make up their minds whether it was the unconscious expression of innocent stupidity, or was a deliberate ruse, a cunning mask behind which he hid the extent to which he was laughing at everyone), that curl had vanished completely. It was last year I submitted my invention, he said . . . l-a-s-t year, and I've still had no news. In the beginning I felt sick when I saw the postman go past, saw him go past every day, but by now I've resigned myself . . . well . . . that is to say until recently, because I'm worried about that war people are talking about more and more, they say it'll be like in 1870 all over again, but I don't really believe that. And ondine was surprised at him, she shook her head at these crazy ideas: what difference could a trifling war make to an invention? They're only big military exercises, we'll see a few soldiers trooping past in their outfits, staging mock battles in the countryside: from your attic window you have a nice view of them advancing and retreating. But vapeur shook his head at Her crazy idea: the times we're living in now and the times to come will be as different as day and night, yes . . . (and he raised his finger, just like valeer did, when he wanted to say something that exceeded his comprehension): yes, even in people's thoughts, in their souls there's going to be a change! But suddenly continuing in a perfectly ordinary voice, he said: apart from that, who'll give a thought to an unmanned rail crossing in time of war? And ondine was about to reply to that too, but it was no longer possible for either of them, her or her father, to go on ignoring zulma: zulma, her mother, who was sitting there at the window twisting and turning in her chair, fiddling with her dress and twisting a button until she'd pulled it off entirely. Another button! cried vapeur, who in the evenings did nothing but sew buttons back on and wash underwear . . . Another one! And he showed zulma the button, thrusting it under her nose. But she paid no attention, she shouted and ground her teeth feverishly: if you're talking about children, look down the toilet, there's one in there! It was as if the heavens had opened above ondine's head, and god himself had descended with the flaming sword of justice in his hands. So it was her! This madwoman had been the witness to her crimes on that night, the night that still haunted her, an eternal specter, poisoning her whole life bit by bit . . . drawing a hot wire through her life, slice by slice. She looked at her mother and could not . . . would not believe it. It's not true! she almost shouted, but she jammed her fist in her mouth and bit down—bit till the blood flowed. But there was vapeur, shaking his head at his wife's ramblings: it gets worse every day, he said quietly . . .

you can see her going downhill week by week, he said almost apologetically. And ondine went on nodding, wanting to retain the last vestiges of polite formality at all costs, forcing herself to remain calm with furious self-control. But meanwhile she was edging a step at a time towards the front door, and then her hand was on the doorknob, and . . . then she charged outside.

A GARDENER'S DREAM

What with the winter and all the rain and bad weather, you haven't even thought of the music master's meadow, where he was going to build himself a little garden and a bit of earthly paradise. The whole winter has passed and you haven't written a thing about it, as if a little garden isn't worth looking at when it's all wet and soggy, and black ravens are cawing over it. But now in this first bit of april sunshine, you walk over to see it, and you find the music master walking around with growing astonishment: the world has been turned upside down and that gardener has gone crazy! he calls out to you. And he puts out his arm like jacob van artevelde, and says: I asked for decorative bushes and fruit trees from that gardener, a cypress and some poplars, pines and firs and flowering magnolia—and now spring is coming, and shoots are coming up everywhere, I see there's a plum tree where there should have been an apple tree, but the apple tree on the other hand has been planted over there, lost among my bit of woodland . . . I see plain old willows where I had wanted poplars . . . oh dear, it's just like a carnival here, where all the trees are disguised as other trees . . . it's just like the garden in a madhouse, where all the trees and shrubs claim that they're different trees and shrubs. And I run to the gardener, although I realize that running won't do any good, since he can't make a pear tree into a silver birch . . . but I run anyway, to express my disappointment. But he's not here, says his wife. And suddenly she starts revealing all the contradictions in her husband to me: sit down for moment, she says. She was lying, he *is* at home, down there at the bottom of the garden, planting tulips and delphiniums and primulas . . . and in her view that's an honorable trade . . . but do you think his thoughts are concerned with those flowers? He comes downstairs in the mornings and puts his hands on the rail of the stove and stares into space, into nothing—and then he finally goes and quickly sows some white daisies where there should have been blue asters, then rushes straight back in and pours over a pile of papers and books, full of things I can't make head nor tail of. Look, there they are . . . what do you think they mean? And I look at them in my capacity as music master, and I see that they are plans for a flying saucer, a flying bomb, and a missile . . . I see that they are calculations for splitting atoms, for manufacturing an atomic bomb. And I put the papers down and rush into my garden, and see him planting primulas and pruning rose trees . . . his fingers are covered in earth, but his mind is full of explosive devices. I stare at him for a moment before voicing my disappointment—and he stares at me, biding his time, ready to listen to my complaints—but from the abstracted look in those eyes, which I had always seen but to which I'd never paid attention, I can see that all remonstrations will be useless: it's a waste of time telling him about my carnival garden. And so I ask him instead what he thinks of flying saucers? And he suddenly stands up and talks and talks, and in the depths of his eyes I see a light and a fire beginning to glow: a reflection of the fire that can destroy the world, and tear the earth apart into atoms . . . the earth, a little of which clings to his fingers, when he's just planted sunflowers.

And the music master looks at you and asks: do you understand people, and their strange dreams?

AND OTHER DREAMS . . .

Well, do you understand people and their strange dreams? you ask mossieu colson of the ministry . . . should we not cast the first stone, because we're no better ourselves? What's the music master like, for instance, who had such trouble understanding his gardener? He's spent all summer walking around his meadow, where he was going to plant a little garden, a bit of woodland, a little earthly paradise . . . do you remember how he was going to plant a single cedar here, and there a thicket of jasmine bushes? He bought posts and wire and made a fence, and every time you saw him he had a spade on his shoulder—he was worried about the wind blowing his trees over, and he was glad when it started raining at the right time. It was a dream come true . . . And then, I meet him yesterday and he says with the straightest face imaginable: I'd prefer to sell the meadow and buy a little villa for the same price. And I look at him quite perplexed, taken aback, and thunderstruck: get rid of your paradise? And he nods: I know of a little villa for sale. And taking me by the arm, he drags me to the street over there in the fields . . . that unfinished street, you know, which is an outpost of the town of the 2 mills extended into the middle of the fields around termuren—and indeed there's an ugly hovel of a house standing empty: it's set slightly back, so that a large section on the adjoining house shuts off the front garden completely, robbing it of all sun and light . . . oh dear, how am I supposed to explain without drawing it? But the other three sides of that ugly house have windows, tall, narrow windows like top hats with glass inside, and there are tall narrow doors, tall narrow rooms, tall narrow walls with wallpaper on which an ugly flower winds its crooked way upwards. In a word: appalling, a dark, appalling cave of a tomb. And while we are standing there in that empty, gloomy, damp hole, I still couldn't believe it and I asked: is it really this house that you mean? It's this little villa, says the music master with the straightest, most unperturbed face in the world. And would you convert it into a more habitable house? I ask. And he looks round us in surprise, to see what may be missing, or what renovation might be necessary. What do you mean, convert? Not at all—with a bit of nice wallpaper on the wall and a lick of paint on the door, I think it'll be fine.

And now I'll ask You, says mossieu colson from the ministry . . . now I'll ask you whether you understand anything about people anymore, when you can't even understand the music master.

BLOODY HELL

Ondine charged out of her father's house . . . She walked and walked right down chapel road past the four villas: oh, so it was impossible to trick god and come to an arrangement with him: he always drew the longest straw—and she couldn't forget that he was the master, the complete master, and had her under his heel completely, indiscriminately, as much and as badly as anyone else. It seemed to her that god himself had committed a sin by revealing the truth to a madwoman. And she wept, wept bitterly there in chapel road. It all seemed so senseless to her, the whole business of life and death and those ghosts, ghosts of the as-yet-unborn or already dead, electricity and politics and the war that was coming . . . and she wanted it to come, certainly she wanted there to be war soon and the world to go up in flames. But what good did cursing do her? It doesn't get me anywhere, she thought . . . because after that war there will Still be someone to cause me problems—I must think, I must try and find a way of shutting up that madwoman. But as she went on, with a heart pierced from all sides, she realized what she had to do: shutting her mother up was not the right thing to do, but exactly the opposite: she should spread it around everywhere that her mother, oh dear, was going downhill, now she's saying there are babies in our toilet! But . . . suppose they started looking. Suppose that some idiot, some brainless fool (valeer for instance) was capable of squeezing his fat head through the opening of the toilet, and they found a tiny skeleton? And in her imagination she saw the little innocent skeleton of a baby that had only lived a few hours . . . and at the same time she wondered whether such a child could have any skeleton to speak of? . . . and wouldn't the immature bones have been consumed more quickly in that case? She didn't know. She could say only one thing: bloody hell. Bloody hell, she repeated again and again, she kept saying it till she reached the front door of the pub by the 1st grimy houses, till she got inside the house where valeer was snuggled in a corner with little judith on his knee—because though he wobbled his fat head through life, argued with oscarke and said that nothing was worthwhile, that everything was hot air and lies and deceit and delusion—but he was human too, he needed affection and friendship: he had a heart in his chest like everyone else, not a block of ice. No one knew what he did for sex, he didn't talk about women, he never left the house, he didn't talk about that time long ago when he had wandered through the fields with cousin maria (or later, when like a poor starving man he had stared at her lighted window, behind which the fat lollipop held her in his arms—he didn't talk about it). Perhaps he didn't even think of those days. Perhaps the days fell from him like dead leaves from a tree—and what one had to call his affection, the grain, the spark that he'd been given in life and that smoldered in his ribcage: he gave it all to judith. He held his hands over her eyes in play, his fingers were soldiers advancing over the front of her eyes . . . he'd played that same game with cousin maria's children, and it was pretty much the only thing he could do to amuse children—to amuse himself—but if cousin maria's children were frightened of his advancing fingers and had to lower their eyes, judith didn't react at all: she looked straight at his fingers without blinking. And after he had repeated the game countless times, and chuckled quietly about it, he was suddenly seized by the fear that there might be something wrong with her sight . . . oh, and how touchingly he fussed over her, and was tormented by the thought that it was his fault if this child turned out to be Blind. Bloody hell, ondine came home muttering under her breath, and valeer rushed to meet her: judith is blind, I think! She stood dumbly watching the finger game, which he started playing again to show her—she hated god for having betrayed the secret between them to a madwoman, and she hated him doubly now for having made her child blind . . . she hated him because he punished her as if she was just anyone, as if she were just another quite ordinary bitch of a woman. Bloody hell, it went on drumming in her, reverberating deep and loud. But the upshot was that little judith was about as blind as you or I: the doctor laughed at them: her reactions may be a bit slower, he said, but that doesn't mean a thing. He doesn't know what he's talking about, was all valeer said . . . and he smirked derisively and retreated into his . . . well, what could you call it? into his "bloody hell"?

SOMEWHERE IN EUROPE

I read your published letter from tippetotje, says andreus mottebol . . . the letter where she writes that she'd like to do a painting in her new studio of the rats that are gnawing away at our society—and by chance I saw something in a film that has more or less the same theme: it was about abandoned children somewhere in europe. And in my view for the umpteenth time it was once more too much film and too little art, it was too reasoned and constructed to be art . . . and to my taste it was also too much of a melodrama, and also too much of a good thing, and there was a moral tacked on at the end . . . I don't like works of art that start preaching at the end, showing that drunkenness is the root of all social evils in the world, or where the socially aware heroes start a new society in which everyone becomes perfectly content and happy. But what was so cruelly beautiful in the film, what I found compelling and reminded me of tippetotje's rat painting, were the children who in some scenes were depicted as vermin, as ravens in the fields, as rats among the ruins. I know tippetotje meant with her painting that man himself is destroying himself and that finally the rats will leave the sewers to become the lords of all creation . . . that they will squirm and writhe in the appallingly empty rooms and houses and streets . . . that they will sit there with their gleaming beady eyes and their scrofulous skin, with their filthy coats and bare tails, on the thrones where purple-clad cardinals and popes sat, on the throne where kings and tyrants now sit . . . in the cradles where our children now sleep, opposite paintings torn to pieces and manuscripts gnawed straight through. That was what tippetotje meant, but in the film the children themselves were like rats: somewhere in europe houses had been bombed, and the occasional child was left . . . somewhere in europe men and women were dragged off, herded onto trucks and crammed into trains, shot down and raped, gassed and burnt in camps and ovens . . . and only the occasional child, cat, and dog were able to escape. The children wandered around, met each other and grew into a gang . . . it's true that their clothes gradually became rags, rags and scraps of cloth with rips in them, but that wasn't so important: the most important thing for them was to satisfy their hunger and thirst. And they descend on a pond, a pool, a stream, like a flock of starlings . . . They snatch a loaf of bread somewhere and the whole gang of them tears it into crumbs . . . they kill a horse by the roadside, they steal the raw vegetables from the fields. And look, they flock onto the fields like a murder of crows, and people actually shoot at them just as they do at a murder of crows . . . and so they hurriedly take flight, croaking, as ravens do—or they're by a farmhouse, a village pounded to ruins, an old mansion, and they creep round it like vermin . . . they advance on it, like crafty rats, with their beady eyes and filthy hairless tails, Night falls and in the darkness they creep closer with their gleaming eyes . . . they creep in through cracks and holes, they descend into cellars, slip up the stairs, or slide down the banisters . . . they squirm over the charred beams and fill the nooks and crannies. And all this in search of anything useful: like rats they steal what might be useful. And people shoot at them at random because they are harmful vermin, somewhere in Europe, when there was a war on.

That's how I saw the film . . . and with a heavy heart I remembered tippe-totje's painting . . . and I remembered, as if a penny were suddenly dropping, that you were thinking of adding the life and history of the gang of jan de lichte to your story: and I thought that you should depict that gang of thieves as being like a pack of scavenging rats, looking for something, anything, in the flanders of 1750—and that you should describe modern society on the other hand as another pack of rats, but all-consuming, in search of whatever can be destroyed, here in this world of 1950.

IT'S SELLING LIKE HOTCAKES!

Master oedenmaeckers shakes his head and says: it's not in this world that rats are gnawing away, it's in your mind—in your mind it's as if rats gnaw tunnels right through our hospitals and our asphalt-covered squares, right through our carefully designed gardens, our children's cribs, our statues, right through our museums, our uranium mines and our parliament. But in reality it's man—if he still deserves the name—who sits down at the base of the smashed statue, and with a heart growing ever colder sees the others abandoning themselves to bread and circuses . . . to bread and circuses, I say . . . but it's not so much bread and circuses, it's much more human flesh rather than bread that people lust after: now they're all like savages dancing round the victim they're about to devour, like christ who taught us to eat his flesh and drink his blood, like the executioners and torturers of the middle ages, like the fanatical monks of the inquisition, like the concentrations camps where lampshades were made out of human skin. It's not so much the game, the chase that people want . . . but they have a passion, a positive obsession, with seeing the triumph of the strongest . . . it's an almost morbid nostalgia to see the struggle from the jungle fought out again in all its horror: the one who can defeat and crush the most is the victor, and he'll be crowned with flowers. It's not the story of the first cave dweller who held out a helping hand to his fellow human being that resonates with modern man, but the story of cain and abel, who have dashed each other's brains out over and over again throughout history.

And meanwhile the rare human being still worthy of the name sits apathetically at the base of the shattered statue, in the doorway of an art gallery, by the dusty entrance of a deserted library—he sits there and erroneously imagines he hears the rats gnawing, occasionally thinks he sees a hairless tail slipping away, or a pair of beady eyes staring at him. And I can't stand your writing about that because it hurts me too much. Look, yesterday I was in the town of the 2 mills, looking for a book I'd heard about . . . I may have been the only person in the town of the 2 mills looking for a book . . . and I discovered one of the increasingly rare bookshops in town, and they'd painted right across the window: our prices are ridiculous! And I couldn't help but laugh: so one really has to set such a low price on a book, an absurd price, if one wants to sell it. But not finding what I wanted, I went on, to another, even more pitiable bookshop, and there I found a going-out-of-business sale and on the shop window it said: selling like hotcakes! And again I couldn't help but laugh, because it almost meant that they were throwing books at you for free (because that's the only way for books to sell like hotcakes), but alas, despite the window, I saw books lying around under a thick layer of dust: they were hotcakes but somehow they couldn't get out of the shop, they'd bounced off the shop window and fallen back into the display cabinet where they gradually gathered dust . . .

And you reply: I could write a very funny story about that, master oedenmaeckers . . . but unfortunately my laughter would stick in my throat, because again I would hear the rats gnawing right through the display cases with their Ridiculous Prices. Hotcakes! . . . yes, but it's not the books, it's our strength, our faith and hope and love, that are gradually being consumed . . . and it's the rats that tunnel their way through them.

WILL THEY SPIT ON OUR GRAVES?

You spoke to me about henry miller, mossieu colson from the ministry says to you . . . you spoke about him to me as a great writer, an astonishing product of this confused age, who makes books the way we make cars and flying saucers and h-bombs . . . appalling things that force you to clutch in boundless dismay at both your head and your heart: will something, you ask, emerge from all this that brings mankind a little happiness, or will it on the contrary put an end to his existence? And henry miller goes on writing, and goes on talking about things he fails to understand: about going under and being shipwrecked and foundering . . . about being driven, and colliding with whatever happens to be drifting past one: a wreck, a ship in distress, an abandoned child, a man of our time. Only woman counts, and the pleasure one derives from her . . . only reeling around drunk, reveling in intoxication, and living blind to the general doom—and don't talk to him about the sense and meaning of this existence, because meaning is something that has no meaning for him (it would be the same as talking to the rats and vermin about proportion, form, and line), for a rat of a man only money has any value, and getting women is the only goal. Sometimes he mentions the names of christ and immanuel kant, sometimes he says he's read a bit of dostoyevsky, has seen something by rembrandt, heard something by beethoven—but it's obscure and incomprehensible and all too distant from him—it may be painted on canvases or written down in books, but for rats digging tunnels it has no point and no meaning: they go on digging their own way, right through the books and paintings of mankind. Anyhow, if people have written books before him, he writes them too, and his are just as important—they make as much noise as Beethoven, and proclaim prophecies as important as christ's, and hoot as loud as cars, and are just as dangerous as the h-bomb. And henry miller walks among them all and opens his hands wide and picks it all up, the way one scoops up sand, or water, or manna from heaven, and throws it into his books: it's a grandiose spectacle. No flowers grow in his books, and no birds sing . . . it's appalling . . . but we don't know whether it's to the advantage or disadvantage of man to concentrate on the weeds, the cars along the concrete highways, the rats, the uranium mines, and the h-bomb. It is possible that in years to come his books will be stigmatized because they helped hasten our downfall . . . but it's just as possible that they'll be recognized as a warning to us on our way downhill . . . or again it's possible too that they're just a testimony: This is how it was.

And now, mossieu colson of the ministry continues . . . now I've read another forbidden writer—I spit on your graves, is what he called his book—and it's said that he competes with miller, is spoken of in the same terms, is assigned as great a value or regarded as just as dangerous . . . and I read what he wrote, and it's just a bit of pornography. And so I come to the astonishing discovery that even in these matters people can't distinguish between a message, a cry of distress, and a dance on the smoking ruins . . . to today's world they're all the same: but something is either pornography or it isn't: the message of henry miller, or the spitting-on-our-graves of his colleague, or the attractions of paris-soir: they are all exactly the same pornography.

SOMEWHERE IN EUROPE . . . WITH ONDINE

There followed a sad time for ondine: oh, the days when my children were little! she sometimes said, later, when things were better for her and she could look down—look back—with a smile at all that had transpired, on her old sadness and joy and sunshine and new sadness, joy, and sunshine. She had a hernia and needed an operation, but couldn't have one with the child, the third one, she was expecting. And after it was born, and christened marie-louise—because it was becoming fashionable among the bourgeoisie to give their children a double name (or perhaps it had been fashionable for a long time, and it had only now got through to her that it was fashionable, just like it got through that it was fashionable to resign yourself to saying: I belong to the bourgeoisie . . . as if the bourgeoisie were Everything), and so she chose a bourgeois name, because she herself had acquired the small soul of a bourgeois. And after marie-louise was born, she finally had to have the operation: but she didn't do it straightaway, she started wearing a truss first. This was to some extent doctor goethals's fault, since he was old fashioned and didn't want to hear about ultramodern things like operations and such: operating is just butchery, he said. And in addition the abdomen had always been a dark cellar to him. But no one worried about seeing things from oscarke's point of view: what kind of life was there left for him among the piss-soaked diapers, which were obviously never going to disappear from the house, and which had already, as it were, become a permanent part of his worldview? The same as living with a woman who was always saying: be careful, you know I'm in pain. No, he no longer saw the exterior of things, no longer saw What for other men was all-important: a woman's belly—what did that mean to him now? A dark basement, a membrane that could be torn, beyond which hung intestines. Just look at that, that truss! And he was disgusted, he no longer touched her, he Couldn't love a truss and a length of intestines. She didn't understand . . . she understood the world and its people, but pride prevented her from achieving self-knowledge: she couldn't see, or perhaps refused to see, that she was getting old: in her own eyes she was still the girl who'd shown him her breasts in the doorway of a slated house. But apart from that, the doctor's words were like chloroform to her . . . yes, he didn't operate on her, but he did put her to sleep, he calmed her fears, and gave her a trump card by saying that she had to get a lot of rest: when she was lazy, on long, dark mornings after oscarke had gone to work, and she thought of her mother over there repeating day in and day out to anyone who'd listen: look in the toilet . . . and as a result life was empty and frightening, she stayed in bed and told herself that her tummy was hurting again. Meanwhile the children were turning the place upside down, playing "house," or "shopping" (and judith would want to be shopkeeper, and miraculously mariette agreed at once and came to the "shop," behaving like a real lady, tasting a bit of jam and a sugar lump . . . the piece of apple and the bacon that judith had been given by uncle valeer, but had hidden away to play "shopping" with . . . and afterwards, when mariette had bought everything, and eaten everything up, and also, like her mother, hadn't paid—then judith realized that she'd been cheated), and judith would start crying because she was always letting herself be outsmarted by mariette, and as she cried she said: I'll tell uncle valeer . . . as if uncle valeer was somehow a lord of heaven and earth, a god whose right it was to punish and deprive. But what was uncle valeer in mariette's eyes? Someone with a fat head who came and sat in a corner and muttered to himself incessantly hour after hour, or sat on the toilet hour after hour coughing and gazing at his crippled hand that only had a thumb and three fingers on it. I'll tell uncle valeer! cried judith—and mariette squatted in the corner, and coughed and looked at her hand, raising three fingers and a thumb. And ondine, who was watching them from the bed, was convulsed with laughter, so that her belly bobbed up and down under the blankets and started hurting again—so that she first laughed and then started yelling at the children, whose names she kept mixing up . . . especially the second one, their mariette who was imitating uncle valeer there . . . or was that judith after all? Oh, and anyway, it didn't matter what her name was. At any rate she was ondine: even if they had called her jack of spades she would still have made sure she was an ondine—but that second child, she was going to be a new ondine, she already outdid the eldest, and pulled out all her hair . . . she wasn't fully grown yet but she was already kicking the chairs, and flinging things around in rage. Some days ondine could laugh at it, but the next day she would lash out, till both of them, mother and daughter, fell over: hardhead! she called the girl accusingly . . . and then she hit that head as though it were made of wood. And out of pure habit she hit it once when oscarke was home: are you going mad? he asked—there he was again with that appalling question. It was quite possible that she'd inherited something from her mother, but no one had the right to blame her for it: her lips took on a blue sheen, while her face on the other hand went gray . . . she stood with her back to the wall, and with her head thrust forward she leapt on oscarke and hit him, hit mariette again, hit judith who had done nothing wrong, and even kicked the wooden cot where marie-louise was lying. I'm going to drown myself! she said. So am I! said oscarke. And both of them left, in different directions . . . but when she came back late in the evening, a little drunk, she found him already at home: he was sitting weeping among his weeping children.

Yes, it was like she said later on: oh, the days when my children were little!

AN ATTACK

I live by the side of my baron and am in my studio, writes tippetotje in a new letter to you . . . but I don't do any painting: how can that be? I convince myself I'd rather write something to you, about any old thing, maybe about the gang of jan de lichte . . . I imagine that you're describing an attack on the mail coach: and I imagine the passengers as two war profiteers, a squire with a wooden face and a harelip, two french soldiers of louis XV, a notary, a sad little man of the kind you're so good at describing, plus an unbelievably beautiful woman. They're talking about the war, which enables them to earn lots of money, and they're also talking about the ever-increasing plague of the out-of-work, the homeless, the destitute, the soggiest strata of society. The unappealing little man with his melancholy face and drooping moustache, the kind you're so fond of describing, is sitting opposite the strangely beautiful woman . . . stretching out his little arms, which are far-too-short, saying that all these pariahs by the roadside should be rounded up: they're a plague just like rats are a plague, and they can only be gotten rid of with poison. And he asks whether it wouldn't be possible to distribute free food by the roadside: soup, for example, with rat poison in it? And look, as his little eyes sparkle and he tries to spread his far too short arms, all-embracing, all-consuming, all-exterminating . . . the impossibly beautiful woman has let her clouded eyes wander over her own body, from her bare powdered shoulders, over the wide skirts, down to her low-buckled shoes. She notices that the left buckle has slipped out of its fastener and bends towards her foot . . . she bends very deeply and tries to refasten the buckle. And the unappealing little man, quite by accident, is leaning over her corset . . . his gaze falls, falls very deep into this opened chasm—and he spreads his arms even wider, and asks why these proliferating vermin aren't kept somewhere in a forest . . . our forests are wide and deep enough to herd them together into an almost inaccessible place. And while his darting hands wander to and fro across her cornucopia . . . sinking into it with his gleaming beady eyes . . . he reaches a previously unknown state of rapture. It's no longer conscious speech, it's a delirium, the feverish disgorging of confused sounds and words . . . he talks of hunting down vermin in the most inaccessible places, of hanging them from the trees, incinerating them in ovens . . . he describes how they would be branded on their bare shoulders, how they . . . And while his mouth now produces only confused sounds, his little hands open and close convulsively. And while the woman tries to get her shoe buckle into the fastener, and he bends a teeny bit further over her corset, he tells them how in spain, in the house of a grandee, there's a chair covered with the skin of a young, beautiful nun: her contours have been perfectly preserved, and it's extraordinarily perturbing to sit on it. But however much she bends forward, the lovely young woman can't manage to fasten the shoe buckle . . . and so she raises her left foot, and brings it high up on her right knees, and her fingers seize the recalcitrant buckle like hungry snakes. The squire goes pale—in his long wooden face the harelip becomes a purple, trembling wound. The notary feels a pounding pain in his temples . . .

And then, at that moment, we here a bellowing voice and the Report of pistols: the gang of jan de lichte appears. I'll close my letter, and don't know if it will be of any use to you in your book.

THE MADMAN OF WORTEGHEM

Polpoets comes to see you from his so-called villa, to grin and bare his 2 gold teeth at your desk: I'm not going to worry my head about understanding the point and the meaning of your book on chapel road . . . you've got other characters for that, the erudite professor spothuyzen, the omniscient dr mots, the totally skeptical sickwit the student . . . but to my polpoetish gratification I see that in the margins of your pages there are still people present who live on the margins of society. I see that you're still describing the pepperpot and his nocturnal sorties, I see you're still writing about tippetotje, who's managed to bag herself a baron . . . it's just that you're being a bit gruesome, in the most recent pages there are too many rats slithering around, giving me the creeps . . . and also it's too much like henry miller, you know, in whose world there's never a tree growing or a bird singing. Right, and that's why I'm glad I can smile and bare my 2 gold teeth occasionally, and sprinkle some humor on the tails of your rats. Tippetotje writes about that unappealing little man who goes to pieces at the sight of an exotically beautiful woman, and under her spell starts imagining a kind of concentration camp . . . right, I accept that you can't make a silk purse out of a sow's ear, garbage in, garbage out . . . but let me have a go at writing something, let me address the dear reader of your book. The thing is that in my yellowing archives I've discovered a certain jan cottenier, who lived and loved by the side of jan de lichte, just as I live and love at your side . . . and next to whose name a nickname is given: the madman of worteghem. Ha, and I'll tell your dear reader that he must take a good look at this madman of worteghem: the moment has come for you to smack your lips, dear reader, because the character we're about to present has been a favorite subject for all writers . . . a character that provides you with comic relief: a madman who, amid the horrors, the murders, the rats, and the book-burning, among the degeneration and the disorientation, the h-bomb and the authorized and certified terrors, has to provide some diversion. The fool who, after each of the writer's sermons, will have some comic remark to blurt out, will have to let out a fart, or do something similar, the sort of thing that we all appreciate so much. In one book it will be a cross-eyed character who sees everything doubled, and in another book some stutterer who can't pronounce a certain letter . . . sometimes it'll be someone with a stoop, some-times an out-and-out hunchback. And the reader, having been edified by the fine words about drunkenness and nonattendance at sunday mass, which are of course the causes of all social ills . . . or having had his knuckles rapped for having the descriptions of things in books that were on the contrary written to prevent him from straying from the straight and narrow . . . the reader will then be allowed to laugh for a change at the comic antics of the madman of worteghem. That's the way to get dogs to stand on their hind legs, lure chil-dren to some deserted spot, or get half a country eating out of your hands. But we, dear reader, who still dare to smile and bare our 2 gold teeth in a place where everyone is pale with deference and respect, we have no lump of sugar in our hand . . . we can't promise you that the madman of worteghem won't fart and make you burst out laughing now and then, but we're a different type of humorous narrator. And sticking our nose a little deeper in yellowing folio volumes, we discover that that madman of worteghem was able to escape the justice of his time—that he started from the premise that though the law may have a long arm, it also has legs that are far too short. And on the day of judgment (which in the gang's case was the day when there was a gen-eral manhunt, and everyone caught wandering the roads was grabbed by the scruff of the neck and dragged to the gallows), he was nowhere to be found. So, a madman, but a shrewd one. And thanks to his shrewd tricks we've been left a fleeting portrait of him: 5 feet tall, quite fat, black hair and beard, long-legged. You see, dear reader, long-legged! And let the writers make me a cross-eyed sucker, thinks the madman . . . let them have me see everything double, or pronounce some letter or other incorrectly . . . I smile at them and bare my 2 gold teeth: I laugh, but I laugh last and longest.

A PENNY SAVED IS A PENNY EARNED

Judith and mariette slept in valeer's bed, valeer who'd become a manservant (oh, that had been a merry dance when valeer was about to go: judith clung to him and showered him with kisses: hold my hand again, uncle valeer! . . . and then, give me another kiss, uncle valeer! . . . and when he'd finally gone she cried and sobbed and fell asleep still crying, and called out to him in her sleep), and valeer only came home on sunday afternoons. He had the afternoon off, but didn't know what to do with himself, and so just hung around: no longer at home in ondine's place and not really at home in that rich mansion, not at home anywhere, he would just sit there nodding his fat head with little judith on his knee, starting arguments with oscarke, saying things he didn't really mean or understand . . . oh, and that oscarke didn't really mean or understand either. They started arguments because they couldn't just sit there without talking to one another: why else did people have tongues? But the point was that they couldn't use those tongues as they should have, or else they couldn't use their brains properly while those tongues were wagging. And so oscarke sometimes said precisely what valeer had wanted to say . . . and valeer replied that it wasn't true and said exactly what oscarke had wanted to say. And then they would quarrel and couldn't stand each other: god, there sure are some dumb people around! said oscarke. And having tired himself out quarreling, valeer went to bed. But where are you going? asked ondine . . . where are you going to sleep tonight? Well, in my bed, valeer replied sheepishly and without realizing that he had no bed there anymore, that the children now slept in it. Sleep in that armchair! said ondine, although that was another problem, because then where was their marie-louise going to sleep? The sunday afterwards it was the same story, and the sunday after: valeer stopped coming. Still, that armchair wasn't ideal for the child—true, it was pushed up against the wall on one side, and on the other a couple of other chairs had been lodged against it, but it frequently happened that the girl was found in the morning suspended between armchair and wall . . . or on the floor between two chairs. Oh, they absolutely had to buy a bed, but what Didn't they need to buy? They already had three children, but were still using the same junk she'd had when she was first married. So where did her money go? She didn't know: it poured through her fingers, oscarke brought in some and valeer brought in some and in her pub she earned almost as much as the two of them put together . . . and yet she never had a centime in the house. It was like doctor goethals said: no sooner will you have it in your hand than it'll go out again—but what could she do about it? Start saving for a house of her own? She made arrangements, she talked the landlord into letting her pay a little more on condition that the pub would eventually become her property . . . and she calculated, on days when the sun was in her heart, that it could be hers, her own pub by the 1st grimy houses, in about three years . . . but when she was in one of her depressions, and did her calculations then, well it might as well have been thirty years. And also, to tell the truth, she knew that saving wasn't in her blood . . . what was the point? Should she stop becoming a god, a god or a devil, just to step off her pedestal and scrape a few cents together, a few cents to gain possession of a heap of stones? But don't be silly, she told herself . . . buy a piggy bank like little kids do, she said with a laugh (a bitter laugh), but realizing that there was no other way to manage. And as always happened when she became convinced of the truth for a few hours, she started giving orders: she told oscarke that he had to start saving, and she told Judith—who was occasionally given a centime or two by friends or family—that she had to start saving too, and took the child's few cents away from her and put it in the piggy bank . . . but she always took it out the next day, of necessity. She needed some money the following week, and so emptied little judith's piggy bank. But valeer had to save, and oscarke had to save . . . and what they had scraped together they had to give to ondine, who spent it by the next morning.

WOESE THE NOTARY

Johan janssens, the poet and writer for the weekly papers, says to you: even if you're writing about a gang of thieves, you Still shouldn't forget about the social side of things . . . alongside the robber chieftain jan de lichte I would create another character, who I'd call, for example, woese the notary: I imagine this shark of a notary as a very polite and friendly old man in the carriage, with soft, sweet eyes and downy hands like the velvet on a pin cushion. And he would be constantly talking about the old faith and morality that are being lost . . . that the lower classes of society have a tendency to mock the church hierarchy and no longer fear the punishments of hell—that this tendency should be fought tooth and nail: one should expose the common people who no longer blindly obey authority to the severest penalties. And entwining his pudgy fingers he would add that for hundreds of years lewdness and vice had been the sole prerogative of the privileged classes . . . while they all had to be constantly on their guard to make sure that the masses remained within the bounds of decorum and decency. And with his sweet hands raised to heaven, woese the notary continues: but the common people, the soggiest strata of society, with their sickly skin and their clothes stiff with filth, they're no longer ashamed to turn their backs on our ancient faith and traditional morals! And while woese the notary is saying all this in such a masterly way, he would be glancing sweetly at the bare and powdered shoulders of the uncommonly beautiful woman—this sight wouldn't trouble him . . . he'd simply go on rubbing his downy hands together, and start to reveal that this was all part of The system: it's part of The system that the lower classes should reproduce excessively, since sex constitutes the only valve through which their excess pressures can be safely released . . . and it's first and foremost a hygienic necessity if they're to remain healthy and poor, because only by proliferating in this way can their sickliest elements be trampled underfoot by the stronger ones . . . and at the same time, while they're busy conducting a furious and bitter battle among themselves, they're powerless against the numerically inferior ruling classes. From their vast numbers we pick out the strongest specimens and set them to work. It would never have been possible otherwise to realize the great achievements of which our society is rightly proud: how else could we have built our cathedrals and noble castles? How else could we have transformed our forests into farmland? An abundant choice of human resources is part of the system: the poor must go on proliferating if the soil of this country, and the insides of our vaults, are to be made fertile with their young, their sweat, and their dung. And look, somehow or other these people always manage to put a few cents aside . . . and those few cents must always be taken from them, so that they plod on in poverty and according to the laws of our ancient faith and morality . . .

And if I let woese the notary expound all this—says johan janssens—then, afterwards, I would have the cruelly beautiful woman lift her knee very high in order to refasten her shoe . . . so that we see things under her skirt: the . . . whatever . . . towards which woese the notary stretches out his plump hands, his chubby fingers.

TWO WOMEN

And in the evenings your wife too sits with your book on her lap, reads sections and has her opinion about them . . . and in her opinion there are two many pages with cancers eating and rats gnawing at them. There should also be some women in your books who are not only beautiful and cruel, she says, but who are beautiful and also courageous—like me, she thinks to herself. And she imagines a pub, lost among the fields and somewhere on the edge of the woodland, which has the appropriate name of "the lost cave of hunger." And there a meeting of thieves and tramps and beggars is convened, and two women come in: they quickly shut the door and shake off the chill of the night—a little while ago, in the lane, you heard them chattering away, but now they're as silent as a grave, hanging their scarves on a nail by the door and brushing their lovely, luxurious hair. One would have the name anne-marie de clerk, an angel, a devil, a woman: cruelly beautiful and terribly dangerous . . . young and passionate, but coming from aeltert. And, see, the name of that village would make the men draw back the hands which they'd stretched out in lust: ow, from aeltert, where there's first a knife fight for every girl who's turned fourteen: the quickest knife wins the prettiest girl. And this strikes them as only fair: so anne-marie became the sweetheart of simon ysenbaert: woe to the bastard who became horny at the sight of this heifer, woe to the soldiers of louis XV who tried to assault her. She knows this. Wherever she goes her eyes blaze at the men, her breasts provoke them, her coal black hair—scorching hot—wafts into their faces, its smell paralyzes them and makes them helpless: oh, you . . .! the men stammer in dismay, and they have to clench their fists deep in their trouser pockets. She laughs, hoarse and mocking—she knows that three murders have been committed for her sake.

The other woman too is not exactly ugly (your wife says to you): I'd describe her as fresh-faced and blonde, and give her sweet eyes . . . but eyes rather like the eyes of a chattering bird, like trien the whore in fact—trien would also be her name, catherine van den haute—a sweet girl who a few years later will be sentenced for consorting with thieves and criminals . . . and when that happens, she'll start weeping. But whether she'll feel remorse and start screaming, or remain stubborn and proud like anne-marie de clerk, it boils down to the same thing . . . they'll still be our own women, lovely and luxuriant like flowers, stripped naked and having their backs torn open. If a person were to know all this beforehand there probably would have been another war about it. But anyway, there they are in "the hunger": two flaming flowers, two wild, sprouting, and blooming thistles, a world of unexpressed thoughts seething and bubbling deep inside them . . . a world of centuries-old hate, they don't even know against whom . . . against every damn thing and person, the kings with their powdered purses and the cardinals with their holy water . . . against the stone saints that people had the audacity to hold up as examples . . . against the people who never ever got horny or drunk . . . against the people who never felt hunger gnawing in their stomachs or were never rejected anywhere, who were never wet with rain or blue with cold and were never refused a warm fire . . . against the strangers who took them by force and threw them on the ground, one sunday evening, in the dance hall . . . against the eternal dogs who always lick the hand that strikes them, and yet are cruel and cowardly enough to bite the other dogs stumbling along beside them. But I wouldn't have them just express all this in words . . . because it would hurt, inside their heads, if they had to put such things into words. No, the main thing is that they be included—that they live in your books—that creatures roam through your pages who are women, who are beautiful, and who are courageous.

And when your wife stops talking, you add: and who are like you.

THE DEATH OF BRYSKE[1]

Oscarke had to save, and give the money he saved to ondine . . . but she, no, if she had some money on the first of the month she would spend it on a hideous vase— which she thought was beautiful because it cost her so much. But in so doing she made oscarke's life hell: he couldn't care less what she did with her money, for the simple reason that he had no notion of what money was—bank notes were strange birds, difficult to catch and immediately flying off again, as far as he could tell—but it never occurred to him to earn lots of money: it was something that just wasn't part of his life. Vases and sculptures, though, were, since he was still under the delusion that he was a sculptor, that he would one day be able to carve his dreams in stone: he would sit all evening looking at that monstrosity grimacing at him from a shelf, wondering what on earth it could have been in ondine that had enabled her to seduce him when they were young: she had No taste, she had no idea what was beautiful or ugly, and so in a certain sense she had deceived him when she'd talked about emotional and spiritual things. But she couldn't stand to hear this, she insisted the vase was beautiful, that oscarke was the one who didn't understand what beauty was: something that cost so much and was on the mantelpiece in every rich person's home . . . had he ever been to a rich person's home? No, he hadn't, but that didn't mean anything . . . it just proved that the rich had no taste either: and don't talk to me about them, I know who they are, that crowd who come and drink in the pub. And then they quarreled about that: not about the vase costing too much when they badly needed other *things, but because it was ugly, and especially because the rich had no taste. Do the socialists have taste then? she kept asking, whether it was relevant or not—and he replied with something equally irrelevant: and again they were back in the endless loop where people gossiped and argued about things they didn't understand—so that oscarke fell silent and thought that everyone who had a tongue that couldn't be controlled by their brain was a nitwit. And he forgot that the same applied to him . . . oh, he forgot that it was especially true of him: he saw this grave fault in others so easily because it was his own grave fault. But, was it actually true that those kinds of vases and sculptures and knickknacks were in all of the rich people's homes? Apart from monique, who after all was only a bourgeois, and apart from the castle,*

---

[1] This is not about the death of mr brys from the ministry, who unless he dies first has a long life ahead of him . . . but about the other mr brys, who was one of the first socialists, and whose story takes place in the early 1900s, shortly before the first world war.

where she'd spent a few weeks when she was young (and which in those winter months had been more or less empty), ondine had never really penetrated into those patrician mansions herself—and so a rich person's house was something that only existed in her imagination. Since whenever she went to pass on the tidbits of information that she'd picked up here and there (not only to serve the greater good, but also for her own benefit), and spread her intrigues over the town like a net, she was still never admitted into their sanctums: she had to wait in chilly anterooms.

The same thing happened when she brought the latest news to the derenancourts: bryske had been found along chapel road drowned in a canal. He'd probably been drunk again—and the socialist party was going to give him a civil funeral. He'd given his whole life to the party, so it was impossible to speak of him as an ordinary person: he was a piece of history, and to talk of bryske was to talk of the cooperative. And now, after his death, the party still claimed him as theirs: he was a lifeless shell, the pole for a flag that was of no further use and that would have been put in the attic of party headquarters, if he wouldn't have started stinking up there—sure, he had stolen all the co-op's money, but they pretended it wasn't true, they delivered leaflets door to door in which he was praised to the skies as a man who'd died in the service of his ideals. They made speeches about him, but they were banned, they got broken up by the gendarmes: they publicized him as being the first corpse to be buried in the little town of the 2 mills without a church ceremony—because although they wrote that religion was a private matter, they knew that the church was their most powerful and underhanded enemy. The church wanted a world of servility, but they wanted a world of freedom . . . and there was much to be said, much to be argued about between those two opposing views, though it remained an issue that couldn't be resolved through reason alone: it remained an emotional matter. And emotion, what was that? The priests did the rounds of bryske's family to try to prevent him from having a civil funeral: after all, hadn't he been a christian all his life? But the socialists rightly pointed out that in the past the priests had refused him communion. Both sides clung to brys's body, and the band of the 1st socialists decided to accompany him to the cemetery, to bury him without holy water or anything of the sort. Ondine sat in the anteroom at mr achilles's place—there wasn't a fire, and it was cold, but she didn't feel it, there was a fire burning inside her: most probably it was a sickness, this hatred of the reds, it was abnormal, for there wasn't a single reason for her to be so down on them; but she was against them, just because, for no good reason, just like oscarke was in favor of them, and just like valeer was indifferent. She talked about the death of bryske and gradually, imperceptibly, became more and more excited—she had hated him, him and the cooperative and the band that was going to bury him: how dreadful, to bury a human being without calling on the Lord, without doing anything to help him rest in peace . . . although she couldn't care less whether he rested in peace or not . . . oh, on the contrary, she begrudged his resting in peace, because if the priests had managed to purloin him from the socialists, that would have stuck in her throat too, then she would have thought it scandalous that a socialist was being admitted to heaven. Something must be done to stop it, she said . . . something, yes, but what? You had a brilliant idea with st . . . with what's-his-name, said achilles: think about bryske and come back. But the fact was that she didn't feel like leaving right away, she sat her plucking her top lip, knowing that he was looking at her . . . so that it was impossible to keep her mind on the dead bryske. He sat and looked at her—and what was he thinking of? what things from the past was he remembering. . . was he happy? wasn't he just a little bit sorry that he hadn't married her? And it didn't occur to her that while they were sitting there together that he might still desire her . . . and the thought that she might still desire him was inconceivably distant from her, she might as well desire valeer who was washing dishes somewhere in the house. It stinks to high heaven, she said . . . a funeral without god . . . they might as well have a manure spreader come, since without god they're just planting some fertilizer in the ground. She'd been sitting staring at the floor, chin in hand, and suddenly she looked up: a manure spreader? Could we ask a farmer to put a faulty tap on his manure tank and drive a few meters in front of the band? And so they decided to ask a farmer who lived some ways beyond termuren: he came to clear out her cesspit in the pub by the 1st grimy houses: she helped him, she opened her doors and let her floor get dirty . . . but she didn't stay to clean the floor afterwards: she had to get out to see the funeral. First, a hundred meters or so ahead, the manure spreader, spilling its liquid, creating an almighty stench along the street . . . and behind it the band, and behind that the carriage with bryske on it draped in a red flag. They had a lot of fun over bryske's death: here and there one of their clique would be standing at his window laughing—and ondine, whose heart swelled with an almost voluptuous schadenfreude, said later that the musicians had been blowing so hard on their instruments, it was like they were trying to play the stench away.

THE DAMN PAGE

And suddenly bryske is standing in front of you—but it's only mr brys, the other character in your story, character and friend and colleague . . . and he stands there reading your report on the death of bryske—the other mr brys, who was one of the 1st socialists, and one of the 1st to have a civil funeral—and mr brys says: I can't say exactly why, but I've got something against that page: it jars me, it hurts me, I think you should take it out of your book . . .

And you reply soothingly: come now, mr brys . . . you too? Look here, when I had to give a reading from my work on the radio, I sent in this page about the death of bryske and it was rejected. Every week there's a mass on the radio, every week there's a sermon on the radio, and the 1st time when there's a description of a civil funeral, it's rejected. And so I sent the page to the most liberal magazine being published, which has established itself as an ark of the covenant dedicated to Free Expression, and at the top of my page I wrote: rejected for radio—and the magazine of Free Expression also rejected it. And so I sent the page to the most revolutionary and radical left-wing weekly that's ever appeared in this country, with the note: rejected for radio, rejected by the magazine of Free Expression—and they rejected it too!

And mr brys, trying to put his finger on what exactly in the death of bryske offended him so much, says: no, I tell you, there's a devil in this page, I can't make head or tail of it.

IT'S NOTHING

And andreus mottebol says to you: look, when I hear that tippetotje is going to start painting again, the urge to start again myself sneaks up on me. Sneaks up, I say, like a highwayman stalking an honest traveler, pouncing with a blackened face and wielding a knife: your money or your life! That's how the urge pounces and threatens me: paint or your life! I try to fool the urge . . . I tell it I first have to choose a subject: the courtyard of a prison perhaps . . . or no, a white hospital ward. And I try to imagine those 4 white walls, lines increasingly severe, colors increasingly sober . . . but it's impossible for me to be sober, always, always I'm too full of all the things my eyes have already seen, and I see my painting starting to fill up, starting to pulse with life. I see the white, deserted corridors (the word "corridors" has a solemn ring for the people of termuren, filled as they are with a fear of pain in its many forms, betraying their awe of death), I see the flowerpots on the windowsills, I smell the wisps of ether escaping from the operating room, and I also smell the polish that's spread copiously over the wooden floors . . . yes, and I see the plaster saints calmly opening their hands, and I see the nuns carrying thermometers and urine bottles in their hands with equal serenity. And I no longer know how to paint all that, unless I were to build an entire puppet theater, with wooden creatures moving woodenly inside. Can you see that world of wooden puppets? They're made of patches and scraps of cloth, their arms are far too long or their legs too short . . . they have stuffed balls for feet and botched, misshapen hands, and faces carved from wood. A nun with a sharply etched wooden face, wearing a pair of wire spectacles . . . and a nun with a fat, round face, with a dab of red paint on both cheeks. But again I'm too full of everything I see and hear . . . I hear noises, I hear whispering and laughing and weeping, I see many of the puppets recovering and going home, and I also see puppets who die and are put in wooden coffins. And it's no longer a painting, it's a novel. There in the second bed in the line lies a young puppet who thinks she doesn't have long to live—puppets can think this all they like, but that doesn't make it true—and in her fear of death she calls for a nun . . . the one with the sharp wooden face, with the wire glasses leering from it. And the young puppet in the bed expresses her fear, and says that as a puppet she has lived such a bad life: I've lived such a bad life, sister, and I'm so afraid. And the nun's wooden face opens and she too speaks: she says that it's nothing: it doesn't matter that you lived a bad life, jesus will forgive you, so you mustn't be afraid. But the puppet in the bed continues to struggle with her fear, and asks if she may confess the whole of her bad life to the nun . . . it becomes a faint, persistent whisper (something I'll tell you about another time, under another title), and amid the whispering one hears the same repeated response from the puppet dressed in a nun's habit: it's nothing, dear, it's nothing . . .

And then (this is turning into a novel that demands a satisfying ending . . . and so I'll give you the ending), although the puppet with the wire glasses said it was nothing, nothing at all, it Was something! Because the puppet in the bed doesn't die, doesn't die despite her fear and despite her confession . . . but all the nun-puppets stop speaking to the puppet in the second bed: the puppet with the wire glasses gave such a graphic account to them of her confession that they ignore the puppet in bed now and don't even deign to look at her, because she's lived such a bad life . . .

That's a good puppet story, andreus mottebol . . . and is there a moral attached, as with every good story? And andreus mottebol says, quite seriously, that there is: the story ends with a nice puppet moral: child, never confess the truth to anyone, not even when you think your last hour has struck.

THEOCRACY

So tippetotje writes to you to say she's bewildered that everyone becomes solemn and silent when they hear she's going to start painting again. And to tell the truth, that gives me an uncomfortable feeling . . . a feeling like I'm deceiving everyone, the feeling that someone has tied a solemn mask over my face, and that I'll sweat to death in it. And then I think of those men with their holy jesus faces who wander the world with their pamphlets on the kingdom of god—the watchman on the tower, the riders of apocalypse, tobias and the angel—and one of whom found his way into my place, into my studio. And wearing his clean-shaven mask he came to sell me the peace of the lord . . . and I looked at his mask with interest and asked if he wasn't sweating to death under it, as I usually do under mine at carnival time. And he said in reply that he sweats only under god's burden and out of fear of the horror that is about to be unleashed: it's written here, in st john's gospel, for sale at only 2 francs, that within 7 months and 7 days all mankind will be smitten with a flaming sword, and that only 7,000 of them shall behold the kingdom of god. And I asked if he'd never heard of democracy . . . because it struck me as rather fascist to lock millions and millions of people in the concentration camps of hell, cast them into eternal fire, run them through with a flaming sword . . . only in order to allow just a tiny elite to triumph. And I also said to him that it could only be weaklings who'd devise such a system, people who because of some weakness in their minds have never dared to live . . . who in their sick thoughts want revenge, and want to see everyone else in the world slaughtered with a flaming sword . . . that only the nazis, the weak, and the mentally ill can't imagine a world of freedom, equality, and brotherhood, but are filled instead with the desire for revenge and more revenge and the eternal gnashing of teeth. And he stared at me with his perplexing eyes in his serene mask, and said that they were not democrats but theocrats: the kingdom of god must be established here on earth, and a flaming sword must smite the sinners, and that only 7,000 . . .

And I slammed the door and was about to go on painting. But you see it was hard to go on painting, because despite everything, that spiel kept buzzing round in my head . . . I'm a woman, and occasionally I feel weak . . . and yes, I'd actually like to be one of those 7,000 who stand watching with a grin while the millions of others go into the mincing machines of hell. Say what you like, but I wouldn't like any monsters to pounce on me with their flaming swords while 7,000 others enter the kingdom of heaven with their holy jesus masks on. No, no, I want to be by their side, if only for that one day of revenge, and then seek seclusion and go on painting as if nothing has happened.

And believe it or not, later on that god-anointed fake calls again with his theocratic ideas, and I jump up and ask if I can be included in the list of the chosen. And he says that it's written in the gospel: within 9 months and 9 days, 90,000 will be saved. What do you mean, I ask . . . wasn't it within 7 months, and wasn't it 7,000? And he looks cautiously into the street, and holds his hand over his mouth so no one can hear, and says: yes, but in the meantime the theocrats have recruited lots more members.

WITHOUT FAITH SALVATION IS IMPOSSIBLE

So that day ondine went around and had to tell the story of bryske's funeral everywhere and to everyone, and she didn't get home till evening, almost the same time as oscarke: she said she wasn't feeling well, that her hernia was hurting again . . . and indeed, this was true, because of all that walking around and hardly resting for a moment, the lump in her groin had started bulging again. I'm going to the doctor, she said . . . although the doctor couldn't help her, and she was back so quickly that oscarke was doubtful whether she'd actually been to see him at all. I've got to rest, she said, just rest . . . and she went to bed: you clean the house for a change, oscarke, and look after the kids and cook some food. But she wasn't sick anymore the following day when she wanted to savor the spectacle of the townspeople who must still be congregating in little groups and discussing the bryske affair. But as she walked round she was upset to find that everything was continuing just as before: no sooner had something happened than it was forgotten: everyday something or other happened, and she would have to dream up something new for every hour of the day if she wanted to make an impression. People lived only for themselves: so bryske had died, oh well, ok, and so he'd been buried without a church ceremony, oh well, perhaps that was ok too—all right, there had been a bit of a commotion about their disposing of him like a dog, true, a socialist dog, draped in a red flag, but shouldn't everyone just do as they liked? It was only strange because it was the first time something like that had happened, but if there were a second or a third time, well, it would soon become a habit, a tradition, just as the church was a tradition now. Answers like that flabbergasted ondine: she tried in vain to remind people that there were ideals at stake!—and people agreed that one couldn't live without ideals, but it was equally true that one couldn't live on ideals. And ondine had the impression that our lord had died in vain for mankind: he hung there on his cross and had opened the gates of heaven—but heaven was something far off, something after death: these people were alive, they needed food to eat, a bed to sleep in, and someone in that bed to keep them warm. That was life—and no, they couldn't understand why ondine wore herself out for something that was so far off, and had no practical importance: they made sure that they had some warmth in life, and they also made sure they had some warmth in the hereafter by going to church, maybe putting something in the offertory box. Ondine swam against this tide, although day-by-day she was forced to experience the truth of their views . . . the bitter but necessary truth. And even that word "bitter" was redundant. It was natural that people should cling to the present, that they should meet the needs of the present . . . they would be meeting the needs of the future when it came. That all stood to reason—and whether bryske had himself buried with or without the church was up to him. And then someone made the very sensible comment: after all, he hadn't even been able to choose for himself, and probably god couldn't care less how they all had fought over his corpse, like dogs over a bone, or which dog had won: bryske would get his just desserts. But it was no good using logic with ondine, she couldn't bear other people's wisdom, she couldn't stand the fact that everyone had his own thoughts, and acted on them: she'd been brought up to believe that salvation was impossible without true faith. Man shall not live by bread alone, she said

. . . but that very day she had to go and buy bread like everyone else—and what was worse, others could afford that bread, and she could not: she had to go to a shop where she wasn't very well known and hunt for her money, finally saying in surprise that she'd forgotten it.

THE LAST NOOK

And while ondine has been brought up to believe that, without the one true faith, salvation is impossible, and her husband oscarke is becoming a small, frightened, skeptical socialist . . . Meanwhile the elections are gradually approaching and leaflets and manifestoes are being pushed under the doors of the 1st grimy houses. Ondine hastens to read the ones with a 3 on them, and confidently tears up the others, while oscarke reads them all, small and frightened, skeptical of everything. But while all this is going on, unnoticed by the people in the 1st grimy houses, may has arrived . . . the snowdrops will bloom and the wood anemones, the yellow broom will come and the fragrant lilacs . . . the fat snowballs will start to melt, and in their place will come orange blossom, with a scent so powerful you dare not go too close. And the music master hurries over the unmanned crossing, down the winding path into the country, straight to his bit of garden. And don't talk to me today about jan de lichte and his gang of thieves, he says . . . I know many years ago it was a purgatory and a hell here in flanders, with plague and smallpox and famine, with omnipotent lords of the manor and the domination of monastic orders. And don't talk to me about ondine and oscarke and the new elections either, where the issue is whether we're headed for a new age of omnipotent monastic orders and the domination of new lords of the manor. Keep quiet about that stuff for a second, for just one brief second—and instead take a walk with me, help me choose the spot I've been dreaming of to build my cottage: it doesn't have to be anything special, it can be made cheaply of wood and pebbles or concrete blocks . . . I'll drape some wild vines over it, blossoming flowers and creepers, which will hide the poor state of the building: none of that matters, as long as it's there and has a nice name: The Hunger perhaps, like the pub where jan de lichte's gang hid out, or Malpertuis, or the Lost Cave, or the Last Nook. I even know someone who on his garden gate wrote the words that dante saw on the entrance to hell: Abandon hope all ye who enter here. And the music master, wandering round his piece of earthly paradise, searching for the spot of his dreams, walks past the jasmine bush, not a branch of which has given any sign of life . . . past the weeping willow, which has some kind of disease and only grows a few wild shoots from its trunk . . . past the fir trees that were put there by mistake, in the spot that was actually intended for the poplars . . . past the cedar in mourning, and the apple trees that in may are still dormant . . . past the spot where the solitary fir tree stood that was chopped down by a christian in order to celebrate the birth of christ by stealing. And he can't he find the spot of his dreams anywhere: the most suitable spot is up there on the slope, but then he'd only have a view of the grimy houses on the unfinished road that runs through the fields—and if he goes further west he'll have no sun through his window, and if he goes east, a wonderful beech tree will wind up in the middle of his bedroom . . . a tree he'd have to uproot, the one tree that that really wants to be part of his garden, and that now stands there flaunting its dark red leaves. And finally the only place left is the one he doesn't want to use under any circumstances: it's the lowest part of his plot of land, where it's always wet and soggy, even now, in these may days . . . and where in winter there's a bog, a flooded miniature lake, a frozen river.

And the music master goes back down the winding country path over the unmanned crossing . . .There are problems everywhere, he says . . . taking the election manifestoes out of his mailbox, but thinking about his bit of earthly paradise . . . but I wouldn't want to live out there in that mess. There are problems everywhere, you reply . . . having already forgotten about his garden, and thinking of the elections . . . but I couldn't live in the shit of a pro-monarchist government, armed with guns and clubs.

A FAIRY TALE FOR MAY DAY

Sometimes there's a whole world alive in me, johan janssens says to you on this may evening . . . a private, unreal world of wooden puppets—and up to now I've felt helpless and haven't had a clue how to express this world . . . should I cut it up like masereel did, or should I add movement, as happens in the eternal puppet show of punch and judy, or should I describe it like kafka did in his strange books? And I can't imagine any event in this unreal world, any tragedy, any catastrophe, any sunny may day parade, any birth or illness or death, that doesn't take place near an unmanned railway crossing—that pair of gleaming rails like taut iron ribbons, like long gleaming worms . . . the signal box in the distance, the poky little station positioned for maximum profit on the border of 2 villages—and in the winter the rain that lashes down on it, and in the summer the sun that stews everything, and in may the cool shade behind the station and the blossoming gorse along the railway embankment. That's all I need to write my book of fairy tales, in which the wooden puppets would come to life. A strange, unnatural world where the stationmaster, for instance, would be the hero . . . a new stationmaster who arrives at the station of agterdenbergh-waaiendijck late one may evening. Yes, just like the hero in kafka's book: it was very late when k. arrived . . . a heavy covering of snow lay over the village. I'd do it exactly like that: it was very late when the new stationmaster k. arrived . . . the yellow gorse was everywhere along the railway line, flaming, flaming . . . And you see because it's an unreal world after all, I'd make the station dark and grubby and dirty: gray and stinking of tobacco smoke, the walls leprous and crumbling because they haven't been whitewashed for years, the floor tiles covered in the dust and mud of all the travelers who've made their way to the station from the 2 villages . . . the heavy, muddy shoes of those who work on a distant building site, or who leave for the mines very early, before the sun is up, and among them the lighter shoes of children who with their schoolbags and student train-passes ruin the trains for everyone else, the hobnail boots of gendarmes coming to chase poachers, and the lopsided shoes of smugglers who've slaughtered cattle or distilled their own gin. And the stationmaster k. arrives there, and looks around, and is enraged at all this gray desolation, and goes in search of a bucket of whitewash and a brush, puts his stationmaster's cap under a piece of gray paper, and whitewashes his own office. And the other wooden puppets, who are the booking clerk, the conductor, the signalman, the crossing attendant . . . they avert their heads in shame, and also hunt out a bucket of whitewash and brushes, in silence . . . they all stand there whitewashing without saying a word or looking at each other. And retrieving his cap from under the gray paper, the stationmaster k. goes round while they are eating their lunch . . . and without a word he bends down to pick up some wrapping paper that's lying on the station floor . . . and the booking clerk follows him and, shamefaced, picks up the empty sardine tin that he's thrown on the ground . . . and the conductor follows silently in their wake and, shamefaced, shovels up the trash that's been swept into heaps in the 4 corners of the waiting room. And everything is suddenly white with whitewash and yellow with blossoming gorse and red with may day.

And on this may evening you listen to johan janssens, and say: but that sort of thing can only happen in that world inside you, johan janssens . . . and even then only on may day, when the yellow gorse is blooming, and the fairy tale of the world of the future can be told.

REALITY OF MAY DAY

But the shops where ondine wasn't well known weren't so easily found anymore—every time they needed more food it was quite a problem figuring out where she could exercise her nefarious practices. She had to wash properly and curl her hair, which became more difficult week by week—the days when she was full of expectations of a better life, hoping for a miracle, had become as rare these days as the shops where she wasn't known. In the store she entered now she started in immediately about the death of bryske, and the socialists, and about knowing mr achilles so well—but for the first time in her life she encountered someone who didn't know who she meant by mr achilles: which mr achilles was that? Derenancourt, she said with a laugh, since she was on such intimate terms that she only used his first name. But they didn't even know a mr derenancourt in that shop. And when she went on about the socialists? Everyone has his own opinion, they said, and they didn't mind if ondine was of a different persuasion, but they themselves were in favor of socialism: my father-in-law represents the socialists on the town council, said the woman behind the counter. On the town council? asked ondine, looking pensively out of a little window at the street. On the town council? To the best of my knowledge there isn't a single socialist on the town council. Then the woman explained the whole setup to her, which oscarke already knew about, as did all the people who traveled up and down to brussels, but which ondine had never heard of. My husband's father, boone, you know, boone from by the station, was on the liberal lists as a socialist candidate, the woman began. And ondine, who listened in silence, and understood everything, realized that the encyclicals had been fooled after all, despite the business with the stone saint. She asked for a loaf of bread and a few bits and pieces, and she forgot to pay . . . no, this time it wasn't a ploy, she really did forget, and she went home, where she started thinking. It was as if she could think better at home . . . could bear the blows of fate better. And snuggling up in a corner she was again forced to the appalling realization that everyone had their own opinion about everything, and not only that—because that wasn't so bad in itself—but that everyone was right in their own way. When she had stood there with oscarke and the priest by the newly-built wall, and had listed to their absurd conversation, she had already realized: everyone has his own bit of truth, his own small, stupid version of the world and everything else—and every little truth could be weighed equally well against another: oh, it was enough to make you weep, the way all those notions were equally small and equally true. Now she'd met some socialists, and it was the same with them: they were little people in search of truth, believing one thing and doubting another. Everyone was right . . . except her. Because she was a victim of circumstances, a victim of life, since she had wanted to enter into a life-or-death struggle with the little truths, and as a result hadn't noticed the enormity of the situation. Of course it was true—you see, another little truth!—that everyone had to look after themselves: she'd suggested smearing that statue with filth, and what had been her reward? Being called "madame," ha, as if that was all she cared about. And now with this funeral of bryske's: she'd had to supply her own filth, she'd had to lead the attack, all at the risk of getting a bad name, and the others had laughed behind their open curtains—catholics and liberals and socialists had formed coalitions, pursuing their own interests, and she . . . she, ondine, had to go round begging, telling lies about having forgotten her purse. Oh, her battle against *socialism, wasn't it foolish? It was foolish of oscarke to call himself a socialist and swallow big lies in the service of his little truth—but it was also foolish for her to get all worked up and spread lies in the service of the little truths of the gentlemen. And again, again she realized that she had lost her way, that she had lost sight of her great aim in life, and had got worked up and wasted her happiness, allowed herself to be sidetracked.*

A JOURNAL

You've read lots of books and write books yourself, says the old skeletal hunchback . . . I can't read or write because I started working in the mills at the age of eight. And I hear they're writing a lot about cruelty these days—I hear there's a literature of cruelty—faulkner in america, they say, and sartre in paris. But life is still a bit different and a bit more than what writers can make of it in a book. And what I want to tell you now is every bit as good as what those writers can make up . . . it happened many many years ago, when I was still living in brussels—I lived by the van-praet bridge where lots of people throw themselves into the river, I lived on the small island where the gas burners are and the senne flows past, and I lived in lots of other places besides—brussels is beautiful, in all its ugly nooks and crannies it's beautiful. But when I was living in brussels many many years ago, I'll never forget, in a small, ugly room on the sixth floor, there was someone else living right over my head, an old woman who sat patiently waiting to die. And one nice, cool morning at the beginning of june, I won't forget that either, she sent for me and gave me a handwritten book: it was the journal of her husband, she said, who'd been crippled in both legs and had tried to run off on those two crippled legs and had fallen down the stairs and died. Here is his journal, she said. And that bit about his falling down the stairs is obviously not in it. You can have the journal, she said. What good is it to me? I asked. I can't read or write. That's exactly why you can have it, she said: keep it till I'm dead too and until me and my husband with his crippled legs have both vanished from people's memories. And years later I came and lived here in chapel road, on the edge of the town of the 2 mills (it was at the time of the great Strike), and one fine day I thought of that journal again, and I asked the father of the music master if he would read those handwritten pages aloud to me. And a hidden life was opened up to me, the old hunchback, the hidden life of that crippled old man and his wife . . . so unbelievable that faulkner in america and sartre in paris couldn't match it—how he, the cripple, lying there with his paralyzed legs, pondered how he could torment and torture his wife, afterwards noting down the result of those torments in his journal . . . as a chemist writes down the results of his experiments in a book. I'm not going to tell you everything, it's too cruel (you modern writers don't know what real cruelty is), but I'll give you a small, insignificant sample, something trivial, but that'll give you an idea of the man. His wife had bought half a kilo of coffee beans and he wrote in his journal: counted the beans, 2,843. And after she'd made coffee in the morning and had gone to work, he wrote: counted the beans again, 2,790 left. I'll stop there, because in a minute I'd have to go on with the story, and you'd stick your fingers in your ears and run away. He was a monster. And so, unable to stand it any longer, going crazy with fear at having to go home yet again, with him getting up to heaven knows what while she was out, the wife went to see a doctor . . . and the doctor went with her and shortly afterward called for the Van: but when the Van arrived and the 2 men in white coats came up the stairs, the cripple realized he was going to be taken to the madhouse. He immediately leapt up on his legs that had been paralyzed for all those years, and walked 3 meters . . . then fell down the stairs and was dead.

So you see, says the skeletal old hunchback, that's the story of the man whose journal I still have in my possession . . . but the day after the father of the music master read that book aloud to me one evening, the great Strike began, and that story of cruelty receded into the background: the life of an individual is sometimes submerged in the life of the community.

ATTACK ON THE CASTLE

Johan janssens said to you that even in a folktale about the gang of jan de lichte, you have to pay attention to the social side of things. And he also said the following to you: of course I'd tell people a few things about that formidable crook, because people enjoy reading about that—but I'd still point out that people only started robbing and stealing, and subsequently burning and killing, out of hunger and deprivation. And since in those days, as always, it was the nameless masses that were starving, I would pay particular attention to depicting those nameless masses. For example, if in your book you were to describe the sacking of a castle by the gang, you could first of all (in order to satisfy the reader) have the most undaunted thief force his way in through the gate, peering round cautiously. But then, just as it's inevitable that ravenous wolves will all follow the same scent, and that the black spots of ravens will all alight on the same field . . . so the starving and neglected masses are like rats that always know when there's food hidden somewhere. They flock from far and wide, those scurvy creatures with their gleaming eyes and their disgusting hairless tails, and advance on the castle. They're not part of the gang, but are poor, destitute creatures who were dying by the roadside . . . there are cowards among them, and desperate souls, and people who don't know how to make arrows from a piece of wood or how to make ends meet. There are real criminals among them, but also well-behaved ones who sit in their shacks waiting for a miracle from god, or else some assistance from the devil. And somehow they've all heard that this castle is about to be sacked . . . how do rats hear that there's something decomposing in a sewer nearby? They don't hear, they smell. And everyone who's caught a whiff of this smell comes running from far and wide—so those who now force their way in through the gates are strangers. True, we recognize this woman with a black patch over her eye as a female member of the gang. But the rest are nameless—they are women with skin drooping over their frames, with hair and teeth falling out . . . they are emaciated creatures without name or sex, and whose scrofulous scabs or abnormalities make them shun the light of day . . . they are young boys on spindly legs that are too long for them . . . and they are mostly children, children. They slip in, one at a time, and spread out through the inner courtyard garden of the castle, among the flowering rhododendrons and beneath the fragrant lilacs, closing in, ever nearer, on the spoils. They lower themselves into the mouths of the cellars, turning every doorknob, trying every lock and every window latch. And then they stop—they're waiting for something special—they sit everywhere, in every nook and cranny, and hide as much as possible the glitter in their eyes, the fidgeting of their hands and feet, and are quiet as the dead. Each of them has chosen the place where, to the best of his knowledge, he's both safest and best able to pounce on the waiting feast. They sit there and wait . . .

And then the man after whom the gang is named appears. He may be disguised with a black patch over his face, or as a nobleman with a twirled moustache, or as a monk in a brown habit and rough beard. For a split second he's visible to all—from his monk's cowl comes the imitated cry of some startled nocturnal bird—and at that same instant everyone detaches themselves from their safe and dark corners and charge forward. Those who clung to the dungeon mouths force their way in, window latches are broken, door locks twisted . . . glass is broken and wood splintered. Sometimes a knife gleams. The woman with the patch over her eye crawls through the bushes on her hands and knees . . . and there are so many of them, and their hunger is so frenzied, that they could kill each other in this writhing heap.

You see, johan janssens says to you . . . that's how I would describe the attack on a castle in your popular novel about the robber chieftain jan de lichte. Now and then a ray of light may strike some robber or other . . . but I would pay most attention to the nameless ones: and among these I would include many honest and upstanding folk who hate to hear glass shattering or see a knife gleam, but who are forced through necessity to drag off the spoils to their poor, rundown shacks.

And see, there he is again, johan janssens! Forgive me for disturbing you again, he says . . . but it's about my world of wooden puppets—I sometimes sit for an hour or so, when I have nothing better to do, with a book of my son jo's on my knee, with photographs of the puppet theaters in this country, a book that is so strange and so beautiful that I forget all about my collection of Masterpieces of Painting: photos of creatures who live without moving, with their floppy legs and rag arms, and with their rigid blank faces, so that it drives me to despair that I'll never be able to represent anything so perfect myself. One of the illustrations in that book is of the wheel of fortune . . . you know, the wheel that's dragged along in processions and parades and cavalcades, and that as it turns shows first the rich man, then the farmer, the soldier, the priest, or the beggar—and I think of that old print where the farmer says the following to the judge, the soldier, and the priest: you may fight or judge or pray, but the farmer lays the eggs, I say—and all those characters hang there limply and with no will of their own, and are moved only by the wheel of fortune. And whether they're rich or poor, famous or despised, decorated or locked up in jail, they all have the same rigid, blank face: and that makes them a true representation of our people, living under the delusion that some kind of fate determines which of them will be rich or poor . . . and with dumb, submissive faces endure that fate to the end of time. And that book of my son jo's shows the wheel of fortune, lying slightly askew on the cobbles, so that the rich man is hanging forward with his rag arms in front of him, and the poor farmer is moving backwards, his limp arms crushed against his blue smock: a painting, a masterpiece, which I've already sketched five times, without ever succeeding in capturing it so poignantly in all its simplicity.

And leafing further through the book I also find a picture of a puppet play from the area of mons, in which a policeman comes to arrest a housemaid . . . and under his stiff uniform he's exactly the same, a perfectly ordinary puppet of sawdust and rags, dumb and speechless with his wooden face, resting his rag hand on the shoulder of the housemaid as he arrests her in the name of the law. And she too looks stiffly and silently straight ahead, although dishonor and shame are hanging over her wooden head—she stands there in her white apron with red dots, the very image of the eternally cowed race of servants and housemaids—which is what we all are—who listens dumbly and speechlessly to the judgment of the court, the imprecations of the church, the sermon of the priest and gendarme who say: in the name of the law. She's silent and isn't even capable of feeling shame: she lives under the firm delusion that the world has always been so and will be so forevermore, amen. And beside them stands her husband the servant in his red-and-white striped livery, staring straight ahead in dismay, and with an eternal polite grimace round his mouth that he carries with him everywhere. He listens with the same dismay to his father's orders, and makes the same polite grimace whenever he's chastised—and so, when he's old and sick, he'll wear the same polite grimace as he ekes out his meager pension, and with the same polite grimace he'll face death. But now he stares straight ahead with wide, terrified eyes, and bares all his teeth in a grin, while next to him his impassive wife is arrested by the impassive gendarme. It's a drama . . . the drama of our people, in all its politeness . . . so cruel, so chilly, that I attempt time and time again to paint it, and if I ever succeed, I shall entitle it: flanders, the race of servants and maids. For the moment, though, I sit there dumb and speechless, with dismay in my eyes and a polite grimace on my lips, staring at all these puppet plays.

PEOPLE IN FLANDERS

So what did ondine do? She had wanted to dominate, and so had chosen the side of those who happened to be dominant—but should she go on taking their side? Certainly not. She should take no one's side, she should only look after herself: that was the great aim in her life, that was the great law in nature. Everyone must look after themselves. And she was surprised that again it came down to "oneself": she had been frightened of the devil, like oscarke and her father too perhaps, and had realized just like them that she herself was the devil. First she'd discovered that everyone was his own devil, and now she discovered that everyone had to look after themselves: soon everyone would be his own private god as well. But there was Something she couldn't stand, and that was everyone finding out about this: imagine what would happen if her mother and valeer and vapeur and oscarke and that little witch mariette—that horrible second child of hers—knew that they themselves were the devil, and that they only had to look after themselves . . . god, what a world that would be! Still, having all these thoughts, ondine stayed exactly the same as she'd always been—since she couldn't as yet adapt to practical life the ideas that had dawned on her with such harsh clarity: she didn't want to, she didn't dare. Or, rather, it wasn't a question of daring, since she went right on brazenly taunting everyone around her, forcing them to arrange their lives according to her own little truth.

But she felt a strange attraction to those people from the socialist shop, why she didn't know. It wasn't affection—far from it. I think it's curiosity, she said. But it wasn't wholly that either . . . she went there and was on her best behavior, and even paid for the goods she'd bought a few days previously . . . and immediately brought up the subject of that father-in-law, boone, "who was on the town council." Isn't he on it anymore then? asked ondine. And the woman, skinny but wiry, and radiating an energy that one could feel a long way off, told ondine the story

of her father-in-law, who had no sooner got onto the town council when a social-
ist knocked at their door: he worked in the sanitation department and had a wife
who couldn't work because they had nine or so kids, and what he earned emptying
dustbins, god, it was ridiculous . . . and you might think he could have worked
somewhere else in the evenings to earn some extra money, but no . . . mr achilles
whom ondine had talked to them about yesterday (ha, I said we didn't know him,
but that's not true of course—we know him only too well), well he made the men
from the sanitation department work in the garden of his castle on chapel road at
night under threat of having them dismissed from their jobs with the sanitation
service. The man had said all that to boone, and boone had protested about it in
the town council: ha, now he had those nice catholics on the run: there must be an
end to making people work for starvation wages, he said, and there must also be
an end to municipal employees having to work after hours for private individuals,
unpaid, and with the constant specter of being fired hovering over their heads. Oh,
they laughed at that socialist liberal, they didn't believe him: all fairy tales! And at
the next session the little man, that fearful and hesitant socialist, was summoned,
and he stood there before the gentlemen, cap in hand, and they asked him if it was
true that he earned only half a franc . . . and he replied: no, gentlemen, it isn't
true, I earn one franc. And they asked him if it was true that he had to work in
mr derenancourt's garden after hours, and he replied: no, gentlemen, I go of my
own free will. Oh, it was obvious he'd been coached beforehand, that he had been
threatened, that he may even have been promised something. And after that, boone
had retired from politics. You see, said ondine . . . that's what the socialists are like!
Of course, replied boone's daughter-in-law, that's what the socialists are like! And
she inveighed against them and said they stunk like rotten fish, even though they
themselves were socialists. And ondine couldn't understand: why would you speak ill
of yourself? That's not speaking ill, that's telling the truth . . . the truth must always
be told. And even the fact that the socialists were all just little cowards wasn't proof
that socialism itself was no good, but on the contrary just one more proof of how
craven and stupid ordinary people had been made in this country—and you see,
her father-in-law had left the town council, but not the movement: he was now a
librarian, because the socialists already had a fine library. And she invited ondine
into the back, into the kitchen, and made coffee and showed her books by zola and
sue . . . and ondine drank coffee and sat with her feet up on the stove, and felt more
at home than she ever had before. She left with the books under her arm, and then,
after the gentlemen had gone home that night, she sat up reading zola in bed.

DEAD SOULS

It's an early evening in july, the sort where you can't tell whether it's going to
rain or not—just like with the skeletal old hunchback, who asks you everyday

what's going to happen about the king, is he going to come back or not? And johan janssens strolls up to your front door, looking indifferently at some unfamiliar passerby, and says: another new resident of chapel road, a stranger, someone who has absolutely nothing to do with us . . . recently I been feeling as though I've lost my way here, like the ugly duckling in andersen's fairy tale. Everyone I had anything to do with is taking flight from chapel road, as if plague and cholera and famine and catholics already had chapel road in their grip. Tolfpoets is way over there in the country in his so-called villa, and the music master is also building a cottage in his little garden . . . tippetotje and maitre pots have gone to brussels, and now mossieu colson of the ministry is going to move there too. And so chapel road is turning into a no-man's land where the weeds of clericalism are springing up, where the new residents put a photo of the king in their windows, and on sunday mornings have their children go about in hitler youth uniforms.

And you say consolingly to johan janssens that chapel road isn't completely lost yet: you still live here, and so do I, and so does kramiek. And johan janssens looks at you with a face like the july evening outside, the sort where you can't tell whether it's going to rain or not, saying: don't talk to me about kramiek . . . don't talk to me about him, because he's seen and heard for years how I live, and yet he still feels he has to number me among those like himself: the dead souls. One evening he was going to give a lecture, about one more something that was going to turn out to be a big Nothing . . . in which he was going to drape and dress himself and those like him, the dead, respectable souls . . . in which he was going to talk for two solid hours and say nothing. The subject was, I think, the necessity of kramiek and the kramiek-ness of necessity. But when that evening came I didn't feel like going anywhere, didn't feel like having to mouth polite formulae, listening to something that was Nothing . . . and the next day I meet kramiek, and he looks the other way and doesn't talk to me anymore: he's angry because I still haven't become a respectable citizen, because I remain what I've always been: a wild card, an unmanageable child, an unpredictable human being. And I can't really understand kramiek anyway: he should really be angry with himself, should never talk to himself again, should turn away when he meets himself in the street: because as a respectable citizen he wants to be friends with someone who'll never behave like a respectable citizen. But no, instead of that he's also a big pain to my wife because she's married to a man who's not respectable: he meets my wife and turns away. And now not only is kramiek angry, but so is my wife: she scarcely speaks to me anymore because the likes of a kramiek turns away when he meets the wife of someone like me . . .

And at that moment kramiek comes out of one of the 4 villas on chapel road . . . the one where mossieu colson of the ministry once lived, but where that stranger lives now, who has nothing to do with us . . . and johan janssens says: actually, I'm annoyed and angry with myself, because I can't follow tolf-poets and the music master far into the country over there, or because I don't want to follow tippetotje all the way to brussels . . . instead being doomed to live among all these dead souls in chapel road, which becomes more and more catholic everyday.

THE DREAM

Tippetotje sits in her studio, but she doesn't paint: she writes you a letter about everything she'd Like to paint. I've picked up the pen, she writes, because for days and days I've been wrestling with a dream, so beautiful and so strange that I wouldn't be capable of painting it anyway. I don't know why, but I was dreaming about the pepperpot . . . that strange hero of your book, who in the evenings lurks beyond the castle stream waiting for his prey. And I dreamed that the pepperpot had moved into the hot fields beyond termuren, and was now lurking on the footpath winding between two tall fields of corn. The corn is high and the path is narrow, so it's a long corridor in semidarkness, with a line of clear blue sky up above . . . It's silent and still, so still that a golden oriole can shuffle close to his feet . . . and in that silence, that solitude, the mysterious shade, he walks on: and suddenly the Thing he has imagined for years, the thing he's wanted to happen for years and years takes him by surprise: he approaches from one direction with a red poppy in his hand, and from the other direction a young woman approaches holding a blue cornflower. And look, the woman who approaches has nothing in common with all those other creatures that are called women and that one can meet in any street at any hour of the day . . . no, no, she's a dream woman, she's so terribly beautiful that it's not really possible: I don't dare describe her, just as I don't dare paint her: with eyes in which first the blue of her cornflower is reflected, but where the yellow sheen of the corn is also present, and in which one can also find the mysterious gloom of that narrow path. I'll say nothing about her body and all the rest, my pen is all choked up and already lost for words: but what approaches the pepperpot, blue flower in hand, is a poem of a woman. And, you know, the pepperpot has been dreaming about and longing for something like this for years, but has never seen it happen. Now it's happening. And now he is paralyzed by it: his hands hang by his sides, his legs have turned to the rag legs of a puppet, and he doesn't know where to turn: he actually staggers and stumbles to meet her, and with every step he grows more aware of his impotence—and he understands One thing in particular, that they'll pass each other and Nothing will happen. A strange pain gnaws at him, a stupid long-ing renders him helpless, and impotently he stumbles closer and closer to the place where they'll pass each other by—where they have passed each other by. And the pain pierces his veins like nails: he looks at her with all the pent-up longing of many, many years: now she's there with the blue flower in her wet mouth. And he passes her with leaden hands, leaden feet, with something inside that renders him impotent: yes, something can be so beautiful that it makes us tired and cowardly and impotent. And yes, I'd like to paint that moment: the woman with the blue cornflower in her mouth, coming towards us out of the shade of that wedge in the cornfield . . . and a little further on the pepperpot walking away from her, his back towards her, silent and ashamed, sad and cowardly, with the powerless legs of a puppet: impotent.

That was my dream, tippetotje writes to you . . . but won't my mind be just as impotent when I'm painting something like that?

THE SILENCE

And then there's the silence, andreus mottebol says to you . . . sometimes I get up in the middle of the night and creep on tiptoe to the patch of garden behind our house . . . and if there isn't a freight train trundling past in the distance, at great length, and if there's no nocturnal plane droning high in the sky, and if over on the main road no cars come chugging and puffing and banging along . . . and if no people come chattering and chirping down chapel road—and no one chattering to himself and slurring a song or kicking a jar . . . then . . . then . . . I sometimes catch the silence, as one catches happiness, as one catches the miraculous phoenix: by quietly, quietly, on tiptoe, finger on your lips, sprinkling a little salt on its tail. And then, when for another brief moment I've been able to hear the silence, I work out how long it's been since the last time . . . and if I'm not mistaken, it was last year, that night in the Ardennes, before those campers arrived with their loudspeaker. And I wonder what it is that people have against silence—is it fear? Is that why many many years ago in the forests they started roaring and shouting and smashing stones, terrifying all the other animals: making them tremble and retreat: here is the creature that makes noise out of a fear of silence—man. And since then man's gone on making noise—he's cast off everything that reminds him of the past, except his fear of being alone in the silence. He's gradually led a life separate from life, an artificial life, a rubber or glass or gleaming metal life, where there's no room for silence: silence would mean the end of that artificial life. He must go farther and farther along the path he's chosen, the engines and the machines must bang and rattle and chug and drone and explode: so that no ominous silence will frighten him.

And although I don't care much for cinemas—says johan janssens—mr brys cajoled me into going with him the other day: and we were sitting there before the film began, and in the silence the audience looked at each other uneasily . . . until they started playing records down at the front, amplified by six loudspeakers. And the audience was immediately reassured: they whistled and growled and sang and stamped their feet in time with the sextuple amplification: they were still alive, there was still noise. And although I don't care much for the radio, because all that comes out of it are meaningless sounds, parasites, talk programs, sunday interviews, pop songs, and other kinds of noise designed to put even the stars themselves in awe of the creature that can't bear silence . . . although I don't care for it at all, I say, it was my son jo who obliged me—morally—to buy one. And so a man comes and installs a radio in our house and makes the noise flood in . . . and I take a step back and look at him in dismay—but he nods his head reassuringly, telling me that it can go even louder if I want, and turns the knob further and further so that earsplitting noise fills my house, and a piece of paper on my desk trembles and curls. And I retreat still further, and look at him and his noise box full of horror—but he says to me, reassuringly, that there is another special knob: a sound booster: and he turns that up too. I think I started screaming at that point. But, I asked, doesn't it play any quiet music, a lonely tune, some lonely flute in the wind? But that wasn't possible with this man's radio: and he looked at me like I was crazy because I changed my mind and didn't want to buy it. And stepping outside with the box under his arm, he looked back at my house as if it were the house of an idiot, someone abnormal: someone who's frightened of the sound we human beings make.

And something else, andreus mottebol says to you: I told someone about this just yesterday, a very intelligent man as it happens, and I admitted to him that like tolfpoets and master oedenmaeckers that I'd like to live in a little cottage on the fringe of the forest. And he looked at me in dismay and said: but . . . but it's so QUIET there.

BOONE'S INFLUENCE

Ondine was in her pub with the gentlemen, and noticed how people served themselves and cheated her and were actually making fun of her . . . but she pretended not to notice. Once she'd longed hopelessly to be like them, and now who were they, what did they know, what did they understand? Not a thing. And whichever way her thoughts turned, it always came down to the same thing: it was all nothing, the whole world with god and the devil and poverty and luxury, was all nothing at all. She realized that her efforts to reach their stature were grotesque if for no other reason than the fact that the gentlemen had no stature at all: it was a mirage, the so-called ruling class, they just had a bit of money, that was all. If she started really looking after herself, stealing and cheating and killing and breaking open all the offertory boxes, they would have bowed down in front of her: if she had more money than fat glemmasson, he would grovel in the dust. Still, that was precisely the problem: what she lacked was money—and there was no point in further philosophizing, money was everything and wisdom was nothing. And so she still felt they had the upper hand and were superior to her. And because she couldn't attain their stature (admittedly, their false stature), she tried to bring them down a peg or two: she told spiteful gossip, she depicted the misery of the poor, lacing her story with smutty language, telling them how the poor all lay in a heap and made babies, and . . . Yes, suddenly she understood that it was precisely That that they came to her place for: the impossible situation: sitting in a shabby pub, round a stove that really belonged in a workhouse, and laughing at her ugly vase and piss-soaked diapers. It hurt her. She saw that they'd taken bottles from the bar over there and emptied them into the coal scuttle: right, she thought . . . they're only doing that so I'll go broke, and they can enjoy my going broke. And she resolved to cheat them in her turn: she got a kid drunk who had plenty of money to fritter away and who was openly attacking the others for bringing him there, because he was frittering his money away and getting no pleasure for it—and she knew very well that for him pleasure meant bare flesh. Oh, she said, shall I show you my ass, you might get some pleasure from that. She let them go through bottle after bottle, but whenever one of them rolled under the table she took a few bills out of their wallets.

THE SAW

Yes, chapel road is becoming increasingly abandoned by all the characters who used to make themselves at Home at your place . . . and because you can't stand all those empty chairs in your living room any longer, one day you escape for a change and look up everyone who's have deserted you: if the mountain won't come to mohammed . . . And you meet mossieu colson of the ministry, and he asks you why on earth you want to go on living your life in that chapel road: just because godmother mie and godfather sooi lived there years ago . . . just because ondine was born there, and grew up there during the rise of socialism . . . just because you've started to confuse chapel road with your own road through life? You don't hear or see anything there, you're not really living in the real world there, but in front of stage flats on which the world has been copied. And when I was still living there I didn't realize I was living between stage flats either, they'd been put up so cunningly . . . but now that I've left I'd like nothing better than to put chapel road on canvas as an image of flanders: I'd paint a gray, sad landscape, an overcast sky and rain-sodden countryside with tall lamenting trees, and running through it all the muddy chapel road . . . but far away on the horizon the inside of a

barred window, and between the heavy iron bars a more spacious, more colorful sky. Just as if the whole of that chapel road, the whole sorry landscape,
all those people of flanders kept deliberately stupid, were nothing more than
the painted walls of a prison: a cell with a small window, where between the
heavy bars one can catch a glimpse of a wider world.

And speaking of putting something on canvas . . . yes, I live and work in
brussels now, and I see tippetotje painting, and it has a bit of an encouraging
effect on me—so, speaking of putting something on canvas, I'd like to paint
johan janssens, who lives and works over there in chapel road, and goes on
writing his columns from there: I'd like to paint him as someone who can
only concern himself with his small and insignificant problems, even if the
world is being sawn in half in the meantime . . . and I would paint him just
like that, sawn in half: the lower half of his body still sitting at his desk, with
insignificant books and insignificant papers . . . but the upper part perched
on his windowsill, from where he studies the chapel road cell of his flanders
prison. And against one leg of the table an upright saw, painted red in an
outrageous style. Like with the singers at the fair, like with the fakir at the
circus . . .

And you answer mossieu colson of the ministry: for goodness sake don't
tell that to johan janssens, since he's quite capable of leaving chapel road too
. . . and who will be left then to go on sawing through the thick bars of the
prison of flanders?

THE CONVERSATION

Yes you'd Like to paint all that, you say to mr brys . . . you want to, but you
don't do it. And apart from that, what do you do here, and how do you live
and how do you kill your lonely, regret-filled hours?

And mr brys tells you that here in the rue saint-hinoré he's surrounded by
strange furniture that he still has to get used to, and that he conducts long, serious conversations with himself. And suddenly I see the way I present myself
to the world, folded open like a cardboard box, as though I'm unveiling the
secrets of life and death, hope and love, him and her. I catch myself leaning
slightly forward, with a deep frown on my brow and a fixed look in my eyes.
I hold my left hand like an orator, forcefully raised, the fingers spread wide,
to display the secret. But the right hand I hold pointing towards me with the
same fingers spread in exactly the same way, as if to protect the revealed secret
after all, at the very last moment. So I talk and talk, but suddenly step out of
character and realize that there's only an empty chair to listen to me. And I
feel ashamed and apologize to myself . . . and also a little to the empty chair.
And only afterwards do I start wondering whether my whole life and all of

our lives aren't just a series of conversations with empty chairs? The chairs where the others sit, invisibly, the dream creatures who are exactly the same as we are, but don't exist . . . and yet listen ever more intently to what we feel we have to say. And a little later still I start wondering whether this might not be a poignant subject for a painting: an empty room, preferably with white-washed walls . . . or no, with some monotonous wallpaper, in which a small flower repeats itself, crablike, in a diagonal pattern . . . and in that empty room a man sitting in a chair, revealing the secret of life and death to No one . . . only an empty chair turned to face him. And he stares at that no one with a profound frown on his brow. But look, I'm sorry if I'm capable of finding a subject for a good modernist painting without really being able to paint it: my draftsmanship is still at the stage where I drew little figures on the wall with a lump of chalk as a child: a big round head with two eyes and a nose at the side. But suddenly, in the no-man's land of this tenement block in the rue saint-honoré, the amazing idea came to me of simply photographing my subject: what god or what law has decreed that subjects must be painted and not photographed in order to be art? And in that same moment of inspiration, I realized that problem of its appearing to be just some old photo of a man in a room could be solved by tying a mask over the face of my model . . . or better still, by fastening a white handkerchief over his face, giving him a faceless face, reducing him to a kind of articulated artist's manikin . . . so that the sharpest focus is on his orator's hands: the puppet in the empty room, conducting a conversation with no one . . .

And so mr brys sits there surrounded by furniture that he has to get used to . . . himself speaking to someone in an empty chair, that creature with whom he'll conduct conversations to the end of his days, without ever getting used to it.

ONDINE SAWN IN HALF

But the next evening ondine was Another ondine again: she longed desperately for the miracle, the miracle that had appeared to her since her childhood like a will-'o-the-wisp, and had as it were eaten away at her bones and perhaps poisoned her blood. She told norbert that oscarke had never been able to satisfy her in this respect: I don't know what sort of a husband he's supposed to be, he just comes home and putters around a bit and goes to bed, and then in the morning he's off again . . . you never hear him say anything, but don't try and tell me that he's not thinking anything: it's as if he's living somewhere else, it's as if he has a soul somewhere else and hangs that soul on the hat rack when he comes here—and it seems impossible to me that he could ever die here or even fall ill: it would be unnatural: when the time comes to die he'll do it Over There. And I also feel as if he's a customer in my own pub, just one who has a few more privileges, since he's allowed to sleep in my bed. And the thought that only There could anything happen to him, and that he'd left his soul behind there, norbert found these very beautiful. Actually it's like this, he said: it's almost a case of possession. And without fully realizing it she found herself in that special state again, became the ondine of her youth, who hadn't figured out yet that one only has to look after oneself, and that one should be a little contemptuous of all those little truths out there. Without her being conscious of it, her childhood took hold of her, particularly the time when she stood on the altar and dreamt of being a divine creature. Yes, she said, you talked to me ad infinitum about those things when we were young, but it got no further than words . . . She watched with her heart in her mouth as he went silently over to the top curtains and closed them. Her hands were squeezed tight between her knees, and she knew that she always sat like that when she was deep in thought or intensely happy, or when great worries were hanging over her head . . . in short, whenever she was alive. *She watched him place a small table in the center of her pub and put some chairs round it, she saw him bolt the door and heard him ask—in a matter-of-fact voice—if people would be seated. But only ondine saw that a strange pallor hung over his face and that his hands were clutching the back of one of the chairs. She had expected, had worried that there would be protests, or that fat glemmasson at least would have objected, but no, they beat her to the table and she had to hurry to try and grab a seat next to norbert—which she was too late for anyway, and so had to sit between glemmasson and that rich kid. Norbert turned off the light and asked if they would all place their hands on the table—and the moment he asked if the spirits was there, ondine felt something creep up her thigh. She was close to screaming but lacked the breath . . . and afterwards she didn't dare, she felt something crawling higher and higher, and she also listened to her heart, which at the start had beat a rolling march, but which now went up and down more slowly, as if it were tired, as if it were exhausted. And then, she screamed after all—because no one could trick her for long, it was no ghost, it was one of them, however much norbert droned on about the other side. Light! she cried . . . put the light on. And she didn't see who turned the light on, but in the general confusion she looked under the table and it was that rich kid who'd crept under her skirt: she had to pull him off her, because he was clinging to her like a tick, like a leech. They would have laughed but it was too tragic to see the kid's face—and ondine wanted to be furious, but at whom, at that little rich kid? At fat glemmasson, who (as was perfectly obvious) had no part in it himself, and was looking flabbergasted at the kid? The only really guilty party was norbert, once again, the pig who had deceived her twice now with his nonsense about ghosts, ghosts which had always been norbert himself. But, no, in the final analysis ondine was the only guilty party. It was her own grave, stupid error, allowing herself to fall again and again for those lies about things on the other side. Still, she had to do Something, they were all sitting huddled together like sheep, like chickens in the rain, although she'd never actually seen chickens in the rain. In one stride she was standing next to norbert, he was sitting in a perfect position to be given a slap: she raised her hand . . . but at that moment he looked up and looked at her, looked at her with sad eyes that were weeping without tears . . . exactly the same eyes as his brother achilles had shown her when he'd done her wrong back then, and wanted to make it seem that he himself was the victim. So that she didn't know what to think, so that she realized once again that she didn't understand people at all: was he the culprit or was he the victim? Had he really wanted to organize a séance, and it was just the others who had dispelled the miracle with their . . . oh no, there were no words to describe their stupidity—or had norbert fixed everything himself in advance? We'll turn the light off and someone can sneak under her skirt! And as she stood looking at him, hesitating, trying to read those eyes of his, she was suddenly overcome by the bitter thought that this evening was, as it were, the image, the synthesis, the perfect précis of her life . . .*

THE PICKPOCKETS

Johan janssens gets annoyed when they say that he stays there in that insignificant chapel road and goes on filling his insignificant sheets of paper while the world is being sawn in half. Termuren is not just any village, but the image, the synthesis of this world, surrounded by walls that block every view and bar every escape . . . and chapel road is not just any village street down which father munte and smee the blacksmith walk, but a road on the 38th parallel that cuts the earth in two. And as I write my columns I am sawn in half along with it . . . Sitting at my window, I see the people weighed down with packages and bags, with sugar and salt, with bacon and lard, and especially with rice. There's a war in korea, they say. The world is being sawn in half, and all that matters to the people of chapel road is that it's going to be difficult to get rice and that they'll have to lay in supplies for the drought. They'll have to stock up and look to their profits. Those are words that are in the ascendant: no pity, no sympathy, but charity begins at home: only profit, and worrying that there may be no rice tomorrow. And in particular the possibility that, if we stock up now, we may be able to make a profit.

And look, says johan janssens, I go on studying chapel road, which runs not just through flanders, but a little farther: and there's been another gas explosion in the mines, again there were choking fumes and seams of earth and coal came crashing down. Just like in the miner's song we learned back in school: your father, sweet children, sang hardly at all, behind the old clog pile death waits for his fall. And what the song describes really happens: grit and dust and gas, and the earth closes up. And above ground there's an equally large explosion: in the hearts of the women that the mine took with it when it collapsed. And with trembling lips and great startled eyes they stand watching by the gate: their lovers are brought up from the rubble of the mine and the rubble of their hearts: behind the old clog pile death awaited his fall. And against that iron gate a woman sobs—and meanwhile there's no pity among those standing by and watching, no fellow-feeling, just those fashionable words: we have to stock up, we have to find a way to profit: look at this photo from the daily press—a pickpocket caught stealing the purse of the weeping woman. The thief also waits behind the old clog pile.

I see all this, says johan janssens, from my window overlooking chapel road, and my sorrow is great at these disasters in the world . . . but not quite so great as my fury at seeing the way most people react to them.

THE UPSIDE-DOWN PAINTING

Mr brys has fled from chapel road, and now lives in the rue saint-honoré where things have only gotten worse for him . . . and to make matters even worse still, tippetotje drags him around with her on all her excursions: in the evenings she tucks her baron into bed and takes brys with her on her nocturnal jaunts. She shows him the open wound that is brussels, just as the hero of the dutch fairy tale "little johannes" was shown a cemetery, she shows him round among the scrofula and the mould, and shows him how the flower called art blossoms in the middle of a rubbish dump. And she also pushes his nose into the flower itself, the breathtaking orchid that grows on rotting trees, whose roots are set in corpses from which it distils its life essence—even if the Disease from the dung heap already affects it. Tippetotje drags mr brys along with her at night and introduces him to mr maecken. And mr maecken, who is a pathogenic bacillus living on art, which is an orchid, which grows on a dung heap . . . mr maecken stares in dismay at mr brys who still smells of the simplicity of chapel road: with a slight jolt he remembers how, many years before, he also lived in chapel road, and he wants to address mr brys in his native flemish, but when he opens his mouth it's an english, a spanish, a swedish word that's on the tip of his tongue: he's completely forgotten the language of chapel road, and being a little drunk he bursts into sobs. And mr brys asks him: what are you actually doing now, mr maecken? And mr maecken dries his tears and says: I promote nonsense, I destroy nonsense . . . I'm what you could call an art impresario—because it's a simple fact that a gap has appeared between the artist and his public. And the moment something interesting happens, some crafty guy pops up and wonders if he can earn a centime or two from it: only an idiot would ask how the gap can be filled—the wise man asks himself how he can profit from the gap. And I, mr maecken, have discovered that on the one hand the public is divided into 2 groups: those who maintain that incomprehensible art is no longer art, and those who on the contrary maintain that art only begins to become sublime when it's incomprehensible. I, mr maecken, have nothing to do with the first group . . . but the other group contains snobs, nouveaux-riches with a castles that need decorating, barons who want to dazzle you with important names, idiots frightened of being thought illiterate . . . and I produce nonsense for them, I destroy them: I palm off modern paintings on all those suckers.

And as they leave mr maecken, tippetotje says: it really is true . . . the other day he palmed off a painting on my own baron, and when he came by a few days later with the great painter salvador klee, the artist looked at his own painting on the wall and exclaimed: but it's hanging upside down! And mr maecken burst into thunderous laughter, and said: well then, voilà . . . it's hanging just right.

ONDINE GROWS FAT AND OSCARKE THIN

She had believed in miracles, in god and heaven and all that other stuff, she'd led a pious life and had even committed momentous crimes like a joan of arc, like an avenging angel of god, but the outcome was always this: they fooled her so they could creep under her skirt. And as if a flaming, agonizing sword had cleft her stupid head, she saw that there was nothing else and nothing more: just illusions that men conjured up for her eyes in order to get to her cunt. And at the same time, just as that notion was just taking hold, she already rejected it: it all might be the fault of human stupidity itself; boundless human foolishness was obstructing the advent of greatness. She stood looking at herself in the mirror and finally said: all I know is that I don't know anything. This realization made her resentful, made her jealous and malevolent, she felt a new attack of unreasoning anger against everyone . . . although it had been months, years, since she'd hated everyone so indiscriminately: and anyway it had softened into a contemptuous tolerance, a mockery of their faults, a chance to profit from their stupidity. And the fact that she hated them again now, wildly, revealed that, in fact, she couldn't do without them . . . that she couldn't yet do without them precisely because of the miracle, because of god . . . she went round blackening everyone's name, sewing discord and confusion, trying to turn everyone against everyone else: she said that such and such were not christians, that madame van wesenborgh had two husbands, one for the daytime and one for the night, and she spread the news that a schoolgirl was expecting a child by . . . well, which honorable man should she mention? She hunted down valeer, who came to her less and less on sundays, and took his money god knows where—and she discovered little by little that he'd been going to spend his sundays with a tart on the edge of town . . . at a place called "the pool," though there was no pool to be seen for miles around, just that huddle of poor people's shanties. That slut, a woman with only 1 leg, had as many children as could be: girls who were far from ugly, but who one knew from the age of thirteen onwards had nothing to hope for but the brothels by the station. And could you believe valeer was actually going to that widow, to that one-legged wonder . . . god, she was happy because it was so disgusting. She would lure valeer home, she would send word she was ill . . . or rather, that little judith was ill, because he would only come back for her (perhaps because she was a little like he was, the ass: silent and withdrawn, and willing to allow other people's mistakes to be lain at her door), and she remembered how he had waved colored scraps of paper in front of her, saying: you see this, it's red . . . and shortly after asking: what color is it? And ondine sent word that little judith was seriously ill, and was asking for him. He came, he fell into the trap like a mouse, and the things she accused him of, and the way she stripped him naked, emotionally, spiritually, were truly horrible: the fact that he, who'd never before so much as looked at a woman, let alone felt one, who'd even gone through life ignorant that horses were divided into stallions and mares, he was now suddenly going to the "pool" to peek under a skirt at 1 single buttock (or is it 2 buttocks but just 1 leg?), and to throw away his week's wages on that, haha, just for a look—a look!—when after he'd gone home there was a line out the door of men who'd come for a proper ride. Oh, ondine must have been a sadist deep down, because otherwise it wouldn't have been possible to beat him down like that. It kept her going for a day or two, but when the hunger to see other people's suffering began gnawing at her again, she took oscarke in hand: she said that there were men who were interested in children, Very interested, while they had a home, had little girls of their own, and she wondered whether those men ever asked themselves what it would be like if a stranger who liked children assaulted their own daughters? And as with valeer, she used the most vicious words that came into her head. Oscarke sat and listened with his head bowed, he didn't understand that she was thrashing around trying to find out what it was that was going on with him Over There like a blind person gropes for an egg: that she was only trying to hurt him, and that she'd moved on to inveigh against the women of brussels, who are all diseased . . . thinking, realizing, suspecting that he couldn't have caught on any other kind of hook over there but a woman—that it was the same with him as with all men, dreaming of this and longing for that, believing and doubting, living and dying, but in life not being able to cling to anything but a woman's skirts. He didn't understand, he was too dismayed by her words to understand . . . because really, really he'd no longer been able to restrain himself over there, and now sat wondering fearfully day and night whether he hadn't gone too far—she was so young, she was so inexperienced in these things, his jeannine, and now (no, he didn't dare think about it) he'd heard the mother say today as he was washing his hands in the washroom: jeannine, do you still not need a sanitary napkin? And her "no" had come out so hesitant and anxious that he had not been able to move, and had washed his hands over and over, he didn't know for how long, but it could have been hours. Ondine laughed at his bowed head, and she hated him for his cowardice: defend yourself, for god's sake, she said . . . say one thing or say the other, but don't sit there like a wet chicken. And again she had to laugh, because everyone looked to her like wet chickens nowadays, because because . . . Oh, in the morning she sat in church and in the in evening in her pub, which was a little worse than a brothel (because in a brothel people went upstairs and paid and what happened up there was the most natural thing in the world), but what happened at her place were sins against the holy ghost, as the priest says. She became fat from her intrigues, from her malevolence—and oscarke became thin with torment and doubt.

WALK A

It is now the time of paid vacations, and in termuren it's empty and quiet and all the blinds are shut . . . and the postman walks down the deserted chapel road to put a brightly colored postcard through the mail slot of every sleeping house . . . from rome and capri and even further afield come the cards with strange stamps on them, and drop through the mail slots into echoing and slightly stuffy halls: from the castle of bouillon people write to their neighbor who meanwhile is admiring lake lugano, and when they get back they two of them will find their postcards waiting. And going down that empty and deathly quiet chapel road, knowing that kramiek has chosen the balearic islands, and that master oedenmaeckers has taken off for the south of france, you're left on your own, having been declared fair game, and never having enjoyed a paid vacation. And you stroll up to the home of andreus mottebol, your spitting image, your equal, who says to you: it's a shame you too can't escape the daily routine and these too-familiar faces for a change, in order to rediscover the daily routine and too-familiar faces in some holiday resort or other . . . you'd see a world of commotion, shorts, sunglasses, and empty-headedness—in the grand duchy of luxembourg you'd find the people who live over there behind the labor weaving mill, and on lake lugano you'll find a man who just bought a car, bemoaning the fact that his business isn't flourish-ing. Ha, and do you remember the man who runs the coffee business here? (no, not the character from multatuli's novel *max havelaar*, but the one who before the war was dirt-poor, and now has a car, and is always bemoaning the fact that his business isn't flourishing?), well, that's him, he's in switzerland, sitting on a hotel terrace, and the landscape stretches away beneath him and his family—*walk A*—and pointing to that *walk A* with his outstretched arm, like napoleon pointing at the pyramids, he says to his daughter: elise, just look at everything your daddy can offer you . . .

And you say to andreus mottebol: stop joking around . . . because I feel myself getting a little bit bitter, because I myself am a father, but I have to say: elise, just look what other fathers, who aren't writers, could have offered you.

TRAVEL BROADENS THE MIND

And as you stand at your front door in the evening kramiek comes walking along, clearing up the 1,000 and 1 things that are getting in the way of his intended trip to the balearic islands. Around the castle of bouillon there are signposts: *walk* A: shout and you will hear the echo—but kramiek shouts instead in the many offices and departments that are getting in the way of his intended journey, and up to now has heard no echoes back from the sunlit regions where the rich walk around wearing sunglasses, hold car races, and display their empty minds. However, kramiek won't take no for an answer, and will not be diverted from his path: he is inexhaustible in politeness, uses long winding sentences which envelop and mollify everyone, and anyway belongs to the race of the thick-skinned. He'll reach the balearic islands for sure, and bring back a few things that may be of great use to him . . . for instance, a degree. The thing is, kramiek collects degrees like your son collects postage stamps. And as he comes walking down chapel road in order to remove all the obstacles from his path in his polite, thick-skinned way, he sees you standing at your front door and he is suddenly torn: should I walk past with a short but friendly greeting, thus proving that I'm a little too busy to stay and chat? Or should I on the contrary go up to him and talk over his last bitter remark about my getting to the balearics while he stays home? And deciding at the last moment that it's after all better to have one enemy less, he comes up and says: as for that trip to the balearics that I have to make, at the government's expense, you know, you could go there too . . . but now that we're discussing it tête-à-tête, it's really a shame that you haven't got any degrees. Why? you ask. Well, he says, shuffling his feet . . . well, you sit there and write and write, but what are you actually doing? why do you spend your time on that kind of literature? Well, you say, interrupting kramiek . . . it seems to me that you're a little involved with literature yourself, since you're studying at the university. Oh, but that's Quite different! exclaims kramiek . . . that's a course in literary history which leads to a degree, employment, social status—but that's not the case with you, your writing doesn't help you learn anything about literature, you add nothing of any importance to the history of literature . . . just a little creative prose . . . and anyone can write creative prose, everyone living here in chapel road could start writing at any time . . . but all that creativity doesn't move literary history one step farther. Literature is a subject, a science that's totally unknown to you: you know nothing about the structure, the rhythm, the movement, or the significance: you haven't even the humblest degree in the field, and so it's impossible for you to gain any social status or to get to go to the balearics at the government's expense. You just write novels. Why on earth do you do that?

And you stare at kramiek, thunderstruck . . . and you can't think up a reply that would pierce his elephant's hide. All you can do is close the front door and bend over your papers, over your heroes oscarke and ondine, in order to talk to them as one talks to a beaten dog, calming them, stroking their backs: hush now, dry your tears . . . you're My babies.

DEAD NOVELS

So you find out andreus mottebol is painting again, and you hurry over to his house and find him there surrounded by illustrations of our national puppet plays: his dream is to evoke an unmoving world in his paintings: puppets that begin to live only when someone else pulls the strings, that begin to speak only when someone else opens his mouth. And realizing how he's struggling forlornly to achieve a technique of his own, a technique with which he could depict the world as experienced by him, you say to him: in my view you're moving mountains that needn't be moved, you're struggling to achieve a unique style of painting, when you've long since attained your own unique style of writing . . .

Don't talk to me about the dead business of writing, andreus mottebol replies . . . don't talk to me about all those dead hands in books that smoke a cigarette, grasp this or that, rest on a car's steering wheel . . . don't talk to me about all those dead eyes that in books look at something, stare straight ahead, look at her, look at him. And because you look at him quizzically (you see! looking again), he replies that recently he's been investigating the way other writers put things down on paper . . . he says that he also met a dutch friend who showed him the dead technique of modern novel-writing in the most glaring light . . . and in that harsh light all the corpses of those novels lay there so gruesomely that he had to run away in disgust. You find only hands and eyes in those dead books of caldwell and steinbeck and hemingway, of sartre and malraux and st. exupéry . . . they all give you characters who don't even have bodies . . . no bellies, no armpit hair, no throats, no legs that are too short, just eyes and hands and sometimes a mouth too. Whereas in the psychological novels there were still eyes, eyes that were occasionally tearful, piercing, quizzical, staring into the distance, flashing . . . but all they have to offer in the modern novel are eyes that look. Try reading those caldwells and steinbecks and it'll drive you wild: he stood there, looking at him—she was looking at him across the table—they looked at him. It's so dead and cold and chilly, it is just a dead system that will soon start decomposing—because you can't go on presenting characters and making them Look from time to time whenever you don't know what else to do with them. She looked at him across the table while his hands grasped the edge. No, I'd sooner pack it in, because when the page of this century is added to literary history, it will say in it: steinbeck, caldwell, and andreas mottebol, typical examples of the eyes-and-hands novel. I'd rather just paint my puppets.

And you storm out of andreus mottebol's place, straight back to your own, to your own heroes ondine and oscarke . . . to make sure they weren't also always looking at each other the whole time: ondine looking at oscarke, and oscarke gripping the edge of the table. But thank god they weren't . . . you realize that in one of the last sentences you wrote, *ondine and oscarke went on rowing against the current, and day by day they experienced a new truth . . . a truth they'd forgotten again the next day.*

DEAD BLOSSOM?

And then the war . . . sure, people could see perfectly well that something was about to happen, ondine couldn't go out into the street without seeing soldiers, and oscarke couldn't come home at night without talking about what was happening in brussels—because brussels was the heart of things, and the heart was the best place to listen to what was happening down in the depths: there were posters and there was talk of mobilization, and suddenly out of the blue, germany declared war on france, requesting the right of passage through belgium. And everything that was important to people yesterday was no longer important today, because it was war, a new age had dawned. And it was as if the new age brought new people with it: electricity and all the other things that had preoccupied people suddenly vanished from their minds, oh, people even forgot that there had been liberals and catholics and socialists . . . it became an intoxication, a madness that infected everyone, and ondine too went round urging everyone to join the army, because she liked the war: she liked everything that was big and inflamed people's feelings. If oscarke weren't married! she said . . . you'd see he'd be first in line, but as it is I've got to stop him because he'd be leaving me with my three kids. Valeer, who dropped by again occasionally now and looked absolutely lost, twisted and turned to make his fat head invisible, fearing that she would persuade him too, and dream up reasons he couldn't possibly dismiss: he walked around with his hand in the air, so that she would see his missing finger. But she poked the stove hard and kicked the children out from under her feet: do you know, she said, that even men with only one hand have volunteered? Our country is in danger, they're coming to burn down our houses and assault the women and rape the children . . . if I were a man, oh, if only I were a man, even if I had no feet I'd drag myself to the border . . . but, well (and her sarcastic laugh made him blush red with shame), you can't do it, can you? you've a finger missing, and even though that coffin-maker probably has something wrong with him too,maybe his hearing isn't too good, and someone else is a priest, and another person is a schoolteacher . . . oscarke can say that he's an artist, a sculptor, and so the enemy will arrive and find men like old women waiting. What could valeer, with his simple way of thinking, say against that? That's just the point, he said . . . no one is going and again I'll be the victim and have to sacrifice myself for everyone else. No, said ondine, you don't have to . . . just stay with that widow and her wooden leg and her daughters with filthy sores in their mouths . . . stay in bed there and come over to our place for coffee so that we can catch the same diseases and have to go to the lime pits. And she dug her finger in her eye and wept. You stay here and let your old father go in your place, she said. Don't go, uncle, cried judith who had been listening in . . . don't go or they'll shoot you, you'll die and we'll never see you again. He stood there silently balanced on one leg and heard the word "shoot," and had exactly the same feeling as on that long-forgotten day when cousin maria got married—when she sat by the lollipops at the top table while he had to help with the washing up in the kitchen. Oh dear, what else could he do but report to the recruiting station and hide his severed finger? But he didn't have to worry: in the general frenzy people didn't look that closely—who could have foreseen that war would be like this? There were police to stop the socialists when they wanted to go on strike, and in addition there was an army to parade through the streets of brussels, to stand guard with a plume in their hats at the king's palace and to do just about everything with their rifles, salute, shoulder arms, eyes left, and so forth—and apart from that there was a mounted martial band that was world-famous—but they were at a loss because they had to shoot their rifles, and didn't know how. They shoved a rifle in valeer's hands too and sent him over to liege to stop the germans—their position was in a forest and they saw some cavalry in the distance and they waved and called out: where are you riding to? But they were germans, and, really, they were surprised when the germans started shooting at them. And then a plane came over, one of those old-fashioned '14-'18 machines, tied together with string, and they all fired at it, bang, bang, and the plane went away and shortly after hundreds of grenades fell on the copse. Then they had to run, run in their clogs, and throw away the packs that contained absolutely nothing of use, a knife and a comb—who on earth felt like parting their hair while chunks of mud were exploding round their ears?—so that they saw valeer again in no time in the little town of the 2 mills: he suddenly turned up at ondine's pub, one wooden clog broken, and he and his comrades looked utterly wretched, they borrowed some tobacco from oscarke and said they *would give it back after the war. And yet it wasn't valeers fault that he said some-thing so dumb: which of them knew that they were going to be floundering around in the mud for four more years? They left, limping and bleeding, and no sooner had the last of them turned the corner of the 1st grimy houses, the first germans arrived: and those soldiers shot at each other, and that was all ondine got to see of the real war, of blood and mud and terror and fire. Now a different war began for them, the german headquarters having been set up in the school, they had to keep the pavement clean and pull out the grass from between the paving stones—and a boundary called a stage area was drawn between brussels and the little town of the 2 mills, so that none of them got to go to brussels anymore. In a certain sense oscarke was glad, because he was out of work now and could just lay around, and he thought of starting to sculpt in the pub, since no one went into pubs these days. The place was empty, he put his clay on a small pub table and waited . . . because he could feel it, it would be a long time before an idea took shape. Something was stopping ideas from coming: he heard that in leuven whole streets had been set on fire, and that this had happened here, and something else had happened there, and god knows how they had fared in brussels at jeannine's place! Jeannine who'd stopped having her periods. Oh, he walked round the empty pub, his studio, and groaned and dreamed up a hundred ways to break through that german wall of barbed wire: he stood patting his clay with a lath of wood and didn't feel like start-ing anything . . . and yet, what wonderful statues he could have modeled! Jeannine pregnant, jeannine giving birth, jeannine murdered—the dead jeannine lying with a snapped off blossom slipping from her hands.*

WHERE HAVE WE GOT TO?

Johan janssens meets you there in chapel road . . . he's coming from brussels, which is in an uproar, and where the 1st cobblestones are being dug up—and you're coming from behind your desk, where you've gone on writing your-self silly, working on your everlasting, never-changing novel. And he asks: where have we got to? And rather hesitantly, rather unhappily you answer: ondine and oscarke are now experiencing their 1st world war, germans have put a local headquarters and a military police station in the little town of the 2 mills, and with spiked helmets on their cropped heads they've occupied chapel road: there's order, the streets are clean, and an edict was even given to remove the grass from between the paving stones. There is order in occupied chapel road, and there is quiet in the hearts of the people living there. But oscarke paces up and down past the ridiculous, grotesque wall he built in his house . . . and something stops him from sculpting: he's heard that in visé people were tied together and thrown in the water, that in leuven whole streets were set on fire, and that dendermonde is going up in flames—oh and he walks around in the silence of his house, hands intertwined in desperation: how is he to model jeannine now? Jeannine who is dead, perhaps, murdered by those spiked helmets. And johan janssens turns away and says: actually my question wasn't about your novel . . . I meant that brussels is in uproar, and the 1st cobblestones have been pried up . . . so I meant the attitude of the gentleman in the castle, who only ventures out as far as his balcony door in the evenings, despite his military . . . no, his regular police. And who spends all day amid the overpowering scent of orchids, which will soon fill him with disgust when they start rotting. That's what my question was about: where have we got to?

And you answer johan janssens: yes, that's what I meant too . . . oscarke is now experiencing his 1st world war, when there's quiet and order in the streets, and barbed wire and spiked helmets. And yet for us who are recording his adventures the 1st world war is long since over—there's been a 2nd one too, and indeed people are talking quite openly of a 3rd—but the wall of barbed wire, of order and quiet, still stands in the streets of brussels: it's only the helmets that change. That where we've got to with our novel: we're constantly making mistakes: *oscarke, who is actually experiencing only his 1st world war, thinks there is still a local headquarters and a military police station in brussels to this day . . . oscarke, who in our book sees the advent of the spiked helmets, thinks that the same spiked helmets are still occupying the streets of brussels to this day.*

AN EXPLORER

These days you would knock in vain at the doors of the 4 villas in chapel road: they are empty, hollow, and stuffy: the people have gone to the seaside or into the country on paid vacations. Only the music master will have stayed at home, because of the cottage that's being built for him, over in his little garden . . . and feeling a bit tired (and also feeling empty of inspiration), you walk over to see him to take a rest. Unfortunately, though he's stayed in town because of the construction of his cottage, because of the construction he's never at home, always out seeing bricklayers and carpenters and plumbers: you find only his wife, his child, and one of his pupils. A pupil who's young and exuberant . . . who in increasingly clerical chapel road remains our hope and our strength . . . who in these days of tumult surrounding a king went to brussels and was ready to stand on the barricades. And when you tell him you feel a little tired and empty of inspiration, in all his exuberance he stares witheringly at you: how can you feel tired in these days of struggle, he asks . . . how can you be empty of inspiration at a time when every day brings something different and something new? And he's right, sure enough . . .

yet it's precisely all these events racing by in such an astonishing way that gives you a feeling of emptiness: ondine and oscarke are experiencing their 1st world war, and valeer is somewhere in the mud of the trenches along the river ijzer . . . while we ourselves are preparing to face a 3rd world war. It makes you tired . . . it gives you the uncomfortable feeling that you have no more to say and simply go on repeating yourself: that you've been writing the whole time about one and the same war, from 1914 to 1950. And look, at that moment the music master pushes his muddy and battered way into the house, flops into a chair and says: I'm . . .

Yes, we know, his pupil interrupts him . . . you're a little tired, and you probably also feel empty of inspiration! No, it's not that, says the music master . . . I'm a little indignant that some writers and painters are still not impressed by the things that affect our world every day anew . . . but go on enthusiastically making their products, and making them in exactly the same ways. Over in that cottage that's being built for me, there will be a large piece of flat wall where I'd like to hang a painting. And so I went to see the last landscape artist, who has rented the last farmer's barn way over beyond termuren, and now paints landscapes there. And he was terribly excited: he had made a discovery, he said: he was painting a calvary, and just made the unbelievable discovery that he could set his calvary in the landscape around termuren. And after he'd explained that to me I still looked at him expectantly, thinking that the significant part of his discovery was about to follow . . . but no, that was It, not a jot more. Thousands had painted that calvary before him, and hundreds before him had set the calvary in the landscape around termuren: baby jesus was born in flanders, the counting of the innocents took place in brabant, the lord jesus addressed the woman taken in adultery in kempen, and the flight into egypt took place through west flanders. Meanwhile the world is threatening to split into two great pieces and we're all holding our breath . . . and feeling tired and especially empty of inspiration: but those who experience and feel some of this can still become enthusiastic about a trifling discovery, about a discovery that someone else made years before him.

CLAY IS CLAY

Oscarke walked back and forth. From the top curtains to the ridiculous wall: stop that pacing or I'll walk with you, all day long from one wall to the other, said ondine. And she looked at him but couldn't laugh, because although she thought he was ridiculous and small in the face of fate, most of all it hurt her, because his pacing made her see her own helplessness walking to and fro in front of her. Because no one came to the pub anymore, oscarke didn't earn a centime, they were in the direst poverty—and savings, no, they had none—they'd paid the landlord in installments in order to have a house of their own, but now ondine saw just how crafty that doctor goethals was, how crafty the whole bourgeoisie was—saving for a house of your own! Ha, as if they could now start eating stones. And she went to the landlord and proposed that he return the money that she had paid on account, and so had in fact overpaid—but again this money wasn't as simple a matter as she'd imagined: that sly old rat of a landlord laughed in her face: give her her money, and probably let her off the rent too, because everyone thought they didn't need to pay rent now that there was a war on . . . as if landlords were supposed to starve: she was hungry, she said, but what was he then? and now he was supposed to give her her money back? And he came up with a proposal: that she could have the sum she'd already paid him, provided she paid interest on it as if it were a loan . . . and also provided that he could first deduct the rent due. And ondine might say, first imploringly and then threateningly, that he had no right, but in the end she had to accept defeat: she didn't have two cents to rub together at home. In those days she went round, through streets full of spiked helmets, boasting here and complaining there, because that empty pub and that cold kitchen and those crying kids . . . she couldn't stand them anymore, and she chattered on till it drove you mad in every house she visited, so that she became confused and complained where she'd boasted the day before, and vice versa. When she went to the priest she wept and came away with either a loaf of bread or some potatoes, or she was allowed to go to the catholic school to take a bucket of coal with the priest's compliments—and of course she sent oscarke on that particular errand. She also wept at the doctor's, but all he could give was a mere pittance—my boys, he explained—and offer to make the occasional free visit. She laughed in boone's shop . . . she was still doing well, she still had money in her savings account—and she pulled out her last banknote, the last of the ones that doctor goethals had given her, to pay for the items she'd bought. Or rather, not to pay for them, because she put the note away again, remembering she had shopping to do elsewhere too. And the following day she visited again and wailed and said she didn't know how to make ends meet: because she was trying to draw them out, to see what they actually lived on. Your husband, she asked, does he have a job? My oscarke paces around and doesn't earn a thing . . . right, we've still got savings, but that can't last forever with children who've got to have a decent education . . . I understand, you have no children, you're socialists who defy god . . . and if you did have children you'd let them run around with their hair hanging loose, whereas I . . . I . . . And meanwhile she sat with her feet up on the stove so that they could see her new underwear, petticoats she'd sewn out of curtains from the church. God helps us, she said. But she was surprised that boone, the man from the shop, was never there. God cares for us . . . yes, but she knew that god also cared for those who knew that he didn't even exist, that he cared for everyone, for encyclicals and socialists, for saints and villains. So where's your husband got to? she asked. And to her growing irritation she heard *that boone had been taken on to help build a town park on mr derenancourt's marshy land over on chapel road. And irritation was not quite the right word, it was more discouragement: she knew nothing about town parks, she knew nothing about the group that used to get drunk at her place and had behaved like animals, and was now starting to stir again and do things . . . things like building municipal parks on their marshiest land. No, they hadn't said a word to her about that: they had already fallen on hard times, through women and horses and perhaps even worse things—so that glemmasson had had to sell his last coach, so that norbert had had to become a traveling wine salesman—but now that there was a war on, they were starting to build parks, though no one thought of her, no one thought: can't we help ondine earn a centime or two by making her husband supervisor? Or if supervisor was a little too grand, at least making him a foreman? And she was also ashamed of having said here that she and mr achilles derenancourt were as thick as thieves . . . and now having to learn from the socialists that he had given away that neglected land, those bushes on chapel road, to have a park built on it. It's not true! she said. Not true, good god woman, they're digging a round pond, you should see boone when he gets home: 1 great clod of mud. Then it can't be derenancourt land! ondine countered ingeniously . . . but she kept fidgeting at the stove, still moving her legs to show off her new bloomers, but her peace of mind had gone: building a park to get the unemployed off the street, but wasn't oscarke unemployed just as much as they were? And besides, he was used to working with clay: over there, digging that pond, he would have been in his element.*

JAN DE LICHTE ARRESTED!

Permit us, dear reader, in these tumultuous days of war and occupation—or rather, in these deathly quiet days of iron order—to call attention to our other hero, jan de lichte: he's suddenly been captured through betrayal, and he's now imprisoned in the tower. And now the whole of termuren and the town of the 2 mills should be in a great commotion, all the people should flock together, to gape at the tower window on the market square: the hero of the lumpen-proletariat captured! And the good citizens should flock together singing and dancing: they who see in jan de lichte only what the priest has told them from his pulpit, or what the official crier has proclaimed. The others on the other hand, the nameless masses, should stand silently in the market square, dismayed and pale . . . hesitant and with mixed feelings . . . because for a few moments they had dared to see jan de lichte as the ultimate messiah, because they once again have seen the bottom knocked out of a vague hope—like, for that matter, every other fleeting hope.

For example, the people from the 1st grimy houses should have stood there . . . the people who live outside the town walls, and who in times of war and plague and famine don't really have a right to protection. The people who, like rampant weeds, have started to grow beyond their allotted land, and now serve as a sacrifice for every advancing foreign army . . . as a buffer, and as fodder for the most disgraceful, excessive lusts. Those people might at least have stood there. They might have left their huts, built right up against the town walls, where they now live and die like finches in their cages, finches whose eyes are put out to make them sing all the more sweetly. They might have hopped around restlessly on their perches—where they'd already struck their wings against the clay walls of their dark, stinking hovels . . . where they'd heard, from afar, the winds bringing them the song of the revolt . . . where they'd heard the drum of the beggar-rebels roll

> beat on the drum-a-drum durumadum dum dum
> beat on the drum-a-drum durumadum dum
> battez le tambour durumadum dum dum
> battez le tambour durumadum dum

and sorrow may have crept into their hearts when that rolling of drums was suddenly stopped and the songs broke off with: jan de lichte captured, jan de lichte locked up in the tower! And a sudden silence may have fallen among those grubby people of the 1st grimy houses, in which they listen with a chill round their hearts . . . perhaps with despair . . . and in the worst case, with resignation. And there may also have been a blare of joy on the other side of the barricade, a triumph that can only make us more bitter—and would make us retreat even deeper, like a mollusk into its shell, like a rat into its sewer, into the mud. They may, in the seclusion of their drawing rooms, have taken to the bottle because the godforsaken villain was about to be drawn and quartered by justice. Foreign soldiers may have fired a celebratory salvo. In the vast and imposing church, with its double row of blue-stone pillars, a te deum may have been sung . . . a paean of praise, a gloria . . . incense and myrrh may have risen to heaven because the lawless had been brought back to the straight, numbered, and clearly marked path.

That is how it should have been. Unfortunately history itself, with all its contradictions, confuses the picture . . . it comes up with something else, which is *more* important to the people of the little town of the 2 mills. Jan de lichte was arrested, but no one had time to pay attention to it . . . in their eyes, something far more exciting awaited them: it was almost fair time.

FAIR TIME IN THE TOWN OF THE 2 MILLS

The light that shone in the age-old darkness of commandments and laws, of order and discipline and manifold regulations, that light is threatened with extinction—the banner of Nihil is torn from our hands . . . and the man who managed to become a symbol in the history of flanders of our will towards space, freedom, equality, and a host of other trivialities that we can't recall at the moment, that man is clapped in irons. But the people of the 1st grimy houses can't stream to the marketplace to stare in dismay at that tower window: they're busy stirring the filling for the fair flan, they're busy cooking rice pudding and cutting their ham into slices. It's doubly tragic, if you want take the dismal background of the fair into account—if you realize that these flemish fairs are part of the plot that keeps us poor and stupid. Because it would be impossible to keep dogs chained up if they weren't thrown the occasional bone—children are promised a lollypop to keep them well behaved, and the simpleminded are promised the kingdom of god . . . and once a year those who have survived gnawing on hunks of bread must be offered rice pudding and sausage and flans. Offered . . . don't make me laugh! For a few days a year the people of the 1st grimy houses delude themselves that they're partaking of a cornucopia. They've gone hungry, they've done penance and fasted, they've bowed in sweat and tears beneath the yoke of original sin—but once a year it's fair time, and then they root and toil twice as hard for months in advance: they deny themselves the most urgent essentials, a shirt to cover their nakedness or a bandage for their wounds, just so they can throw money away on the fair days, and spill bits of flan and french toast and ham everywhere.

And also there's been word, vague and from afar, of an additional attraction at the fair: it seems that jan de lichte has been locked up in the tower. And only here and there has someone from the 1st grimy houses—where people are reeling about, drunk and fighting, and where they've also been baking flans—heard the news with dismay. Someone here and there . . . someone who perhaps deep down had considered joining the gang, but didn't quite have the courage to take the big step . . . and so preferred to wait until fate drove him to it, or chance. And such a person is exactly the type who thinks, at the beginning, that it must it must be a fair show, like the fireworks, the jousting, and the egg dance . . . he thinks it must be a fake, an imitation jan de lichte in the tower: perhaps even a straw doll, which will be hung high above the street on sunday evening to general jeers, and set on fire.

HAS VALEER . . . TURNED INTO OSCARKE?

And suddenly ondine kicked her legs off the stove and, muttering something, hurried off: she hurried to the mansion where achilles lived—but as she went along her belly started hurting, and her hernia too—and in her haste she stumbled over a stone, since her eyesight was also starting to fail: it's the war, she thought . . . we're bound to have more to eat after the war. And she pinned all her hopes on that: the end of the war—and perhaps she also thought that her hernia would be cured too at the end of the war, that everything that had been denied her in life would land in her lap. A park! she said sulkily . . . those 4 villas of course did nothing to turn that wilderness into a building plot—but now things will get better, now they'll all want to live by the park: where do you live, madame van wesenborgh? By the municipal park! ondine said, imitating the voice of madame van wesenborgh outloud in the street, with lips so finely pursed that a passerby stopped to watch her go. By the park! Right, oscarke could work digging clay out by the pond—he could make statues, christ yes: a statue at each corner of the pond, summer and autumn, spring and winter, a woman with young leaves round her head and a woman with a pick and a woman with a bunch of branches, and a woman with . . . with . . . well, a woman who was growing old, a woman whose eyesight wasn't too good anymore and who might need glasses, who had a hernia, and always had a bellyache when she had to run. And she stopped. Am I getting old? she asked . . . and then she continued more slowly, fretting about this new topic. Old—a woman in winter—a statue to be placed by the pond—and she would impress on oscarke that they should go and see and make it clear that he, oscarke, was the foreman around here. Meanwhile she'd reached the gate of the derenancourt mansion and rang the bell—yes, he was mayor now, mr achilles, and ondine had fought to make him mayor . . . but were things any better now, did they ever think of her now? He was mayor and something had to be done about the unemployed who during the day stood in line for a cup of soup, since the devil still found work for idle hands—and ondine didn't touch on the fact that his building land had to be sold, that joke would have been in poor taste. She stood and listened to him in silence, since he hadn't found it necessary to offer her a chair, she was only ondine, true, madame ondine—he himself had given her the name, heaven knows why . . . and she looked him in the eye and heard him say that while he had donated the land, he didn't want to find jobs for anyone or concern himself with anything at all—it was a project controlled by the occupying powers, and he didn't want to collaborate with them under any circumstances—and meanwhile he wasn't thinking about the fact that the filature spinning mill was working flat out . . . that fat glemmasson was buying up leather and starting to make boots with his sister, madame derenancourt's, money, which she had put into his business. No, no, said achilles . . . and he spread his long pale fingers as if warding off the thought . . . There was no way he was going to collaborate with them, let valeer apply through the usual channels, and if he's unemployed, he'll be taken on! Oh, valeer . . . valeer's at the front, said ondine. And though his hands were still warding her off, the look in his eyes changed: at the front? he asked. He had intended to disappear into the depths of the house, but now he turned round and looked at her uncomprehendingly. She too looked at him uncomprehendingly for an instant, but then a flush of shame rose into her cheeks in waves—she thought

237

she might faint in the vestibule, because it was suddenly clear to her: he thought that valeer was her husband; he'd come to see her at the pub and had seen valeer, and afterwards glemmasson had sent valeer to him, and now . . . he had employed valeer here as a manservant (and she could imagine what a clumsy manservant he had been, bumbling about this grand house, stumbling and breaking cups, god knows what fun they'd made of him here, just as she herself had made fun of him), and this man here, this achilles, had thought the whole time that this impossible fathead was her husband. He had thought: she lies in bed with that, after she . . . And she saw valeer more clearly than she had ever seen him before with his three fingers and thumb, his neck with the head wobbling on top—she bowed her head and didn't have the courage to explain it to him. What was the point? She turned and went out of the gate, and walked on and didn't know what street she was in.

THE MISTAKE

The music master's pupil is young and exuberant . . . and before rushing back to the thousand thunderous things our times have to offer, he drops by for a moment to ask if he can quickly skim through that big book about oscarke and ondine. And in the book he reads about mr achilles's mistake, thinking that ondine was married to valeer—and after the music master's pupil has skimmed through it, he bursts out laughing: mistakes like that happen, he says . . . when there was lots of commotion in brussels about a king, I saw lots of people marching and I joined them . . . we went to the castle and cheered to the rafters the man who lived there: I'd made a mistake, and found myself among the pros rather than the cons. And making a virtue of necessity I got into a discussion with the man standing next to me . . . who was getting very worked up because over there in the distance, right at the bottom of the big garden, we could see a shadowy outline in a window. Why, I asked, does he never come any closer, so that we could see him? He does come, said the man next to me, but only after dark. Why, I ask, does he come only after dark and only when his supporters surround his castle? And eventually, when he didn't know what to answer, it gradually began to penetrate his thick skull since I didn't share his opinions, I thought differently about things, and hence was his arch-enemy. And you don't chat with enemies, you beat them to death: walloons are traitors, kill them all! And he started sounding the alarm at the top of his voice, so that all the lads from the clerical colleges hemmed me in to plant a few decisive arguments on my chin. And gloating at my predicament, since nothing could now save me, the man next to me said slowly and emphasizing each syllable: he's a red! And the faces around me went white with anger, fists were clenched and sticks raised: all for flanders and flanders for christ, kill him! And I replied: no, I'm not a red, I'm a liberal. And there was a sudden hesitation, a silence when the crowd tried to process this sudden turn of events: a liberal, what was that? There had been nothing about that in the parish newsletter. And making use of their confusion I ducked out of sight and a few moments later rectified my mistake by joining a demonstration that really was a con.

SO AREN'T THERE ANY SOCIALISTS LEFT?

But wasn't it all oscarke's own fault? It showed what an insignificant gnat she was married to: people came to her house and didn't even notice the difference between her husband and valeer—he was supposed to be a sculptor who was going to carve her in every possible way, and exhibit her, and win honor and fame for her and make her rich—and instead he was a mouse, he was like his mother, ha, a baby mouse, That's what he was. She came home and couldn't find him: are you behind the wallpaper by any chance? she shouted with a bitter laugh. No, he was sitting in the pub, but amazingly enough he understood her: strange but true, he'd just been thinking exactly the same thing—with bitter self-knowledge he had realized that his life amounted to nothing and that he was wandering aimlessly round the house while ondine was heaven knows where getting up to heaven knows what, stealing a piece of bread or a shovel-full of coal. And tormenting himself with thoughts of jeannine he went on chipping away at his head of christ—it was no longer to chip away his doubt, since whether he was right or wrong about there being a heaven or not, or about heaven being a future world on earth . . . whether it was an approaching golden age where people could live happily, or a place where souls of the dead found eternal rest . . . it was all the same to him, lazy good-for-nothing, ditherer, worthless sculptor: there was to be no salvation for him. And besides, he'd found an easy way of evading all doubt—valeer had taught him a lot, valeer had taught him this crucial point about life: that one can go round without thinking, silently, acting as if one was too stupid to live . . . and meanwhile pick someone with a wooden leg who you could lie next to in bed without fretting about whether anything was good or bad. And the fact that he was sitting there chipping was still something . . . more because he liked chipping, because despite everything it was his vocation—although something in him or about him, perhaps his brain, or else his pathetic hands, made it impossible for him to give form to the images that proliferated in his head like bedbugs. And apart from that, if he'd dared to push his thinking to the limit . . . well, he would much rather have died between jeannine's legs than come to this. And he said out loud: no! . . . although he knew that it was true. He listened to what ondine had to say about the municipal park—and bowed his head, he'd been expecting it, knowing that it couldn't Last, sitting alone making vague plans—and suddenly knew that he actually liked sitting here in the empty pub tormenting himself with everything, and he also suddenly knew what he had to sculpt: a man bent double looking motionless at a length of rope in his hands. But that was over now . . . that park then . . . what park? he asked. And he went down to the park: they were all old pals, they were almost all men who'd taken the train from green avenue station with him, and in the winter had frozen and in the summer had stifled in those pre-war trains: they treated the work on that park as a joke, since they earned only their war allowance and a bowl of soup, and it wasn't work they were used to: uprooting bushes and digging up tree stumps and pushing wheelbarrows to and fro—they looked up and shouted: hey, if it isn't oscarke over there!—and oscarke felt happy, forgot his chilly empty pub and his clay, and started cursing with them, although he wasn't really one for cursing—and he helped them dig out the pond and build hillocks. And as they pushed those wheelbarrows to and fro they occasionally went for a drink at the tap, and there they played rough jokes on one another, for example smearing shit all over the handle of the cup—and then they shook with laughter, and forgot that they were plodding about there in the mud for a cup of soup and a bit of charity. And had they been socialists before the war? You couldn't tell by looking at them—the germans were there, one was walking about over yonder with a rifle on his shoulder, and there was another one sitting in a sentry box—and as for socialism, it was as if it had never existed, it was as if when the war came there were suddenly no more people fighting for a loftier, better existence.

BIRDSONG

Mr brys is forever wanting you to write to him, wanting you to send him pages daily about ondine and oscarke and life in chapel road . . . since he's lonely over there in the tenement on rue saint-honoré. Living in chapel road, in the hamlet of termuren, he was never as lonely as he is now in the metropolis of brussels. And when you send him the latest pages about ondine and oscarke, he writes you an alarming letter: I understand that oscarke has suddenly become unemployed, that people don't sculpt when there's a war on and hobnailed boots are marching through the streets—and I also understand that he's been taken on to build a park down there at broeck: that for a pittance and a bowl of soup he trudged to and fro with wheelbarrows through the mud. But when you describe that whole business to me, it's not about that brook, the park, the bushes . . . but about the water tap where they played crude jokes on each other. And from my place on rue saint-honoré I must inform you that you have no eye for nature: I can only assume that it rained there again yesterday, and so they're plodding round in the mud outside. That's all. You can't criticize henry miller anymore—your work is chaos, cacophony, a microcosm and a macrocosm, but nowhere is there a flower blooming or a bird singing.

And you reply that you're sorry that oscarke hasn't yet heard a bird sing in that park while he was spooning up his bowl of war soup. Still, there was a time when what you liked most was sitting and writing in the very early morning, when the first morning trains thundered vaguely in the distance, and when all the birds suddenly began twittering. And considering that a bird screaming like that is actually chasing its prey—shrilling and twittering, it's hunting down its breakfast . . . and the little hunted creature doesn't know which way to turn, petrified with fear at all that earsplitting tweeting: so that this famous singing of the birds actually consists of war cries: all those poetic effusions about the concert of birds, about the dawn chorus, are about the struggle for existence, like everything else. And you ask mr brys if he wants you to pack oscarke off to the park at the crack of dawn? You might be able to think up a reason for him having to be there so early—a mistake about the alarm clock, for instance . . . or rather a fight with ondine, so that he can't get out of the house soon enough . . . so that stubbornly and stupidly, rather naively, like a child, he sets off for work hours too early, and there in the solitude of the landscaped park hears the birds starting to twitter. Yes, he could make a striking comparison between the birds, chasing after their prey with their war cries, and the spiked helmets who have driven him into the mud of the park . . . between the birds with their earsplitting twittering and his wife ondine, in fact, who appalls him with her noise and clatter . . .

But mr brys replies: no, please, don't bother, better not describe the dawn chorus . . . it's already grim enough in your book without that.

THE COTTAGE AND YOUR NOVEL

You walk past master oedenmaeckers's bit of garden, where he's having a cottage built . . . and you see him over there in all his oedenmaeckers excitement, waving both arms, having a heated conversation with a fat, red-faced man in faded velvet trousers: the bricklayer . . . and a thin man in a tattered vest: the carpenter . . . and a tall man drawing red pencil lines across a soiled piece of paper: the architect. And while master oedenmaeckers waves his arms this way and that, a man with a clod of earth appears, leaning indifferently on his shovel: the builder . . . and someone who knows how to put up a cottage better than any of them sits on a pile of stones: the spectator. And noticing that you've entered his bit of garden, master oedenmaeckers drops his arms and comes over to you—and imitating the language of literature with scathing sarcasm, he declaims the last page about ondine and oscarke: he tore out tree stumps, and plodded through the mud with wheelbarrows, and at a water tap they played crude jokes on him. Ha, you can cross out oscarke's name and go ahead and insert my name instead—and you can add that bricklayer and

241

that carpenter, that architect, that workman, and that all-knowing spectator, they all played crude jokes on master oedenmaeckers . . . and finally to cap the bitter joke, you can add that the park (or rather the cottage) turned out to be pretty different from the cottage he saw in his dreams. Only now do I under-stand how true the popular expression is, when people belittle and deprecate someone by saying: he's an architect, you know! Look, he's over there, this one's an architect too! Just draw me a dream of a house, I told him . . . and now it turns out he drew a dream all right, but a bad dream, a nightmare. First, below ground there's a cellar, so big and with so many compartments that I've got a separate cellar for my coal, my wood, my potatoes, my carrots, and my peas . . . and I've also got a spare compartment to pile all my old hats in. And aboveground—don't faint—I have rooms that are too big, rooms that are too small, and rooms that serve a purpose that's a complete mystery to me. And in all these rooms there are doors and more doors leading into them . . . in the living room there are four, and in the kitchen five . . . and in the little room where I'm supposed to shut myself away and think, there are six . . . no, I'm wrong, three . . . one to go through to open the front door when there's a knock, one for taking out the kitchen garbage outside, and one that has no use but to stand there and be a door: but a door is never amiss, says the carpenter. And next to my house is something they call a storage shed, I can't think of a single thing I'd need to store in it—except for perhaps the secondhand car I'm going to buy—but the storage shed is too small for that. And can you see them over there, the bricklayer and the carpenter, the architect, the workman, and the spectator? They're building me another shed, a bigger one, next to the existing one that I don't need! And then my lovely wife lucette also wants to have a door to the garden put in where I wanted a window, and in addition she wants an extra door alongside every existing door just for her: I can have a wonderful time slamming doors when I'm in a bad mood, she says. And yesterday she talked about what she would do to the house if she ever won the Lottery . . . and I said: if you win the jackpot we'll share it, and you can build a house to your taste and I'll build one to mine: I'll send you a postcard: greetings from termuren.

Still, I don't think it's all that bad, you say to master oedenmaeckers. And he looks critically at the thing under construction, and says: oh well . . . after all a person is only at home to eat and sleep a bit—just like oscarke was only in the park to get a bowl of soup and a bit of war charity.

GOOD DAY, FATHER!

As he was digging and pushing wheelbarrows oscarke happened to look at the back windows of the 4 villas: that was where his mother lived! And for the first few days he was embarrassed, thinking that she might recognize him among the squirming heap of male humanity in the mud: a sculptor pushing a wheelbarrow, who was digging up tree stumps instead of sketching the models for 4 statues at the corners of the pond, 4 women, for example, representing the spring and the summer, the autumn and the winter—but for all he knew someone might have thought of that already—but what were the odds of that? People were too stupid to have that good an idea. And his mother . . . of course, a person became what fate made him, nothing could be done about that . . . but for some people, for jeannine, for example, for his mother, he would like to have counted for something more in the world. Although what did that mean, for oscarke, "counting for something"? . . . So he kept a bit in the background and he pulled out bushes crouching low, and if a foreman did occasionally send him over to the 4 villas, he stood laughing and talking as if he were Someone Else . . . acting as if he were happy, acting as if he had more to say than the people giving the orders. Go over there and pull, oscarke! they said . . . and he went over there and pulled, with an expression like he was the boss, a benevolent boss who let his men boss him around. Yet a gray head never came and looked out of any of the windows, so that eventually he actually began to long to see her from a distance—and at midday he went over there to eat his sandwiches. But as for knocking at her door and saying . . . well, what would he say? He couldn't just push the door open and say hello—how are you?—after he'd hadn't set foot here in 4 years. Still, she hadn't deceived him in his childhood anymore than any other mother would have done, certainly no more than ondine had done. Everyone fought for himself in life, everyone took advantage of others as far as he could—and who could change that? In this way he constructed the harshest theories about life, sitting there longing to be back in his parents' house—until sitting there at lunchtime eventually became a habit, and he forgot why he was sitting there—or first he tried to forget, and then he finally did forget, and then he found other things to occupy his strange thoughts. For example, the girls coming from the labor weaving mill, where they helped make blankets for the german army—it was midday and the foreman gave the signal and oscarke went and sat down by chapel road, and soon afterwards the mill girls came past on their way to termuren—he looked up at them, at their legs, under their skirts, or at least as far as he could see under their skirts, and meanwhile thought of jeannine's legs—but he didn't want to know that this was what he was really thinking. And when they stopped working in the evening, he came home all the way from chapel road alone, with his head a little bowed and with that same tuft of hair on the back of his head sticking up, and already starting to go gray. One day boone from the shop would be five or so steps ahead of him, the next he would be five or so steps behind him—oscarke saw that he must live somewhere nearby, and he watched him as he went and guessed what sort of man he must be: a rather thick, round head and round shoulders, and a moustache that seemed to say: I'm a bear with a sore head

. . . which of course he was not, bears with sore heads and such round shoulders didn't exist. And every day oscarke noticed something new about him, but he still didn't speak to him, although he must be the boone that ondine had talked about: boone, who was a socialist . . . a socialist before the war, of course. One evening he hurried to catch up with boone, and the following evening he strolled so that boone would catch up with him *—and all the things he told boone in his head about socialism were incredible: one day man would no longer be a predator, one day this and one day that! And in so doing he rediscovered the world, god, and the happiness that's the harmony of all things. And suddenly, by chance, he did after all arrive home together with boone: the hairs on the back of his head trembled and he launched straight in with his very beautiful thoughts, so that boone glanced at him from the side and walked on, and looked at him again—and finally said that it was all bullshit, that beautiful world: there will always be factories and people will always have to work . . . just imagine a thousand years from now, won't you have to wear clothes, and won't there be a filature spinning mill and a labor weaving mill? Of course, said oscarke, but . . . boone cut him short, because he'd had more than enough of these arguments with his father: well, he said, so what are you going on about? And so how exactly is this boone a socialist, oscarke wondered: he was probably one because his father had also been one. And it suddenly dawned on him that it would be the same with that new movement as it had been with everything else in the world: socialism would become something one was a member of out of habit, because one had always been one—just as christians still went to church. And it made oscarke so disconsolate, so heavyhearted. So what's the point of this game here on earth if nothing will ever change? Oh, that's what the catholics say too, said boone: what does life down here mean if there's no heaven. And by this time they'd almost reached the 1st grimy houses. Boone said: look, speak of the devil! And oscarke looked up, since he had been walking along looking at the ground and wondering why why why . . . he looked up and saw it was the priest coming out of his and ondine's place: he was a little embarrassed, actually, and immediately looked back at the ground so as not to have to speak—but it was boone himself who shouted from a distance: good day, father!*

THE LAST PAGE

And so for the umpteenth time a chapter of our life and of our book about chapel road has come to a close—you wonder where all those chapters keep coming from—and you reflect as well that your life is as short as the book on chapel road should be never-ending: one should go on writing such books, passing them down from father to son, for 200, 300 years. Only then would your novel become a book of books, a bible, a document, a testament. Only then would it become something in which one felt one had an integral part:

your book and your life together like siamese twins. Each word would pulse like the pulse of your blood, and every sentence would have the rhythm of your breath. And whenever you felt tired, and felt absolutely empty of inspiration, you would have reached the final pages of a chapter. Now, however, that's not the case—now there are anomalous relationships, mistakes and shortcomings on all sides: your characters were wandering around in some of the gloomiest surroundings precisely when you yourself felt as light and free as a bird . . . they were sad, sick, and wretched, when you yourself were brimming with good humor . . . they were engaged on large-scale works when you yourself felt tired and fainthearted. You started on this chapter so confidently, so proud, so full of courage . . . and you gave it that far-too-beautiful title: your happiness is something you have to fight for. And after you'd written that title, the chapter developed . . . but it began to look as if all the characters who had to fight for their happiness would be defeated in that fight. Ha, it was valeer, with that wobbling, monstrous head on his shoulders, who said in his clumsy way that we would have to fight for our happiness. And where is he now? Somewhere in the trenches along the river ijzer, covered in mud, and again with a bloody rag round his hand: a strange way of fighting for his happiness. And also, whenever they talk about him, they now confuse him with his brother-in-law oscarke—that's how insignificant he is. And oscarke himself is unemployed, and is forced by the spiked helmets to trudge round in the mud of the park to earn some war soup. And his new friend boone, a lifelong socialist, a fighter, a rebel, also works in that park for a little war charity—and he talks about man not needing very much to find a little happiness in life—and just as he says that a reverend father comes by, and he greets him politely: good day, father. Him, boone! It's enough to make you weep. It makes oscarke so disconsolate that he wonders: what meaning does this ridiculous game have, if we no longer dare fight for our happiness? No, looking back we would have done much better to choose these words of oscarke's as a title. And all the other heroes in this chapter live accordingly: mr brys has literally fled chapel road, tippetotje paints rats alongside her baron, polpoets has withdrawn into his so-called villa, and master oedenmaeckers into his bit of garden. And finally, something dreadful happened in this chapter: jan de lichte, the great outlaw, that pirate . . . the only one who grasped with both hands for his own happiness and his own prosperity, is thrown into a dark hole and locked in with heavy bolts.

That's what the chapter looks like, and now, feeling tired and actually rather empty of inspiration, you realize that you've worn yourself out in vain, that you've written yourself dry for nothing: everything that you planned to write at the beginning of that chapter—when you felt so cocksure—stuck in your pen, while everything that flowed so easily from it ought to have been thrown away. Your happiness . . . well, what does it amount to now? But you feel too tired and too empty of inspiration to change the title at this stage. And deeply ashamed you draw a line under these pages, and resolve to start a new chapter as quickly as possible. A more beautiful one. A better one.

A LITTLE MISTAKE AMONG MILLIONS OF OTHERS

THE NEW CHAPTER

You'd like to add a more beautiful chapter to this book on chapel road . . . this book that you've called "summer in termuren" . . . a more beautiful, a better, a more perfect chapter. But look, the page is still empty and blank, and you're looking in vain for a reasonable title for this new chapter. A chapter that would be like a flaming sword, to drive the fallen readers from the paradise of our book on chapel road. A title like the red-and-white crossed arms on the unmanned railway crossings in belgium, which warn walkers to beware. And also a title that would be a summary of everything that your book's heroes and heroines experience, think, do, do wrong, and then do totally wrong in this chapter. Your paper is still empty and blank and you can't find a title for this new chapter . . . but the rain hits your window, reminding you that the title of the book itself was already a mistake: summer in termuren; and again winter is approaching, and again all your heroes and heroines will be going round with runny noses and their hands deep in their raincoat pockets. And then, it's not just the title . . . you don't even know how to start this chapter. Come on, let's take oscarke for the time being . . . let's have him enter this new chapter and also his cottage, there at the corner of the 1st grimy houses behind the weaving mill! Ondine, his wife, may have one of those rare moments of affection and say: hello oscarke . . . what's going on that you're always walking with your head down, looking at the ground? And this will move him, even though it's only his wife ondine who's asking. But he won't be able to answer her. Because your characters have become such an integral part of you that oscarke would unconsciously blurt out what's actually wrong with you yourself. And so this new chapter, twisted and contorted, is already getting underway: oscarke, your hero, will have to invent some specious reason. And since he's a little person who occasionally needs a friendly word, he'll try to think up something else for which he can be pitied . . . something that's just as sad, but that he *is* allowed to say: for example, the fact that he has to do work that is far too difficult there in the mud of the park, and doesn't earn an appropriate wage, when they're living here in poverty and he would much rather sculpt, but he can't sculpt because he's too tired in the evenings. This is what oscarke will say, though there's a quite different reason for his unhappiness. And so the comfort he might be given will be a false comfort . . . ointment on

249

a wooden leg, and on top of that the wrong ointment for the wrong wooden leg. And beginning with oscarke in this way will only lead to confusion, and one mistake will follow the other. Confusion inside him, confusion between him and his wife and his family . . . between him and his friend boone, when they both want to say the same thing, but both express it wrongly . . . between him and jeannine, who's over in brussels at an inaccessible distance, and is probably already letting herself be interfered with by the spiked helmets. That's what's wrong with oscarke. And it strikes terror into your heart when you think of the confusion that will reign between all your other heroes and heroines. They've all retreated into their refuges: tippetotje painting her rats, mr brys exorcising his ghosts, polpoets grinning, and master oedenmaeckers struggling to regain control over his earthly paradise: all wrapped up in the struggle for prosperity and happiness, and a few other things that don't occur to us at the moment. And since not a single character in a single one of your books so far has succeeded in what he undertook, they'll probably all fail as well . . . they'll all fail as they struggle. Failure, error, confusion. And while your characters ondine and oscarke are still experiencing their 1st world war, your other characters are preparing to face a 3rd world war: tippetotje and her rats, mr brys and his ghosts, polpoets and his two grinning teeth. Mistakes and confusion all through time . . . confusion in the minds of people who want to start a 3rd world war in order to preserve peace. And in addition a mistake in the weather . . . where you write that the rain lashes against your window, and you've called your book "summer in termuren" anyway.

OSCARKE ENTERS THE NEW CHAPTER

Oscarke entered his house and couldn't believe his ears, hearing ondine singing and walking round laughing at her children . . . hello oscarke, she said . . . and she asked what the matter was: you still walking around looking at the ground, dear? It touched him, even though it was ondine who was asking. But he couldn't really answer that between their town and brussels—and actually he should have said: between him and jeannine—there was an iron wall of german spiked helmets. He didn't have jeannine, and the new world of socialism had again been moved a little further away from him . . . it must be hanging on a string, that future world, and it was pulled two steps back whenever he took a step forward to rush to meet it . . . but was he supposed to tell ondine that? But because he actually needed a friendly word he looked for something else to complain about: it's because over in the park I do hard work and don't get paid well for it, while we're living here in poverty . . . and while I really ought to be able to sculpt, the head I've been working on just sits there, because I'm too tired in the evenings to do anything . . . and even if I wasn't so tired, I still couldn't go on with it, since I haven't got a model, I don't have anyone to pose . . . but if I could just make a start, if I could just get going again, then I would feel capable of expressing anything and everything. So he stood there pouring out his heart more exuberantly than ever before, saying things that he didn't mean, things he'd never even thought about before. I'll model for that head of christ, ondine said . . . and after rummaging about in a drawer, she came back with a card with a crucifixion scene on it. He was a dreamer, he didn't understand people . . . he had the idea that everyone was like him, and this idea was the only thing that had gotten through to him by way of knowledge of the world. Still, he held his tongue and started chipping, and she came and looked over his shoulder, and she thought that the neck was too long. So, it was just more stupidity after all . . . she couldn't see how this emaciated neck was meant to express all the nonsense he had just confessed to.

But she knew nothing of his thoughts, really . . . she was in a good mood and told him that the priest had just been over, and had told her that he was going to help them . . . oh, he's going to help us, oscarke! . . . and she was so happy that there wouldn't be any more problems for her, that she couldn't believe that anyone else had any real problems either. That neck . . . oh, saw it off, she said. So the priest, then, had put their names down for a poor people's soup kitchen that was going to be set up, where you could get potatoes and vegetables and meat—shut the door or we'll blow away in the draft!—for only a few cents. The first time it was open she rushed over in excitement . . . but what kind of people was she mixing with there? . . . with no one who was her equal, with beggars and tramps and people from the tenements . . . that beggar woman, for instance, who came to her door every saturday, was standing next to ondine and talking to her about the war and her wretchedness . . . which was ondine's wretchedness too, she could see that, but this made her even more furious. She was no different than a beggar woman! And that other woman there, with her uncombed hair! . . . and suddenly ondine groped for her own head, where the hair was also hanging in tousled streaks and where a pin on her shawl was dangling, ready to fall on the ground. And there was a woman with a child clinging to her skirts and another baby in her belly! They should be thankful that they . . . that oscarke at least . . . and she turned her head away from all those in whom she recognized herself. But the further she turned her head the more specimens she saw, cross-eyed men with caps pulled way down over their red, inflamed ears. So, the priest thought she was one of these: a woman from the tenements. And she hated that priest, that bastard of a priest, who could see her as a woman from the tenements because he felt himself too exalted to understand the fate of a tramp, a beggar, a tenement-dweller. Oh he was the reverend father, and that's what he would always remain. But her life went uphill and downhill, yesterday she was madame ondine, and today she was penniless ondine from the tenements and they could jeer at her and spit in her face: the priest remained the priest, the representative of god . . . and the mayor remained a derenancourt, the

anointed one of that same god. They earned money, they grew richer and richer,
war or no war . . . a poor person went hungry in peacetime and doubly hungry
when there was a war on, but the rich had parks laid out and talked about the
unemployed as if they were paper dolls . . . names that were entered in the records
of the town hall, but not people who were standing in line here for potatoes and
vegetables . . . oh, vegetables, something out of a can, whoever could have imag-
ined such a thing before the war? And that meat, she didn't know what prevented
her from throwing it in madame derenancourt's face . . . because it really was her,
madame derenancourt . . . there she was, walking around on her flat feet, sniff-
ing the ladle and running her tongue round it . . . running her tongue round it,
shameless hussy, although she knew that this was the most unspeakable rudeness,
the lowest insult one could inflict on anyone . . . to lick the ladle clean and then
put it back in the tub of gritty meat and gravy: look at her making a face like she's
about to fall on her ass, it tastes so good! She, madame derenancourt, rolled her
eyes, and the people laughed and said: look at that mrs derenancourt, eating the
same crap we eat! It made ondine feel sick, but she still didn't throw it in her face
. . . she pushed her bowl in between two other people's so as not to be noticed, and
hurried home with her soup and her few potatoes that went cold along the way
. . . and when it had been served up, she could scarcely eat it, but the children stood
round the table craning their necks and mariette ate and ate: yum, the reverend
father's food is so good, said mariette, and ondine slapped her face.

IT'S THE OTHERS

While in chapel road the women rush home with baskets full of the goods
they're hoarding and sickwit the student is telling mr brys that he has to rejoin
the army . . . while you go on writing about that 1st world war, when germans
with spiked helmets brought order and silence to termuren. You write about
mr derenancourt, the clerical mayor, who earned money and became richer
and richer, war or no war . . . and about ondine who stood in line at the workhouse soup kitchen, the kitchen for the needy and ravaged of the 1st world
war: and she gave her little mariette a smack in the face for saying: yum, their
food is so good! And when you've written that, andreus mottebol pops in,
reads it, and says: I wonder how children always manage to hit the nail on the
head . . . how they invariably find just the right word to drive you crazy, or to
put some situation in the most glaring and embarrassing light. Only yesterday
I was standing by the unmanned railway crossing in termuren, and there
were children playing . . . they were playing trains alongside that railway line,
chugging along in a long trailing line, one behind the other. And the moment
their train started making a turn, a little boy started screaming and shouting. Immediately a woman poked her head out of a window, duster in hand,

and asked what on earth the matter was: why are you crying, leopold? And leopold screams and shouts that his sister mariette stepped on his toes. Why are you stepping on your little brother's toes, mariette? the woman asks. And mariette replies that she couldn't help it, she stepped back and didn't know that leopold was right behind her. And then little leopold starts screaming and shouting louder than ever, and cries: it's not true, mother, I wasn't standing right behind her, I was standing right in front of myself. And the woman at the window laughed, and I, standing by the unmanned crossing, laughed . . . and you, aren't you laughing too? And then andreus mottebol puts down the page about ondine and her little mariette, and adds in a rather weary tone: he wasn't standing right behind her, she was standing right in front of him . . . and I suddenly thought of many things that happen nowadays, in religion and in politics and the war in korea, where people say: it's not my fault, because I wasn't standing behind him, he was standing in front of me. And it's the same everywhere else . . . everywhere one person is not standing behind another, but the other person is standing in front of the first person. And also people never speak of war but of peace: they only arm themselves in order to preserve peace . . . the defenders of peace attack only to prevent war from breaking out . . . and very soon they'll be saying that this 3rd world war must be unleashed in order to avoid the selfsame world war.

And andreus mottebol hurries out onto the street again, where the women are rushing home with their baskets full of hoarded goods, and where sickwit the student is telling mr brys that he has to rejoin the army. Perhaps he's saying: I'm not standing behind the others, mr brys, it's the others who are standing in front of me.

THE DEAD BIRD

And when sickwit the student has gone, mr brys comes over and peers through your window: hey, are you working? And you look up in surprise and ask whether today is sunday or a holiday? No, mr brys shouts back, but it's one of those rare fine days when the sun is shining, and you start realizing that there's something else besides work: there by the 1st grimy houses behind the labor factory the menfolk are sitting with their backs against the warm wall and are sunbathing, and a bit further away, in Africa, there are whole tribes of unknown peoples who have nothing to do but sunbathe. Come along, lend a hand! And because you mutter something about your work, he replies: those who don't work are still alive, as the saying goes . . . and what popular sayings tell us is the truth. And mr brys coaxes you to come with him, down the winding country road to master oedenmaeckers's garden. He's having a cottage built and it's just been finished. Can't you see, can't you see, cries mr brys . . . can't you see that today's a holiday: no one's working, and where they *are* still working they're filing out and celebrating! The lovely lucette stands behind a couple of crates of beer and gives everyone a bottle . . . the bricklayer and the carpenter, the floor-layer and the plasterer, the laborer who leaned on his shovel the whole time, and the spectator, who was only there to criticize everything he could. To my mind that's not a house, the spectator always said . . . my picture of a house is something quite different! But now he drinks his bottle of beer and joins in the celebrations for the completion of the building. And suddenly, you don't know who found it, there's a dead bird in a corner of master oedenmaeckers's garden. It's a beautiful radiant day, those who aren't working are still alive, and the one who's done nothing but criticize is given his bottle of beer like everyone else. But alongside lies the dead bird. It lies there cold and stiff under the sun's rays. And it looks rather unnatural, since birds were not designed to lie cold and stiff in a corner of a garden: its wings are still spread wide, the wings of a creature that in death still wanted to go forward but no longer could . . . the head is turned away, so as to no longer have to look at the tragedy of its fall with its own eyes. With its own eyes, repeats the lovely lucette . . . it doesn't even have eyes anymore! No, the beetles have come, the cockroaches and the spiders, and all the other vermin, and they've crawled in through the eyes of the bird, and have eaten their fill . . . perhaps they quarreled about the booty, and went away grumbling if there was nothing there to their taste. The soul, the spirit of this bird was not to their taste: they were unable to violate the line of the wings still outspread in their flight, or the pain of that head averted because of its own impotence. And andreus mottebol draws the dead bird in his sketchbook, and master oedenmaeckers gets his notebook and writes the first line of a lovely poem: O dead bird this and that . . . What kind of bird could it be? asks the lovely lucette, and no one knows. Mr brys is still bent over his files, and master oede-nmaeckers over his lessons. Andreus mottebol fills the weekly papers with his articles, and you write your books . . . and no one knows what sort of bird it is. It's a golden oriole, says the bricklayer's assistant, who's been leaning on his shovel and watching the birds. It's a golden oriole, repeats the lovely lucette. In the popular idiom, oriole means: a jay of a woman, a stupid bimbo, a stupid hussy, a flighty fool. There you lie, flighty fool, says the lovely lucette with pity. And then they all return to their bottles of beer and the house is finished off. There's sun and celebration, and those who don't work are still alive, as the saying goes. There are so many sayings. One says that an oriole is a flighty fool of a bird. And you quietly quit the party, and go back to your work. For you it's not an oriole but the Dead bird, it's this book itself, a book like a bird that's crashed in mid-flight . . . it's this new chapter—it's this age and these people, and beetles and spiders and all the other vermin crawling around.

Those who don't work are still alive . . . but the crashed bird, IS it still flying?

THE CATERPILLAR

In master oedenmaeckers's little garden the cottage is finished, and the roof has been topped off, and everyone present is given a bottle of beer. A shame that the weather is suddenly going overcast: and as they drink their bottles people cast grave looks at the sky. Let it rain, we've got a roof over our heads now! cries polpoets . . . and baring his 2 gold teeth in a smile, he sticks his head out of the window. It's a fine house, say the bricklayer and the carpenter proudly. And the architect agrees . . . and the laborer, who was always leaning on his shovel . . . and the spectator, who could do nothing but criticize, also agrees. A bottle of beer does wonders. But suddenly you hear a scream from inside the house . . . a scream let out by the child of nature maria, hung with ribbons and bows. Ugh, a creepy-crawly! she cries. And the architect rushes up with his red pencil, the laborer with his shovel, the spectator with his criticism . . . all of them to help, or perhaps to kill the creepy-crawly, but perhaps much more to take the opportunity to gaze admiringly at the child of nature maria. But no sooner have they all got in than she adds a little more calmly: a caterpillar! And all of them look in relief at the crawly green creature . . . the architect and the laborer, the spectator and master oedenmaeckers himself, and they all add: a caterpillar! And you who again have to be the simpleton, the eternal corrector, the moralist, the defeatist, you correct them: a patercillar! And they all look at you in surprise, anger, and scorn: a patercillar, ha! I can't imagine there's any craftsmanship in any of your books, says the architect . . . if you can't construct even a simple stone of a word correctly. The people of termuren pronounce many words wrongly, you say in your defense . . . for ham they say ahm and for a caterpillar they say patercillar. And polpoets laughs, baring his 2 gold teeth, and says: I imagine that in your books you commit one error after another . . . that there's suddenly talk in ondine and oscarke's house of a new child, without us knowing how or from where it came . . . that you call your book "summer in termuren" while it's pouring with rain . . . and that one hero of your book is still experiencing his 1st world war while the others are already preparing to perhaps experience their 3rd. It's a speech impediment, you say defending yourself . . . the people of termuren can't possibly pronounce the word ham, and so turn it into ahm, and they can't possibly pronounce the word caterpillar, and so turned it into patercillar. But the architect points his red pencil at you as if it were a revolver . . . and master oedenmaeckers, who carries the language in his trouser pocket, gets out his dictionary and reads: caterpillar, caterpillar egg, caterpillar harvest.

255

And you turn away in shame because you have again been deceived about the people of termuren: instead of ham they say ahm, but that's no longer a speech impediment, just willful ignorance . . .

But with the caterpillar on her outstretched finger, the child of nature hung with ribbons looks at you uncomprehendingly, and says: oh it's not our wrong words that count . . .

And rather confused by this sight, you repeat: no, it is not our wrong words, but our wrong deeds.

A CATERPILLAR OF A CHILD

But judith didn't like the food from the soup kitchen, judith led a separate life just as her father oscarke did, young as she was. She'd transferred her veneration for uncle valeer to her father oscarke, as if she'd gone from one saint's image to another with her burning candle. And now she only ate something when oscarke made it for her, she only ate a slice of bread if oscarke had cut it . . . and once when her father had made soup, she asked: is that pa's soup? . . . and she ate till she was sick. Mariette ate her sister's portion and ondine's, all the while looking at marie-louise's plate, marie-louise who couldn't hold her spoon yet. Yes, it was still a bit early for marie-louise to be eating potatoes and soup . . . she was still at the age when she had to be fed with milk and some porridge, but there was a war on and where was ondine supposed to get milk from? And ondine shouted angrily at mariette: keep your hands off marie-louise's plate! She's not allowed to have this anyway, replied mariette . . . she'll swallow it and then it'll go right out the other end. And ondine couldn't help laughing: it was true, and actually she would have argued the point in exactly the same way . . . but because oscarke sat looking at her over his tiny scrap of meat—oh, was that meat? It was much more like the scraps that used to be left over after eating a decent cut, many years ago in termuren—she controlled herself. It's true, you know! she said . . . and she shook her head at that marie-louise. Marie-louise couldn't walk yet . . . perhaps she was like valeer, perhaps a miracle was needed first . . . she lay on the settee and slept or howled, but it couldn't be compared to another child's crying: it was more like a dog's howling. And oscarke and ondine didn't know what to make of it, they trusted in doctor goethals who had said . . . well, what had he said? Perhaps with a child like that it's hard to tell, perhaps it would all turn out all right in time . . . didn't everything turn out all right in time? But they no longer spoke about it, they avoided the subject . . . and ondine couldn't do anything about it anyway, but whenever she looked at the child she thought more and more of valeer. Of valeer? Oh, how she was fooling herself: she was thinking of her mother. You see! she thought deep inside . . . however far you go, thinking you're going to trick fate, it's actually fate itself that has lured you wherever you are, just to play a trick on you . . . I never let my mother be godmother, I never wanted to give my children my mother's name, the demonic name of zulma: yet she's lying here, zulma, the new zulma, howling like a dog, pissing like a dog, eating like a dog. Dog! she said to the child. Or when she was alone with her: zulma! she hissed . . . hello zulma, how are you today, shall we go and look at the smothered babies in the toilet? And then she turned away from the child, terrified. Die, she said. And then she banged her head against the wall, but couldn't cry: marie-louise, sweet little marie-louise, what terrible things am I saying to you?

YOU WORRY TOO MUCH ABOUT EVERYTHING, OSCARKE!

Ondine no longer went out for the priest's food, she became ill and asked oscarke if he could make a small detour from the municipal park to the soup kitchen: so at twelve o'clock he left his wheelbarrow where it was, just as he left his wooden head of christ in the evenings, and carrying a black basket in which a couple of bowls where hidden he hurried to the leopold II home. But once he had his basket in hand, he hurried after boone, who disappeared round a corner ahead of him . . . boone, boone! he shouted, and hurried . . . well, what's wrong? asked boone . . . nothing! replied oscarke. And they walked on together, and of course, oscarke started in about socialism again: it may be that that beautiful world will never come, he said, but speaking of war, surely you can see that the sole object of war is to squash the workers' movement. That's possible, said boone, but then that's the fault of the working man himself, who only gets what he asks for: the working man wanted to be able to eat chips and steak, drink a pint, and give his wife a child, nothing more . . . and he's got what he wants . . . and now he has to work twelve hours a day and join the army, and that won't stop because he's content with it . . . but once he no longer feels like playing soldier or only wants to work eight hours a day, well, then he'll only work eight hours a day. Eight hours! Oscarke couldn't believe it. Eight hours, he said, that means if I start at six in the morning, I, let's see . . . eight from twelve is four . . . so I'd be finished by two o'clock? That would be a whole afternoon and a whole evening for messing around with his clay and stone and forgetting he was oscarke and forgetting that the world he dreamed of hung by a thread: that can't be true! he said, because it was too beautiful to believe. Look, said boone, let's be honest . . . there's no luxury at my house, but that's because I don't want any luxury . . . my wife earns a bit from her shop, I can't fault her for that, she does her best, and the moment when all the shops run out of things to sell, she starts selling anchovies, because what else have people got to stuff in their mouths nowadays but two cents' worth of anchovies? . . . but me? . . . I'm too fond of a drop of beer, I don't need luxury, I need my comfort. Oscarke nodded, and because boone had revealed something about his household, he wanted to reveal something too . . . but he wasn't as sophisticated: once he started, he blurted

*everything out. He lifted up his heavy basket and said: look, we're obliged to go
to that soup kitchen, because we haven't so much as a potato in the house, and we
haven't any money either . . . and the rent we have to pay and that interest we
have to keep up with, and all the rest that my wife talks about day in, day out,
but that I forget because I have no head for money. And boone looked at him in
surprise . . . not because oscarke had no head for money but because they were still
paying rent in the middle of the war, when no one was paying rent. No? asked
oscarke. Of course not! said boone . . . that whole bunch of grimy houses behind
the labor mill don't pay a centime. And he shook his head: I was wondering why
you were so skinny, 'cause you see, it's a tic of mine to observe people and wonder
what they're like and what they are and how they got that way . . . and I noticed
that you torment yourself too much . . . with socialism, for instance, I'm a socialist
too, but I'm not stupid enough to worry about what things will be like after the
war, or to get all bitter about a priest . . . good day, I say . . . but you, you torture
yourself about far too many things . . . about your rent, for god's sake, and about
eating from a soup kitchen . . . let your wife worry about all that, let your wife
scrimp and scrape and make ends meet, that's her job, and you'd do much better to
have a drink! And oscarke, who once he'd started nodding had to go on nodding,
because everything boone was saying was true . . . he went with boone and had a
drink and became a new man. That is to say, he remained oscarke, but as a result
of that drink he felt like a different oscarke.*

THE SLUG

While that 1st world war was still going on, and there were germans with
spiked helmets in termuren, oscarke and his friend boone came home from
work every evening to the 1st grimy houses behind the labor mill. And it was
an obsession of oscarke's to size everyone up, and wonder what they were
like, and then to worry about it. Oscar worried about absolutely everything.
And having written that you put your pen down and push your chair back a
bit: you go and rest a bit in your impossible little patch of garden . . . a rock
garden, that is, about as big as an apron . . . and under one of the lumps of
sandstone there you find a snail. And the boone's last words are still sounding
in your ears, the words he said to oscarke: you worry too much about everything, oscarke! And repeating those words again and again, savoring them
like the last lines of a poem, you say them to yourself: you worry too much
about everything, oscarke! And squatting down by your rock-plants, whose
names you can never remember . . . by that yellow herb popularly called rice
pudding, and by the hard leaves popularly called thunder leaves . . . squatting
there, you see a snail come out from under a stone: a great slimy gray snail.
In master oedenmaeckers's garden we found a bird, a golden oriole that had

crashed to earth, and in the finished cottage polpoets's wife found a green caterpillar—or are you getting it wrong again, and it's really a patercillar?—but
all you find in your impossible patch of garden is a snail. You worry far too
much about everything, oscarke! And your wife is walking round the house
with her bad nerves, back and forth, upstairs and downstairs, around your
desk when you're writing, and around your impossible patch of garden when
you're are out with your rock-plants . . . and walking around with her nerves
she makes you nervous: so is there going to be another war? she asks. And
you grab a sandstone and throw it on top of the snail. A fat slimy gray slug.
You kill it . . . crush it . . . destroy it. And the slimy gray pulp splashes over
your hands. You worry far too much about everything, oscarke! said boone,
while they were walking home from work in the evening. And wherever you
twist or turn, to the sink to wash your hands, to that yellow herb they call
rice pudding, or to the hard leaves called thunder leaves: you get a headache,
migraine, nausea. And your wife walks round and asks . . . And boone keeps
on speaking to oscarke inside you . . . And sitting down on your front step,
you see women rushing home with hoarded goods from the shops, and you
hear sickwit the student saying to mr brys: I've got to join the army again, mr
brys! And you sit there, while it's one of those very rare, beautiful evenings,
after all that rain and rain, and you've got a headache and feel like throwing
up. And you don't know if it's because of that snail, or those words that boone
keeps repeating inside you, and in your mind it's actually everything mixed
together. So if you see another snail, a slimy gray slug, will you think that
there's going to be another war? . . . And will you hear boone say that you
worry far too much about everything, oscarke? And if there does turn out to
be another war, will you then see everything made into slugs? . . . dirty gray
slugs whose pulp splashes on your hands?

And you return to your desk . . . and oscarke listens to boone, and says
rather desperately: you're right, boone, I worry far too much about everything,
I worry over far too many things . . . but what can I do about it?

A SYNTHESIS

I've got to talk to you about that hoarding that was going on, says master
oedenmaeckers: in that patch of garden, my cottage is finished now, and on
the great flat wall of my living room I'd like to hang a painting: a painting
that is the reflection, as it were, of our people and these times . . . that is, as it
were, the synthesis of everything that has been thought, felt, and experienced
here. And with the money I had saved for it, I went from painter to painter
. . . but one paints nothing but a cow and patch of meadow, a crossroads or a
pot of flowers, while the other paints something abstract, something absurd

that I can't understand, So the world is divided once more, in painting too: with one person there's still the old faith in an antiquated religion, and with the other a blind obedience to science gone astray . . . on the one hand a corpse that people still bow down and burn incense to, and on the other an aimless, absurd, and almighty cerebration that's grown into a monstrous sore. Just as god was once almighty, technology is now becoming almighty. And just like I had no trust in a life after death and beyond the earth, I have no confidence in a life that aims for nothing but speed, explosions, and tooth-paste ads. And not finding the painting that's actually a reflection of what we've become over the years, that is as it were the synthesis of what we've already seen and experienced, I decided to paint my own picture for myself. After all, everyone else paints, why shouldn't I paint too? Poets and doctors paint, lunatics and novelists . . . henry miller paints, and winston churchill too. And so I bought a square meter of canvas, some paint, and a few brushes . . . but look, I'm a person who changes from day to day, evolves from hour to hour: what was the sum of all my thinking yesterday, today no longer adds up: something new has already been added and something else subtracted. But a verse can be added to a poem, or a chapter to a novel, but a painting is a square surface that's stuck once and for all in its frame. So I should either just start writing about what I'd like to paint in the bottom corner of my painting . . . or better yet, I should just leave that square meter of canvas blank, until I've grown so old that all my feelings and desires have atrophied, and no new ideas can be added. That is to say: till the moment I die, and so no longer need any paintings.

Yes, but I thought you were actually going to talk about the hoarding? you ask, interrupting the schoolmaster. Well, he says . . . so I was sitting at the window, with a few brushes and a palette in my hand, and coming down chapel road I saw people rushing home with baskets stuffed full of food. There was a woman who had bought a 1,000 nutmegs, while my own wife admits that she uses only 1 nutmeg a year . . . and so clearly that woman thought she could survive the new war for a thousand years. And seeing them hurrying along with all those things, I abandoned my virgin canvas, and went and shouted at them from the front door: and you know, I said, you won't be able to get any more paintings either! And look, for a split second there was hesitation in the crowd hurrying home: the woman with the 1,000 nutmegs stopped, wondering desperately what she should do, but a man with 1,700 boxes of matches burst out laughing and cried: that's a good one!

Certainly it was a good one . . . I had to laugh myself silly about it: if I wanted to make a synthesis of all our longings and desires, of all our dreams and reflections, then I didn't have to take the trouble to paint a painting:

it would be much easier and quicker to hang some nutmeg and a box of matches, a pat of butter and a can of chicken soup on my wall.

THE STRANGE WOMAN

But in master oedenmaeckers's finished cottage that great, flat wall remained empty: there should be a painting on it, a synthesis of his life, as it were, should be displayed on it. And unable to conjure up this sum of his life, he paints something that's just temporary instead. Temporarily he's created himself a god in his own image, temporarily he's dabbled in art and science, temporarily he's thought up a philosophy, and temporarily he's tied the mask of morality over his face . . . all the while also playing with fire a little, and splitting atoms a little too. So master oedenmaeckers, who's like all of us, is waiting a bit before doing his real painting, and is first playing around a little with his paints and brushes. And you ring his doorbell, and his lovely wife lucette comes to the door and says he's up in the attic: wait, I'll show you the way . . . over there, go in and have a look at his painting. And the painting represents a rather archaic landscape: the edge of an ancient road paved with great flat stones—stones that had been carved in the time of the egyptians and greeks—and which are already starting to crumble and crack with age, where moss and tough grass are starting to spring up in the cracks. The road goes higher and higher, slow and winding, to the summit of one of the mountains that one sees in the distance. But on one side of the road is a wondrous expanse of lake, with such calm and clearly reflecting waters that it seems to call out to you: leave this road that people travel and keep traveling, come instead to my shore and lose yourself in beautiful, aimless reflection. And on the other side of the road is a house, or, anyway, the remains of a house, battered and damaged, with a roof that's had its tiles torn off, where the clouds and rain, the sun and the snow, whirl right through. It's the house that man has built for himself temporarily on the long road he still has to travel . . . a house where he can temporarily warm his feet, cool his passions, worship his god . . . sometimes put on and then take off his morality like a shirt, like a hat, like a mask, depending on the circumstances . . . a house where he temporarily plays with a little fire so that the walls are scorched black, and also where he temporarily splits some atoms so the roof is blown off. And between the calm lake and the battered house is the long road which man has yet to travel. But look, on the threshold of that house, in the black scorched opening of the door that's already been torn off, a woman stands and waits. She's naked, beautiful, and waiting. And the lovely lucette notices that you're finally looking at the naked woman, and she says: you see, that woman . . . is me!

And master oedenmaeckers, who up till now has said nothing and gone on painting, suddenly looks up, silent and indignant, first at his own wife and then at the woman in the painting . . . and he dips his brush in the yellow paint and gives the waiting woman yellow hair, where a moment ago it was black.

The road is long and meandering, and if man grows tired . . . if he were ever to stray from the path . . . the miracle that lures him onward must be not only beautiful, but especially strange and unknown.

OSCAR IS GOING TO HIT ONDINE

Oscar went with boone for a drink: he drank at a bar where smugglers lit their cigarettes with banknotes . . . he asked for some money, but wasn't given any, though all their pockets were crammed full, and the stuff was bulging right out. He stood right next to these men and drummed on the bar to get his drink . . . and sure enough, no sooner had he downed it than he remembered the night when he'd been able to finish the dregs from ondine's bottle . . . and he also remembered that the bottle had never been paid for . . . he remembered that afterwards he'd felt like all his troubles were over, just like they felt over now: the world was as it was, and it was fine as it was: and he started to sing the red flag, and klokke roelandt, and o scheldt, just as if he were singing his eldest daughter judith to sleep. The smugglers at the bar listened to his songs, and asked him if he was a socialist or a flemish activist . . . I'm a dirtyist, he said . . . and it was amazing how much like his father he suddenly was. He'd always been like his mother, and now he was suddenly like his father too: he was a little bastard who made eyes at the daughter of the pub—rosa was her name—and he took rosa on his knee and started groping her breasts: you've already got a lot hidden in there, he said with a gleam in his eye . . . let's have a feel. But she knocked his hand away and ran off, and afterward stood looking at him from the kitchen with the tarty smile of an underage girl. Boone stood laughing at him and shaking his head: you'd be a good neighbor, I could have some fun with you . . . and, you know, the old cunt next door just died and the house is empty . . . come and move in, you can live there for nothing! You see, oscarke said to himself . . . you see, there were absolutely no problems anymore, or there were but they were all solved. And oscarke wanted to sing louder, but they'd got into an argument with the smugglers, one of whom, malgré, claimed that boone had called him a cunt: you said cunt! Oh for christ's sake, said boone, I said that the cunt next door had died! But the smugglers were determined to pick a fight: and you stole ten marks from me! added another man, taking his money out of his pocket and starting to count it. You see! I'm ten marks short: thief, bastard . . . But oscarke jumped up like a young dog on its hind legs, with the tuft of hair on the back of his head sticking out more than ever: take that back, fucker, or I'll kick you right in the balls! he shouted, forced to look up because the smuggler was two heads taller. Now, now! said boone, and he had to pull oscarke away. But when they got outside, boone laughed: you idiot, he said, anyone can see that you can't stand up for yourself, and still you want to fight! Of course, it was all because he was drunk, but oscarke didn't want him to know that, he walked along with his hands in his pockets and stopped every five steps: I'd have kicked him to death! he said furiously . . . and made as if to turn back. Now, now! said boone, laughing louder and louder . . . and oscar took his clenched fist out of his pocket and extended it towards the pub round the corner . . . but what was that? Clutched in his fist was a ten mark note. Ten marks? asked boone, and suddenly he understood . . . and looking him up and down, sizing him up, he saw something else wrong. Oscarke looked at his hand and saw that his basket was no longer hanging from it: we'll get it tomorrow, oscarke said, and I'll buy a round. And when he got home he was like his father again, in the sense that he was a little judas . . . and when ondine asked about the food, he answered: food, food . . . I'm not hungry. And he told the children that their mother paid rent when no one paid rent anymore, when they could go and live for nothing over there round the corner in the 1st grimy houses. And ondine was too surprised even to answer back . . . and he was rather surprised that she didn't fly into one of her rages . . . since the fact that he'd become a little judas was only due to the drink he'd had, and that had made his vision a little foggy. What was wrong with her then, not getting furious? . . . oh, nothing was the matter with her except that she should've married someone who could stand up for himself, someone who could put her in her place occasionally, and occasionally hit her. And oscarke went up to her through the fog of his drunkenness and said: I'm going to hit you.

JAN DE LICHTE'S WIFE GETS HIT

Polpoets is sitting bent over the archives that mention the gang of jan de lichte again, and he says to you: shut up about the termuren of today for a moment, and shut up about oscarke and his termuren of 1918 for a moment . . . wait a moment before you have oscarke hit ondine, and see how jan de lichte's wife got hit in the flanders of 1750: they not only sentenced and broke jan on the wheel, but they also flogged and banished his wife. His wife, called maria van dorpe, aged 29, from heuse near audenaerde. She toiled and labored for the gang like a horse, and yet not one of them took her work seriously. There wasn't a single one who could hear her name mentioned without a smile playing round the corners of his mouth: she was given the nickname of mie gendarme . . . and mie gendarme she remained for all who knew her. And yet, and yet . . . she was probably the only one who more or less understood the true meaning of jan de lichte's gang. Or at least who had a sense, vague and distant, of its significance. No one understood her inhuman labor . . . but neither did anyone see the disproportionate growth of the gang as clearly as she did. If one really looks at it closely, the gang outgrew itself. Which is to say . . . those ever-widening circles, already convulsing the courtrai region, may have been the result of a particular stone that was dropped into the water with a plop . . . that long-forgotten day when jan de lichte first talked about his gang. But it's equally true that the times were ripe for such things . . . that on all sides the people, driven by hunger and need, were overstepping the all-too-narrow bounds of law and order, to appropriate for themselves some of the bread that had grown scarce. The gang is growing . . . but in such a way that no one can control it anymore, that people can no longer remember all the names and facts. The rising tide, in higher and fiercer waves, overturns all the names and facts. There's talk of the gang as far as the courtrai region . . . or about the Thing that as yet doesn't bear the name of gang, but that's a seething and a bubbling, a boiling over of what's been simmering too long. Perhaps these hundreds of people do have the vague impression that they're still affiliated with a gang, a gang whose name they don't even know . . . but their aim is to rebel against all the parasites that live off this dunghill of a people succumbing to famine, wars, the pox, and typhus. These hundreds know nothing about the organization . . . they know nothing about the tramps, the neglected children and boozy old wives who, laden with packages, are links in an endless chain. They don't know the origin of these strange convoys . . . all they know is that they're filled with plunder, and that they too can get their mitts on it. And so it happens that the chain is overwhelmed . . . that the links, already too loose, fall apart: things still get stolen, but the proceeds don't always come back to camp. Now there's a problem around peteghem, at a bridge over the leie: there's a market there, and it's a total mess . . . but it's not jan de lichte's gang that's responsible, they've already been swept away by the swelling flood. And mie van dorpe rows and rows and works and slaves because she doesn't want to see jan de lichte's gang submerged in the great, general, all-embracing tide. And if she'd received more help instead of that covert mockery . . . and had her bitter and unforeseen end not been so close at hand . . . perhaps she would have succeeded in the task that, however vague and confused it might have been, she envisaged. She was too great for her surroundings, too great for flanders. And on the other hand, she lost herself in details, and wasn't smart enough: that was the fate of the woman they mockingly called mie gendarme.

And polpoets pushes his papers aside, and says to you: if you want to describe jan de lichte's gang—even if you only describe it to escape this world of today—then you will have to pay attention to the part that this woman played in the flanders of 1750: how she, with her peddler's bag over her shoulder, and a wooden clog in her hand, tried to drive the rebellious tide down channels chosen by her alone.

THE LAST FLY

It's everybody else who's growing old, polpoets said to you a while back . . . it's the others around me who are growing old and dying, while I always remain polpoets, and I am exactly the right age. And suddenly, when you least expect it, you get a letter from tippetotje . . . a letter that hits you like a punch in the face:

right, let me hit you, like oscarke wanted to hit his wife, tippetotje writes . . . you didn't know it, but while you thought I was safe with my baron, instead I was wandering around in your neighborhood . . . lonely and forgotten and no longer recognized by anyone, I wandered round in termuren, while the fair was going on. And you know that termuren has one of the latest fairs of the year: they say that in termuren they bake the flies into the carnival bread, since after the fair is over there are no more flies left and winter is here. And having tucked in my baron in brussels, I suddenly thought of you, and how the fair was in your neighborhood. And like knitting needles, like barbed hooks, memories came back of days gone by, when we were still at art school, you and I . . . and we were young, and we helped catch flies to stuff them into the carnival bread. Do you ever still think about that?: it's evening, a few lamps are lit, in the bar of the 1st grimy houses they're playing cards on a crate for a rabbit, the merry-go-round with its music drowns out the music of the ferris wheel, old paerewijck is walking round completely drunk and tomorrow in drawing class wouldn't be worth a damn. Old paerewijck, who was the goddamn old man we reluctantly used as a life model: we should have had a girl. A girl. But the fair's on in termuren, so old paerewijck is drunk, and in the evening and the falling darkness the girls leave the dance tent. Oh tell me, do you still remember the girls, do you remember mimi, juliette, and what's-her-name, oh dear, what was she called? I can't remember her name, but I can still see her, with skin a little too small for all the meat bursting out of it . . . I can hear her rather hoarse laugh in the falling darkness of chapel road. And now . . . I was in brussels and carefully tucked in my baron, wrapped him up like a precious instrument that must not be damaged. And I slunk off then on tiptoe, grabbed my raincoat and hurried by the train to termuren. It was still dark there in chapel road, and they were still playing cards on a crate in the bar of the 1st grimy houses, and the girls were still going by in the lamplight outside. I'll stop . . . my pen simply doesn't want to go on writing this letter to you . . . my pen is trembling in my hand that's suddenly grown tired: another

mimi, another juliette, another what's-her-name . . . what was she called? . . .
walked past me, as beautiful as in the olden days that went by too fast, when
we were still at art school. It's everyone else who grows old, polpoets said to
you. Ha, that's a laugh, a bitter laugh: it's Us that grow old, it's us that are
the last flies that are baked into the carnival bread in termuren. There were
still girls walking by, but they were Different girls . . . the girls we knew have
grown old and haggard, they've long since married some vinegar-pisser of a
husband, developed neuroses and lines round their mouths . . . and they've
forgotten that dance hall near perre. Oh, you know . . . that dance hall's
been closed down for years, I saw it for myself. Nothing is left. Nothing of
what we knew is left, and yet everything's stayed the same . . . the girls walk
still along out there, always young, beautiful, and fresh. But they're different
girls and it's a different dance hall. Their wet mouths still gleam and their
eyes still have velvet depths. There's still one whose skin is too tight for all
her meat . . . there's still one who's so woundingly beautiful, so achingly
beautiful that I ran off without daring to drop in on you. It's the others who
stay young, and it's us that they're going to bake into the carnival bread: the
winter, the last fly, your tippetotje.

THERE ARE PARIAHS WITH A CAPITAL P
AND PARIAHS WITH A SMALL P

Andreus mottebol has been nowhere to be seen or heard, for the last few days
. . . he's at home by the stove and has something he calls the flu but isn't: it's
the approaching winter, the falling leaves, and it's also in some sense that his
own leaves are falling: a person is like a tree after all. And visiting him, you
see him there fighting his fever. Andreus mottebol has fought his whole life,
first against this and then against something totally different, but most of all
against himself. And he sits there, fighting his fever, with some book that's
been sent to him: the pariahs.

Pariahs, says andreus mottebol, are writers who have been expelled from
literary cliques because they're actually too big for them: after all, ants don't
drag elephants into their anthill . . . pariahs are unbusinesslike writers who
can't find a publisher . . . pariahs are writers who have no time to learn to
write, but are seized by writing as one is seized by a disease: yesterday they
were normal people, but today the writing flu has taken hold of them . . .
pariahs are writers who don't regurgitate the same set of commonplaces for
the 147th time, but live with their eyes open, and see things for what they're
worth . . . pariahs are writers whose style looks strange, bitter, and hard,
not because they aren't able to master existing forms, but because—wait, it's
here in the book—because from righteous anger they take up the javelin of

the word in order to pierce its many hardened layers . . . pariahs are writers whose work doesn't fit the existing pattern. And taking up the pariahs one by one—william blake, proust, d. h. lawrence, james joyce, anaïs nin, henry miller—andreus mottebol adds this: the world around us has a religion and a morality, a philosophy and a science, and above all a goal: yonder lies the goal we must seek, says the world. And if you try to cast doubt on that goal in your work, you're immediately expelled: you become a pariah. And the world as we know it now is an atom that man has managed to split: an eastern and a western electron that each want to pursue their own opposite courses: a cell that's broken into 2, each part living a separate life. And the writer who tries to point out their separate mistakes to each of the halves, is expelled by both these halves. There's a peace of the east and a peace of the west, there's the science of the east and the science of the west, and there's also the traditional art of the east and the traditional art of the west. And the artist whose work doesn't happen to fit any of these categories . . . the one who walks around with his eyes open and takes things for what they're worth . . . he who takes up the javelin of the word to pierce the hardened hides of east and west, is expelled: he becomes a pariah . . . a pariah on the left, a pariah on the right, a pariah everywhere.

And see, you forgive andreus mottebol these harsh and bitter words, because he's sick and has a fever . . . he doesn't see things as they are: he exaggerates a bit. Because the pariahs he's reading about are no longer pariahs. And you say to andreus mottebol: you like pariahs, andreus mottebol, but the moment you and the others have promoted them to Pariahs, they have ceased to be pariahs.

OSCARKE GOT LOST IN THE FOG

I'll hit you! said oscarke to ondine . . . and ondine shouted: come near me and I'll cut your head open! But the fog in front of his eyes made him go near her anyway, and she put the knife that she'd pulled out of a drawer back on the table and cried and asked: oscarke, you're not really going to hit me, are you? But the next day the fog had gone and he was the usual oscarke again, who found the ten marks in his pocket, and though yesterday he'd resolved to hold up the money to her and say: I don't need rich people to get hold of cash, I don't have to go running to mr derenancourt or clinging to the priest's cassock—now he found the ten marks and put them on the table without a word. What's that, oscarke? ondine asked, and she was subservient, as humble as other women were towards their husbands. But she didn't see that he was ill, that he was frightened and was a coward. She talked about that empty house . . . go over there, she said, and ask if we can have it. God, it was easy enough for her to say, but did she think he could go into a stranger's

house and make demands? say: listen, that house that's standing empty, give it to
me! What was it boone had said? You worry too much about everything—let
your wife make ends meet. But in the evening, when he came home with boone,
he cautiously raised the question of whether boone himself might not ask the land-
lord on his behalf. Buy me a round like you promised yesterday then, said boone.
And they went into the bar, and oscarke paid, and he got a warm feeling round his
heart again, and put the owner's daughter rosa on his knee again, rosa who made
dark eyes at him like a little whore, and pushed the hair from her temples so that
her bare earlobes brushed his lips, and he started singing a song from the train for
her: and when it rains in brussels the rain comes down in pails, and all the little
ladies walk round with bushy tails . . . and he sang lots more, so that eventually
she walked off again, and stood listening and laughing in the kitchen, and said he
was a dirty old man. And boone, who'd seen the game with rosa, had to laugh at
oscarke's innocent face: you've got to come and live next to me, he said, if anyone
else comes I'll beat his brains out . . . I'll go to the landlord in a while and I'll ask
him for you. Ask for me? said oscarke . . . no one has to do anything for me, tell
me where he lives and I'll go myself. And sure enough, he did. He threw open the
landlord's front door and shouted out: that house there next to boone's, can I move
in there? But there was only a maid at home . . . although she could just as well
be the lady of the house . . . but no, he couldn't tell with that fog in front of his
eyes. Now are you his maid or are you his wife? he asked . Both, she replied. And
she had to laugh about it, and so did he. There was something funny about her,
something that he couldn't really explain . . . it was in her eyes, which has such a
funny look that he couldn't stop laughing. She led the way, and he followed and
meanwhile gave her a pat on the bottom.

AT ROO-KAUTER

Sitting down next to you, polpoets says: I was telling you about the role maria
van dorpe played in jan de lichte's gang . . . can I also tell you about another
episode I found in the old archives?

Of course you can tell me, polpoets . . . but you'll have to hurry, because
that book about jan de lichte is nearly finished . . . andreus mottebol has
helped with the social aspect, and tippetotje has written me letter after letter
where she quoted the cruelest, bloodiest things. So now, polpoets, these are
the last pages we can spare for the robber chieftain and pirate. His role in the
2nd book on chapel road has been pretty much played out. Very shortly he'll
be taken to the scaffold, and then there'll be nothing left for us to do except
go into hiding, put on a mask, find ourselves a baron, make the sign of the
cross piously and hypocritically every evening, and unleash our own devils
into the balance of what is and is not permitted.

I'll hurry, says polpoets. So mie van dorpe, then . . . mie gendarme as she was called . . . she spends the whole day walking and trudging down winding and turning roadways that are supposed to take her ever closer to that distant river, the leie. And evening slowly falls over flanders: one must think of sleep. But sleep is no problem for her . . . with her skirt squeezed tight against her legs, she'll bed down anywhere—somewhere in the undergrowth, perhaps, if there's no farm to be seen for miles around, somewhere she could nestle unnoticed in the straw in the barn. Now, though, there's no question of lying down . . . evening is falling, but the work for today is far from finished. She hurries through the fields, and comes out on the edge of roo-kauter, where anthon van simois and catharina de bouver live, in a less-than-humble hut. She's sent word to say that that she will arrive there this evening . . . and many destitute people, suckers and slobs, will come and bemoan their plights to her. They'll be those kind of people one can only have a vague kind of pity for, who are too immature, too poor to even be accepted into a gang of thieves. They don't belong to the real gang, but perhaps they do to hers . . . mie gendarme's. First and foremost, that anthon van simois: he's fifty-seven now, and his wife seventy-five, and they've both grown too old and too indifferent to have anything to do with the gang. The gang has come too late for them . . . it should have been there ten years ago, when they were so hard-up that they arrived in roo-kauter one dark night ready to steal anything they got their hands on. They didn't get their hands on much. But over by the brook, by the row of willows, someone else showed up, a certain jan de metter, who to make matters worse might have seen what they were up to with their rather meager booty. And what if, grumbled anthon, we fucking well got him to hand over his money too? And with his hungry stomach deaf to reason, no longer knowing what he was doing, he jumped out from behind the gnarled willows to "attack" that jan de metter. You go through his pockets while I hold him, he supposedly said to his catharina. And that old bag, a good eighteen years older than her anthon, supposedly went through jan de metter's pockets with her old trembling hands. That was ten years ago. Now they don't really need much . . . trousers to cover anthon's skinny ass, a little soup of turnips and carrots, a few worthless trinkets. But they are sympathizers. Your jan de lichte has come years too late, anthon sometimes says to mie van dorpe, when she visits roo-kauter at set intervals . . . when she comes by to see how *her* gang is faring. No one takes that work of hers seriously, because her plans always get bogged down in trifles. It's more of a social club than a gang: it's brimming over with goodwill, but it has no vision, and it plods along till it drops among all sorts of unimportant trivia.

And when you write your book about jan de lichte's gang, polpoets says to you . . . then you shouldn't waste too much time on that, since there are greater things to describe: whole rows of houses will go up in flames, and the leading members of jan de lichte's gang—the real one that people in the region of aalst still talk about to this day—will in their crazy fury and blind hatred commit the cruelest murders imaginable. But alongside the man sentenced for having set fire to over twenty-two houses in the space of a few days, there will also be the woman who took a few pennies from a cupboard. They will all stand next to each other: the most hardened murderer and the most insignificant sucker who stole a loaf of bread out of hunger. And you, who want to be the truthful biographer of the gang, you will have to pay attention to both one and the other.

THE THEFT OF JOHANNA TANGE

And polpoets asks: can I, before you return to the modern world, tell you about one last episode from the life of the wife of jan de lichte? And you say in answer to polpoets that he's still talking about that jan de lichte book in the perfect tense, though it's almost time to use the past tense . . . because it's over and done with . . . the book is almost written, and it no longer has the slightest importance in our story about chapel road; we know that it's useless to try to escape this society, as jan de lichte tried to do: all of us, in running away, would run right into a brick wall. No, no . . . let's take the world as it is, and let that jan de lichte go ahead and perish on the scaffold.

And polpoets looks at you rather sadly with his ingenuous face . . . that's a shame, he says: I had another nice episode to tell you about from the life of jan de lichte's wife . . . an episode that you may find unimportant, because it's about the theft that a poor woman committed in her dire need . . . but don't forget that this woman was flogged for it, flogged and branded and banished from the country. Johanna tange was her name and being pregnant she comes to lament her bad fortune to mie van dorpe in that shabby hut. She's twenty-nine now and comes from the bruges region, from oedelen. And the story that she's about to tell mie van dorpe we can find summarized in the minutes of the trial. It's a touching little story . . . she'd already dished it up, insipid as it was, to all the other suckers and slobs waiting to tell their troubles to mie van dorpe. She told the story to old anthon and the even older catharina . . . but they've become like very old trees, their sap flows slower, and their bark has grown thick and unfeeling: you could drive nails into it without their feeling a thing. And afterwards she tells it to a certain vekeman, who in the trial will be accused of having stolen an iron hammer. And johanna tange would tell the dogs, and even the dogs would be moved . . . but she knows there'd be no point. She's begged her way along the roads, homeless, with no food, pregnant . . . a man wouldn't understand, but a woman worries about all

270

kinds of things out on her own. And wandering past the outskirts of quadrecht, near wetteren, one sunday morning, she knocks at the door of a farmer named jacob verhoesten. We've no time, we have to hurry to go to mass, said jacob verhoesten in all his dignity and bluntness. Right, they both went off to mass, he and his wife . . . and suddenly it dawned on johanna what that meant: she turned back, and quite innocently she went into the farm, across the living room, playacting and pretending she'd been invited to sit down. Yes, they were safely in church, praying and praising their Lord with the fat beads on their rosaries. And in the silence of that empty living room Johanna could hear her own heart pounding, and even her belly rumbling from pure fright. A flogging, a branding, and several years' exile were hanging over her head. She took the key to the cupboard and fiddled with the lock. Her hand was sweating, and at first the key went into the lock at the wrong angle. She stole everything there was to steal: fourteen or fifteen francs. A pittance. And in her haste she went and banged her belly, twice . . . first on the corner of that damn cupboard, and then again on the open door as she walked out. A pittance. And then I came here! johanna tange concluded her story.

Certainly she's there, anthon and his wife catherina see it, and so does vekeman the hammer thief. But you can't meet a woman in flanders without her being pregnant—it's a fertile country . . . but it's a poor country: all that fertility of the land and the people just makes the poverty worse. Certainly they see . . . but anthon and catharina don't need to be told—they only remember their own story. Stop telling us about it, woman, and tell mie van dorpe.

And it's a shame you don't want to know any more about jan de lichte's gang, says polpoets . . . because then you'd have mie van dorpe come along and listen to that story and make johanna tange a member of the gang. And when she'd done her work, mie van dorpe would lie down and sleep the sleep of the just . . . the sleep of those with a clear conscience who have, in virtuousness, completed their day's work.

OH . . . BOOKS ARE ONLY BOOKS

And so oscarke stood there next to his new landlord, in the kitchen and the living room and what have you . . . and all the walls were covered with books, from floor to ceiling . . . do you read all those? asked oscarke, not really knowing who he was talking to, so shocked at seeing all those books. Don't you read? asked the landlord. Oh, books! said oscarke . . . I'd like to read, but I have no time . . . and besides, it's all just fantasy and dreams. Fantasy and dreams can be wonderful, said the landlord . . . there are people who worry too much about everything, and can't see anything nice about the world, and so they can then run away from that ugly world in books. And he looked deep into oscarke's eyes and smiled, and oscarke felt as if he were standing there naked. That's possible, he said . . . but I have my own fantasies, my own dreams, all I'm missing is the time to describe them. And the landlord admitted that such a thing was also possible: don't you live in the bar of the 1st grimy houses? he asked . . . and he also asked if norbert derenancourt still drank at their place: I heard that he gives séances in your bar! Oscarke didn't know anything about that. No? asked the other man in amazement, and looked at oscarke in the eyes once again . . . no? well, in future don't you have anything to do with that sort of thing, because that sort will all go mad, they're looking for something and they don't know what they're looking for, they're playing with fire and they'll get burnt. And it made oscarke happy that someone agreed with him, someone who thought the derenancourts "were just scum" . . . as a result he forgot where he was, and sat down on a chair, and told the landlord all about his life with ondine . . . and suddenly he was listening to himself in amazement, as if someone else were telling the story, because it was about all his problems and all his strange ideas . . . that the earth was a woman, that man was the devil, that all human beings were fragments of a god who'd exploded . . . but after he'd blathered on a bit about the lack of morals in young girls today—for example that rosa—he mainly talked about the woman who was his only and inexpressible love: about jeannine: how I've loved that girl! he said . . . and he couldn't go on with his story. Well, said the landlord, I'll give you the house, you can have it for the whole war, but you have to come and see me now and again and tell me about these things. And he took out book after book, and showed oscarke what others had thought about the same things, about that exploded god, but it didn't surprise oscarke that others had thought and described exactly the same things . . . he didn't even attach much importance to it . . . he just nodded a bit superficially, because, well, the way it was put there in those books, it was someone else's problem, not his . . . and it didn't interest him to know what other people thought about god or what other people thought about beauty, it was as if those books were talking about a different god, a different art from his. And everything the landlord with his book learning told him, things for which ondine would have given ten years of her life, went in one ear and out the other with oscarke, not affecting him in the slightest. The fact that there were ghosts, that the dead went on haunting the living for a while, and all that other nonsense, well, it didn't matter a bit to him, he was only interested in what was tangible and visible in the world, and especially in what he himself experienced, felt, and thought. He got the house, and sometimes dropped by because the book sage had asked him to . . . but he mostly went there because of the funny face of the landlord's maid, or was she his wife? Both, she had said. And he still didn't know what it was about her eyes: they had such a funny look . . . you're a funny one, he'd said . . . and he didn't read the books the sage gave him, he took them home and put them on the sideboard: ondine picked them up, and her fingers started trembling just from seeing their title pages: get another book, she said, get another book . . . but she read so hastily, so voraciously, that most of what she read escaped her completely . . .

CHILDREN ARE BEAUTIFUL

Andreus mottebol shakes his head and says that you just write and write, and set up cardboard characters around you like you'd arrange props on a stage . . . phantoms, reflections, puppets . . . and at first their function is to depict a part of your own self, but gradually, perhaps without your realizing it, they've shriveled into marionettes. Mr brys with his files and me with my social hobbyhorse: we're not people anymore, but caricatures of people . . . we play one-sided roles, we're either too wry like master oedenmaeckers, too comical like polpoets, or too cynical like tippetotje . . . we have nothing but wrongheaded ideas like sickwit the student, or we can't do anything right, like kramiek. Me, for example . . . me, andreus mottebol, I only pop up when for the umpteenth time there's been some social injustice, and having voiced my righteous anger I must disappear back into silence, I must disappear back into namelessness, into nonexistence. Is there nothing else in me then, is there never a little human joy, a few human shortcomings? Other people experience terrible, tragic things, but then they get over them, they recover from their wound, and are able to laugh occasionally. But not me. In your pieces I just ride my social hobbyhorse, and you never, ever let me talk about anything else. Certainly it's true that I tend to concentrate on the social background of people and things, always and everywhere, but I still have my own little joys, my own little happiness. In the first place there are the children: children are a constant source of joy to me. Once when a painter was dying, he wanted to say a few words, something he had to get off his chest, something that summed up—as it were—what he'd experienced in his life, and he said: snow and sunshine, they were so beautiful. I imagine that I, andreus mottebol, would say: children, they were so beautiful! My son joke is 12 now, and a while ago I went out with him, way beyond termuren, far beyond the garden of master oedenmaeckers, to the place that the farmers still call in old flemish: the last nook. And it really is the last nook in flanders, because beyond it begin the vaulted woods, beyond it a new land begins: the land of brabant. And as we went on our adventure my son joke picked up a couple of hangers-on by the roadside . . . They chatted and dawdled and either fell way behind, or acted like indians on the warpath and went on far ahead of me. Yes, they soon forgot me . . . I was too old, too dried-up for them . . . I was actually a grown-up, an enemy. And as we arrived in a lonely place in the last nook in flanders, there was—of course, there had to be—another unmanned crossing over the railway, and one of the hangers-on began telling us with sudden enthusiasm that there had been a big accident there, last year, when an express train surprised a group of playing children. And the main thing he heard and saw at the time was contained in the unexpected question: and do you know how long it took the train to stop? And well, none of the others tried to answer . . . although he was waiting with eyes sparkling to see what they'd say—on the contrary they bombarded him with questions about other things: they don't want to know about those incidental facts: they want to see the accident happening all over again, want to see blood and hear the confused cries of the participants. And then, when there was nothing more to tell, I finally asked him: well, how long did it take the train to stop? But all those questions from the others had made him lose the thread, made him shift the focus of the thing: he too had realized that figures and facts are the most interesting thing . . . and that the poetic description, the strange quality that had caught his imagination at the beginning, had now lost all interest for him too. He actually looked at me uncomprehendingly, so that I had to remind him of that question of his just a few moments before . . . and then he shrugged his shoulders, saying indifferently: well, quite a while. And when I laughed at that answer, they all looked at me in surprise: what funny behavior. What's he laughing about? And they also started complaining because I wanted to go further and further: they couldn't understand that either; because that is where they wanted to be, where things were going on, where one could get run over by the train, where it was dangerous. And they gave me disgruntled looks, and one of them said to my son joke: don't bring your father along next time.

And andreus mottebol wants to add a moral, a moral lesson, a conclusion . . . but you shut him up and say: what a shame I can't say the same to your son, andreus mottebol!

THE PROBLEM OF WORN-OUT SHOES

Polpoets is so lonely in his so-called villa, desolate out in the middle of the fields, that he—even more so than mr brys in his tenement in the rue saint-honoré—has started hearing ghosts gnawing at the wallpaper. And grabbing his hat he hurries like a bird down the long winding country road, to the shop of the old master-painter, for paint and paintbrushes and canvases: now he's sitting there in a corner of his so-called villa and staring at an almost completed painting: a pair of worn-out shoes. Yes, just like van gogh did, he paints a pair of worn-out shoes in a corner . . . but with him they're not a pair of shoes kicked off by some poor devil of an exhausted farmer . . . they aren't social shoes. Or, at any rate, polpoets's social problem has become something different than van gogh's social problem. Because he's no van gogh . . . the missionary, for whom life had no value if there were no cross to be dragged to golgotha . . . that priest who wanted to make everyone as unhappy as himself with his religion. No, no, he is polpoets, he belongs to this age, where every belief is fading, where people only shrug their shoulders, where people take things for what they are, and only occasionally smile and bare their 2 gold teeth. And so he stripped these shoes of their social significance, placed them with their toes towards the viewer, and gave them a quite different meaning: from these shoes toes suddenly start growing in a strange and incomprehensible way . . . toes that are actually self-contained beings that, groping around, hesitantly exploring the world around them, grow forwards: rather frightened of this world that they don't understand, they hatch from the shoes like chicks from an egg, like a child from the womb, and they grope around then in the cold and unpleasant atmosphere outside. They are warm, alive, and red—their surroundings are chilly, artificially lit, and indifferent. Will they soon wither and die in this atmosphere, like young trees whose roots grope around in the wrong soil, like plant matter that must have been brought here from another planet, and so can never thrive? And while polpoets is busy painting all this, you knock at his door, sit down next to him, and stare rather anxiously at these uncertain forward-growing toes. But polpoets lays a calming hand on your arm, and simply says: all I'm worried about is what to call it. And in terror of those toes growing toward you, you blurt out: the urgent problem. But polpoets jumps up like he's been bitten by an adder: ow, do be quiet . . . never mix one with the other, never confuse painting with literature. Up to now only books have been banned, never paintings . . . a book is something which everybody more or less knows what it's getting at, and for that reason is more or less hated, abhorred, and censured. But a painting is something whose sense and meaning can't be completely grasped, and is therefore seen as something comic: the writer is a menace, but the painter is a clown. Give me a title for this comic painting, but not a title that's an explanation, or a title that turns it into something cruel and oppressive and cold. And especially not a title with the word Problem in it. The word problem is something sacred . . . it's attached to religion, the fatherland, and the flag—morality, morals, and the Future: things for which one has to put on a serious face: beware, no laughing here. But I'm polpoets . . . I paint something comic, and if my jokes make you feel something serious, I can't help that . . . if you see a problem in my painting, that's not my fault: no, help me find a title, a more innocent title, a title that fits a painting that up till now hasn't alarmed anyone, a painting by polpoets who up till now hasn't alarmed anyone . . . for example: a pair of worn-out shoes.

Evening falls over brussels, and tippetotje and mr brys are sitting together in the studio on the sofa that was bought for her by the baron. The ghosts are gnawing at the wallpaper in the tenement in the rue saint-honoré, says mr brys. And tippetotje replies that something is always gnawing everywhere: the rats are gnawing at the world my baron lives in, and bitterness is gnawing at my heart like a disease. But she says this rather absentmindedly . . . she gets up off the sofa and runs her fingers over the luxurious furniture she lives with, writes her name listlessly in the dust on this polished furniture: she draws a heart with an arrow through it, and below that, her name and that of her baron . . . she throws a couple of thick books into the wood-burning stove, since the evenings are gradually getting chillier, and her above-mentioned heart is also growing chillier. And then, absentmindedly, she runs her fingers across the keys of the grand piano. It's a street song that she starts playing without thinking. And mr brys joins her at the piano, and asks her to play something . . . something with the melancholy of long, sad sundays brooding. And while tippetotje with rather reluctant fingers, rather absent-minded fingers, starts playing "come sunday," she tells him that the keys on this piano remind her too much of the teeth of her baron: mr brys, it's as if I'm actually hitting his teeth and making music out of it! And going on playing "come Sunday," she says: sometimes he comes and lowers himself into the sofa over there and I have to play him something by ludwig van beethoven—beethoven, yum yum! he says licking his chops—and as he sits there melting in the blissful rapture of classical music, it seems to me more and more horrific, as if I'm banging out beethoven in his open mouth. His eyes roll back as if he's about to faint, his mouth hangs open . . . all we'd need is for him to start drooling like old men do. And when I finally stop beating out budwig van leethoven on his teeth, he looks at me like someone drunk, and raises his thumb and forefinger in a sublime circle, and says: ha, art, my darling . . . art! And then my fingers casually bang out a final chord on his teeth, as if I have to wipe away the saliva, and I say, so nonchalantly: could you lend me 3,000 francs perhaps, I'm so short. But look, the ghost of ludwig van beethoven immediately disappears and his face goes painfully stern . . . yes, he's actually annoyed that people should dare pester him at such exalted moments with something that has to be expressed in francs. And still playing "come Sunday" for mr brys, tippetotje goes on with her story . . . her fingers go on touching the keys, and she goes on and on talking about her baron: ha, art, mr brys . . . art! And while one hand hurries from left to right over all the keys, she raises the thumb and forefinger of her other hand in a sublime gesture: and then he hurries away, my baron, while the last notes of beethoven are still resounding in his fat head . . . his head is fat and empty, but his fat wallet is fat and full. And beating out a last chord on her baron's teeth with irritation and no little horror, she gets up and gives the polished grand piano an unexpected kick . . . a kick that makes all the strings suddenly vibrate, and a strange high-pitched sound to resonate.

Did you hear that, tippetotje? asks mr brys . . . it was a ghost groaning! And tippetotje bursts out laughing, and says it's not true: it was just a string twanging, listen! And she gives the underbelly of her baron's polished piano another kick.

ONDINE UNMOVED

Ondine and oscarke and their litter of young ones moved next-door to boone, onto the long terrace of the 1st grimy houses . . . but it was more like if they'd moved in with boone himself: ondine spent more time with her feet up on their stove than she did at home . . . particularly now that a child had arrived at boone's house too. Ondine went pale the first time she saw that little fellow on boone's wife's lap . . . and she immediately started talking about people who brought up strange children, if only to earn a centime or two, because what with the war and everyone rooting around everywhere to find a few cents. And she laughed, sarcastically. For goodness sake, woman! . . . said boone's wife . . . it's our child, it's our little louis! Louis was a very delicate child, it had actually been born with one crooked, dangling leg, and boone's wife sat with that leg in her hand all day long holding it straight: I'll put it right, she said. Ondine, then, sat there or dropped by, and after work oscarke went straight from the municipal park to boone's shop: I expect ondine's here? he asked . . . and then he stuck around there too. He also spent a lot of time with their landlord, and with that woman with her funny eyes: malvine, she was called. He was given a book by the landlord and forgot it there . . . where's my book? asked ondine . . . and then he looked under his arm, oh, he'd left it by malvine's bed . . . but of course he didn't say that. With malvine he gave his senses free rein, she held him tight and asked what he saw in her . . . yes, what did he see in her? . . . she was no jeannine, far from it. And when he looked at her closely, well, to be honest, there was something wrong with her eye, it looked in a slightly different direction: he thought she was looking at him and it wasn't true, she was looking past him, and that's what had made it funny. It must have been like that even the first evening he'd seen her, he'd thought she was ready for a laugh and so had given her a fleeting pat on the ass . . . but it wasn't true, there'd just been something wrong with her eye. And now, what did he really see in her? He thought about it . . . perhaps he didn't see anything in her, apart from the fact that she didn't have a hernia and didn't wear a truss, and her belly wasn't a dark cellar but warm flesh and blood. He no longer touched ondine, and she didn't make a fuss . . . she was discovering a new bit of truth in those borrowed books: that one must be chaste in life . . . that if one wanted to know more about life and death than what an ordinary person knew, one must become more than an ordinary person. And she looked up in astonishment . . . yes, that was true, if you lived like an animal you knew no more than an animal did . . . just look at oscarke's father! . . . and those who wanted to fathom the secrets of flesh and blood must first master them, must rise above them. So she lived purely, she lay down and pretended to sleep . . . they played hide-and-seek together: oscarke didn't touch her because he was hot for malvine, and ondine didn't want to be touched so that she could become more than what she was. And then she also learned from those books that one shouldn't get angry: everything should wash over her without touching her, without her being moved.

ANDREUS MOTTEBOL MEETS THE BARON

Andreus mottebol happens to meet master oedenmaeckers as he's coming back from his bit of garden, where he's had a cottage built. And when will you be disappearing for good into that refuge of yours? asks andreus mottebol with a mildly sarcastic laugh. And master oedenmaeckers shrugs his shoulders vaguely, and says: oh, there's so much left to do to my cottage, but, well . . . I'm master oedenmaeckers, not a banker . . . because, speaking of refuges, you'd have to be a banker for that too: unfortunately I'm poor and stupid: despite everything I still live with the crazy illusion that my vocation consists of showing young people the way to beauty and freedom and democracy, and a few other things that don't really have any value anymore . . . when I should long ago have become a businessman earning lots of money.

But andreus mottebol immediately interrupts him, saying that those are two different things: a businessman and someone who earns a lot of money. Even a businessman, he says, doesn't have it cushy nowadays . . . see for example tippetotje's baron.

But master oedenmaeckers obviously doesn't care for the baron, because he says that in each of us, at this moment, there's a perceptible hesitation: we're all dominated by the feeling that we're on the eve of something totally new and unknown . . . a fear seizes us, we know not how or why . . . we begin to realize that the values that up till now gave the world its purpose and meaning are gradually turning out to be worthless: the foundations on which our civilization and our morality were built are rotting away: everything that for centuries had been a rock and a support is staring to wobble: the old is worn out, the new that's inevitable frightens us and makes us hold our breath: is this a dusk or a dawn? . . . is this the end of everything or are we, on the contrary, about to take a heroic step forwards?

Yes, but what has the baron—sorry, tippetotje's businessman—got to do with all that? asks andreus mottebol. What that businessman of a baron has got to do with is precisely that he has nothing to do with it, replies master oedenmaeckers rather preciously: he has in fact nothing at all to do with it . . . he has absolutely nothing to do with the change of values, and yet he's at the vanguard of this change of values . . . that's what is funniest or most tragic about it . . . tragic if you remember einstein's last message, in which he says more or less that men of science have already become the office assistants of the world's businessmen—in the west they're the office assistants, and in the east the disciplined followers of a new god—and at this moment therefore there's a fear, a doubt, and an uncertainty in us. But what am I going on about again, as if I were at the blackboard in front of my pupils . . . all I wanted to say is that tippetotje's baron-businessman is the only one who can make a proper refuge. And I'd also need to be like him if I'm ever to have money to build my cottage right, and if I'm to be able to live in it with a clear conscience.

But looking up at andreus mottebol, he asks: why are you looking at me with such a pitying smile? And andreus mottebol replies, oh, I'm looking at you with pity because I've just been able to meet the baron himself . . . not in his factories, where his workers were working feverishly, black and dirty and perfectly designed for suffering, or in his offices where the telephones were ringing and the calculators rattling and a mechanical brain was just being installed . . . no, he himself had turned his back on all that and was locked away in his domain . . . his earthly paradise, his refuge, his haven . . . and he was sitting there at the center of his wild garden, with his head in his hands, and when he noticed that I'd caught him in the act, he said with a sigh: yes, I need this . . . with all that glass and steel around me, those ringing telephones, those rattling calculators . . . sometimes I feel fear, I don't know why or of what, as though something in the world was changing . . . and then I come here and have a good cry.

LONG LIVE THE VICTOR!

Somehow or other then andreus was able to meet the baron: the man who's at the head of something he has nothing to do with, namely society . . . the man who's made every man of science into an assistant who has to split atoms for him . . . the man who's made subordinates of priests and philosophers, doctors and professors, poets and thinkers . . . the man who, finally, as master oedenmaeckers thinks, feels none of the fear that seizes the best among us, when we see this society of His going the way it's going. And yet . . . this last thought, that he himself feels no fear: it was dead wrong. Andreus mottebol met the baron during the rare moment when he sat crying in his garden, when he felt split and torn, after he'd helped turn the world into two opposed hemispheres.

Somehow or other. And it was because the baron wanted to talk to him about art and the like . . . he was right at the center of the garden of his castle, in which the already overgrown park was much more like a forest, and where he slept in what had once been the coach house. Only now the walls disappeared behind bookcases, containing for example the complete works of the marquis de sade, illustrated with uncensored photos, and bound in human skin. He was listlessly reading some verses when andreus mottebol came in, and the baron was the living image of someone who believes in nothing, nothing and no one anymore. And he talked to andreus mottebol about art and the like, about the poetry he was reading . . . he would like to write poetry himself . . . but hasn't the poet become a clown, a pariah, andreus . . . er, oedenmaeckers? And andreus mottebol replies that art is indeed disappearing: it's just something that will survive it's own ignominious death a little. But when andreus mottebol says this, it's pervaded with regret . . . and when master oedenmaeckers says it, it's in the desperate hope of being able to change it one day. But now the baron agrees and nods his head indifferently: good, yes, I'll take that into account. He's sitting there having a bit of a cry, and yet his attitude is the attitude of someone who must always be ready to get going . . . a tired captain, a conqueror of el dorados who's tired of life . . . but this tired man, drunk and tired of life, always consults his instruments before moving: the realistic attitude of someone who was never allowed to miscalculate. No art then: art is doomed. And by the way, andreus mottebol, what is your opinion on the international situation . . . about korea, china, the UN and the soviet union? And he asks this in an unperturbed way, just like a seismographer records the vibrations of the earth unperturbed, and a barometer any kind of weather . . . he also speaks about them without passion, without hate . . . he doesn't really believe in these things, and simply tries to assess their commercial value. He's not decidedly left-wing or right-wing, he doesn't go to church, and he's not anti-catholic; he's not a democrat and not even a fascist, because none of these concepts has any value to him . . . only the first one to the finishing line will be the victor . . . and whoever the victor is, whoever crosses the finishing line first: the baron had to bet on him, and through him Remain master of the situation.

And he asks andreus mottebol: who, do you think, will cross the finishing line first? And andreus mottebol looks at the baron in silence for a moment, from his dirty teeth to his ever-open and stained fly, and leaves, to never return.

VIOLENT BLOWS

But was everything supposed to pass by ondine without her getting angry? Oh, that was asking too much . . . that would have been all right on days when she was seized by a blind lethargy . . . but the day afterwards? . . . the day that marie-louise made her first attempts to walk, but stood there drooping as she had done in the chair, with her head down by her knees? Oh, she went pale, ondine did, she . . . she . . . call doctor goethals, she said to oscarke with her voice breaking, and the doctor came and looked: there's something wrong with her spine, he said . . . and he also talked of sending her to a home for abnormal children. A home? And they all looked at him as if he were the abnormal child. A home? Because she couldn't walk yet, because she was a little bent over with her mouth open? But ondine suddenly dropped her head onto her breast and wept: she thought of her mother, she thought of that night, she thought of all the saddest moments in her life. Of course, she'd just read it there in a book: that each of us receives what's coming to him, since there was no escaping the law of cause and effect. And that law of cause and effect . . . wasn't that actually another name for god? So that her father was proved right after all: god would become science. And look, here was proof . . . what used to be called god's justice was now called the law of cause and effect. Nonsense, she said . . . in a wild and desperate attempt to throw off the yoke of truth . . . nonsense, the fact that she's a little bent over comes from hanging between that chair and the wall all night, it's distorted her growth a bit, it'll be all right. And she thought this mainly because the crooked foot of little louis boone actually had been all right, they'd massaged it and put ointment on it and put it in splints, and now he was walking and no one could see anything wrong. And that had happened to socialists too, so why shouldn't it be all right for her, with her children? But it was strange, the more she tried to stay calm, the more violent blows she received: oscarke came home and said the work was finished over in the park: boone of course had been lucky, he'd been able to start working there on the corner for that taxi-man . . . he's going to drive coaches and take the german officers to their whores at night . . . but me, all I can do is say again that it's all over for me over there. What do you mean, over? asked ondine, who couldn't, wouldn't believe it. Well, do you think that digging ditches lasts and lasts till the end of time . . . or did you think the germans were intending to dig right through the earth and come out in america? And he stood there laughing quietly at his supposed joke . . . and at the violent blows that ondine was receiving.

WELL-BEHAVED IDIOTS

Evening falls and tippetotje is still sitting in her studio, when mr brys drops in without knocking . . . the wood stove is on and the reading lamp is also on, and on the floor on the luxurious bearskin rug is a small naked girl. Come in and close the door quickly, says tippetotje . . . this is my little sister, and I'm drawing her. And the little naked girl looks up in astonishment and says: it's not true, I'm not your sister! But tippetotje hastens to muddy the water with lots of words that bury this naïve exclamation. Oh come now, be quiet, you don't know what you're saying, you *are* my sister! And so it's my little sister that I'm drawing and drawing, over and again, but with less and less success . . . I'm losing momentum and all I can paint is rats . . . I draw her and think of the little naked tippetotje I once was, and wonder whether little gerda will also one day be obliged to get hold of a baron . . . and forgive me mr brys, but I have the idiotic feeling I'm going to start crying about little gerda, who one day will have to tuck in a baron and milk him—like a farmer milks his cow—to get a little money, to be able to live. And I draw her and think too much about all that . . . and I also wonder bitterly: is everything always the same, or does the same thing never really happen twice? . . . what do you think, mr brys? . . . is there never anything new under the sun, or can we never bathe twice in the same stream? But mr brys doesn't answer tippetotje with some plagiarism or some cliché . . . for that matter he doesn't even get the chance, because the little naked gerda has already hopped onto his lap, and is telling him that she had oh such a strange dream: we were all birds, beautiful strange birds but with human bodies . . . naked human bodies but with strange blue and green and red wings—look, in my dream I was just like I am now, but I had lovely blue wings here on my shoulders—and we were living in a big room in a house that was all alone in the world, and we flew into that house through the open window, and greeted each other by moving our beautifully colored wings up and down . . . wait, I'll draw it for you. And little gerda goes over to where tippetotje's paper is sticking up and takes the artist's pencil out of her hand: go away, go away, she says to tippetotje . . . go away so that I can draw my dream for mr brys. And mr brys looks at the little naked tippetotje . . . no, that's wrong, looks at the little naked gerda, and can't quite decide how old she is . . . she's only this big, but she has enormous eyes from which the two hemispheres of the earth look back at him. And on tippetotje's paper she draws a house such as all children draw: a triangle roof with all the tiles and a chimney with all its smoke, a crooked road, a rectangular door, and the open square of a window. And mr brys asks where all those birds with their beautifully colored feathers are? She points to the square hole of the window and says, almost whispering, with a raised finger in front of her mouth . . . shh, quiet . . . they're inside: oh they're so beautiful, so light, so happy, and they're waving to each other with their wings. And mr brys feels like a barbarian, because he can't see little gerda's marvelous strange birds . . . he's so sorry that his eyes are too old to see the wonderful strange birds of little gerda. And tippetotje notices how sorry he is, and as she strokes the naked little gerda's young rosy bottom, she says: come on, gerda darling, mr brys and I aren't capable of seeing dream birds . . . I only see rats, and he only hears the ghosts behind his wallpaper . . . come on now, and comfort yourself, I'll turn the reading lamp off and show a film. And onto the virgin canvas of a painting not yet begun, tippetotje projects a film in the darkness, a film with charlie chaplin and his lopsided feet. But mr brys has eyes only for little gerda, lying naked on the bearskin rug looking up at that crazy little man with his lopsided feet . . . and he asks: what do you think of charlie chaplin? And little gerda looks up at him in the darkness and says: he's crazy, but he's good. And mr brys stares at tippetotje, and she stares at him, and suddenly both of them see the world anew again, so that tippetotje gives a wry laugh: it's true mr brys, he's crazy but he's good . . . your writer from termuren, polpoets, kramiek, and I, we'll take violent blows just as ondine and oscarke took their violent blows . . . we'll allow ourselves to be duped by others, but we're good, and also a little crazy . . . and the others, who tear off one ball and then the other, they may not be good, but they are behaving sensibly. And though mr brys knows that it's true, he says: those dirty words . . . that they tear off one ball and then the other . . . I don't like that kind of thing, tippetotje! What don't you like? asks tippetotje . . . for them to tear off one of your balls and then the other, or for me to use dirty words? And on her bearskin rug little gerda replies: in my dream my birds can't have first one ball and then the other torn off, because they haven't got any.

THE FISH COMES AT A HIGH PRICE

Together with his son joke andreus mottebol has climbed aboard the train to brussels, and his son joke says: when the boy in that book went to diest on the train with his father, he pulled the cap off a farmer's head . . . so shall I pull the beard off the chin of the phony santa claus at obomarché, father? And andreus mottebol says: it's more than enough for you to pull those false beards that I myself so laboriously try to tie on every day . . . and it's lucky tippetotje doesn't live in termuren anymore, because under her pernicious influence and following her appalling example, you'd probably dare to pull the heart right out of my body in the long run. And so andreus mottebol barges into tippetotje's studio, where she's doing a few sketches of cruel and cold-blooded fishes with wide-open mouths. And by the way, asks tippetotje, how did it go with the priest, who fixed it so that the prize for the best book of the season didn't go to the person entitled to it, but pretty much into his own pocket? . . . wait a minute, what was his name again, it was the name of a fish too! And joke mottebol answers: his name was eel. But tippetotje shakes her head with a laugh and replies: he certainly was slippery enough, but his name was more prickly . . . ah, I've got it, his name was perch. And going on drawing her cruel fish with their open mouths, she adds: yes, it was a perch, a fish with hard red spines, I think it's a predatory fish that's native to our rivers . . . have you never caught a perch in the dender, andreus mottebol? I'm not an angler, replies andreus mottebol gloomily. I once saw a perch float to the surface, says his son joke . . . waste from the factories had killed it. I don't believe that, answers tippetotje . . . it's more likely he died because he thought he was doing his duty to swallow his share of factory waste. And andreus mottebol says almost in a whisper: how you must hate the world and human- ity, tippetotje, to be able to talk about them so harshly and so mercilessly! But tippetotje, still going on drawing the cruel wide-open mouths, replies: on the contrary, I don't even know what hate is . . . it's just that my sympathy has moved a bit to the wrong side. I see in myself the girl who picked up a baron, and I feel well disposed to anyone who finds themselves in the same boat . . . for example that perch, who instead of a baron picked up a book of moral literature. Do you know that the nicest pages from the story of jan de lichte's gang, the bloodiest pages, the cruelest pages were written by me? My heart went out to the robbers and bandits, and with my refined bloodlust I had him murder and burn, lie and deceive. My heart goes out to the vermin, to the rats with their bald tails, to the birds of prey with their unfeathered, slippery necks, to the predatory fish with their insatiable, wide-open mouths, to people who are sly and shrewd and double-refined like it says on the sugar boxes: double-refined. My heart goes out to this perch, which was able so cunningly to profit from people's aversion to their own dirty and humiliating bodies. Oh, just like him I could urge everyone to malnourish their sinful bodies, to beat them with sharp rods and make them disappear on the stake in flame and smoke and dripping fat. I would urge them all on, the idiots and fools, the timid and the shy, the weasels, the asses, and the charlatans . . . who have become hateful because they never received what's due to them, and whose days are numbered, without hope of reprieve. I would urge them all on to burn everything that I dislike. And it would be gruesome pleasure to my vicious soul to see all those immoral bodies burning . . . I wouldn't know what to do with my hands, or where my head would be, as I watched—with great excitement!—all these immoral things crumple, shrivel, and collapse in piles. Hold me back, or I'll make a start tomorrow, no, today . . . peter the tippetotje instead of peter the hermit, preaching his crusade against immoral books . . . shivering with pleasure at tracking them all down, squirming with pleasure reading every page where I can catch a glimpse of naked flesh, my fingers grabbing at every word that strikes me as taboo, and with drooling lips weighing every book on my scale of impurity.

And the main thing, says tippetotje with an unfathomable smile . . . the main thing . . . But she no longer needs to say what the main thing is, because andreus mottebol's son rubs his thumb and forefinger together in a meaningful gesture: when I'm grown up I'll set up a gang too, he says . . . the morality gang. And tippetotje laughs: the gang of the predatory fish. And only andreus mottebol shakes his head in dismay: the two of you will pull the heart out of my body yet, he says.

THE LIBRARY

Rather shaken up, andreus mottebol gets off the train from brussels, and after he's taken his son joke home, he drops in to see you, and comes straight out with it: what do you do with the books you no longer read? And before answering, you try to retrace his train of thought . . . there must have been a library involved, but although you've written about all the books owned by oscarke's new landlord, that can't be it . . . no, he's upset, he's returned from brussels and he's met tippetotje there! And you answer: oh, did tippetotje fill her stove with books again instead of coal? And silent and dismayed, andreus mottebol nods: he couldn't see which books they were anymore, but the top one was still unburned, and it seemed to be goethe's faust. And you mutter in agreement: that's a thick book, I expect it gave a lot of heat. Be quiet, exclaims andreus mottebol . . . be quiet, how can anyone throw such a masterpiece in the stove? They say man is ashes and will return to ashes, andreus mottebol, and so it's only logical that faust and his mephisto should have risen from the flames of hell to return to the flames of a wood stove. But andreus mottebol covers both ears with his hands and says that in the bible god was furious at mankind, that wasted the seed of its body in the fire . . . so how furious will he be when he finds out that we're now casting the seed of our spirit into the fire? Oh come on, andreus mottebol . . . the seed of our spirit, you say . . . I've picked faust up many times, and always put it away again pretty quickly. It was there in my little library and everyone said: hey, so you've got a faust too? And it seemed to me that they meant by that: hey, so you've read that too? And then I became ashamed and said apologetically: yes I've got it, but I haven't read it. Because I was terribly afraid that they would take me for a goethe expert or something . . . someone who knows nothing, can do nothing, has heard and seen and experienced nothing, and so hasn't thought anything about anything, but has read goethe. I was afraid people would identify me with a politician, that businessman-investor-minister-of-a-baron, for instance, tippetotje's baron, who earns lots of money and doesn't give a damn about anything, but does know a few quotations from goethe—quotes that he found in a very practical work: a thousand easy-to-remember quotations for all occasions. And I was also afraid that people would confuse me with old paerewijck, who shook his head sadly when he once heard people talking about goethe's faust, and afterwards said: what kind of world is it turning into when people don't even know that faust is by gounod! And so I'd actually like to do the same as tippetotje, andreus mottebol, but unfortunately I haven't got . . . Any books? asks andreus mottebol. No, a wood-burning stove, you say.

But, no books? Andreus mottebol looks around your living room, where there isn't a single book either upright on a shelf or anywhere else, and he says: I hear you talking about all your books, but where are they then, what do you do with them? And you reply that you actually have 2 kinds of books. The first being the books you love, and have gathered together to choose from every evening to read a page before bed . . . the most beautiful, the best, the purest . . . but anything you want to read, the others want to read too, and so they borrow them and then pass them on to each other and just throw them around . . . they're lying in heaps in the rue saint-honoré at mr brys's place, in polpoets's so-called villa, and also in master oedenmaeckers's cottage that's still under construction . . . yes, they fall out of my little library like autumn leaves from a tree, they flutter away in the wind and are picked up by god only knows who. Just last week I met kramiek with a book under his arm, and he said to me: I've found a lovely book, would you like to read it? And I open it and on the first page I read from the Writer to his friend boon. And then there's the second kind of book, those I never read and no one else ever will either . . . I've already put them up for sale but no one wants to spend money on them . . . I took them to an antiquarian book dealer, and he shrugged his shoulders: haven't you got an old bike for me? And I fetched your son joke and told him he could have them for christmas, and he looked at me and said evasively: sure, but if I take them I'll never see the walls of my room again. So what do you do with them then? asks andreus mottebol. I send then to tippetotje, you reply . . . that copy of goethe's faust? It was mine.

THE MEDICINE

Oscarke thought he was being witty, asking if the germans there in the park were making the unemployed dig a pond right through the earth to wind up in america. But that word "America" . . . true enough, a shop had opened in the little town with the 2 mills where they distributed american bacon for occupied belgium. Well, "distributing" was overstating it a little . . . when ondine arrived she had to pay like everyone else, but at least they weren't black-market prices, there were tins of sardines and there was bacon and there were blankets too.

Someone from the derenancourts was sitting there at a sales desk . . . yes, it was norbert . . . and she hurried to get in the line at that table. He gave her something, without looking up . . . no, she said, give me a tin of sardines! He looked up and she was immediately given a blanket, although they were for distribution to war-victims only. Ha, war victims, that was another joke, because real victims never saw a blanket, or weren't in a position to buy them . . . and so the blankets lay there for a while until a new consignment came and the old consignment was sold on the black-market. How are the spirits? she asked . . . and she leaned over towards him: I know almost as much about them as you do now! He beamed and asked if she'd discovered them for herself, and because she shook her head in denial he smiled rather pityingly. She went outside, and thought he was probably right to condescend, because it wasn't exactly the truth that she knew as much about them as he did . . . firstly she could scarcely guess how much he really knew . . . and secondly . . . and, damn, what was she thinking of? She'd had a chance to ask about work for oscarke and she hadn't remembered. She retraced her steps . . . it was a mansion with a large gate and stone steps, and lots of poor people milling around, all lining up for some bacon . . . she fought her way through again, was pushed sideways and forwards and backwards and suddenly she found herself being pushed face-first against a poster: auxiliary policemen required. After endless struggles she reached norbert's table again . . . listen, she said, can't you make oscarke an auxiliary policeman or something? Of course, norbert said . . . get oscarke to send his application in writing, and by next week he'll be appointed. Appointed, appointed! She went home beaming . . . next week you'll be an auxiliary policeman, she said, and she produced her tin of sardines, opened it and swallowed the whole thing, big as it was. Oscarke looked at the empty tin . . . and what about me? he asked . . . what, you always used to say you didn't like sardines! ondine said . . . yes, I used to say that, before the war, but it's three years since I saw sardines, and apart from that, shouldn't the children have something? What good are they to the children, said ondine, they've never even seen sardines. Do they taste nice? asked mariette. No, they're not nice, it's to make you go to the toilet, it's medicine from the doctor.

A MISCARRIAGE OF JUSTICE

Polpoets is suddenly standing there in front of you and forgets to bare his 2 gold teeth in a smile: I've sat bent over those old archives for days and days, to be able to tell you a few more things about that pirate of a jan de lichte, he says . . . and now you're telling me you've got no more use for him—that it's too late—too late again—always too late—but I haven't told you anything yet, not really, just a few marginal observations, and I've said scarcely a word about jan de lichte himself. I've told you nothing about the hour when I stood bareheaded in the market place of aalst, and the priest raised his crucifix and the executioner prepared his wheel. I've said nothing about the great manhunt . . . I should at least have been able to say that we'd grown too bitter to describe the excesses of his persecutors, so we had to turn our backs on it. That we heard shouting and screaming, the clogs of the farmers, and the hobnail boots of the soldiers of louis XV as they trotted back and forth chasing down all the people we'd once called our friends. We heard their confused cries, and when they once again managed to overpower a pregnant woman, and we didn't look round . . . we couldn't watch the way this woman, with bloodshot eyes, tousled hair, and rumpled clothes, passed through their hands. Perhaps it's that lioness, that heroine, the uncommonly beautiful woman anne-marie de clerck . . . or perhaps it's marieke bleecker, that child . . . or perhaps it is jan de lichte's wife herself, mie gendarme, from whose hands a whole group of men wrest the wooden clog, in order to hit *her* in the face with it.

And something also happens that makes us grin, with truly sadistic joy: a certain jan willock, who willingly helped track down many members of the gang, much too zealously in fact, sees one of the fugitives coming to drink from a stream at nightfall. And taking off his clogs, he creeps after the kneeling figure, and falls on it with his full dead weight. It was a child . . . it was anneke van de wiele, the daughter of marie van audenhove, who last year had stolen an apron somewhere. And the way he comes down on top of that child, she almost cracks. He drags her up onto the road with him, and the closer he gets to the town gate, the prouder he gets: he's a hero, a courageous fighter for law and order. And so the people who see him entering the town gate cheer for him enthusiastically . . . but jeer at him just as enthusiastically. Because that's how it goes with a mob: it cheers and jeers at the same time. At the front they cry bravo, and at the back people aren't really sure what all the fuss is about, so they cry: boo, go back where you came from! Someone asks: what's happening over there? And someone answers: they've caught some more members of the gang, a man and a girl. And the mob jeers at them, and pushes forward, and wants to tear them to pieces. Because that's how it goes, yesterday and the day before there were many who were well disposed towards them, because they stole the money and the property of the gentlemen in their castles and distributed it among the poor. And the poor felt nothing but pride because they had such a great protector. But now they're bringing in those protectors to justice and killing them, and the poor rally and cry out: down with jan de lichte's gang! And they push forward, and are going to kill the prisoners themselves on the spot. Fortunately there are soldiers of louis XV at the town gate, and they drive the crowd away, and they themselves take charge of the two captured members of the gang. They

seize hold of anneke van de wiele and jan willock and take them on. This
is accompanied by hysterical shouts and jeers . . . a stone and a flowerpot are
thrown at them from a window. And the farmer, jan willock, tries in vain
to make this mob realize who he is: jan willock, a member of the farmers'
watch, who's zealously helped to track down the gang. But amid this commotion people can't properly understand what he's saying: he's got the nerve
to give a speech! cries one person in indignation. And the soldiers give this
intransigent prisoner a kick in the ass. En avant! And together with anneke
van de wiel he's kicked into the dungeons of the belfort. And jan willock
loses his respect for the law, and calls their high-and-mighty Lordships all
the names under the sun. But we, dear reader, rub our hands and grin with
devilish glee.

And polpoets bares his 2 gold teeth in a smile and says: well, I was sorry
I hadn't said anything in your book about jan de lichte himself, and here you
let me speak and once again I say nothing about him . . . it'll keep for next
time. For the next and last time, polpoets, because what's the good of writing
about people who managed to escape society when we ourselves shall never,
ever be able to do so?

GLOOMY DAY

That's certainly true, says polpoets . . . I can see myself that there's no point
anymore in talking about jan de lichte in this book . . . it was a mistake to
start talking about him in the first place . . . a mistake among millions of
others. But because I won't be speaking about him anymore, I'm going to call
this last piece "gloomy day." Gloomy because I won't be able to say anything
about him . . . and doubly gloomy because it's also his last day . . . his last
day in our book, and also the last day in his brief, heroic life. I can only
raise my far-too-short arms in regret, and say: don't blame my pitchfork for
being too small to take on all that hay. For I would have liked very much to
tell you just how jan de lichte was arrested. There was a general manhunt,
and one part of the gang fled deep into the hilly country of brabant, while
the other chose to flee towards antwerp. And however much I'd love to tell
you about it, there's no point in my describing how we grabbed them by the
scruff of the neck, one by one, and beat them up—guilty or not: that would
be decided later—and all kicked together into the clammy, chilly dungeons.
But we know virtually nothing about the arrest of jan de lichte himself. Only
a bit of a legend, some ancient stories, some memories of him that have been
preserved. Some ancient men will tell you that they were there themselves,
although it's two hundred years ago now, and so they could only have heard
about it from their great-grandfathers. Legend has it that jan de lichte was

arrested just outside the town gate, where he'd hidden in a hollow tree. And that same old guy we were just talking about will be happy to point that tree out to you, though as far as we know, a hollowed-out, pollarded willow could never stay standing for two hundred years. But no matter. Let it be that tree or another that's grown in the meantime, and grown old and hollow in turn. Every piece of worked land, every boggy meadow in flanders and the aalst region, is bordered by a line of pollarded willows, and countless trees are old, wrinkled, hollow, and canker-ridden. And it's not important which tree is actually the one in question . . . yes, it's not important whether a new tree has meanwhile grown old and hollow in its place. The most important thing is that the memory of jan de lichte has been preserved, that something is still known of him, something, however little—however pathetically little—of those illustrious days that we've recorded in our hours of disillusionment and sweet, imaginary revenge.

But if it's true that jan de lichte was found in a tree, then he must have lost all his friends in the confusion of the manhunt. All that running this way and that, the shooting and cursing, it must have been jan de lichte that they were chasing. They were fighting against the whole army of louis XV, and the united farmers and citizens of flanders . . . but they couldn't defeat them with just a handful of men. You surely don't want that, dear reader. You surely don't want us to pull the wool over your eyes and describe to you how a few men cut whole armies to pieces? Come, come! And having lost his friends, he wanders round, pursued by hundreds. And yet, as you've heard, he comes running to aalst, all alone, to rush to the aid of his imprisoned friends. But he must have been too late . . . his bosom friends must have all been herded inside already . . . and the farmers' watch, helped by the brigade criquy, helped by the regiment-royal-rossillon, are now hunting for the third man. They've cordoned off a wide area, shoulder to shoulder, and the noose that they've formed is being pulled tighter with their every step. And yet, once again, he's too slippery for them: they've already passed his hollow tree. But blind chance, as we've already seen often enough, lends the mob a hand: some merchant or other has to take his cart to town, and his dog starts barking at the hollow tree. Dogs bark for the benefit of their masters even when they're worn out under a cart. This dog licks the hand that beats it, and barks as the wagons pass. And the soldiers retrace their steps, and from the hollow tree retrieve a man with red, inflamed eyes: our hero, our jan de lichte.

Amen, says polpoets. Although he knows that it can't be anywhere near over yet, since jan de lichte must first be jeered at, spat on, kicked and tortured and scourged before finally being broken on the wheel. But polpoets will be silent about that once and for all now. And that's for the best . . . instead of seeking consolation from the footpad jan de lichte, we should have compassion for him . . . compassion for others, though we ourselves have yet to reach the end of our misery.

THE ARMBAND POLICEMAN

So oscarke became an auxiliary policeman . . . he wasn't given a uniform, he had to go round in civilian clothes with an armband on—armband policeman, people called him. Winter had come, and as an auxiliary policeman he stood on the bridge in the freezing night, asking people for their papers . . . but as soon as he got used to the police a bit, he asked for the post on the unmanned crossing, close to the 1st grimy houses, although it was more dangerous there, since there were professional smugglers around who had to be stopped. He'd always been a little coward, but recently he'd developed into a little bastard . . . now he confiscated smuggled bread or a bit of butter or fat from simple, hungry people. And he also sometimes said to ondine: I've got to do nights again. But that was only so he could creep into the landlord's house, and spend the whole night with malvine with the funny eye. But still he didn't dare abandon his post entirely for her . . . he stood listening in the cold and walking to and fro, imagining the warmth of malvine's bed . . . and suddenly, there was a german walking back and forth on the other side of the railroad tracks, and he slowly came towards oscarke and his partner: there was some mist, and when oscarke saw that gray shadow with the rifle over the shoulder, he shivered: he suddenly remembered having seen exactly the same image years ago—although this was his 1st war and he'd never been in the army, so how could that be?—but he remembered, remembered slowly: hadn't he dreamt it once? Yes, that was it, the night when ondine had taken ill with her belly for the first time, when he'd drunk that bottle, he dreamed that a soldier with a rifle over his shoulder was coming towards him through the mist. How amazing that was. And what was even more amazing, and was something he knew nothing about, and would never know anything about . . . was that the same thing had happened once in one of ondine's dreams. It was unbelievable that they should both experience so much that now turned out to be exactly the same . . . that they were both so to speak unwinding the sample spool of yarn, had exactly the same thoughts, drew exactly the same conclusions, and yet never knew what the other was doing or thinking . . . on the contrary obstinately clinging to the idea that they and they alone could possibly have such thoughts. Oscar stood looking at the german in bewilderment and didn't know what to say . . . could he really say: I saw you coming towards me out of the mist of a dream years ago? But these thoughts that were rather too strange still didn't stop him from confiscating people's butter and tobacco. He took them to malvine, and sometimes also took a little something to ondine . . . and ondine sold it on the—well, he was an armband policeman, and it allowed him to smuggle what he'd confiscated from the smugglers.

In these wintry days chapel road is wet and cold and foggy, and as it says in the schoolbooks, it's full of dead leaves. How beautiful they are! But even more beautiful is the car that sometimes drives over these dead leaves, and suddenly stops at the last of the 4 villas. They're visiting andreus mottebol's house says the lovely lucette to herself. It's a packard, no it's an oldsmobile, say the children of chapel to each other. It's a dutchman and he's rung our bell, says andreus mottebol's son. It is an impressive event: what might it mean? And when the dutchman comes out again at long last and disappears in his gleaming automobile . . . so that all the leaves that have fluttered down fly away into the air so as not to be run over again . . . the children and the lovely lucette approach the last of the 4 villas, and look at andreus mottebol expectantly, who's stopped by his open front door: he was a publisher, he says, slightly upset. And the lovely lucette claps her hands with glee, and adds excitedly: and he came to ask you to publish all those hundreds of books you've written over the years, and you said yes, and he wrote out a check for a hundred thousand francs! But with a melancholy smile andreus mottebol turns towards the damp fog of chapel road, into which the publisher has disappeared, and imitates the way he came in, the way that publisher set everything on stilts. And do you know what stilts are, lovely lucette? They're wooden legs that help you see the world from a higher perspective, she replies. Yes, but they're also crutches that you can fall from and break your neck, says andreus mottebol . . . and they were exactly the kind of tall and dangerous legs that the publisher put me on. He asked me why every writer has a book published but I don't. And inwardly I repeated the question to myself: have I got nothing to publish then? And I surveyed what I'd written in recent years, books and booklets, novellas and stories and newspaper columns . . . why, every nook and cranny of my house is stuffed full of columns from the weeklies . . . and can none of that be published? And while I was wondering this, the publisher went on tell me more and more about the business . . . about one writer who's turned seventy, or perhaps eighty, and has written another novel, a novel he is now going to publish . . . and about another writer who's only twenty and has already won a literary prize with a particular novel, which he's now going to publish . . . I publish everything, I publish everyone—you're the only left who has nothing to publish! And meanwhile I take a look at all my books and stories and columns in my mind's eye . . . and I say: everything I've written and have yet to write is fated not to be published . . . one publisher thought my long books were too long, and my short books not long enough . . . because a book has to have exactly the right thickness if a reader's going to buy it, he told me . . . another publisher thought there was too much clutter in my books, although, I said, my wife is poor but clean: she never tolerates any clutter. And the publisher you've just seen driving off had to laugh at that: they didn't mean actual clutter, he said, but mental clutter. And brushing aside all my concerns with a single wave of his hand, he said: no, no, I publish everything, I publish everyone. And finally I allowed myself to be persuaded and gave him the ridiculous manuscript of our impossible book on chapel road . . . and he opened the first page and read the first word, and his face clouded over: the reader, he said, always opens to the first page in a bookstore and reads the first word before buying—if he doesn't like that word, he'll put it right back on the shelf . . . can't you change the first word? And I took our manuscript away from him and put it right back on the shelf: you saw what happened from there: he drove back to where he came from.

And the lovely lucette looks pityingly down the wet and misty chapel road, down which the publisher drove away. But andreus mottebol leaves her no time to look for words of comfort: every spring publishers set all their new hopes on a new book, lovely lucette, but in the autumn that hope shrivels, and falls like an autumn leaf, and they have to throw the book into the leaf pile of all the other unsold autumn books, and with it our hope of ever seeing this book in print.

But although oscarke started smuggling it didn't bring them a better life . . . ondine, no, she wasn't the kind of woman who could keep a household in order. They had a bread ration card and she sold it, she sold the stolen bacon and butter and tobacco, and apart from that they all still went to the soup kitchen . . . that is to say, she sent her children there, small though they were. The 2 little girls could scarcely speak up for themselves, and sometimes they got lost on the way . . . sometimes they even stood outside their old pub by the 1st grimy houses, forgetting that they'd moved away . . . and because the soup kitchen was in the center of the town of the 2 mills, mariette wanted to see everything, this shop and that one, and judith, though she was a year older, cried and said: we'll get lost . . . No, said mariette. But sure enough, they were already lost . . . it was already about 3 in the afternoon and they were still turning corners, and found themselves in streets they had never seen before.

THE WHEELBARROW IS NO MORE

No, life isn't easy for andreus mottebol, the poet and painter: he sings and writes songs, writes articles and paints canvases that no one wants to buy, and now and then to earn a crust he paints the doors and windows of some house on chapel road. Would you paint the doors and windows of my cottage, over in my little garden? asks master oedenmaeckers. And andreus mottebol goes there in the early morning, along the winding country road beyond termuren

. . . but the days are much shorter in this month of december, and in order to save some time he comes back on the trolley, which he waits for over on the main road. He stands there at the stop in a dark corner, it's raining, the cars roar past over the wet asphalt with the sound of a lashing whip: shoosh, shoosh. On his left he sees the double light cones of their headlights, and on his right he sees their red rear lights reflected on the wet gleaming surface of the road. How is it that more accidents don't happen? he wonders. And he also thinks: where on earth is the trolley? And as if it's been waiting for this signal, the red warning light comes on, the electric wires start humming and over there on the bend it appears: the trolley. It sways on the bends and glides up over the points, and at the same time figures emerge from the dark doorways and from behind hidden corners: they're wet and black and they hurry over the small section of highway in order to stop at the same time and in the same place as the already-slowing trolley. The trolley: a machine, a mechanical vehicle—and man, someone who willingly accommodates this mechanical creature. But look, together with the approaching trolley, a heavy, dark truck also approaches. Towing an even heavier trailer . . . one of those monsters that recognize that only might is right, and that destroy whatever's foolish enough to get in their way. The trolley gasps, swerves and is about to stop . . . and the people emerge from the doorways . . . but the heavy truck is still going as fast as it can. Stop! Stop! the waiting people shout at andreus mottebol, and andreus mottebol in turn shouts at them: be careful! And there's no room anymore for the truck and it rears up onto the pavement at full speed, among the people fleeing this way and that. But because the truck swerves onto the pavement, the trailer angles in the other direction . . . and this angle smashes into the side of the trolley. Crashing glass and wood, a shower of slivers, the groaning of a single human voice. And then there's the silence that can be heard after every disaster for a brief, oppressive, breathless moment: the moment in which one remembers all the heroes who've perished in all those road accidents, and in which one feels one's own wretched body up and down and then rejoices that everything is sound and unscathed. And immediately thereafter all hell breaks loose, and everyone tells everyone else how it happened: I was so close, this and that . . . But in the evening and the rain andreus mottebol walks home, while the cars whisper shoosh shoosh in his ear. And he gets home and says to his wife: you almost lost your andreus mottebol.

And his wife asks: but what did that truck driver say in his defense? He said, says andreus mottebol, that he was convinced he could still get through. He said that . . . but meanwhile I looked at his expressionless face, a face like the puppets I always paint, and I realized that it was something quite differ-ent: he was the servant of the machine, the obedient slave of the creature that he himself brought into the world: the machine, the mechanical creature that already rules the world. The car, the missile, the a-bomb . . . these are the creatures manufactured by man, but which have carried out a silent coup and taken power from mankind. And as another writer predicted: only here and there will a machine remain loyal to man, for example the wheelbarrow. Alas the master of the wheelbarrow is no more, he's long since given way to the slaves of the car, the blueprint, and the a-bomb.

LITTLE LOUIS BOONE

Ondine had been waiting at boone's house for her two children to come home from the soup kitchen, and in order to kill time she'd been needling everyone at boone's place a bit . . . especially little louis boone, whose crooked foot might have got better, but who must have had some other problem too, a crooked foot in the mind, so to speak, because he would just come in and sit down in a corner and cry, and no one knew why. When they asked him what he was whining about, he would say: I don't know. Ondine looked at him and said: I think he's got worms, let's have a look at your bottom, little louis. It was quite possible that he had worms, but it was also quite possible that he was just too highly strung. He went to see his father in the taxi yard . . . and on the corner where wittepennings the taxi-man lived, a man was shot down by the germans . . . a puff of dust came out of his coat, he spewed a stream of blood, and looked right at little louis, who had fled into a doorway. Oh, that was a wound cut with a blunt knife into little louis's soul. It was like a wound he'd once painted, with watercolors, and ondine had said: I'll ask oscarke what he thinks of it . . . and oscarke, who was a sculptor, a real artist who had filled the parks of brussels with statues, oscarke laughed at it: did you paint that in the dark, little louis? he'd asked. Or louis would go onto wittepennings's property itself, through the open gate, across the empty courtyard, and finding that whole big house was deserted, and feeling himself a little anxious, he went into the kitchen where wittepennings's daughter was standing completely naked, with blood dripping from between her legs. Oh, that was something else that made him cry, and he came back home and there sat ondine, whom he hated . . . he cried, and he had to show his bottom to everyone so ondine could look for worms.

But ondine left little louis boone there with his trousers pushed down and his shirt pulled up . . . she was thinking of her own children now: where on earth were they?

OH DEAR . . . LITTLE LOUIS BOONE!

Yes, you've got to the point in your ondine-and-oscarke novel—that endless and endlessly accursed novel—where a new hero has appeared in its pages.

A strange hero. A little fellow with large bewildered eyes, and a rather weak, rather melancholy mouth. A mouth that will gradually change over the years . . . that will become a little more sensuous, but also bitter. And eyes that will become duller, with bags under them, as if they were retreating into a fortress. But you're getting bags under your eyes! little louis boone's wife would say later—much later, when this book about ondine and oscarke comes to an end . . . if it ever comes to an end. And little louis boone will nod his head in agreement and say that she's right, as an idiot usually does: nodding his head in agreement and saying that everyone is right: you're right! Yes, little louis boone appears in these pages for the first time. And he looks at ondine and oscarke, and he looks at you, and he looks at the whole wide world with his large, bewildered eyes. I can still see it as if it happened yesterday, says ondine . . . the war was on and little louis boone was playing there, opposite my door, opposite the door of tinne from the shop, and the germans with their spiked helmets were herding, into the police station, the people who'd been drafted. Little louis boone was standing there looking with his bewildered eyes. And suddenly he was knocked over, 2 times, first by a draftee with a battered cap, who was running away, then by a german with a spiked helmet who got down on one knee and started shooting. Bang. And little louis boone heard that bang and started running too, as children do: they do something and they don't know why. So I called out: watch out, little louis boone! And right next to him the man with the battered cap fell down outside the door of tinne from the shop. And a little puff of dust came out of the coat of the man with the cap. A tiny puff of dust, nothing at all, like someone had thrown a pebble at him. And the man with the cap lay down, and doctor goethals came, and the priest too. The inevitable doctor and the inevitable priest, the inevitable last people a man sees. No, the last one was tinne who had to scrub her pavement clean afterwards, since blood stains are so hard to get out. So little louis boone makes his appearance in your book as a little bewildered person. He plays with little polpoets and the even littler tippetotje . . . that is to say, he stands watching their games . . . he watches their games and asks: did you see it? It was a little puff of dust, that's all. But little polpoets didn't see. There are children who see everything, and children who see nothing. There are children with big, bewildered eyes . . . and there are children who from birth smile and bare 2 bad teeth . . . bad teeth that will be replaced by gold. Little louis boone tells everyone in the street what he's seen, but no one's interested. Everyone sees things, they say. Everyone sees something different. But despite this, little louis boone tells everyone everything he sees: it's his vocation, telling them what he's seen. And perhaps it's the vocation of the other people not to listen to what little louis boone tells them. Over the years his mouth becomes a little bitter, and his eyes a little dull: bags form beneath them. He's told them almost everything that he's ever heard or seen. He's made a lot of enemies and very few friends. Sometimes he says to his wife: people who don't see much are lucky. Sometimes he also says: people who can hold their tongues about all they've heard and seen are lucky too. He sits there and sometimes feels the bags under his eyes, and wonders whether all the things he's seen and still hasn't dared talk about aren't what's hidden behind them. So little louis boone, this new character, will come and play a part in your book. Ondine will make fun of him. Sometimes she looks at him and says to his mother: he always looks so sad, I think he's got worms!

Worms, oh dear . . . and big, bewildered eyes: it's little louis boone.

THE HARLEQUIN

In the winter my so-called villa over there is completely bare, says polpoets to andreus mottebol . . . and although he tries to bare his 2 gold teeth in a grin, he shivers. It's so empty and bare there that, with a little goodwill, you can look right through things, he says. And andreus mottebol replies: you've said that already, polpoets . . . that one should look at things till one has seen right through them . . . but people don't do that, people run away and try to talk over it with someone or other . . . but you would have done better to go and call on kramiek, polpoets, because as it is you've come to the devil to make your confession. And without mercy he shoves the first sketches for a new painting under polpoets's nose: an almost comic painting of a harlequin. Look, he says to polpoets . . . this man wandered through the streets at carnival time in a crazy outfit, with a cardboard mask on . . . it's one of those vacant masks without any real expression, strange and stiff and impersonal, just like a machine would have. Except that for a moment, round the mouth, there's something that you could almost call a smile . . . a vague trace . . . a faint semblance of a smile . . . a smile that heightens the strange, stiff, and impersonal effect, and may well just be the result of an optical illusion: perhaps it's just a crease in the cardboard, a fold, a dent. But whatever it is, this impossible smile gives the stiff mask a stupid, idiotic quality. This harlequin reminds me—against my will—of the people I see around me, polpoets, who become afraid when they realize that the things surrounding him are made of glass . . . when he sees that one can look right through all this glass. . . when he notices that all these glass things are so brittle and fragile and so worthless. And with this false smile he makes his way rather woodenly down the street . . .

But polpoets raises his hands in self-defense: no, let me go, andreus mottebol. I got the wrong door and I'd rather go and call on kramiek now. But andreus mottebol stations himself with his back to the door and will not let polpoets out. But look, he says, the comic thing about this painting is still to come . . . this harlequin may be wandering through the street, but the street itself no longer exists, it's nothing but a little rubble left over from the bombings. Just as strange and unreal as that figure from a carnival wandering there is the rubble lying everywhere around him . . . and in the background the walls still left standing rise up, with the dead eyes of their windows—oh, polpoets, have you ever noticed that even the dead eyes of the windows of bombed-out houses have an empty smile across their mutilated faces? And with his own face averted, trying to get hold of the doorknob, trying to get back his smile and to reveal his 2 gold teeth, polpoets says: none of those things exist, andreus mottebol . . . and if they Do, then they don't have the slightest significance.

It doesn't have to have any significance, replies andreus mottebol . . . a painting doesn't need to have any significance, it just has to give you a shock . . . an electric shock that suddenly goes through you when you unexpectedly see right through things . . . when you unexpectedly see all the glass in the world fall and break. And anyway, apart from that, it *does* have a meaning . . . it means that man still doesn't dare to admit to himself that transparent, worthless things multiply around him only to fall and break and then multiply again, and that man walks among this rubble with an unreal face, and a set smile on that face that's only the result of some optical illusion. So he walks through the ruination that he's created, he walks through the things he's broken: man is his own enemy, man is a creature that's only on this earth to bring his own enemy into the world. Just as we look at the monkey and smile, one day there will be a creature who will look at the harlequin and smile, smile at that crazy figure walking around among his own ruins.

But in a desperate effort to regain the optical illusion of his grin, polpoets says: let me out, andreus mottebol—this winter your heart is even emptier and barer than my so-called villa.

LORD LISTER

But man is who he is. You can show polpoets the as-yet-unbroken glass world, and he'll shiver a second, then shut his eyes quickly enough to say: I didn't See it. Polpoets didn't see the harlequin that andreus mottebol is about to paint . . . so in his memory, in his polpoetish consciousness, all that is left is the following: andreus mottebol is going to paint something again! And he manages to find something funny in that, so, wonder of wonders, his cheery smile reappears on his lips. He forgets that the world is made of glass that has yet to be broken . . . no, he's never known it . . . and he bares his 2 gold teeth in a grin when he sees all andreus mottebol's unsold paintings leaning there in the corner. And with this smile he says: I remember reading an article in the daily paper recently about a painter who was moonlighting as a burglar. I don't know what kind of person he might have been, but if he was a relation of kramiek's he would have painted charming landscapes and domestic scenes . . . and if on the contrary he was my polpoetish brother he would have painted comic-surrealist things, shoes with toes growing out of them in some miraculous way . . .and if he had something of tippetotje in him he would have painted rats gnawing at our civilization . . . and if he was going round with mottebolish notions he would definitely have put carnival clowns and puppets on his canvases. But whatever he produced, in order to live as an artist he started burgling at night, And you, andreus mottebol . . . why don't you start leading a double life too? . . . why don't you wash out your brushes as evening falls, tie one or another of your favorite masks over your face, and sneak through the streets with the same fixed expression you like your puppets to have? And andreus mottebol is so flabbergasted at this suggestion that he sits down on the chair where his palette is lying, and then looks at his sketches and paintings with unseeing eyes, and says, stammers: I could certainly try it, polpoets . . . I might as well, really, considering all the other things I've already tried. Up till now my life has consisted of nothing but trying. From my childhood on I've been trying things, in order later on to cling once and for all to whatever revealed itself to me as the most beautiful, the best, and the most lasting idea . . . but now I'm almost forty, and I've never stopped trying things: will I know on my deathbed what the most beautiful, the best, and the most lasting is, or will dying itself be one last try? You won't understand, polpoets, but in my life I've tried love, art, science, religion, and politics . . . I've tried to be sensible and wise, to think, to reason, to solve mysteries and to understand. But all I achieved were so many spectacular failures . . . and they felt like even bigger failures when my name was occasionally mentioned in the local paper, or if I was awarded a government subsidy to encourage me in my work: after all, someone who's well-ahead in the race doesn't need encouragement—it's the ones whose handlebars have broken or who've had to change wheels . . . they shout at him: come on, you can do it! you can still catch up! And I rode in the race of love and art, polpoets . . . I rode in the race of religion and politics, and heaven knows what others. I've danced and yodeled and sung songs, written and painted . . . sometimes I've flattered and sometimes I've kicked . . . sometimes I've begged like a down-and-out tramp for a slice of meat on a slice of bread, sometimes I've growled and showed my teeth like a dirty, treacherous dog. And now burgling: why not? I'm only frightened of one thing, polpoets . . . That you'd fail in that too, andreus mottebol? he asks. No, says andreus mottebol . . . I'm frightened that I wouldn't be a painter or a writer anymore who breaks into places at night to earn his living . . . but that I would become a burglar who writes and paints a bit during the day to pass the time.

IN WHITE SNOW

Polpoets is still in andreus mottebol's house, and despite everything is still reluctant to go back to his so-called villa: it's so desolate and bare in those silent fields, andreus mottebol . . . and look, now on top of everything it's starting to snow, I'll be snowed-in over there, and I won't be able to find my front door . . . I'd like to stay here and wait for next spring! And together with joke, andreus mottebol's son, polpoets goes over to the window to look at the twirling snowflakes, while andreus mottebol goes on working on a painting he'll never find a buyer for. In fact, I'm living in the middle of a forest myself, says andreus mottebol, more to himself than to the others over by the window . . . I crawl out of my cave every morning and creep through the forest, club in hand, to whack some defenseless victim on the head. A man has to live. A man has to provide for his wife and young with food and fire and light. And in my forest there's no social security, no welfare. There are no unemployment benefits, no help or sympathy because of accidents or illness—like in paerewijck's shop: closed on account of marriage—and if I can't find anything to kill anywhere, in the evening we'll all sit staring miserably at our empty hands. Even my son joke experiences this struggle in the forest with me . . . going to secondary school and learning fractions, french, and history, he'll be right in the middle of forest himself if he sees his father come back to the cave empty-handed: when I put my hat on the hat-stand, and put my club in the corner, he looks at me with his dark eyes and asks if the pickings were good today. And only if I answer in the affirmative—since, well, however hard the struggle in the forest is, sometimes I do find myself on the winning side, sometimes I've been able to give someone a surprise on the back of their head—when I answer in the affirmative, he immediately comes out with his wish list: a kind letter to santa claus: though, unfortunately, one that's still left over from last year.

But although joke has been watching the swirling snow, he's also been listening to his father's swirling words . . . the flakes fall inaudibly, and the words fall almost as quietly the from andreus mottebol's lips . . . and joke comforts him: some things we always get for free, father, such as snow. And polpoets has also been listening to andreus mottebol's swirling words . . . though he's only been thinking of his so-called villa becoming snowed-in out in the fields, he's still been listening, and he replies: everyone gets the life he deserves, andreus mottebol, and you deserve nothing because you won't listen to good advice. I suggest you become a painter-burglar, and you don't want to

. . . you thought you'd become a burglar who only amused himself by doing paintings. But it doesn't matter what you succeed or fail at! Look, after the newspaper report about that burglar, I read something that was more like a fairy tale: some young guy, together with a couple of friends, smashed in his wife's skull with a wine bottle . . . and as an insignificant aside it was mentioned somewhere that he earns the tidy sum of 60,000 francs a month! And now I have to ask you, andreus mottebol . . . do you also earn the sum of 60,000 francs when you hit some sleeping victim on the back of the head in your forest? And while polpoets is asking this, still staring at the snowflakes, andreus mottebol looks at his tired, empty hands, and he lets the whispering snowflakes of his words fall in front of him: I earned the sum of 60,000 francs once in my life, polpoets . . . but that was over an entire year . . . and my wife and I still talk about that year, that sacred year of 1900 and such-and-such. My wife was working then from morning till night, until she dropped, and I was toiling and slaving till I dropped too. And I collapsed, polpoets, and my wife collapsed beside me, every evening. In that sacred year such-and-such we earned 60,000 francs . . . earned, but not saved . . . received but not kept . . . and the . . .

But his son joke interrupts him, and asks: did I collapse too, father, or wasn't I big enough yet to collapse?

THE CROSS-EYED WORLD

So ondine waited for her children, and finally she went out into the snowy town of the 2 mills, walked through it like it was her living room, in her slippers with her stockings round her ankles. She bumped into her children, and almost walked past them, not recognizing them in the street: those two snot-nosed kids couldn't possibly be her children . . . but then she looked twice, and even forgot to give them slaps . . . she was, she had to admit, almost ashamed at the way they were walking along: emaciated, with scarcely any clothes on them worth the name, while she herself waddled along fat as a snail. Yes, ondine looked greasy with fat . . . it was almost as if she'd needed all those difficulties and hardships in her life to feel at ease . . . like she needed all those tragedies around her like a fish needs water . . . the coal problem, for example: they didn't have any, so she went to get warm at boone's, and then every night she said to oscarke or judith: cold . . . how can you be cold? Aren't you ashamed to complain so much! And when oscarke was just out the door on his rounds, ondine went into the empty front yard where the chill took her breath away and looked at the christ that had been chipped out by oscarke . . . the christ with his neck that was far too long and who came along with them from the old house . . . and she took the saw and sawed the head off the christ to make the neck shorter . . . then she stuck it back together again and sold it to doctor goethals: oscarke didn't care about it anymore anyway, it might be months before he thought about it again. But it was as if he knew there was something up: he came home looking for that head of christ after work . . . he didn't say a blessed thing about its having gone, but because he was a sulker he didn't want any dinner . . . and ondine took advantage of this to eat everything, and he stared at her in disgust, with loathing, wondering what on earth he had in common with this woman: it would have been far better if he were married to malvine: she didn't understand him either, she didn't even know what a soul was, but she was warm and kind and laughed when he came to see her: oscarke, honey, is that you? But if he'd flown into rage and cursed and hit her, ondine would have learned her place . . . but now, what a little coward he was! . . . Sulker! she said sarcastically when she'd eaten everything, and asked him accusingly what she was supposed to live on if she weren't allowed to sell his stupid head of christ: you sculpt in order to sell, and then when I'm able to sell, you're upset, fucking idiot. And no sooner did he open his mouth to express some feelings about art, about sculptures that have been tampered with against their makers' wills, than she started on about the landlord: go and live with that landlord then, if you don't like it here anymore! What do you mean with the landlord? he asked. Yes, with that cross-eyed floozy! she said. With that cross-eyed floozy . . . so . . . so . . . she was cross-eyed, that was all. His whole theory about her eye . . . ha, it was ridiculous, she was just looking at him cross-eyed. And to think he'd never noticed! He hadn't noticed anything, he hadn't seen anything, or he had seen but he'd been blind, and suddenly he started telling his life's story to the children, just as if ondine weren't there: well, your mother has four children, he said . . . and he waited a bit. Three, answered ondine. No, that can't be right, are there only three? he asked, and looked round, and started count-ing the children around him. Then he looked at ondine, but she looked away, her head close to the wall . . . then she banged that head on the wall . . . so, everyone, oscarke, her mad mother, and the whole fucking world knew what she'd done. Oscarke! she groaned. He got up and came over to her. Oscarke! she repeated. Ondine! he said . . . and she began to cry, with her head on his shoulder. And just for a moment, he, with jeannine in his heart, and the cross-eyed floozy too—yes, the cross-eyed floozy—and she, ondine, who had never loved her husband or chil-dren, were one.

But the next moment he was alone again. He digested the fact that malvine was cross-eyed. The notion of being cross-eyed, which up till now had been some-thing vague, began to encroach on him, became part of his little view of the world. He applied it . . . he tried it out with his theory of the exploded god, about negative and positive polarities—and in the beginning he had to laugh, and then he became furious . . . no, a bit irritable . . . at the thought that cross-eyed malvine might see two separate oscarkes when he was in her bed. And while ondine, who still felt one with him, told him about spiritualism, he looked at her and shook his head.

Spiritualism is intellectually cross-eyed, he thought, but he didn't say it aloud. Spiritualists see doubles in everything: a crude and visible body on earth, and a more refined invisible body in the ether. We, and the spiritualists, and everyone in the world have eyes, but our vision is far from perfect . . . we have double-vision: life and death, good and evil, day and night . . . while in reality there is no life or death, no good or evil, no day or night: we're just looking at the world cross-eyed. And he could have wept because of his helplessness, he could have hanged himself right then and there out of grief at human imperfection. But all that could be seen of his great sorrow was that he sulked a little in bed with malvine that night: he was rather annoyed at her for being cross-eyed.

FOR REVIEW

Among all those white falling flakes, a black one comes fluttering down to andreus mottebol's front door: it's the postman with a letter from tippetotje! I take up the pen, writes tippetotje, to tell you that I've heard you don't want to become a burglar-author, and I'd like to give you a pat on your mottebol mothball-head for that decision. For example, I . . . through my baron . . . have managed to get a job reviewing books in the free weekly journal for art and other cultural matters: I know a lot about books, since I burn them every day in my stove. Of course, I know that you write books, and as a result you start from the false assumption that books change and improve people, or at least mean something in the world . . . and if I were also to start from that false assumption, I would now be receiving lots of books that I wouldn't know what to do with . . . books that would be getting under my feet, and slowly and surely embittering, poisoning, and ruining all my beautiful winter evenings. They would be like smelly leftovers, like flat beer, like discarded old shoes, like my baron's dirty teeth. Oh, I imagine the disgust with which I'd have to pick them up . . . And either the editor of the free journal for art, etc. would ask me at long last where my review is—didn't I send you a tearstained handkerchief of a book by the well-known author stein von goethe two months ago?—or else I'd write with my reluctant pen that the book of the above-mentioned von goethe is nothing but some artificial fertilizer, and make myself a bunch of enemies . . . just like you, andreus mottebol, have already made more than your share. But no, I derive a great deal of pleasure from these books . . . first and foremost I receive them free, and hence save a lot of coal . . . and in addition I receive a little extra pocket money . . . so why shouldn't I do my best then to say that these books that for centuries have been like discarded shoes and that I couldn't bear to actually read are really tremendous works of genius, and should be in everyone's possession? Look, in front of my stove at the moment there's a tragedy in verse, by no one less than shagspear, and in so-and-so's translation . . . the hero speaks and says to his sweetheart that she must stay innocent and ignorant a while, until she rejoices in what has happened: the light grows dim, he says, the crow wings home to his nocturnal refuge, and the good things of the day fall asleep. And when he's said that, he asks: do my words surprise you? Oh, andreus mottebol, if my baron were to say something like that, I think it would surprise the hell out of me. And precisely because of that I wrote in my review that this tragedy will really give a lot of pleasure to whoever reads it . . . people will admire the way the feet of the words are played with—good things doze off as day darkens!—ha, it's even better even than "boon's bitter deliberations" . . . though I would have preferred it if the writer had said "dumb things doze daily as the dark deepens" to bring out the effect even more: maybe it works better in the original. Shame that it's such a thin book. And after writing this review, I threw the tragedy in the stove, andreus mottebol . . . a shame indeed that it was such a thin book. As a result, through my baron, I've asked the editor of the free journal of art, etc., to send only thick books in future. Postscript: I'm sitting here amid the extravagant and rather barbarous luxury of my baron's house and see snow swirling outside . . . with you it's probably black snow that falls . . . am I right, andreus mottebol?

THE ALBUM

Last christmas eve everyone—simply filled, as we know, with goodwill—went to polpoets's so-called villa: everyone with their own newest paintings under their arms: andreus mottebol with something showing living puppets, master oedenmaeckers with an unfinished painting intended to be the summation of all his thinking, and polpoets himself with something that he made with the tip of his tongue sticking out of his mouth, as children do when they're working on something serious. Only you yourself, boon, have no painting. Everyone paints but me, you say gloomily . . . the things I see around me are so gripping, so cruel and immense and tragic . . . they're countless, but connected, so I couldn't possibly single out a specific subject . . . and they also succeed each other with such amazing speed that the canvas I have to paint on stays empty and blank, like the white screen in a cinema after a showing. And mr brys—who's also arrived without a painting—lays a thick album on the table instead and says: the things around us are certainly too poignant, too innumerable, and succeed each other too quickly to capture them in oils . . . but I've found another way to preserve them. Look, hundreds of illustrated weeklies appear, and thousands of photographs are printed in them, and now and then there's an image among them that shows people in all their cruel and tragic reality . . . a photo taken by chance, some living cliché that's printed there as a human document. And as I just happen to be mr brys, you know, who as the result of my professional training must clip out everything I see to save it in boxes or file it away—I cut out a number of photos and saved them in an album. The majority of what appears in those illustrated magazines I throw away, of course, immediately and forever, because they're only the eternally repeated shots of athletes, film stars, and fashion models—picturesque kitsch, the UN meeting, and the first snow in brussels. I throw that stuff in the garbage. But now and then there's an image hidden among them, just by chance, without my knowing how or why, that seems like it was taken backstage, behind the cardboard scenes of this shrouded world . . . a picture that was taken at a rare moment when the mantle fell and the veil of the temple was rent: naked, wry, and poignant. Here is the album in which I've collected these images: there are photos of the atrocities of war and the horror of the bombings, the prisoners-of-war and the population on the run. There are photos of prisons and houses of vice, alleys and passages and black ghettoes . . . I have blind and tattooed people, and all kinds of grinning masks. There are pictures of everyday life that were taken at random in the streets . . . and it's mainly the children who are depicted so poignantly, so tragically and so cruelly—since the street is the stage on which children act out their dramas: and the sewer, and the gutter. And mr brys shows a photo in which children, dressed in rags and tatters, and with thin, careworn faces, are playing in the gutter, while behind their backs is a huge department store, and above the great shop window one word: food. And look, this is a lovely one! says mr brys with the enthusiasm of a stamp-collector showing a rare specimen . . . look, this is a very good one; a picture of a bombed train station in China: a flattened area of brick dust, with a tall twisted iron frame in the background, and in the foreground the quay swept utterly clean . . . and on this quay, lonely and desolate and bleeding, a small Chinese child putting both fists in its eyes and weeping. And I'd like to use this photo as the first in my exhibition, says mr brys . . . I'd like to give my album a title, like one gives a book, a painting, or a film a title . . . a rather hesitant and restrained title, like: man, who on earth are you? And you look at all these photos and say, mr brys, I've wanted to write and paint many things recently, but now I see most of them here in your photo album, cold and chilly and motionless.

THE WAR IS OVER!

No, the war ended before it had a chance to break madame ondine . . . it had just been a squall, a storm that passed over her head and that left her in some disarray. Wait until the war is over! she'd said . . . and with that she was unconsciously expressing her inner life: that she was tired of chasing after figments of the imagination, that she wanted to rest, though she didn't want to admit this to herself. So she waved her hand and said: I'll do it later, after the war. And just like she'd only seen a very small part of that global struggle . . . a belgian soldier disappearing round a corner, and a german soldier springing out from behind a hedge and going bang-bang . . . so now she only saw a little of its glorious ending: a few bloody german soldiers who came back from the front, trying to drag a cannon to the fatherland with a paper rope. They were singing because the war was finally over . . . and if there was one of them who realized, who had a premonition, that there was a new war waiting for them at home, without mud or trenches—but in which his search for sums of money with more and more zeros at the end, finally exchanging a bed and typewriter for a single dried herring, was to become more and more hopeless—well, if there was one of them who realized this, he didn't ruin their song. He distributed sugar cubes to passersby from a tub that they had to break up and destroy under the railway later, and he stood there rather awkwardly on his one leg, picking his nose, looking at madame ondine's children, who were lying on the ground scrabbling for these lumps . . . mariette had already filled her pockets, and the way she looked for some secret spot to hide them, behind the hedge in the dark street, digging a hole with her little black hands, she wasn't much more than a dog hiding a bone . . . Judith, the eldest, went and called their mother, but the house was empty: the old lady, ondine herself, had also gone to look for carrion. On the corner, where the long terrace of the 1st grimy houses ended and thrift street began, where on one side doctor goethals lived and on the other was wittepennings's taxi yard, the field kitchen had driven in and the soup was steaming. It was still the same as 4 years ago . . . their field kitchens rolled in and their soup still steamed: it steamed in vain for their soldiers, since they were all drunk and only thinking of the end of the war . . . rolling cigarettes and lighting them with bundles of marks, and so soup was dished out to the poor people of the 1st grimy houses, who had been hungry four years ago and had stood in line to get welfare money. Certainly, someone would always stand and watch with a triumphant laugh, and say he would rather drop dead than accept anything from those gray bastards . . . but the rest kept quiet, and would cheer and jeer when the complainers had gone . . . and now got into profiteering as well. Give me those marks, said ondine. And they laughed at her, they offered them to her, and when she grabbed for them, they yanked them back. Come in! they said . . . and they lured her into wittepennings's taxi yard . . . she went . . . oh, she wasn't afraid of those poor defeated soldiers: she was capable of killing a couple if need be and just stealing their marks—although she too had gone downhill physically and had acquired a neck that was too long and thin, crowned by a bird's head. But her great strength lay in her soul, in her brain, in her cool gray eyes that could have forced them to do anything. She followed them into the kitchen where everything had been thrown around, and cognac was being drunk out of beer glasses . . .

gimme! she said . . . drink first! they answered. She drank, even sang, because they wanted her to . . . she danced for them. Danced, yes! They laughed . . . dance! And she raised her arms, twisted them in the air . . . she swayed a little on her emaciated hips, and now and then raised a foot off the ground: well, that was her dance. But her eyes continued watching them coolly and were also watching their marks. These soldiers didn't understand her any more than the gentlemen had understood her when she was young, any more than god himself had understood her all through her life: she took the marks off the table and looked at their bewildered faces: she laughed, silently and bitterly.

MARKS WITH LOTS OF ZEROS

Ondine listened to a soldier, who stopped her at wittepennings's gate, telling her that those marks had become worthless: he held up a note and made a gesture as if it were fluttering off in the wind, and then he shrugged his shoulders contemptuously. She understood, but didn't believe it: worthless—was that really true? And when she got home she did just as mariette had done, she dug a hole . . . she scraped a space clear in a drawer, among a nest of dreary and haphazardly folded handkerchiefs and lots of other garbage, and tucked in the marks. There was going to be new money, the people said in the street . . . belgian money again, over there by the church the germans were just giving their marks away. She went to the church, and took some more . . . although it was too late, since the bulk had already been distributed . . . and she returned and silently stuffed the drawer even more full of marks: it was money, money, money. She lifted it with both hands and let it flutter down to the floor . . . did it again and again, and then she shook her head incredulously: had it really become worthless? In that case it was no better than when her children cut an old newspaper into pieces and scrawled a whole bunch of zeros on it with oscar's red pencil: a thousand francs, ten thousand francs, a hundred thousand francs. And as they did it the children said that they were playing, that this money was just for show . . . oh, so they were only for show, these marks, you couldn't even buy sweets with them: so that's how money was—today it's everything and tomorrow nothing. Some mysterious power decides, some human being like oscarke or achilles derenancourt, they decide that it's going to become worthless, and then suddenly it was *worthless. So in real life it was just like with the children . . . she'd always laughed at the children, and yet! . . . people played and acted as if those notes were everything, and then all at once, just like the children, they tired of the money game and the notes were left to rot like strips of newspaper. And it didn't only apply to money: virtue and goodness, a christian life, god, socialism: it was all just a show. A game. Today god was everything and tomorrow he was nothing, tomorrow they would leave him lying there like newspaper . . . And she stared into space for a moment, for the first time in her life into a pure void, into a pit, into a deep, deep abyss where the darkness of Nothing gaped at her. Another person would have closed her eyes, or got drunk, or gone off, if need be,with a man—because that was what human beings did: they wouldn't have stared and gone on staring into the depths of eternal death and endless night—but ondine did: her head spun, but still she bent over that abyss. It was enough to drive you mad.*

THE EMPEROR IS COMING!

You stood staring at mr brys's album, in which the most beautiful, cruelest, most poignant photos from the weeklies are collected, and sadly turned your head away and said: I've wanted to write lots of things recently, mr brys, but it's all already in your album, even colder and more impassive, even more naked and more objective than I could ever describe it. But as discouraged as the album's made you, it's much worse for andreus mottebol, the poet of the weeklies. He can't bear to tear himself away from that album, and stammers: tell me why it is that I didn't think of this myself, mr brys? Because I've looked countless times at pictures I've said I should frame and put on my wall . . . which I of course never did, so that those photos are hopelessly lost. But now! . . . And he looks at mr brys with his eyes sparkling, asking whether they could maybe work on this album together, as if it were a collaborative novel, a film, a human document: can I join in the game, mr brys? First of all I already have a photo showing a crowd as the emperor goes past . . . it's a japanese crowd, and as you know they believe that their emperor is a sort of distant relation of god in heaven. Because crowds of people, who from antiquity down to last days of mankind will always want to believe in fairy tales, allowed themselves to be fooled into thinking that their leaders, seducers, and misleaders were chosen in some way by god in heaven: moses was able to receive the stone tablets from god's own hands on mount sinai, the egyptian pharaohs were sons of god, the pope is the representative of god on earth, and the emperor of japan is his cousin. And so the emperor comes past and the crowd stares at him. There's a woman with a child on her arm, and she points to the emperor with a trembling finger, and she says: see, here comes the one who makes the sun shine and makes our rice ripen. And there stand the old priest, the rough soldier, and the tender young girl . . . and in their faces that you can read like an open book, you see how every human instinct has been led astray: this old monk has been led up the garden path, and his human longing to immerse himself in reflection and meditation was abused in order to get him to tell the crowd the lies it wanted to hear . . . and that soldier was led up the garden path as well, the human instinct in him to fight and overcome difficulties made him murder, burn, and rob, all in good faith, for the benefit of the cousin of god. And the instinct of the young girl is to love, to give herself, to feel ready to receive . . . and this human instinct too was abused, twisted, and distorted, so she now receives the seed of lies and deceit, she now receives a sly japanese emperor, a moses with stone tablets, a representative of christ on earth. And among them stands the worker too, the working men and women . . . they laugh and rejoice and are moved as never before, having never been so affected by what little happiness, freedom, and prosperity they've managed to acquire for themselves. No, it's the son of god, the emperor, the Master who brings it out in them, passing by. It's someone who's been raised far above them, who they can worship, and who they can also blame and curse, when necessary . . . a higher being who cares for them, thinks for them, clears obstacles out of their path—for they are small and stupid and afraid, and can't look after themselves or think for themselves or clear their own obstacles out of their paths—and also someone they can blame when everything goes wrong. And andreus mottebol falls silent, and gives his photo to mr brys to add to the album.

And yet . . . mr brys takes the photo, but says: sometimes you're indignant, andreus mottebol, because the people of this age are becoming cynical and no longer believe in anything, and then sometimes you're indignant because they're hysterical and believe everything blindly. And andreus mottebol replies: that's true, mr brys . . . man never wants to keep things in proportion . . . for centuries he's knelt before whoever presented himself as a relation of god's, but laughed cynically at people who wanted to bring them a light, a lamp in their darkness. A hirohito is hysterically acclaimed, but a gandhi is gunned down, a george bernard shaw is seen as an old fool, and an einstein is made to address geese. Let's keep this photo, mr brys, it's the bitter witness of our unheard-of stupidity: on your knees, the emperor is coming!

MEN WAITING

Now andreus is in search of a photo that he knows must be somewhere in a drawer. And as he searches he mumbles that mr brys's album can become an image of today's world, the world as it's become: crazy and cruel and tragic. So crazy that no malaparte has yet managed to describe it in all its cruel jollity . . . so fragmented that no picasso can depict it in all its chaos . . . so tragic and dismaying that the work of hieronymus bosch, with those impossible monsters and animals devouring each other, pales by comparison . . . and the work of goya, with all its war, its madhouses and cannibals, is becoming worthless: reality has caught up with all those nightmare visions, thinks andreus mottebol. And hastening to mr brys's house with his find, he apologizes for its being a little creased and damaged. Yes, replies mr brys . . . but wait for a bit before you bring me any more photos, and let's discuss first how we're going to stick them all in. Should we just stick them in as they fall into our hands, higgledy-piggledy in any order, yesterday a photo of prisoners-of-war, today the newest fashion trend . . . so as to show the world exactly as it presents itself to our eyes in all its confusion, its lunacy and its tragedy, its cruelty and its jollity, its bewilderment and its insanity? Or should we on the contrary follow a certain order and regularity, stake out a few clear sections and determine a number of motifs, so that our album becomes a novel in images, a symphony of photos . . . a film . . . a work of art that slowly but surely climbs to a zenith, a climax, and a resolution: to a conclusion that must not be a conclusion, but should remain an open question, and that perhaps will end with the photo of a high blank wall where someone's daubed the last sigh of mankind in whitewash? And because andreus mottebol says nothing and seems lost in thought, mr brys goes on: look, we began this album with the question: man, what kind of a creature are you? And we immediately came up with that weeping child amid the rubble. And now to support this initial chord, I'd like to have 3 more images of ruins. These pictures were taken in berlin I think . . . but it doesn't matter, it could as easily have been vienna or warsaw . . . it may have been paris during the nazi occupation, and it may be peking or moscow or brussels in the future: in our album it will remain a nameless city. And the 1st of these three photos shows the entrance to a cinema which has over-optimistically opened its doors amid the rubble, and where people are waiting in a long line . . . but the main thing is not the rubble or the people, but the caption that astonishes you with its sobriety: people who haven't eaten for two or three days line up outside the cinema. And in the 2nd photo I have an image of the same city—that same city anywhere—showing a bombed avenue, which has become a great ruined plain . . . and the main thing, the craziest thing, the cruelest and most cheerful thing, is that at the edge of this avenue that has become imaginary, the shoeshine man has once again taken up his position. And the 3rd photo shows the shapeless mass of what was once a tenement, and on the other side the scorched and cracked wall of a warehouse . . . and between these bits and pieces of walls barely standing, a young woman has strung a clothesline and is now hanging out her rags . . .

Well, says andreus mottebol, then let's add the photo I just brought you . . . the already rather stained and damaged image of a red-light district, where the narrow pavement is strewn with brick-dust and the men stand waiting in groups: eight or nine men crowd around a house with a big number, whose windows are broken, whose curtains are hanging out in tatters, and has holes in its walls covered with nailed-up planks . . . a broken chair lies by the door, and the fragments of a chamber pot have been thrown on top of it . . . four sol-diers are in conversation with a civilian . . . and a man with a cap on his head looks reflectively at a cigarette in his hand. And the caption reads: numerous men are waiting outside this house, and every 10 minutes 4 are let in.

And mr brys sticks these 4 photos at the front of his album: man, who on earth are you, that walk around like an uncomprehending animal among the ruins of your life, hanging out your washing, having your shoes shined, lining up despite the hunger in your belly for the movies and for a brothel where they let 4 of you in every 10 minutes?

WITH THE CURRENT?

Then you take up your pen to go on with the story of ondine and oscarke, to go on with your book about chapel road, with your eternal book that wriggles on like a tapeworm and bubbles like a sore—like a cancer, which is the plague of our time . . . and you take up your pen and write and write, and andreus mottebol says to you: stop for a moment and ask yourself where your tapeworm-cancer-sore of a book is crawling to. Ask mr brys what its course is, or should become . . . since he alone knows how to keep track of these things, he who supervises dossiers and papers and memoranda, who records and classifies everything. You write your books and I fill in the weeklies, polpoets bares his 2 gold teeth grinning at everything, and master oedenmaeckers treats us to his odd and usually wrongheaded observations—we write and paint and act—we act and don't look back, as in proverb. But I don't think the best way to write a book is to go ahead and not look back . . . a book must have order and structure and regularity and everything else . . . so how far have we got with the structure and form, with the point and the meaning of this book, mr brys? And mr brys frowns so that his forehead is full of thick folds, which means that he doesn't know either, that he's also lost the thread—or let's say rather, lost the tangle of many, many threads. We got to the point where . . . where . . . and he says nothing more. And polpoets says: this chapter is called "a little mistake among millions of others." And he says it innocently, as though he thinks he's helping. And he also says: we thought we were retreating into our refuges . . . I moved to my so-called villa, and master oedenmaeckers into his cottage in his bit of garden. First we tried to stop the machine that was racing towards the abyss, but we were in the minority and had to withdraw, to try and preserve and rescue whatever could be rescued in our haven. We tried to escape this monstrous society, but we couldn't escape, because the age of the robber chieftains—the jan de lichtes and the cartouches—has gone: we couldn't go back to their world of 1750 . . . or anyway, we figured out that it's just the same now as it was in 1750—and we started resigning themselves to it: the world is as it is, some of us started to say, and we're wasting our strength by trying to row upstream all alone. I prefer rowing with the current, tippetotje said to me . . . I much prefer to be carried along, she said, to milk my baron like a farmer with his cow. And polpoets looks at you and says: you see, in my view, that right there is the point and meaning of your book, at least up to this point. And andreus mottebol stares straight ahead pensively and says: yes, it's hard, and it hurts my eardrums when I hear things like that, but it turns out to be the truth: we're wasting our strength by always rowing against the current. Or else, let's say, the machine is racing towards the abyss, and there we are in front of it, trying to stop it with our bare hands . . . an avalanche of a hundred thousand maddened animals is charging down to plunge mindlessly into catastrophe, and we try to stand in their way and cut off their advance. Maybe we'd do better to run with them, get to the head of the stampede . . . and in that way redirect the course of the maddened herd. But polpoets bares his 2 gold teeth in a grin and says: hey, that's always been done by the people who over the course of time have misled the masses . . . it was always the cold, sober, and calculating realists who rode the blind beast or onward-speeding engine to their objectives, regardless of the consequences . . . And we were, on the contrary, the idealists, andreus mottebol interrupts him, the foolish and impractical dreamer who preached in the desert and allowed themselves to be crushed by the speeding realist machine. So stop. Stop writing your book on chapel road, stop going on without looking back . . . and ask yourself for a moment whether you wouldn't rather stop rowing upstream and wasting your strength, wouldn't rather have us all swim with the current instead?

IN WINTER AND BAD WEATHER

The child of nature, hung with ribbons and bows, who is polpoets's wife, is far away in their so-called villa, snowed-in in the middle of the country: it was 1 big white plain out there, with a croaking raven master of all he surveyed. And that child of nature, polpoets's wife, feels quite in her element: she's a small figure, a small black moving dot, amid the snowy world of pieter brueghel the elder. But suddenly the snow has gone again, and wind and rain have come, and she's hurrying down the winding road to termuren to do her shopping. And at the unmanned railway crossing she meets the lovely lucette. And she says: I'm sorry I didn't visit you when all that snow was here . . . our so-called villa was lying bleak and forgotten, and when I breathed on a frozen window and made a small peephole, I saw your snowy bit of garden with that cottage that was being built . . . and I thought: it's a shame that the lovely lucette doesn't live there yet: I could have called out to you across all that white swirling snow, and I would have heard your answer. As it was, I only heard the answer of the croaking raven. And also you could have helped me to pull a ladder, like a sleigh, across the snow, over to the distant highway where the coalman lives—the milkman and the coalman, right next to each other—but in the whiteness of the snow you can do without the whiteness of the milk, but you need the coal really badly. As it was, I had to pull the ladder like a sleigh across the snow all by myself, and return with only a small, 25 kilo bag . . . and anyway I had to be all alone, a small white dot in the whiteness of a pieter brueghel winter . . . and I also had to bear the beauty, silence, and discomfort of the winter all alone. A person shouldn't have to bear, enjoy, or fight her way through something all alone, she should do it together with other people: so when are you going to move into your cottage in your bit of garden so that we can see snow and rain together in the winter, like we saw the corn and the white scudding clouds in summer?

And the lovely lucette stares at that child of nature with great alarmed eyes, and lays a hand on her troubled heart: go and live there? she asks in alarm. And gazes down the muddy country road that winds and winds into the distance, out to where the cold and the rain, the wind and the snow and the ice, and also the black croaking ravens are the masters. Go and live there? And her great troubled eyes turn away in alarm from that landscape, where the cottage must be. I'm not going to live there, she says . . . like a frightened little child that doesn't want to go into a dark room, and that already feels some of the burdens of life shifting onto her delicate shoulders . . . I'm not going to live there, she says stubbornly. And that child of nature of a polpoetish wife looks at the lovely lucette with a strange smile: why's that, why did you have a cottage built in your little garden, if you didn't want to live in it? And the lovely lucette is silent, like a small and stubborn child is silent when it's confronted with the sober things of life. She regarded that garden as something that was a long way off, that you speak of like eden or noah's ark: something that may have happened thousands of years ago but that one doesn't really need to make up one's mind about. And so she knew a cottage was being built in that garden . . . but it was only a place where they might possibly go and live in a dim and distant future. Come to think of it, it hadn't ever really been a question of living there: at the beginning lots of plans were made, and plans are dreams, and dreams are deceptions: plans are made specifically never to be carried out or transformed into tangible realities. The architect showed her the plans, but they were plans on paper . . . and she'd borrowed his red pencil and put in many more doors than had been drawn, but they were doors in red pencil lines . . . dream doors in a dream house. And, in addition . . . it had been summer then, with waving corn in the fields, and red poppies.

And so the lovely lucette lays a hand on her heart, and looks with large, dismayed eyes at the rain and wind across the distant plain, and she says like a small frightened child: I'm never going to live there. And when that child of nature of a polpoetish wife laughs, the lovely lucette is silent and still refuses to come to terms with the realities of life.

THE REVOLUTION OF '14–'18

And while ondine stood there and couldn't believe that her money wouldn't have any value any longer . . . the front door opened and oscarke came in: he saw her in the front room in the middle of the scattered marks and laughed: he kicked at them and the notes fluttered back up into the air: there's a revolution in germany, he said. And he told her what he'd seen in the street, in bits and pieces, incoherently . . . because he was someone who noticed quite a bit, but usually kept quiet, who had such a detailed world in his head that he'd forgotten how to use his tongue. In the street, he said . . . and at the same time he made a gesture to show what the street was, what the street was in his thoughts—a hubbub, a struggle for existence, a clash of ideas, a . . . a . . . anyway, the street—but anyone listening to him couldn't possibly understand what he was talking about. And in the street then, over there in the street where the landlord lived, he'd seen a car—one of those cars that were still like tiny horseless coaches, with big copper headlamps and a box and an iron running board, and perhaps still had a tray to put a whip in—and in that car there were some german officers, but some german sailors came and stopped them and made them get out so they could drive themselves around instead. And as he told the story oscarke stood looking at ondine with big, blinking eyes, while his hand made wild, ridiculous movements, for example beating a drumroll on the corner of the table, or running through his hair that was standing on end, or pointing to something . . . he didn't know what—so how was ondine to know? And, he said . . . and . . . And then he fell silent, and looked inwards with his blinking eyes. Inside him it all meant the dawning of a new age, an age in which the gentlemen are chased out of their coaches and the workers get in and drive on . . . it meant revolution and socialism and justice, everything that he had always hoped for . . . and the world, that new world that he'd believed would come, must come—perhaps after hundreds of years—was already there, was there now, and he himself was going to experience it and see everything himself. And he rejoiced and danced and sang . . . inwardly, in his little oscar-like thoughts. And the fact that his hands were trying to convey something—perhaps the new world itself— the fact that his fingers beat out a drumroll on the corner of the table, well, they were the regiments of the future, the new men, who were lining up. But at the next moment his hands were ruffling his hair that was standing up, and thereby perhaps expressing that . . . that . . . he was also afraid of the new age, because despite everything he was still a little person, and new things always scare little people. The blinding light, the first ray of the sun, the first licks of fire, the first turns of

the wheel, it must have always have sent a shudder of fear through the ranks of
mankind. Something at the back of his head trembled, shivered, sang, and wept:
he grew, he belonged to the revolution, he had seen it with his own eyes . . . and
he also held his hair and let his shoulders droop: damn, damn, what're we going
to do? Ondine didn't understand him . . . she couldn't make any sense of his few
hesitant words, apart from the things she herself knew and had seen: so it was the
revolution, and money was no longer worth anything . . . life and death were
worthless too . . . the borders of countries were paper borders and people's feelings
were paper feelings. They looked at each other, they were oscarke and ondine, two
o's that oscarke had once wanted to intertwine into an ornament, two worlds that
he had wanted to bind with a little cement, with a rope, with a bit of yarn.

WHICH BEAK DO YOU CHOOSE?

How it happened you don't know, but tippetotje, andreus mottebol—on
her left—and master oedenmaeckers—on her right—have all magically
assembled in tippetotje's studio. A fine set of mantelpiece decorations we'd
make! laughs tippetotje. But look, master oedenmaeckers can't laugh at this
important moment: this is an age in which people no longer laugh and in
which laughing is actually forbidden, he says . . . this is an age when we look
with fear, with horror, at the things that are happening around us . . . this
is an age when every person, together with the world, is split in 2 . . . and
moreover it's a time in which one has to choose to belong to one side or the
other. And however much one stands there invoking this, stopping that, and
shouting that this shouldn't be allowed: it simply is. It simply is, like spring
and summer and autumn, like day and night, like the tiny single-celled creature the amoeba suddenly divides in two. There's already a peace of the west
and a quite different peace of the east . . . there's already a philosophy, a science, and a logic of the west, and a completely opposite philosophy, science,
and logic of the east. There is finally, which is most important for us, the art
of the west and the completely opposite art of the east. And which art do you
choose? I don't choose anything, says andreus mottebol . . . I have more than
enough with my own art. I sit there and write . . . the lamp glows, the paper is
blank and empty, and it's so wonderful letting words drip onto it . . . I have no
particular art form, I just sing and I just write and I just paint, whatever I feel
like doing at that moment. But master oedenmaeckers shakes his head and
says that it's no longer possible to twitter with whatever beak you like: there
are 2 beaks, an eastern beak and a western beak, and before long one of those
beaks will be tied over your face . . . and then you'll sing, and you'll listen
in astonishment to the song that resounds through the beak you've tied on,
your beak that's been tied on by east or west. No, don't cry, don't complain,

don't launch into a jeremiad: it is so. It's coming. This society is a tree in the autumn, and the fruit of the atomic tree is the atomic bomb, and the atomic bomb is ripe and will soon be picked . . . and no escape from the orchard of the earth is possible . . . the orchard is as big as the earth, and hanging over your head is the ripe fruit that will fall from the tree of this society. But you're a poet, a painter, a writer . . . so all that you can do, all that you're expected to do is to celebrate, describe, and paint the fall of that fruit. Just as past writers and painters described the birth of jesus christ, you'll describe the birth of the atomic bomb, and this world split in 2. And it won't be long before you sing through your eastern or western beak, whichever gets tied on. And don't say: I don't want a beak, because that would be like a fetus saying: I don't want to be born. You are going to be born, and so the only choice you have is whether you'd like to be born with an eastern beak or a western beak. So which beak do you choose?

And andreus mottebol, master oedenmaeckers, and tippetotje sit there listening to the voice coming from heaven, from hell, from the deepest depths of their blood, of their brains, of the finest fibers that linked them to the earth, to the splitting atom . . . they hear this question and are lost for an answer. You speak first, andreus mottebol, says master oedenmaeckers. And andreus mottebol, the man scorned, beaten, and kicked by life, kicked by the world—this king of the jews, this INRI, this artist—he stands up and speaks.

THE BEAK OF THE EAST

Andreus mottebol is the first who wants to say which of the 2 halves he'd rather belong to. And looking at the polished parquet of tippetotje, he says, it's true, there is a western art and a completely opposite art of the east . . . the art of the west is the art of the nobel prizewinners, of blowing first this way then that, and of saying things in such a way that they can be interpreted however you like . . . it's the art of arguing about politics as little as possible, since politics is a finger with which the western writer pokes out his own left eye . . . and where one must always be careful never to speak the blunt truth, but to dress it up with decency, since indecency is the finger with which the western writer pokes out his own right eye. No, anyone wanting to write for the west in the future will have to preserve decency, and not put any revolutionary, socialist, or anarchist thoughts on paper. And the art of the east is equally restrictive: in the west art must for the time being be defeatist, negative, and destructive, but in the east it can only be clear, trusting, and constructive . . . there, thou shalt talk only of the worker, who in the west collapses dead at the factory gate, but in the east looks towards the future full of confidence and laughter. Between them is my own art: my own doubt and

316

my own atheism—my own dream of beauty, my own idea of freedom and personal happiness. And all these things that are mine and mine alone, they belong neither to the east nor to the west. And perhaps the real essence of my art consists in my having to stand between these two halves, raising both hands imploringly . . . to die between the two . . . like isengrim the wolf, who tried to act as a an arbitrator between the charging rams and was left lying half dead among them. And yet, I know all this and still I can't stop. But . . . you tell me that that one day I'll have to stop singing with my own beak, and that they'll tie an eastern or western beak over my face, and that henceforth I'll have to sing through one of these two beaks. So which alien beak would I rather wear? If I think long and hard, and have to answer honestly, I would answer that I'd prefer an eastern beak. This society is going under through its own errors and mistakes . . . korea, china, and soon africa too: those are the ripe fruits falling, they're the harvest that we've sown: you always reap what you sow. And thus the west will get what it deserves: a punch in the mouth, a kick in the pants. We've given the yellow people and the black people a kick in the pants, so now the time is approaching when we'll get one in return. And besides, in the west there's no room anymore for the poet and the writer . . . while in the east there is. In the east the writer and the poet are national heroes: workers who have a right to exist, are useful and necessary members of society. In the west he's not. In the west the poet and the writer is a pariah and lunatic, someone forced to live on manna from heaven . . . and has 1 chance in a 100,000 of winning the nobel prize: one of them wins a 1,000,000 francs and the other, who's just as good and maybe better, gets nothing. Assuming you can make yourself look towards the future with laughter and confidence, the poet in the east is no longer a pariah, but a recognized member of society. As for me, I live my own life and my own art emerges from that . . . but if ever, out of necessity, I have to accept an alien beak, I won't allow them to tie on the beak that just keeps everything the same: I would be less and less able to sing what I wanted to sing, I would be less and less able to talk about injustice and oppression and the hope of a better, socialist world—to talk about my hope for one, and also my doubts about it—and despite everything I would remain a starving pariah. Singing through the eastern beak I would sacrifice just as much freedom, but at least I'd be relieved of that humiliating fate.

THE MASK OF THE WEST

Tippetotje is still sitting there with her polished furniture, between west and east, between andreus mottebol and master oedenmaeckers, and she's listened to andreus mottebol, who's just accepted the beak of the east in the event that he is not allowed to sing through his own anymore . . . and, he adds, in the event of my not be allowed to show my own face, I'd prefer to tie on the face of the east, he says . . . of course I'd resist as much as I could, and try to be myself . . . and of course I'd try to show my own face as much as possible behind the mask—like in the days of the persecution of heretics, when atheistic painters continued making calvaries for cathedrals, but in one little corner of their canvases would paint themselves in as a mocking devil, as a smiling unbeliever, or as an indifferent onlooker. And thus far master oedenmaeckers has listened and said nothing, until tippetotje says to him: now it's your turn to choose, to tell us which beak and which mask you'd prefer to have tied on, if you couldn't walk around with your own voice or face. And master oedenmaeckers says: in the event of my having a mask tied over my face, I certainly wouldn't want the mask of the west. I'm walking around now with the mask of the west, and I wear it against my will . . . I'm ashamed to belong to the west . . . I think the ground would swallow me right up if I were suddenly summoned to appear before a tribunal of chinese, before a court of blacks, and all I could say in my defense was: I wash my hands of it! But still, I wouldn't want the mask of the west to be ripped off—for the strange and unfamiliar mask of the east be tied on in its place. Some time ago I was talking to a great painter who's put on the mask of the east, who's begun to sing through an eastern beak that he's tied over his mouth of his own free will . . . but the time when we spoke happened to be a rare moment of despair, and he said to me, in a slightly embarrassed, slightly dispirited way: if that's the world that we're building, I have everything to lose and nothing to gain . . . and I'm afraid—this new world that they're building is not My world: if I were to start painting only what they want to see painted, well, I might as well break my brushes. That's what that painter said to me, and a few days later I heard that the work of our writer, boon, despite his sympathy for the east, won't be allowed there: he wrote his books here for the working man, he's protested against injustice and dreamed of a better and more socialist world, and he's expressed that protest and that dream in his books countless times . . . and yet those books can't be published in the east. And if that's what happens with the green wood, what will happen to the dry? And with the mask of the west tied over my face, I've been allowed up till now to speak and act however I like . . . but once the mask of the east has been tied over my face, I'll have to march forward, one man in an unending line, looking towards the future with laughter and confidence, to starve and die as I'm ordered . . . dressed in the uniform of the new society. Up till now you've been able under the western mask to choose whether to write or go hungry . . . but under the eastern mask you won't even have any choice about that: you'll have to write, and write what you've been ordered to.

It'll be just the same as in russia, said ondine . . . and she shivered . . . and oscarke shivered. During the war they'd heard a few vague things about russia, but it had been so distant-sounding, they scarcely remembered: wasn't it something about people dropping dead by the roadside, and maybe heaps of corpses, and also people eating human flesh rather than starve? But over there was one thing, and here was something else: yes, people had lined up for soup, and . . . yes, they had danced and sung for a few worthless marks . . . but now, no, there was a revolution here now too—now they were going to have to shoot each other to get hold of a loaf of bread. And oscarke's fear of the revolution got bigger and bigger, because in his mind the new world had been a world full of milk and honey and free cakes, a dreamland with rows of jeannines standing panties in hand. He didn't understand that a new world is born the same way as a child . . . for as above, so below . . . it's always and everywhere the same: what we see with our tired eyes, what we see with our old, tired, aching eyes: wasn't there something in the scriptures about a new man being born to us, or he was going to be born to us, well, anyway . . . but still something joyful, something new, something glorious? . . . but no, people forget that every birth comes with fear and pain and blood. So why wouldn't a whole world be born in the same way? And suddenly oscarke thought— oscarke knew—that it was exactly the same with the earth Itself: the earth was a being, a living, androgynous creature that had been born in blood and pain, and that had to struggle through its years of adolescence fearing things that made no sense at all, and then getting up to mad, childish pranks that were against mother nature, and meanwhile torturing and tormenting itself and others—and now perhaps the earth was at the stage where it had begun to long for great and beautiful things, when it was fighting to make a living but still longed for a . . . a socialism perhaps, a . . . well, for everything that oscarke himself longed for. Oscarke, a tiny particle of an exploded god, a tiny particle of the earth, born in blood and pain—a tiny bit of something great, something about which he could say: I'm a part of that, I'm a particle of that . . . but also part of something alarming and upsetting, something to retreat fearfully into a corner from—since being a small particle, he was still a separate entity, a living thing in and of himself. A thing with its own thoughts and its own sorrows to bear. And he already saw himself in a situation like that in russia . . . in russia, where you were shot for a trifle and still couldn't overcome your hunger, and where apart from the fear and hunger people lived as if in a fever. Exactly, that was it: a fever. And everyone was affected by that fever—every small and independently thinking particle, or independently Living creature, had been seized by that illness, that fever of the earth's. Revolution in russia, revolution in germany. Revolution in hungary, new world, blood and mud . . . or no, no, blood and mud meant war . . . blood and hunger. And the germans were still retreating and the first newspapers of liberated belgium started to appear.

. . . BUT A REVOLUTION WITH SNAGS

Yes, the papers were already appearing, filled with the victory, the fatherland, the king, our boys back from the front, our Heroes. But the most important things was this: revolution in russia! There were photos of corpses and more corpses, whole mountains of corpses piled on top of one another, corpses being scooped onto carts with a shovel, like garbage, like old shoes, like worn-out buckets. And a title: the czar, our little father, the beloved and anointed by god—murdered! And ondine, slowly recovering her breath, closed her eyes on the absolute nothingness she'd discovered—yes, those great strangers had decided that money would be worthless, but they were also working to ensure that the abyss that'd opened up in front of all the ondines (and also all the other oscarkes and boones) would be immediately filled up again. Oh yes, the money was paper money, but honor and reputation and good morals, true faith and virtue . . . poor but honest, work ennobles, idleness is a curse . . . All of that remained. They were tired from playing and tired from waging war, and because too many people had earned money from smuggling, well, the money was destroyed: it's no longer valid! they said. So ondine could breathe again—the world was changing, but as it changed it still remained the same: people kept watch, they misled the new, they kept their eyes on the verities, like Good and Evil—oh, and look how quickly bryske had started drinking, and look how quickly old boone, who'd sat on the town council as a socialist, had become fed up with things. No sooner had the germans gone than people realized that revolution meant hunger and decay . . . while on the contrary behaving well and allowing oneself to be led around by the nose without thinking meant happiness and comfort . . . but no sooner had people become convinced of this than something else happened—the world was developing far too quickly, or no, the world lived its own epic life, but man was rather small, his gray cells were too tiny to be able to take it all in at once: all oscarke or ondine or boone or anyone had to do was finish one thought—like: revolution equals pain and blood—and four or five other things had happened in the meantime: things they'd never manage to understand. The germans had gone, and the belgians weren't yet there, and so the country was indeed completely Lawless for 24 hours. Oh, it may have been on purpose, to let the little people have their little way for once—after all, they'd said for four years now: wait until after the war!—we'll do this to you and that to you!—and you couldn't take them straight from one compulsion to another, from a german military administration to a belgian military administration—no, they had to be given a bit of slack, and so everywhere the houses where people had consorted with the germans were invaded and ransacked.

Yes, everywhere they broke into the collaborators' houses . . . But that's putting it a little too grandly! Everywhere the little houses of a few little people—a little woman who'd allowed her hole to be used to earn a crust of german bread . . . a little smuggler who'd said: to hell with belgium and to hell with germany, I'd like to earn some money for a change!—poor little folk who'd managed to earn a few francs from the thunderstorm, a few marks that were now totally worthless, and who really were honest enough in peacetime (oh honesty, honesty), or maybe just who didn't have the shameless audacity to hang a belgian flag on their houses after the liberation . . . Well, people in disguises invaded their homes, men with dirty, multicolored skirts and old flowered caps and stockings with holes in them over their heads, holding up umbrellas white with fake snow, hitching up their skirts when they had to step over the gutter: like it was a cavalcade, a carnival. It was the only revolution in oscarke's little town, a revolution in miniature permitted by the powers that be, a revolution in a jester's outfit that couldn't do much harm. Oscar had imagined it quite differently: it was enough to make him cry when he saw that That was the world he'd longed for—stood with his heart in his mouth watching as they smashed down the gate at wittepennings's . . . he was across the street and had to stand on tiptoe to see over people's heads . . . and he wasn't quite sure if his heart was with them, His people, or with wittepennings—oh, who'd only driven around with the germans because he was paid, and who had a whore of a daughter who was married to a feldwebel—a feldwebel or a sergeant or a postman or a gendarme. He was jostled to and fro there on the street corner, worrying, weighing the pros and cons—and it was like his worries were following his skinny body, that they were being pushed to and fro by the crowd, that the rhythm of his feelings was dictated by the ebb and flow of the crowd, from here to there and back again. Yes, he believed that Justice must be done (but meanwhile he thought with shame of the nights when he'd been at the crossing and had stolen people's bacon and tobacco), but he had to find a way to forgive himself first, so he twisted and turned his actions in retrospect until they were something he could attach fine intentions to—but he found no reason at all to forgive other people. Justice! he muttered—and he stood there with a haughty heart, with a dry heart, capable of killing. But he still didn't like seeing those disguised carnival clowns: nameless people, harlequins, devils who were wielding the sword of justice. He saw how they battered down the gate of wittepennings's place, and how one of them was holding a bayonet that a german must have left behind—and that he probably got from a retreating german soldier in exchange for tobacco—and was now making wild and threatening gestures with, as though he was going to destroy the entire world.

If I'm no longer allowed to move my own beak, I'll choose the beak of the east—said andreus mottebol—because wearing the beak of the west I won't be able to write what I want to write, and I'll always be a pariah and beggar. Wearing the beak of the east, I still won't be able to write what I want, but at least I'll be considered a useful worker, accepted by society.

And tippetotje took this in . . . tippetotje who doesn't think or live in either an eastern or a western way, but lives and blossoms just as a flower of a tippetotje should. And she says: this society is, as you say, a dunghill—art is a rare and magnificent orchid growing on the corpses of rotting flowers: the more rotten and poisonous the flowers, the more luxuriant and colorful the orchid of art. That sounds cynical, but That's how it is. A paid and salaried and official artist will produce dead, artificial, ambivalent, and official art . . . and in the west this will win him the nobel prize, and in the east the stalin prize . . . but in both halves meanwhile the true and genuine artist will always remain a pariah. Desperate and rejected, unknown and unloved, in the west and the east he'll go right on running headfirst into every blank wall. In the east and in the west both, it's possible to go on writing what one wants to write, on the condition that one does it in one's teeny bit of free time, late in the evenings and in the deep, quiet night . . . on condition that during the day one remains a loyal and obedient member of society, who only at night throws off one's mask, and safely mocks and kicks and burns what one worshipped and glorified during the day. At night it's possible to paint the rats that gnaw at our world—that gnaw at our eastern and western peace, science, logic, art, and dogma—on condition that during the day you've painted pretty flowers in the west and smiling workers in the east. I am tippetotje, and in this western world I've bagged myself a baron . . . I use the means available to me . . . if I'm hungry I look for my food where I know I can find it, if I'm cold I throw the thickest and most useless books into my stove, and if I need money I milk my baron like a farmer milks his cow . . . because my one and only aim is: to paint the rats that are gnawing right through our civilization. And so I'll go on doing that. I'm not part of the west, because I hate the west that's made me starve since I was a child and has withheld my rightful share of beauty and luxury . . . and I'm not part of the east, which is going to start an even chillier and more painful world, which will kill and crush me. I am tippetotje, the nihilist, the anarchist. I'm concerned only about myself. And apart from that, I do believe that a more beautiful world is possible, provided that people really start wanting a more beautiful world: man gets what he wants: but right now he only wants to kill, to squash, to crush, and to impose his dogma on everyone else, so . . .

And when tippetotje stops talking, andreus mottebol feels his eastern mask and master oedenmaeckers feels his western mask—nervously.

ALL THOSE WAR STORIES

It's almost spring . . . and in the coming spring master oedenmaeckers wants to prepare to move into the cottage that's been built for him out there in his bit of garden. But master oedenmaeckers is a man of order and tidiness . . . he's not like tippetotje and kramiek and me, and all our other characters: impulsive and blurting out whatever comes into our heads . . . no, he thinks things over for a little longer, picks and chooses and finally makes his considered decision. And now spring is almost here and he's getting ready: he rummages in every drawer and noses around in every corner of his house on chapel road—he burns all the things that he thought he would need over the years, and that he therefore stowed away deep in his cabinets, or else banished to the attic, or else hid away in the cellar—and that he'd now have to take with him to his cottage just to banish them to his new attic, or to his new cellar. He finally finds himself in front of his small library, just as you arrive, and he's busy making 2 piles . . . a pile on the left, of books that he bought because everyone else was talking about them, and a pile on the right, of books that he's ruined his eyes with over the years. And on the left-hand pile, the top two books are war stories. And because you leaf through them for a moment master oedenmaeckers says: they're each books that were written by somebody or other, some american, or englishman, or russian: written in the heat of battle, in the teeth-grinding course of a retreat, in the sadistic joy of victory . . . by someone who experienced a small part of the struggle for victory (victory over who? over what?) . . . who then experienced a small part of the supposed victory and wrote his small thoughts, his insignificant thoughts, in a small and insignificant book. And on their first publication each book about this turned out to be The book of the season, and everyone talked about it, and I had to have it, had to read it, if I was to remain worthy of my reputation as master oedenmaeckers. Now here they lie, and the dust of the ages is descending on them . . . they turn out to be two more epics about heroic courage and Morality. They lie there and dust descends on their heroic courage and Morality . . . on all the capital letters that fill us with awe, the dust of insignificance now descends. And master oedenmaeckers pushes one pile even further away from him, and goes to the other pile, on which there is only 1 war book: kaputt. And he says: kaputt is not a book that was written in the intoxication of victory . . . nor was it written by someone or other who counted himself among the victors, who pinned a decoration of victory, of the fatherland, of the flag and Morality on his chest—kaputt is

323

kaput . . . everything is kaput . . . the book of the dead made kaput, the flag made kaput, the fatherland made kaput, Morality torn to shreds. Our civilization is kaput, these people are kaput, this world is kaput . . .

And you stare so gloomily at master oedenmaeckers that he says shaking his head: I see your face clouding over. Like my garden over there clouds over when the dark clouds and bad weather come and weigh down on it . . . are you worried perhaps that I, like tippetotje, will put all these war books by russians and americans and englishmen in my stove? And you stutter in dismay: no, but in my own book I've described the life of ondine and oscarke while they experience the 1918 war—and I'm afraid you'll put my book on that pile too: the pile of the small and insignificant books, written by some insignificant russian, American, or fleming.

THE BITCH OF THE REVOLUTION

Among these revolutionaries in disguise there was also this bitch—there's no other name for her—who'd forced a cap over her hair that was probably hanging loose anyway, and was drunk and performed a strange dance in front of the gate, in front of the crowd. She had a torn-off piece of curtain over her face, and where her mouth was she had cut a hole: it was dirty and stained around the hole, from all the smoking and drinking . . . and perhaps also from the words she'd spoken. Oscarke knew these songs, he'd heard more than enough of them on the workers' trains—and although he'd recently sung a song like that for the bar-landlord's daughter rosa, for the pleasure of molesting her not-yet-mature mind, he'd previously thought: dear little jeannine, I wouldn't want you to hear things like this, I'd want you to drop dead before anyone opened his mouth to molest your mind with this kind of song. He looked at the dancing woman, and hated her—he hated her simply because she was different from how he'd imagined her: she wasn't the young, beautiful girl who raises the red flag and is right at the front and exposes her breast—oh, her breast—to the whistling bullets. He hated her because she was a hussy with a piece of curtain over her mouth, who only wanted to loot, to destroy, and even just vent her lust for murder. She was one of the first to charge in when the gate was forced with much creaking and splintering . . . and in that way she did offer her breast, her withered hussy's breast and her soiled curtain. She was a shield, in her way, between the carnival clowns and wittepennings, who wasn't exactly a hero . . . and yet not a coward either . . . just a perfectly ordinary coachman. But still. So the witch in disguise charged past him—he was standing there and didn't know himself why he was standing there: perhaps he was too scared to hide—and then the man with the bayonet pushed him into a corner and everyone else went past him, and even in the street you could hear the breaking and the smashing. At one of the upstairs windows the hussy came and displayed wittepennings's daughter: she pulled up the girl's skirts and struck her on her bare ass with a whip—for a moment, a flash, they'd glimpsed that white flesh . . . then there was a rushing to and fro, and a few crazy sounds came from a piano—oh, a song, with nothing to it, la madelon . . . not we'll keep the red flag flying here, or the internationale—and a minute later the piano was pushed to the window and crashed down onto the cobblestones, it was one of the cruelest cacophonies ever heard in the vicinity of the 1st grimy houses. Oscarke closed his eyes and shook his head very quickly, as if trying to shake off something that had almost crawled inside: I'm going, he said . . . I'll walk and walk right round the world if need be, but I won't come back till this nightmare is over, till the world and the people are the same world and people as they were before the war began, and I can sit down and relax and carve a piece of wood.

THE END OF THE REVOLUTION

But for the moment, I'll wait here, he thought . . . because wittepennings's daughter might come to the window again, and maybe they'll pull up her skirts. And he was disgusted by himself. Finally he turned away, because someone had tugged at his sleeve several times, and he had nodded, to indicate that he knew that they were tugging at his sleeve to get him away from here, but he wasn't fully aware of it—and finally he turned round, and it was boone standing there, a bit emaciated from the war, and with a piece of his moustache cut off, and with his round, good-natured shoulders a little more sunken, and with an old striped vest on from before the war that was rather baggy on him. Come on, said boone . . . and oscarke tore himself away from wittepennings's house and the furniture that lay in a heap in the street, and then was set on fire. A framed photograph was also thrown out, the shattered glass flew around and the frame was completely lopsided: it was a photo of the daughter with her feldwebel, and the way they both looked: the feldwebel with his domineering face, contemptuous in its prussian stupidity, and she with her airs and graces . . . Oh, and oscarke hated them, just like everybody else, and he followed boone, who walked and walked and said nothing, and took him to a big house on the market square: there was a party, and there was a flag out, and boone stopped and put out his hand silently but significantly: it was an old patrician mansion with a big weathered front, and a copper plate on the gate: norbert derenancourt . . . and then he took him further, to where the blank wall led to the 1st grimy houses, and he pointed to that plate: achilles derenancourt—and there was a flag out there too. And look, a soldier in a strange uniform that people around there had never seen before (and that people still looked at in surprise) jumped off a motorbike and rang the bell. There was laughter and rejoicing at the gate of the derenancourts, and the sister of fat glemmasson, laughing and weeping, threw her arms round the neck of the strange soldier. There was boone on the other side of

325

the street still holding out his hand and pointing, and oscarke understood him: he
nodded, and said that boone could take him to the castle of fat glemmasson now,
and put out his hand and point there too: one of them made blankets and the other
boots, and the 3rd sold the food that was sent to us from America. And do you
know what? asked boone . . . and he stopped, looking at oscarke. They're already
talking about planting a tree, a freedom tree, and erecting a monument there to
the derenancourts, who did so much good during the war.

DREAM

In Brussels, in the rue saint-honoré, where the ghosts wander around behind
the wallpaper of the furnished rooms—you can hear them gnawing behind
the old-fashioned commode and the wobbly bureau . . . you can hear the
flakes of whitewash constantly rustling down—mr brys sits and has conversations with himself about his strange, tormenting dreams. Among the yellowed and crumbling things of his apartment, he dreams that he has to hurry,
that it's imperative that he visit chapel road . . . he rushes out and runs, runs
. . . at least he tries to run, but he can't really manage it: however he sweats
and strains, he stays right in the middle of his furnished room: he's hurrying to chapel road, but the old-fashioned commode and the rotting bureau
remain beside him. He reaches the unmanned railroad crossing, and he can
already see the winding country road to polpoets's so-called villa, and yet mr
brys is still surrounded by all his yellowed things, and he hears the ghosts
rustling behind the wallpaper. There's no escaping those rustling ghosts, just
as there seems to be no end to the winding country road, which is also a little
different in his dream: technical colleges, the whole complex of a car plant,
a huge radio institute, and many other things—other ghosts—have sprung
up on the country road, are rustling behind the wallpaper. And where mr
brys has never met another soul, he now sees countless people . . . and they
too are running along the winding country road, feeling their eye sockets
and foreheads in a dazed way. So he runs, but gets no further than where
he is: a cartwheel turning round, faster and faster, more and more furiously, more and more crazily around its imaginary axis . . . and over there
in the distance stands polpoets among the huge building complexes, waving
to mr brys. And yes, mr brys can see that polpoets is over there beckoning
to him, but he also sees that polpoets is running alongside him: he knows
that polpoets is there twice . . . he knows that more and more people are
feeling their heads in astonishment: and look, look there, it's oscarke from
your novel! Oscarke who suddenly puts both hands protectively round his
head. And mr brys can feel it: SOMETHING'S HAPPENING HERE
. . . something happening to the world and to its people, and he wants to get

away, away from this never-ending country road along which stand all the building complexes of the world, and behind which he can hear louder and louder rustling. And polpoets stands over there and beckons him, and holds his head fearfully. And mr brys wants to get away but can't: there are waves of madness sweeping over the world, like gas, like a mist, like banks of fog . . . and mr brys puts his hand protectively round his head, and . . . screams.

DREAMS ARE NOT AN ILLUSION

Yes, over in the rue saint-honoré mr brys dreams that there's something wrong with the world and its people . . . and although dreams are deceptive, he suddenly feels the need to leave his tenement room, and actually visit chapel road . . . and just as happened in his dream, he sees polpoets standing way over on the winding country road . . . he's standing there beckoning and waving, and baring his 2 gold teeth in a grin he calls out: come and look, something's happening here! You see, thinks mr brys . . . but following polpoets he becomes slightly disillusioned, because he shows him only the trees and the bushes, where the ghosts come to haunt in the spring. I thought you were going to show me different ghosts, he said, rather disappointed . . . I thought you were going to show me people clutching their heads in a dazed way, or holding their heads protectively with both hands . . . a fog, a mist that penetrates us and drives us mad: that's what I thought I was going to see. And polpoets bares his 2 gold teeth in a grin and says that those banks of fog are indeed hanging over the whole world: but that's something perfectly ordinary, mr brys, it's so everyday that no one at all notices how the fog's penetrated his head. This world is becoming a madhouse, mr brys, a world that has defeated fascism, and is now becoming more fascist than ever. Because it's really true that there are ghosts gnawing behind the wallpaper: hitler is dead, and the world that put him to death is now becoming hitlerian—that's how the world goes, mr brys . . . after christ was hung up on the cross the christians worshiped under the sign of the cross . . . and after hitler and mussolini have been torn apart, the world is starting to become fascist. Hitlerism was a danger to the world, and the world rose up to kill hitler . . . along the paved and concreted roads of the world trucks and tanks rolled, and the red cross vehicles, with the sign of the united nations . . . the whole world was dismayed, angered, and horrified when it heard of the atrocities committed by hitler, and the whole world united and charged down upon him. Now hitler is dead, and now the world is becoming hitlerian. And you, mr brys, who haven't started to think like they do yet . . . or at least who hasn't stopped thinking, and who also can't content yourself with The one and only absolute and redeeming thought, you are temporarily barred from every public office . . . you are being temporarily deprived of your living, refused work, pointed at with a hitlerian finger. Temporarily, I say . . . because the world that defeated hitler and is now becoming hitlerian will soon start acting more and more boldly: yesterday you were barred from every government office, today the police will force their way into the homes of people who are in favor of freedom of conscience and freedom of research, and tomorrow they'll drag you out of your house—out of your room in the rue saint-honoré—and shoot you.

And mr brys says, furious, almost weeping: how can you laugh about it, polpoets? And laughing, baring his 2 gold teeth, polpoets replies: I'm laughing, mr brys . . . because for the time being that's the only way to escape the madness of this world.

WHERE IS THE REAL REVOLUTION?

And boone went on, and suddenly oscarke stopped: the world is evil, he said . . . the world is rotten, the world is a fragment of an exploded devil . . . you're no good, and I'm no good, and no one's any good . . . there's . . . And stretching out his hand and pointing to everything boone had shown him, he saw the pointlessness of his words: oh fucking hell, he said. And hearing that fucking hell from that skinny little fellow, boone began to laugh . . . he grabbed onto the railings of the fence around the municipal park: oh fucking hell, oscarke, you make me laugh! he said. They wandered round the little town and came to the socialists' house, the house that had been the headquarters of "justice and freedom" and that had been shut during the war . . . now the doors were open and there were flags hanging out, a red flag alongside a belgian flag, although before the war there had never been a belgian flag there: they'd been against the king and against the belgian state that sucked the workers dry, but now everyone was a patriot: LONG LIVE BELGIUM. And to tell the truth, it was wonderful being a patriot: gabrielle petit had fallen and had cried out: long live belgium . . . and that had been a grand gesture—something, a tiny thing, that stood firm amid the stinking stream of injustice—but on the other hand it was something with which working people allowed themselves to be fooled. Long live belgium—but didn't that mean: long live derenancourt? long live fat glemmasson? They went into the hall and drank a pint, and everyone talked to boone about the library that had been shut, and about all the stuff that had disappeared—and this and that, small, trivial things, and boone nodded and answered with small trivial things, and meanwhile oscarke was sitting on top of a world that was boiling and bubbling and where one moment something shot up sky-high, limpid and gleaming, and the next moment collapsed and sent out an equally high column of mud. No one asked him what he thought about it. Come on, he said . . . and boone looked at him in surprise: come on, okay, but where to? And oscarke suggested going somewhere else where they served

alcohol: some little place where they served big portions. Oh, he's a comic! said
boone to the others . . . and he got up, and with oscarke they went to the unsightly
bar where rosa was, rosa the landlord's daughter. But oscarke paid no attention
to her, his head was too full of other things: we're sitting nice and comfortably
here, he said . . . and they shared a drink that put some warmth inside them, so
that oscarke realized how cold he must have been. How cold and lonely. And his
blood gradually warmed up so that the desire to walk round the world till these
troubles were over vanished, but on the other hand he had the urge to go back to
wittepennings's and shout: stop! that's not the Real revolution!

THE RUBBER-TAPPER

No, it's not the real revolution johan mottebol says to you suddenly . . . and I
could prove it to you just like oscarke wanted to prove it to boone—but what
good is proof?—and I'll be damned if I'm going to go on using chapel road
as an example. Anyway, not a single paper wants articles about it anymore,
because the market is saturated—and I'd rather illustrate my point with a
strange story that happened very far away:

in the past I'd been told all kinds of things about it—it was all in the bro-
chure of the northern rubber bank—there's a future for us, said my wife—
there are hummingbirds in the virgin forest, said my ten-year-old son—and
they both got this nonsense from the circular of the above-mentioned bank—
so they were going to go—afterwards it turned out that at least 50,000 people
had signed on—or should one say 50,000 souls, or 50,000 head?—I'm not
sure, they both sound so stupid—one is so pathetic and the other one makes
you think of beheading—these fifty thousand people, anyway, they were
actually the beginnings of an army—an army that was going to tap rubber—
now it's clear that it's the tree that's tapping us—or is it the northern rubber
bank that's tapping us?—I can't remember precisely anymore—we were
numbered from 1 to 50,000—I was given the number 38,341—my wife was
given the next—my son the number after that—we were loaded onto trucks:
a ramp had been constructed as is often done when animals are loaded onto
trucks—this was in rio de janeiro, and the trucks took us to belo horizonte
or pinapora—my wife would have liked to go to belo horizonte, she thought
the name was so beautiful—my son on the other hand was for pinapora—he
dreamed up all kinds of funny variations—porapira, for instance—it was
monday morning when they'd loaded us up in rio de janeiro—it was scarcely
4 in the morning, it was dark, and it was cold too, and there was even a bit of
fighting—as a result my son was pushed off the ramp at the last minute—I
saw him submerge for a moment and then resurface—he reached out to me
and shouted something—he found himself on a different truck and acted

brave so as not to cry, but his eyes were very big and round—we were given soup that had been poured into empty paraffin drums—the soup was cold, but worse still, they had forgotten to clean the drums—it was then that my wife started to feel that it was all going to go wrong—will he be able to get the paraffin soup down? she asked—and we'd also had an argument over a shawl—she insisted that I wear it—how am I supposed to tap rubber if you're not around anymore? she asked—if only we could give it to him! she said finally—and of course, that was the answer, but he was unreachable and pathetic in the other truck—it had been monday morning when the trucks started off, and it was thursday afternoon when they stopped in pinapora—it's funny, but the only thing I remember about pinapora is that my wife kept saying how happy she was—if he's with us I'm happy, she said—she repeated this again, at night, when she woke up—at the time we were on one of the boats to joaheiro on the borders of bahia and pernambuco—a long, monotonous journey—we disembarked at prolina—our numbers were called out one by one and we had to step forward—there was some commotion a long way up, they were obviously a person short—I believe there was a further two days' journey, days that we were packed on top of each other in trucks—we slept standing up that night—some raw peas were distributed—then we went by rail, in freight cars—or was it first by train, then by truck?—but what difference does it make now?—we arrived in fortaleza—I can't remember fortaleza anymore—I know we were given uniforms—a special hook had been fitted for attaching our number to—when they'd had the uniforms made they'd immediately thought of the number—the uniform was far too big for my son, in fact it would have been too big for me—then my wife's prediction began to come true, that it was all going to go wrong—there were constant arguments—there had been arguments when they distributed the raw peas, and now there were arguments about the distribution of uniforms—I can't remember where it was, but we stayed for a couple of days in the open air—we had to wait—wait for what?—we were called out by our numbers again—there were already people missing here, there, and everywhere—my wife wasn't feeling too well—but there was good news, the authorities had been informed and were going to distribute medicine for preventing yellow fever—now we had to go to sao luis de maranbao, we would be very well treated there—it was a camp, we slept in big tents—there were bitter struggles against yellow fever—it was then that my wife died—I remember very well, a revolt had just broken out in the camp—people were demanding more medicine—the revolt was put down, the yellow fever wasn't—my son went and looked in the communal pit, where his mother had been lowered—his eyes were very large and round—and then we went on the boats again—I remember lots of other names—names of towns, names of boats, names of god knows what—I particularly remember topona, where my son died—the rest doesn't matter—our numbers were called out again—there were still 20,000 of us—my number was 38,341—my wife's had been 38,342—she's lying somewhere in a mass grave that I didn't go to see—my son's was 38,343—he is buried somewhere in topona—sometimes he stares at me in the night, with those big round eyes—sometimes I ask him: please don't stare at my number—the rest doesn't matter anymore—it seems that the newspapers wrote about us—they said that workers who still have some hope of eventual compensation for the privations they've suffered will soon be disillusioned— we didn't see that newspaper—many have fled—many are dead—the rest are now at the mercy of the merciless jungles—sometimes I feel as if I arrived all alone to find a future here—what was once my uniform hangs in shreds around me—I still have a number, it's my son's—they sometimes get the numbers wrong—recently I heard that I'm not the only survivor after all, there are supposed to be a couple of others a few miles away—it's strange, it seems that they've never tapped rubber either.

THE MASK

What about liebknecht? said oscar, and he looked at boone . . . what about the 200 germans who were shot down in the courtyard of a barracks for not wanting to take part in the war? And he stood up and started waving his hand and knocked his glass over: smash it, he said. We've got to smash it, he cried . . . destroy them all, break all their necks . . . let's go over to the derenancourt place, to the glemmassons, to the . . . where are the socialists? where are they? the men who are sitting twittering about a library? And he looked round wild-eyed, and only saw the daughter of the landlord looking at him with fearful eyes—and that cooled him down a little, and he sat down in embarrassment. We've got to smash it, he said again, but already much more quietly, as if he wanted to summarize while sitting what he'd been proclaiming standing up. But as he sat down another idea came back to him: something new must come, something new must be founded: all those who shared his ideas (and surely there must be some, surely he couldn't be the only one in the world to see the truth?) must begin something new together! And boone had to laugh because while standing up oscarke had said that they should smash everything . . . but when he sat down he said that they should build. Oscarke on the other hand Could not laugh, he smiled a little to please boone, but his heart was sad, his heart was bitter. And if the booze had made him into a lion, what was the point: he didn't know what to tear apart. And shaking his head he arrived back home, after walking a bit with boone, past the park where they'd both worked together digging out the pond, and where it was now so wintry and desolate that it immediately enchanted oscarke: I wish I lived all alone in the middle of a wood, he said. And then he got home where the children were all rooting around in the same bowl, it reminded him that he hadn't eaten anything all day—but he had no appetite: where's your mother? he asked. And mariette, both hands full of what she had scraped out of the bowl, pointed upstairs, to the bedroom: so she was upstairs. And after he asked where his food was, and judith (no, leopold) had explained to him that judith had made porridge, he also let slip that their mother had come home drunk. And he laughed, leopold, he laughed and slapped his knees: ha, and sat laughing and digging in to his food and fighting off mariette who wanted it all to herself. At first oscarke was going to go upstairs to see what was wrong with ondine, but . . . drunk? No, he didn't want to see any drunk people, he didn't want to see a drunk ondine—and turning round while still on the stairs, something on the bottom step caught his attention: what was that? A piece of curtain with a hole in it? a dirty hole through which someone had drunk and smoked and sung filthy songs?—and there was also a cap, an old cap that ondine had once bought him, but which he'd never dared wear because it was too big for him and hung over his eyes, and that ondine then started using as a rag for cleaning the stove.

LAUGHING MASKS

And from brussels tippetotje sends you an letter in the manner of johan mottebol: I'm sitting here next to my baron who is a bit ill and pale and poorly, and so to amuse myself I'm writing a story, inspired by ondine's mask:

somewhere in the moselle region in france lies jouy-aux-arches—it's supposed to be beautiful—beautiful and a bit dirty, like everything in france—marie dorzini lives there with her husband louis antoine—they have three children, and the youngest is called monique—but it's not about facts or names—it's about that eternal incomprehensible element in people—marie borzini is a housewife, a wife, a mother—and apart from that she has a strange quality that no one's been able to account for—she collects lovers—they say that there are six, as if the precise number would bring us any closer to her secret—and even more incomprehensibly: there's not a one of these six lovers that she actually cares about—so what kind of longing is there in her that she has to seek out in all these men a Man who doesn't really exist?—well, our women in termuren always have something to do: to the point of tedium they're occupied by something in the household every minute—after all, we're poor but we're clean—but there in jouy-aux-arches, people are not so eager to track down a little dust, to mend a hole in a stocking: instead of taking up knitting, marie bonzini goes to the cinema—she goes in the company of one of the above-mentioned lovers—the daily papers, despite their love of facts, report nothing of the showing or of the film itself—only that afterwards she returned home alone, and went to bed with her husband—and also that she denied him his marital rights—that's what it all comes down to with men and women: men always ask for something, women always refuse something—quite possibly a slight tiff ensued, an insignificant quarrel with all kinds of words spoken that never make any sense and can never explain things—or it's just as possible that there wasn't a quarrel—that louis antoine simply sulked a bit, turned his back on her, and went to sleep resenting her—but marie bonzini lay awake and looked into the darkness—it's a shame that we're told only facts about people—we have too many facts—when it's something else that we want to know about them—our thoughts, those strange thoughts, which are the origins of our incomprehensible behavior—so what is marie bonzini really thinking, staring into the dark?—but she leaves the bed and carries the sleeping monique into the other room, where the two older children are asleep—then she goes down into the cellar—she strikes one match after another until she finds the ax—the ax with which you chop kindling to light the hearth—the hearth!—hearth and home—and chopper in hand she climbs back up the stairs—and then she brings the chopper down three times on the head of the sleeping louis antoine—I won't describe the scene to you—what matters aren't the facts but the thoughts: so what incomprehensible thoughts are going through the head of marie bonzini?—is it only her husband she's striking on the head there?—or is it also all those other lovers that she cannot truly love?—as far as louis antoine is concerned, it isn't thoughts that are going through his head—he was refused something, and then he went to sleep—perhaps he was still sulking in his dreams—or perhaps, on the contrary, he found some kind of satisfaction in his dream—what else is freud good for, after all, than to help us find compensation in our dreams for what was denied us when we were awake?—but then his dream is cut off, suddenly—three blows of the chopper and he's no more—a strange phrase: "no more"—marie drags her late husband out of bed over to the window—she opens the window and pushes the body out—it falls with a thud—it lies there now on the cobblestones of the courtyard—these are all facts, bloody and meaningless facts—the only thing, the true, the real thing . . . up till now it's proved impossible to discover—there lies the body on the stones, and for a few moments now marie bonzini acts as if she is actually her husband—she writes a letter, just as louis antoine would have written a letter—no, not as he actually was . . . but as he ought to have been, for her—forgive me, dear wife, look after the children: I'm putting an end to it—she tucks the body into a tarpaulin and sets the letter down somewhere—and then it all comes out at the same time: overpowering, confusing, and also revealing—when she's arrested she denies all guilt—and more than that, she adopts such a provocative attitude that even the presiding judge becomes furious—it's a shame, a shame for him, a shame for us—how are you supposed to find out what can't be found out if you start getting furious?—she adopts a sarcastic attitude, and enjoys making faces at the crowd—these are all descriptions from the newspapers—there are masses of such descriptions in the press, but well, what do they prove?—marie bonzini answers with a grimace: you're wrong—or: I don't remember—and when she's accused of having six lovers, she replies: I was always a faithful wife—everyone laughs—she makes a face—and you were probably also a good mother!—and with a grimace: yes!—and there are other details, but I won't quote them—again they're only misleading facts: the prosecutor calls her a monster and demands the highest penalty—and the very last thing, the most typical thing, the most confusing thing that hits me like a stone hits a window: she immediately appealed.

WHERE IS MY HOUSE?

So it had been her, ondine, there at wittepennings's! It was inevitable that he should have immediately started hating this revolution . . . that he had wanted to wring its neck, and smash it—smash everything—start something new—yes, something new must be begun, but it need not necessarily be a new world: it could easily just be a new life: going to brussels and staying with jeannine and sculpting and going into the woods and seeing the sun set amid the trees.

And he saw judith sitting there proudly, proud and happy because she'd been able to make porridge—she was still sitting, waiting, she was watching oscarke—he came over to the table and tasted the porridge: that's delicious! he said.

But the soldier they had seen in station street, he was an englishman, or a canadian, he was the first soldier of the allied armies that the people had long dreamed of seeing enter the country, and who had now driven past them before they'd even noticed. Oh, the whole town was up and about, but people forgot to smash everything up, people left their hammers and bayonets and masks where they were and went to the derenancourt house—long live this and long live that—and people sang and rejoiced and almost pushed the gate down. The flag was hanging out of the window and all the windows were lit, there was a party on, and mr mayor came out onto the balcony, next to the english officer, and bent and bowed and read a speech—and everyone who was there, libertines and socialists and clericals and malcontents, shouted and laughed and clapped their hands in unison: long live our mayor. Like it was him who was returning from the front, him who'd made blankets for the allies there: the people stayed all night, and walked up and down the cold, dark street. A few sat sleeping on the pavements: soon, very early in the morning, the first battalion of troops arrived. They slept at wittepennings's place in the wrecked stables, in the straw, and there was a sentry at the gate just like the germans had had—the officers slept at the derenancourt place, where another new flag was hung out: the flag of the regiment. There was a parade, and all the women who had slept with the germans to get a loaf of german bread now slept with the allies to get an allied loaf, and you couldn't go down a single dark street without bumping into a couple that wouldn't get out of the way. And then the belgian soldiers arrived—there wasn't that much enthusiasm, since they were only belgians . . . and also, they weren't quite the same soldiers anymore: they had fled with round tins on their heads, hobbling on cracked clogs and bleeding, and now they came back with iron helmets on their heads. For they came from the river ijzer . . . the ijzer this and the ijzer that, they said . . . and they thought they were going to change the world, turn it upside down, make it better: they immediately founded an association: the association of heroes of the ijzer. But that was as far as it went, they'd scarcely got back before they realized the truth: the world was going to stay exactly the same as it'd always been, one man shut himself away in bitterness, and another looked for work that wouldn't be too much trouble, and yet another stayed in the association—the association of heroes of the ijzer, which soon became an association of drinking and eating, mussels and chips, every year on armistice day. Ondine, for her part, was grateful that the world was still carrying on as before—she was grateful, but she didn't really know why, and she didn't know to whom she was supposed to express her gratitude to. God, she still said—but it had become a very ambiguous concept: for all the good things she thanked god, but the bad she blamed on her fellow men. It was good that everyone still doffed his cap at people with money and power—but it was far from good, for instance, that everyone had been able to earn money wildly and ruthlessly in this war. Everyone, that is, except her. She walked through the street in the same black dress, muttering that she could have earned money too if she'd known in advance that people were going to do so well—and she lectured her children on the subject: see that you smuggle and smuggle for all you're worth if there's another war: buy sugar and cocoa and milk in tins, but don't broadcast it, and be very sweet—say that you don't like business, but that you like to oblige people, etc. And she looked angrily at judith, because she said: honesty is the best policy. And she smacked leopold because he said nothing at all. And she went to boone's wife and said that she could have smuggled and smuggled and earned money, but she hadn't wanted to: she would rather have seen the germans drop dead . . . and apart from that: honesty is the best policy! And she looked spitefully at little louis boone, who looked at her contemptuously with his dreamer's eyes: she hated that little louis boone a little more each day, he was far too quiet a kid. But the shop bell rang, and a boy came in and shouted: mother, a soldier! It was little leopold . . . ondine immediately went out: a soldier, a soldier, who might that be? Hurrying along in her stockings she threw open the front door and sure enough, it was a soldier, he was wearing boots and a helmet—a great big bucket, a bucket on a head that wobbled to and fro: it was valeer. It was only valeer. Oh. It's just you? she asked, and looked straight past him to see if there was another soldier perhaps. The soldier

335

she'd hurried home for. She stroked her chin thoughtfully and didn't know what
to say—because it was true, she hadn't foreseen this situation—he stood there and
immediately understood: he was bringing lots of problems with him. Over in the
trenches he had heard the others curse, beg, and pray, and when they were finally
about to go home he cursed with them and prayed with them, but now that he was
home, where was he going? Where was his home?

WINTER APPLES

You can throw that story about the laughing masks away! writes tippetotje in
a great hurry . . . I've got a much better one here:

I, rosalie petrowska, was on the staff of the old men's home—I smile
when I see you instinctively grab for your hat—I understand that—you're
immediately seized by the modesty with which in your youth you looked up
to the sisters of charity—and a similar aura must hang around me as well:
nurses for old men—I spent my life among old men—I remember that in
the beginning I went around with smiling concern—with compassion for
all these wrinkled faces like winter apples, at all those eyes with their fail-
ing sight, those trembling hands, those hesitant, tentative feet—I also seem
to remember that in the beginning I felt a bit afraid of bumping into those
ageing shells, in case they might fall and break—it made me rather sad—sad
because I saw so clearly and at such close quarters the fragility and transience
of this life—whenever one plumbs this life a little more fully, a little more
deeply, one becomes a little sadder—they say that knowledge breeds pain—I
experienced this, and know that nothing can be done about it—fairy tales
makes children happy, and faith gives us the illusion of some happiness—but
knowledge and experience on the other hand make us melancholy—wiser,
calmer, but more melancholy—in the beginning I mainly felt humility—a
calm, smiling concern for all those old men who'd already gone such a long
way downhill—I knew that for them it was just a short in-and-out stay—after
all, you don't end up in an old men's home to go on living there happily for
years—no, that's a fairy tale—you go there when you can't tell which wood
the arrows are made from anymore—you go there when you can no longer
hold the bow to shoot the arrows from—and they enter trembling, and allow
themselves to be taken to their numbered bed—and a few months later that
number and that bed are available again—in fact there's no point in giving
them a number, but, well—that's how we are, aren't we? there has to be
order—that little bit of humility, that little bit of smiling compassion . . . no, it
can't last forever—you look at it and in the long run you grow a little indifferent—true, you remain melancholy by nature, but you can't just go on griev-
ing indefinitely—you can't feel compassion and go feeling it forever—you get

jaded—I sometimes said: tiens, old jaspers in the corner will hold out for a while yet!—I got curious as to when he'd die—oh, I sometimes found myself making bets with myself—bet he'll snuff it before the week is out! I said to myself—they changed faces, those old men who succeeded each other, but their number stayed the same—sometimes number 6 was a gentle-natured chap who kept muttering to himself—but afterwards it was an old slob who didn't know when it was time to relieve himself—he just did it and didn't even notice—he caused me a lot of trouble—I'm sorry, but I longed for him to get moving and make way for someone else—but, well, people are cruel, you hear all kinds of stories—I once read something in a paper about old men in the congo—the tribe herds them all together and makes then crawl up into a tree—then they shake the tree, and the men who fall out have no further right to the protection of the tribe—at least if they haven't fallen head first—I find that rather barbaric—but I've heard other stories too, about old men here in this country, who sometimes get run over in the street: it seems that they have no more rights, and the insurance companies won't pay anything out for them—since they're no longer capable of looking where they're going, they have no further right to walk the streets—come to that, didn't a minister once say that old men here live far too long and yet go on benefiting from their pensions?—you have to start looking at all these things in a level-headed way—and something else: these are hard times—so many things are manufactured that you can't afford, but that we can't do without anymore—a car, for example, everyone drives cars and no one can really afford a car—not that I want a car that much, but there are so many other things—then, suddenly, a demented old man disappeared from the old men's home—his body was found on the banks of some river—he had a big head wound, and his broken crutches lay next to his body—it was a sad story—particularly because a woman's scarf was found at the scene of the crime, and also the prints of a woman's shoe—this was 2 years ago now—time flies—and no one knows better than I do how time flies: in the course of 2 years a lot of old men fall out of the tree of life—but then 200,000 francs disappeared, belonging to number 12—come on, bet you he's only got another couple of weeks to live?—and what's he going to do with 200,000 francs in his trembling old hands?—and if he suddenly dies earlier than my prognosis predicts, who or what will get the money?—and again something sad happened: the old man noticed at the very last moment that I was slipping his banknotes into my blouse—he was blind enough not to see where I put his cup of milk, and kept knocking it over—but now he could suddenly see that I was stealing his useless money—I was questioned—they suddenly produced that scarf—I had to admit it was mine: I told them that it had been stolen two years ago—but my shoes were checked and it was claimed that only these shoes could have made the prints they found on the banks of that river—I was charged with murder: I was supposed to have beaten the old man's brains out with his crutches—it's a shame—so many old men fall out of the tree of life, like wrinkled and worm-eaten apples—it still makes me so melancholy—is it really so terrible to have shook the tree a little hard?

VALEER SEES ONDINE'S CHILDREN

Well, where was his home? With she of the wooden leg, perhaps? where the german soldiers had stood in a long line?—or with his father, who divided his time between sitting, gnawing his fingers during the day, and at night staring wide awake into the dark . . . but where there was no more bed for him, valeer! He had made a beeline for his parents' house, but in the 1st street in the little town of the 2 mills he'd already started having doubts, wobbling his head to and fro: so he went to ondine: to the woman who in fact had thrown him out—as if he wanted to say: look, I'm back, can I do what I Want now, or are you still going to boss me round? But he came not only for her, but for little judith who'd pulled at his sleeve, and said: don't go, uncle, they'll shoot you dead. Oh, they hadn't shot him dead—they'd done something much worse: they'd brought iron bottles into the enemy lines and opened them, and he and his comrades had had to piss in their handkerchief and hold them over their mouths: he couldn't smoke a pipe of tobacco anymore and he couldn't show people a wound that was inside him, so he just coughed a bit. Nothing heroic, then: there are plenty of people who cough a bit. He came and sat down, and simply didn't see that ondine remained standing—as though she were waiting for him to leave. He sat rubbing a finger that was itching a bit, and with his meek eye sought out judith, in order to pick her up and sit her on his knee like before—maybe to wave his hands in front of her, and worry desperately about her probably going blind. Judith looked at him through her thick glasses: she'd grown, of course, did he think that she would wait almost five years to continue growing, however much he might have wanted it? He also looked at mariette, who was not so pale and fat, and who didn't wear glasses but on the contrary had piercing eyes—where had she got those mischievous eyes from? And finally he looked at marie-louise, who was sitting on a blanket on the floor and playing with a ball of paper—and so he settled for sitting this marie-louise on his knee, and couldn't quite remember if that one had already been there when he'd had to leave—she grabbed at his big brass buttons and tried to put them in her mouth . . . she hung forward as though she were going to break in two. He tried to sit her straight, but he couldn't: that was how she was, bent in two: her spine had grown like that. He didn't realize it at once but tried again, and when he finally realized he looked up at the others, but everyone looked the other way. Except for mariette, of course—she said: that's how she is.

338

He immediately felt sorry, valeer—he made a very funny face at marie-louise, he pulled his mouth lopsided and looked at her cross-eyed, he tried to reach the tip of his nose with his tongue—and when he succeeded (and leopold came and looked at him more closely, and tried in vain to copy him) then marie-louise laughed. It was a strange laugh—like someone, having first drawn breath with great difficulty, had forced the sound out of their throat—the raw, hoarse sound came very regularly, whistling, only to disappear for a moment before reemerging, again whistling—and meanwhile she stayed bent over. Valeer heard the laugh, and looked at her again, as though a totally different child had come to sit on his knee—he shook his head thoughtfully and said nothing—maybe he was thinking of his mother, maybe he was thinking of ondine: the night she'd cut off his finger. And he got up and went back and sat her on the blanket on the floor, pushed the paper ball back into her hands, and didn't look at her again after that, all evening. Because really, night was starting to fall, and valeer was still sitting there as though he was home, as if this house was the haven he'd talked about for four years over there in the mud. Each of them sat gaping at the other, and no one was concerned with what they would usually have filled their evening with: it was as if they were waiting for something. Valeer could feel it, he wasn't that stupid: they're sitting here waiting for something! he thought. And he himself, he was also waiting for something: for some time now he'd been feeling a gradually growing hunger, and had glanced at the table, covered in trash (a rag doll of the children's, and a cup with some water in it, and a crumpled-up packet of headache powder, and a newspaper, oh, there were all kinds of things), and he also gradually got a headache at the suggestion of the packet, but most of all from sitting there waiting for something to eat: when were they finally going to clear the table and cut some bread? And suddenly he understood: they were waiting for him to go so they could finally start their evening meal! And sure enough, at that moment ondine said it: what's wrong with you valeer? she asked . . . I don't understand you, another soldier comes back from the front and can't wait to get home, and you just sit here with strangers! With strangers, that's right, that's what she said—and how often he'd noticed that: that others expressed what they were thinking as if it were obvious, they came out together, the thinking and the expressing all at once. While he on the other hand . . .

A LOOK BACK

Johan janssens is doing what he usually does to fill the evening: he's reading our second book on chapel road, he's rereading all the newspaper columns that mention him, and in which as always he's played a socially conscious role. In the part of the book that takes place fifty years back, oscarke plays the social role, but in the world of today johan janssens shoulders the same task—*as if oscar, so many years ago, were another johan janssens. Oscarke went to work in brussels, he traveled back and forth on the train—he left from green avenue, that gloomy station that was only for workers who traveled to and from brussels with weekly passes—and in that dark station, in those unlit, unheated trains, he read the very first newspaper of the socialists—a piddling little paper called Justice and Freedom. And then the war came, the first war, when the germans with their spiked helmets occupied chapel road, and when there was suddenly no more talk of socialism or Justice and Freedom—what is there to talk about when there's a war on? Hunger and privation and death, smuggling and earning money—and then the war was over and everything was the same as it was before. So what was there, before the war? asks oscarke. What about liebknecht? he asks—and he stares around him, at fat glemmasson's rich-man's mansion, and the castle of skinny mr derenancourt, where the flag is hanging because the war's over and we have won. And who are the we who've won? Who else but fat mr glemmasson and thin mr derenancourt, while oscarke and liebknecht lost.* And among them walks johan janssens, so many years later, when another war is over . . . oscarke with the first war behind him, and johan janssens with another new war behind him—and everything has stayed the same once again: the flag is still hanging out at the glemmasson and derenancourt places, because we've won. Sometimes it seems to johan janssens like time's stood still, that he's actually oscarke and is called johan janssens by mistake, seeing that the same water is still flowing into the same sea. Because while there is social change around him, social improvement, it's all to the advantage of rich mr glemmasson and rich mr derenancourt, on whose castles the flag is hanging because they've managed to win the war—they've won the war, they've won the peace, they've won their social reforms—oscarke and his contemporaries fought for univer-sal suffrage, and as they marched for it their ranks came under fire . . . but now they've had universal suffrage for ages, and with that universal suffrage they voted in the same mr derenancourt. And in the days of oscarke and the first paper Justice and Freedom, they fought to receive aid for periods of sick-ness and unemployment, they fought for pensions and child benefits—or were the children's benefits thrown in for free by mr derenancourt?—and now in the time of johan janssens, mr derenancourt enjoys a pension himself, and can rely on state support in case of accidents, and can write off his children's expenses . . . as the director of a spinning mill and minister of domestic affairs . . . and johan janssens gets nothing. Emiel moyson was there, the student . . . and zetternam, the writer . . . and vuylsteke, the poet . . . all intellectu-als, all poets and writers and students and painters, and they led, supported, celebrated—described in books, painted on canvases, carved in stone, and cast in copper the struggle of the prolerariat—emile moyson, eugene zetternam, eugene laermans, pierre paulus, constantin meunier, and johan janssens. And the director of the steel foundry, of the harbor, of the factories lining the foul waters, they all now enjoy social security and aid from the state—and all the socialists who founded Justice and Freedom, the poets and the writers and the dreamers, the intellectuals, the sculptors, and the painters, they who went hungry because they stood side by side with the very first socialists, well, they (despite everything) still have nothing, still don't have a thing.

That's what johan janssens gleans from reading the last chapter.

VALEER'S FURY

Oh, it was so difficult first to think something: valeer, for example, sat all evening thinking of how it could have happened that ondine asked him to move in with her and even fetch his bed—and how he'd built a wall for her, over there, in that bar that he'd gone to 1st, but where he'd been told that she'd moved and was living next door to boone: that shop over there, you see it? The row of houses with gray fronts and with drainpipes next to their front doors? And so he'd come over and now she said that he shouldn't stay with strangers . . . and what was he supposed to say to that? That it was her after all who'd cut his finger off and then chased him off to war where he'd been gassed and now . . . and now . . . Home? He asked innocently, home, where's that? Ondine, who tried to act indignant and was theatrical in her speech (oh, who'd even started acting theatrically in her deepest thoughts), said that home is where your cradle stood. I haven't got a cradle, but I've got a bed and it's right here! said valeer . . . and he started to stammer with emotion because it looked like he was finally going to be proved right. And because his retort was so effective, mariette couldn't help laughing loudly, and even had to wipe the tears from her eyes, and let a thoughtless curse escape: oh fucking hell! Only a little curse, it's true, and one that had only slipped out because she'd been laughing so much—but really! Go to your bed, and without any supper! cried ondine. Mariette went, and because leopold was giggling, ondine shouted at him that he too must go to bed without supper. All of you to bed! she cried harshly and threateningly. And all of them, including judith, got up and went upstairs. And you, she shouted at valeer . . . you dare to come here and talk about your bed when it's always been My bed, a bed that you were just allowed to sleep in next to me for a while. Then where's the bed that I'm allowed to sleep in now? he asked. At your cousin's place, she cried, that whore of cousin maria, over in brussels. Your bed's there—in brussels with the whores, you can sleep three in a bed there! she shouted louder and louder, as if she were expecting (as if she wanted to hear) a protest. But there was still no sound from the corner where valeer was sitting, and yes . . . also from the corner where oscarke was

341

sitting—the two of them hadn't looked at each other yet. Valeer still had a silent
laugh around his weak mouth, though he was sad that people were Like that, that
his sister was like that, that oscarke and the children were like that—he tried to
soften the blow for himself a little and asked oscarke for a cigarette—and oscarke
replied, just as quietly, that he only had some tobacco and a pipe, but valeer pro-
duced some grubby cigarette papers from inside his uniform. He rolled a cigarette,
and anyone who wasn't watching closely would never have noticed that he had
a finger missing. I'll be off then, he said quietly. Oscarke mumbled something.
And with his fat head wobbling on his shoulders valeer disappeared into the eve-
ning—but he can't have gone five paces, because there was another knock, soft
and modest, and he was back: he'd come to ask for some change for his train to
brussels. Soldiers don't have to pay, said ondine. That's true, he replied . . . but
they don't give soldiers a glass of beer and a sandwich. Are you trying to say that
you couldn't get a bite to eat here? she asked. Oh, he shrugged his shoulders—he
had to answer her again, and that was the last thing he wanted to do—what he
most liked doing was sulking, all alone and quiet: she sends me away without a
centime, without a glass of beer, without a sandwich: I'm going back and asking
for money! And so he stood there and put his hand out like a beggar: a beggar in
uniform. Ondine put five francs on the corner of the table, next to the crumpled-
up packet of headache powder—she smoothed out some paper and wrote on it:
I, the undersigned, valeer bosmans, hereby declare that I owe 5 (but there was a
faint line in front of that 5, so anyone reading it would have made it 15), 15 francs
to my sister ondine. And she thrust the pen into his hand: sign that, she said. He
took the pen and bent over, while everything in him refused to sign—the seconds
passed, slowly and irrevocably, the clock ticked on in the silence, time weighed
down on him, and then: no, he thought, I'm not signing, I've only got 5 francs.
But he didn't dare say it aloud, he made a funny squiggle instead and put the pen
down, slouching to the door without a word. What's this, what did you actually
write here? ondine shouted after him—but he went out, into the darkness—and
came back one more time and drummed on the shutters, and in the street and in
the darkness he called out: it was only 5 francs.

KRAMIEK DRAWS THE LINE

These are the end times, here in chapel road: almost none of your characters live here anymore, almost all of them have left you and your book
behind: tippetotje and maitre pots, master oedenmaeckers and tolfpoets and
mr brys—and now valeer who's going to live in brussels at his cousin's! So
why, why—again and for the umpteenth time—why are you the last man
standing? Why are you still playing the heroic role all by yourself: do you
want to be the bravest, the most honest, the most courageous of all? Why do

you want to perish alone, flag in hand? Your friends have all been ousted by people who are not our sort of people, who we've now described ad nauseam. And look, you wonder about that too, why you go on living among them, go on writing about them with sarcasm and open mockery—after all, they're deaf and can't hear, and all your barbs break on their elephant hides. And one day when you'd fled chapel road to enjoy some freedom, some peace, some little silent joy, and visited master oedenmaeckers in his bit of garden that ends in a bit of woodland, on that day he asked you (oh, be quiet, master oedenmaeckers!), why didn't you come and live there too? Get a cottage, something small, something white, something not really worth anything, lost in the greenery and paid for with what you borrow here and there: come on! And now you creep round your house on chapel road like a thief in the night: your house that you want to leave. Like the last soldier who's stuck to his post in the face of disaster, and is now about to desert with the rest, you stare at all the familiar things: the stones little ondine walked over when she was young and had 2 stiff braids, and across which she passed on the arm of her "sweetheart" oscarke . . . and across which she passed with a string of vagabond children clinging to her skirts—the cobblestones over which the first socialists passed, with their wooden clog music and their first red flag—the cobblestones where there riots and disputes and cacophony, and the clog ball and the carnival, and all kinds of foreign soldiers. Without a word you stare at all that out of your window: are you going to drop the flag, throw away the mask of the hero and leader, and go and live your life over there Out of Town? And are you also—worst of all—going to abandon your book on chapel road? Fail to take that book to its glorious conclusion, to its highest pinnacle where the flag of victory must be planted? Are you just going to discard it, rid yourself of it, draw a line under it and say: the end, amen, and period?

And look, at that moment kramiek comes in—kramiek, the only one who's stuck around and will always stay . . . kramiek, the very picture of the man who can always adapt to his surroundings, who twists and turns depending on which way the wind blows . . . kramiek, especially, on whose lips the slogans bloom and fall like ripe fruit: for freedom and prosperity, for labor and victory, for altar and hearth, for god and country, for prince and mince and something else that we've all forgotten. And he comes in and doesn't notice how you're stuffing all your papers hazphazardly into a laundry basket and are about to abandon your post. Do you know what's still missing from your book on chapel road? he asks . . . I've read the reviews very carefully, and in my humble opinion the critics have a point: what seems to me to be missing from your book is everything that there's too much of. And stuffing the second part of your book into the laundry basket, you say:

you're quite right, kramiek . . . and not just that there's too much in my book, but also that the writer himself is superfluous: you go ahead and draw a line under the project in my place, tell people that I've stopped, thank god, and add a nice slogan and a moral, for example . . . but you yourself know perfectly well what it has to be: something out of Nothing. And send my regards.

FOURTH AND LAST CHAPTER:
WE INDIVIDUALS, IN A WORLD OF BARBARIANS

WE INDIVIDUALS

Away in his tenement building, far from chapel road and everything else we're writing about, mossieu colson of the ministry sits and takes up his pen: another chapter of your impossible book seems to be nearing completion: all of us, your characters, have played a role in it, and in some way or other have come to a conclusion, an ending—a conclusion that isn't really a conclusion, and an ending that isn't really an ending either—because we won't come to an end at the close of some chapter or other, but at the end of the book itself. Or maybe not even then? Will we be just where we are now at the end of your book? Will it be another blank wall that we grope our way along without finding a way out? But no matter—we haven't reached that point yet—in this last chapter almost all of us have fled chapel road, and those who remain are getting ready to desert—to leave this society where technology, science in little boxes—the only belief that brings salvation—and fascism are supreme. I can feel the end of this chapter approaching, because you've sought and not found, and you can't go on seeking without finding: at some point you'll have to stop and ask yourself if you took a wrong turn—at some point you'll have to grant us, your characters, some peace, and let us think, and give us an overview of your wrong turn. And meanwhile, while we've struggled almost in vain against the dogma of salvation, against science in numbered beakers, and the fascism that's stronger than ever (because fascism was fought by everyone, and now everyone is becoming a fascist anyway), meanwhile, I say, the 1st world war has also been wrapped up in your book . . . oscarke and ondine are sitting there, a little the worse for wear after the storm has passed over them. And they've always said: wait till later, wait till the war is over! And now the war is over, and they're not doing any of the things they resolved to do—oscarke realizes that the revolution of '18 is a revolution with snags . . . with some smashing things up, with some boundaries being broken, and apart from that with leaving everything as it was—while ondine discovers that money and god and being good and living honestly are only pseudo-values, but that new money comes in time, and a new dogma and a new honesty, and she is reassured and resigns herself. And oscarke discovers that it's always his kind who pays for the broken pots, while it's always a different sort of people who assume power again—because power always has to be assumed. And meanwhile valeer comes home again, and doesn't feel at home—and we, in today's world, don't feel at home anywhere either: we've been dispersed and forcibly scattered, and scattered we are helpless in the face of the world around us, which has become more fascist than ever: we are individuals in a world of barbarians. Postscript: hey, could that last line maybe be the title of your new chapter?

MODERATO

On your evening walk in termuren you meet johan janssens . . . and he tells you how he wanted to write this section for you, this first section in our final chapter—but how he cannot. He's restless and uncertain . . . he knows that it has to be the final tap of the nail, and that if people want to hit the nail on the head, they don't miss the nail in the last chapter. He knows that every word now places its full weight on the scales, and that every frightening question, every idea supported by 100 facts must swell into a sea of words, sounds, and images, so that, amid the roaring surf of this book—the rock of the 1 dominant idea rises up, the idea that in fact led you to write the book. And yet . . . meanwhile even johan janssens tortures himself with the many other trivial ideas that are involved; for example the nagging question: are we actually writing this book in order to express a Dominant idea . . . did we write it for no good reason, the way some people can't help making money, for example? Or the way wild chestnuts grow in the woods? And so, hesitating and doubting that there is in fact an Underlying idea, an idea that we have consistently forgotten, that we lost sight of from page to page in a mass of 1,001 less important ideas, johan janssens only dared write the title of this short section—moderato—and having written that word, he abandoned the blank page and went back home. He—one of the few individuals left in this world of barbarians—doesn't dare begin this chapter: this double chapter of the double book, in which on the one hand we describe the life of chapel road a few years ago (but with what swift strides they're approaching our own time!), the life of oscarke and ondine and their litter of children, the life of boone with his big moustache and his son louis boone, and the life, in fact, of everyone who once lived in the long terrace of the 1st grimy houses—and on the other we describe the life of today's modern chapel road. And johan janssens, aware that these two chapel roads are constantly merging, are constantly linked like the two banks of a waterway by a bridge, walks unsteadily back and forth across this bridge. He wonders whether in this last chapter we might have bitten off more than we can chew—and also wonders if we'll be strong enough to unleash the storm, the relentless typhoon the last chapter should be. And trying to avoid his own struggles, he visits the music master in his bit of garden and lends a hand in his struggle against wind and weather . . . escaping his own worries, he helps mossieu colson appease the ghosts of this modern age . . . shutting his eyes to his own fear, he stands beside tippetotje looking with horror at the army of rats advancing on our civilization. And now he says to you: I scarcely dare return to that sheet of blank paper, to the story of how the rats, the ghosts, the barbarians, have gradually forced us up against the wall . . . the final wall, where our weapons will be knocked out of our hands . . . the final wall, where this book on chapel road will inevitably end. Our book, and also our last bit of freedom. And also, perhaps, our last little chance to live.

WHO'S A BARBARIAN?

We individuals, in a world of barbarians. And who are those individuals? They are all the people in the world: 50 years ago ondine and oscarke were the few . . . ondine and oscarke and boone with his big moustache, and apart from them everyone who inhabited the long terrace of the 1st grimy houses and chapel road and the little town of the 2 mills—they were all a few individuals in a world of barbarians. And who were those barbarians: why, they themselves were—because 50 years ago ondine was a cow of a woman who spied on and pestered oscarke and her children and valeer, and little louis boone too, and envied each hunk of bread in their mouths: all of them together are barbarians, and they're all out to kill the individuals: all of them together make the world a little more fascist every day—look how a fascist general is dismissed, but the mob acclaims him and throws flowers—see how people only vote for a democratic law to justify antidemocratic, dictatorial, and fascist ideas (no, fascist acts)—and see how in the meantime our books are banned, and the secret police attend our meetings. And so it was good that andreus mottebol began this chapter hesitantly . . . because we ourselves began this book hesitantly: we started from the idea that only the precious little moment counts—a moment of joy, a moment of freedom, a moment of some little beauty, of some little happiness . . . because it's only that which makes life worth living. Yet in that 1st chapter we experienced firsthand how that precious little moment is snatched away from us, and how doggedly we must fight for it—and so our next chapter was called: happiness is something we must fight for. Alas, it was a mistake . . . we were wrong about the way we should fight, we were wrong about constantly wanting to rush back to the age of baekelandt and jan de lichte, and we were wrong about ever making appeals to this world that is becoming ever more barbaric, and finally wanting to combat this ever-more-barbaric world. And our next, 3rd, chapter was accordingly called: a little mistake among millions of others. And now comes this final chapter: all of us, in a world of barbarians—because one can't draw the line now, can't say that this one is an individual now, but is now someone else—because at one moment the little individual is a poor little chap, a boon, and then the next he's an entire people, Yes, at one moment my enemy kramiek belongs to a world of barbarians advancing towards me and wanting to trample over me as if I were a rat—and the next kramiek is himself the rat, and is being chased by myself and all the other barbarians. This book is hesitant and doubting and uncertain . . . because people who are sure of themselves, who are men of action, who know who their friends are and what their ultimate aim is—who, sure of themselves, attain their ultimate goal—they are the barbarians. 50 years ago mr derenancourt of the castle, director of the filature spinning mill and chief of police, was a barbarian—and ondine, who lived in a room above the bar at the 1st grimy houses, was just as great a barbarian . . . and her husband, when he had had a drop too much to drink, when he lusted after little rosa, he became a barbarian too. And valeer, returning from the front, returning home and not feeling at home anywhere, was an individual: a little individual in a dreadful world of barbarians. But he didn't know it himself, he felt a kind of rancor inside, a vague sadness, a feeling as if he'd been done wrong . . . but how could he have explained it? And what did he do next? Ha, you'll see, when we go on writing about him in this chapter: he too became a barbarian . . . Being an individual, hunted by the horde of barbarians, he joined the horde and chased after the rats, the other individuals . . . and so trampled on himself.

This book then, so contradictory, so skeptical of every value, groping around so hesitantly amid the chaos, advancing so cautiously among all those mechanized, cultured, pious, scientific, hygienic, fascist barbarians . . . this book can only be called hesitant and skeptical.

THE CURSE

Valeer felt like an individual in a world of barbarians—he felt it, but couldn't formulate it so clearly. He knew, he understood, from that very first moment, that the 4 years at the front had been of no use . . . on the contrary, they had been 4 years during which his own struggle for a living (a living, some happiness and prosperity) had been suspended, and instead of fighting for that he'd fought for mr derenancourt of the castle, so that he could present himself as being even more strictly catholic, more immoral and barbaric, because he was so small, so stunted and stupid, that nothing that happened in the world really got through to him: just a few weeks after ondine had kicked him out, a car stopped outside their door, from the american army, with massive tires and a small engine, with a cogwheel and treads that ran from the front wheel to the back . . . oh, and all the children in the neighborhood of the 1st grimy houses hung around it, jumped on the running board and looked inside, at the driver, who had a leather cap over his ears, a huge leather cap over a huge fat head. Little leopold soon realized: it's my uncle valeer . . . uncle valeer-traleer! he sang . . . and he crawled into the car and pressed the copper horn. He cried and screamed and lost his mind over it. I'll teach you to drive, said valeer, getting out and throwing his leather cap onto the seat—leopold jumped on it like it was a piece of fresh meat, and he put it on his head and so could no longer see where he was going . . . valeer had to give him his hand so that he could find his way to the door of the house. So they came in together—he said nothing, valeer, but tipped his cap, military fashion, because he thought he still had his cap on, and so was really tipping his disheveled hair—something that wasn't allowed in the army. But they didn't know that here. No, they knew nothing about the army, about the war, about american cars—he felt contempt for them, how was it possible that he'd allowed himself to be fooled by them for so long . . . by that philosophizing oscarke, and that . . . that . . . how had his cousin put it? That hysterical sister of his. From his pocket he dug out the 5 francs she'd lent him: here you are, he said. And he gave a franc to judith, and one to Leopold wearing his big cap . . . and then he pointed to the front window, where you could see the car standing at the curb: our cousin's! he said. And he didn't notice that none of them had said a word, had invited him to sit—he rattled on hesitantly: she smuggled during the war and earned a lot of money! he said proudly. As though smuggling during the war and earning lots of money was an honor and a great achievement, but anyway knocking the bottom out of all ondine's retorts. Because she'd been intending to take a sugary sweet tone: had their cousin earned that car by doing business with the germans? But now this ass was saying so himself—he came from the front, where the germans had subjected him to 4 years of misery . . . and now he was proud that his cousin had helped prolong the war. Oh, what a fucking idiot! was all she could say . . . was all she Wanted to say at least . . . for what was the point of wasting her words on him? No, she should have smuggled too, smuggled till the wheels came off—but it wasn't her fault, she was a woman . . . and him over there, oscarke, oscarke who was the man, what had he done? He'd helped dig out a pond and he'd been an auxiliary policeman: so you see, little mr armband policeman, what other people are capable of! she said to oscarke. Honesty is the best policy, said oscarke. Honesty . . . who's talking about that? she asked—and when she started to rant on about all the things that no longer counted in this world, oscarke turned away from her, and went over to the window . . . but he didn't want to look at the car, he stared over the top of it. Valeer asked if the children would like to go for a drive with him—yes! cried mariette and leopold—me first, cried mariette—no, me first, cried leopold—and while they were arguing, they didn't hear that their mother forbade it. She shouted louder, but the children shouted louder still, and finally

351

she grabbed the stove hook and threw it on the floor with a clatter. She swore, in a high-pitched, piercing voice.

THE OTHERS SHOUTED LOUDER TOO

From over in brussels in his tenement mossieu colson writes to you: So I've read that story about valeer, but what grabbed me most wasn't that he spent 4 years among the rats for nothing. We all know that by now, know that no war whatsoever ever bore any fruit. And it also left me cold that, on his return, he didn't feel at home anywhere—because, after all, that has nothing to do with the picture we're trying to give of our times and the people around us. It struck me much more that he, returning as a hero, actually felt like a rat that was being hunted down by all the rest . . . and that he, out of his human incomprehension, but also in his animal instinct for self-preservation, began running with the pack to help trample the other rats of his species . . . that he went to live with his cousin who had bought up everything from the germans, and he went and acted as a servant and drove their car, and with a grand gesture gave ondine's children a franc each. You see, that's how I have to unravel your stories and separate the important from the insignificant: it was important that he, who had been in the trenches, dug out a coin that had been earned from his own misery and the misery of his brothers-in-arms with such a proud gesture. And again there's a detail that you only mention in passing, but that moved me enormously: that the stove hook clattered to the floor, but that her children couldn't hear it because of the din that they were making, their squabbling about who was going to have the first drive: ondine forbade the children to go, but the children didn't hear . . . and the louder ondine shouted that they couldn't go, the louder they had to continue the argument about who was going to go first, since the children couldn't hear each other over their mother's screeching. And look, after she'd thrown the hook clattering to the floor, and sworn, high-pitched and shrill, you could have added the following: that the children finally looked up, astonished, their faces seeming to say: is she going mad, standing screaming like that about some unimportant thing? Because that would be the most important thing for me, the most important point to make in this last chapter of ours: we raise our voices, but the barbarians will still argue between themselves as to which of them will be first, who'll be able to go for a drive first . . . which of them will be able to act quickest, most rationally, scientifically, and barbarically. And the louder we raise our voices against them, the louder they'll quarrel among themselves . . . until they finally look at us with their astonished eyes, asking: is he going mad to shout so violently? to make so much noise that we can't even hear each other speak? They want to become the most scientific, most dogmatic, most technologically skilled barbarians—they're rising up all over the earth, they fill the ether with their long- and short-wave, the roar of their engines, the rattle of their machine-guns, the successive explosions of their cannons. And the children—the children of this age—hang around at their feet and argue about who's going to have the first drive, fire the first shot . . . the children stand around, and they'll know from the roar what make and date the engine is, will be able to tell from the explosion what kind of bomb's been dropped. And we live among them, forced into our corner . . . we who long for a little silence, a little beauty, a little humanity . . . and we get up and ask for quiet, but in the roar of the world where the barbarians rule, they don't hear . . . and the louder we raise our voices, the more intense their din becomes . . . and the deeper we retreat, the higher they'll crank up their loudspeakers. Because our little human voice actually disturbs their raving—they make all that racket because they think they're doing us a favor . . . so that there'll be no one in their world of barbarians who's deprived of noise. And if they should ever, by chance, hear us speak, they'll look at us with astonishment in their eyes: but he's crazy!

MY CAR

Ondine was burning red—and at that unfortunate moment (or precisely because of it, because of all that din), valeer remembered something: that they should go to the markets, there was money to be earned! You load the car full of sweets and you go to the market square and turn on the loudspeaker and soon everything is sold. And now ondine was almost dropping dead from exasperation, so: you should drop dead in the market! she shouted. At least, she wanted to . . . but in her blind fury she mispronounced the last word . . . oh, a few letters more or less, what did that matter, how stupid it was to mention something so unimportant! But they had to laugh, through their tears, and mariette found a little revenge in it: drop dead on the mat, on the mat! she kept repeating and laughing all the while, joylessly—only intending to taunt her mother (who had spoiled her pleasure . . . because children just weren't allowed to have any fun in life, weren't allowed to crawl on a chair or play in the street, weren't allowed to swear or fart). But even so, valeer had to laugh too—and as he was laughing he choked, and in the twinkling of an eye he was a different man: he looked ashen and clung on to the table: he coughed a cruel harsh cough that sounded tortured and horrible. He had arrived feeling confident, and hadn't thought it necessary to doff his cap to anyone on the streets, where usually he tipped his cap in military fashion everywhere he went—but now he was suddenly insignificant and hollow. He was hunched over the table, and tried to sit down—but the chair next to him was covered in clothes that needed darning, and he didn't have the strength to clear it off . . . he lowered himself beside the chair, and lay on the floor with his knees tucked up. And they all saw now that gas was worse than a bullet: anyone who swallowed any was as good as dead: valeer, to see him lying there, was a doomed man. And leopold, being a child, said what the others were thinking: shall I sit next to you in the front of the car, he asked, so I can take over the driving if you drop dead?—and again mariette had to laugh. But after valeer had lain still for a while, and had swallowed a pill with some water, he stood up again, pale and tired: he took the cap off leopold's head and crawled into his car—into their cousin's car, but he always said: My car—and drove back to brussels.

THE LAST NOOK

There's a party going on in chapel road—a party for something or other that entails joyful salutations and a lot of noise: from the bar of the 1st grimy houses the jukebox blares out, a car comes round the corner with the radio going, and along the long wall of the labor hang more loudspeakers playing records like the ones on the radio. It's the festival of the ascension of the fallen heroes of the battle of the jitterbugs, the festival of the increasingly earsplitting din in which not a word of humanity is heard any longer, the festival of reactor engines and of values that have no more value: the festival of the barbarians who have triumphed. And andreus mottebol, the poet and journalist for the weekly press and what-have-you, he sneaks out, carrying the laundry basket into which his useless papers have been stuffed on his shoulder—and his worn paintbrush lies on top. And it feels like a celebration to him as well, because he's finally getting out, and it marks the final end of his struggle against the barbarians: from now on he'll only write about the blackbird that sings in the rain, and about wood anemones, which . . . which . . . yes, you see, he's going to have to learn. And andreus mottebol walks down the winding country lane that leads to master oedenmaeckers's little garden: he's going to rent a tiny parcel of land from him with a small monthly payment: a trifle that he'll have to work hard for—and as he takes the laundry basket off his shoulder, the paintbrush has already fallen off, and the pile of papers have blown away in the wind . . . but what does it matter? After all, they're the pages of which kramiek said there were too many in the book on chapel road, where andreus was riding his social hobbyhorse—an animal that will now be replaced by some other, maybe guido gezelle's nightingale, by god! And andreus mottebol hacks back the bushes and digs the foundations for his cottage, something low and white that won't cost too much—only a tidy sum that will give him gray hairs. And he gets hold of a bricklayer, just as tippetotje got hold of a baron in the past, and he buys stones and sand and cement, and haggles over the price. The only problem, though, is explaining to people where on earth master oedenmaeckers's little garden is located. And the bricklayer nods, and the stone-man too: they nod their heads and say: oh yeah, it's out there in the place we call the last nook.

The last nook: it hits andreus mottebol like a shot: the last nook into which he's retreating from the advancing barbarians . . . into which he's being driven, like an animal that's become a pest, being forced into with his back to the wall—the figurative wall of this last corner of the world, against which he'll continue to defend himself tooth and nail—because he may say with a laugh that he's now going to write about the poet guido gezelle and his companions, the boatman and the blackbird and the tits' nest—but he'll go on writing about the barbarians who've killed the last remnant of poetry, while poems boom out through the loudspeakers (this is a wonderful poem for broadcasting, an announcer said on the radio recently), and andreus mottebol helps the bricklayer and helps the carpenter and puts in the windows and does Everything—there in his low white house that he is going to call "the last nook"—and apart from that he'll find work somewhere, or live from hand to mouth as poets and weekly journalists do, and apart from that he'll go on running his head into all kinds of brick walls, no one understands why. And apart from that he'll grow more and more silent, and older, and will finally resign himself to the course of events.

And as he's standing painting the name of his cottage on the gate, the postman comes by and delivers his first letter: a letter from tippetotje: I'll come and visit you on sunday, together with my baron if he's a bit less ill and pale and under the weather, and in our car, with our radio . . . and why don't you have a telephone put in, so I don't have to write you any more letters. And andreus mottebol realizes immediately that it was no good retreating to this last nook in the world—where yesterday the blackbird sang but today the telephone jangles, and where on sunday tippetotje's radio will arrive. And in alarm he whispers to himself: I'll run away. I'll run away, but as I run, there will always be a barbarian ahead of me: myself.

ISENGRIM

Johan janssens flees like a thief in the night with a basket on his back—and you creep after him like a shadow: you too leave chapel road, you're going to live over in the countryside. And look, you could never have believed that you had so many friends when it's a matter of getting you away from this damn beloved chapel road: tippetotje designs you a house and johan janssens helps to build it, and kramiek comes and tells you that it's beautiful but will look like no other house ever built—and they all offer you a house according to Their wishes, characters, tastes, and incomes . . . and you walk around help-lessly and don't dare say: yes, but.

All you're allowed to do is choose the name, if you study hard and are good: isengrim—isengrim the wolf who in this life was far too hungry for all sorts of things . . . he hungered and thirsted for righteousness, as christ our lord said . . . but also hungered and thirsted after all those things that the same christ our lord condemned (and are indeed dishonorable, but pleasurable), and also: what's mine is mine. Isengrim, alas, who took the most knocks, and who now walks along with a battered coat, with a crutch under his arm, and with an eye permanently closed as a decoration for courage and great hunger. That's where you live now. And for the first time in your life you hear the trees rustling round your house, and also actually hear the nightingales sing—hey, is that all?—and you write a letter to tippetotje: greetings for the first time from my house here at the edge of the woods, where the anemones are flowing and the silver birches are painted a beautiful gray. And tippetotje replies: I'm returning your letter, from my own woods, my social jungle . . . when the wolf with the poet's pen starts praising the flowers, I block up both ears with all 10 fingers.

WITH HER HANDS IN HER LAP

There sat ondine with her hands in her lap, and 1 day after another she would come out with: so they've got a car over there . . . and that was completely typical of her thinking. Yes, that was my cousin's car, she said in the street to madame ci and madame ça . . . It's a liberty, she said. Madame ci said that her brother had bought a car too, a benz, and madame ça maintained that her brother was indispensable in glemmasson's factory—glemmasson and co—and they were going to buy him a car, no she didn't know what model yet. But they all talked about cars—yesterday they didn't and today they did—yesterday the car was something that was in the drawer of some engineer or other, a figment of the imagination, and today it was something one had to have if one wanted to count for anything in life. Where was the time when people talked about socialism like it was the end of the world, and then about electricity, and then about the war? Now it was the revolution and the money that had been declared null and void, and of course about the car. It tired ondine out—really, really it tired her out. My brother's car is a benz . . . Stop talking about it, said ondine and brushed her hand across her forehead: what she needed was to get sick again, to lie in bed and to issue her orders from there—to sleep a lot, rest a lot and think. Because she really had to revise all her ideas about what had happened in her life up till now, what she'd desired, what she'd given up—given up? And she jumped, she suddenly became wide awake, and saw herself again standing on the edge of the abyss, on the edge of that eternally dark Nothingness: to be young, desiring everything, wanting to possess everything . . . and to fall ill, and so put things off a little . . . and growing old, to give up what she had once desired, but had never actually possessed. And the rage, the impotence, the helplessness in the face of this grinning Nothingness had her in its grip, for a day, two days—she went round and complained, she walked into the walls and pounded on them—and if valeer had been there, he would have said: she'll be in bed tomorrow. And then she was in bed, where she tore the sheets into strips, and said: tomorrow morning I'm going to start again, fresh from the beginning. And once the storm of her madness had blown itself out, she came downstairs and was ondine again: the fading, graying woman who no longer saw things too clearly, and thought about buying glasses . . . and perhaps unconsciously she thought she could fool the universe in that way too.

THE FOREST OF PEOPLE

In the bustle of the streets that you're becoming unused to, the meetings and lectures at which you no longer feel at home (how beautiful, how quiet it is there in your isengrim), you suddenly bump heads with professor spothuyzen. And he puts on a beautiful smile and says: you're a bit like a rat in a trap . . . and out of politeness I would use another animal for the simile, a lion, for example . . . but I know that you like to be blunt. You're like a rat in a trap, running around in your trap, staring round helplessly with its shiny beady eyes, and trying fruitlessly to run up the high, flat walls—you're your own prisoner, and the prisoner of your own work: I'm prepared to bet that you've started a new chapter in your life and new chapter in your work. Your previous chapter, if I'm not mistaken, was called "your happiness is something you must fight for"—and so you started fighting for your own individual happiness . . . you sensed that your own individual happiness was under threat, that your life and your art, your dreams and your happiness were under threat, all your inexpressible and inexplicable contradictions (since following dreams raises both practical and legal problems, but especially makes clear all the contradictions of your heart, which even you can't explain), and you've tried, fighting all the while, to retreat to your isengrim refuge. You've dreamed up a life for yourself, far away and somewhere deep in a piece of woodland—but living in the woods isn't possible, unless you're tippetotje's baron himself . . . you need the others, and the others need you . . . if you fight for your own individual happiness, you're also fighting for other people's individual happiness: you are, whichever way you look at it, socially aware, a social being: you're caught in the trap, but you're caught together with lots of other people—you belong to a group, to a society of rats driven into a corner. At times you've tried to withdraw into a refuge, you've wanted to rush back to the days gone by when robber chieftains and pirates lived on the edge of society—but today none of that is possible. And professor spothuyzen smiles at you, and what can you say to him? You're rushing from one mistake to another, professor spothuyzen continues: sometimes you've said that this society is a jungle, and that you've decided to withdraw deep into the woods in order to escape it. How stupid that sounds: retreating to the woods in order to escape the jungle! Why not live in the woods of this society, withdraw far and deep into the jungle of this society . . . and write your books there for yourself: marcus aurelius boon, all for himself. And having said that, professor spothuyzen disappears into a forest of people, into the jungle of this society.

WHAT ARE YOU ACTUALLY SITTING THERE THINKING?

Yes, ondine really had to buy some glasses if she was going to be able to put one over on the universe: reading wasn't easy, it gave her a headache, sometimes she had to press her fingertips against her closed eyelids afterward. In order to be able to control life she had to be able to be indifferent to life, that's what it said in the book she couldn't read anymore. Certainly, what she read there was true: every goal that had left her cold, she had achieved . . . and everything that she'd longed for heart and soul had been denied her. And yet, suppose that she wanted nothing and was given everything, what joy would that bring her? None at all. She would accept it, and it would be a burden to her—just as everything else that she'd received unwanted was nothing but a burden to her. So she sat there by the stove in the evening, stockings down by her ankles, the hem of her skirt covered in dirt and dust, full of dried mud from the street—and she looked at oscarke who sat on the other side of the stove, a silent and empty-headed lout: a dreamer, a good-for-nothing, a hack sculptor . . . no, an armband policeman—an ex-armband policeman. He probably wasn't even thinking about having to look for work now! Well, oscarke, ondine asked suddenly (and he saw the contemptuous smile round her mouth), what are you actually sitting there thinking about?

MARILOU'S LIFE STORY

Tippetotje sends a story to your small, white cottage in the country, your isengrim, that she wrote at the bedside of her sick baron who's tired of life—a story, she says, that could almost be her own life story:
  you may have heard of me, I worked in the hospital for a long time: didn't my hands wander carefully over your limbs, as your contorted face stared at me!—I was a streetwalker too, perhaps it was there you met me: perhaps it was under those circumstances that my hands wandered over your limbs—I can't remember—but call me by name, tell me what my name is and I'll tell you where you met me—yes, go ahead . . . am I marilou? . . . sister maria of the angels? . . . mrs maria peret?—I remember how the grass waved in

summer, I was a very small girl, the waving grass was a green undulating sea: I let myself drown in it—I remember that I was thirteen: madame zyla took me with her to bourges—you know, they said she was a woman of dubious morals—I didn't really know, I mean I don't really know what dubious morals are: morals are crazy anyway—there shouldn't be any morals, just like there shouldn't be any diseases—they called me marilou in bourges: I experienced lots of love there, I saw many diseases—I saw more diseases when I was a whore than when I later became a nurse—I was 20, I was so mature that I frightened myself: the things I've seen and the people I've stroked—thieves, murderers, cancer patients: I wasn't terrified by their afflictions, I was only terrified of myself—I remember that I spent hours bent over the cracked enamel basin, and that I washed and washed my hands—I stared at those hands with horror: sometimes I thought they weren't mine—sometimes I also heard the bell chime at the nunnery, while the water spurted from the brass tap covered in verdigris—the nuns? I became a nun too: sister maria of the angels was my name there—for 23 years I was known as sister maria of the angels in the corridors and cells: for me it was much longer, it can't be expressed in years, only as a "life sentence": I was born there and I died there, I've lived more than once, but that was my longest life, when I was sister maria of the angels: there were the long chilly corridors, the hours of praying in the chapel, wandering around with an oil lamp when at night I had to go to the little room that we didn't name (oh, as marilou I had seen, named, touched everything), and the hours in the bed that was too short, with the heavy skirts tight against my thighs—did I still have thighs?—the lord that I called out to there will be my witness that I certainly did still have thighs—and the lord, the same one, is also my witness that I was still terrified of myself, even there, even in that life—the things I've done in order not to be alone with my terror of myself—I don't know how many years I was marilou for, but I was 43 when I ran away from that convent: sometimes I went back to that gate and had a look, later: "franciscan sisters" it said on an arch around the gate—I was still one of the franciscan sisters long after I'd fled the convent—I became a nurse in paris, I tended your wounds there too, I touched the whole world—my hands wandered over all your bodies, and I saw again all the diseases that I knew from my time in bourges—I sometimes wonder whether I'd thought that the sick had ceased to exist while I was in the convent?—I don't remember ever having thought about it—meanwhile I've forgotten those sick people again, all I remember is that I was standing washing my hands again: in bourges the taps were covered in verdigris, in the hospital the taps were highly polished: this gave the impression that the water flowing out of them was dirty by comparison—I was on nightshift when they brought in peret, he was more or less in pieces in the arms of the taxi driver who'd brought him: he never became whole again, he remained something made up of pieces—he fell in love with me: he'd never seen anything as heroic as a woman able to see all that suffering, he said—those are the kind of things one should never speak about—he was the first man who wanted to marry me: for 20 years I had been marilou, and for 23 years the bride of christ, and this piece of a man was the first person to ever talk to me of love: I was so overwhelmed, I married him—perhaps you heard how my married life testified to boundless self-sacrifice—I don't understand those words: again I stood for hours washing my hands under the tap—then peret died—once I'd been marilou, once sister maria of the angels, and now I became widow peret—they said that afterwards that I led a wild life, 50 glasses of wine a day, blind drunk somewhere in a steep alley, somewhere in a gutter, somewhere under a bridge—then carron came along: the papers said that he was a degenerate type—I don't really understand those things in the papers: madame zylva was a woman of dubious morals, carron was a degenerate type, and what was I?—carron wrapped some old woman in a sheet and tickled her feet till she choked: now he blames it all on me—I'm back living between the whitewashed walls of a cell, sometimes I feel like one of the franciscan sisters again—I have a different name now: 814—yesterday I dreamed of the waving grass, I was a very little girl again; when I woke up I didn't know who I really was—have I ever known?—and sometimes I'm allowed to wash my hands under the tap.

OSCARKE'S THOUGHTS

Oscarke looked up and shook off his thoughts—he'd been thinking about valeer's car, and madame ci's brother's car, and cars in general: that yesterday they hadn't existed and today were a new . . . a new . . . anyway it didn't matter, but everyone talked about them, everyone earned money from them: even boone, by god! In the war boone had worked in the coach yard, without bothering about anything else in the world . . . which didn't mean: without having his own opinion—the opinion that everything stayed pretty much the same in the world, whether he hurried and got into a state and worried, or on the contrary didn't give a shit—and instead of hurrying home in the evenings, he strolled around a bit in the empty coach yard. He scraped some rust off a coach and pried off the peeling paint with a knife, and shortly after the old boss got boone to smarten up all the coaches with some paint: it didn't have to be immaculate and gleaming and precise, as long it was fairly neat: there was a war on after all. And now the war was over, but boone went on scraping off rust patches and painting over them: one taxi company after another came to him, glemmasson came with his coach, and norbert derenancourt came with his too—and boone, who at first had smartened up the coaches right in the street, right outside his front door, had to knock together a shed for himself from a few planks, across the road on a piece of wasteland, and on it in stiff letters he wrote: boone, carriage painter. Carriage, that's right—but suddenly the car was there, no one had ever heard or seen a car, but suddenly the car was a part of the world—whoever said "world" was unconsciously saying "the car"—and so he changed his sign: boone, car painter. He stood there with his moustache, the ends of which he had trimmed, at the lopsided door to his shed, smiling at people, telling jokes, and shouting out from a distance: good day, mr derenancourt!—and tipping his hat. He was still a socialist, yes, but he was also a car painter. I've got no time, I've got no time! he said . . . and he sliced the air with his hand, and soon shaved off his whole moustache, and he looked fatter and older, and at the same time younger; he was still boone, but somehow he was a slightly different boone: people had to get used to the sight. His wife sometimes looked at him with surprise and shook her head: but she had lots to do in her shop, and she needed help because there were big packages to be fetched from the station (items for her shop, items for boone's car-painting business), but since boone had no time, she had to go herself, and went blue in the face and then almost collapsed—and boone saw her coming while he was standing at the door of his shed, telling jokes to people, saying that even he could scarcely carry one of those packages by himself . . . yes, that's what oscarke was thinking about while ondine stared at him.

AT BOONE'S PLACE

But at boone's place his wife had been in bed for three days, exhausted by all her efforts, her overexertion . . . yes, from nervous exhaustion, as the doctor said. Not old doctor goethals, for whom a belly was a dark cellar, but a young doctor who talked about nerves and drove a car—this was the new age, the postwar age in which everyone was earning money, in which wages went up, but so did prices—and in which a shop was a goldmine—and in which the eight-hour day got started. O proletariat, that is this goal for which we'll perish! sang boone till the walls shook, there in his shed, working on fat glemmasson's car, and calling in the children after school to crawl under the car and paint it all over for half a franc an hour—while during the war he only got half a franc a day, what was the world coming to? But now he himself charged five francs an hour, and he suggested to the children that they convert their half franc into sweets and chocolate in his wife's shop—oh, chocolate, for their half franc they got a gobstopper, just like in the days before the war: they used to get a centime and now they got a franc, but they could still buy just as little with it. Little louis boone stayed home from school and also helped paint cars, but he remained there what he'd been at school: not exactly a poor pupil, but a dreamer . . . someone who wasn't really sure if he was in the world or not—perhaps he knew, but he was too quiet to say: *when someone said anything about him, he hid behind the car. He was well behaved—exactly, he was a good little boy, he was born to be kicked and say thank you. Oh, our little louis, he's a good kid! said his mother—and that would have made ondine furious, she hated good kids, she would have liked leopold and mariette and judith to be good kids instead of shameless bandits. It's ondine's gang of bandits, people said—and now she had to make up all kinds of excuses for them. She had to spin all kinds of yarns to wrap the deeds of her bandits in, till people couldn't make head or tail of it anymore. She looked at that little louis with her cool gray eyes: still waters run deep, she said . . . I prefer someone who laughs now and then to someone who's sneaky . . . look at that dog of sander toppe's, it doesn't bark, but all of a sudden it's in your skirts. And she rattled on, about that dog, about sander toppe himself who drank and drank and walked round with his fly open . . . my dear, I went pale when I saw him standing there like That—you can imagine what a bear of a man like him must have down there: makes oscarke's look like a kiddie toy. And meanwhile she looked round that house of boone's, where they had a new stove, a new kitchen table, and where the back kitchen was done in oil paint: something one didn't see even among wealthy people yet. In her house there in termuren the walls were still whitewashed—and afterwards she'd bragged, because in her place the walls were hung with paper: but here they were painted pale green, and the doors were painted to look like oak: our louis did that oak! said his mother. Although it looked like oak he'd just pulled a piece of jute over it. I'll call oscarke, he's an artist! said ondine—and oscarke laughed, he asked little louis if he'd done that in the dark? Just as he'd done with louis's watercolors. And ondine too laughed and laughed, and they went out together and went on laughing there Too.*

WORLD WITHOUT WOMEN

Tolfpoets finds johan janssens there in the living room of his "last nook" with a hand over his sleepy eyes. I've come all across the fields to visit you in your new house, says tolfpoets . . . I listened in astonishment to a crowing cockerel, to a gang of twittering sparrows, and I didn't know what to make of it: it's already february, and soon it'll be march, and soon there'll be a new virgin spring . . . a new spring and a new tune, johan janssens! he says, quoting the poet gorter. And johan janssens says: I can't tell, tolfpoets, that it'll soon be spring again, although, as you say, I'm a poet and a journalist for the weeklies . . . I've been a poet and a weekly journalist and a housepainter, plus the other things that I've forgotten . . . jobs for a few days, a few weeks or months that I don't remember anymore. And in my life I've ridden the social hobbyhorse, since I experienced the social side of things at first hand—you've bared your tolpoetsian teeth in a smile, and strewed a little humorous salt on the tail of things . . . but you can't strew salt on the social side of things, tolfpoets; you're hanging high up there from a gutter and are cold, or feel tired, or know you're in danger. And now, tolfpoets, in order to be able to afford this cottage—this country cottage—I work in a strange town for a strange firm . . . I don't really know myself how strange a firm it is yet —all I know is that I have to catch the train at 5:20 every morning, so that I'm walking along the winding country road before 4 . . . it's still cold and dark, and only when I reach the terrace of the 1st grimy houses do I sometimes see a light on—somewhere, I think, where there's someone ill . . . a nightlight for someone from the terrace of the 1st grimy houses who's about to die or about to be born—have you noticed, tolpoets, that people tend to die or be born at 5 in the morning, when it's dark and cold and lonely? And in the same never-ending terrace of the 1st grimy houses an alarm clock starts to ring, in the house of someone who like me has to go to some obscure job or other, and now hurriedly rubs the sleep out of his eyes, drinks some coffee, and shortly after comes out to shatter the silence and the darkness with his footsteps and his cough. I only hear that cough in the darkness. And in the darkness I also hear the telephone poles humming . . . it's a strange world, so quiet that you can hear the telephone wires buzz with the conversations that have passed along them—messages, figures, and a thousand meaningless conversations. And over at the corner of the street, where the terrace of the 1st grimy houses comes to an end After All, and where it's a bit closer to the station, 2 other male figures walk hurriedly along—I hear one man say something, and the other man answer something—strange words that have no meaning for me—and they also hear my steps and stop their strange conversation, and look at me in bewilderment: who's that, and what's he doing here so early in the morning—because all the male figures who hurry towards the station in the morning, before 5 o'clock, know each other by sight: for them I'm still an intruder, someone they're not used to meeting here. And you see, tolfpoets, I remember the products of contemporary painting, remember all those dream landscapes, those surreal, expressionist, cubist, and futurist landscapes of the mind and our dreams, where only a naked woman wanders round slightly groggy and uncomprehending—I think of them as I myself walk through that strange world, and I see that their paintings are lies: this strange world, where it's cold and silent, still dark and still lonely, is a world Without women.

DEAD MOTH

From his tenement over in Brussels mossieu colson wonders if he might also contribute a story—it seems that our refuges have become superfluous, he writes, and that people prefer to read stories, so:

it isn't always as clear as crystal: let's follow in the footsteps of one anne-marie griolet for a moment: she's a 30-year-old primary-school teacher and takes the train to bordeaux but gets out at toctouan, telling the conductor there that she's feeling unwell—because conductors don't like it when you buy a ticket for bordeaux, but get off halfway: it seems to be against the rules: should he actually allow her to get off when she's really supposed to continue her journey?—it's lucky that he doesn't know that she's also left her hat and suitcase on the train (it's as if she's saying goodbye, giving things up: good-bye to bordeaux, where she was going, goodbye to her hat and her suitcase, which after all are things with which one maintains a certain contact with the world)—she tells the conductor that she'll hitchhike the rest of the way: she owes him this explanation because though she's had to say goodbye to her hat, he hasn't said goodbye to his official cap: a conductor's cap covers the head of a conductor, let's never forget that!—quite possibly she isn't even thinking back to arachon, since anyone saying goodbye to their hat and case (and to the purpose of her journey itself) can easily bid farewell to the village where they live—and, for that matter, anyone who throws away his identity card is thereby throwing away his place of residence anyway—yet it's a mel-ancholy day, there's has been a chilly, unpleasant drizzle hanging in the air, a curtain of chilly, misty rain, the fringes of which clung to the windows of the train—but as anne-marie griolet makes her way along the road, without a hat, without a suitcase, the drizzle begins to fall more and more heavily: soon it's pouring rain: a devastating rain that flattens everything—she's soak-ing wet, she knocks at the door of a farm and asks if she could take shelter there till the storm is over—the farmer's wife doesn't ask too many questions, and when the squall is over anne-marie gives the woman a golden brooch as a present, another thing less in her possession—and since she was already without her suitcase, we can assume that the golden brooch was part of her outfit: something attached to the neck of her blouse—in the papers it was emphasized that it was gold; we understand that: we realize that the reader attaches more importance to its quality than for example to its shape: for most people gold is the most important thing anyway—but it's more important in this case to know what the brooch represented: was it a gold butterfly, or was it on the contrary a beetle?—no, I must delete that phrase "on the contrary": butterflies and beetles are actually exactly the same, they're both insects and both metamorphose into a different kind of insect—I think of ancient egypt, I think of kafka, while anne-marie herself is metamorphos-ing—from a crawling insect, sitting in a train, into a fluttering butterfly: she gives away the gold butterfly in order to become a butterfly herself—now she's left the farm, to wander through the woods . . . it's been raining all day and the woods are dripping wet, and apart from that, night is falling: it was chilly and wet, and now it's getting dark as well—anne-marie griolet, metamorphosing into something other than What we are, must also have thrown away her blouse at this point—and all the rest—but I'm not going to describe things in immoral detail like literature does: a naked wandering woman in the soaking wet wood—she now has a certain similarity to the women of surrealism: wandering around as if in a dream, with a flower in her hands perhaps—but for her all this is reality, not a dream: the wet boggy floor of the wood that her naked feet walk over, the bushes and low branches that clutch at her loins, at her breasts—only the flower in her hand is missing—but . . . surely that's a symbol! The flower means poetry, fairy tale, the dream itself—so this woman doesn't have to carry all this so clearly in her hands; she carries it inside her, hidden from us, hidden from the farmer's wife to whom she gave a gold brooch, hidden from the conductor to whom she gave a sweet lie—she wanders all night like that: at the end of the woods she lies down in a ditch, near the main highway—in the early morning a walker finds her: she's dead—sadly, butterflies don't live long—but it's disappointing, when one reads the comments in the newspapers—it's assumed that she must have died of hunger, cold, and rain—it's true, all That may have been partly responsible . . . or else something completely different—because there's always a reason—but what I mean is this: it's disappointing that they ignore the strange mood that caused anne-marie griolet when she left everything behind, or just gave it away, to finally die naked in the woods—like a butterfly.

OSCARKE LOOKS FOR WORK

Yes, when they came out of boone's place they were still laughing; oscarke talked about beauty, feeling, line: you can see they're not artists, he said. But ondine was no longer laughing now; she swore, she accused him of being an idiot; she had only called him in to make that boone look ridiculous, but apart from that she was dying of jealousy: they weren't artists, no, but their walls were finished in oil paint. And they had a new stove. Miserable idiot! she said . . . you better start doing something with cars too. And because he realized how she'd exploited him again, how she'd used him again like a weapon because it suited her, he turned away from her and returned to his worrying. With cars? he asked . . . what am I supposed to do with cars? Everyone's doing things with them, said ondine . . . at our cousin's they're doing business with them, at wittepennings's they're hiring them out, boone is painting them, the doctor does his visits with one—you do something too! What? he asked . . . and the word came out so poignantly and desperately that ondine started looking round to see if she could find the answer lying in the street. Paint them, she said hesitantly. Sure, and you'll drive round to all the neighbors in one and go on letting your children grow up to be crooks, he said in his desperation—because a car, what in heaven's name could he do to earn money from a car?—unless he copied one in clay: ha, that would be a subject, a car in clay! But meanwhile ondine had got on her high horse: and you'll drive to that cross-eyed malvine! she cried. They had a terrible fight, oscarke went off and got drunk, and then came back to show her who was boss, because he was now that other oscarke, the oscarke with blood on his torn coat . . . but she'd already gone, she'd left the front door open and stationed judith on the threshold—and the next day when he was sober, when he was a quiet little oscarke again, she started on at him again: cars mean nothing to me, he said quietly and primly, I'm a sculptor. Then ondine laughed so hard, so cruelly and unnaturally that she had to hold her sides. A sculptor? You're nothing, you're rubbish, you're a nothing. And she went over to the dresser and picked up a dead bluebottle and hurled it in his face and shouted: look, That's what you are. Oscarke picked up the fly and looked at it, and suddenly began to cry: tomorrow I'm going to brussels, he said, tomorrow I'll look for work . . . and he tried reluctantly to swallow his supper, he tried, but he had no appetite.

THE BARON IS NO MORE

Suddenly a letter, a story, and a mourning card from tippetotje:

may I inform you that mr harry kendal, my baron, has passed away? Oh, keep your expressions of deepest condolence to yourself, get on with your life: he was old enough, 67—he died at lanapoule, on the coast, in the south of france: no flowers, no ceremony—anyway, lanapoule itself is 1 huge flower—in his final days he walked alone as far as the balustrade of the raised garden, and gazed out over the bay—sometimes he'd tell me a bit about his life, sadly not very much: he was one of those people who immediately forget what they've experienced as soon as it happens—he had committed a murder in paris, for instance, and his case was heard no less than 10 times in 9 years, and the press photographers all agreed that a nicer man had never posed for them—he wasted a fortune trying to persuade the judges he was insane— and afterwards he wasted another fortune proving to the doctors that he wasn't mad at all—he really wasn't mad, he was just as crazy as the world around him, that's all—he was loveable, rich, and a little crazy: for 20 years he went on giving away money to girls who were able to please him—and he pleased them too, according to the law of reciprocity—unless perhaps they only accepted the money, and were actually afraid of the craziness of the situation? Who knows? We know so little of what happens around us—and apart from that, it hasn't the slightest importance—when he was 36 he married a chambermaid in some hotel or other, and when he was 41 he gunned down the well-known architect stanford in the theater—it seemed that stanford had

366

put a sedative in mrs kendal's champagne before carrying her off to his apartment—for 20 years mr harry kendal had slipped the sedative of his 8,000,000 marks into the champagnes of all sorts of women, and the one time the same thing happened to him, he shot stanford the architect—and then? mr harry kendal wasn't thrown into prison just like that: for 8,000,000 one pleads diminished responsibility—responsible enough to have millions and seduce all sorts of women, but not responsible when he shoots someone: for the first time there was talk in the world of the "unwritten law": he spent 9 years in all kinds of mental institutions: it was difficult to find the ideal madhouse for him, a place where only millionaires and murderers were admitted. Yes sir, said the nurses—it's damn difficult putting a straitjacket on a fortune—and then he started spending money to prove he wasn't mad: irresponsible, but by no means insane: there's a fine distinction—finally he escaped with "the help of a bunch of con-men"—but what kind of expression is that? You've said "bunch of con-men!" on more than one occasion: were they the same con-men, or different ones?—still, one thing is certain: once out of the madhouse he got divorced from his wife—he had no objection to her having been seduced by someone else, but he resented her being the lover of someone he'd murdered—and then he traveled round the world: in every country he visited he had a brush with the police: he collected women of all nations, like stamps—yet he lacked the application and self-sacrifice of real collectors: he simply bought his specimens—he had a weakness for dancers and his method of conquest was always the same: I sent them a bouquet containing a 1,000-franc note, he told me—and I believed him: say what you like about him, he had no originality, only money—I think back to that evening with sadness, when we stood by the balustrade and gazed at the golden coastline, while the pearls of his extraordinary memories fell—I never interrupted his rare confidences . . . anyway it wasn't necessary for me to answer him: for me he was just a dog that one has to take for a walk in the evening—and although I stood all alone by the open grave yesterday, I couldn't help giving the usual graveside speech: "just as those who fear the lord and have lived righteous lives, whose life has been a succession of sacrifices and whose examples of true piety and the loyal performance of their duties have etched a blessed memory in our hearts, so he received the crown of old age and silver hair: he attained the general esteem that great fortunes are able to command"—I did not inherit his fortune, by the way: there was one last visitor to his deathbed, who was able to cherish him—yet I retain a pleasant memory of my baron, since he taught me a great deal as regards my view of the world: she, the very last one—she who inherited his whole fortune—didn't even go to his open grave—why should she?—"I've got his money, and anyway . . . he's dead for christ's sake," she said.

367

Tomorrow oscar was going to brussels . . . and the Thing he'd been thinking, fearing, torturing himself about for days—how was he going to find jeannine?— meant he couldn't get down a single potato. It gave him a headache, and he had to take a powder and go to bed. He slept all day, got up in the evening with his hair in a mess, and wound a scarf round his neck. Where are you going? asked ondine, who had long since forgotten the argument—she'd argued and made a fuss, turned round and forgot about it, was already preparing for a new and different argument. But for oscarke it meant two weeks of headache, stomachache, diges- tive problems, constipation. I'm going to get a season pass, he said—but he took a completely different direction, he went to the landlord's house, to see malvine: the landlord came to the door and said: ha, it's oscarke! You'll have to wait a bit, because malvine has gone shopping—and he returned to the kitchen where he went on reading a thick book. Have you read this, oscarke? he asked. Oscarke said: no, what is it? But he didn't hear the answer, he'd only asked out of politeness, and was sitting there wondering why he'd actually come to see malvine—and it seemed to him that he had to drop in to see malvine before he could go back to jeannine—it seemed to him that he had to tell her that from now on she couldn't be for him what she'd been during the war: and suddenly he realized that all his strange behavior might be stemming from politeness: he lived for politeness. By the same token, he ought to apologize to jeannine for having crept into bed with malvine during the war. And he silently left the house and walked down the street looking down at the ground, and without realizing it wound up After All at the station: there weren't that many trains and it was already late morning when he arrived in brussels. On the way there he thought more about jeannine than he had done all through the war: he had almost forgotten her, as he'd needed to forget many things in his life—no, he had never thought about her: during the day she had disappeared from his conscious life, but he knew that he had dreamt about her a lot: he closed his eyes and sank into sleep and jeannine would immediately be there. And then he would wake up, and live his wartime life, his life with malvine and ondine and boone, and he wouldn't think of her. But suddenly he'd have a dream in which he . . . but he buried the dream deep inside, to hide it even from himself—because it was a dream people would have cut off their own hands for having, it was so utterly filthy. And reaching the old stonemason's lane he searched from a distance for the corner house where his boss had lived, where jeannine lived—and as he approached it he retrieved the dream, and felt it. Oh, what could have happened to her in those 4, 5 years? She had been 15, she would now be 20—and he almost wept because those 5 years would have turned her into a different person, and she'd have gone through her 5 best years without his being able to devour her with his eyes. And so what was the point of his going to see the

ageing jeannine, perhaps married, gone to seed, her hair in a mess, with wrinkles,
with gray hair—yes, he imagined her, aged twenty, with gray hair. And there was
no question any longer of his devouring her with his eyes: he should turn away
from her, like a dog turns its back on food that's been in the bowl for two or three
days and has mould on it. But she wasn't old yet! Nineteen at most—at worst she
might have a sweetheart. Oh, have a sweetheart: jeannine and her sweetheart! And
oscarke would have to smile, and with a smile shake the hand of some cute young
guy: look, oscarke, that's our jeannine's sweetheart! Ha, good day . . . good fucking
day! And he made that last remark aloud, repeating it again and again aloud . . .
and getting closer to tears. Because no one had to tell him how old and old and
old he was getting . . . how polite he'd been to his mother, saying: no, mother, I
won't draw any naked women at art school . . . how polite he'd been to ondine,
and polite to jeannine and malvine—jeannine, malvine, just stick it in between.
And he smiled at the rhyme and was deeply, deeply unhappy.

TWITTERING SPARROWS

And tolfpoets says: I'm sorry, johan janssens, for showing up just like that and talking to you about all these poetic things, like the approaching spring, for example . . . I live over there in my own refuge, my so-called villa, and forget that in the mornings there's a dark, cold, and lonely world out there . . . a pre-5 A.M. world, a world without women. And johan janssens replies to tolfpoets that no one needs to be sorry: I too would much rather stay where I am in my "last nook," in this piece of soggy meadow, this piece of overgrown woodland: I've still got to whitewash this cottage, and plant roses or acanthus around it, I've still got to screen it with firs and silver birches so as not to cast a curse or a shadow on this last nook of brabant. But alas, in order to live here I've had to borrow money, and in order to pay back that money I can't live here: I get up before 5 in the morning to go to that strange town and do that strange work . . . because I have to live, tolfpoets, and my wife and my son joke have to live too . . . and as it says in the bible, I gird up my loins, and make my heart haughty and cold: I forget that I'm a poet who would much rather stay here and watch your new spring from the end of a winding country road in the last corner of brabant. But look, in this dark world there's the station, still lit up, with the trains that stink of people's tobacco—and the train rattles on through the dark, cold landscape, from station to station, and picks up silent and coughing and cigarette-smoking men. And at last I arrive in that strange town—one of the grayest towns in the country, tolfpoets, where the stones are steeped in age and history, where the houses bear the scars of countless wars, famines, and dreadful diseases, of oppression and rebellion: I arrive in that town, and suddenly—I don't know where they come from—there are gangs of twittering factory girls. It's the time of day when around your so-called villa, and around my last corner, the sun hatches like a chicken's egg, and whole gangs of sparrows suddenly start twittering and twittering. And there in the station square of that strange town whole gangs of factory girls suddenly start twittering. I said I didn't know where they all came from so suddenly, but that was my poetic stupidity tripping me up again, because I know only too well: in the train, tolfpoets, there was a special carriage for the twittering sparrow-girls: it's right at the front of the train. You know that the middle carriage is the safest . . . you know that because your father taught you and your mother always said: make sure you sit in the middle carriage, little tolfpoets . . . and sure enough that's what you do, you make for the middle carriage, the safest one, a second-class one. But the carriage in which the twittering factory sparrow-girls are locked tight is right at the front . . . they have to go furthest down the platform when it's still dark, and when they arrive at their destination they have furthest to go . . . they have to run way down to the first carriage so as not to be late, and from way down in the first carriage they have to run to work in order to be locked up tight on time in the factory. And they run and leap and twitter out of the station and are always a little late for their streetcar. They push and shove—they are pushed and shoved—and one of them curses, one of them laughs, and all the rest twitter and twitter. They too have tender young bosoms, tolfpoets, but they are late for work and only room enough on the crowded platform for those tender bosoms to be crushed together. They too should have young, fresh faces, tolfpoets, but for that too they are too late: they've spent too long in the first carriage of the train, and stood too long on the rear platform of the streetcar, and their young mouths have been crushed against rough jackets, and against gleaming raincoats. And look . . . for this streetcar ride they pay the trifling sum of one franc, tolfpoets, because in the dark before 7 o'clock it only costs one franc on the streetcar, but after 7, 2-francs-50: because there are social laws, you know: safety and security, and therefore reductions on the rates before 7 o'clock . . .

Meanwhile, a similar gang of sparrows twitters round your so-called villa and my last nook.

THE HOUSE IN HARLEM

And from johan janssens's last nook tolfpoets comes to your isengrim house, and says that he's also written a story . . . just like tippetotje and mossieu colson would do, in masterly fashion, if only they didn't forget to bare their 2 gold teeth in a grin on occasion:

in 1909, harlem was not yet the busy district, the black heart of manhattan, that it is today: it was a suburb of new york, a nameless area under construction—there was a house there, one of those machines for living in that provoke no more horror than all the others around it, but in the middle of that no-man's-land, it was bewildering—it had tall, narrow windows strangely offset by an exuberant concrete balcony, adorned with the flourish of an iron railing—and the lives of those who lived there were also more bewildering than fantastic—the papers didn't say much about them: one never dwells on such things for long, one quickly skirts round it and forgets it—water behaves in the same way, seeking the easiest course: it flows around the stone, and babbles on its way—hence, in a variation on the well-known saying, this building was a stone of contention, a blot on the landscape— behind the flourish of the iron railing lived two brothers, homer and langley: estimates put homer at 20, and langley a little older or a little younger—but that's irrelevant—the rest of the world was the water flowing away, and the brothers were the stone: they shut themselves up in the house that stood for-lorn in the mud of no-man's-land—they didn't have themselves connected to the city's gas or electricity, so as not to have the bill-collector on their doorstep every month—their shutters stayed closed, and the concrete balcony became totally useless: it still thrust bewilderingly into the air, but only to catch water and dust, and also the seeds of all kinds of weeds: yarrow and wild mustard soon took root—and also the tough kind of grass that's so fond of ruins—and around the iron railing twined something that looked like creeper: a jungle in miniature, with a concrete base—though homer and langley could only sur-mise: they never saw it—they only came out after dark . . . especially of late, when more and more buildings began sprouting up around them—the two of them took turns doing the shopping, stumbling through the mud and mortar in the dark: the purchases were made as far away from home as possible, and if possible never in the same store twice: after all, the people out there talked about things that weren't of the slightest interest—for instance about a war, the first one—and homer or langley trudged back through the mud and darkness, and getting home forgot to mention that there were things happen-ing out in the world—in a world that had nothing to do with them, and in which people were stubbornly trying to involve them: the grocer started chat-ting again! Langley would say indignantly—while meanwhile harlem just got bigger and blacker: harlem became a black neighborhood—no longer just an anonymous suburb, but a real city neighborhood full of teeming life—and actually as a result it became easier for homer and langley, as far as the choice of stores went—but it also became more complicated not to let oneself become involved in other people's business—sometimes a black person or a visitor for-eign to harlem would look in bewilderment at the house, which had become shut in by monstrosities of a different style and taste: the house in itself no longer raised eyebrows: at most there were occasional looks at that comical jungle of a concrete balcony, which already had ivy hanging from it—and it was then (we've reached 1933) that homer, who'd always been sensitive to bright light, went completely blind, and Langley henceforth had to do all the shopping himself—sometimes he still remembered how he'd had to trudge through the mud and darkness, but now he had to be careful not to get run over when he crossed one of the busy intersections—but he wasn't particularly worried about harlem, he was more worried about the looks that people gave him, the pushy questions they asked him, the strange stories they tried to tell him—for example, that there was going to be another war, the 1940 one—and this confused langley momentarily, because he remembered that in the past people were trying to tell him the same story—and so he hurried back home through the brightly-lit evening streets, and at last he saw their jungle of a balcony, illumined in the strange light of a series of neon advertisements—and to this discovery another was immediately added: that their no-man's-land of the past had become a street, which had its own name, 5th avenue—and getting home, he really swamped homer with too much news: you know, we've got to clean up our balcony sometime, because it raises eyebrows, we live on 5th avenue, and people want to buy our house . . . and yes, something that I forgot to tell you about years ago now: there was a war going on then and there's going to be another war—and the blind homer stared somewhere in the direction of his brother, and asked: does it really raise eyebrows?—he meant the balcony—but the balcony wasn't cleaned—instead they took other measures . . . langley began digging a hole immediately behind the front door: anyone trying to get in was bound to fall into that hole—he also dug more complicated passages, tunnels, and dead ends under the whole house—but he forgot the proverb: if you're in a hole . . . and since homer was blind and didn't dare offer to help in the treacherous passages—he contented himself with calling out: everything okay, langley?—but one fine day things were not okay with langley . . . so homer started asking less and less—it went quiet in the strange house on 5th avenue—then the police received an anonymous phone call—the door was knocked down, the fire department was called in to find a way through the trash and the traps: the daily press noted as a curiosity that over 100 tons of their decaying possessions had to be cleared away in order to find homer and langley . . .

Well, that's my story! says tolfpoets. And you stare at him in horror, and ask where the humor in this story lies? And baring his 2 gold teeth in a grin he produces the newspaper clippings:

Some papers spoke of filth, of quite worthless Rubbish—but another listed this Rubbish more precisely: fourteen grand pianos, two pipe organs, various clocks, violins, two cellos, thousands of books and other papers—and another funny detail: the papers called the two brothers Oddballs, oddballs who played violin, cello, organ, piano, and read books—and a smaller, sensationalist paper simply wondered: who made the anonymous call to the police?—and so the water flows around the stone of contention, and babbles on and on.

OX

Oscarke stood on the corner of the lane, by their old shop, and didn't see that it had changed: that it looked dilapidated—the big window where the tombstones had stood, and the crosses with their stone flowers, and the angel that opened their stone wings: that window had gone . . . wooden planks had been nailed over it. And the window of the door in the center had partly gone and had plywood nailed in front. Wooden planks, and plywood, and cardboard that had covered a chicken run, that was the kind of thing the house on the corner was made of now—and it still didn't surprise oscarke: there had been a war and so much was wrecked, the whole of leuven and namur and dinant and dendermonde, it was All rubble. He peeped through the small piece of glass that was still in the front door, and looked into the shop, where everything was broken too: there was still a smashed angel there . . . one of the angels that oscar had made back then: it must have his signature still on it: o.x.—and jeannine had had to laugh so much at that: ox! she had said. But hadn't her laughter sounded rather mocking, rather disappointed? Hadn't her eyes, oh her eyes, looked at him rather reproachfully? There'd also been a long argument, with the stonemason himself, as to whether he should carve Their name—and he looked for the piece that had been knocked off, it was there in the corner, he held his hand over his eyes in order to be able to see the interior of the shop: and sure enough: there were the letters! Not "ox," but Their name. He pushed at the door, which was closed, and then went round the back, through the gate . . . and he imagined, he was afraid, he hoped he would see jeannine skipping there—which was of course impossible: a girl of 20, still skipping.

WHILE ROME BURNS

If you really don't want to hear our opinions about today's world anymore— says the music master—I might as well give you a story too for god's sake:

I still don't know which of the two is more important, karl nagelli or maurice caramel: for most people it's obviously karl, since he was one of the biggest international embezzlers, and maurice caramel only appeared to be his accomplice—but the rank we're assigned in life, the decorations with which we're honored, and even the rung of the ladder to which we've climbed . . . these all only have an illusory importance: for me what's most typical is also most important—so, which of the 2 is the individual that most precisely characterizes this age?—karl was the most cunning . . . he was swiss but was

sentenced to jail 6 times in his own country and finally deported—how lucky
that there are borders: just like a gardener will throw a stone over the hedge
into the neighbor's yard, karl was thrown over the hedge too—in marseille
he set up various companies that existed only in the imaginations of the gullible—but in this world only the smartest can triumph, and karl turned out
not to be up to the job, since in the midst of his huge frauds he was outma-
neuvered by an even more sophisticated fraud—it makes me smile, because of
the nice lesson that can be drawn from it—but it's easy for me to draw lessons,
since after all it wasn't me who was outshone by an even greater swindler: but
karl, bewildered, ashamed, fleeing the place where he'd been made to look a
fool, came to paris: it was there that he met maurice caramel, and chose him
as his accomplice—a man has to be careful in choosing his accomplices—so
he started up again in paris, but on a larger scale, in the same business he'd
failed in in marseilles—he could pull the wool over people's eyes because he
knew that with everyone it all just boils down to a bit of illusion: the fact that
you and I haven't been swindled out of millions is only due to our not having
any—so alongside him there now lived maurice caramel—I don't know the
extent to which he had to act his role of accomplice . . . to tell the truth he
remained by nature nothing but a common thief: he would walk innocently
out of a bar, taking a fur coat or handbag from the cloakroom—however this
commonness too proved only illusory: he showed himself to be a typical product of his time: he stole the fur coat only to be able to wear it himself, he stole
the handbag just to get his hands on the lipstick and the powder case—rouge
baiser, poudre tokalon, a trifle, a nothing . . . all the things that are so desired
by women were prized by maurice caramel too: he powdered himself—he
wasn't ashamed of it, he did it in public—why not? Because when rome is
burning one must not fail to powder oneself—this is a century of technical progress . . . the skyscrapers and the deserts are growing ever larger, and
because of erosion fertile land is disappearing, and man is gnawing ever deeper
into the bowels of the earth—even atoms can be split ever more intensively
and precisely—and maurice could testify of himself that he actually contributed to the general downfall: so if we have to disappear Anyway, it's best to
do it with a dab of perfume, with a little rouge baiser, with a few trifling
bows and ribbons—yet karl tried to outdo maurice . . . I mean to outdo him
as a typical phenomenon of our age: he stood as a candidate in the elections,
and succeeded in legally being married to 2 women at the same time: he wed
a certain galen, and also a certain rosa de blonde—and meanwhile Maurice
remained with him and powdered himself—and the question arises: which
of the trio was karl's real wife? While maurice continued to work for himself, galen and rosa had to hand over their earnings to karl—in addition he
got to know more ladies from the same circles, and soon there were at least

10 people being sent out to work—he didn't even marry them anymore, he treated them just like the 10 foolish virgins that the scriptures speak of—and maurice also continued to distinguish himself in this babel, this niniveh, this rome: he sat on a café terrace and powdered himself; there isn't a single law that forbids such a thing—come on, how long will it be before there's a sign hanging in our living rooms saying: real men do it with powder?—but, the fact of the matter is that it's against the law to do it with a stolen powder compact: Maurice was caught out, as they say, when an inspector of police asked where the compact had come from—and to make matters worse, karl was caught together with him: inevitably one drags the other down with him to destruction: either we stand together or we fall together—and one day we shall all be caught out by this civilization, together with the most perfect and typical inhabitants of our burning rome.

GRAY FLOWER STREETS

In the old gray town to which johan janssens travels in the mornings, he takes up his pen to write a letter to tolfpoets. Out there around our refuge—he writes—it must be misty and cold and damp now, on this rather chilly february day . . . or at least you probably think that . . . you think that it can be sad and gray round our refuge, but you err in this like the heretics. Because whatever the weather, you can see the horizon there, the countryside that is always beautiful, and the trees that are never the same in winter or autumn or spring. Here in this town, which is old and blind, you see only the houses, the cobblestones, and above them a narrow strip of sky like a piece of grubby sailcloth. Sad and gray, I write . . . but I know that those words don't look sad and gray enough to describe the stupidity of it, always the same houses, the same cobblestones, and a never-changing strip of sky. I arrive at 7 in the morning, when the streetlamps are still lit, dawn is beginning to break, and on every side factory sirens are beginning to wail over the long terraces of the grimy worker's houses, to my left and to my right—in termuren the 1st terrace of grimy houses is behind the labor, but here there are innumerable terraces of grimy houses, right and left—they lie there like horizontal stone rulers, interrupted only by identical stone rulers at right angles. And you, tolfpoets, who see spring approaching around our refuge, can't imagine anything so stupid and soul-destroying—you can't imagine those corpse-like streets, laid out next to each other in innumerable rows like in a cemetery . . . And I must also describe to you the dead-end streets, the cités as they're called—suddenly one of those corpse-like streets will end in a stretch of wall, a row of posts, in a fence of sheet iron. Now and then you find yourself in the wrong cité, and come to a dead end in a crumbling, moss-covered old wall, and you know

375

you've made a mistake: this is cedar street instead of fir street—because yes, tolfpoets, in order to prevent any mistake they've given all these gray streets, all those city-corpses lying next to each other, the names of flowers, the names of trees. So around your so-called villa, and also around my last nook, there are some firs and some silver birches . . . but here there's only the signs for fir and silver birch streets. Not a branch, not a leaf, not a flower is to be seen—in spring only the cobbles bloom, and in autumn instead of fruit there are only the same stones, still called hazel or walnut street. The people in cedar street have never seen a cedar, tolfpoets . . . they've never seen how the hazel starts to bloom with dark red buds, they've never felt the smooth bark of cherry trees, and have never caught the scent of blooming lilacs around them. No, the streetlamps are still lit for a little while in the world before 7 o'clock, the gray morning twilight breaks, and on all sides the factory sirens sound . . . and the people from magnolia street and rose tree street hurry along the gloomy, ruler-like dead streets. Meanwhile I start my strange work, which I still don't fully understand, and dream of paying off my bit of woodland, and of going there to eavesdrop on spring undisturbed.

SEE YOU SOON

Oscarke stepped under the small glass lean-to, which was also broken, but he didn't see that either: good day! he said to them, and at first they didn't recognize him, but when they realized who it was: It's oscarke! And they immediately wept, they showed him the house, where nothing was in one piece. Nothing. And as they explained their war to him, he realized that they too had consorted with the germans—how was it possible that the same thing had happened in brussels as had happened over in termuren?—but as they explained it, it wasn't as if they'd really collaborated with the germans, they'd just behaved properly and the germans had behaved properly too . . . everyone behaved properly, except of course for the people who had smashed up their house: men and drunken women in disguise, with curtains over their faces. And why? Solely because their jeannine had married a feldwebel during the war—and in the final days of the war that feldwebel had fled back to his country, he'd been part of the retreat and jeannine had followed him. Now they were without jeannine, without windowpanes in their house, without furniture, without money, without anything: we've got to start all over again, oscarke, and we can't start again—could we get a new jeannine? And they cried—and oscar nodded and nodded and wept with them. Of course, they'd got what was coming to them—why on earth had they fraternized with the enemy and married their daughter off to them, just as wittepennings had done?—like glemmasson had made boots for them, and derenancourt blankets?—like the priest had sung masses for them, and he, oscarke, had stood by the tunnel as an armband

policeman? But he didn't think of those things—he laid his arm on the broken
wobbly cupboard and buried his bird's head in it, with its tuft of hair sticking up.
The pain was tearing him apart. And they . . . they tried to tell him that it was the
socialists' fault, that the people who had smashed up their house had been social-
ists, communists, bolsheviks—although that wasn't true, the people who'd smashed
up the houses belonged to the scum, to the nameless ones who lived in the gutter
and had seen their ranks grow so terribly thin. But the stonemason and his wife
were confused, they called everything that was no good "socialist," and went on to
live their small and insignificant lives right up until their small and insignificant
deaths. But no, they couldn't even tell oscarke that it had been the "socialists" . . .
because there he stood, oscarke, and he was a socialist too . . . and he was weeping
with them. He thought of boone's stories about wittepennings's daughter—and
wittepennings's daughter immediately became for him the stonemason's daughter
as well. He remembered that she had been brought to the open window with her
petticoats hitched up, and that they had drawn a cross on her bare bottom—and
thinking of wilhelmus he saw the big handlebar moustache of wilhelmus and the
bare bottom of wittepennings's daughter . . . no, not wittepennings's daughter—he
saw jeannine, jeannine and that dream. And lifting his head from the fold of his
arm, still crying, he noticed jeannine's wedding-day photograph in front of him,
with her feldwebel beside her—he was big and blond and carried his spiked helmet
on his arm, and next to him stood jeannine carrying her wedding bouquet on hers.
He knew that he would never be able to see white flowers again without seeing a
spiked helmet along with them—he eased the photo out of the frame and put it in
his pocket. He put on an old apron of the stonemason's and started tidying things
up a bit—he cleared out the yard and hung the gate straight and made an orderly
pile out of the bricks from a low wall that had been kicked over. He worked till he
dropped, until about noon, and then he ate his sandwiches, went out into the lane
and said: see you soon.

BITTER RICE

My baron is dead but that doesn't mean a thing: I'll get by—tippetotje
writes—but instead of telling you what I'm doing, I'd rather tell you a story:
    of course it's an Italian film, but it's set in paris, anyway it doesn't matter,
it could just as well be an american film set in berlin: what's the point of
trying to distinguish them?—I simply mean that both heroines happen to be
italian: one is called eva and the other vitale: of course they're both very beautiful—girls in advertising and film have basic obligations in this respect: who
can enjoy a movie if the heroine isn't drop-dead gorgeous? Eva and vitale are
exactly What the public wants: not the trace of a pimple, and eyes like knives
that take one's breath away—and there's also another co-star, but he doesn't

377

get a name, he'll remain unknown throughout the film—and that's how it has to be: since he's an industrialist: the nameless financier comes and goes, having what the cultural exponents lack—the poet, the thinker, the philosopher . . . they have the flame in their hearts, the halo around their heads, the lamp in their hands: they point the way—the way that no one follows—while everyone flocks round the industrialist, who has money—though the thinkers and the poets are men of renown, while the financier always remains anonymous—that's precisely the drama of eva and vitale: both are beautiful vases into which some content must be poured—in reality they should go to the poets, the philosophers, the men of science and knowledge: they'd give eva and vitale what they're missing . . . alas, the exponent of culture, the giver of content, has no value . . . that is to say, no monetary value—that's the way it goes, you present yourself as an exponent of culture with no money, or else as a financier without culture: neither is to blame; both might be men of goodwill, each building their tower of babel—since, alas, we know they speak different languages—the thinkers, the poets and the builders know approximately what the tower should look like, but it's the financier who tells them what to do—but let's return to our two breathtaking vases, eva and vitale: they stand there and are beautiful, they're the most successful product ever developed by mankind—they stand there without knowing why or what for, but they long to do something, to communicate something, to receive something: but unfortunately they receive nothing but what the financier has in abundance—but what do you know, it makes them still more beautiful and desirable, and at the same time emptier and more hollow: still everything feels like Nothing—so at his wits' end the industrialist takes them with him to paris, but while there they meet neither einstein nor miller, neither picasso or le corbusier: they wander around lost in the appalling emptiness of a universe in which the tower of babel was never completed—he takes them to the most luxurious hotels with every conceivable comfort: bathroom, telephone, television—he meets them only at meals: the moment when there's something to chew on is the only moment when he really counts: it's the only content that he can offer: cold turkey with salad, crab with dancing flames around it—after a few days he can't help noticing that his vases are even absenting themselves from those meals—he leaves the dining room and knocks on the door of their room—they don't open the door—he enlists the help of a maid, who opens the door with her spare key: eva and vitale are lying in the bathroom, unconscious because of an overdose of drugs—and to name the substance that they'd taken to replace their missing content: it was encodale, something heroin- or morphine-based: the only kind of dream one can acquire with money—but now things become even more complicated (up till now the film was fairly simple in structure), since a difficulty arises: the doctor who's called in discovers that they've taken encodale, but the police, who are not called in, but come in anyhow, discover . . . that the girls themselves have smuggled a large amount of encodale into paris—and what does that mean? That they not only want to use up the money the financier has been offering them (which only stands to reason), but that they in turn have become their own industrialists, financiers, brokers, smugglers—and we're now nearing the end of my story, but I should just emphasize a few statements that have appeared in the papers: one comment was to the effect that it was lucky the police were able to intervene—and I look around me, and I know that this is a stupid lie: we're not lucky: our content has still been poured out, and all tower-of-babel-builders must still listen to the ignorant financier: and the vases are still there, breathtakingly beautiful, but perfectly empty—and something else, the very unusual happy ending of this film: despite their protests, eva and vital are placed in custody—I can imagine that they protested! Because why them and not their financier? Why the empty vases and not those so unable to fill them with content? Why eva and vitale, and not this whole society that has money but no culture?

A PLASTIC CEDAR

From a letter to tolfpoets in his so-called villa from johan janssens, over there in that strange gray town: as it says in the bible, my voice should cry from the depths, tolfpoets . . . from the depths of this gray life in which I'm buried alive, tolfpoets, I write to you . . . I write and I don't know why, except perhaps so I can say to myself: you're really still alive, you're really still a human being. Because all these dirty red bricks and all these gray paving stones are lying on top of the grave I've been shoved into, the grave where I do work I can't understand: how people work and work without understanding a thing about what they do! How much is done that has no use or meaning in this world! I write "in this world," but I mean much more the world of the others: in this world that surrounds me but is not my world, the world of other people, people who work and toil without any idea how or why or for what . . . there are factories and factories, tolfpoets, ports and warehouses and planta-tions, storage depots and companies in which we're shut up like small cogs buried alive in the guts of a machine—technology and automation, rubber and nylon and plastic, sodium lighting and laxatives . . . all that, and to what purpose, to what end, for what point and meaning what, tolfpoets? I don't know. And in order for nylon and sodium lighting, plastic, and all the other indescribably insignificant things to exist, people work and toil, fight, murder, disarm and rearm (is it true that they're talking about moral rearmament in the schools, tolpoets? . . . that is to say, that they're already drumming into our children that they must get ready, to advance one day bayonet in hand and hoist the a-bomb above their heads and charge?), all for sodium lighting, plastic, synthetic car paint, and toothpaste and laxative factories? And is it because of that and only because of that that there are ruler-like streets laid out like corpses alongside each other . . . streets that should actually be given a number, as the dead in cemeteries are numbered, or soldiers in barracks, or prisoners and the condemned—but that instead have ironically been given the names of flowers . . . that have been called, as a sick joke, fir street and silver birch street? Is all that for the benefit of modern science, of synthetic kitschy lampshades and stockings? And I wanted to describe to you the women from fir street and silver birch street . . . I wanted to show you them, squinting and twisted, crooked and with a hunchback from their work, and how they only have money—a few insignificant cents—from saturday evening to sunday morning. Because on saturday mornings they get paid in all those storage yards and depots, in those innumerable factories of synthetic modern science, and by sunday evening everything has gone. Apart from that they live on credit, they're squinting and deaf, twisted and with humps or steel-rimmed glasses. There are social reforms and social improvements, there's safety at work, there are bathhouses, there's synthetic soap and synthetic contraceptives . . . and soon there'll be a synthetic fir tree and a synthetic silver birch in front of fir street and silver birch street, and they'll be growing babies in bottles—but meanwhile it remains gray and sad, the women are old and dried up, with stumbling feet and steel-rimmed specs. And they have no money to buy all this synthetic science, the plastic, those nylon stockings. They live in the depths of a grave, and the gray stones of their streets are the stones of the grave they were born into, that they stumble around, that they work and work and will die in. And from the depths of that grave I cry out unto you, tolfpoets: from the depths of that grave I write you my letter. Postscript: is spring really coming out there at our refuge?

HEART AND GLASSES

And look, oscarke saw the streetcar just come trundling along: he stopped, should I get on too? wondered oscarke—and when the streetcar finally started up again, he broke into a run and was just able to jump aboard. He gasped and wiped the sweat from his brow, arrived in the center of town and walked around, sat down on a bench somewhere and asked a policeman the way . . . the way, but he didn't know to where, he muttered something and the policeman turned away. He strolled on and found another bench, and sat there for quite a while watching a truck being loaded—there were marble sheets and there were men on tall blocks with aprons that were white with stone dust: masons. Hey, oscarke was amazed, and he strolled across the wide avenue towards them. It was a large, imposing house, covered from top to bottom in slate (well of course, they were stonemasons after all), and through the open gate he could see the courtyard over there, full of slate and marble, and men sitting on top of the blocks playing cards and chatting away: it was lunchtime. They looked him up and down and realized that he was wasn't a customer, a rep, a gentleman—they pointed him towards a french sign saying "on demande," and a cardboard hand pointing the way: office. He was forced inside as it were by the finger. It was his mother's finger, and also the threatening finger of ondine. He went in, but it was lunchtime there in the office too: there was only one girl sitting there, who might have been jeannine, if she hadn't been so . . . how could he put it? so artificial—with neatly colored hair and colored eyes and colored legs . . . just as if she were made of wood, of iron, perhaps she even had an iron what's-it there between her legs, and it was painted, imitation . . . done up so it looked a little like jeannine's, which had been warm and real. She looked at him with her iron eyes and spoke french while looking at a clock, and from that oscarke understood that he was too early: he rejoined the men in the courtyard, who had been waiting just for him: they gathered up their cards and started work. It was work that oscarke knew, but by hand, whereas here they did it with a machine. He strolled back out of the gate, because though the masons might have gone back to work, the clerks were still away . . . he sat looking at the boulevard, boulevard montbernard where lots of girls were going past to their offices, offices on other boulevards. And as he was watching 3 girls go past—the one on the far left was the most attractive—their legs and backs and asses swaying slightly, it suddenly dawned on him that he was now here in brussels, in the heart of the world, and that everything was passing him by . . . science and politics and religion and brand-new ideas, none of which he had a clue about: to his mournful senses the world consisted only of flesh. Malvine and jeannine, stick it in between, and that iron girl there behind him and the 3 girls in front of him. He tore himself away and went inside, it was 2 o'clock and he turned immediately to that imitation girl . . . but she had nothing to say, she worked and was silent, and oscarke had to direct his question to a little old office lady with glasses. She wrote down his name and asked for his pension card, and though he had no pension card, he was still allowed to start.

JEANNINE'S PHOTO

There was a lot of fuss in the boulevard montbernard . . . it was quite different from jeannine's father's place: the boss stood there and pointed out what had to be done: you do this and you do that. And oscarke went up to him and said: I'm starting work—so he was given a task too, he had to sweep up stone dust and brush off a finished statue. The boss . . . or rather the foreman . . . explained to him how to do that, how to get the dust off the statue—oscarke said nothing, but nodded and got on with his work. He cleared a table and rolled up papers, plans, and picking up the plans he saw that it was to be a monument—the barrel of a cannon, and a woman with cannonballs in her hands: to the fallen artillerymen. He was the dogsbody, the errand boy, the lowliest workman . . . and he noticed that one of the other workmen was talking and didn't have a clue about masonry—and then it was time to go, he put his coat on and went out with the others, about 30 of them. 30 stonemasons, how was it possible? He came home to the terrace of the 1st grimy houses, there with ondine, and hung his coat on the hat stand, and then ate in front of the stove. He said nothing, and ondine didn't ask, and when dusk fell he went to see malvine—he'd wanted to go yesterday, to say he was returning to jeannine, and now he wanted to go and say that it was all over with jeannine—and suddenly he remembered the photo! He had a photo of her! He felt dizzy and could scarcely get the photo out of his coat pocket, he stopped under a lamppost and looked at her and the spiked helmet: he ripped the spiked helmet off and tore it into tiny pieces which he dropped as he went on: he would have liked, liked so much to be alone somewhere with that half photo, but he didn't know anywhere to go. And then he looked for the bar where he'd sat with boone, and where that daughter was, what was her name again? . . . no, he couldn't remember her name. That bar—it had remained the same yet was somehow different, the war had drawn a curtain across all existing things, the bars had become cafés and the drinks cost francs instead of centimes . . . but apart from that the core, the soul, remained the same. And in that café he Still wasn't alone enough to look at his photo: the daughter had meanwhile grown up, and all the studs of the town crowded in to be near that bitch in heat. Oscarke went into the yard, where there was a very dim light, and looked at the photo. He looked at her. He had never seen her like this, 19, beautiful, beautiful, beautiful. He ran his hands, his lips over it. He stood still leaning against the wall. The daughter from the café came into the yard, didn't see oscarke standing there, thought she was alone, and in great haste peed without even crouching down—standing straight with her skirts hitched up, like a monument in brussels, like a spouting fountain . . . oh, oscarke suddenly remembered her name: rosa! Rosa lowered her skirts and went back inside—oscarke's heart and spirit had suddenly died, but his manhood on the contrary was very much alive: he'd never known it to be so big, and undoing his trousers he pressed jeannine's photo against it—jeannine on her wedding day, marrying the feldwebel who'd been torn off.

PLEASED TO MEET YOU, MY NAME IS RABBIT

Oh god, oh fuck, now you've got a story from kramiek too: I, kramiek, who've played a role in your book that I never liked, am now writing you a story that you won't like—meanwhile, though, best regards, and yours truly, rabbit . . . sorry, kramiek . . .

My trial has begun: I've already been asked all kinds of questions I can't answer . . . I'm being asked about my actions, about the numerous twists and turns I've taken in my life, and that I myself cannot possible tell apart—the only thing they don't ask me about is the one thing that's preoccupied me for so long: what I really think about life—the presiding judge: what is life?—I (rather hesitantly): it's a kind of bewildering joke—yes, that's how I'd put it—I've never had a lot to do with religion, but I've been told that, for the Chinese, life is merely the dream of buddha himself (perhaps buddha ate a little too much cheese the evening before) . . . I've also been told that according to the egyptians it's a conjuring trick of osiris: this whole world is just the rabbit that he pulls out of his hat—but I maintain the belief that it's all just a bewildering joke, that the gods are telling each other: soon the joke will be over, and when they get to the punch line they'll burst into Homeric laughter—now and then I've wanted to call a halt to all those twists and turns, not so much to change or improve, but rather to step back and get an idea of the whole: I've never succeeded—why didn't I die in some concentration camp like so many of my race? Why did fortunes fall into my lap? Why am I now on trial?—but . . . can't you see that I've lost the plot during all those twists and turns?—oh yes, I'm a jew . . . I'm a german jew, and besides that, a nazi—you laugh? Yes, if you want to go on listening, you'll find it gets crazier and crazier—I was a jewish nazi, I was water and fire at the same time: I was the quarry being relentlessly hunted down, and I was also the relentless hunter himself—I once heard the following story: a jew was brought before the nazis, and an unloaded revolver was placed against his chest . . . and just as the trigger was pulled, he was hit very hard on the head with a plank from behind—and when he came to they convinced him he was dead (hadn't he been shot?) and had gone to hell—I was also brought before the nazis: I expected the terrible blow behind my back with the plank—but instead I was asked to organize several houses of ill repute for wehrmacht officers— I started work in astonishment, and perhaps it's true that I was a little too rough with the girls: but come on, sometimes we get a plank on the back of the head, sometimes we hit others on the head with a plank—apart from that I had nothing to do with them—I supplied all kinds of provisions for these houses: liqueurs, coffee, and chocolate . . . things that were no longer available, but that I still had came up with though as if by magic—one thing leads to another, eventually it became textiles, and then wood for mines . . . eventually it became so complicated that even osiris, the great conjurer, could no longer make head or tail of the rabbit—for christ's sake, I even joined the gestapo . . . my real job became to track down stray jews and hand them over to the nazis—according to Rosenberg, the jew was to blame for everything, a stain on our civilization, a patch of decay to be cut out: and I, a jew, was given the knife: the cornered animal had a hunting rifle thrust into its paws—I tracked them down, wherever they were: sometimes they had fortunes, sometimes they had fabulous treasures of jewels and precious stones—it seems I was supposed to hand these over too, but on the way they went astray in the most improbable places . . . first in the soles of all the old shoes in my house, and then when there was no room left, in cavities in the walls where I'd made holes—sometimes I tried to work out how much I'd already amassed, I can calculate amazingly fast . . . yet I was never fast enough to keep up with the fantastic growth of the figures: they raced ahead of the tip of my pencil, they multiplied even as I sat gazing at them—and at one such moment the gestapo burst in—and so I arrested myself, sentenced myself to pay several million to myself—sometimes I wondered whether I hadn't really been hit over the head with the plank after all—and only the fact that I was able to give the girls a good kicking saved me—so now, when the war is long since over and done with, a new trial against me has been begun—what's being said all sounds so improbable to me—I wonder to myself, why am I actually on trial? Is it because I was arrested as a gestapo man by the gestapo? Or is it because the gods have reached the insane punch line of their joke?

UNFATHOMABLE VOID

Oscarke went back into the café . . . he was white as a sheet, his hands were trembling . . . he was trembling all over, he didn't even have the strength to lift his drink. Aren't you well? asked rosa. No, he replied . . . or at least he tried to, but he couldn't even open his mouth, his lips had stuck together. Then he paid, and went wandering through the evening streets. And lo and behold, jeannine was pushed slightly to the back of his mind, since he felt annoyed that he could scarcely pay for his drink . . . ondine still gave him the same allowance as before the war, she still reckoned in centimes, and didn't know (or didn't want to know) that the world worked with francs. Everything cost thousands. And that's why they had to fight for higher wages, but the higher the wages became the more expensive everything you had to buy became: it was a never-ending catch-up race. But he still didn't tell ondine that he needed more pocket money—and he remembered boone's saying: the workman will get what he wants . . . yes, he was going to get it, but they would have to fight for it, there were strikes here and strikes there, there were fights between workers and gendarmes . . . but the 8-hour day was only a few weeks away. But for oscarke . . . oscarke as a little person, as a little fellow in the grip of life . . . for him everything remained only so-so: he was given 20 francs pocket money by ondine after making an almighty commotion and threatening to drown himself together with judith . . . but out of those 20 francs he had to pay for his

season ticket on the train, 13 francs, leaving him only 7—and out of those 7 francs
he had to pay for the streetcar in brussels . . . because ondine didn't understand that
you couldn't possible go anywhere on foot in brussels. And the rest went into his
lunchbox, on some mincemeat, or salted bacon, or a herring . . . the stonemasons
sat there in the yard and looked at each other's lunchboxes, louis-paul always had
eggs, and someone from zotteghem always had some local sausage (the dialect
word for it always made the men from brussels laugh—it showed how petty life
was and with what small ridiculous things people filled their small ridiculous
lives), and oscarke sat among them and he had nothing to spread on his bread.
No, it was a choice between coming on foot from zotteghem . . . oh, what was he
saying . . . between walking from the north station to boulevard montbernard and
buying some cheese—or taking the streetcar and having nothing. And with the rest
you can buy yourself some tobacco! ondine had said. With what rest? But it was
useless trying to make her understand: it would have been like filling the unfath-
omable void: the void around and above and under him that couldn't possibly be
filled—that was what ondine was like—that was what her actions were like: she
was part of this unfathomable void. With the rest, which was a figment of her
imagination, he could buy himself some tobacco! And someone would sometimes
ask: don't you smoke, oscarke? . . . and he would have to reply, with the yawning
hunger in his eyes, "no." She, ondine, knew nothing about it . . . or perhaps she did
know, but just didn't Want to know.

AN EXAMINATION

Mr brys is still walking round town before returning to his room in rue saint-
honoré . . . and he drops by to see you while you're working feverishly on
your book about oscarke and ondine—at the beginning you weigh things
up, hesitate and doubt, and your pen tries to find its laborious way through
the labyrinth of still-unwritten words . . . but gradually the incomprehensible
fever of writing seizes you, as if your pen were afraid of not having written everything down, as if it were afraid that something irredeemable might
happen to it before the very last word has been said. And mr brys comes in
and sits down, as he always does, gazing with his calm eyes at his equally
calm hands. Is that a mask of his? you wonder fleetingly as you go on writing about oscarke and ondine . . . is that a mask too, like ondine and oscarke
also wear? Is he hiding heaven-knows-what under that mask—what we all
hide—what we really are, and that we're afraid of Being?—and you stop
writing a moment in order to hurl that question at mr brys. But just then,
noticing that you've stopped, mr brys hurls a question right back to trip you
up: you've already reached page such-and-such, I see, but do you know yet for
whom or for what you've actually written your book?

The thing is, mr brys, as far as I understand it myself (since who really understands the sense and meaning of what he does?), the thing is that I'm worried about that little bit of happiness and that little bit of freedom that people like you and I have . . . people who have a little humanity . . . in a world of creatures not yet worthy of the name human being, and yet who are the masters, and have all the power, make laws, draw borders, who constrain us, watch in hand, run us over on the street, squash us, shut us up in camps and prisons, will shoot us down because we're different from them: because we don't fit in to this—their—world. We don't fit into it, mr brys, and so we must disappear from it: we are a few individuals against the horde, against the legion of robots—and because we realize deep in our hearts that we really don't fit into their world, because it's a wrong world, a derailed world, we must prepare to defend ourselves as best we can. We must retreat to a kind of spiritual refuge, and from there continue the struggle for some beauty and humanity, for some rationality and some human feeling—among these creatures who are not yet people, and yet are in control, we must live like the survivors of a shipwreck, saving what we can. This then—I think, I assume—is the aim of my book, as far as I understand it myself. Because what do we ultimately understand of things, mr brys, what do we ultimately understand of ourselves?—except the vague sense that we, latter-day greeks in a world of barbarians, must cover ourselves with some mask or other. A mask to avoid being recognized, so that these other creatures, who prescribe rules and laws to us, and who are not yet like us, won't find and catch us. And mr brys drops the mask of his smile and says: a while ago I dreamt that a strange, powerful creature had entered my room in rue saint-honoré, rustling behind the wallpaper . . . and when I tried to flee, it grabbed me as one grabs a beetle or an earthworm, in order to find out just what kind of creature I was.

A PAIR OF CLOGS

And when oscar sat by the stove in the evening, and saw his girls sitting on a blanket in the corner, making themselves a world with a few rags, some cardboard or bits of wood for the stove . . . and then leopold destroying that world again . . . when he saw how they howled and wept and laughed and fought—and ondine on the other side of the stove sat partly knitting, partly reading her book (and only did both things halfway, her reading and knitting, and so did neither), then, oh, he bit his fingernails to the quick. Ondine sat there and was having another dream—oscarke could tell, and if he waited and was quiet, he might be able to feel and eavesdrop on that dream . . . because unconsciously ondine would let it issue forth from her mind. He sat and was silent and dozed off, and tried in that way to flee . . . but at any moment he would be jerked back, it wouldn't take much, all that would have to happen would be for the children to stick the scissors in each other's eyes, the way they were carrying on, and he would have to put on his coat and go to a doctor, to the hospital, and see blood and curse and tear his hair out. Don't stick those scissors in the air like that, mariette, he said. But he said it tonelessly, still far away in his other world. And then ondine began to project her dream like a film onto the screen of his restlessness: across the street from us is that piece of wasteland, which they should fence off . . . the way courting couples wrap themselves around each other is a real scandal, these days people have no er, what's-it anymore . . . and now she's showing him boone's shed, where he paints cars—and if we were rich, oscarke, we could build ourselves a house there. And she went on knitting and reading her book—he thought it was stupid, reading books, stuffing yourself with other people's dreams when you were chockfull of dreams yourself. And so that was her dream: to build over there—a bourgeois home of course, covered from top to bottom in slate, with carved staircases and carpets and vases. Oh, he traveled back and forth to brussels, he walked from the north station to boulevard montbernard and bought an onion to eat with his sand-wiches—an onion or a radish or a stinky cheese, which he divided into six pieces: a piece for each day of the week—and they were such small pieces that he first ate his sandwiches and then the piece of stinky cheese. Oscarke and his stinky cheese, they said at work—oscarke and his radish. And he gave a rather embarrassed laugh, he didn't tell them that it was the only way he could buy a bit of tobacco, the worst and foulest smelling tobacco that could be found. What on earth is that terrible smell? asked ondine. And in bed he had to lie with his back to her: I keep getting your breath in my face, she said. Right, he crawled straight into bed, with his back to her . . . he thought about the likelihood of becoming a foreman at that big stonemason's, the possibility of setting up on his own and becoming the biggest stonemason in brussels. And so he fell asleep—and the new world that had to be carved out, and the girls who still troubled his senses, all that was far away. Oh, he was a chump, there was no changing that . . . was he alive, or was he not really living?—he dreamed that he lived, he thought up a life for himself . . . he wanted to achieve some sort of clarity about the sense and meaning of life—and suddenly he had a terrifying thought about life, and just as suddenly he remembered having had the same thought before. And in that way all he was doing was to dodder round in a circle in his thoughts. But sometimes everything went to his head . . . for example now he heard that the daily pay-rate was going up . . . the daily rates were constantly getting higher and higher, and still that made no difference to his life, to his bad tobacco, to his radish or stinky cheese. And ondine also came to this peculiar realization and wrote to his boss to ask why on earth that was—she wrote to his boss, yes, but to his old boss, the one out there on the avenue, where jeannine had become a woman and gone to live in germany with a spiked helmet—and had word from brussels that oscarke had only been there for a few hours, and that they *would pay him for those hours, and that they were still a pair of clogs of his there, and Please, when was he coming back?*

She was surprised, a little annoyed even, because he'd worked for a few hours for nothing and had left a pair of good clogs behind . . . and half amused, even half proud, because oscarke had found another job in brussels all by himself and still hadn't mentioned it—as if it wasn't worth it.

BUOY COME ADRIFT

While I'm sitting here all alone and still haven't decided what to do—tippetotje writes—I've knocked together another story for you:

I'm a trader and I've got problems . . . no, don't shrug your shoulders and say to yourself that you've got problems too: I know, but as a trader I've had to listen for years to other people's problems: the customer is king—show the same accommodating attitude to me for once and listen, if only out of politeness: I'm in a jam, I sometimes do deals that, while they aren't exactly forbidden, aren't really allowed either—you know what I mean, times are hard and only the smartest people can keep their heads above water—only the smartest people can scrape fortunes together, and those who are less smart don't get a chance—life is complicated . . . I can't explain it all very well, but light and shadow, for example, they intermingle so much that eventually you can't tell one from the other—but there always remains some Something you believe in: people need that, in the midst of all this something has to stand out like a beacon . . . not so much for you to hold on to, but to help us check now and again how far we've drifted off course—the flag, for instance . . . now that's something you can really go to town with—hence my admiration for men with decorations: it really affects me, those medals remind me immediately of the flag, flapping above the chaos—I remember the battlefields where so much blood was spilt . . . it doesn't matter that there was absolutely no reason to spill that blood, but it's the image that I find uplifting: the moment after the victory, for example—victory over whom or what, well, that's all immaterial: it's really the victory over oneself, the flag that's borne back from the battlefields, a little tattered, smeared with blood . . . the national anthem rings out, the monument is unveiled, the medals are presented—I'm working myself up into ecstasy, I'm mixing everything up . . . yet after all, it's the only thing we have left, the only thing left that obviously (or should I say "apparently"?) has any value—no, for god's sake don't start relieving yourself in the corners of the altar or the hearth . . . don't make me see that the beacon, that flag at their feet, is starting to rot: in the midst of my deals that aren't exactly forbidden but aren't allowed either (you know how it is), I really need such a thing—and now from this line of honorable men

388

alexander damat came towards me : three rows of decorations were pinned to his chest, he was bolt upright, his hair was starting to gray slightly at the temples—it made a big impression, in his presence I felt how far I'd already strayed: I confessed all that to him, I confessed my fear that all those deals of mine might come to light—yet he was able to console me: he belonged to the french deuxième bureau, and was in touch with the american intelligence services, he had great influence and could easily talk round the police and if necessary the courts—oh, what a relief: the nation paraded past, the "attack" rang out, the flag dipped for a moment: and all to help a woman out of trouble after she'd strayed too far—it was just that a few palms needed greasing here and there, the altar and the hearth, the fatherland and the flag too . . . it's quite a difficult thing, you know, it needs lubricating to make it run as well as you want—colonel damat asked me 1st for so much, then so much more—he telephoned me from london and urgently needed 3,000 francs: by now I'd given him a cool 1,000,000 pounds all told—so I hung up the receiver and left the phone box . . . and who should come along, on the other side of the street, but colonel damat, also out of a phone box!—so the graying hair that I loved so much was a sham . . . as were the rows of decorations, that waving flag, that beacon . . . everything fell apart around me, I cried a little, and called in the police—although I distrust Them too . . . at the end of the day, is there anything left one can trust?—an inspector collars him, and when he's brought face to face with me he gives me an affectionate tap on the cheek—he says: come on sweetie, don't worry . . . unfortunately it was my job to cheat you out of your money—and it's true, I don't blame him: it's my job too to cheat people out of their money . . . after all, the burning question for everyone is: how is other people's money, sitting in their pockets, to be transferred to my own?—but things have become bleak for me, now the beacon too is bobbing away over the water, now the threadbare flag has also become a business—there seems to be no end to my troubles: I'll never be able to calculate how far I'll sink in future.

HALF A FRANC

And ondine wondered: where could he be working? A tingling sensation went through her, because there was again something to which she could devote her energies, and she went and stood at the station to find out what men oscarke came home with—and in the group she saw the husband of . . . liza, by god! Lisping liza, from the days in termuren, when they were kids, when she was still so crazy about boys that she sat down and peed in the street: does she still live in termuren, then? and oh how fast life is going! And where were the days when she was queen of termuren, a queen in clogs who was still called "madame" by everyone. The

world endured and the world passed away, and people changed without their real-
izing it: she was amazed: she'd almost lost sight of the great aim in her life, perhaps
because neither her eyes nor her brain were big enough to comprehend the purpose
of an entire life—and so instead of that one great purpose, she'd always found a
little daily purpose, and had pursued it, and perhaps all those little purposes added
up After All to a life's purpose, in the end? She saw oscarke turn into factory
street, and liza's husband instead take labor street, and she followed him: do you
remember me? she asked. Of course he remembered her: she was ondine, vapeur's
daughter, who was married to oscarke. And are you still living in termuren? she
asked. Yes, I've been back for about 2 weeks. And although the reply made her
laugh, it turned out afterwards to be something staggering: we lived all that time
in the rooms above the café of the 1st grimy houses, he said . . . you know, where
you used to live, and ran the café! Ondine shook her head in astonishment at such
a strange coincidence, liza coming to live where she had lived, and their never
meeting each other—but she had no time to let this sink in completely, there was
something else that appalled her: he had said "café," the café of the 1st grimy houses,
when it had always been the pub of the 1st grimy houses. I don't suppose you know
where oscarke works? she asked. Yes, I know, he replied . . . in brussels! Well, she
knew that herself, but where *in brussels? He didn't know, he thought and thought,*
he frowned and walked along with his chin jutting pensively into the evening sky.
Did you ever know? asked ondine. No, he replied. Then you won't be able to
remember, idiot! she said, and would have liked to box his stupid ears. Oh, woman
. . . he was thinking of someone who would probably know, what's-his-name, look,
he was coming from the station over there! And so ondine learned that oscarke
worked on boulevard montbernard—she went back home and was annoyed with
the men for having called her "woman" instead of "madame ondine." And the next
day she wrote a letter to boulevard montbernard, and received a reply saying that
oscarke earned 4 francs but that from next week on, in accordance with the this-
and-that act, he would be getting a half-a-franc raise. 4 francs, that was right . . .
so he gave her his wages as he received them—very low wages, because he had of
course started work without asking how much he would be earning, and without
ever asking for a raise. And she was curious to know how he was going to tell her
next week that he had earned 50 centimes more . . . perhaps he wouldn't say any-
thing at all, handing over his wage, and leaving her to smell out the difference.

But oscarke had heard about the raise too, it had been reported in Justice and
Freedom as yet another victory for the workers . . . and at the beginning it had left
him indifferent: 50 centimes more or less with that pittance that he handed over to
ondine, no one would notice it—whether he was a sculptor who earned nothing or
an armband policeman who confiscated people's packages, or a laborer in the park
earning 2 francs a day, or a stonemason in brussels earning 4 francs an hour, things
remained the same at home: dirty, cracked cups, children with heads full of lice, a

broken stove, and a bed that was a mess. A dirty unmade mess that one crawled into with a sheet rolled up here and a blanket there. And as he sat holding Justice and Freedom, the idea emerged of keeping those 50 centimes: for ondine it would only be a drop in the ocean that flowed through her fingers, and for him it would be . . . no, he couldn't immediately comprehend what it would mean to him, he had to work it out first: it would come to 30 francs a week. Such a pile of money overwhelmed him, it even struck him as Too Much—but if he withheld only half, she would notice, and so he was obliged to keep the whole thirty francs, and take the streetcar to the boulevard, and buy ham and eggs and tobacco . . . good tobacco . . . and a pint. And warmth radiated right through him, from the inside out—the warmth of the world, of the universe, mingled with his own warmth—he sat silent and happy listening to the song: 50 centimes! And he came to the conclusion that a person doesn't need that much in life: he swept away the dirt made by the others as they chiseled, and slept with ondine (with his back to her, because of his breath) instead of with jeannine, and there were a few other things besides—and yet he was happy.

NOVEL OF THE FUTURE

Mr brys dreamt that the man of the future grabbed him, as one grabs an earthworm, to try and determine what kind of creature he was. And you shake your head skeptically: I think you were wrong about your dream, mr brys! The creature that grabbed you is the man who controls the situation at the moment . . . the creature that tries, watch in hand, to measure our dreams, who's going to lock us up in prisons, who's going to step on us as one steps on an insect. And yet, mr brys, we must keep up our courage . . . we must remain convinced that We are the real masters, and that the others are inferior creatures—we've always talked about humanity, of respecting each other's ideas, of allowing everyone freedom; but now it has reached the point where they've gained the power to say: these individuals are not like we are, and so they must disappear. And yet it's us, mr brys, who must view them as barbarians, who must keep them at arm's length with a contemptuous smile—we must be cunning where necessary . . . we must be sly when nothing but slyness will help . . . and bare our teeth when people are out to kill us. A typical case, mr brys, is that of kramiek, who drops in now and then to see me with some new plan or other for an impossible novel . . . or let's say, with the kind of novel that's always been possible: the image of the world to come, or the society to come, seen in the light of science: new discoveries, progress, technology, advertising, and the growing of embryos in bottles. It's interesting, exciting, scientific, says kramiek. Development, progress, encouraging statistics, and especially the soothing feeling that this world of technology will still exist in the year Such-and-such, and we shall all be exactly the same . . . just a little more complex, a little faster, a little more machine-like: bravo, ha ha!

And kramiek rubs his hands and thinks that's the best story, the most representative story I could tell. But much more representative is kramiek's own case: the novel, the tragedy of kramiek, which is the tragedy of everyone like him: the mechanical, scientific, test-tube spawned, stupid, quick, and punctilious barbarians. So kramiek is the desired prototype, the numbered copy of a modern world of hygiene, sodium lighting, white-tiled swimming pools, and fascism. And we, mr brys, who long for a bit of beauty, for some truth, some peace, some freedom . . . who still know what it is to be moved, who can still rejoice at a pure thought and a beautiful image (a mere nothing), can weep at something that's lost, and be saddened by all the scientific samples in test tubes . . . one day soon we, mr brys, will be grabbed by kramiek and his millions of clones as one grabs an earthworm, and squashed underfoot as something inferior. The man of the future, ha! You make me laugh bitterly, mr brys . . . the man of the future is this same stupid, scientific, and fascist creature—and we are the worms who have stayed human, wrongheaded poets and dreamers, pitiable thinkers and philosophers: the redundant and the harmful.

AIMLESS HAPPINESS

And, well, oscarke came home and ondine looked at his wages and said: where's the 50-centime rise? It was like a slap in the face . . . no, it was more than that: it was as if that little bit of happiness had been torn out of his body, out of his soul, with a pair of pincers: he was being operated on, but without anesthetic. If you're not in league with the devil, they can pull my head off my shoulders! he said. And he flew into a rage—he would have preferred to say nothing and sit in a corner . . . and he fully intended to, but as he sat down, the pain at his lost happiness yanked him upright again. That bit of extra food and that tobacco and that pint . . . everything that other people took for granted, like arms and legs and a prick, didn't he deserve it too? No, no, it wasn't to Be: I'm getting out, he said, I'm going to drown myself—and aware that he still had all his wages in his hand, he left . . . but he walked past judith without daring to look at her . . . because if he had done that, he would have stayed—he was already sorry, wanted to turn back and ask . . . or say . . . But he walked on because she wouldn't have understood him anyway. He went into the café where rosa lived, and blew the 50 centime rise, the 30 francs that was to have been his happiness, on drink—and once drunk he was again strange, different, just like his father: a little shit who leaned up close to the daughter and immediately started groping her under her skirts—a little shit and a troublemaker, because at the bar was a plainclothes policeman, one of the most wretched, dissolute people you could find, whose nickname was "the pimple"—and the pimple was looking for trouble, and oscarke was looking for trouble, and soon they were in a fight: he, little oscarke, against the big pimple of a policeman. People had to pull the pimple off him, or he would have squeezed oscarke to death. Yet oscar pushed rosa away when she tried to clean the blood off him and kiss him, and picked a fight with her too: monument! he cried . . . fountain! and no one understood what he meant. Covered in blood he wound up in jail, and called the police bastards: you stand at the bar and pick fights and then throw us in jail! . . . and he insulted the town council on which libertines and clericals had sat and cheated the working man: and now there were socialists on it, who also Help to cheat the working man—and he said that everyone who secured a top post was a fucking idiot, a sneaky bastard, an ass-kisser: here you don't need people who know what's to be done, you need rags you can wipe your feet on. He raved in the courtyard of the town hall while three policemen held him and hit him in the face—but he wouldn't admit defeat, he didn't notice the blows, he didn't feel the blood and the foam streaming from his mouth together with the truths he was bawling out. Yes, they were truths—it was a tiny kind of truth, truth seen from only one side, but truth nevertheless. In the morning he was let out of jail and he didn't dare look anyone in the face, he didn't dare go home, so he just went to brussels, without eating, groggy from the blows, and the whole of his coat covered in blood—the yard sent him to place malou, where a monument was being erected. They were putting up one monument after another: it was as if they wanted to put up a monument in every street, by every house—for the fallen heroes, airmen, artillerymen, and infantrymen, for gabrielle petit and miss edith cavell, for the invalids and the deported—while the invalids and the deported had as much as possible docked from their pensions . . . perhaps to pay for those monuments. There were riots almost every day, and demonstrations, and strikes—yes, the strikes were increasing day by day . . . and the stonemasons, the monumental masons had also gone on strike, the last general strike to secure the eight-hour day and also for something special, oh, a stupid incident, a mason who'd been sitting carving on top of a stone woman and fell off, and now got no compensation or pension. But oscarke who'd sat blind drunk in the courtyard of the town hall and screamed and hadn't felt the blows raining down on him, he didn't dare to join the strike: when drunk he was a troublemaker, but sober he was a little coward: he went on cleaning away the dust around the monument, and when there was no more carving going on, there was no more dust for him to sweep up, so he started carving himself. He carved letters: homage to our heroes . . . and he also carved the face of a hero—he who was a coward carved the face of a hero—and it was so beautiful, he himself went pale when he looked at it. Behind his back a gentleman stood nodding in approval—oscarke had never seen the gentleman: what do you think of it? he asked, like a great artist might have asked some passerby, some insignificant character, without paying much attention. And that gentleman . . .

was the boss himself, the great owner of the stone-yard on boulevard montbernard, whom oscar had never seen. He got the plans and looked at the hero on paper, and then at the hero in stone and they were identical: in the future you can do that permanently, said the boss. Oh, and oscarke couldn't contain himself, he wanted to be at home, he wanted to be somewhere else, to tell them what the big boss had said about him—and so he rushed to the train, and arrived back there, and . . . well, he suddenly remembered what it was like at home. He walked around aimlessly, full of great happiness at henceforward being allowed to carve permanently—and full of restlessness, full of doubt as to whether he was always going to be so wonderfully successful . . . and also full of resentment, fear, the gnawing of his conscience, about home . . . home for christ's sake, with ondine.

THE COLD LITTLE STOVE

Oscarke walked down a few streets, to malvine's place, but walked straight past . . . he walked straight past everything, and finally he actually went to chapel road, to the 4 villas where his mother lived—his old mother welcomed him in tears, kissed and pampered him . . . it was still the same bare house as when he'd left, and in his old room, which was empty and chilly and dead, he fitted out a studio for himself as best he could. Yes, he sat there in the evening and looked out over the park that he'd helped lay out, and where 4 stone female figures had been placed around the pond by a sculptor from brussels—yes, while local stonemasons like himself had to go and work in brussels. And he was sorry not to have shouted That too in the courtyard of the town hall: you let your own artists starve and dig out a pond for 2 francs a day, and bring in lice from outside, look, to put 4 ridiculous statues round the pond: just look at that winter up there, that woman with her bundles of branches, but also with a dress that hangs open and reveals her shoulders—her shoulders, but not her breasts, because that would have been too indecent, and one must not offend the children's nannies who came walking round the park. Is that really a winter? And he thought of how he would have done a winter: a shivering jeannine, who had fled to germany, and was perhaps being beaten by her spiked helmet, who was enduring hunger and misery and had to beg and spoke german in a garret in berlin or a slum neighborhood in hamburg—he would have modeled her, shivering, naked, and cold, under a blanket that she wrapped round herself. And in that empty room he went on dreaming, and supposedly arranging a studio for himself—to dream up his statues but not to give his dreams shape . . . because what he imagined he would never have been able to achieve anyway. He made himself a studio . . . but apart from that continued traveling up and down to brussels: he gave his wages to his mother, and his mother gave him twenty francs pocket money, out of which he had to pay his for his season ticket and the streetcar and his extra food, and then with what was left he could buy himself tobacco—it was just the same at his mother's as it had been at ondine's—and his mother also wrote to his boss, to ask he if could be given a raise. Oh, it was all the same—and all the theories and problems he thought up, regarding people and society and the world and god . . . that a child was born, but that there was a road mapped out above the child's head that it had to travel—whether it stayed with its mother or married an ondine or fled with a jeannine to the ends of the earth . . . He resolved never again as long as he lived to love another human being . . .and, anyway, whom had he ever really loved? Love began with oneself . . . only if one had an excess of love could one give any away, just like it was only when a stove was fully warm that it could start giving off heat . . . but could he, cold little stove of an oscarke, radiate any warmth?

A CHIP OFF THE OLD BLOCK

But one evening when oscarke emerged from the station as usual, and was about to head automatically to chapel road, there were three girls standing in the station entrance—three devastated and careworn children—one was bent double while saliva ran out of her mouth, which hung open . . . the other, who was about twelve, had hard, mischievous eyes . . . and the eldest, judith, had a pale, puffy face with glasses. Hello, daddy, said judith. And he looked at his brood. What are you doing standing here? he asked. Waiting for you, said judith . . . mother said that you were coming home today, that your great work in brussels was finished. It's not true, said mariette . . . our mother can lie so well she believes it herself. And little marie-louise laughed with her crazy, ridiculous laugh. He went with the children, and he bought them a doll . . . one doll to share between the three of them, and with their arguing and fighting over the doll it was broken even before they got home: give it to marie-louise! said oscarke. But mariette didn't want to: she smashed the doll to pieces, kicked it. Give it! said oscarke. And she only gave it after she had torn it open so that the sawdust ran out of it: she cried and swore at the same time. Are you swearing? asked oscarke threateningly . . . he got worked up, became furious because he was frightened to death: a girl of twelve who said "fucking hell," what would become of her?—she would . . . no, he couldn't imagine what would become of such a girl. And he wanted to hit and kick her, to kick it out of her: did you swear just then? he repeated. Oh, kiss my ass! said mariette. And his rage, his fear, and whatever else it may have been was suddenly dispelled by that imperative: he didn't know what to do about It—for a simple curse he could have slapped her . . . but now, what was he supposed to do? . . . When he got home it was sweet as could be: is that you oscarke? asked ondine—looking at him with the smile she'd had before she was even twenty. They sat by the stove all evening, and she talked and talked: she felt faith, hope, love, and remorse—and he told her about brussels, about being able to carve for himself: and one day I'll

395

carve your head in stone! he said. Although he wondered how he was supposed to do that now that she'd started wearing glasses—and ondine smiled too, replying that it shouldn't be a head but just a big long neck that they could saw pieces off. This immediately killed their reawakening love, no, not the love they'd known in their crazy youth . . . but a love between mature people who've been through so much poverty, and already have a litter of kids. But the upshot was that ondine got pregnant again, with her glasses and her hernia.

MARCH WINDS

A letter from you to tippetotje: it's lonely on chapel road, tippetotje, just as your studio must be lonely now that your baron has died . . . it's lonely here on chapel road in these march days, when the tender blossom of the approaching spring is already being snapped off by snow and hail and spring storms. March is a strange month, tippetotje . . . it's the month I was born in, and it gave me something of its capriciousness, its restlessness and instability—it's the month that presages spring, a new spring and a new sound, but that nips the life out of the first blossoms with ice and snow. It's the time of march winds—and as you may remember (if you remember anything about termuren), the people of chapel road talk incorrectly of march "swings" instead of winds. And I assume they're referring to the fact that the month keeps swinging first this way then that. That's the kind of month I was born in, tippetotje, swinging first this way then that—oh, my whole life has been 1 march swing, swinging first this way then that . . . 1 march swing, full of expectancy about something that was always just about to happen, but never materialized: the spring, the earthly paradise, happiness, the golden age . . . I expected them, with my capricious nature, and then with my bitterness snapped off the first blossoms. And so I sit here lonely in this month of march and am writing you a letter because I've nothing else at all to write about—my days used to be full of writing . . . I wrote so much that I forgot about you, it escaped my notice when you hooked yourself a baron. Early in the morning the sun came from the north, and towards evening the sun came from the west, the shadows lengthened, and finally the lights had to go on, and I would sit there and write. And now, tippetotje, I stop and look round for the result of all that writing. And there is no result. The only change is that the paper that lay blank on my left now lies on my right covered in dead letters, the corpses of words . . . full of thoughts that are not My thoughts, or which I didn't intend to write down. And I don't know how it happened—I sat there and wrote, and whenever I saw the result afterwards I got upset, flew into a rage, stamped my feet and my eyes filled with tears: That's not what I meant to say! I would cry out. And to myself I would say: that surely wasn't what I dreamt in my loneliest, bitterest, most painful hours! Surely it was something quite different that I wanted to say! Why on earth is that? And the being hidden deep inside me, the being that's really me, stamped its feet too and its eyes filled with tears too—and lamp in hand I'd like to climb up into those uninhabited attics, descend into those abandoned cellars, enter those never-visited rooms deep inside myself, would like to return with arms piled high with treasures to be poured out over the blank pristine pages. But as I write, I lose everything that I retrieved from the depths and heights of my Self—and if, as I'm writing, I try to return to those rooms in my thoughts, I find all the doors shut. I should have written in a completely different way, tippetotje—and now, now it's almost too late: now I've grown sick of writing, and the march wind of writing has changed . . . now I must tell you that I'm written out, that I don't have a single thing left to say. Oh, how could that happen, tippetotje? I've nothing more to say, and I haven't said anything yet: can you make sense of that? I sit here lonely, whimsical, full of march winds . . . and I look up and realize that you've left me. I'll close my letter, just as the rooms inside of me have always been closed.

THE GATE CLOSES

One afternoon cross-eyed malvine came round, supposedly for the rent, but really to see where on earth oscarke had got to—and an argument started, the two women got into a real catfight, so that leopold sang outside: my auntie malvine is a murderess. He thought that she had to be a relation, since he saw his father on his way to see her so often. She was forthright and mischievous, that malvine—ondine, though, was the champion of making accusations and thinking up vile ideas . . . rolling her eyes and changing her voice, speaking with a guttural sound in her throat, and acting as if the whole world was hanging on her every word. But cross-eyed malvine paid no heed to all her words . . . a word gets spoken, reverberates a bit, and then falls back into the great void: a word is just wind. And she didn't like wind, so she shot straight forward and gave ondine a bang on the head: ondine's glasses flew off, and she collapsed in shock—she tumbled into the chair, first pulling over little marie-louise with her on the way. But her feelings were very powerful! She who had done this and that in life . . . was it all to end with her coming to blows with some insignificant cross-eyed bitch? And for what? For oscarke? Ondine slowly stood up, she was an irresistible force rising up, she was god descending from mount sinai to smash the stone tablets—and with her belly already swelling slightly, with her hernia and her glasses, with her hair hanging down in strands and going gray here and there, she went up to cross-eyed malvine: go away, she said, and because cross-eyed malvine couldn't understand that god had descended into ondine, ondine put her hands around malvine's neck: in the same flat voice in which she'd said "go away," she now said "I'll kill you." She wasn't furious, she didn't rant and rave—no, a sea of indifference surrounded her . . . her and cross-eyed malvine, who was firmly in her grip. The children howled, and judith shouting in the street without really shouting anything in particular, drawing people to their front door: they came in and extricated cross-eyed malvine from ondine's grasp. And now one might have thought that there would be a reaction from ondine . . . but no, she had no time for it all to sink in, or perhaps she had just a little more substance than other people, and so was . . . Oh, who knows what she was?—but now that she'd got excited (excited, yet still feeling her god-like indifference), she was capable of averting fate, of putting destiny to flight, of unleashing a revolution. So she washed and combed her hair, put on stockings, and paid a call on norbert derenancourt in that old-fashioned, by now rather dilapidated mansion—it had a great many windows and a gate, but they were old windows and it was a gate gnawed at by decay. She rang the bell and took up her position in the shadowy hall . . . it stank, as is usual in an old, empty house . . . but to her surprise a hushed shadow came to say that mr derenancourt would see her now if she wished. It was the first time that she'd ever been admitted to the inner rooms of a posh mansion, and there she found norbert, squatting in a little nook where it was dirty and grubby, and where an electric lamp was burning all day long: in that electric light he looked very aged, very changed: there were bags under his eyes, and his thin hands with their slightly trembling fingers lay expectantly on the desk. Here I stand! she said. And he sniggered briefly, surveying her. Here I sit! he said. And she nodded, she pulled up a chair and sat down, resting an arm on his desk—they understood each other, she thought: we're two of a kind. And what she thought, he put into words—but after that they said nothing. At least get me some money! she said after a long period of silence. Oh, money, he replied . . . you're ondine, and you happen to have no money, but if you were to have money, you'd still be ondine: with glasses and gray hair, with a swelling belly and with a hernia. How do you know I've got a hernia? she asked. Oh, I'm just assuming that, because I've got a hernia too. The gate closed behind her again, and she realized that she . . . oh, that she'd lost sight of her main objective again! She hadn't come to ask about his assumption that she had a hernia . . . and not about his theories that an ondine with money would be the same as an ondine without money . . . but to say that he should have provided her with that money himself, regardless—money and work—respect, happiness, and fame—immortality, heaven, and earth—and more besides. That's what he should have provided her with: everything she had never known in life.

DARK ROOM

You write about norbert derenancourt's dark room, says tolfpoets . . . so may I also offer you a story, as all the others have done?:

in all of our hearts there is a dark room, an unused niche where there's nothing but some gossamer-thin spiders' webs, stretching from corner to corner—once I didn't know that such a room existed, yes, in fact I knew very little about what lives and roots about in the dark inside man, hidden and unknown—I've no need to be ashamed of that, since most people around me are not much wiser, and know nothing of the existence of this dark room either: I now wonder whether man isn't a house, most of whose rooms are still unentered—one doesn't need to read learned or profound literature, just the daily papers (those polyps that extend their tentacles towards everything that smacks of the unusual) because everyday in their columns they deal with the door of a room that's never been entered—yesterday I read something of the kind, and today the papers came up with something almost identical, but which happened in a quite different part of the world—but let me begin with the story of the sisters irma and estelle, who were born in about 1870: estelle was never seen again after the 1st world war, and when there were visitors (but how often did someone visit?) irma would tell them that her sister had become shy of people and didn't like to be disturbed—such a thing is possible: it may be strange, but it is possible—but a few days ago Irma, by now 87, had an unfortunate fall on the stairs, with the result that she died from her injuries—relatives, however, searching the now-empty house, found a small area in the basement where the 82-year-old Estelle was living: she'd become 'shy of people' when she was 44, and now she was discovered in the cellar aged 82: she was dressed only in a pullover, but was covered with all kinds of vermin—one is never naked: either one wears clothing or all kinds of vermin come and cover us—she lived in the cellar for almost forty years, with nothing but that pullover and a chair—it's strange, but have you noticed how so many rather odd stories and also rather odd surrealist paintings have chairs in them? A chair on which one sits for forty years, and has long conversations with oneself: it's a pity estelle didn't keep a diary, to record her conversations with herself—and may I point out a secondary circumstance? Namely that the rest of the house was well-furnished and maintained, and also that irma was universally regarded as very distinguished—so I can't help thinking about Man himself: man is a fairly large house, well furnished and maintained, and universally regarded as very distinguished, but with a dark room somewhere, where someone is sitting in a chair for forty years and having strange conversations with oneself—and look, I'd no sooner cut that story out of the papers than they were there again the next day!—a strange noise was heard in the residence of the 84-year-old miss louise tucker (and just compare the age of miss tucker with that of miss irma), who attracted attention by throwing bottles and gold coins out of her window into the garden: on forcing entry into the house, the authorities found not only the old lady, but also a man in a the corner who tried to hide his nakedness behind a beard a meter long—and now compare this man, who wore a garment of hair, with the woman who wore a garment of vermin!—but unlike the elegant bourgeois house in the first story, this place was disgustingly filthy: the dirty curtains hung in tatters, while all kinds of birds fluttered round the darkened rooms—but the rest is completely identical: neighbors testified that a young man had once lived in this house, but had vanished without a trace after leaving school: no one ever saw him again—so the man had been living for 25 years in the dark rooms of that house, naked, with a beard that had grown a meter long, and living among all kinds of birds that twittered around—and speaking of those birds, they concluded the report with the news that the birds were placed in the care of the society for animal welfare—but that's not what I'm getting at: I know very well that the papers have to see things in this light: putting out a happy ending to satisfy its readers, a happy ending in which miss tucker and the man with the beard are taken to the hospital, and the birds are given a good home by the society for animal welfare—but I'm not talking about the birds, I'm talking about the room itself: about that dark, empty room in which we squat for 30 or 40 years, and have lonely conversations with ourselves . . . in which we sit on a chair, and nothing happens except that our beard grows: I've cut out both these articles, but I bet if I ask you about them, you won't know the answer either.

MUSSELS AND CHIPS

She went on, did ondine . . . she called on glemmasson, who had become the richest man in town—he, together with his sister from the comptoir et credit bank, together with this sister's husband, who had become the principal owner of the filature spinning mill, and who was also mayor. The trio controlled the town, they formed as it were a gang that had occupied the strategic points and had a small army of police at its disposal: he, fat glemmasson, had two castles and a wife in each castle . . . he owned stables and luxury coaches, and most important of all: he had a jester again, a very amusing one. They went into a restaurant opposite the town hall and from there rang all the mayors in the surrounding districts to say that the governor wanted a word with them—and so all the mayors arrived there at the town hall, one in an old farmer's trap, one in a dressed-up ex-army car, and even one on a bike, panting and sweating. Mr glemmasson had a wonderful time, but never laughed. His gray lips leered as he imagined them standing gaping at each other—and when they came out again, indignant, waving their hands around and crawling furiously back into their farmer's traps, then he smiled his chilly smile—chilly and with downcast eyes, as though to keep all these inferior people from staring at his smile. But when he looked up and noticed that the owner of the restaurant was looking down at him, his pleasure was completely punctured. He got up and his jester promised at once: we'll play the same joke on that guy. And they went to another restaurant, and from there telephoned to place an immediate order for chips and mussels for fifty people for a general meeting of the church board at 7 tomorrow evening. And that evening, at 7 on the dot, he went into the restaurant with his jester. His car waited outside, with his uniformed chauffeur at the wheel. But as the door closed behind them, the owner went deathly pale and had to grab hold of the nearest table, particularly when he looked up at the clock. It's 7 o'clock, said fat glemmasson, also looking at the clock. And the jester asked if he could have a plate of mussels and chips. But mr glemmasson! stammered the patron . . . mussels and chips for fifty people, do you realize what that means to me? But the jester whispered something in his master's ear, got into the car and drove to the outskirts of the town where there were nothing but wooden huts and emergency shanties—only scum lived there, thieves and beggars, drunks and womanizers . . . they huddled together there, and the high-class people in town shunned the mangy place with the shanties—each shanty had a sign saying "Emergency dwelling Albert I, number such-and-such," creating the impression that the germans had set fire to lots of houses, but that the king of the belgians had put houses up to help his people, for the time being . . . just for the time being, till things improved, and they were all given brick houses—but the war had been over for some time by now, and the wooden huts were still there, decaying, developing cracks you could put your hand through, and clouds of vermin infested them. Only the rabble remained there, only thieves and murderers could thrive there, those who'd come from the reformatory and those ready for the madhouse. That was where mr glemmasson's jester drove too, and he selected the choicest specimens, 50 of them, to eat mussels and chips in a chic restaurant. For christ's sake they almost died with excitement, they swore and punched each other in the face to get there first, to be one of those 50 chosen ones—they came, and the cloud of vermin hung around all their heads like halos: lice were dropping off them, and everything they touched went black: they arrived in the restaurant then and knocked over tables and chairs, broke crockery, and slipped ashtrays into their pockets. They stumbled round and roared at each other, and shouted at glemmasson: hey, fatso, are we turning your stomach?—but tipped their caps and looked sheepish if you stared at any one of them individually.

EMPTY BOTTLE

Tippetotje's reply: here among the polished furniture that my baron left me, there's a cupboard that I have christened "the bar"—because in the late evening I'm fond of hunting for a bottle in it and pouring myself a large glassful. And at the bottom of that cupboard lie the many empty bottles, boon my friend . . . they lie there with the openings of their decorked necks pointing towards me: they have been emptied, when in lonely nocturnal hours they have provided a liquid anaesthetic, oblivion, and a treacherous rose-tinted view of things: they are empty, and they now have only the last remnants of some scent, to remind me of what they were. And so that's what you are too, boon my friend . . . you're an emptied bottle that has poured out its contents, and has finally found its way to the bottom of the cupboard that I have dubbed "the bar." But that's not the question: the question, from your point of view, is *why* you're an emptied bottle—but the question from my point of view is, who filled you in the first place? Not me, though I've been close to you all my life, ever since childhood, since my childhood when I was poor and hungry, told polpoets fairy stories to get a piece of his sandwich . . . To make polpoets happy with my fairy tale, and watch him bare his 2 rotten teeth in a grin. And first I had to borrow that fairy tale from you . . . with you the fairy tales bloomed like flowers in a garden, and all I had to do was come and pick them, armfuls of them, without even having to thank you—because it seemed to be your vocation, just as it's the vocation of the natural spring to flow until it runs dry. First you were a garden in which flowers were there for the picking . . . first you were a brand-new bottle, still full to the brim, with a gold collar round your neck. But now you've written and written, and you say . . . you've let the bottle empty, you say. But I wonder who you've poured the content out for? Surely not for me, surely not for poor thirsty tippetotje: day after day I've read what you've written, and day after day I've put it aside, and said to myself: no, it's still not from that marvelous bottle with the gold collar, he's keeping that back for later—oh, and do you know what that means, boon my friend, "for later"?—your contents always made me tremble with excitement, with constant expectancy, and whenever you sent me one of your books I shook my head, and thought: still not the real thing. And now . . . now you write to tell me that the bottle has emptied. And I get furious, stamp my feet on the waxed parquet of my studio, I kick the grand piano, I kick everything that my dear late baron left me, I scream . . . I weep. You've run dry, and you haven't poured out anything for me—you've said all you have to say, and I've heard nothing. You've emptied like a bottle, you tell me, and I find that it was the wrong bottle: that's why I'm crying, boon my friend . . . and at my wit's end I kick the polished item of furniture I have named "the bar"—and out rolls an empty bottle, and breaks.

THE OTHER GLEMMASSON

That was glemmasson—but not all of him. There was of course another glemmasson whom no one ever got to see, except for his jester perhaps: a glemmasson who couldn't get out of bed in the morning and cursed when he was woken: because what was the point of living, or what was the point of his being woken up? And as he crawled to a sitting position in bed, he had to begin by considering whether there was anything happening on that day that was worth leaving the bedroom for—and he thought of his castle here and his castle there, of a horse, a car, a woman . . . always of some treat that would make him feel like starting life anew that day. And if there was nothing new, god help his jester! Shall I summon the king to your bedside in his shirttails? asked the jester. Yes, said fat glemmasson. But of course the jester couldn't, he fetched someone called king and got him to enter the bedroom in his shirttails. Oh you idiot, said glemmasson. And at long last he crawled out of bed, gasping and groaning and with a head hurting so much he'd have liked to put under the wheel of one of his cars. And then ondine arrived: madame ondine! the jester announced her solemnly —but he quickly closed the door and mimicked her, with her pregnant tummy and her glasses: she's an ugly one, he said. Show her in anyway, said fat glemmasson, she was my sweetheart once for a while . . . oh, by saint anthony and his flute, what a long time ago that was! Ondine came in and pleaded her case: he needn't trot out any philosophy like norbert, because she had no intention of being put off—and meanwhile glemmasson sat nodding very slowly and with his eyes shut. Yes, yes, he said at five-minute intervals . . . since she prattled and prattled and he couldn't possibly keep up with her. But . . . he said suddenly, but . . . that's all your own fault! My fault, how do you mean? Because you've never ever seen or heard of in our circles . . . every thursday there's what you might call a "gala evening," and you never show up. The jester stood behind her listening . . . but suddenly she turned round: get rid of this freak from behind me. And both of then, ondine and glemmasson, suddenly recalled the time when he'd had her covered in shoe polish. She'd been young then . . . she'd been beautiful and naked and black and shiny. Come along next Thursday evening, he said—and he accompanied her to the door of the room, but not a step further: you'll find your own way out, he said. She had to go along a hallway, and at the end of it was a black lacquered table with a gold dragon painted on it, and on the black surface lay a gold coin—lay two gold coins, in fact, that were hard to see at once, certainly for her with her glasses . . . and as she went past she looked around quickly and seeing no one, took hold of a coin. Yes, she took hold of it and could have immediately dropped dead from exasperation and rage: it was stuck to the table: it was a joke. And they were all certainly watching her stupidity from some crack in a door. But still she went, the next thursday evening—there were lots of guests, the cream of the town was there: all thieves and murderers, drunks and womanizers. Yes, exactly the same as the ones from the huts—because both the highest and the lowest in the land were thieves and villains, and in between were the little people who worked and grubbed and saved and were honest, and came to nothing. For a while ondine *stood watching a pair of gamblers at a table with amusement: they're playing for matches! she thought . . . that's what the rich are like, they've got millions and they play for matches! But one of those matches represented the sum of 500 francs, and there were about 30 of them lying by that tall thin man, a pharmacist, mr van droogenbosch: he laid all his 30 matches in a pile: raise you 30! He said. And a master-mason (oh, ondine knew him, he'd been a millionaire twice, and twice a beggar, but now he had billions instead of millions, having bought things for the germans, no one knew exactly What), he raised 60. Ondine had to be pulled away from that table by glemmasson and by norbert, who'd come over to her immediately, as soon as he'd noticed her.*

SELF-DELUSION

A hastily-written new letter from tippetotje: tear up my first letter, destroy it before reading it—because no, it's not true, you're not a bottle that's been emptied by mistake or been broken . . . it's just that up till now you haven't said a word of what you really had to say. I know how that happened. Here among the polished furniture that my baron left me, everything I abhor and hate and yet can't do without, I've sat up all night and thought helplessly about it: you're written-out now about the things you shouldn't have been saying in the first place: the time is now approaching when you finally unlock the door of the room you've never dared enter; the time is now approaching when you take the cork from the bottle with the gold collar. I know how it happened, how everything went so wrong—and sometimes I could weep with rage, with regret, with god-knows-what: your very first book was uncorking the wrong bottle, and instead of starting anew from square one, you continued on down that wrong road, you soldiered on and just churned out one book after the other—and you also started writing for the daily papers, the weeklies, the monthlies (aren't there any annuals?), and it was just a stupid merry-go-round, a deadly never-ending circle. The time has now come when you suddenly come to this realization, this painful, bitter realization—and I curse with you, I race furiously with you among my polished furniture . . . sometimes I stand at the window, when I think that you must also be standing at the window, and clench my fists. And yet, and yet: I'm happy, I laugh through my tears. I thank little jesus on my bended knees, because I know that you're not hopelessly lost. I'm happy that you're crying and cursing and are full of remorse at the books you've written, and are standing at your wit's end at the window and clenching your fists: the time is now approaching when you write what you really had to say. Finish your book quickly, end it some way or other, draw a line under it and send it off—or give it to me to burn in my stove. And open the bottle, the one with the gold collar.

*At fat glemmasson's "gala" there were women who smoked cigarettes in long hold-
ers, and wore skirts that brushed the floor—but who when they sat had half their
bottoms showing. Ondine dared not look at her own dress, which was a quite
ordinary poor-person's dress, brown, because brown didn't show dust or dirt or
margarine stains: she was standing with these thoughts in her head looking at a
platform that a woman had mounted to sing a song. You sing us a song too! said
fat glemmasson. And she smiled faintly: why not, he insisted . . . why shouldn't
you show us what you can do? But sing, she wouldn't have known what she was
supposed to sing, unless it were the song of her poverty, and of her . . . lapse . . .
alongside oscarke. I've never sung in my life, she said. They drank a bit, and they
ate a bit, and as soon as she could she rushed back to the tables with the matches
on it. They were playing poker. The master-mason lent her a little, she joined in
the game and was lucky, as always happens with beginners: once she had four
aces, and then she had a . . . well, she didn't know the right name or it, because
it was an English word, but it meant that you had a full run. I'm full! she said.
They fell down laughing, and looked at her rounded belly. But she still won—she
laughed and was bright red, her eyes sparkled, and she put her glasses away to look
around the room where one of those women had started to sing a song again: if
you call that singing, I can do that too! said ondine. Right, give us a song then!
they insisted. I'll sing and I'll dance, she said. But glemmasson didn't want her to
go up there in that brown dress: there was a black silk dress lying around somewhere. She was carried off and something diaphanous was placed in her hands,
and one of the women took ondine behind a curtain. You won't be able to get into
that dress like that, they said to her . . . and they stripped her naked, down to her
truss, and then put the black dress over her head. Ondine stood there on the stage,
and a large floodlight had been set up behind her . . . she sang, she was a little
drunk and didn't really know what she was singing—she swayed her old hips a
bit . . . and perhaps, without being aware of it, she sang What she had sung when
the germans withdrew, what she had sung with her mask on at wittepennings's
gate. At first it went deathly quiet down there in the darkness, but immediately
afterwards a high-pitched, cackling woman's laugh rang out, a chair was knocked
over, and a door slammed. But that was down there in the darkness—she was
living in another world, she sang and didn't know what she was singing about, just
like she was living and didn't know what she was living for: she was alone now,
she was a queen, she was god. And she didn't realize what a dreadful trick was
being played on her: the black dress was made of extremely translucent silk, and
the floodlight behind her bored right through it: for everyone sitting below, she was
naked—she swayed a bit and they could see she was pregnant and wore a truss.
And in the darkness they screamed with laughter, they howled so loud they almost*

kicked each other over. When ondine had sung, plaintively, the final notes of her half-whispered song, and comically, dramatically bowed, people couldn't look at each other in the hurriedly relit room. That woman over there, with the high-pitched cackling laugh, was ashamed now and sat flapping a fine silk handkerchief around her face—oh, anything to hide it. Ondine had no idea what had happened to her—she was still a little drunk and in her thin fingers she was still clutching the money she'd won at poker: she had sung and won money at poker, that was her story, that was her life, and all the others who now were sitting and gaping at her were experiencing a different story, a different life. If only she really had been god and was able to control it all . . . but as it was, her little life was played out among other little lives: the money won at poker, and the money from oscarke's work as a monumental mason, plus the little that she'd earned from complaining or bragging, that money just ran through her fingers—money, days, and life . . . hers and other people's . . . and she was helpless to do anything about it.

The time soon came when she had to withdraw upstairs to the bedroom, and how many times did that make? To await the arrival of the baby. It was a boy and they called him mauriske.

LEAVES OF GRASS

Here's a story for mauriske, says johan janssens:

children, they grow up around us, they're a new, ripening harvest, and for a long time I felt at one with them, felt myself shooting up and becoming something new, something different, something more beautiful: I'm no longer exactly sure when the rift opened up between them and me—they still shoot up like the leaves of grass walt whitman sang about . . . but it happens quite independent of me, without my partaking in it—perhaps I'm getting old, perhaps I'm turning into that dead wood mentioned in the scriptures—still, these young people . . . they sometimes send a shudder of surprise through me, like the sixteen-year-old boy who hanged himself in his foster-mother's wine cellar . . . in his pockets a note was found containing the following words: there's no point—it's now being said that he didn't like his work—true, there's always a reason, just as with another twelve-year-old boy, who disappeared mysteriously: he had hidden away in the attic in an old suitcase and burst into tears when he was discovered a few days later: I'm so unhappy, he said—certainly, there's always a reason, it's said that he never dared open his heart to anyone—though the latter is only an expression, since nobody has ever yet opened his heart: the heart is a muscle whose function is to pump the blood through the arteries, and the moment one opens this muscle, one ceases to exist—but let's assume that something else is meant, what would that boy actually have said? A bagatelle, a mere nothing—only if one compares his words with those of the other boy does a perspective open up—I, the dead wood, scarcely dare look in the direction in which these leaves of grass are pointing me: I can still see the note left by the sixteen-year-old boy, I can still hear the words of the twelve-year-old, while I'm already staring at another article: thirteen-year-old boy commits suicide—just a few lines of newsprint, and circumstances are added that make it even more painful: the reporters in the news-in-brief section are so fond of that: adding details that make things so painful for me, but don't answer my questions, for instance: what on earth is going on with all those leaves of grass?—it was also reported that the police have launched an inquiry into the motives that led the thirteen-year-old boy to decide on this course of action—I doubt whether the police will look in the direction of the perspective I have outlined—but was it in the same paper that I also read something about a fifteen-year-old girl? She committed suicide by throwing herself under a train—in her case too they searched for a reason . . . but look for a moment at this difference: I wrote "she threw herself under a train," but the papers wrote "she threw herself under a train that crushed her to death"—I know that the reader is hungry for sensation, I know that similar lurid descriptions are constantly found in our newspapers—but I sometimes wonder if the world isn't becoming too cruel and too gruesome . . . I sometimes wonder if all this iron and steel, this glass and concrete, this dizzying speed, this constant fear and tension, don't weigh too heavily on the young and tender leaves of grass—I sometimes wonder if the step from the fairy tale to reality is not all too abrupt for them—because look, I've lived with them for a long time, and I know that Their fear is growing too—but perhaps I'm looking at things too gloomily, perhaps it isn't necessary at all to feel sympathy with the leaves of grass that are trodden underfoot, but rather sympathy for me, for not having a correct view of things.

MY CHILDREN

And here is also a story for mauriske, says mr brys:
I love my children: my children, lovely children—they're living more or less all over this old young world: I recognize them from their deeds, I occasionally see news of them in the papers, and then I know that they're still alive—I love them, and so I won't hear a bad word spoken against them . . . I tenderly extend a hand, while they're being snarled at by everyone, interrogated, locked up in reformatories—because it's not only *their* fault that they are as they are : it's also partly my fault, it's also partly all of our faults . . . and it's even partly the fault of the god who's worshipped by all of you, who obviously wanted it to be this way—I read about them, when they've hidden 79 marks in a garden in hartlepool . . . oh, and I even remember

once finding a gold brooch with little albert, and having buried it by the long blank wall of the labor weaving mill: it was our big Secret—but those two boys in hartlepool buried 79 pounds in a garden, and they too refused to give any explanation: the juvenile court sent them to a reformatory (the papers wrote "reform school," but I can't quite believe that distinction), and yet they gave away nothing of their Secret—work began immediately, they attacked the mystery with shovels and pickaxes, rooting around in the garden: there are still 38 pounds missing—yes, dig up the whole garden, if necessary root around in the very hearts of my children: stick the spade in, set to work with the pickax: what do two children's hearts matter, if they can help recover 38 pounds?—I heard something else: little ivette was caught red-handed trying to break open the offertory boxes of the Hospital Chapel: the young thief was handed over to the police—that's what it says in the papers, literally—she's 11, and I try to imagine the hands she was handed over to, big rough hands that a moment ago were wielding a truncheon, and to which she has now been handed over: did this young heart beat as we hear the heart of a sparrow beating in our closed fist? The Hospital Chapel of the Ordered World, all of it in capitals . . . the little eleven-year-old girl is caught, handed over, made a ward of the juvenile court—the offertory boxes will be surrounded with special care . . . oh, I know, it's not very nice of my children to hide 38 pounds in the ground, to break open the collection of Lawful Possession . . . but I wouldn't have said anything about all that, and would simply have thought of them with affection in my heart: but now circumstances oblige me to speak out—in fresnay an eleven-year-old boy disappeared, he ran away from home because he was given a severe reprimand by the state police: he has not been seen since—the state police . . . I repeat the word under my breath, I repeat it and try to imagine how it must sound to my children—perhaps I'm a little over-sensitive, but admit that it sounds rather authoritarian, cruelly beautiful german words: they wouldn't be at all out of place in the mouth of a prussian—imagine that you are "iron order" incarnate (yes, chest out, hand on the butt of your weapon), and now say rather vaingloriously: state police!—and in order to find my eleven-year-old boy, they used police dogs . . . that's the way: using dogs that have patchy muzzles and bloodshot eyes—a diviner has also been consulted, but that was probably a contribution from the parents themselves: the police arrive with bloodhounds, the parents place their hopes on a teller of fairy stories—hocus pocus—according to what this man has seen in his dreams, my eleven-year-old boy is lying half dead by a barn—johan janssens spoke about the children who commit suicide (their numbers are constantly growing), and today I am talking to you about the children being tracked down by the police—we don't choose the most cheerful subjects, I know.

A different doctor had come for mauriske's birth, because ondine didn't like the thought of calling in doctor goethals, she didn't know why—perhaps because almost no one went to him anymore . . . the boones, for example, called in a young doctor who listened to you and felt you, while doctor goethals scarcely looked at you at all: "I'll write you a prescription," he said, while you still had your hand on the doorknob—but this young doctor injected you, and gave you boxes with skulls on them, "poison, do not exceed the recommended dose," and people liked that. Tell him to come and see me too, was the message ondine sent to the boones—and he came, that young doctor, and you could easily see that he belonged to the new age. Once there was only 1 doctor for the whole town of the 2 mills, and now there was a doctor's nameplate on almost every street: there were doctors for the eyes, and doctors for the skin, and doctors for the intestines . . . they meddled in everything and they were no longer so easygoing. Take this doctor, he took off his gloves, and washed, washed again, and examined ondine and gave her an injection, and felt and tapped her all over. She became frightened precisely because a belly was no longer going to be a dark cellar: you've got a hernia, he said . . . you should have an operation—and he had to laugh and shake his head because she clung obstinately to the notion that a belly had always been a dark cellar: where do you get an idea like that from, there are x-rays, aren't there! You see . . . there was electricity and there were x-rays, and there wasn't a corner left that was dark and mysterious and wonderful: god was becoming science, as her father had predicted. She realized it all too well, and it pained her: it was growing chilly in this world, where nowadays one could only talk about miracles to children—to children, but they mustn't be like hers, like mariette or leopold. And while this young doctor, this doctor of the new age was still examining her, she thought about how they already had a radio at boone's house . . . what was that again, a radio? a new miracle of the new scientific god—and they told her they were waves in the ether, and an artificial ear that could listen in on the world (and you should have seen little louis boone, the way he twiddled the knob and waited till the current came through . . . radio brussels here, ici radio paris, norddeutscher rundfunk . . . and he wrote it all down, and it made him feel important, but he didn't show it: he was a little brat and he thought the world revolved around him), and wait till something happens with those cars, thought ondine . . . because she had seen so many times in her life that things first go up and then go downhill again, that every summer is followed by a winter . . . that today there's plenty of money coming in but that tomorrow you'll have to spend even More, that today you're very lucky but that misfortune is already at the door waiting to come in: and what were they going to do with that radio tomorrow when their misfortune arrived, what were they going to do with that artificial ear that listened in on the world? She thought this over, in front of the doctor . . . but he took little marie-louise between his knees and examined her thoroughly, he looked in her ears and mouth, he checked her teeth and counted them, he pulled back her eyelids: she must go straight into a home, he said. And when ondine asked what the great hurry was, he replied that it was in the interests of science. Science. He pronounced that word like the first christians, who muttered the name of their savior and happily went to their deaths. He brought lots of papers with him, and interrogated ondine about who her parents and grandparents were, and oscarke's parents too, and all the diseases they had had—he was cold and unfeeling, he was a machine that recorded things . . . just a needle, a pen moved by science. Ondine couldn't possibly resign herself to this, and consequently answered evasively. Nor could oscarke resign himself: he didn't want to be a guinea-pig . . . science could write down whatever it wanted, but it didn't write down what concerned oscarke himself—it couldn't make gold out of lead, or secure everyone their rightful share of happiness . . . so that one no longer had to walk from the gare du nord to boulevard montbernard, and was only allowed one stinky cheese every six days (he ate a stinky cheese in six days and on the seventh day he rested), and oh he laughed, but wasn't it sad to laugh at it? Now they were trying to calculate everything, even the incalculable—but look, if he didn't go to malvine, it would supposedly be out of love for jeannine, out of respect . . . though on the contrary he hated her (for hadn't he carved her in stone, hadn't he loved her, lusted after her, and finally possessed her? . . . yes, so that he could stand there in the pump shack beside himself with fear as he heard her discussing those things . . . well, how can one say, those things that are normal for women . . . and hadn't she—just like that and for no reason at all, without giving him a second thought—followed a spiked helmet deep into germany, where famine and misery and revolution were bound to erupt?), but he was allowing himself to be distracted, the main question was this: how were they going to record and enter on their charts and forms all the impossible and confused feelings of his and jeannine's and in fact everyone's? And also: how could you write down dreams? He was an artist, he chiseled his dreams in the stone, but how could they explain that scientifically? With the great exploded god of his imagination, yes, it was possible with that . . . but not with science: science was technology, and technology wasn't a component of the exploded god: you needed feeling, intellect, to play an unreliable game with the powers of darkness, to create a work of art—and science couldn't yet put something like that on a chart.

EVENING IN THE RAIN

Your reply to tippetotje's last letter: my sweet liar of a tippetotje, I no longer recognize you in your letters . . . did I cast off all self-deception just so that you (you of all people!) could come running with new blindfolds? With all kinds of lies, inventions and fantasies, that you yourself don't believe? And don't you wonder where I'll find the courage, the time, the gusto, and the audience, to start all over again from scratch? I'm walking in the evening rain down chapel road, which I constantly revisit, and am composing my letter to you word by word . . . I walk here in the evening rain, where I used to sit and write by the light of my desk lamp: I'd forget you then, like I forgot everyone, I'd receive letters and wouldn't answer them, I was asked things and didn't reply, people knocked at my door and I didn't open: I had no time: I'd let the wrong bottle empty. Now I'm walking here, and I see that you've all gone . . . I see that around me people have died, the people who were actually the ones I was writing for, and that others have been born who do not know me and for whom it was never my job to write: everything around me has changed, and yet has remained hopeless in exactly the same ways. I walk here and stare at things . . . the rain and the clouds, and the last streetlamp over there by the unmanned crossing . . . and I think of you, and my estranged wife, and my son who's grown away from me. And if I, hesitantly, sadly, not knowing what Else to do, were to feel like returning to my study and desk lamp there, I don't know what I could possibly have to write about—the way you search desperately for words of comfort, tippetotje, for ointment, for a bandage for this wooden leg. And if it's true that it's only the wrong bottle that emptied, who will give me the courage to uncork a new one at this late date? No, I prefer to walk around here, evening after evening, and it rains a bit, or it's windy, or there's snow or hail, or sometimes a little late sunshine—and I say hello to the people from the long terrace of the 1st grimy houses, I greet oscarke and ondine, who've grown very old by now and don't know that I'm writing a book about them—once more the wrong kind of book, once more a large glass, the last glass poured from the wrong bottle—and I stop and talk a bit about the weather and the times and people's illnesses; yes, it's pretty cold for this time of year, yes, these are strange times with all those wars and atom bombs and science in little cartons, yes so-and-so died suddenly and his wife did this and that—and I meet mr brys and polpoets and kramiek, and I talk a bit to them about art and politics and philosophy (ha, don't make me laugh, philosophy!) and I reply: yes, that poem by sander toppe isn't bad. And meanwhile I think about what I Should have written, tippetotje, but why should I inflict pain on myself again, torture myself, make myself lots and lots of new enemies? Why should I see myself banned and burned, make my wife cry, and heap infamy on my son's head? Now I can rest on my laurels a little . . . on the laurels, tippetotje, that I won by emptying the wrong bottle—so now the people from the 1st grimy houses can still see me as an honorable person and a nice man . . . now kramiek can still regard me as someone who is someone—but meanwhile I'm walking here through the evening rain, and behind the mask of my honorable face I display, for myself alone, as willem elsschot puts it, godforsaken grimness in my eye.

WITH HAMMER AND SICKLE

And just as oscarke was about to explain that to the young doctor, ondine's father, vapeur, suddenly came in: oh, and the things the three of them discussed! That is: oh the things vapeur discussed, while the young doctor nodded (oh, if only to find out what that vapeur was like, so that he could note it down afterwards on his chart), and finally what oscarke thought and felt, but couldn't express and so sat gnawing his fingernails . . . or his fingers themselves, since he had no nails left. The beginning and end of vapeur's reasoning were always those unmanned railway crossings and his invention and the railway company: now he'd finally had word from the company, telling him that his invention was theoretically acceptable but in practice would be vastly expensive. And he, vapeur, now maintained that this was obvious: there were a hundred thousand unmanned crossings and the company couldn't possibly place a ruinously costly installation at every crossing—however, looked at from the other side, it was undeniable that there were fatal accidents everyday. And he took a wallet from his inside pocket (not a leather one, but an imitation leather one . . . because that was another characteristic of the modern age: everyone had everything, but everything was imitation—and something else: people had once laughed at the alchemists for wanting to make one thing into something else, but now everyone thought it the most normal thing in the world), and from this imitation leather wallet he produced a wad of newspaper cuttings, to which he'd added dates in ink: express train surprised by car, cyclist falls under train at unmanned crossing, playing children hit by train at railway crossing. What was to be done about it? And vapeur looked at them all, and all of them looked back in silence: the railway company, he said slowly and stressing each syllable . . . should be nationalized . . . look at russia! Russia? That was a bombshell . . . was he a bolshevik then, the kind who ate his own children? But vapeur shrugged his shoulders: have a good look at me, he said . . . and I'll tell you how they used to think that the socialists would never march past the chapel of termuren—and maybe I thought so too, till the day when I saw their band marching right past it . . . and also, to start with, they said the socialists were going to murder everyone and set fire to everything . . . and now the priest tips his hat to the alderman of public works . . . who's a socialist.

NEEDLE AND MAN

And vapeur went on and on, especially since the young doctor was listening and sometimes jotted something down—unfortunately, however, though he was as unfeeling as a recording needle, he was also forgetful like a human being . . . so he went off and left his papers behind. And on them oscarke read about his father-in-law vapeur: delusions, imagines he's an inventor, prone to altruism.

RIDICULOUS DEATH

And so mauriske had come, but marie-louise left: the night she died was a strange one. The young doctor was there, and boone's wife was there grinding coffee and boiling water, and madame d'haens was there looking for clean linen in the cupboards: an enlightened and scientific doctor, and the wife of a socialist, and the widow of a liberal, and then oscarke with his crazy theories, and her father with his . . . his . . . how COULD it be otherwise than that god was punishing her, punishing the whole world? She had been born to strengthen discipline and make faith prevail, and in the night the devil had come to sow tares among the wheat, and now those tares were growing wild even in her own house. It had become a new tower of babel, with a chaos of tongues: one person was a christian who only wanted to help his neighbor, and the other was a socialist who wanted happiness and prosperity for the workers, and yet another was a communist who wanted a more just distribution of worldly goods: and they worked together at the tower of babel and were at each other's throats: they would never be able to build a house that reached the clouds and drove god from his throne—so god himself must not want there to be happiness and prosperity among human beings, because if they started to be happy, they would . . . they would no longer need god. And ondine faltered in alarm at this thought, she became afraid to think it through to the conclusion that mankind was its own god: she stared distractedly at marie-louise, who was preparing to reenter the darkness from which she'd come . . . to again become part of the intangible element from which she had emerged. And she cried, ondine, in her frenzy she pulled her hair out—oh, there were already lots of gray hairs in the bunch in her hands. She fell flat on the wooden floor and rolled back and forth . . . Crying out again and again: oh oh oh. And they were all bent over her and no one looked at the child—and once ondine calmed down for two minutes, and they could look at the child again, well, it was already dead. Ondine clung to her: tell me where you are, she wept . . . tell me where you're going. And this was rather ridiculous of ondine, since marie-louise had scarcely been able to speak when she was alive . . . how could she be expected to talk now that she was dead?

STONEMASON REQUIRED

And the next day while ondine was still a little dazed from her grief and her atheism, or rather her doubt, luck knocked on the door—because it's not misery day after day, it's misery today and perhaps luck tomorrow. Such is life. It was some *flunky who knocked at the door, having been sent by mr achilles derenancourt, who needed a sculptor. Oscarke went along after returning from brussels and having a bite to eat—and ondine waited for him like a cat on hot bricks: she went into the house and read a book, she stood at the front door and killed time in boone's house and in madame d'haens's house. And tired from waiting she returned to her book, just as oscarke came home: he hung his coat on the hat stand and started gnawing his fingers. Oh, take your fingers out of your mouth and say something for a change! cried ondine. Well, it's for his house, said oscarke . . . and then went back to nibbling his fingertips. For his house, which house? For the house he's living in, what other house could it be? So she had to drag it out of the reluctant oscarke, in dribs and drabs. So the job was to face his old mansion in slate from top to bottom, with two pillars by the front door with wreaths of flowers carved in them, and a balcony that also had to be framed in a stone garland of flowers. Oh, oscarke! she said . . . and she laughed, and she cried: oh, our marie-louise! She said. Still she wanted to know what mr achilles had said and what oscarke had replied . . . and going by what oscar said, achilles had conceived the idea of having his old mansion completely renovated—and looking for a stonemason he'd asked boone, who was repainting his car, if he knew of one anywhere—but of course, there's oscarke, right next door!*

FOREVER BEGINNING ANEW

And suddenly kramiek turns up there in your small, white house in the country—he comes in pleased with himself and rubbing his hands, and talks about your book, as if there were no kramiek in it. He plays the role of a man, thick skinned, slippery, oily, off whose back the deluge of your words simply roll—the model of the kind of people who are the stones that the world is made of, and with which the streets are paved . . . who are tough and solid, and play the stock market, who are industrious and work away to get degrees in diplomacy, and keep on everyone's good side . . . and who even, in their way, are honest and follow the golden mean—who, like dry-stubble, that pompous character in multatuli's novel "max havelaar," live in fancy houses and are brokers . . . who lie there side by side, like the secure, familiar, smooth-worn cobblestones, over which generations upon generations have passed—or did they just walk back and forth a bit, without making any real progress? There they lie in their neatness and their order and their regularity, over which multatuli's hero shawlman still stumbled . . . they lie there and keep the street neat and safe, but between them no more flowers can bloom, and among them every dream and every hope is doomed to wither. And kramiek comes in and rubbing his hands asks you: but who on earth is that, that kramiek, that deluded, half-baked idiot? And as he stands there in all his sincere naivety, your finest thoughts stumble over him, and all the flowers of your poetry wilt. Yes, it's only through the hundreds and thousands of specimens of the creature called kramiek that the world keeps turning, turning in the same place—because he's everywhere, kramiek, and he keeps the world in balance, but also keeps it from becoming something finer and better . . . he's at the board meeting but also in the trade union, he belongs to the animal welfare society but also sits on the abattoir's board of management, he's on the church board and in the left-wing socialist party, in the army of the Jesuits and the federation of freemasons, he's at the UN sessions, and he populates heaven: blessed is kramiek, for his is the kingdom of heaven, because he's simpleminded and manages to adapt to anything, everywhere. And he was annoyed with you and your book, because all you do in it is indict, because things are undermined, and capital letters are avoided—but suddenly he hears someone say somewhere: why, that's the attitude of a nihilist. And he immediately comes in, rubbing his hands, and is glad that you too have a name, that you too have had a label stuck on, and so belong in an ordered world where everything can be pigeonholed. Pigeonhole: kramiek. Pigeonhole: nihilist. And now he turns up, just at the moment you're about to write the very last pages of your book, and he exclaims: halt. Halt! Because I've still got something to add. And then he says that the title of this last chapter was very well chosen: we individuals. We individuals . . . says kramiek. And now for you, everything has to be done all over again, because the world of kramiek, the world of barbarians, the world of increasing insanity, of indomitable dogma, of dreams of the future and the belief in ultimate victory: it's all turned on its head again by kramiek's attitude; he comes to you and counts himself one of the individuals in a world of barbarians. So they are becoming the individuals, and we the barbarians—yes, you must begin again all alone.

THE LAST MONUMENT

And so what was your answer to mr achilles derenancourt? ondine wanted to know. Oscarke had said that he was working in brussels on a monument to the fallen sailors, but that he would be able to take care of it in the evenings after work (after all, his free time was gradually growing longer). And the following week, starting on monday, he came home and had a bite to eat and then went to the old house, fitted slate and carved and sang, and got leopold to help a bit—when dusk fell they returned home, both singing, and they had a pint in that café . . . the only café oscarke went to at moments of overwhelming joy or sorrow . . . and little leopold sang and swore and walked on his hands for at least five meters, because he was drunk. And at home there was a steak waiting, a small one: you've got to have some meat, oscarke, said ondine . . . because you're as skinny as a bird on a stick. He fixed the front of the house, and everyone came to see the flowers, and the satyr's head, which he had copied from an old book and enlarged and carved in the stone—and he made a drinking fountain at the back of the courtyard of the old house. And fat mr glemmasson, who saw it, had to have a drinking fountain too, in the garden of each of his two castles. Oscarke became famous, he walked through the streets on sunday mornings, with Leopold holding his hand, to be seen, to greet everyone hat in hand—and then he received a commission, the largest, most beautiful commission, to crown his life's work: a monument for the fallen heroes of termuren that was to be erected at the end of chapel road.

HAT IN HAND

Yes, a monument had to be put up even there—no village wanted to be outdone by any other, although only about 8 men had left termuren for the front, and almost all had returned . . . but things were not that precise in termuren, and when oscarke went to discuss matters, he asked if he could consult the plans—but they didn't even have plans, they didn't even have an architect's drawing: hadn't they just asked Him to do it when he'd put those fountains in mr glemmasson's garden? So oscarke made a drawing himself, a pointed column, and at the foot of the column a fallen helmet: to our fallen heroes. He'd come to hate that word—he'd had to carve it in almost every street in brussels . . . And as he carved, he thought of the kid who'd got stuck over there in the mud of the river ijzer. They had fallen—and for what? For glemmasson, for derenancourt's castles, for comptoir et credit—and just as oscarke was now carving "for our dead," it was as if it were for all the dead . . . for those who'd fallen at the ijzer, yes, for them too, but also for those who'd fallen in the strikes, for those who'd caught diseases in the factories, those who were worn out or were left without pensions or support—for all the nameless christians and socialists and liberals and anarchists, for fanatics and those condemned to death. And it turned out beautifully . . . he'd given up his job in brussels and every morning he went down chapel road with an imitation leather briefcase containing his sandwiches and his coffee jug, a postwar coffee jug, a thermos bottle, which you only had to look at to break—a modern convenience, that is. Everything you reached for was broken, like the furniture made of plywood and the stockings made of artificial silk—everything prettier, expensive-looking, but worthless. And mean-while he carved—and suddenly someone came and congratulated him, a gentle-man, an artist, saying: finally someone with some notion of order and moderation and clear lines, finally someone with restraint who doesn't defile our dead with a monstrosity! And that gentleman said so many other things that oscarke had never thought about . . . he stood there speechless, and when the gentleman had gone he couldn't go on working, but went to the café . . . he pulled rosa onto his knee and told her everything the gentleman said: order and moderation, clear lines and restraint. And he sang. And the next day someone stood behind him and laughed: what's that supposed to be, a smooth piece of stone . . . and what about that there? And this someone pointed to the fallen helmet that had just rolled from the head of a fallen hero, as an eternal indictment. It's just like a chamber pot! said that someone, laughing. And so oscarke went to the café again and drank, but did not sing, and sat gazing hungrily at rosa and could have impaled her till he lay dead on top of her—he was drunk and swore and fought, and came home bleeding. But these were only isolated incidents, petty anecdotes, passing things that washed over him: one person showered him with praise, and the other mocked him: his helmet was called a chamber pot, and one of the satyr's heads on mr achilles's gate had a crack in it . . . but to tell the truth, these were passing things: the main thing was that he was earning money, that his wife was called madame ondine, that he became self-satisfied, and made passes at that rosa from the café—nothing much, just a bit of poking, and occasionally groping between her buttocks when she was sitting on his knee . . . the main thing was that he tipped his hat to the alderman for public works, who was a socialist, and that the socialist alderman for public works reciprocated by raising his hat to him in turn. He could sit at his front door in the evening, and look round haughtily . . . he could say to leopold: go and get me a packet of tobacco, the best there is! And then as he sat smoking his best tobacco at the front door, the folk who worked in brussels came home from the workers' trains . . . they came past the long wall of the labor with the Justice and Freedom newspaper in their pockets—and the struggle that had once been the center of his life had become very far removed from him.

THUNDER IN SPRING

And while the final pages of your book remain to be written, the music master comes to your small, white house in the country, and sees you working in your bit of garden: you root round in your muddy clogs, like an ant, like a gnome, like a human being . . . from the nearby wood to your bit of garden, back and forth, because you're looking for wild cherry trees, whole colonies of which seem to be shooting up in the forest—but you have to know them or you walk right past them, just as we have to know the individuals, the wild-cherry-like individuals, in this wood of barbarians. And crisscrossing the wood in all directions with the music master, you say to him: over there at the bottom of my garden I'd like to plant a copse of wild cherries . . . just imagine, in spring when a copse like that blooms. But look, while you plod together through the still-wet woodland floor, it suddenly starts thundering. Is that thunder? you both ask . . . though both of you heard it perfectly well. It's thunder in this delicate month of april . . . it's thunder in spring, thunder amid this tender weather—and it starts raining so hard it's like a thousand flat hands striking the trees of the wood . . . the silver birches, the young oaks and the slender hazels—and a bolt of lightning strikes so we can see that we can't see anymore, and at the same time your ears almost burst from the thunderbolt—that was close!—but where do you run to when you're in the middle of a wood in a spring thunderstorm? I recently read a collection by an English poet, says the music master . . . and it was called "thunder in spring." And I thought it was a well-chosen title: something impossible, to show that the world is upside down—but, as you see, it isn't impossible: the world *is* upside down. The world is upside down, you reply, because kramiek came to see me, and he said that I should really give this last chapter of our book the name: we individuals in a world of barbarians: *we* individuals, said kramiek. And the music master stands there soaking wet, and bursts out laughing because of kramiek's indestructible belief in himself. Tear this temple down and three days later kramiek will rebuild it . . . and kramiek will also be the first customer, who comes to pray in this new temple. There's a thunderstorm in spring, and the world is upside down—and on top of this topsy-turvy world sits kramiek. And now turn this new world upside down, demolish and rebuild it from scratch . . . and kramiek—amid the rubble of what's been torn down, among the mountains of sand and lime set aside to rebuild yet again—will come trotting up as usual, as he always does, invariably does, to sit on top. And with a laugh you answer: in this spring thunderstorm he'll get wet up there! But the music master shakes his head and says that kramiek never gets wet, never gets tired, never feels rain or cold, hunger or shame, kicks or pinpricks. And kicking open an emerging toadstool, this kramiek of the woods, this kramiek that shoots up in the space of a few hours, amid the wild and blossoming cherries . . . who looks around him in bewilderment, and feels like an individual toadstool in a world of blossoming barbarian cherries—and kicking open this toadstool, he says: but still we must go on fighting, even though they turn the world upside down and call Us barbarians—even though they call Us the devil, who roams around at night to sow the tares of unbelief among the wheat of their complacency, their certainty, their unshakeable dogmas.

THE DOG IN THE STRANGE KENNEL

Indeed, it's just as the music master says: we must go on. But with what? There in our refuge, around our small, white house in the country, there are other things to do than writing a book—we've got to plant and dig and do the farmer-only-knows what else. But we're stuck with the story of oscarke and ondine . . . oscarke sits there puffing on the best tobacco and sees the men from the workers' trains returning home—what are we supposed to do with that? Come on, let's get it over with as quickly as possible, and write a big chunk about him, the last chunk, and end our book with that—for good:

Oscarke smoked his best tobacco, and went to mass but didn't listen to what the priest preached from his pulpit—every sunday the priest had something to preach about, and it was never anything new . . . it was still the same as when oscarke was a little boy: about the corruption of morals that was increasing alarmingly, and about the communists who had forced their way into a convent and abused the nuns—the communists, the priest said now, just like he'd once said it about the socialists . . . but now there were heaven knows how many socialists themselves sitting in church listening to the priest: oscarke was there, and boone was there, and such and such: all socialists and children of socialists. And while oscarke half listened, he thought of his father-in-law vapeur, who the day before yesterday had told them how the first bunch of socialists had needed to fly over the chapel of termuren, since they were living devils who couldn't pass a bowl of holy water . . . and now they were sitting in the congregation, and the holy water had no effect on them. He thought of other things too—he thought a lot, he was still that all-doubting, all-pondering and all-combining oscarke—but he no longer let it show as much. He no longer gnawed his fingers, but smoked the best tobacco and doffed his hat. And ondine had also got him to enroll in the trade union, building-industry section, as a sculptor-stonemason—yes, it had reached the point where the dream of that student and of the late lamented bryske had finally been realized: everyone belonged to a medical union and a trade union, but it was a clerical medical union and a clerical trade union. Oscar had joined the church social club, a room with a dartboard and a backgammon set—and they played darts with the curate, the priest in charge. He was a very pleasant fellow, that curate, someone who could take a joke and himself told The joke about the priest and his maid. Oh, it was just as well that oscarke was satisfied with so little—and, amazingly, that all the people playing darts were satisfied with exactly as little as he: they played for five centimes and drank one pint an evening—that is, on sunday evening, because during the week they drank nothing at all. And in their view adam and eve had eaten from the apple tree, which had been the root of all the misery in the world. And this-and-that and the workers' trains? oscarke sometimes asked. Oh, that was because of adam and eve, they said. And he soon fell silent, suddenly feeling that he didn't really belong there—he was the dog lying in a strange kennel, and had a vague sense that there was another kennel somewhere. He drank his pint in silence and listened to the curate's jokes, oh, always the same jokes, at first you could laugh at them, but when they were always about the priest and the thief, the priest and the sexton, the priest and his maid—god, you felt like kicking him. He left early and had a bite to eat at home, and then sat at the front door. He liked being alone best, with his own thoughts, and when it was time for bed he lay down next to ondine, looking at his dreams with his eyes open, and falling asleep, always with the same feeling that he really . . . really . . . no, it wasn't so easy to explain that feeling. A dog in a strange kennel, yes, there was something to that, but it could be better explained, though in a more roundabout way, by saying that there are actually two oscarkes: he was one of them, lying next to ondine with the curate's wet jokes in his head, vaguely remembering that there must be another oscarke a very long way away from here—and that the other oscarke was as aimless as he was restless, and was lying awake thinking of this oscarke—and that the two oscarkes should really be fitted together to form a complete whole. And there was more: looking round the house he noticed that something was not quite right about that either: he was now earning good money, and he could afford to go out and buy himself tobacco, but what had changed? Nothing. And in fact, didn't even that tobacco still come out of his 20 francs pocket money? Anyway, he no longer needed to buy himself a train ticket, or pay for streetcars, and that was the only reason he was able to buy himself some tobacco and drink in a sunday school . . . no, a social club . . . because sunday school was for children. And the social club was for big children like him, who believed in adam and eve. And he also noticed that his children had only the bare essentials—when all the other children were playing with tops, leopold had no top: he had had to steal the top of a little boy whose mother came and made a stink. And when the top season was over, and the marble season began (since children's toys also had their set periods: first they played with balls, then with marbles, and then hoops . . . and you might think that these were just childish whims, but no, oscarke had noticed that they played marbles in brussels too at the same time . . . and that when they suddenly had a new toy, a diabolo, and he came home from work, and passed the park, by god, look: there were children playing with a diabolo here, too), ondine had asked little louis boone for a top: anyway, you're far too big to play with one! she said. And ondine had hurried home and said to leopold: look, now you've got a top, I got it from santa claus. But what good was a top to leopold now all the children were playing marbles? And apart from that, he looked it up and down and waggled the spindle: it's louis boone's top! he said. This made ondine so angry that she tore the top out of leopold's hands and threw it in the stove: that would teach him not to believe in santa claus . . . that would teach him to be a boy of his time, the new, scientific, irreligious time. Even though it's louis boone's, I still got it from santa claus! she cried in a rage. But leopold shrugged his shoulders: oh, a top, a pathetic top . . . louis boone's got a movie projector now! And sure enough, that very evening louis boone gave a screening in his cinema, admission 1 franc—and all the children made for boone's shed, where the cars were painted, and where a bedsheet had been stretched over a wall: all the children were there, except for ondine's children, who weren't given a franc—they stood outside and tried to peep in through a gap in the wooden wall. They shouted and screamed to kick up a commotion, and leopold threw a stone at the door . . . and suddenly mariette's voice changed and she called out: I've got a much nicer cinema than this! And that made leopold laugh till he almost choked. Oh, all the children came to school in the morning with a centime, with which they bought a slice of bacon . . . but ondine, who was always talking about learning to save, and saying things like, "you can't always have what you want, you'll turn into slobs," stood at the front door and suddenly called out to all of them: come and look, come! They all came, judith and mariette and leopold and little mauriske. Look, said ondine, and she showed them the little orphans who were coming down the street in a long line: look at those children who have no mothers anymore, no woman who loves them like I love you, who don't have the sign of the cross made over them by their mothers at night, and who can no longer have their faces washed by their mother . . . but have to do it all for themselves, have to clean their faces with harsh, stiff paper. And she cried and she pulled at her children's heartstrings. Give them something, mother! said leopold, who didn't really have a hard heart, but on the contrary, who despite all his mischief and pranks had a heart no bigger than a bean. But ondine, still crying, replied: what can I give then, we've nothing ourselves! And she hurriedly shut the front door. But of course, she could cause hopeless devastation in their little souls, but she couldn't fill their hungry stomachs with all that claptrap about orphanages: judith and mariette stole other children's biscuits . . . they collected children from all over the neighborhood and took them to school in the morning, and for that they were given a franc by the mothers every saturday morning . . . and besides that they ate the bacon that these mothers had given their own children to take with them. On the way to school they stole a turnip or a carrot from the greengrocer's display: their bellies were insatiable . . . and their bellies were the least of their problems, it was mainly their eyes that were insatiable: their eyes were wild with longing.

Whatever does she do with that money? wondered oscarke. Oh, in a final helpless attempt she put together franc after franc, centime by centime—first the money she had won at poker, and then the money that oscarke had started to earn from sculpting—now she would bend down whenever she scrubbed the floor and saw a stray centime—whenever she scrubbed the floor, but actually it was judith who scrubbed the floor, and mariette who mopped and ondine who gave the orders. It was very strange to see judith scrubbing, her sight wasn't very good despite the glasses, for which she had to have thicker and thicker lenses—put two pairs of specs on, one on top of the other! leopold would cry—and in the corners of the kitchen the dirt and sludge lay two inches thick. She never moved the coal-scuttle, she never shifted the armchair, she scrubbed round them—she gave the floor around them a bit of a lick, just as she gave her face a bit of a lick instead of washing properly. She was clumsy and knocked everything over, and then ondine would cry: leopold, tell her about those two pairs of glasses again! Mariette mopped, and when she'd done the inside of the house, she went on mopping endlessly along that bit of passage, the threshold, the pavement—and the people in the street got to know mariette's ass almost as well as her face. Ondine didn't see—she was counting her cents, she was sitting upstairs in the back room with the money tin between her knees . . . oh, not because of some little scrap of dirty paper money: it was another of those periodically recurring struggles of hers, her struggle to get on top of things, to achieve her life's goal. And if that goal changed, if it shrank constantly and became more and more humdrum, the means of achieving it remained, invariably, that same damn precious money. Her current life's goal at the moment was still as follows: to own a bourgeois mansion there on that patch of empty ground across from the terrace of the 1st grimy houses. Every night she went to bed early: I like to have the bed to myself for a bit, she said—but it was to see her dreams become reality: in her imagination she bought the land, saw the builders digging the foundations and lugging bricks and scaffolding. And the next evening they plastered, furniture was put in, and carpets were laid. She became sleepy and catty, since she dreamed during the day too . . . she became lazy, and apart from her increasing meanness she had no other passions, no other desires. Oscarke, who must have seen something in some street or other that had roused him, was greeted by her without enthusiasm: are you back already! she said. But he was wild, he was lusty, and chased the devil: she was finding her new pregnancy very difficult, she lacked all energy, and let everything go: all she was concerned with was that house in her dream and that child in her womb—and she had the rather dreamy notion that they would both come at the same time. And she imagined that the child was going to be her favorite child . . . because what did the other children mean to her now? They had just slipped out without her really thinking about it—always having had other problems on her mind. She paid no attention to her family, judith and mariette and leopold, and not even to little mauriske: they were strangers to her, just as oscarke had always been a stranger to her . . . they were creatures who had names by which one could address them, but apart from that they were ghosts that led an incomprehensible life of their own, completely different from her own. Oscarke felt this alienation in his heart: I'm a dog in a strange kennel! was his constantly recurring thought . . . it was may day now and the socialists took to the streets: it was a huge procession: they had a people's hall and and a cinema and a library and a hospital, a trade union and a pharmacy and a bakery and a printing press: they were a world unto themselves. And oscarke knew that he really belonged to that world. And when he met boone on may day, with a red flower on his lapel, they went to their local and had a drink and oscarke took boone's flower and put it on his own lapel . . . and he looked everyone in the face, especially rosa, as if to say: do you see, I'm a socialist too—although he wasn't: he was christian democrat. And boone started on about socialism, saying that it wasn't exactly perfect, because behind all those fine rooms and cinemas and music there was lots of injustice and fraud and bribery: they were dreaming now of finally getting a socialist mayor, and who do you think they should choose? . . . who among the socialists has the right to become mayor? . . . boone, by god, my own father, who was the 1st socialist—I well remember how they came and smashed our windows everyday and daubed our doorway with shit—but there's no chance of that now, if there were ever a socialist like that, it would be one of those new-fangled socialists, a stranger, an opportunist: the world stayed the same, after all, but the world was also What you made it: a drink, a steak, an hour sitting in the sunshine. And oscarke drank and nodded and spoke his mind too—and he got drunk, and lost control, and picked fights with children and old people . . . in that state he'd come home covered in blood and smash all his windows. Ondine rushed out with mariette and leopold and mauriske and stayed at boone's or with madame d'haens—or with a new neighbor, a butcher, where she propounded her ideas about people and the world and the universe, and where she bad-mouthed everyone and said: just you wait till oscarke sobers up! Judith stayed with her father, drunk or not, since she had remained his favorite—she had sat on his knee in the past, in his most desolate hours . . . he had made her porridge and washed her diapers back when a small child was still a miracle for him. Now she washed his bloody face—and drunk as he was he barricaded the front door, and swore he would live for little judith alone, and never let anyone else in the house. Oh, that was just the drink talking: once he'd fallen asleep judith went to get her mother at the butcher's—yes, always from the butcher's now, because whenever ondine was taking them to boone's, mariette would say: let's go to the butcher's, I like it better there. And ondine would laugh, here was a younger version of herself, a new ondine through and through. The butcher would give them a sausage or some ham trimmings and would play with mariette, and occasionally smack her bottom when it was bare again—and she looked at him with her hard, mischievous eyes. Judith came to get them, and ondine went home and kicked the sleeping oscarke, who tucked in his legs and grunted.

The baby arrived: another boy, and his name was albert—and with him the time had arrived, that time about which they had said: I'll do that "later." Now "later" had arrived, and ondine didn't really know what she was supposed to make of it—she still felt a bit tired, a bit listless. She could still see the importance of overturning idols, but it was as if the time had come for Others to overturn the idols—when she, ondine had done enough in life. It seemed as though she were more fond of reflections than actions: sitting somewhere, talking without getting excited, sleeping and dreaming of that bourgeois mansion there on that empty plot—oh no, even that dream house was slowly starting to bore her. She was still saving . . . but every now and then she dipped into her savings, to buy a mat for the hall, to buy chocolate for little albert who was to be her favorite child . . . supposedly chocolate for little albert, but really for her to gorge on herself. Then she would look up in surprise when her thieving girls started asking for dresses—they had never worn much else but a few patched rags, or clothes she had begged for elsewhere . . . now they whined for a purse, an umbrella, a Kodak, a bike. Up till now they hadn't known that there was any other kind of food but porridge and potatoes, and dry bread to take to school—but at boone's they cooked steak and chips, and mariette who sometimes went along, until she was suddenly thrown out: that hussy, they said. It was boone himself who had thrown her out, and he'd said to her: mariette, pull your skirts down a bit! She had sat looking at him with her mischievous eyes, with her bottom almost bare. And boone didn't like that: it frightened him—having a drink and sitting in the sun for a bit and reading a book by the stove: but not That, that sort of thing destroyed your peace of mind. And mariette was capable of saying: give me some money in return for what I'm showing you. She wasn't bad, though: she just wanted to be dressed like other girls—while ondine on the other hand bought linen, or bought a gold watch and a gold penholder from a peddler, all for 50 francs: I've bought you a watch, oscarke! And oscarke wouldn't be allowed to wear the watch: she had to show it off everywhere first, she had to wear it in fact, but alas, the gold watch turned out not to be gold, and aside from that it soon broke. She bought material from a peddler and visited a fortune teller who had parked a caravan on that patch of wasteland—and when the fortune teller came to her house with the cards, her children forced their way into the strange caravan—leopold made mauriske keep watch while he stole some money . . . afterward they had to go to the police station to make a statement, and believe it or not, on the way there leopold stole another carrot from the greengrocer's.

Ondine knew all the priests, she was on good terms with them and always brought in more work for oscarke, confessionals and communion pews for repair— she schemed and planned. But suddenly she realized that she had miscalculated. First and foremost she'd miscalculated over valeer: he acted as chauffeur for her cousin in brussels, he drove them to the markets where they earned lots of money, but he couldn't really take standing there in the wind and rain: he was coughing himself to death—and apart from that, he'd come back from the front, where he'd spent so much time imagining what things were going to be like after the war: sitting by the stove, feeding on one's memories of the muddy trenches, and coughing a bit. And so things were far too hectic for him there at his cousin's place: he came back to termuren to live with his father, and sat himself down there by the stove—and it was as if he brought luck with him from brussels, as if some luck had lodged in the folds of his clothes: no sooner had he arrived home than he received word that he was now going to draw a pension as a full war-invalid. And he was more grateful for the badge than for the money—now that he wore that badge every serviceman had to salute him, he said. There's always a special seat on the train for me and I go to the front of the line everywhere! This was the crown on his conception of life—and he waxed philosophical about it: a man always gets what he deserves, he said to his father . . . but you, you're asking for the impossible! But now that luck had flown over termuren, and had knocked on their door for shelter, there was suddenly also news for vapeur himself: a letter from the railway company. Oh, he almost went out of his mind, he didn't dare open the letter— imagine if they gave him 50 francs for every unmanned railway crossing, and there were a 100,000 of them in belgium, that would make . . . that would be . . . And he sang and danced and kicked something. And finally he tore the letter open: they asked him if he would sell the land on which his house stood, because they wanted to build a special station for termuren on the site . . . a goods station, from which the finished products of the 2 mills could be dispatched. Oh, and the land's value had risen enormously since the war, and what vapeur was being offered could be called a small fortune: he paid off all his debts and felt like a lord—but he still remained a bolshevik and a nihilist (no, not a nihilist, because there really was something positive in his thinking: the sense that the world was advancing towards a goal that we cannot comprehend). And there was also work and more work . . . a house had to be built with a spiral staircase, and the plate still hung on their gate: specialist staircase builder. He made the spiral staircase, he had a special knack, but, you know, you had to know what was what—and two Architects came from the city and asked him how he did it: that's a secret, he said. And then they asked valeer if he would help out in their factory instead, saying they would pay him so much an hour—but valeer earned enough with his 100% invalidity. We'll make you foreman, they said . . . and vapeur sat and stared at them and valeer with a grim smile—he knew that they were trying to wheedle the secret out of his son . . . but it was all useless, valeer knew about as much about building staircases as that coffee jug over there. The workshop became too small, and in two months they were going to have to leave the house anyway, so vapeur went for a walk every evening to see where he would move to—he passed by where ondine lived and chatted to oscarke about the lovely winding staircase he had to make, and about his workshop that was no more than a barn . . . and immediately afterwards about all those things that both their minds were full of, but that never produced any- thing tangible. And then on his walk he found a house, a long way past ondine's, by the remote karrebroeck stream: it was an appalling ugly shack, built of ash stone and cement—and in fact it wasn't habitable, it had been a lemonade fac- tory that had gone bankrupt: there were just a couple of places for living in, and the rest was factory. And to crown it all, it was again by an unmanned crossing. It was a desolate area, but vapeur, whose eyes were turned inwards, didn't notice: whereas he'd used to take his evening walks past the crossing and along the rail- way line to termuren, where he looked at the yellow brush, he now walked here in karrebroek, again past a level crossing, again along a railway line, and again looked at the yellow brush. And to zulma his wife, whom they had moved to the new house, still sitting in her armchair, it must have seemed as if she had just been out for a pleasant trip and had returned to termuren, because she sat at the window there in karrebroeck, and what did she see? exactly the same stuff. They had bought this ugly factory for 8,000 francs, and the houses were still rising in value: he had only just moved there when he was asked whether he would sell it for 20,000: oh, he'd become a rich man, not by working or calculating or inventing, but just by being stupid: that's the kind of society it was. And ondine? Yes, she had completely miscalculated. She came and looked at the cement hovel, and still felt she was the dominant woman in this family, the queen who gave the orders—who tried to trip them up, and wanted to cause trouble. She believed through thick and thin that it was her money that they were doing business with, and she talked about valeer stealing from her, and she talked about . . . oh, what didn't she talk about? No one could follow what she said anymore. She managed to get them to the point where they promised her a share in the profits—and at first she was so happy about that that she couldn't stop hopping in bed with oscarke . . . although she had read a book about neo-malthusianism once, and had described that book to everyone as blasphemous. But although she disapproved of it (was disapprove the right word to describe the shock that had gone right through her, right through her soul, through her whole being?), and although she was shocked—from the tips of her toes to the tips of her graying hair—she applied its theories. But as the days passed, she realized that her share of the profits over in karrebroeck was a bird in the bush . . . so she took steps to try to get her hands on that pension of valeer's, on the grounds that she had always taken valeer into her home. She failed in that too, she failed in everything. And oscarke, who knew nothing of her machinations, came to bed as usual to fuck, and she cried out in a rage: listen to me, albert must be the last, if not I'll chop it off—and mariette, who was in bed with judith behind the partition, burst into such hysterical laughter that immediately afterwards she had to try and save herself with all kinds of excuses. Because ondine, who was herself capable of saying the strangest things, couldn't bear to have others talking about them, and definitely couldn't tolerate her children speaking about them. But judith, who was now sixteen, hadn't understood what made mariette laugh so much: I'll chop it off, their mother had said . . . but what would she chop off? And mariette laughed even louder: you should go to the butcher's, he'll soon show you what has to be chopped off. In bed they had the strangest conversations about it, but in the living room they talked more primly than nuns—in the living room they behaved as morally as can be—but during the day mariette was always out and about in the town, and ondine sometimes came home drunk, hair loose in the wind and her faded cheeks flushed. And meanwhile oscarke sat all alone with judith, whittling a piece of wood. Ondine had gone out, and didn't say where she was going—and then mariette took off, to the butcher's, she said—and leopold went off, for a walk with mauriske, he said. It was just as well that that leopold had gone out, oscarke couldn't take his pranks—he did nothing but get up to Mischief, putting pins on chairs and suchlike, all those tiresome things that weren't funny, and which no one could laugh at but him. And another of his jokes: farting. He had a thin, birdlike face, just like ondine in her days of illness and doom and regular periods: when oscarke looked at leopold, he saw ondine with a period. But one evening oscarke had to go out too: an art dealer had invited him over to discuss a commission: a big commission, a beautiful commission, four statues were required for placing in a park, to the design of a very famous modern sculptor. And since it was a sober commission, with simple, expressive lines, oscarke saw himself as being in complete control—oh what a lot ondine had to say for herself in those days, how she walked and laughed, and made the people of the neighborhood jealous—oh and how oscarke sang with judith. And when the statues were finished, there happened to be an exhibition of artists from the little town of the 2 mills: the statues that oscar had made were going to be included in the exhibition! And the whole neighborhood of the 1st grimy houses went to see them—boone went to see them with little louis, and madame d'haens and the butcher—but he couldn't help laughing, because they were naked men. But there was a snag: that famous sculptor, that genuine artist, had come to see his statues, and thought they were really good: he had given them the odd tap and chip and put his own name underneath. Oh, and he made off like a bandit from them too . . . as far as money was concerned, there was no shortage of that here: after all, these were the gardens of glemmasson's castle. Oscarke of course came to see his own work exhibited, holding leopold by the hand: your father made that, he said to leopold. But there was the sculptor himself talking in the hall to the mayor achilles derenancourt, and mr glemmasson and the others nodded as if they knew all about art . . . and as oscarke went past, mr glem- masson greeted him very cursorily, and said something to the artist, and the artist smiled briefly at oscarke. The mayor remained impassive and oscarke raised his hat and went on. But he dawdled around the staircase that led to the room, and there he saw boone and little louis. And boone said: I thought that You had made those statues, oscarke? That's right, said oscarke. Those statues there. Those statues over there? repeated boone, pointing to them with his finger . . . but there's another name carved on them. I myself didn't see it, but our little louis noticed. And oscarke went and looked, and yes . . . Then he left, went downstairs, while his world exploded, dropped dead—not because of the name, but because of the atmosphere. Who was depicted in those statues? The men from the workers' trains, the beggars and the unemployed and those transported to germany, the miners and the name- less clerks and the traveling salesman. But who is allowed to carve them in stone? Artists who stand talking to mr glemmasson and mr derenancourt, smoking cigars: with mr derenancourt the clerical mayor, and mr polflit the socialist alderman for public works—and who for money, for a bit of grubby money, carve their names in the finished products. Yes, the statues were now going to be erected in mr glemmasson's garden, and mr glemmasson's whores would look between the legs of *those far too skinny young men, and point to their far too low-hanging balls—and then laugh with their stupid whores' laughter. He, the artist, isn't bothered, he doesn't even see them—and what the eye doesn't see the heart doesn't grieve over . . . and apart from that he's been paid. And oscarke, who forgot that he'd come in with leopold, went out all by himself, went into the same café as always, and drank and drank . . . he was alone in the place with the daughter of the café, with rosa: take me upstairs with you, he said. And in the bed he lay with his head between her legs, and cried, and whispered: I'm a dog in a strange kennel.*

ALTHOUGH OUR BOOK HAS ALREADY COME TO AN END,
A FINAL END—WE SHALL WRITE, BEYOND ITS LIMITS,
ONE LAST CHAPTER: TWILIGHT OVER THE WOODS

CAN YOU KEEP A SECRET?

It's a beautiful spring afternoon, and you're with tippetotje in the woods at marode, which are full of a slightly moist, dark odor. She squats down and wipes the beads of blood off her legs, cut by the brambles. Tippetotje—who let her baron choke on his money, who left him to his fate and to his death, and didn't inherit a centime—she sits there and looks up at you. I'm thinking about your book, she says. I'm thinking of that gigantic, thick book that you're letting choke to death, just like here in the woods everything is choking under the brambles . . .

That's how it is, tippetotje, is all you reply. You left your baron to choke and I'm leaving my book to choke. One thing chokes after another. All of us who wanted to be of good faith almost choked to death in this world of barbarians—but luckily we were able to escape at the last moment!

But tippetotje removes a drop of blood from her leg with the tip of her finger, and tastes it with the tip of her tongue. OK, OK . . . that's a satisfying ending to your book: your characters retreat before the advancing barbarians, before modern, routine, specialized, and mechanized barbarism. But . . . now we're all alone in this damp wood that's quickly becoming a rather *dark*, damp wood—far from the world, far from the barbarians who can't hear us, and especially far from the literary world that demands an acceptable ending to your book—now you must be honest, and admit that you've ended it too quickly, made it too rushed—oscarke is lying there between the legs of rosa from the café—sst!—but can he stay lying there till the end of time? No, you have to make a final effort, must add something like a hammer blow . . .

Can you keep a secret, tippetotje? you ask. Can you be as silent as the grave? Well then: I got rid of it. I told myself it was more than enough of a good thing, that I could just as well draw a line under it There as I could five or five thousand pages further on. But if you'll be keep it to yourself, keep silent for forever plus three days, I'll let you read the bit that I excised from our novel, the bit that's no longer included, but already had a title:

WORLD TO COME

Ondine, who in earlier years had cherished the illusion of being a child of god, gradually discovered with growing alarm that she was actually a child both of the devil and of god—discovered that god and the devil were one and the same—discovered that white and black, good and evil, day and night, were changing manifestations of the same thing. And after that? After that she wanted at least to be the center of these ever-changing manifestations, which nevertheless while constantly changing constantly recurred. She wanted to be the god and devil of this world herself . . . or of her world at least, first of termuren, then of the neighborhood she had moved to, of her household with oscarke and the children. Oh, of the children, whose names she couldn't even get right! But didn't she also discover that, to her equally great consternation, everyone in the world forced their own way through to these same truths in the end? Or . . . if they didn't force their way . . . if they had no clear awareness in their minds . . . that they all had a vague inkling, a faint sense? Or let me take a broad view—she thought—and assume that they nevertheless unconsciously act in accordance with something that could be called a law? Look at oscarke, she said. Look at the children, she said. And she looked at the children, who crossed themselves a lot or farted a lot, depending on whether god or the devil spoke, but who did as they pleased and remained their own gods or devils regardless. She understood, but didn't resign herself to it. She wanted to continue to embrace Everything, she wanted to continue regarding these eternal laws as HER laws. That's why she was always here and there, running around and chattering and gathering Everything to her. Like an industrious ant she kept bringing new grains of sand to her anthill—but though she might have completely unraveled and spun out the life of madame d' haens—and though she might have fathomed the financial difficulties and the cracked cups and the nocturnal onanism going on in all these households—though she might have kept in her memory a chronicle of every marriage and death and illegitimate child in the town: there were still things that escaped her. And you see, that was it, the things that escaped her! What value did one thing have if another thing could escape her? It was one more proof that it wasn't she who led the dance, that it was she . . . oh, she wept with impotence, she ran round even more restlessly instead of resigning herself to the facts. Resigning herself! She hated that word, resignation; there could be NO question of that.

Also, too many novelties appeared that were none of her doing. No sooner had she finished or thought she'd finished with the thing people were wont to call spiritualism, than the car and the radio appeared at the other extreme. On the side where she was expanding her world, things were shriveling, and on the side where she had neglected the world—the side of her father vapeur—the specter of modern technology loomed up. She had tried to fathom the madness, the nocturnal terror, and all the weird things relating to her mother—and meanwhile the things on her father's side had developed into a monstrous excrescence. Cars had arrived, oh yes, and radios, and everything else that made a racket, and together with all that the new mental illnesses had arrived. She had no part in the advent of all those things.

She hadn't noticed when they first arrived and didn't know where they'd come from. And yet she refused to see that the world was headed towards a particular goal, and WITHOUT her. She refused to see, because the day had come when she HAD to see. And to her mind, oscarke and boone and valeer and for that matter any other fool were all welcome to rack their brains about what that goal was. For all she cared it might be the downfall of the world, hell, general devastation, or a far chillier and ignominious end in Nothingness—it wasn't the goal that affected her, but the fact that the goal had been set independently of her. Still, she accepted the car and the radio and onanism, she accepted the mental afflictions of madame d'haens and madame boone—though it was ridiculous to hear those two forever chattering on about their mental problems—plus the inflamed ovaries of the butcher's madame. The ovaries, the womb, and the rest of the filth that people talked about in this modern age—instead of leaving it all where it was, in the dark cellar that was a belly, in that place that should be taboo. But no, she accepted it . . . she struggled against it but ended by accepting it.

Oh, and she suddenly realized—just like all the other things she'd discovered and forgotten, and discovered again but hadn't applied—that everything WAS after all relative. Whenever things didn't go as she wanted them to, whenever the wishes of others were carried through instead of her own . . . whenever her children returned home after endless quarreling and fuss and finally got their way—she said . . . she thought (for there was not the least discernable sign of her saying it aloud), after her curses, after her tears: all is relative.

But what she wanted and desired, unconsciously, in the midst of this relative world, in this neighborhood of the little mill town as it went its own way, was to be called someone of significance. Oh, to be "madame" ondine was not enough. Not the mistress of everything, not the queen, just a madame! It was for that that she skimped and saved, and it was crazy of the children to ask for a film projector, and it was ridiculous of mariette to come and tell her that something like that was "all the rage"—and it was a stupid idea of oscarke's to want to buy a book on sculpture, "you who've never read a book, you who've always been satisfied with your own thoughts, I wonder why you want to own a book now!"

This embarrassed oscarke, since actually he was wondering too. But, in general, what reason can one give for wanting something? Why did he insist on keeping a ripped photo of jeannine, although it was dangerous since ondine went through all his pockets? Why did he dream, for instance, of having an album—an album of sculpture, as he called it, to collect pictures from books and magazines in—when actually he was only playing hide-and-seek with what he really wanted, because what he really wanted was an album of miniature jeannines? Oh, he'd noticed that others had depicted miniature jeannines too, he'd seen an illustration somewhere of what was it again—easter, or spring . . . no, it had been april—and it had been a little jeannine, with very young breasts, who was sitting perversely and alluringly

*playing the flute. And he wanted to collect those things in an album, and wanted
to call them Testimonies—he wanted—he longed—his life and the life of boone
and the butcher and more or less everyone he knew was passed in longings: being
a Human Being meant longing. Voilà . . . there was the answer to ondine's question "why did he want to own X?": because it was human to want. But he also
realized that people's longings were relative—the longings, and the fulfillment of
those longings—oh, the fulfillment most of all! He no sooner longed for something
than he encountered ondine as the eternal stumbling block on the road to fulfilling
that longing . . .*

*But how difficult life was for ondine in those days, being the stumbling block
for oscarke and mariette and leopold—it was only with judith, the eldest, and
albert, the youngest, that she had real problems—since they wanted nothing more
than to scorch their shins on the stove in the evenings and grumble at having to go
to bed so early, and in the mornings to nestle in bed and stay nestling there, and
grumble at having to get up so soon—those were longings too, but it didn't cost
ondine any money. The longings of the others, however, did. On the one hand she
had to have money, and hence save money, in order to be someone . . . but on the
other hand she had to spend money lavishly, if she wanted to prove she was someone of significance. Hm, it wasn't easy! Madame d'haens bought sausages from the
butcher, a whole line of them that hung up to dry above the stove and which she
didn't dare eat—and if ondine wanted to count for anything, she was obliged to
buy a similar chain of sausages—she was obliged to wait until madame d'haens
was in the butcher's shop, to say: give me a meter or two, I'm not fussy. And then
the sausages would hang to dry, and dry, until leopold became ravenous, until
mariette could NOT look at them any longer, and went out into the yard in the
darkness and stuck her finger in her mouth till she was sick. Mauriske, that secretive
lad, was much shrewder: he showed his elder brother leopold how the meat could
be removed and replaced by something else—sawdust, for instance, or chippings
from their father's sculpting. He ate his share and apart from that was silent. He
wasn't arrogant, and even listened without speaking when leopold told the story of
their tricks in the neighborhood, sitting over the cellar door at madame d'haens's,
bragging and smiling with his sharp bird's face—and meanwhile mauriske sat and
looked at him with silent disgruntlement. He was the choicest comrade–in–arms
for leopold, who liked to boast about his heroic exploits—it was quite possible that
their mother ondine would today or tomorrow find out about what had happened,
but since there were two of them, one could accuse the other, or they could rush
out and hunt for their carrion elsewhere for an afternoon or evening. But ondine,
who actually did find out, but who found so many things out—one thing followed
hard on the heels of the other—and in blind fury threw the fake sausages into the
stove, again had other things to worry about: the rent for the house, for example,
and the rate at which the house could be paid off, and finally—after a period of*

time that was difficult to calculate—become HER house. But she didn't pay the installments: with money in hand she could bluff, but not with a paid-off house. And anyway, who could tell if a lot or a little had been paid off? She had a place to live, that was the main thing, and she carried weight there in the neighborhood, thanks to her tongue. She simply lied through her teeth: oh yes, the amount that oscarke has earned from carving monuments, carving flowers in wardrobes and front doors, eventually you don't know what to do with it all! And madame boone nodded: things had gone pretty well for her too, but you know what boone's like: a cup of coffee with a cake after lunch, a glass of wine and biscuits in the evenings . . . and on top of that, things seem to be slackening off with those cars lately . . . and there's also something amiss with little louis, I don't know what's got into that boy. He's got worms, said ondine: get him some worm powder and give him a good thrashing regularly . . . and what about your house, my dear, I'm shocked, is it true that you've paid it off? And ondine went away and talked everywhere about the house that was now completely hers.

Oh, and meanwhile she stood there in her old battered shoes that were worn down at the edges—because wherever she went her feet faced slightly inwards— that idiot leopold collected pictures, the animals of the wilderness, and on one of them there was a monkey with its feet in EXACTLY the same position. Leopold laughed and choked and farted yet again, "look, mother!" and the next day he had slipped her photo in with the beasts of the wilderness. Those were his usual tricks, tricks that no one else could laugh at . . . neither judith, who never understood anything, especially not leopold's jokes, nor oscarke, who didn't understand his humor either, nor mariette, who could only laugh when she was out to hurt someone, or if she could conflate some innocent saying with something smutty. And ondine didn't WANT to laugh at it, and didn't want to think about it: godless boy, was all she said, godless boy, thinking his mother comes from a monkey . . . Darwin and malthus and spencer, you have to read them, but you must not forget your catechism. And she laughed, rather bitterly. But meanwhile she stood there again with her feet lopsided! And she turned on oscarke in a rage, because he pointed this out to her . . . because he sat there and observed everything, and again was out of work. Out of work? How strange that sounded. He carved and chiseled ornaments, and carved flowers in wardrobes and beds—at the bottom of the yard, next to the coal and the toilet, he had turned the little shed into a studio full of cobwebs—but now there'd been no work for a day or two. A strange fashion had arisen for manufacturing furniture without carving, and erecting buildings without sculpted decoration . . . and in the sunday paper there were articles about order and neatness, about housewives who had too much work to dust properly— and how dust was a breeding ground for bacilli —and how undusted, detailed carvings and moldings were therefore breeding grounds for the tiny creatures that brought disease—and so everything was much nicer and healthier, much cleaner and easier to maintain, if it was smooth. Smooth, that was the new thing. Ha, flat and soulless was what oscarke called it—still, whichever way he looked at it, however much he stared himself silly at it or closed his eyes to it, "smooth" was one of the words he'd used for a while to define his world, the world of the future. Hadn't he imagined that one day a time would come when every obstacle to happiness, every confusion, twist, lie, or illusion, would be swept away?—a time when there would be an end to the eternally repeated and eternally revamped lies of the priest?—a time when neither stupid faith nor idiotic sermons would thwart freedom (and at the mention of freedom he made an ample gesture with his skinny hand) . . . freedom then, and happiness? Thwart, exactly! And when there would consequently be no more borders between countries. And how strange, now that those plans were beginning to become vaguely discernible in reality, and his dreams and those of a few others were beginning to assume a more concrete form, it brought him, oscarke, no benefit, but on the contrary harmed him. He sat for hour after hour gnawing his fingers, trying to refute everything, trying to push the guilt onto others. And one evening, when he lay down but could not sleep, he expressed to himself the profoundest thought he had ever produced, but whose real profundity he did not appreciate: people long for things that bring people no benefit. And what he really meant was that that people want things for themselves and their fellow human beings that aren't good for them as individuals. But having thought this up, he immediately fell asleep. And all that was left the next morning was his resentment at there being no work: and ondine said it was his own fault: others are earning, and you're not . . .

That's right, I'm not! said oscarke, conceding all her pronouncements in advance. What was the point of trying to explain to ondine all the things he could barely explain to himself? And so he went to see boone and talked to him a bit about things—boone stood there and nodded and nodded gravely, and then came out with a truth of his own—exactly the same truth that OSCARKE had discovered—that this new society, in the midst of the old society that went on existing, would bring nothing but misery. Oh, and the terrible realization that oscarke suddenly came to, seeing boone nodding there with his fat head? That everything was relative in life, this was more or less his discovery. A franc is relatively a lot and relatively a little. A girl is relatively beautiful, but her beauty doesn't bring unalloyed happiness, but on the contrary trouble and torment. And that the world to come is only relatively desirable, because when it comes it brings trouble and worry . . . And—what remained the primary issue for him—it brought a new fashion that no longer wanted carving. Oscarke mourned because of this new fashion, and ondine scoffed when that new fashion was mentioned—but (since one thing led to another) with this fashion for smoothness, something else occurred as well: no more craftsmen like oscarke were needed, and everything could be done with machines, so mass production was born. Suddenly you heard people talking about mass production

. . . slightly deprecatingly, but still!—mass-produced items were flat and ugly and without ornamentation, but they were cheap and no more dust lodged in those scrolls and curls, as they used to, and boone bought a kitchen cupboard like that. Oh, it's mass-produced, said oscarke and ondine. Yes, but it was modern—true it was just like a box, but boxes WERE precisely modern. Oscarke got a job for a bit for a gentleman with a drawing room, louis-quinze, where some of the carving had worn away, and while he worked there he proclaimed his horror of boxes. And he fiddled around somewhere else too, another dirty, difficult, and tricky job that didn't pay very well—and there too he declared his disgust. Wherever he went he talked about those horrific boxes, but wherever he went those boxes were ousting him. They were silent and mechanized, they were mass-produced, and they were ousting him. It was useless for him to express his hatred, because the next day—or no, the same instant, while he was elaborating his theories—the door opened and mass-produced goods were delivered: smooth, flat, and enameled.

WILLY-NILLY

There's the music master in his bit of garden, in his bit of earthly paradise, mowing his grass—it's a beautiful and monotonous song that the scythe sings for the falling grass. I thought so, he says, I thought you felt there was something missing from that novel, and that you still didn't feel at ease in our refuge: tippetotje told me, swearing me to silence forever, how you had to make oscarke realize one last time that his world to come would bring nothing but new trouble and bother and difficulties.

That wasn't nice of tippetotje, you reply . . .

It's not nice of you, replies the music master. It's not nice of you to go into the damp and darkening woods alone with her like that, and only to reveal to her that a bit of your novel had been left out, a bit that's now appearing beyond the finishing line, beyond the End. A bit that you've only written to soothe your conscience: that world to come, hell, that will come to Nothing too! And the music master sharpens his scythe and feels its edge with the tip of his thumb. But you didn't put things sharply enough, he says . . . you would have done much better to put the emphasis on that last discovery of oscarke and ondine and boone, and for that matter of the whole world there: that everything is relative, that everything will remain just so-so. We have withdrawn into our refuge, and even here it's all much the same—here too happiness is incomplete, here too the outcome of our lives is only a relative outcome. And living in our refuge, we in turn see the world of the barbarians with different eyes: living among these barbarians, and feeling ousted by them, we thought that their world was heading for the abyss, that their world was no longer redeemable and that cancer had already taken hold of it.

But here, far from that world, we see how relative our diagnosis is and how relative the scope is for its barbarians to operate in.

And something else, the music master continues . . . with that fragment of a story about ondine and oscarke, you've not only exceeded the limits of your novel, but also the limits of the time allotted: ondine and oscarke experienced things as they were, and we things as they are today—and now you're bringing ondine and oscarke over that limit, and having THEM experience what we ourselves have been through: the new fashion for smooth lines makes its appearance, and the modern mechanized world of the barbarians is now also advancing on THEM . . .

And then? you ask in a whisper, in an anxious whisper.

And then! says the music master . . . and then you're also obliged to evoke all the other things from modern life, together with mass-production. Now you have to go on writing, willy-nilly, and bring ondine and oscarke to the point that we ourselves have reached . . .

I can't write all that anymore, you stammer.

You've got to! says the music master. Whoever invokes demons must also be able to exorcise them. You consciously exceeded the bounds of your novel, and now you must bear the consequences.

RELATIVE WORLD

Oscarke went home, slightly stooped, with the gray tuft on the back of his head that had always stood upright, but with the passing of time was finally beginning to lie flat—and as if he and ondine, together, and yet without being aware of it, could only have the same thoughts, he said: this time it's a radio. A radio, a box, a mass-produced item. Nevertheless, despite ondine's loathing, it evoked a different sound at the back of her mind, deep in her heart: a radio, an artificial ear that eavesdropped on the world, were they going to start selling that as a mass-produced item—shiny, smooth, cheap? And that same afternoon, with the haughty and hurtful tone of someone crossing into the enemy camp, she said to madame d'haens: we're thinking of buying a radio. Or she twirled the knobs of the antiquated set at boone's: the final chords of some brass band music poured out over the modern kitchen cabinet and boone's unsold merchandise, then silence, and then the weather forecast for the next day was announced—moderate showers of rain, or moderate wind—and ondine listened and thought her own thoughts. She suppressed those thoughts and made a joke of them—"moderate windfall" she said—but would you believe it, meanwhile those other suppressed thoughts returned, in a different form: moderate wind and moderate windfall, moderate this and moderate something else, moderate god of a moderate heaven and earth: everything was moderate and everything was relative. And boone said: look, ondine, you should have one, a radio! And little louis looked at her, and boone's wife looked at her—yes, it was a momentous moment. We'd have had a radio long ago, but oscarke can't stand that mass-produced stuff, she said. Yet as she dashed around the town she said to herself: what nonsense, maybe you can't stand mass-produced stuff that doesn't need carving, but you can have mass-produced stuff in the house if it benefits you. She noticed a new shop, and pretended to be surprised—oh, although the shop was her only goal: it was a completely converted and modernized property, with a smooth flat frontage, large mirrored windows, and a revolving door. Good gracious me, a revolving door that you passed through like a mill, while the sounds of a radio poured over your head—you heard the merry widow, said a voice—and ondine was inside and saw all those radios, and didn't know from which one music was actually coming: it was if they were all playing music and broadcasting the weather forecast. There was a large banner above these musical boxes—Credit—and a gentleman approached ondine, he was elegantly dressed, spic and span and very correct, and handed her a leaflet telling her how many valves the radio had, what improvements had been made to the condenser, the loudspeaker, the coils. The gentleman went on and on, and ondine nodded but couldn't understand any of it: she studied the circular in which there was a photograph of the very same radio that was playing there in the shop, in the corner of a modern room, next to a cactus plant. Very beautiful. Oh very very beautiful. And in great sorrow she averted her eyes, because what else was there for her to do but turn away and go? Moderate wind. Oh yes, and moderate poverty, moderate rent and electricity, oscarke's moderate earnings from carving a bit on louis-what's-his-name stuff. Then the gentleman's finger slid over a series of very small figures: she could take the radio home, music could flood over her own rooms, and she wouldn't have to pay anything. Or rather: she would have to pay 60 francs a month, which came to 2 francs a day. Many people gave their children 2 francs to take with them to school every day—she could give 2 francs a day and have a radio. She could scarcely believe it, she had lied to and deceived so many people in her life that now, WITH sorrow in her heart, she couldn't wait to wink slyly at the gentleman and say in an understanding tone: oh yes, oh yes! But the gentleman remained very serious: no, no, he said. And then her eyes—admittedly eyes that were growing old and tired, but that were now astoundingly sparkling—flew over the figures: 6,980 francs for the radio next to the cactus plant, 12,960 francs for the radio photographed next to a bookcase. They cost thousands, these radios, and yet one only had to pay 2 francs a day, and meanwhile it was in her house and playing, playing. She felt really feverish and tried to think—I have to think it over, I must try and see everything that's involved, she thought—but she COULDN'T see everything, it was too powerful, too huge, too overwhelming. No sooner had one thought been dealt with than 3, 6, 12 others already presented themselves. The gentleman produced a form on which everything was again confirmed in writing, and also took out a pen—he gave her a pen. And she looked helplessly into his eyes, because that was her last resort: trying to see in his face whether it was a fraud . . . or whether it was not, at least, a TOTAL fraud . . . But no, he smiled, he was correct, she took the pen and signed, and her eyes were a little moist. She picked up the radio, a little box, beautifully smooth and polished—that is your radio, madame! he said—and he twiddled the knobs for her, and she saw brussels and paris and london gliding past on the dial, but it didn't play yet, it first had to be connected and provided with a grounded antenna. She couldn't take it with her, although she tried to put it under her arm, tried to press it to her bosom . . . it was HER radio, which she was forced to leave here: she dawdled and couldn't tear herself away, she saw the gentleman put a sign on her radio: sold. It's best if you come and collect it this evening, madame, together with your husband, when he gets home from work. And despite herself she replied, proudly, in an almost automatic reflex: my husband works from home, he's a sculptor. Of course, of course, said the gentleman. Then she was out of the front door and in the street, and she was seized by fear, overwhelming fear.

Everything she hadn't been able to gain an overall view of was closing in on her. 2 francs a day, it was scarcely possible: was that the new age? In the olden days people saved for something till they had out the necessary money together—but now that had all changed, people no longer saved, people no longer worried, people turned a knob and had electric light, gas, or water—and also a magic word had come into being: Credit. And suddenly ondine stopped somewhere in the middle of the street, looking at people, looking at the shops, and shaking her head she thought: I was born too early, I should have been little ondine now. And she went home and looked at mariette, and kept shaking her head at this very odd thought: she would . . . oh, she would have liked to be mariette.

Oscarke helped her collect the radio. She had to pay 500 francs up front, and she also had to purchase a few things before the radio was ready to play, the aerial and the plug, the ground-wire and also a lightening conductor—she had to pay a man to crawl onto the roof and attach the aerial. These were all the kinds of things she had suspected, but hadn't had an overall view of, and it was from instinct that she had brought her purse with her, under her skirts, pressed close to her thighs that were growing scrawny—because she was afraid that they would take it all away from her, that the money would all flow away this way and that—and that she would be left naked and penniless. She placed her hand on her thigh: right, I'll pay you, tomorrow, next week, she said—and haggled about a centime here and tried to get something for nothing there. She even maneuvered the man who fixed the antenna on the roof outside . . . very dangerous work . . . maneuvered him out of the house and treated him as though he had done it for fun, as though he liked climbing over roofs: when the work was finished and a suspicious discordant sound flooded into the house when the knobs were turned (no, still no music, something must be wrong), she steered him outside: I don't think you've done it right, and she closed the door behind him. Little louis boone came and twiddled the knobs, short wave and long wave, bremen, breslau, brussels—there was a valve loose, he said, and he opened the box and fixed it. The radio played. Someone was speaking in a foreign language and they laughed at it: what did he say, little louis?—and little louis said it was english, london regional.

Ondine set aside 2 francs every day, and then forgot about it after a while, and had to find 90 francs on the first of the following month—because she had also bought a washing machine on credit, a washing machine that ran on electricity—since they had only a wooden tub that had to be rocked to and fro by hand, and she COULDN'T rock anymore with her hernia, with her belly that hurt for 6 days a week, and with her legs that were worn out. Yes, she was beginning to walk around rather oddly with her lopsided feet, and whenever she stubbed her toe on a protruding stone the pain shot through her, here in her groin, and there in her side. And then it was judith who did the washing . . . judith and mariette, supposedly . . . but judith rocked and scrubbed and rinsed the linen, and all mariette did was hang it on the washing line to dry. She bent down deep into the basket and half her ass was showing. Then came the electric washing machine, and judith washed by herself and mariette went into town. Oh, boone watched those goings-on at oscarke's from over the wall, and laughed about it: he told his wife and his wife told madame d'haens, and they all amused themselves about that radio and that washing machine at ondine's. But . . . looked at closely, the same thing was happening—in a different way—at boone's. He had actually gone with oscarke to get the washing machine, they had looked for a car but hadn't found one, and so had been forced to use sander toppe's wheelbarrow: first they took the wheelbarrow into the center of town, and drank a glass of beer without hurrying too much—since oscarke had no work—and only then got the washing machine. And there boone bought, on credit, a mandolin for his son, for little louis boone, because it was ridiculous all the things they gave you for 2 francs a day—and with the washing machine in the wheelbarrow and the mandolin on boone's chest, they went for another pint, and boone played a bit on the mandolin, just plucked strings at random and produced discordant notes, and a string broke, bit it didn't matter since he had been given a whole bag of spare strings—and then they went home. But look, he had bought a mandolin for little louis, just like ondine had bought a washing machine and a radio, and meanwhile oscarke had said: we're not that short on time, since I've got no job. But was he, boone, so busy then? He had said that the car was the wave of the future, how every new job would be a job in the service of the car—the car is overwhelming the world and you must send your boy to a technical school, oscarke, where they learn about cars! Boone was not a fool. But consider this: at the beginning, when cars had just been invented, people drove then for a good twenty years . . . every year through the rain and mud and wind, or under the burning sun, and the paintwork blistered or cracked, so that *people called in boone to repaint them. All very well, let there be lots more cars, let everyone drive a car, so boone would have to buy the whole of that empty corner to build a workshop as big as a factory! But now, they not only mass-produced radios and washing machines and mandolins, but also cars—cars especially. And cars were also sold on credit—and one driver didn't want to be outdone by another, a question of model—model this, type that—no one wanted to drive an old-fashioned model, last year's type, because every year there was a more urgent improvement, a handier gearbox, a nicer streamlining. Streamlined: how oscarke hated that line: smooth, elegant, gleaming. How often boone had had to swallow this complaint from oscarke, so that he finally said: oh for christ's sake, oscarke, will you shut up about your smooth lines?—and now it was being applied to the car too! They were mass-produced, they were made of tin and sheet steel and plywood, and didn't last very long—but why should they last long?—after all people bought a new, better, more beautiful one on credit. They were painted at the factory, and there was nothing more for boone to do—true, he occasionally had to beat out some dents from the fender and did a bit of repainting, but this just kept him from realizing the truth: he had been slow to see that recently there'd been nothing but repairs. And then a year came when cars were no longer painted but had leather, imitation leather of course, modern leather. And boone laughed inwardly: it will crack and hang loose and be ugly, he predicted—and his prediction proved true, haha!—but over in the factories they worked feverishly and came up with another innovation (oh how did they keep making these innovations?), and started painting with a gun. Spray painting, technology, mechanization, modern age, credit. And anyone who bought a car from the factory got a car complete, painted, upholstered, with an ashtray and bouquet of flowers, and—to crown it all—with a working radio in it! Boone shrugged his shoulders, and went on repainting the occasional fender—but most customers who came to him with a dented fender asked if he was using a spray gun yet. They asked just like that. And spray painting became boone's nightmare—he told oscarke about it—so oscarke droned on and on about the modern line, and boone droned on and on about spray painting. There they sat of an evening, agreeing with each other, each with no work.*

MAY RAIN

A soft, silent rain in the month of may—and your living room fades into your patch of garden, and your patch of garden fades imperceptibly into the bit of woodland—it's just like a surrealist painting in which the wood is a sea, and the green of the leaves are the waves that break on the beach of your living room. And tippetotje sits there beside you and her regret is tangible: how does that work? she asks . . . you happen to write a word too many and I happen to utter two too many, and suddenly everyone knows that the novel about oscarke and ondine didn't end between the legs of little rosa from the café. And she looks away from the flooded wood and stares at you from the side with her regret. And because you don't say anything, she goes on: and before you realize it, you're up to your neck in trouble, in technology, mechanization, the smooth line and spray painting—and something new, Credit—oh, I'm sorry, I'm more sorry than I can say. And I'm especially sorry for you, because it's become such an unhappy ending with no way out: oscarke and boone are sitting there on their thresholds, just as we are sitting here behind the glass wall of your living room, and they're out of work. And again you've got write another section, something that injects some courage, that makes them turn to see some brilliant sun in the distance—the heaven promised to everyone with goodwill but poor in spirit—the future, which shines for everyone not satisfied with today, who are unhappy and sick, downcast or embittered . . .

Yes, tippetotje, yes . . . but I'm not of goodwill, nor am I poor in spirit, I'm not unhappy or sick, not downcast or embittered . . . it's so beautiful, that drop of rain in this month of may, the wood that comes washing into my living room, and in addition your beautiful regret that is almost tangible—leave it like it is, let oscarke and boone just sit there together on their doorsteps: it's more than enough, we've said all there was to say.

True, replies tippetotje . . . it's all been said, but the last page has still not been written, the last page like a hammer blow, that is a conclusion and an end and at the same time a return to the very beginning: a beautifully closed circle.

It can also be a book like an overflowing wood, you reply . . . it can run aground like all that greenery around us here, it can go out like a penny candle, it can . . .

Yes, but not on boone's threshold there . . . says tippetotje obstinately. Not there! Come on—while we're here alone, and while this soft, silent rain is falling—let's look for an ending together, a tippetotje ending, a conclusion that is acceptable and yet challenging: it's all right for everyone to know who and what we are, and how we may have withdrawn but still remain proud and stubborn and challenging. Come on, let's try to find a title for it that says more than enough . . . for example:

OSCARKE'S SHITTY WORLD

True they sat there in the evening, agreed with each other, and mostly had no work. But . . . no sooner had oscarke sat down than ondine was there with something or other to make his life—the evening life on boone's threshold—a misery. Oscar, go and do . . . and she racked her brains—tired out from talking—to find ways of making his life sour—chopping wood for the stove, moving the coal, which is to say: taking the bit of coal piled up here and piling it up over there. And when oscarke had gone she sat down on the threshold herself: do you sell a season ticket for this doorstep, boone? she asked. And unbelievably she asked only jokingly—for in the past, oh in the past she would have savored real schadenfreude—in the past she would have said: he who laughs last, laughs longest: it won't last with those cars—and now, it HADN'T lasted, but she still didn't have the last laugh; she felt no triumph because things were going badly for boone—she didn't feel victory as she had imagined she WOULD feel it. She did feel some satisfaction that things weren't all sunshine for other people, that they too sometimes found a punishment . . . an ordeal . . . oh, what was she rambling about—human misery on their door-step. But the awareness that everything was relative, that everything had a light and shadowy side had already penetrated too deep inside her: she could only grimace rather bitterly when boone's wife came to the front door too, and suggested that she and the butcher's madame probably had the same affliction—she grimaced bitterly about those strange words, womb and ovaries, with which boone's wife too was going to beat her around the head—first madame butcher, and now boone's wife, and who would be next? Soon everyone in skirts . . . soon even the priest would be talking to her about his ovaries and his womb. She laughed at that idiotic image and no longer felt so rebellious about it: she really wasn't worried that much anymore. There were others, younger than she was, to turn things upside down now, to tease madame this and madame that, to halt the world in its sinful course, and throw a veil over every belly so that they became dark cellars again. Others had to be found, because she herself (and today, today especially) only made a face, and turned away, and wanted to sit on her own doorstep and give herself over to reflections on the relativity of everything.

And sitting there on her own stoop—after having quickly stuffed something into her mouth in the house that the children must not know about . . . after having drank a bottle of beer that she had fetched from the pub—no café over there—she grimaced at boone, grimaced about madame d'haens. She felt a little sunshine inside, and thought: don't let me start thinking that everyone carries their own sunshine within them! And she laughed—and yet clung on, with both hands placed against her heart over the little ray of sunshine in her, as if it were a bird that might soon try to fly away. Madame butcher appeared in the doorway of their shop and came over to her, most probably to talk about those disgraceful things again: ow, my ovaries, and the doctor says and I replied and the butcher himself, my husband, decided that, if it all HAS to be removed, they should do it as soon as possible, but I don't dare I don't dare. Oh, let her go fuck herself with her womb, thought ondine . . . let her have her ovaries removed and put on sale in their shop, the world IS relative, for me the world remains WHATEVER I make of it. She saw the butcher's wife approaching and held on more tightly to the sunshine in herself. Do you know what, ondine! said the other woman . . . that empty corner

444

has been sold to an american who's going to put up a cinema. A cinema? And it staggered her, so that she called inside: oscarke, come here, they're going to build a cinema here. And oscarke was staggered too, he called the children and pointed to the wasteland and said: a cinema! And the children, oscarke, and ondine stood pointing at the wasteland and picturing a cinema to themselves. The children soon went off to play, to play cinemas, oscarke went inside and as he carved his work his thoughts also carved a cinema, the butcher's wife went back to her ovaries, and ondine sat alone, there on the worn front step of their house. She remembered the dream house that she had placed on that corner: oh god, she said. She looked at the wasteland, she looked at the children playing, at leopold who was both the projectionist and the hero of the film: sometimes he turned the handle and made a humming sound, then he leaped around with his feet askew, made ugly faces and fell on his ass. The other children sat around and laughed and jumped and made wild cowboy gestures—they shouted and trampled little albert under-foot. Ondine turned her head away. Yes, she did. She turned her head away from boone's troubles, because everyone had their own troubles—she turned away from the obscene things that had to be removed from the belly of madame butcher, for it was no longer up to her to stop the course of the world—and she turned away from her dream house, since everything is relative. Everything was relative. And with her realizing this, she no longer got so annoyed, no longer got so annoyed it could have killed her when someone in the neighborhood didn't go to church—just as long as she went to heaven!—and apart from that, going to heaven was another impetuous expression from her youth . . . and so it would be better to say: as long as she went to mass, the priest was well-disposed to her, and the repair of confes-sionals and communion pews was given to oscarke.

You should be seen a bit more in church, oscarke! she said, while she held a card from the fellowship of the sacred heart, on which he drummed her fingers thoughtfully: they sent this card and you didn't go, how are you supposed to repair confessionals and pews if you don't go and wear them out first! Oscarke was about to reply that, well, it wasn't a matter of a man more or less, that those confessionals would wear out without him, but . . . thinking about it . . . it was just her imag-ery. He stood chisel in hand, ready to carve a wooden flower, and didn't look at her standing there holding a card from the fellowship of the sacred heart: she won't understand anyway, he thought . . . that a person can be self-sufficient. If I were to start explaining to her that everyone has a little sunshine in their own heart and must cherish that sunshine and try to maintain it, she wouldn't understand. And he nodded in agreement with her, to be rid of her, to see her leave his shed where cobwebs draped the little window. Go away, he thought, and leave me alone with my bit of sunshine, I can do without the sunshine of the church. So ondine saw him nodding his head thoughtfully: he understood. And she turned away towards the door of his shed—his studio, she said elsewhere—but seeing judith in the yard

*who had been peeling potatoes and came to throw the peel in the dustbin, singing
as she worked . . . singing ave maria, as if she were in front of an altar, perhaps
with pleading eyes behind her thick lenses . . . gave ondine an idea! And she turned
back to oscarke: of course she said if something in the church is to be repaired, it
first has to become worn out, but . . . why don't you join the church choir, since
you can sing the stuff they play on the radio so nicely? This staggered oscarke all
over again, just as that cinema had staggered him—the number of changing things
there were in the world, of . . . what should he say . . . phantoms! A cinema, a
chorister in the church, an american, a priest. And looking at the wooden flower,
and cutting with his chisel into that cinema, into that singing church, he ruined
the flower, dammit. Dammit, he said . . . you see what happens with all your . . .
things? Now my church is ruined, now . . . now . . . Oh for christ's sake, chorister
in the church, all the nonsense she came out with! And he thought partly of the
world to come, his world of the future, into which a church chorister didn't fit,
where it was all going to be smooth lines and planes and boxes, and . . . hadn't he
just had the idea (since his world of the future could no longer be purely a sedative
for his appalling questions) that that world of the future no longer mattered that
much to him? A world of the future, future said it all, it was something for the
future, for those who came after him—after all, it'll be the kids who have to clean
it up! said boone whenever he encountered a setback in life—and also, hadn't he
also thought that people long for a new society, or for a heaven when they're about
to die, without realizing that this heaven or this new society was already inside
them? Inside was a bit of sunshine, inside was heaven, inside was the new society.
So why go to church, and sing? In honor of the god and the heaven inside him?
And on the other hand didn't singing in church mean being a kind of failed priest?
Like so-and-so, what was his name again? who walked down the street with a
sanctimonious, prim expression, with a thick prayer book under his arm and his
eyes fixed on the toes of his shoes, almost without lifting his feet off the ground . . .
but who had produced and continued to produce offspring one after another, and
it didn't seem like he was going to stop in the near future. And oscarke would like
to see that zealot in bed sometime, with his eyes piously closed and his church book
under his arm, making babies with his wife. So that was what he, oscarke, was
going to become too, the church chorister, a zealot with a church book under his
arm. But, on the other hand. But, on the other hand—or again on the other hand:
how many other hands are there on a simple little, innocent little question like (for
instance) singing in church?—and from there, how many other hands were there
on the millions and millions of other little questions of which the world was made
up?—and thinking of the millionth other hand on that millionth little thing . . .
being a church chorister, singing while everyone sits listening, raising your voice
and reaching the high notes, or with a deep deep growl producing the lowest notes,
as he was so fond of doing—it made his spine tingle around the lower vertebrae,*

so that the sun, a small piece of sunshine, began to vibrate in him—and he made it vibrate, he sung some low, some very low notes—and then, afterwards, when the high mass was over the people would rush out of the church, and say: did you hear oscarke singing those low notes there? Happiness is inside you, and singing in church could be part of it. He went. And ondine, who thought—no, who had vaguely imagined to herself without really thinking about it—that the church choristers were saints, who just sang a bit at mass, soon learned that such things had to be learned: the mass of this and that, and of something else: all kinds of names of composers who had written masses—as oscarke was able to tell her—and who were composers whose work she heard on the radio sometimes, but immediately turned off. Because though she was catholic, she couldn't listen to catholic music, and though she was against the merry widows—what a filthy term that was, what a host of lewd things it conjured up: a merry widow?—but she put on the merry widow music instead. But all that music that she couldn't bear had to be learned by the church choristers: they had to have rehearsals: and it soon seemed to her as if oscarke's life consisted of nothing but wood chips and rehearsals. Evening after evening he had to go, and evening after evening they went for an informal sing-song, a chat and a discussion, in a pub—oh, when was she going to move with the times? In a café—and played cards and the priest sometimes bought them a round. And the priest sometimes told a joke about the-priest-and-his-maid—oh again that joke about the priest and his maid, the never-changing and already permitted and even respectable joke about that priest who slept with his maid—but hadn't oscarke heard that the previous priest what's-his-name . . . had been dismissed, or transferred, or put into a home where priests were sent who had transgressed, and who were never heard from again?—but whatever the finer points, the previous priest had gone, and no one ever mentioned his name again, and so in fact he had been lowered into a deep dark pit, a trap—and this new priest stayed up all night long drinking and boozing, and came into church in the morning half-plastered and celebrated mass. And oscarke knew a joke about that priest too, but it was a forbidden joke, which the butcher's wife had once told him after swearing him to secrecy . . . which he now told himself everyday having sworn himself to secrecy . . . everyday to start with, and later occasionally, and then sporadically, for example when the priest told his joke about the-priest-and-his-maid. I know a joke about the priest too, said oscarke. Tell us! Tell us! cried the others. Oh, I can't tell jokes, when I tell one nobody laughs, he replied.

Ondine was only sorry that it was a very respectable and very catholic café, because she couldn't say anything filthy to keep him from going—but she didn't know that oscarke had a pint from the priest and then immediately left and went to that other café, where rosa was: rosa, who though she was already married, still remained the rosa who had been willing to listen to the story of his life for the price of the pint that he came to drink: rosa, who as a very young girl had sat on his knee while he sang smutty songs for her: rosa, who had let him sob his heart out between her legs. And so when oscarke asked for money, it was actually to cultivate his artificial happiness further in the presence of rosa, and to tell the forbidden joke about rev. vanderklincken. He cherished his sunshine there with rosa and her husband who stood rinsing glasses behind the bar, and with the child on her lap and the child that ran in and out and slammed the doors: he worked at building the heaven inside himself, the new society, for himself alone. Right, that was it, he had a new society for himself alone. And coming home from that café he liked looking at the girls in the street: he looked at the girls and he liked it—he used to be ashamed about liking young girls, but no longer, he had begun to realize that it was a misguided kind of heroism to fight and go on fighting against it. Apart from that, a bud was more beautiful than a rose, because it always had the potential to become an even more beautiful rose—and apart from that, the fact that he liked roses-in-bud more was ondine's fault, who had been an overripe and overblown rose when he . . . oh, when he had discovered jeannine. And what he no longer knew . . . because he had forgotten, because he had forgotten jeannine herself . . . was that he was unconsciously looking for jeannine! Or rather, that he was unconsciously looking for the days, the bygone days from his life, with jeannine. And looking at the girls in the street, he thought again of his album of "testimonies," and looked up the reproduction—april—oh, and there she was, little jeannine, little rosa, and christ how sweet! He immediately made a folder, at the back of the small shed, and put "april" in it. Then came something else, and then . . . then came something that he himself scarcely dared look at—what could you say about ondine, who suddenly appeared in his shed looking for a piece of cardboard to cut an insole out of for leopold's shoes—leopold's shoes that were too big for him, he said, and when they had an insole in them were too small, he also said, so that ondine didn't know what to do and hit him on the head with the shoes—"can I have that bit of cardboard?" she asked and meanwhile she already had the folder in her hands and all the "testimonies" fell out. Oh, oscarke . . . oscarke, what is THAT? And afterwards it was his kids who had found the folder—because what didn't they find, where didn't they poke their noses?—and leopold took it into the street, he sat on the butcher's stoop with the folder on his knees, and all the children in the street hung around him. But the artificial armor in which oscarke kept his world of the future, his heaven, his bit of sun, was only brittle armor: the slightest thing knocked holes in it. For example, the eternal distraction of ondine, who was always trying to impose her own will, her own foolish ideas on him, although he knew—and she should also have known—that everything always remains as it is: if she kicked a stone a little further, it would STILL come to a stop, a little further on, and would still REMAIN a stone there. So ondine could kick him wherever she could, but he would still stay oscarke, with his own little will, and his own crazy ideas . . . The distraction of ondine, *who forbade him to keep his nicest pictures in the book of testimonies, so that he had to hide them where they were liable to get damaged, torn, and nibbled on by mice. The distraction of the children, of leopold, who took his father's little bit of happiness, his father's little bit of sun into the street, to show to the neighborhood children. And also, especially, that there was no work again. The priest couldn't go on having chairs repaired forever—because however often he went to confession or communion, however loudly he sang in church, that still didn't produce enough wear and tear for him to have work every day—and besides he still wouldn't be the "church sculptor," in the same way that he was a church chorister, in the same way that there was a church upholsterer and verger and a church priest. And he thought about it, fearing that he might have to look for work in Brussels again—because those things were fine for young lads who LIKED traveling on the train, who liked going back and forth to brussels, supposedly to look for work but actually in search of adventure. But oscarke and adventure? Oscarke and looking for work in brussels? That little tuft on the back of his head was already completely gray—and sometimes he had to borrow ondine's glasses for a moment when he had to copy or enlarge an ornament—and also he always had a pain in the small of his back when he had stood for too long, could it be his kidneys? People had kidneys. Young people didn't know that—young people who traveled back and forth to brussels thought that a body was something like the world itself, eternal and everlasting, hard as iron, and existing solely to pin girls against a blank wall somewhere, and to rush towards adventure—but as one got on in years a little, you began to understand that that a body is a machine that can show wear and tear, a mass-produced item following hard on the heels of the previous item and ousted by the mass-produced items that would follow it—and with kidneys in it that start hurting. And there was also a problem with his leg, a particular vein always swelled up if he stood upright for too long, carving away at his new world . . . no, carving away at his work and dreaming of his new world, and meanwhile the vein swelled and his leg puffed up and hurt. Now he sat down, lay around a bit, rummaged a bit in a drawer, or read the paper. But over there in brussels, assuming that he was going to look for work and assuming that he was also going to find work, which was a completely different matter: he wouldn't be able to sit down over there. He couldn't say to his boss: I'm going to stop working now and go and sit and look at the street, at the girls who don't yet know they've got kidneys and veins, but assume that they only have feet for dancing, and young breasts to make married men forget that they have a wife and kids and a god—and who will not know till much much later that they also have a womb and ovaries that will hurt.*

No, those things could never happen in brussels . . . brussels had become an impossibility for him . . . for him brussels was the center of this whole damn shitty world.

Now it has stopped raining, and you can hear the grass grow—the grass and the weeds together. Never having to put another letter down on paper, but to be able always to look at that garden and wander through that wood!—to be able now to chase all your characters into the Nothingness from which you conjured them up! But no sooner have you thought that than johan janssens is standing on your small terrace and tapping on the glass wall of your living room: it's me! Right, you're there dammit, and have come to be a nuisance again, have come to tell me this or that is wrong with my novel, and that it's still not good enough, when WILL it be good enough?—eternal, tormenting demons, eternal damn demons that you are, begrudging me my happiness, my bit of sun, my bit of heaven on earth, my bit of world-to-come-for-me-alone . . .

It's your fault . . . how could you try to end your book with only that tippe-totje with you? Why try to end a book with something that was intended as a challenge, and yet wasn't? No, no, you conjured up johan janssens, me—you had me mount the social hobbyhorse, had me ride it towards social reforms and changes—and now you end your book with a church singer making an album of testimonies, for whom the world is a shitty place that he has nothing more to do with. Not like that! Your book will end where it has to end: where it began. On the last page, your book will once more and for the last time be a mirror of everything I have lived and fought and been tortured for—or my name is no longer johan janssens . . .

Your name isn't johan janssens, you say—you don't even have a name—you don't even exist—you're just a reflection, a ghost, a shadow of an illusion . . .

All the same, you still have to listen to me, and I insist that your book not end by saying that the world is . . . is . . . No, you'll go on writing, go on writing just a little longer, and only when it's to my liking can you bury yourself in this patch of garden, in this patch of woodland.

And what if I don't want to? you ask. And johan janssens laughs pityingly. Come on, he says . . . let's start, let's write a definitive final page—not a tippetotje ending, but a johan janssens ending: something about . . . well, about something that's always fascinated me, and which I've constantly had to fight for: theories. So let's mention:

MARIETTE'S THEORIES

Brussels had become an impossibility for oscarke. But, as always happens—as it always happens in life, that when there's is no room for something, room is found for something else, something small—and also to reinforce his theory that

450

everything was relative, he might have had less work, but on the other hand, judith found work. Oh, it was odd, he'd looked all around town: he and boone and other people in the neighborhood had almost no work, but on the other hand there was more than enough work for the women. Almost every woman was working in a factory and came home in the evening and cooked something in a mad rush, and also washed and cleaned, and so did Everything, but the men were out of work and just sat around—or the man did the housework by himself—the woman went to work and the man did the housework, the man washed the children's diapers and the woman worked in a factory somewhere—soon you'd be hearing about women coming home drunk from work and men having periods—soon the man would get pregnant and would have to bring children into the world, while his wife sat in the café talking dirty to young . . . young . . . well, would there be young men serving beer to the women? And oscarke smirked at this, but the fact remained that he was sitting around while judith on the contrary had work. But then in itself that work of judith's was also relative—she worked but she didn't earn anything. At the end of the week or the month, what did she bring home? And oscarke didn't bother to work it out, because he didn't like working things out or calculating or facing truths that were too painful—but if he HAD worked it out, he might have seen that judith's work was actually costing *them money: she had to be neatly dressed and had to have something to put in her sandwiches, something different every day, sometimes ham, sometimes egg, and she earned scarcely enough to buy even one egg a month—this was a little exaggerated, but nonetheless. She worked in the big store where they'd bought the radio and the washing machine on credit. Everything on credit, and the revolving door spun round, and the radio played the merry widow music, and people came and bought everything you could desire on earth, provided they could put aside 2 francs a day: judith stood there in the shop and showed people pianos and washing machines, stoves and radios, and something else, something new that no one had seen yet: a jazz band: something with black musicians playing, and everyone came and looked and had to laugh: what on earth is that? But judith wasn't there long, they were afraid that her swollen head would frighten people away, and shook their heads at her short-sightedness, which got worse every day. Even with the strongest glasses in the world she still bumped into everything, the counters and the revolving door, that brand-new novelty with the black musicians playing, the jazz band. She came home and bumped into everything there—but wasn't it somehow like leopold said: that she didn't see anything when she didn't WANT to see anything? In particular she didn't see the dirt that was on the floor—because it was still her job to wash and scrub—mariette was supposed to help her, but she just sat on the toilet, or was sick, or had an errand to run in town. Recently she also spent a lot of time standing at the front door, looking at the american who walked back and forth across the patch of wasteland: he arrived in a car and slammed the door so* that everyone in the street jumped, walked back and forth a bit from the wasteland to boone's shed, and got into an argument over the shed, because it was actually on His land, where he was going to build a cinema. Boone talked big when the american wasn't there—but now that he stood there with his feet wide apart, rolling cigarettes like a cowboy, giving orders to the people he was paying to transform the empty site into a tower of babel, boone wisely remained indoors. Oh, boone had taken things a little too easily, had collected some planks and sheet metal and built himself a shed on that empty site, the land was unused anyway, and now he was frightened of being taken to court: he wasn't taken to court, but the american, who was a calculator, started working out how long the shed had stood there since he'd bought the land, and boone had to pay rent in arrears. Mariette watched all this—she swung her hips and flashed her eyes a bit, till the moment when the american arrived with his wife. Oh, that was her?—everyone knew her, she was from over there by the pool, the daughter of that cow with the wooden leg, a snot-nose who'd run away from the pool, and—could you imagine it—had wound up in america. Mariette got a bit of a shock. But the next day she forgot that he was married anyway—judith washed and scrubbed, but mariette came out to swab the pavement and again bent over too far with her ass half bare—figuratively, that is, since she was now wearing trousers: trousers her mother had bought, with long legs, which she however had cut down so that they had become shorts that were far too short and onto which she had tacked some lace edging, very roughly. Yes, just as she did everything very roughly: washed roughly, but powdered herself and applied rouge to her cheeks very carefully. Something that caused an uproar every day: I never did that, said ondine. Ondine measured everything in the world by what she had done or hadn't done—her children weren't allowed to do anything she hadn't done, but they weren't allowed to do anything she had done either: I did that, and I'm sorry I did, and it's been enough of a lesson to me, she would say. Oh, but all those words were lost on mariette. And if judith had been smart, she wouldn't have washed in the yard, behind walls where no one could see it, but she would have taken the washing machine out into the street, onto the pavement: then mariette would have helped.

Occasionally ondine would meet someone who said to her: that daughter of yours, what's her name again, judith, you should keep her indoors a bit more, because she's always over there by the edge of the park, and the way they carry on is really a disgrace! Our judith? thought ondine. But she soon realized: it was mariette. And so she said to mariette, who was starting to powder her face and curl her hair with tongs: where are you off to, down to the park? Mariette promised not to go to the park anymore, and not to hang out with that boy—but in the next few days ondine heard that mariette had been seen down by the arsenal, or down karrebroeck way, where ondine's old father vapeur lived, the specialist inventor . . . no, the specialist staircase builder. She had been walking with a man, *in jodhpurs, who looked like a cowboy: isn't it that american, who's going to build a garage right opposite your house? Oh, first it was judith, who had actually been mariette—then it was an american who was going to build a garage, which was actually a cinema. A cinema and a garage, judith and mariette, and on top of that . . . with a married man! It was a little much for ondine, who wanted a little peace and quiet, who wanted to hold on to the sun inside herself, and wanted to live in peace with things. But how could she live in peace with things, with those fucking kids, those street brats? Street brat! she shouted at judith, who looked at her in astonishment. Oh, said ondine, it's really our mariette that I mean. And then she had another of her nasty turns and had to lie in bed, had to have the doctor called in, who prescribed expensive medicines, special remedies, and she had to count her money, which was dwindling, had to spur oscarke on to look for work, had to smack leopold for breaking a window somewhere that she had to pay for—and because he'd started a fire somewhere way over in karrebroeck—what business did those brats of hers have over in karrebroeck?—and had burnt down a haystack too. And she also had to find work, both for mariette and for judith: she found work immediately for judith, who had always been the victim: again in one of those shops, not selling jazz, but coffee and sugar and hairpins and children's toys, and the devil knows what else: a large department store that had been built in the little mill town. Judith became a junior sales assistant—and the white collar over her black apron was just like a white dish on which her swollen head and alarmingly thick glasses were displayed. All she had to do was wrap things up, and give the customers a bill to go and pay at the register: very easy work—but work where, once again, she earned almost nothing.*

No one had to ask where that department store was, because you could see it blocks away, see the throng of people trying to get in and out. There was an unbelievable range of products available and everything cost virtually nothing, how could they sell it at that price? And as a result people's attitude towards small shopkeepers changed somewhat: the piles of money they must have made in the past! Because look, a box of matches that had always cost 1 franc fifty from boone cost only 90 centimes from the department store—but people didn't consider that in the department store the boxes were much flatter, and that therefore they paid less but also got less—and also that if you saw someone trying to light a cigarette with a match that kept going, and then another one with one that went out, dammit that makes three, people would say to the other one: I expect you've got department-store matches! People laughed, but went on shopping there. And the same thing went for the made-in-japan electric lightbulbs: oscarke and boone had no work (what on earth does it mean? your man and mine have no work—are we supposed to live on manna from heaven then? Lucky they've opened a big department store where everything is cheaper!), and people bought bulbs made in japan by people who lived on a bit of rice, didn't need an eight-hour day, and didn't need any benefits or pensions, so that those bulbs could be made for a song and be sold for a song in the big department store. And so you bought a bulb, but six times out of ten, the same evening: bzzt and it went out, it was useless. But it was mainly the farmers who lived far beyond termuren who flocked to the department store—the call of the department store had spread from the town far across the countryside, to country people who lived in great poverty—and they came on foot, or sitting on their carts, or riding their bikes—the whole street was filled with bikes, and the people in the neighboring houses hung notices in their windows saying: do not place bicycles here. Because there were also shops around that couldn't do any business at all with that damn big department store next door, so that the owners were infuriated by all the bikes, but still remained polite in their fury—the polite fury of a shopkeeper, who must always beware of his customers and so expressed his fury as follows: PLEASE do not place bicycles here—but this didn't do any good, because even if the farmers parked their bikes in bike racks while they were in the big department store—they were still in the big store buying trash for next to nothing that they had no use for when they got home—and if they got hungry, having come to town from so far away, they bought biscuits in the big department store, they bought black or white sausage or doughnuts. And when they got back to their fields, they'd spent a lot of money on trash. Boone had no more trade in his shop: everyone went to the big department store. But he himself wouldn't dream of buying a lamp from the electrician round the corner, he also went to the big department store, where lightbulbs were much cheaper—and people bought radios and kitchen cabinets in that other department store, in the credit shop, instead of ordering a cabinet with hand-carved curlicues from oscarke. The whole world had been turned on its head, the world was rolling towards an abyss of cheapness, and everything and everyone was a link in the chain pulling everything and everyone towards that abyss.

But leaving that aside, judith was an assistant in the department store—she earned scarcely anything, that was true—but at work she was called miss, and that was equally true. Ondine tried to get mariette into the department store too, she worked there for a week on probation but was thrown out unceremoniously without receiving a centime: she let her lace edged knickers show, she snacked on the biscuits that were for sale and she stood flirting with every man who happened to come into the store. Everyone had their own department: judith was in the comb-and-hairpin department, and in the millinery department was the daughter of a small manufacturer who had gone out of business because he could no longer compete with the department store . . . and mariette was in the school-supplies department. Mariette and school equipment! Mariette and children! And she abandoned her school equipment and went over to the biscuits, and went somewhere else if there happened to be a man standing there, a farmer, a gentleman, a student, it made no difference to her. And her trial week was over then and she

454

didn't go anymore: no, she simply stopped going of her own accord, because they weren't going to take me on anyway, she said. She had sensed it infallibly, she had the nose of the young ondine: and she also had invisible feelers on the top of her head, antennae, an artificial ear that listened in on the world: she lived by her feeling without feeling, and yet she was infallible in her feelings. She knew about everything wrong going on in town, and there was never a scandal involving this person or that without mariette being friends with those involved, or mariette being involved herself: it's incredible! she would sometimes say, shaking her head, while the appalling case was discussed in her presence—while she lay back with her feet on the stove, while she sat with her feet on the top rung of the chair, and her skirt was as ever too short to cover her thighs. Now she became pals with this wild slut who worked in a milliner's by the park—that's right, that same damn park where derenancourt's monuments stood, full of dead leaves, full of dead memories of things that had long since passed, and that no longer counted for mariette and the other girl . . . who worked in the milliner's next to the park.

You don't have to look for any work for me, mariette said to her mother . . . I've got work in a milliner's on the park. But her work was just a game; it would have been better if she'd said: I've gone to play *in a milliner's—it was curiosity that drove her there, and the boys who worked there, and the boss who was said to like working girls. And two weeks later she was pals with another . . . well, "whore" wasn't quite the word, but what other word was there?—who worked in a stocking factory, and so mariette suddenly also worked in a stocking factory. Then it was somewhere in a knitting shop on the outskirts of the town, somewhere around nievekerken, and then, for the next two weeks, she was in a shoe factory just down the street. Mariette didn't want to have to commute by train to another town—because there were problems on the trains; because scandals happened on those trains . . . or so she'd heard. No, mariette wasn't a bourgeois—that attitude and that life of hers, and all those factories, and all those scandals, who knew better than ondine that it was far from bourgeois? But what was the point of her fighting and going on fighting all those . . . all those . . . Our mariette working in factory? Yes that's right, but she's in the office, said ondine. She types in the office, ha, that was something bourgeois—yes, and before mariette got back in the evenings and ate a sandwich while standing up, powdering her face, and then flying off to the darkest corners of the town, the most suspicious cafés, the seamiest dance halls, then she typed there in the office: I type in an office, said mariette, who began to believe her mother's lies. And she started despising all those farmers, all those factory workers, those who modestly worked at home, and tradesmen too, she went around with assistant pharmacists, young schoolmasters, and sons from rich families: in the past she'd been involved with soldiers, and now she was involved with students. With students at the university who were socialists or something even worse, or else were completely the opposite. Like the son of madame van wesenborgh—he was a tall,*

pale streak, the Pear Tree they called him, because as he walked he wobbled like
a young fruit tree in the wind, and if you touched him he collapsed. But he had a
student's cap on his head, carried a club, and talked of nothing but politics: he was
in favor of a strong hand that kept the world under control, of a new order that
would clear away the muddle of the present: he talked of nothing but this clearing
away: on his lapel he wore a small gold pin depicting a street sweeper. He talked
mainly french and mariette was obliged to learn french too, which she did quickly:
she began to enjoy speaking it and getting her big mouth around that foreign lan-
guage . . . And strange to say, ondine, ha . . . she also spoke french and they started
parlez-vousing, mais-oui and bien-sur, all day long. And mariette expounded her
political ideas—that is to say, the political ideas of madame van wesenborgh's
son—and they were, however unbelievable it may seem, the ideals that ondine
had when she was young and lusty and religious. But mariette wasn't religious, or
in any event clericalism didn't affect her: she was a fascist, she said. And she broke
it off with the pear tree, and in order to taunt him she courted a distant relation
of the gourmonprez's, a socialist of the top rank, and he explained the world as it
appeared to mariette: a monstrous thing full of injustice and corruption, that cre-
ated fascism in order to provoke war and dissolve the trade unions, and to allow
injustice and corruption to persist: he spoke of the great financiers and the trusts,
about the most bestial slaughter of all time, the first war . . . And mariette suddenly
interrupted him to ask why he was actually a socialist, and saw syndicalism as the
solution to every problem: he who after all was a rich man, and would see his
wealth being taken away by the syndicalists. That doesn't mean anything, he said
. . . and he talked and talked till he no longer even understood himself, but if you
wanted to summarize it, it boiled down to the following: the world had to become
something like it was in russia. And his friend, who was walking beside him and
beside mariette, said: in that case you're not a socialist, but a communist! Mariette
almost fainted with shock, really, because a communist, what was that?: a beast
that raped nuns. And then she went home, and proclaimed the precise opposite of
what she'd been saying the previous week—or she mixed socialism and fascism
and communism together into a hodgepodge that became a true picture of the
world: a mishmash that not even the devil could fathom.

SOME PEPPER AND SALT

A foolish young guard dog comes running from the woods and puts its paws
against the glass wall of your living room—so that in no time there's the
filthiest mess there you've ever seen—and after it runs off right through your
flowers, which it tramples underfoot, tolfpoets says to his idiot of a dog: why
do you have to come here and make everything a mess? And tolfpoets says
it's so lonely over there in his so-called villa: when we used to live within the

town walls of termuren, I longed for silence and peace, but now that we're living out here I've discovered that we actually need other people's noise—if only to be able to get mad at them—to put up garish signs and boom forth furiously from our loudspeakers: please be quiet! And tolfpoets smiles and bares all his gold teeth: it's a long time since I've found a joke like that in your book: you're writing more and more pages Beyond the finishing line of your novel, and I see my humor has a smaller and smaller part in it. The music master is angry, tippetotje is cynical, and johan janssens is too—but tolfpoets's humor no longer seems suitable; I was good enough to add the occasional touch of spice, to sprinkle some pepper and salt over your pages, but now . . .

Oh tolfpoets, please, leave me the fuck alone—it's forbidden to come and unsettle me from here on in! The 2nd book on chapel road, the book that we've called "summer in termuren," was ended you-know-where . . . And it's only for the critics, for the reader, for convention, and for the 1,000 different formulae required to be able to live and write nowadays, that I've consented to write a little Beyond the finishing line. I only did it to introduce oscarke and ondine into our modern world . . . and to acquaint them with the world of the barbarians. And finally to satisfy the music master, and tippetotje, and johan janssens . . .

And tolfpoets shoos away his young idiot of a guard dog, which is walking right across the pages of your book, and he says: exactly, to please them you've put oscarke and ondine and judith and leopold and mariette right in the middle of technology and mechanization and politics—but is that supposed to be the postwar period? Come on now, those days were totally different! All you've described are indignant, embittered, and cynical details, and again you didn't notice the essential point: humor! And one last thing: you've written a deadly serious book, so why not give it a humorous ending, a funny conclusion—you've written a book aimed at raising hell on stilts as we say, and that was good: stilts are humorous legs that are too long—well, let's push on to the bitter, humorous end, and write a few final pages . . . about for example those legs that are too long . . . or no, something better:

SHORT HAIR

Mariette sat telling them about her adventures, and judith could only gape at her: then she sang the ave maria by schubert or gounod, no one could distinguish the two—and then she cried a little because she wasn't a success, didn't know french, and couldn't talk to students about music . . . no, about politics. She also wanted to walk around town, and say that she typed in an office, in an office in a department store, and that she could sing the ave maria by shunod. These days not an evening went by at ondine's place without a fight: judith blamed mariette and

mariette blamed judith . . . and ondine, who had to listen to them, blamed them
both—and besides that there was always some trouble with leopold and mauriske,
who were turning into real vagabonds: oh, there were frightful scenes. Oscarke
was in the middle of it all and fought for his bit of happiness: I'm going for a
walk, he said, and he strolled to the outskirts of the town and watched the sun set
somewhere behind an unmanned crossing, a farmyard, and a horse in a field—or
saw the arsenal and the gray houses around it and over along the railway, soaked
by some rain. He let the hubbub of the kennel that had penetrated his head waft
away. And as he walked along he sometimes heard mariette shout something, so he
turned around on those slightly uneven cobblestones, which were taking him away
from the town and the grubby houses there—but when he turned around he saw
no one: it was only that noise, that shouting of judith's and mariette's and ondine's,
and leopold's outright screaming, and mauriske's whining: all echoing in his ears
now that he was walking in silence down this country road.

And strolling through distant karrebroeck he dropped in to see his father-in-law
vapeur and valeer, who were in their workshop making things without straight
lines, neither the old line with carved flowers, Nor the modern line that was reminiscent of a flat box—but something nameless, shapeless, tasteless: something that
could only be made by a dreamer of an inventor of a vapeur while he went around
with such strange things in his head—and which valeer helped him make: valeer
who was valeer, who just rocked his fat head back and forth let his own strange
ideas rock along with it. Oscarke talked about line, the old and the new lines, and
suddenly, after oscarke and vapeur had been arguing for hours, just For the Sake
of argument, just to hear their own voices, valeer got up off the floor where he'd
been sitting and carving, and intervened: and oh, the things he went on about,
while his fat head swung from left to right more drastically than they'd ever seen
before! He gave a portrait of oscarke, a very well-observed and depicted portrait,
and then a portrait of his father vapeur, also such a perfect portrait that oscarke
nodded and said: everything you say about your father is true, although you're a
bit wide of the mark about me—while vapeur said nothing, since he'd been going
to say: everything you say about ondine's husband is quite true, but the picture
you paint of me is a bit exaggerated—and valeer then said that they were fools,
curved or straight lines, what difference did a line make to Them?: we're not in
a palace here with curls and ornaments and antique statuary, nor are we in a
modern house with smooth, flat lines, but . . . where are we in fact? And as oscarke
and his father looked up after being brought down to earth, he gestured around
them: we're in a shed built of cinderblocks that used to be a lemonade factory.
Voilà, those are the facts . . . those are facts. And he stumbled over his words a
little, and gestured with his mutilated hands, and repeated himself two or three
times, but what he was trying to say got through very clearly: don't look at shape
and form, at principles and theories, but get on with it—don't keep looking back.

Right, let's look ahead and not go round in circles, let's take the cheapest wood there is and make mass-produced items out of it—something not too difficult to make, that doesn't need too much time or trouble, for example dressing tables: let us make dressing tables by the thousands—mass, mass, mass-produced—with children who'll help knock the parts together somewhere far away, with someone else who'll fit the mirrors, and with oscarke who'll carve 1 flower in every table, always the same, and then off we go! But the way he said it, they were in stitches: 1 flower, he said—and looked sideways at his little finger, which was supposed to represent that 1 flower. And oscarke laughed at him: you know nothing about carving, he said . . . carving this and carving that . . . and he brought in all kinds of impossible objections that had nothing to do with the matter at hand. But they failed to see the main thing—the big advantage. There could have been a fortune in valeer's proposal . . . but, well. And oscarke walked on, past the wet scrub, down the road, past a girl who looked at him, simply looked at him, since oscarke was a little guy with graying hair who was a bit skinny and a bit this and that—and oscarke looked at her . . . and he looked round again, just as the girl herself looked round again, thinking: that old guy is giving me such a look—and he looked and smiled and felt a touch of happiness, felt a bit of sun. And when he got home, well, there was another fuss: he shouldn't go for walks anymore, there was enough work to do in the house, a bit of painting, whitewashing the yard, digging up the floor and then resetting it with the same stones—since there was a dip in it where the water gathered whenever it was scrubbed—check the washing machine and run an electric cable to the little shed—but ondine wouldn't let him buy any tools, he had to do it all with his bare hands. He had to paint without paint. And then he went and borrowed tools from boone. He fiddled with the lock on a door that no longer closed after having been slammed too many times in previous fights or kicked shut when leopold had one of his tantrums—and he tried to get a plug of paper out of the lock, which mariette had stuck in when she went to bathe behind the door . . . when she finally got round to bathing and stripped down naked as if she never intended to wear a stitch again. Oscarke stood there wasting time, messing around amid the fights that went right over his head: it was still a fight about a boy, the same as he'd been listening to for ages now, and since he'd never paid enough attention to fully understand it, it seemed to him that it was still about the same boy: and he asked, what boy they were actually talking about? And they laughed at him: oh, what a dope of a father they had, thinking there was only 1 boy in the whole town. Mariette had a striking body and the most beautiful legs you could find anywhere—anyone could see that, since she didn't exactly hide her light under a bushel: every five steps there seemed to be something wrong with her garter, she would hitch up her skirt and straighten her stockings—and she was also one of the first to help bring the immoral fashion for short skirts into vogue. She'd been nagging on for days about getting a new dress: I'll save up for one myself, she said finally—and eight days later she had enough. She'd saved that money up pretty quickly. The dress was being made and every evening she had to go for a fitting: there were endless descriptions to judith as to what the dress was going to look like: she would stand there with a broom in her hand, striking the most impossible poses, twisting and turning her body, looking over her shoulder with her eyes closed, and meanwhile constantly swiveling her hips—so that leopold started screaming with laughter, imitated her movements and meanwhile let out a great stinking fart. A scuffle broke out, and after the scuffle mariette went on telling them about the dress. And when the dress was ready and was brought home and mariette tried it on—well, it came to just above the knee. Ondine looked and looked: oh, they got the size wrong, what happened? And she laughed at the girl who had brought the dress—but afterwards it turned out that it really was the latest fashion in dresses: ondine was furious, laughed and wept—and suddenly she grabbed her own brown dress covered in margarine stains and hitched it up far above her knees, and strutted about with her backside bare—with her old, rather flat thighs in dirty, torn, long-legged bloomers, imitating the new fashion. And while still prancing around like this she called mariette a whore: ondine who'd always been so decent. So mariette in her new dress in the latest fashion began raking up the whole of her mother's youth—and when ondine made some retort about the park and the milliner's, mariette had countered with termuren castle, and when ondine mentioned the commuter trains, mariette cried: vapeur's bitch . . . vapeur's minx! Because if mariette had lovely legs, she still had a hard face with piercing eyes, and too much to say for herself—especially in a fight.

Oh, oscarke was still puttering around on the floor, taking a stone out and tamping down the earth, spreading cement and reinserting the stone—on his knees with the stone in his hands, staring at their two great mouths in amazement. The harsh, provocative laugh of mariette cut right through his skin, through his soul, as if someone were scraping iron on iron—it reminded him of ondine's laugh at the most appalling moments of their lives, when he had wondered: is that really ondine, the ondine I married? But the laugh cut ondine to the core too, right through her brain: she clasped her hands to her ears and fled outside: it reminded her of little marie-louise, who had died, who had passed away on the saddest, most tragic night of her life. She fled into the hall, out of the front door. And she stopped there on the threshold, looking round to find something to switch her senses, her thoughts, her whole being to some new wavelength. Yes, switch, wavelength, just like the radio inside could be tuned to some different station: and then she looked at the empty plot on the corner of the dark street. The empty plot, she kept saying . . . but it was no longer an empty plot, it was a scene of desolate devastation, the greatest chaos imaginable, now that the american's builders were going full speed ahead: a café that was going to do car rentals, and a garage where a taxi service was planned. That's right, a garage—and not a cinema. Who had got that into their head in the first place, a cinema? Perhaps since there'd been mention of an american, someone had immediately dragged in a cinema—but even apart from that, he wasn't an american, how could he be, he was a belgian like the rest of them—he was from the same town, but he had gone to america, to the state of ohio as he said—where he'd met that snot-nose from the pool, that slut with her flaming eyes. And now, having grown rich over there, he'd come back to the empty space where ondine's dream house should have stood: she looked at it and told herself the story of that american to shake off mariette's laughter. As soon as it had quieted down a bit, she went back inside—oh, but soon, at the slightest spark, the argument flared up again. Judith intervened with the silliest and most absurd arguments—and sometimes mariette thought it was an argument against Her, while ondine on the other hand thought it was to Her disadvantage: and they both came down on judith like a ton of bricks. Judith would then fall silent, she was ugly and nobody loved her, her sight was poor and she was the slave—she was the slave more or less everywhere, at her job in the department store, and in the yard at the washtub. She occasionally accompanied mariette on her jaunts, but had no luck—and funnily enough mariette had no luck either. The boys didn't like judith's hydrocephalic head with its glasses, and kept away from both of them—and that body, what kind of body was that? Shapeless, with a dress that was taut where it shouldn't be, was baggy here and tight there: and she also went out in a dress that only came up to just above the knee, but it still didn't look immoral on her: she could have gone out naked and it Still wouldn't have looked immoral. And so mariette, with judith in tow, had no luck at all: she didn't dare go anywhere, neither to the students who discussed socialism and fascism and activism, nor to those dives where there was dancing to the rattling tones of a pianola and where love was for sale. She usually played around and gave the students a taste of her big mouth, and the soldiers and the married men from the factories too—but with judith she avoided all those places and went to completely different venues, for example to the outskirts of town, where there was a local fair, and a temporary dance hall had been set up. Mariette thought: no one will know me here . . . but no sooner had they got inside than everyone knew who was there: it's schatt's daughter mariette! And who was the other one, that one with her hydrocephalic head and glasses? No one knew judith. And when they left the dance hall in the evening—the tent full of holes that had been put up on an empty building site, or the garage that had been slightly tidied up, and where the bar and the barrels of beer had been placed next to old tires and empty gas cans—when they left, they had to make do with the worst that was on offer: in the throng they hadn't sized up their beaux too well, and outside, in the falling darkness, they still didn't see too clearly—but then as they walked along, judith in front with her "sweetheart" and mariette behind with the other boy, when they came under the light of a street-light: christ almighty, mariette held onto the post to keep from laughing: judith's *admirer was someone with a limp in his left leg. And the strange spectacle of the limping shadow in the lamplight! She hung onto the lamppost laughing hysterically: judith, look! The young men hurried off into the darkness in embarrassment, and from a distance, from the black cavern of the evening, they shouted something about "whores"—but mariette immediately shouted back something like "horny gimp!"—and as she walked on she noticed that judith had stopped, had stayed leaning against the lamppost and . . . was crying. Finally she followed in silence, sat in her corner, and then went on crying quietly—oh, after all, it was such a fluke for her to have had a sweetheart in the first place, and if he had a limp, what did that matter? As if she was a catch herself!*

But when mariette had done the rounds of those shoe factories and knitwear shops, she started from the beginning again, and went to the milliner's over by the park. She'd only just arrived when she asked for a raise—and as though she actually deserved a raise, a raise for her cheeky mouth and her lovely legs . . . and because of the way she went to the office and sat herself down on a chair . . . no, not even the boss could resist: she was given a raise, and now had to come and help him in the evenings with sorting or filing or some such thing—and of course at home the story was exactly that: she stayed late to check the books. But those were strange books that he sorted with mariette: soon she became a supervisor, and walked around in a white coat, patrolling the area between the warehouse and the toilets, chasing the girls back to their stations and making them work harder. But then she was discovered by the boss's wife, sitting and filing with the boss. Oh, that was a fine business! And so mariette was sent to brussels to stay with cousin maria. And her life now revolved around the forestoise mill, where she was soon set up in a café, or became a barmaid for the hell of it, or she took the streetcar to the city center and walked around the department stores, or went to the cinema, or leaped around in the bobino dance hall, or went and had some fun with a streetcar conductor in a hotel room: she gave free rein to her demons and was drunk and horny but never satisfied: cousin maria wrote to ondine that they couldn't stand it any longer with mariette, she brought a bad atmosphere with her that affected her husband and children and apart from that the whole neighborhood by the forestoise. Mariette came back home thinner, with black rings round her eyes from drinking and smoking—she spoke brussels dialect and pretended to forget what they called a mop at home, but suddenly she tripped on one that judith had left lying by the back door, mariette got tangled in it and fell flat on her face: goddamn fucking mop! she cried . . . so she did know. And in brussels the fashion for short hair had been introduced—which actually issued from the war and the modern age, from the age of the smooth line and mass-production, of credit and heaven-knows-what else, when girls had to resemble boys. But mariette didn't go into it that much: it was the fashion, that's all, and she wanted to be in fashion—actually she wanted to launch the fashion: what she would have liked best was to become a model in brussels and compete in a beauty contest: she had submitted photos showing her legs and her thighs, but still with her hopeless long hair. She raised hell at home to be allowed to get a tomboy cut—and ondine burst out that it was the whores who'd gone with the germans whose hair had been cut off, but the war and those whores, they were long ago—and the younger generation, mariette among them, didn't remember. And one evening when ondine had gone out somewhere again—to her father's house, perhaps, where valeer had made three or four dressing tables and put them in a line, as if they had come off the conveyor belt, as if they had been mass-produced—or to the house of madame butcher who had sent for a famous doctor, a specialist, who had told her that those ovaries of hers had to be removed . . . and who was now ill in bed, desperately ill, and still didn't Dare have the operation—or to the house under construction where the american walked around, day and night, morning and evening, looking at his garage and café under construction, leaping into or out of his taxi and slamming the door hard—one of those evenings when ondine had left her kennel and oscarke had gone to the church choir, or to rosa, or to look for illustrations for his album . . . mariette went up to the attic, where she slept with judith, to cut her hair herself. Judith went with her to watch the spectacle, shouting after mariette: do you have the scissors with you? Meanwhile mauriske and leopold were downstairs, with little albert between them . . . and maurice, or leopold, who was it actually? . . . came up with the amusing idea of tying little albert to the table leg: they danced round it, screaming and cursing: they were bandits, they said. They went around hunched, with handkerchiefs over their mouths and knives in their hands, and made threatening gestures at albert who was crying and scared to death, as if they were about to murder him. They hunted through drawers and cupboards, maurice found 20 francs and put them in his pocket, then they rushed off, into the evening—it was a game: they would give back the 20 francs, and they would untie little albert, but meanwhile they had disappeared into the darkness, forced their way into the café under construction and kicked over a newly built wall. So that there was no one left in ondine's house but the crying albert, tied to the table—and those two way up there, who didn't give a damn. Ondine came home and had to slap little albert in the face, since he couldn't stop crying, and was already turning blue and starting to choke—and then she called out in the hallway, by the toilet, at the foot of the stairs: oscarke? . . . leopold? . . . mariette?—no answer. And at long last the trap door was raised and she came down: mariette! Ondine almost died from fright and screamed and kicked her legs as if she was going to choke too: mariette looked like a shorn rat, with a head like those whores who'd consorted with the germans. It was dreadful. But it was dreadful particularly because judith had started to do the job—and first and foremost her sight was poor, and in addition she was paralyzed with fear: in some places she'd cut off too much, and in others her scissors had slipped: and finally mariette had

had to do the cutting herself, standing in front of the mirror, while judith held a pocket mirror behind her head. And where is judith? ondine finally stammered, when she'd finally more or less recovered the power of speech—well, judith was upstairs and stayed upstairs, not daring to come down, and the next day she wore a scarf over her head: no one ever saw her *tomboy cut.*

BY THE HAZEL BUSH

Just now you've discovered a bush full of hazelnuts in the wood and you guide tippetotje down the overgrown path, hush-hush: here it is, just growing here, a bush full of hazelnuts! you whisper . . . back in the autumn, and then back in the spring, I could have transplanted it—but the fact is that once again I've discovered it too late to transplant it into my bit of garden . . .

I'm sorry, says tippetotje, that you're filled with poetic emotion every time you . . . oh well, it's quite normal, and the most natural thing in the world, but I urgently need to relieve myself, wait a minute . . . And she sits down, asking you if you'll keep a look out for any barbarians who might show up. Then she smoothes her skirts, and says, well, what were you so excited about just now? . . . oh yes, about the hazel that you were going to transplant into your bit of garden—transferring, changing, renewing—from long skirts to short skirts, from curls to the tomboy cut—not letting anything grow and blossom as it wants, not being able to leave anything alone and interfering with everything: rooting, fiddling, being Human. And she nods in agreement: all right, go ahead, I won't stop you . . . go ahead and transplant bushes when it's already too late, damage the wood in order to bring something into your garden that'll die anyway—go on writing pages and pages Beyond the limits of your book: because johan janssens asks you to and would have preferred to see more of the social side of things, because tolfpoets asks you and would have preferred something humorous. Jesus, tolfpoets's dire humor, the tiresome humor of people who want to laugh, yet don't Dare . . .

Now *you're* exaggerating, tippetotje! you say . . .

The tiresome stories of people who write and don't Dare to write! Tippetotje continues as a furious sparkle appears in her eyes. Put an end to your book! Draw a final and Irrevocable line under it, or write something, something . . . And she looks round desperately, furiously, as if she might find that "something" there in the wood. The end of the book should have turned into a diabolical pantomime, she says . . . the barbarians should have advanced with banners waving and drums beating, and all your protagonists and antagonists, ondine and oscarke and valeer and mariette and leopold—all, all of them—should have leapt and danced and cursed and screamed around the advancing barbarians: a last judgment, a collapse of the tower of babel, the fall of sodom and gomorrah, of niniveh, of rome and pompey:

THE GANG OF BARBARIANS

No, judith wouldn't leave the house, she didn't even go to mass on sunday, but sang the high mass at home—she sang the high mass in the living room and screamed the high notes, while her father sat in the loft booming out the low notes. This was how it went: judith had a lovely voice, and apart from singing there was nothing that had any meaning in the world to her—the church choir, the radio, this singer and that composer—that was her life, singing was a stone that had fallen in the water somewhere and made ripples. And mariette, she was another world entirely, another stone that had fallen in the water and made ripples that bisected judith's ripples. They all fought over the newspaper, but judith only wanted the radio programs, oscarke wanted to be irritated by politics, and mariette wanted sports and film news: movies, movies, one of these days you'll turn into a movie yourself with your rat's head! said ondine. And leopold would smirk, because he remembered mariette's words, which she had uttered long ago: I'm a cinema unto myself. And ondine wanted the newspaper for the local news—a new curate, an accident in koolstraat, death and stillbirths—although she realized that it didn't really matter, although she had a vague, gnawing sensation of having gone off the rails, heaven knows how. She thought: I'm damned if I'll get involved in anything else, if I'll lift a finger over anything else—but when she read the reports she couldn't WAIT to form an opinion of her own about them, to get involved in them—even though she also realized that she still wasn't able to control oscarke, whom she didn't understand, or mariette, who was a monster, or leopold and maurice, who . . . who . . . oh, she turned away from her own problems, and read about other people's problems in the paper. She'd always been ready to bang two stones against each other, but now she wondered what pleasure she could still get from that—and whether the trouble she had to take was worthwhile. She watched as they fought over the paper in her house, and bided her time, listlessly. Or no . . . it wasn't listlessness, it was more her being content: sitting there with her hands in her lap, complaining and getting irritated at the bunch of them. What on earth was wrong with her? Look, she thought, other women think of something to do in the house, for example . . . for example cleaning the windows, how long has it been since they were cleaned? And she started griping at judith, who'd just gotten hold of the paper, for never cleaning the windows: I'll get some ammonia, that's good for getting them nice and shiny, make sure that you make a start this afternoon! And off ondine went, to see if they sold ammonia at boone's! she sat there by the stove, with her hands in her lap, wondering how or where she could have gone astray—not realizing that this thought was growing and choking the feeling that she had a little sunshine in her heart. And she asked for ammonia for cleaning windows: I don't expect you've got any of that, boone? And boone nodded his head solemnly: Sure I have, sure I have, but I can't sell you any unless you have a bottle. So she went back home and found an empty beer bottle, and got it filled at boone's and also put out a bucket of water, and a sponge. And then . . . well a few things happened, a bricklayer fell off the scaffolding on the café that was being built for the american, so she left her bucket and rushed outside, squawking, The bricklayer wasn't badly hurt, the american drove him off immediately in his car, and yet . . . ondine rambled on, discussing how it had happened, and how she remembered that during the war . . . no, it was before the war . . . And she forgot that the time was approaching when the children came home from school . . . and leopold had been thirsty all day, so thirsty that during playtime he'd licked the iron pillars under the gallery in order to cool himself down: he came home and saw the beer bottle and drank . . . and immediately afterwards he came outside crying. The neighborhood children, who had come straight home from school for sandwiches, and with the sandwiches in their hands had rushed straight to the american's half-built garage . . . they saw leopold, limping and crying like a dying animal. They had seen him go inside, and said to each other: leopold will come out crying!—because he was a crook: wherever he went he did things that weren't allowed, but this still didn't stop him going round crying and with a snotty nose. And then he was there, really crying, and the neighborhood children started laughing at him. But he fell down, started writhing on the pavement, tearing the skin from his mouth and throat with both hands: and boone came out of his workshop and got his wife, and she immediately took leopold to a doctor. He was a an ultramodern doctor, a specialist: he was a specialist in x-rays, and was attached to a clinic where he took x-rays of everyone and everything: he took x-rays all day long, and so was actually more of a photographer than a doctor: he came and looked through his office door, but didn't even examine leopold, who was filling the whole of his office hallway with bestial noises. Squeeze a lemon and pour the juice down his throat, he said . . . and he closed the door behind him.

Ondine came back home that evening, very late: she'd been to brussels to see their cousin, since she wanted to know the full story of what mariette had really got up to there—since letters were still arriving from soldiers stationed in brussels, from streetcar personnel, from the devil knows who else—and some of them were in the crudest handwriting, but clear enough: when I think of your hot spot my thing starts rising and there's no stopping it. But it was such a mess over in brussels, even worse than here with those factories: one ripple crossed another. And the things they told her, things here and things there: there must have been at least 2-dozen mariettes that had gone to brussels, since 1 mariette couldn't possibly have got up to all that. Ondine arrived at the station and walked home past the empty site—oh, the same way that oscarke had walked an infinite number of times,

every dark morning and every dark evening, in the days when he worked in brus-
sels—and there by the empty site mauriske came to meet her, he jumped up and
clung to his mother and cried: our leopold's in bed, he drank the ammonia! Oh,
what did he say? And he was immediately slapped. Leopold, who was indeed in
bed and had cried himself to sleep, was also slapped: that'll teach you to keep your
hands off things! And she turned to mariette with her tomboy cut, thrust the letter
from the man who wrote about her hot spot into her hands, and said—harsh,
bitter, and sincere—I can't raise my hand to you anymore, you're more than I can
handle. But then she turned to the other kids, to all her offspring, and she shouted
furiously and loudly: but it won't happen with you, as true as our lord is hanging
on his cross, it won't happen to you . . . I'd rather slash your "hot spots" to ribbons!
Oh, but the day after? The day after mauriske and leopold had stolen candles
somewhere way over by karrebroeck, and they came back home with their pockets
full of them—albert looked at them longingly and wanted some too, and then
they cut the wicks and spread them over the pavement, and said that if he could
gobble them up like a chicken he could have some candles. The butcher stood
watching their game and doubled up with laughter, but madame d'haens came
out and turned the whole street upside down: oh this and oh that!—as if someone
had been killed. Ondine locked them in the front room upstairs and bolted the
door—and the boys, who had matches in their pockets, set fire to the bed. Then
there was something else, and name of schatt became known all through the town:
because of his wife ondine, and his daughter mariette, and his sons mauriske and
leopold. Meanwhile the two vagabonds no longer dared go home, they stayed out
and wandered past the factories along the river dender, and past the empty freight
cars in the switchyard—and between the gasworks and a coal depot they found
an empty corner with tall wild grass—that was the prairie and they were indi-
ans—and when they walked between the tall grass they created passageways that
were very mysterious, and this mysteriousness added to the fear of what awaited
them at home—something that they tried in vain to put out of their minds—and
it made their bellies rumble, so they sat next to each other and shit on the ground
out of fear. The day is long, said leopold. And treading down new passageways
through the wild grass, they found a wooden shed with a sloping roof built against
the high back wall of the coal depot. They forced their way in, and mauriske talked
of staying and living there, living there forever, and during the day going out and
looking for food. The day crept on, the factory whistles blew, and gradually the
clanking and rattling died away—twilight fell on that bit of wilderness and the
wooden shed that was lost in it. The boys swore never to leave each other. And it's
hard to say how it came about . . . but mauriske actually came up with the idea,
and then leopold expanded on it and put it into words: they decided to form a
gang: "we have formed a secret alliance to stand by each other unto death." And
although he couldn't fully comprehend what death meant, all the same it was a

grim word the way leopold spoke it. For ages they searched for a name for their gang, and as night fell, and they were huddling together on the rotten floorboards, almost falling asleep, but constantly woken by leopold's cough, and mauriske said: the gang of Two! But what in their first panic had seemed like an impossibility, "going back home," nevertheless became a reality: in the morning they arrived in their street as if automatically and crept to the stove, and as the beneficent warmth of the stove sent them back to sleep, they heard—as if from afar—their mother first threatening, then weeping. Their fear subsided—and so the idea of having to live forever in that shack and survive on stolen provisions didn't become a reality: but what remained nevertheless was the secret alliance, the gang of Two. They returned to their wilderness almost every evening, and the whole desolate sunday. They emptied ondine's food cupboard, they went and stole turnips from the fields or fruit from the orchards far beyond karrebroeck, or took a string of sausages from the butcher, and hid it all in their shack. And once they even lured a very small boy along with them, then stripped off his shirt and trousers and made him run around naked and serve them—and as he was bending down in front of them, leopold stuck a plum stone up his ass: the little boy cried and knocked in vain at the barred door, and later they could scarcely extract the stone from his ass.

But they weren't the only ones who'd formed a "gang"! Mariette, who for the first few weeks regularly trimmed her hair Herself, or went to brussels and found a salon de coiffure, finally saw a salon open in the little town of the 2 mills, where they actually knew about the latest fashions. For a while she was their first and only customer, but gradually a few others joined her—first a fat matron from down by the station, and then a girl who'd run away from home—and finally a flamboyant character with a real boy's face whose hair had to be combed with a part: she told them about a woman athlete who'd had her breasts removed so that they didn't get in the way when she was playing. And that's True actually, she said . . . it's the same with me, what's the use of those two lumps anyway? She would have much preferred to be flat, like a boy. And then the matron from the station said something in reply, to which mariette replied with something hysterical, with her big mouth, which the flamboyant girl couldn't laugh at. However, in 1 thing they all stood shoulder to shoulder: in their love of short hair, which for them meant the new world of the future. The hairdresser seemed to be the shaper of this new world, and the girls his priestesses: they formed a new religion—in their fashion they formed, like mauriske and leopold, a secret alliance, a gang of the Short Hair. Judith on the other hand let her hair grow, she was so ugly she was just like a nun who'd cast off her wimple on those rare occasions when that shawl of hers came off her head—and meanwhile she sang, not a day went by without the ave maria bubbling from her throat. She had a silver throat, so to speak, where notes welled up from the depths and then hung in the air and trilled—oh if people hadn't known that it issued from judith's ugly face, they would have listened and stayed listening: a gentleman came and rang the bell and he listened to judith's voice, nodding his head and with his forefinger raised. Oh, the gentleman just had to see that girl, and so talked his way into ondine's foyer, eager to see her: but how astonished he was to find himself in such a madhouse! He came to listen to judith, but ondine said: stop that singing, judith, we can scarcely hear each other—and ondine wanted to tell one story after another, she wanted to reveal her whole life to the gentleman. And so it was actually ondine who sang, who rattled off the litany of her rich origins, of her childhood among the gentlefolk, the invention of her father who had a dressing-table factory: we're expecting a legacy from that! Meanwhile the boys were creeping around on the ground and fastened a white reel of thread to the gentleman's trouser leg with a pin. But he didn't see that—instead he saw little albert relieving himself on a newspaper, and mariette laughing dementedly with her backside bare. Only oscarke behaved himself, because he too wanted to steal the limelight, wanted to talk about his sculpture, about his monument on chapel road—but he didn't, he pushed judith forward, his favorite, made her center-stage: now sing the Welders' Song, judith! And while she drew out this song, which was really for a male voice, from somewhere deep in her silver throat, and her shawl had slipped, revealing that head that the rats had gnawed at, and she was ugly ugly ugly—meanwhile the gentleman slipped away, without saying a word. Judith stood singing with her eyes closed, oscarke gaped at her, and no one noticed that the gentleman had gone, although the reel of thread unwound and rolled out into the hallway after him. No, it was inexpressible, oscarke's sorrow, ondine's rage, the crazy joy of mariette, the dejection of judith. But while ondine's rage subsided, as did judith's dejection—she was after all accustomed to resigning herself to things and being silent, and then immediately launching into a new song (now a song in which she expressed her dejection)—sorrow and shame continued to gnaw at oscarke's heart. At first he sat and sulked and refused to speak, refused to eat too—he'd always used his appetite as a weapon—and even refused to go to the choir: and when evening came he didn't want to go to bed and lie next to ondine, or next to the boys and mariette and judith. Yes, he was sulking at judith too: he was sulking at the whole world, himself included. His suffering soon became the world's suffering, and while everyone prepared for sleep he left for the choir after all (or so he said), but went to rosa's and got drunk instead, walked through the dark streets cursing and accusing that gentleman, that unknown gentleman, whom he swore he would find and tear his throat out. The next morning he still hadn't returned home, or the next day either: and ondine told everyone that a gentleman had come from brussels, the director of a great theater, and that oscarke had gone off to sign the contract for judith. But mauriske said that it wasn't true: he's with his mother, minnie mouse, on chapel road. And it was true: oscarke had burned his bridges in order to start a new life: and while he was there his mother died, minnie mouse, and he shed a tear, and got drunk again, and in the dark evening he came down chapel road all alone, with his fly open and his thing hanging out—and while he was there, a little fellow came down chapel road one afternoon, crying that he wanted his dad: my dad lives with minnie mouse who's dead, is living with lots and lots of crosses. He didn't know where his dad lived, nor did he know his dad's name, it was little albert who'd got lost playing with mauriske and leopold, and who vaguely remembered something about chapel road. Oscarke was living there now, almost completely alone—because his father, where was he, or where was he living?—in that cold and drafty house, shut in by white plastered walls turned black by smoke and soot and many dirty hands—and now with albert too. He felt sad, felt like a different man, an oscarke split off from himself and forced to look for his lost double. And if rosa hadn't been married he would have asked her to become his mistress, to come and live with him there in that cold and gloomy house on chapel road: he wandered up and down the muddy road to termuren, looking for a rosebud, but what bud would be inclined to let itself have its petals removed by a ghostly, skinny little man? Then he dug up the crumpled piece of a photo of jeannine out of his pocket and stuck it on the wall with a pin.

More or less at the same time, the american's café and garage were complet-ed and he organized a free-drinks evening to show people the way to his door: the whole neighborhood turned up that evening for free booze—even madame d'haens with her poor nerves was there sipping a glass of mineral water—and all of them listened to the fantastic stories about america, and how you could earn huge amounts of money there. But in fact people were only half listening: he'd earned a pile in america and he was a good fellow, because he was providing free drinks, so the details weren't that important . . . the state of ohio, for example, who could remember that, or who could see the point of remembering it? It was the stories from their own town that interested them, down to the smallest details: sander toppe was drunk, and told the story of why he'd never gotten married, since his sweetheart had panicked after he'd had sex with her the first time: because you can't imagine how big and hard it is, like iron. And he went behind the bar and showed it, and all the women who'd seen it came back from behind the bar with slightly flushed cheeks, and biting their bottom lips in dismay. And the butcher was drunk and told them about his wife, who was lying in bed and wouldn't let them operate on her and so was going to die: and if she Had to die, let her do it quickly, because I can't go on waiting and waiting, he said. And ondine was drunk and told them about oscarke who was living alone over on chapel road where his mother had died: I'll leave him there a bit longer, then we'll have the villa sold. And mariette was drunk and told them about her first sweetheart, with whom she'd gone to the park, and who she'd loved more than any of the rest . . . and then she also told them, in the strictest confidence, whispering, without really knowing to whom, how she'd known a married man in brussels: christ, the way he could do me, they don't do it like that anymore. And everyone made their own confession,

470

talked about things that were usually hidden, and sat listening in dismay to their own stories coming out of their mouths—and so people only remembered everyone else's confessions later on, after they'd managed to forget their own.

RAIN OVER THE WOOD

It's a mild morning, with a quiet rain rustling over the wood, and from there comes rustling over your garden, towards the glass wall of your living room—but then to its surprise finds the glass wall open, and hesitates, and doesn't dare come inside. The stove is burning quietly, and the rain is rustling quietly at the open wall of your living room, which as a result has become a part of the woods. And you sit there and stare at the quiet rain, which has acquired purpose and meaning—in the town, rain is something melancholy and unpleasant, but over the wood rain is something that belongs, that makes things unspeakably beautiful and unspeakably fragrant. And listen to the birds singing! You said yesterday evening to kramiek: listen to guido gezelle's nightingale! In the twilight of the late evening to kramiek . . . because, yes, he was suddenly there, and you had to say Something—something trivial, about the poet guido gezelle and his nightingale. And kramiek agreed with you, as he always agrees with everyone and everything: I'm really pleased, said kramiek, that you're returning to nature and can talk about it . . . it gives me pleasure, because it means that I'll soon be able to find something about nature in your writing—about the birds singing—because yes, I regret more than I can say that up to now it's been mostly the opposite: the birds were being hunted. I'd reread the last thing you wrote there, about those confessions of the drunken neighborhood—but I don't dare reread it, and the first time I just skimmed it anyway . . . I mean, what kind of writing-method is this, if I can put it that way? What kind of behavior is this, going on writing a book after the End's been reached? That's like going on boxing after the bell sounds: you don't know how ridiculous you are: the bell's already sounded and the referee has counted to ten, and you go on boxing in a vacuum—to the great amusement of the crowd. And what are you adding after reaching the finishing line in your book? Nothing substantial. Nothing that I, kramiek, didn't already know.

And gradually the resentment that you'd always felt towards this kramiek welled up in you, but which, now that you've withdrawn into the silence and peace of your refuge, you wanted to control. And now kramiek has gone, but the resentment of him has remained, while the rustle of the rain over the wood is monotonous and soft and persistent. That book of ours is the same way, monotonous and persistent—so does kramiek say that the rain doesn't communicate anything new or substantial either? And now you sit there and write and write: it can't be the kind of ending that everybody wants, an ending that's like a hammer-blow, an ending that's a final explosion, of shouting and screaming and the advance of the barbarians with banners and drums. Oh come on, it's all nonsense, the world will go on turning with or without us, and with or without the barbarians . . . I prefer to end the book like a candle that's snuffed out, or like rain that falls persistent and gray and ever more quiet, so that at some point it stops without your noticing—the extinction of all your characters, the merging of all your themes: a . . .

TWILIGHT OF THE GODS

The american had been in ohio, and so the sign painter came and put "café ohio" in big, modern letters on the windows, and it was as if that café ohio brought a new spirit into the neighborhood, a spirit of pleasure and dissipation, of drunken orgies and riotous behavior. Although . . . no, it was an illusion, this dissipation was equally a consequence of the new postwar period—the priest had always said so from his pulpit, he was still going on about the growing moral decay, the same as he'd been doing for years and years—but now it was really true, and now you couldn't even go out to drink without seeing the priest. Apart from that there was a feeling around, like any day now war might break out again: it wasn't really peace right now, it was an armed truce: the great and the good, for whom ondine had always had such tremendous respect, knew that perfectly well! The same battle would begin again after people had recovered a little from the hunger and the loss of blood, after they'd got good and drunk and made some new children, and joined a union. It's a truce, said the ordinary people, like well-drilled and christianized monkeys—but perhaps they were confusing truce with peace, because they sang and drank and went to mass on sunday morning, and on sunday evening walked around with their flies open, and put out the flags when someone got married, and forgot the war completely. Forgot it, yes, but still lived instinctively as if war might break out again any day—and looked in astonishment at the socialist youth, who wore blue shirts and carried clubs, and shouted "no more war"—and they thought: you see? They're talking about war again!—and so they started to profit from the present. They didn't think about things too deeply. That's how they were, no reflection. And they had a good time and sang the lewdest songs. They sang "Justine Agathe Marie," and at the same time they went to church and lit candles and promised the impossible to god, whose existence they doubted. It was an ambivalent time. It was a time with a split personality, somebody said—but mariette, who happened to hear that, nearly died laughing: so many things are split! she said. But ondine, who also heard, just kept nodding: do people really know what they want? she wondered. And she forgot that she'd once realized that human beings would never get to the point where they knew or understood anything at all—that

472

humanity was not a thinking, organic being, but on the contrary was something like a jungle—that is, something like nature, something like the river dender (because what did jungle mean to her? It was a scabby word that evoked a wood full of whores), yes, something like the dender then: every person was a drop of water, and all the drops together making up the dender were mankind. Every drop of water could have its own thoughts: first and foremost those contradictory thoughts within themselves, and then the thoughts that contradicted the thoughts of others, which in turn . . . Oh, stop it! But all of them together were flowing somewhere, and as they flowed people never talked about themselves, people said: the dender. Because the dender itself had no thoughts, it allowed more and more new factories to be built along its banks and dump polluted water into it. It allowed itself to be straightened at one point, since shipping was being impeded by its curves—and so it was actually a bit like the flamboyant woman who wanted her breasts removed, because they got in the way of playing sports. Such was the modern age. It was modern, they said. Everything people didn't understand, that was confusing or worthless, was modern. The older people shook their heads, but the young ones believed in it like in a religion without a god. Lies and fraud were modern, like that man from america, who had a car—right, but it was going to be used as a taxi: at first people thought he was a gentleman, but now they saw that he was parked at the station like an ordinary coachman for hire in the old days. But his customers were mainly just drunken louts, or whores from down by the station, or sons of postwar parvenus who wanted to paint the town red, and whom he took to the café ohio in his taxi. The café ohio became notorious. And ondine didn't want to go there anymore: the house stood there in all its smuttiness, its freedom, and its godlessness, as a symbol of the modern age: students and soldiers and streetcar workers, stokers and train drivers, gendarmes, beggars, and rich men's sons, All of them came in, and danced and roared and filled the empty place with vomit. They vomited alongside each other and in so doing erased the distinction between classes—the class distinction that ondine had observed all her life— and now, with that gentleman who drove a car and was also a servant at the station, the whole lot had been so shaken up that ondine could no longer understand any of it, and no longer Wanted to understand it. But, wasn't it also a little because the american had destroyed her dream, because he'd built a café where she had wanted to put her dream house? Now she had to choose another plot of land to imagine her dream house on—but this was impossible, she couldn't imagine a dream house in a place where no one knew her: it must be here or nowhere. So it was nowhere—and the american also pulled the wool from her eyes: it was not with an oscarke who today sculpted and tomorrow was out of work that one could build dream houses . . . but on the contrary by going to america and making one's fortune. It wasn't by saving, by bending down and picking up every lost centime, by worrying and moaning and trying to make the world catholic, but by Daring

473

to cross the ocean. And she never went into that café again, or spoke to the american—and she hardly ever talked to boone . . . because boone, with his stupid talk
and his shaved-off moustache, had gone for a pint and told them all the story of his
shed, and he'd slapped the american on the shoulder, "give us another pint," he
said, and then asked if he could rent a bit of the garage to paint his cars in. And a
few days later boone stood at the entrance to the empty site greeting everyone at
the top of his voice, just as he had done previously at the entrance to his shed. He
didn't have much work on hand, that was true, but he still had plenty to say for
himself. We may not be earning much, but we still have a good life! he shouted to
everyone. Or he would say in jest: only one more pint to drink! And he called out
to ondine too: hello ondine, nice weather today! But ondine didn't answer, she just
stood there in her doorway, with a brush in her hand, looking across the street at
the big windows with the yellow patches of the letters painted on them: café ohio.
And madame american, that former snot-nose from the pool, who had gone to
america alone, to ohio, also came and stood in her doorway with a brush in her
hand . . . or no, again ondine was too quick to jump to conclusions: it wasn't
madame, it was the maid who came out with a brush in her hand, the waitress,
while madame looked on—and without a word madame ohio and ondine looked
each other in the eye. But one evening madame de wesenborgh's son was sitting
there, that pale streak of shit, that student . . . that is, ex-student, since in the
meantime he had become a lawyer, maitre henry van wesenborgh. He was sitting
there with the doctor goethals's son, who had also finished his studies and was now
a doctor too, dr paul goethals, and who told the most scandalous stories about illness and operations that had ever been heard for miles around. They were sitting
close to the window and occasionally looked into the street—and lo and behold, at
that moment mariette came out, backwards, mopping the hallway. It's mariette, I
recognize her by her ass! cried paul goethals—and they jumped up and invited her
into the café: you'd sit there drinking and amusing yourselves and don't so much as
offer me a drink! said mariette. You'd mop the whole street with your butt in the
air, and not warn us to watch out! replied paul goethals. And henry said nothing.
He was a pale lump, and could only open his mouth when it was about politics,
about fascism and sweeping the whole filthy bunch away for good. But you always
have to watch out for the quiet ones! laughed mariette, leaning back in her chair,
legs crossed very high—she emerged from the café later in the evening, thoroughly
drunk. And ondine used this as a pretext to rush to madame ohio and blame her
and vent her spleen and all her hatred—she gave the blind-drunk mariette a slap
in the face and went across the road in her stocking feet: who on earth do you think
my daughter is? My daughter is respectable, and had a bourgeois upbringing, she's
not like some person who goes off to america all alone . . . But to her surprise
madame ohio wasn't even in the café, there was only the waitress on paul goethals's
knee, and henry de wesenborgh. Aren't you doctor goethals's son, and aren't you

madame de wesenborgh's son? And she rattled on and cursed them, recalling the whole of her youth and telling them about their fathers and mothers in those days. She sat down: because I'm not as young as I was and can't stay standing up. She drank a cocktail that was offered her—and later emerged into the night just as drunk as her daughter. From that day forth there was always someone from ondine's household in café ohio: ondine herself, or mariette, or occasionally judith who went there to sing, but was shunned by madame ohio and the waitress because she was ugly—she could sing, but she was ugly—and leopold also went occasionally, with mauriske, but through the garage door to steal things. But in the gloom they hadn't noticed that the american was sitting in his taxi repairing a few things: leopold was grabbed by the scruff of his neck. Whose brat are you? asked the american—but of course leopold didn't want to say, he was sniveling and his eyes were bloodshot like those of a cornered rabbit. I won't do it again! he screamed, and meanwhile he looked for a way he could escape, and suddenly dashed for the garage gate and out into the street: fucking hell! he cried from there, furious and seemingly drunk, as he was almost fainting . . . bloody hell, I'll kill that american. Meanwhile his mother was sitting in the café listening to madame ohio's stories, to stories from america, but she would have done better to keep quiet about america, because ondine also knew how to tell a story, knew when lies lurked beneath the truth, and with her feelers could sense the slightest distortion—and soon ondine knew, as if she had been through it herself, the whole story: they hadn't earned money in the great factories of ohio by working hard—it was only blacks and polacks and italians who worked on the conveyor belts, and only the blacks who could stand it (he, the american had told them that!), so they couldn't possibly have amassed their fortune in the factories. And then she heard that the wife had run a café and a garage, close to the factories: ha, thought ondine, just like here! Ha, she was a slut! A slut who was modern and could say what everyone wanted to hear and go to church or not go to church: she laughed at the church with madame d'haens and went to church like madame ondine. She was a slut and she could look at you like some kind of mystery, like a slut's black mystery from a café in ohio. Of course, the younger generation looked at the waitress, who was a young thing with blonde hair, in a tomboy cut, who smoked cigarettes (oh, if oscarke were here now), and next to that young thing, madame ohio looked like a slut of a matron, looked like the lady of the house, the watchful madam—but as was said, in the beginning students and soldiers and streetcar workers and gendarmes came . . . but gradually more and more gendarmes came, and more and more frequently. True, soldiers and beggars came occasionally, but once any of them had seen the gendarmes, they stayed away. The gendarmes came after work, in civilian clothes: they had gray, pockmarked faces, they actually looked like crooks when they weren't in uniform—and taking that strange thought a little further, they seemed to be in disguise: criminals dressed as gendarmes. They had nothing but contempt for that blonde, cigarette-smoking young thing of a waitress, to whom the last student was still clinging—but on the other hand they were all the more attracted by madame ohio, the mystery slut. And if they were occasionally obscene with that little waitress or with mariette when they were drunk, madame ohio on the contrary was treated like a goddess, whose favors had to be begged for. And as she got drunk and horny, those days in ohio came back to her, with blacks draped round her in clusters—in ohio it had been blacks who occasionally smashed the place up, and in the little town of the 2 mills it was the gendarmes. Mariette laughed and kicked her legs, and egged them on to smash up more and more—she laughed with her hysterical cackle, so that she could be heard miles away in the quiet street, and people started awake, turned over, and muttered: mariette's off again! One evening, however, oscarke turned up again, hand-in-hand with little albert . . . and what was his reason for coming back, only the devil could tease it out—oh, oscarke could tease it out himself, but once he started telling a story, there was no end to it, he would bring in some other issue, some other theory, and more and more, till it became a tangle in which he'd become lost and confused. He closed the door of the chilly house on chapel road, and threw the key inside through the letterbox: perhaps he was more or less imagining his homecoming, how ondine would be standing there, and how she would grab little albert (who was supposed to be her favorite, as she'd said before, before he was born) and smother him with kisses—and then look at him, oscarke, who . . . And he pushed open the front door, which was ajar, and went in: but the place was completely empty, as empty as the cold dead house on chapel road, which he had just left. And yes, that had been one of the reasons for his return, the emptiness over there: the first day when he'd arrived at chapel road, his ears had still been full of the racket at home, and after that there'd been a kind of peace, and then a kind of unease—so that he had started to long for some kind of little rosa—and after that, the silence had become a kind of grip throttling him: a sandbag hitting his head. The place was empty, was silent—and madame d'haens, who'd seen him arriving, came to tell him that ondine might be at café ohio. At café ohio? And he stayed in the dark deserted house, at the dead window, looking at the lighted windows of the café. Then judith came in, and without wanting to explain the details of his flight, he asked her, still full of remorse but also rather annoyed, what it was like there at café ohio? Judith told him: in the café it's like this and that . . . And he pushed little albert into her lap and crossed the street. Yes, even if only to peer through the windows, and to stand hesitating by the glass door of the café . . . because he was a little coward when he was sober. A little coward, who was unhappy. And so first he went and drowned his sorrows elsewhere, and gradually became furious with ondine, who didn't stay home as she should and patiently wait for his return: patience, who has patience anymore? he shouted, drunk and with his gray tuft of hair sticking up again, as it used to. I haven't got any patience and you haven't got any patience, he called out at random to an old man who jumped and dropped his clay pipe. And oscarke's rage immediately subsided, and for an instant he had to laugh, and said in a slurred voice: a clay pipe is easy, if it falls you don't have to bend down and pick it up!—but his laughter soon turned back into rage. No one has it anymore! He shouted again . . . no one has a clay pipe! And it was actually patience that he meant, but he had forgotten. And he came back to their street, swearing that he would fucking well smash a clay pipe in her face: no one has a clay pipe, but I'll make sure they have a clay pipe. And he threw open the door of café ohio—and it may be that he saw a few things that weren't acceptable, and it's also quite possible that he saw nothing at all, but no sooner had he gone inside than the uproar could be heard out in the street. You could hear the breaking of glass, the frightened screams of ondine, no, the cruel screams of ondine and mariette . . . or was it after all . . . well, anyway, the screaming of mariette and ondine together. The neighbors came and stood round the café and listened but didn't get too close to the windows, because they might break and fly out onto the pavement and into their faces. They never went in anymore, the neighbors, because they got in the way of the gendarmes: at first they'd shared the occasional glass with the gendarmes, but for christ sake while they sat there they were given a ticket, oh, for god knows what . . . weren't there enough laws and regulations and ordinances without a person having to worry about getting a ticket from some gendarme at any hour of the day? And so at first the neighbors went, but ondine did not—and then the gendarmes arrived and ondine went, but the neighbors stopped going. Ondine went back every day to sing the praises of that good man from america, who'd earned his money there in such a respectable way, but they answered: you lie so well that you believe it yourself, ondine! And the butcher said: his wife ran a brothel where the blacks came and did their black business. And sander toppe said: they stole money out of the pockets of the blacks. And boone said nothing, because he was still renting a bit of the garage, although he was thinking of getting into a different trade, and he thought: once I'm no longer in the garage, I shall spill the beans about that american and madame ohio. But ondine shook her head, now gray, and asked where they got all that nonsense from—though she knew well enough that in the past she herself had spread those stories. But right now oscarke was selling clay pipes to that good man from america—and just as people had foreseen, the yellow letters of "café ohio" flew into the street. Oscarke fought like a lion: because he was drunk, he would take on the whole world. And suddenly the light got smashed and they were left in darkness, and they heard the cry of the blonde, cigarette-puffing thing, who was pissing on herself with fear in this darkness. And without telling each other, a few people took advantage of the darkness to sneak inside and give oscarke a hand, and sell a few clay pipes in turn: the butcher was there, who hated the gendarmes because they could drink and hitch up mariette's skirts and show her ass without thinking about women who had sick insides and couldn't be touched in bed. And sander toppe went in, that giant of a man, with his iron fists, with his iron dick that all his sweethearts had run away from. They fought with him, and punched everything they ran into in the darkness—and it's quite possible that they occasionally pounded oscarke himself. And leopold and mauriske arrived back from their scavenging expeditions downriver—they saw the open gate of the garage and heard the noise—and with mauriske behind him leopold slipped into the café, where everyone was in a heap, panting, cursing, and wrestling. Pushed up against the bar, leopold pulled a knife from his trouser pocket, a knife that he had stolen-found-bought, and opening the blade he thrust it into the air at random. Oh, he was still the same pinched little boy he used to be, with his mother's bird-like face, with his father's tuft of hair sticking up—with the occasional fit of dry coughing from the time when he drank ammonia. No one knew who was stabbing, and no one knew if anyone had been stabbed, but the cry of "they're using knives!" made both sides (oh, could one talk about sides in that darkness?) fight on fiercely and bitterly. Someone grabbed hold of the bar itself, raised it up, and brought it crashing down, splintering—it was probably sander toppe, you could almost tell from the deep growl of laughter . . . almost, but who would dare later to swear, under oath, that it had really been him? But in the darkness the gendarmes left one after another, put their uniforms on at home and came back to café ohio as the restorers of order: the butcher had gone and sander toppe had gone, the american was lying with two huge black eyes—and oscarke, all alone, was still dishing out clay pipes. The time had come for him to be given a clay pipe himself.

GRAY AND SOME PINK

And you stop writing, stop writing about ondine and oscarke and the rest of them, and stare through the glass wall of your living room at your bit of garden, where the rhododendron is in flower—a great pink patch against the gray of the silver birches in the wood—you've always loved that, gray and pink. The grayness and monotony of life merging with the pink, arousing some sexuality, some hope, some modest delight. And you leaf through your book for a bit, and review the titles of the chapters—and yes, they too are gray with a bit of pink: the very first chapter was called "only the precious little moment counts." And the second "your happiness is something you have to fight for," and the last chapter "we individuals, in a world of barbarians." And that's how it should be. It was good that the novel ended with oscarke, where we know it ended . . . and it was good to write this last chapter Beyond the finishing line too, as a final echo of all your themes, quiet and muted, with some blossoming pink among all that gray. No, let tippetotje say what she likes, let johan jans-sens and the music master and even kramiek go on kramiek-ing as much as they like. Tomorrow I shall finish, tomorrow I shall finish once and for all, and

478

irrevocably—like the late mr god determined to pass his last judgment once and for all, and irrevocably—and I'll write about how oscarke and ondine, together (oh, for the last and only time Together) were taken to court—and how for the first time a socialist became mayor in the little town with the 2 factories . . . so that ondineke's novel merges with johan janssens's—and how the world nevertheless goes on turning, heading for a goal that is not a goal—and how meanwhile everyone remains the same as he always was and will be: look at mariette, look at you, look at me! And now judith talks about getting married, and mariette reenacts her mother's life—all that ondine has experienced in her little bit of life, mariette will now experience too, an eternal repetition of something that always remains the same, with a few variations of course, a few unimportant little details . . . just like there's a difference between one little leaf of grass and another little leaf of grass.

And meanwhile evening falls, gently and a little sadly, over the wood, over your bit of garden, and the rhododendrons stand flowering against the gray of the silver birches in the wood, Twilight over the wood. Twilight over the lives of your characters, twilight over your book. Very early tomorrow, at about five in the morning when the birds are already singing their loudest, perhaps with a little rain so that the blackbird is at its best, we shall write the

END

Ondine and oscarke had a whole lot of summonses . . . malicious damage and defamation and moral turpitude and god knows what else . . . and ondine walked and walked and was unaware of her belly and her problems, she made plans, tried to foment dissent and to mollify everyone, went to the priest and the curate, to sander toppe and norbert derenancourt—who immediately referred her to his brother achilles. But what was it like at achilles's place? The catholic had needed to answer a committee of inquiry about a state school that needed enlarging, and which he had said could not be enlarged—especially at the front, since it would have ruined the view of the ancient square with the ancient trees—but what about the rear? Why, that land belonged to the derenancourts! And this wasn't the end of the distasteful story: there was a coda: the state had offered an incentive for every- one starting to build this year, and because of all the deliberations the building of the school had to be postponed and so the town did not receive the incentive. Achil- les derenancourt had to answer for all this to the socialists and liberals on the council—now that it was a matter of a state school, they were all pulling in the same direction, but no one knew whether the next time they might not be pulling in opposite directions—and so the mayor was keeping his gate shut. Ondine's knocks fell on deaf ears. She finally seized her chance when a maid came out to go shopping: mr derenancourt is not receiving! said the maid. I know that! replied

479

ondine, slipping inside and making a fuss in the gateway, because she Had to see mr achilles. He came, still tall and upright, but oh so gray already, and with lines round his mouth, lines everywhere, oh god! And ondine explained her case while he looked at her, tall and upright. There was nothing to be done about the law, he said. Ha, we shall see! replied ondine—and she tried to remind him of one or two things from both their youths, but there was nothing more to remember: really, he no longer remembered her. He asked if she weren't what's-his-name's daughter . . . what's-it, what was his name? Oh, something collapsed in ondine's soul, creaking and raising clouds of dust. What's-it's daughter! And she looked at him haughtily with her old, dull eyes—for a moment she was an anarchist and a nihilist. She walked and fumed and went to see boone—boone who had given up the lease on that bit of the garage, and had bought a ladder and was now a housepainter—and boone told ondine about the business with the school, and that the mayorship of the derenancourts would soon be over: it's our turn now, because the people are in-dig-nant! And boone said in-dig-nant in his best flemish. Yes their time had come, although the catholics pulled a last trick on the eve of the elections: they stuck up posters everywhere showing a mother with a crying child on her arm, a child that was crying because it didn't know who god was: for the soul of the child, vote catholic. And people who were finally going to vote socialist saw the poster and were moved, and voted catholic After All—voted catholic everywhere—except in those little factories where they were fed up with godless children, where they were fed up with mr derenancourt . . . and where they weren't anymore socialist than anywhere else, but where they wanted to see the dance halls that the catholic mayor had had shut down opened again, and there they voted socialist: the first socialist mayor was elected and that evening there was a procession, a torch-lit procession, with a hired coach in which the new mayor sat surrounded by flowers: mayor boone. Old boone, dammit, and the folk from the factories walked in front and behind, singing "O people o scared ideal." And along with the people from the factories were the people from the emergency dwellings on the edge of town, thieves and beggars, all that grubby lot joined in, and sang "o people o sacred ideal," although they had no other ideal than to fill their bellies and steal and murder and whore, just as the rich bastards had always done, and which they now hoped to be able to do themselves, Now, when the socialists were in charge—and not when they were dead and in heaven, as the catholics had promised them. Ondine stood watching the procession, and no longer knew who was actually right: she had been an anarchist and a nihilist, yes, for a few minutes, and only because she'd been regarded as the daughter of what's-it (what's-it who?). But what did that mean? And at the same time . . . at the same time . . . she felt as if she'd been a nihilist all her life: believing in neither god nor his commandments as soon as that faith got in her way at all, but running around with god and faith like a cannon to blast anyone who was trying to steal her thunder—swooning over god or worshipping the devil, whoring, trying to stop the world in its course. She had been like the priest, that devil in his white surplice, standing in the pulpit to keep people in ignorance. That was how she had been—that is to say, in many ways she had been a bit like That. And now the torch-lit procession made for the "justice and freedom" meeting rooms and held a party for boone, Our boone: he was so moved by the crowd, the sea of lights, that forest of red flags, that he could no longer get his words out and started to stammer, started talking about the time when he lived by the wharf and people had come to break his windows, and there was also a party at the other boone's, his son's, next door to ondine—and ondine herself brought flowers: she cried a little and congratulated them all. Almost the entire world was becoming socialist, and she had to resign herself to that, she said. And meanwhile she thought: my purpose in the world is rather different from yours: looking after my kids, providing for my old age, understanding a bit of what there is to understand—and most of all, ensuring that they weren't ruined by that court case! Yes, she cut her coat according to her cloth, and went to see the new mayor where she explained her case: but the new mayor spoke just like the old one: if it had been the police, he could have intervened, but with the gendarmes . . . no, justice must take its course. And she also learned somewhere that a gendarme was always under oath: everything a gendarme said was the truth, and everything ondine said was a lie. She held her head high and no longer spoke to anyone. But look, injustice is not all-powerful! There was a teacher living in her neighborhood, and also a customs officer, and they too were also both under oath, and both testified Against the gendarmes: then other things came to light, and oscarke and ondine had to leave the court since proceedings were to continue behind closed doors. They went back home, oscarke and ondine, both already gray, both a bit old, but inwardly rejoicing. And the worst crook of a gendarme was transferred, no one knew where to, and the other gendarmes must have been denied access to café ohio, because they never set foot in there again. And ondine and mariette never set foot in there again either, they went to the butcher's as before and talked about socialism—but the butcher, whose sick wife lay in bed upstairs stinking of medicine, could talk only of smut. The whole world was now starting to become socialist—such was ondine's vague, distant opinion . . . although she wasn't particularly happy about it, that's how it was and she had resigned herself to it. But no sooner had everyone started to become socialists than the world deteriorated as a result: everyone now had a radio, and everyone had this and that . . . and if you saw the factory girls walking along in their silk stockings, and if you saw the children of poor people doing their first communion in tulle and lace, if you saw someone from the slums getting married, god, what luxury! Of, course, it was all on credit: ondine too had a radio, but no one knew how much she still owed on it—and if you saw mariette walking along, she was a queen, but it was an open secret that she'd had to let the bosses or the foremen in all those factories between her legs.

And ondine, who didn't wonder too much anymore, wondered: have I grown old and has the world changed, or have I simply changed and has the world remained the same? Oh, the world Had changed, in the past there was one queen, queen ondine, and now they were all queens out there: now all those young things rode shiny cycles, with a kodak on a strap, and let their multicolored skirts billow up revealing their beautiful asses. It was no longer a sin, it was the new age, the age that oscarke had waffled on about. But things didn't get any better . . . not with her at least. Mariette was a queen, and leopold got a kodak with the vouchers they put in cigarette packets—five hundred vouchers entitled you to a kodak and a thousand to a dinner service—but oscarke was out of work again. And boone? Boone was out of work too. Everyone only had to work eight hours a day now . . . supposedly, but sometimes people didn't have to go to the factory at all . . . first one day a week, then two days a week, then three days a week . . . And people amused themselves by painting the doors and the windows—but that didn't matter, boone's old father had become mayor, and boone himself went to the town hall and became something like supervisor of public works. So things improved for boone, for a few people here and there—but for everyone?—no, on the contrary, they got worse. The policemen still walked around in their faded uniforms and guarded the money of the rich, of the old rich and the new rich, against the growing army of the unemployed—and the mill chimneys of the filature and the labor still belched out smoke over the little town, although there was no work in those factories, except here and there, for someone tending some monster that spewed out mountains of mass-produced goods . . . sitting by that monster made you neurotic. But by god, no, it wasn't as simple as that! The world was proceeding, turning and in fits and starts, moving towards a goal that no one could understand—the catholics appeared to be giving free rein to the socialists, who were going to create a new world, but again something different intervened: the new alliance, of which henry de wesemborgh was a member, came up with a ridiculous idea for a new and stupid program—they all wore black shirts and small badges in the shape of a street-sweeper's broom: the street was dirty, the street was full of socialists, and they were going to clean it up—and they called a meeting that fewer than ten people attended, and there they declared that socialism meant the downfall of civilization: it brought revolution and disorder and unemployment with it. Certainly that was true: socialism came and unemployment came with it—but unemployment came from something entirely different, through overproduction. So then the socialists called an anti-meeting. And the catholics too held an anti-meeting. Achilles derenancourt spoke about the park that he'd had laid out and the workmen's homes he had had built, and the others spoke of order, of the strong hand that must govern the world, and the socialists spoke about the poor working man. And a few troublemakers also came, wild men, communists from the capital—and they turned everything upside down and fought the gendarmes. Oh, the whole little town of

482

the 2 mills discussed the fascists' meeting, some people were against them, others for, and most people wondered: what kind of world are we headed for? And mariette too had been at the meeting and had announced that she agreed with fascism: she was in favor of order and an iron hand, and she was especially in favor of henry van wesenborgh. And now she argued with oscarke everyday, with her old father, who remained what he had always been: a little socialist skeptical of socialism. But the arguments that mariette put forward, they were some arguments! Apart from which, no sooner had oscarke made a good point than she simply changed the subject: she said to judith that there was going to be a beauty contest and she was going to enter. She forgot, or she had never known, that achilles derenancourt had had all those new-fangled postwar things banned, and had worked against them for as long as possible, and that she now had the socialists to thank that she was able to pit her beauty against others': she won, she became miss termuren. In fact only three girls had taken part in the competition: three girls who were as ugly and slutty as mariette was: the daughter of a fishwife, the daughter of someone from the shanties, and that slut mariette.

Ondine went to see the butcher and talked about socialism, about which the butcher said nothing, and sulked about the beauty competition which the butcher couldn't stop talking about: he had gone to the contest and the official presentation of mariette's title, and had clapped thunderously when the sash had been placed over her bare shoulders. Ondine listened reluctantly, and preferred to talk about the madame from café ohio, because he couldn't stop talking about her either: looking from his attic window into madame ohio's bedroom, all the things he had seen! And he took ondine up to that attic window, but all they saw at that moment was the blonde waitress, who was dusting. Ondine also sometimes went up to the room where the butcher's wife was lying, amid her rumpled sheets and medicine bottles—she was just like a doctor, the way she talked about the things inside her belly—but ondine was over that, she said, half laughing, half melancholic: yes I can see, a belly used to be a dark cellar, but you've had electricity put in. And sometimes it was mariette who sat there, and it was mariette to whom the butcher told the things he'd seen in the bedroom of the café ohio, and it was her whom he took to the attic to look into that bedroom—and eventually it would have been more interesting to look from that bedroom into the butcher's attic. And when his wife asked: but what are you doing up in the attic the whole afternoon?—he replied: oh, I was with ondine . . . fine goings on in café ohio again! And then mariette would go out, calling out good evening, imitating her mother's voice. But miss termuren looked for fresh pastures—although the butcher was the butcher, he couldn't take the place of a whole audience who would make way for mariette and whisper: that's miss termuren. She started visiting a dance hall, where things were a bit different from that pathetic little tent she'd once been to—it was a venue for the rich, for students from the polytechnic, graduates and doctors in this and that,

and for those making careers in the army, lieutenants and sub-lieutenants. Mari-
ette knew all those positions and all those ranks, she knew all about the army and
the university and sports—but her mother didn't let her go there alone too often,
because they drank champagne like water: ondine went with her—ondine drank
champagne and was miss termuren's mother. And she took judith along, oh, in her
final illusion, thinking perhaps of marrying off both her daughters to some slob of
a rich man's son. But judith was too stupid, too stupid and too ugly—and she was
also too lazy to dance, too lazy and too tired. And dancing didn't mean anything
to her: dancing was something you did with mariette's legs, but could judith dance
with mariette's legs? Or could mariette dance with judith's voice? And also, no one
asked her to dance anyway: you see, mom! And mariette on the other hand was
too imposing, she frightened the boys: she was all right for teaching the facts of life
to inexperienced students, but not for catching a husband. So that it was actually
ondine herself who started courting for her daughters. But she was applying the
tactics from her youth, and by now all that was hopelessly outdated—and all three
of them came home arguing, tired, hungry, and with headaches, came home to
oscarke who sat whittling wood for little albert—making a dagger and revolver
and a cannon for little albert, all from wood. And he also made him a tank, a real
tank that moved slowly forward on its own, because inside there was a camshaft
that was set in motion by a length of taut elastic—a piece of elastic from mariette's
garter. In the morning mariette looked for her garter, which was nowhere to be
found but which she needed in order to go out, to go to work. And suddenly some-
thing happened to her, something that surprised her, and then rather frightened her,
and finally infuriated her: what was the meaning of that, eh? She had set her sights
for that dead, white, anaemic henry van wesenborgh—he was the richest of them
all after all—but things didn't work out: she got pregnant, but when there was
talk of marriage, there was ample evidence that mariette had been out with half
the town, and even further afield in kwaatwijk, and further still, in brussels. When
ondine went to visit madame van wesenborgh, her daughter's record was set out for
her—it shook ondine—and so she came home and interrogated mariette. Oh, of
course she was only guessing—for all she knew, there were all kinds of contributing
circumstances: I don't mind that, but you should have told me: you're making me
play cards and giving all the trumps to the other players. But no matter who was
responsible, ondine locked her daughter up at home and with a cushion under her
skirt went herself to see the priest and the mayor—that is, the ex-mayor—and she
wrote long, long letters. It was without any hope of success, but just for the sake
of it, because letter writing had become a passion with her that made her forget
everything else: she even forgot what had been the initial impetus for writing, and
wrote out the whole of her life in her letters: how she had once been such and such,
and how she had slowly changed, come round, and had resigned herself. Yes, that's
really how it was, she had once and for all irrevocably resigned herself to everything.

484

And so it was ondine who brought the child into the world, instead of her daughter—and her boys, leopold and mauriske and little albert, they believed her, and would already be grown-up by the time they heard about it, and from strangers at that, before they finally heard the whole truth about their sister mariette. It had to be a henry, after the child's father—and ondine told everyone how unbelievable it was, mariette loved her little brother so much! But it didn't live very long, it caught something or other and died. Leopold and mauriske went around with black armbands, playing their filthy pranks—and mariette was in black, a long black dress, taut around her body, and with a black veil that muffled her piercing eyes and her big mouth. And when she sat down, and without her realizing it, her skirt went this way or that, and you could see her thighs again—how was it possible that she was wearing such a long dress and still couldn't sit down without your being able to see I don't know how far underneath it?—and that black dress, with those black knee-length stockings, and then those white buttocks, christ, there wasn't a man who saw her who didn't feel like tearing down some walls.

SUMMIT

You still have a few notes left about the future life of ondine and her household. They haven't the slightest importance for your book—anyway, most of them are only scribbled in pencil, and mostly illegible—but it may interest a few readers to know what happens:

Leopold turned 14 and had corrupted all the boys at school and oscarke decided that leopold should go to art school—but leopold had more cunning than intelligence, and was too good at furtively learning things it would be better for him not to know. What he had learned at school was how to smoke cigarettes, and on saturday evenings how to peer in a window to see if there were any women bathing—but his drawing was hopeless, and in pottery all he could do was make little balls to throw at the ceiling. At her wit's end, ondine sent him to her father, and there in the cement shed he seemed to have found his place: he told his adventures to valeer—and then valeer told him his adventures. And he hadn't been there long before he got his hand caught in an antiquated machine and lost a couple of fingers: so there they were, the two of them, valeer and leopold, waving their mutilated hands at each other. For the rest of his life he was the odd-job-man, the one who had to do everything, and he began to fall in love with a girl whose garden adjoined the workshop—but he didn't dare say a word.

On her side the girl came into their garden and was always annoyed at the workers who just came out there to piss—and she thought leopold was pathetic, afraid to piss, and wore a rag round his mutilated hand.

With socialism firmly established and communism on the rise, the bourgeoisie felt itself rocking on its foundations: they who had always paid for broken pots clung desperately to their privilege to pay for broken pots.

Leopold revised his stories to valeer: he confessed to him that it was all mauriske's fault: they don't make devils like him anymore!

When judith returned home she set out her demands: marriage, or being allowed to join a theater company—and ondine gave in.

It seemed like ondine was going downhill and growing old, because recently she'd been giving in a lot—it seemed like she was getting lazy and didn't want to exert herself. Judith joined a theater company (oh, it was a very catholic theater company, no danger there), but after rehearsals her sweetheart was waiting for her, and they talked about getting married: no power on earth would stop them. I've got to see this sweetheart of yours first, said ondine—and so judith fled to grandma zulma and . . . married from there, and went to live in rented rooms somewhere or other, and never showed her face at home again.

And suddenly mauriske was in the limelight—up till now he had come home quiet and well-behaved, blaming his sneaky tricks on others, but now he was looking under the skirts of his own sister mariette, and thinking up all kinds of excuses to get out of having to find work. When his time came to leave school, ondine suggested that he go to the butcher as a trainee. Mauriske wept, and not able to come up with a better excuse, said that he was sick—yes, he looked sick, he was thin and pale, but that wasn't because he was ill. And finally he claimed he would prefer to go on studying: I'm like our leopold, I'll make you rich and happy one day. Things like that moved ondine—she started telling him the high points in her life, with a strange frankness: you're like me, she said. She started behaving piously, although her faith was long gone by now, and made public penance—she did the rounds of monks and priests and spent hours in the confessional: mauriske followed her on those trips, and they finally found what they were looking for: he went into a monastery to study to become a monk. When he had gone ondine wept, she shut herself away and wanted no more to do with anyone . . . especially not with mariette, who said: it's just as if you're in mourning. In mourning, yes, that was the right word: she shut herself away as though there was a dead person to be mourned.

Meanwhile mariette wound up among the communists, but remained the old mariette even there: she hitched up her skirt and slapped her thigh: this is my fatherland and my passport! But she was still the one who paid the bills . . . almost every evening she went dancing in a distant hamlet where many social outcasts had gone to live, because life was cheaper there, and land cost almost nothing—all those people worked in town and brought their high wages with them . . . and there they built houses wherever they felt like it, by asking a bricklayer to give them a hand after work. They were the strangest shacks imaginable, put together unsystematically: a new town, without the slightest reason for existence, an excrescence that had only come about by accident . . . or no, in the way that a real excrescence is formed: a disease erupting: first the crisis, then the flight to find somewhere cheaper to live. It was like a cowboy town from the movies. The few farmers who lived there lost their heads completely, and it was there that mariette turned the head of an old farmer with her legs and her hysterical laugh. She brought eggs and bacon home, and oscarke blessed the depression that prevented him from working anymore, but allowed him to retreat into a corner and mess around with clay to his heart's content. But even that wasn't perfect, since 2 days a week he had to do some work for the town for his unemployment benefit to continue. But he didn't want to: I don't want to do any work that's outside of my profession, he said. And if they actually did give him work that was part of his trade (repairing the statues in the courtyard of the town hall, for instance, which had been damaged by wind and weather), he didn't want to do that either, without being paid the full rate.

Meanwhile, touching letters arrived from the monastery, and everyone read them: first the priest and then the doctor, and then a lawyer with no money, and the butcher, and finally all the residents of the café. Then a letter arrived with a photo: mauriske in a black habit. Ondine got her umbrella and her black satchel and headed straight for the monastery . . . yes, she brought him back home, because what would he have been there? An insignificant little monk. Mauriske was even quieter now than when he'd gone, and he found a position in the office of the lawyer with no money, and became the biggest skirt-chaser for miles around, coming out with the crudest language that had ever been heard. But if you dared ask him what really went on in that monastery, he would lower his eyes diffidently, and say: I swore an oath never to talk about it—and apart from that he told his dirty stories, so that even people who never went near a church were obliged to ask: hey, could you cut out that filthy talk of yours?

Here and there the petty bourgeoisie, becoming uncertain, began to lean towards fascism—although they didn't even know what fascism was.

Oscarke had finally become a proper socialist, and immediately had an argument with boone, who had been a socialist all his life: boone made a list of all the people who had become socialists recently: almost all the better-off people in the town of the 2 mills—and so finally the whole world is becoming socialist, yet there was

*nothing of socialism to be seen in the world. And oscarke the brand-new social-
ist became annoyed and called boone's attitude: nihilism. That's not true, replied
boone: it's a simple observation.*

*Mariette too talked of marriage: she spent time over there with that old farmer,
but wanted to marry a poor boy who she'd once made fun of—she was already
getting on, with nasty lines in her face from staying out too late at night, smoking
and drinking—but her legs were still in good shape. There were evenings when
she didn't go out at all but crawled right into bed—and since ondine was out and
about in the neighborhood, and the house was deserted, mauriske crawled into bed
with mariette . . . they lay there and told each other their life stories, each trying
to outdo the other . . . and sometimes, despite her extremely unsavory reputation,
mariette had to turn away in embarrassment at what mauriske whispered in her
ear. There in bed he also advised her to go about things quite differently from the
way she was planning: marry the man with money, and let yourself be loved by
those who love you. And that was what she did, she married the farmer but went
on allowing mauriske to come to bed with her—and in the very first days of the
marriage, ondine practically cleaned out the entire farmhouse, she and mauriske
came back each evening to the terrace of the 1st grimy houses laden with bacon
and ham and eggs, with butter and milk and cheese. Meanwhile, mauriske told
very pious stories about the monastery.*

Little albert, the youngest, had become a fascist.

*Ondine received news of their judith: that she lived on the road to that cowboy
town, and that her marriage was far from a bad one, since her husband with his
lame foot was a tailor who earned a lot of money. Ondine went to see her with
her black satchel on her arm, and asked for a glass of water from the madame
who lived there, since she didn't realize that it was her own child—then she cried,
and asked if she would have to spend her whole life with all her children wanting
to have nothing to do with her? But she had come at a very bad moment: judith
asked her very respectfully if she would be godmother to her first child. Then
ondine cried still harder and talked of depression and decline, and of not having
any money to be a godmother. But once granny zulma dies we shall inherit something, said ondine . . . and then you'll be better off than all my other children. The
upshot was that the matter was settled without ondine having to put her hand in
her pocket . . . and that judith came back home every week to scrub the floor and
do the washing, just like she'd always done in the past.*

*But her parents' estate kept preying on ondine's mind, and so she watched the
concrete shack like a cat watches a mouse: whenever she'd had setbacks in life,*

that inheritance served as opium. And when her mother died, ondine searched everywhere for the money, including the cold corpse. Fear and shame? Oh, come on: she had a family, there was a depression on, and soon there would be a new war. She had to live—that was the main thing. But she searched in vain for the money . . . and oscarke, who'd been left alone the last few nights and had cooked his own supper, saw a broken ondine returning home: my father must have stolen the money, she said.

And suddenly oscarke and ondine got into a discussion—both of them sitting there in the almost empty house, grown old and gray, on this very rare occasion in their lives they compared their ideas. And it emerged, hesitantly, full of detours and circumlocutions—each almost embarrassed at the other—but it became clear from their words that neither of them, one religious and the other socialist, believed in anything anymore.

The last to leave home was little albert. And then the nations finally began to do battle with fascism, which like a plague-sore began spreading its infection further and further round it: and little albert, who was a fascist, was mobilized to fight fascism along the albert canal. During the mobilization ondine also saw her old father die—and as a last trump card in the card game of her life, she tried to lure valeer to live with them: sell the house and the machine and come and live with me. Then valeer said that if he had to move he would prefer to go and live with their cousin in brussels. Right, go then, said ondine quietly and dejectedly. And everyone who heard her looked at her rather pityingly: the god of thunder that she had always been had clearly ceased to exist. Then the second world war broke out—but what she had claimed all her life she would do: smuggle, steal, buy in bulk and get rich . . . she didn't do any of it; it was all different from the first world war, new tactics had to be devised for everything: vast fortunes were being made out of nothing around her, but she had grown too old, her strength had faded. She lived from day to day, and sat by the stove and said: oh, it is as it Must be. She no longer resisted, she waited for the end of the war . . . the end of the war, or the end of her life: it remained to be seen which of the two would come first.

SELECTED DALKEY ARCHIVE PAPERBACKS

PETROS ABATZOGLOU, *What Does Mrs. Freeman Want?*
PIERRE ALBERT-BIROT, *Grabinoulor.*
YUZ ALESHKOVSKY, *Kangaroo.*
FELIPE ALFAU, *Chromos.*
  Locos.
IVAN ÂNGELO, *The Celebration.*
  The Tower of Glass.
DAVID ANTIN, *Talking.*
DJUNA BARNES, *Ladies Almanack.*
  Ryder.
JOHN BARTH, *LETTERS.*
  Sabbatical.
DONALD BARTHELME, *The King.*
  Paradise.
SVETISLAV BASARA, *Chinese Letter.*
MARK BINELLI, *Sacco and Vanzetti Must Die!*
ANDREI BITOV, *Pushkin House.*
LOUIS PAUL BOON, *Chapel Road.*
  Summer in Termuren.
ROGER BOYLAN, *Killoyle.*
IGNÁCIO DE LOYOLA BRANDÃO, *Zero.*
CHRISTINE BROOKE-ROSE, *Amalgamemnon.*
BRIGID BROPHY, *In Transit.*
MEREDITH BROSNAN, *Mr. Dynamite.*
GERALD L. BRUNS,
  Modern Poetry and the Idea of Language.
GABRIELLE BURTON, *Heartbreak Hotel.*
MICHEL BUTOR, *Degrees.*
  Mobile.
  Portrait of the Artist as a Young Ape.
G. CABRERA INFANTE, *Infante's Inferno.*
  Three Trapped Tigers.
JULIETA CAMPOS, *The Fear of Losing Eurydice.*
ANNE CARSON, *Eros the Bittersweet.*
CAMILO JOSÉ CELA, *The Family of Pascual Duarte.*
  The Hive.
LOUIS-FERDINAND CÉLINE, *Castle to Castle.*
  Conversations with Professor Y.
  London Bridge.
  North.
  Rigadoon.
HUGO CHARTERIS, *The Tide Is Right.*
JEROME CHARYN, *The Tar Baby.*
MARC CHOLODENKO, *Mordechai Schamz.*
EMILY HOLMES COLEMAN, *The Shutter of Snow.*
ROBERT COOVER, *A Night at the Movies.*
STANLEY CRAWFORD, *Some Instructions to My Wife.*
ROBERT CREELEY, *Collected Prose.*
RENÉ CREVEL, *Putting My Foot in It.*
RALPH CUSACK, *Cadenza.*
SUSAN DAITCH, *L.C.*
  Storytown.
NIGEL DENNIS, *Cards of Identity.*
PETER DIMOCK,
  A Short Rhetoric for Leaving the Family.
ARIEL DORFMAN, *Konfidenz.*
COLEMAN DOWELL, *The Houses of Children.*
  Island People.
  Too Much Flesh and Jabez.
RIKKI DUCORNET, *The Complete Butcher's Tales.*
  The Fountains of Neptune.
  The Jade Cabinet.
  Phosphor in Dreamland.
  The Stain.
  The Word "Desire."
WILLIAM EASTLAKE, *The Bamboo Bed.*
  Castle Keep.
  Lyric of the Circle Heart.
JEAN ECHENOZ, *Chopin's Move.*
STANLEY ELKIN, *A Bad Man.*
  Boswell: A Modern Comedy.
  Criers and Kibitzers, Kibitzers and Criers.
  The Dick Gibson Show.
  The Franchiser.
  George Mills.
  The Living End.
  The MacGuffin.
  The Magic Kingdom.

MRS. TED BLISS.
  The Rabbi of Lud.
  Van Gogh's Room at Arles.
ANNIE ERNAUX, *Cleaned Out.*
LAUREN FAIRBANKS, *Muzzle Thyself.*
  Sister Carrie.
LESLIE A. FIEDLER,
  Love and Death in the American Novel.
GUSTAVE FLAUBERT, *Bouvard and Pécuchet.*
FORD MADOX FORD, *The March of Literature.*
CARLOS FUENTES, *Christopher Unborn.*
  Distant Relations.
  Terra Nostra.
  Where the Air Is Clear.
JANICE GALLOWAY, *Foreign Parts.*
  The Trick Is to Keep Breathing.
WILLIAM H. GASS, *The Tunnel.*
  Willie Masters' Lonesome Wife.
ETIENNE GILSON, *The Arts of the Beautiful.*
  Forms and Substances in the Arts.
C. S. GISCOMBE, *Giscome Road.*
  Here.
DOUGLAS GLOVER, *Bad News of the Heart.*
  The Enamoured Knight.
KAREN ELIZABETH GORDON, *The Red Shoes.*
GEORGI GOSPODINOV, *Natural Novel.*
PATRICK GRAINVILLE, *The Cave of Heaven.*
HENRY GREEN, *Blindness.*
  Concluding.
  Doting.
  Nothing.
JIŘÍ GRUŠA, *The Questionnaire.*
JOHN HAWKES, *Whistlejacket.*
AIDAN HIGGINS, *A Bestiary.*
  Bornholm Night-Ferry.
  Flotsam and Jetsam.
  Langrishe, Go Down.
  Scenes from a Receding Past.
  Windy Arbours.
ALDOUS HUXLEY, *Antic Hay.*
  Crome Yellow.
  Point Counter Point.
  Those Barren Leaves.
  Time Must Have a Stop.
MIKHAIL IOSSEL and JEFF PARKER, EDS., *Amerika:*
  Contemporary Russians View
  the United States.
GERT JONKE, *Geometric Regional Novel.*
JACQUES JOUET, *Mountain R.*
HUGH KENNER, *The Counterfeiters.*
  Flaubert, Joyce and Beckett:
  The Stoic Comedians.
DANILO KIŠ, *Garden, Ashes.*
  A Tomb for Boris Davidovich.
ANITA KONKKA, *A Fool's Paradise.*
TADEUSZ KONWICKI, *A Minor Apocalypse.*
  The Polish Complex.
MENIS KOUMANDAREAS, *Koula.*
ELAINE KRAF, *The Princess of 72nd Street.*
JIM KRUSOE, *Iceland.*
EWA KURYLUK, *Century 21.*
VIOLETTE LEDUC, *La Bâtarde.*
DEBORAH LEVY, *Billy and Girl.*
  Pillow Talk in Europe and Other Places.
JOSÉ LEZAMA LIMA, *Paradiso.*
OSMAN LINS, *Avalovara.*
  The Queen of the Prisons of Greece.
ALF MAC LOCHLAINN, *The Corpus in the Library.*
  Out of Focus.
RON LOEWINSOHN, *Magnetic Field(s).*
D. KEITH MANO, *Take Five.*
BEN MARCUS, *The Age of Wire and String.*
WALLACE MARKFIELD, *Teitlebaum's Window.*
  To an Early Grave.
DAVID MARKSON, *Reader's Block.*
  Springer's Progress.
  Wittgenstein's Mistress.

FOR A FULL LIST OF PUBLICATIONS, VISIT:
www.dalkeyarchive.com

SELECTED DALKEY ARCHIVE PAPERBACKS

CAROLE MASO, *AVA.*
LADISLAV MATEJKA AND KRYSTYNA POMORSKA, EDS.,
  *Readings in Russian Poetics: Formalist and
  Structuralist Views.*
HARRY MATHEWS,
  The Case of the Persevering Maltese: Collected Essays.
  Cigarettes.
  The Conversions.
  The Human Country: New and Collected Stories.
  The Journalist.
  My Life in CIA.
  Singular Pleasures.
  The Sinking of the Odradek Stadium.
  Tlooth.
  20 Lines a Day.
ROBERT L. MCLAUGHLIN, ED.,
  *Innovations: An Anthology of Modern &
  Contemporary Fiction.*
STEVEN MILLHAUSER, *The Barnum Museum.*
  In the Penny Arcade.
RALPH J. MILLS, JR., *Essays on Poetry.*
OLIVE MOORE, *Spleen.*
NICHOLAS MOSLEY, *Accident.*
  Assassins.
  Catastrophe Practice.
  Children of Darkness and Light.
  The Hesperides Tree.
  Hopeful Monsters.
  Imago Bird.
  Impossible Object.
  Inventing God.
  Judith.
  Look at the Dark.
  Natalie Natalia.
  Serpent.
  The Uses of Slime Mould: Essays of Four Decades.
WARREN F. MOTTE, JR.,
  Fables of the Novel: French Fiction since 1990.
  Oulipo: A Primer of Potential Literature.
YVES NAVARRE, *Our Share of Time.*
  Sweet Tooth.
DOROTHY NELSON, *In Night's City.*
  Tar and Feathers.
WILFRIDO D. NOLLEDO, *But for the Lovers.*
FLANN O'BRIEN, *At Swim-Two-Birds.*
  At War.
  The Best of Myles.
  The Dalkey Archive.
  Further Cuttings.
  The Hard Life.
  The Poor Mouth.
  The Third Policeman.
CLAUDE OLLIER, *The Mise-en-Scène.*
PATRIK OUŘEDNÍK, *Europeana.*
FERNANDO DEL PASO, *Palinuro of Mexico.*
ROBERT PINGET, *The Inquisitory.*
  Mahu or The Material.
  Trio.
RAYMOND QUENEAU, *The Last Days.*
  Odile.
  Pierrot Mon Ami.
  Saint Glinglin.
ANN QUIN, *Berg.*
  Passages.
  Three.
  Tripticks.
ISHMAEL REED, *The Free-Lance Pallbearers.*
  The Last Days of Louisiana Red.
  Reckless Eyeballing.
  The Terrible Threes.
  The Terrible Twos.
  Yellow Back Radio Broke-Down.
JULIÁN RÍOS, *Larva: A Midsummer Night's Babel.*
  Poundemonium.
AUGUSTO ROA BASTOS, *I the Supreme.*
JACQUES ROUBAUD, *The Great Fire of London.*

Hortense in Exile.
Hortense Is Abducted.
The Plurality of Worlds of Lewis.
The Princess Hoppy.
*The Form of a City Changes Faster, Alas,
  Than the Human Heart.*
Some Thing Black.
LEON S. ROUDIEZ, *French Fiction Revisited.*
VEDRANA RUDAN, *Night.*
LYDIE SALVAYRE, *The Company of Ghosts.*
  The Lecture.
LUIS RAFAEL SÁNCHEZ, *Macho Camacho's Beat.*
SEVERO SARDUY, *Cobra & Maitreya.*
NATHALIE SARRAUTE, *Do You Hear Them?*
  Martereau.
  The Planetarium.
ARNO SCHMIDT, *Collected Stories.*
  Nobodaddy's Children.
CHRISTINE SCHUTT, *Nightwork.*
GAIL SCOTT, *My Paris.*
JUNE AKERS SEESE,
  Is This What Other Women Feel Too?
  What Waiting Really Means.
AURELIE SHEEHAN, *Jack Kerouac Is Pregnant.*
VIKTOR SHKLOVSKY, *Knight's Move.*
  A Sentimental Journey: Memoirs 1917-1922.
  Theory of Prose.
  Third Factory.
  Zoo, or Letters Not about Love.
JOSEF ŠKVORECKÝ,
  The Engineer of Human Souls.
CLAUDE SIMON, *The Invitation.*
GILBERT SORRENTINO, *Aberration of Starlight.*
  Blue Pastoral.
  Crystal Vision.
  Imaginative Qualities of Actual Things.
  Mulligan Stew.
  Pack of Lies.
  The Sky Changes.
  Something Said.
  Splendide-Hôtel.
  Steelwork.
  Under the Shadow.
W. M. SPACKMAN, *The Complete Fiction.*
GERTRUDE STEIN, *Lucy Church Amiably.*
  The Making of Americans.
  A Novel of Thank You.
PIOTR SZEWC, *Annihilation.*
STEFAN THEMERSON, *Hobson's Island.*
  Tom Harris.
JEAN-PHILIPPE TOUSSAINT, *Television.*
ESTHER TUSQUETS, *Stranded.*
DUBRAVKA UGRESIC, *Lend Me Your Character.*
  Thank You for Not Reading.
MATI UNT, *Things in the Night.*
ELOY URROZ, *The Obstacles.*
LUISA VALENZUELA, *He Who Searches.*
BORIS VIAN, *Heartsnatcher.*
PAUL WEST, *Words for a Deaf Daughter & Gala.*
CURTIS WHITE, *America's Magic Mountain.*
  The Idea of Home.
  Memories of My Father Watching TV.
  *Monstrous Possibility: An Invitation to
  Literary Politics.*
  Requiem.
DIANE WILLIAMS, *Excitability: Selected Stories.*
  Romancer Erector.
DOUGLAS WOOLF, *Wall to Wall.*
  Ya! & John-Juan.
PHILIP WYLIE, *Generation of Vipers.*
MARGUERITE YOUNG, *Angel in the Forest.*
  Miss MacIntosh, My Darling.
REYOUNG, *Unbabbling.*
ZORAN ŽIVKOVIĆ, *Hidden Camera.*
LOUIS ZUKOFSKY, *Collected Fiction.*
SCOTT ZWIREN, *God Head.*

FOR A FULL LIST OF PUBLICATIONS, VISIT:
www.dalkeyarchive.com